ILLUSIONS OF LOVE

Lou slipped into his coat and walked toward the door. As he was about to undo the lock, Pearl called after him. "Lou, please don't go. With Jake in the hospital I can't bear to be alone."

His hand fell to his side. Slowly, he turned around. Her eyes were misty with tears. Somehow, the pins at the back of her head had fallen loose and the auburn hair waved softly down onto her shoulders.

"Don't leave me by myself." Before it had been a statement. Now it was a heart-wrenching plea. Levitt walked toward her, raised his arms as he drew near. Two steps away, she moved forward into his embrace. She clung to him, seeking comfort. He drew her closer, held her tighter. Before his mouth pressed against hers, he murmured, "Pearl, I still love you. I always will."

"I know." From deep inside, a voice screamed at her to stop, to think what she was doing, what she was allowing Levitt to do. She was a married woman. Too desperate for the comfort he could offer, she ignored the voice.

Holding his hand, she led him toward the bedroom. At the last moment she listened to that inner voice, but only enough to choose the second bedroom instead of the one she normally shared with Jake. "Love me," she whispered as she fell back onto the bed. "Love me."

Lewis Orde

THE TIGER'S HEART

ZEBRA BOOKS
KENSINGTON PUBLISHING CORP.

ZEBRA BOOKS

are published by

Kensington Publishing Corp.
475 Park Avenue South
New York, NY 10016

First printing: June 1987

Printed in the United States of America

For Manny and all the Mitchell Mob of Toronto

Prologue

The old-fashioned oak bureau was a permanent fixture in Pearl Granitz's life, a square and heavy piece of furniture which had accompanied her through three homes since her wedding day more than forty years earlier.

Always the bureau had stood in Pearl's bedroom, dominating lesser pieces around it. The first bedroom had been in an apartment at the lower end of Fifth Avenue, where Pearl had lived for fourteen years. The second bedroom had been in an apartment on Central Park West. The third bedroom, where the bureau now stood, was in a house in Sands Point, which belonged to Pearl's son and daughter-in-law.

When Pearl had moved to Sands Point, both her son and daughter-in-law had argued against her bringing furniture from the apartment on Central Park West. Sell it, they had told her. They would buy more. She remembered laughing at their generosity, and answering that you did not sell furniture that had nothing wrong with it.

We don't want you to sell it because there's something wrong with it. We want you to sell it because of the memories.

And Pearl had answered that the memories were the very reason she wanted to hang on to the old bedroom furniture, especially the oak bureau. The bureau contained too many poignant memories to be so thoughtlessly discarded, sold in some consignment shop to a buyer who would never be able to appreciate the laughter and the tears which had permeated the rich wood over the years.

Pearl stood in front of the bureau, a petite gray-haired figure who was dwarfed by the furniture's solidity. She inclined her head slightly, listening for noise from downstairs. Minutes earlier there had been bedlam, two elderly men yelling at each other, hurling accusations back and forth with such violence that Pearl had felt that her head must be torn apart. Finally she had screamed herself for them to stop, and then she had left the room and made her way up to the house's second floor, walked to the bedroom to stand in front of this heavy piece of furniture with all of its memories.

7

She heard no noise from downstairs now. Had her absence made them stop? Were they waiting for her return before resuming their battle? She would not let them. She loved both men too much. And yet as she stood and stared at the oak bureau, she knew that her love for one man was based on nothing but a hill of sand.

She pulled open the bureau's bottom drawer. The accumulation of years rested there: birth certificates, her own wedding certificate, picture albums. She moved them aside, for once disinterested in the chapters of her life that they contained. She was searching for something else, another memory that was hidden in a polished walnut presentation box. She lifted the box from the drawer, opened it and saw a card covered with scrawly handwriting. Beneath the card, resting on luxuriant velvet, was a matching pair of ivory-handled revolvers, a cleaning kit and ammunition. Without hesitation, she removed the revolvers from the box, inserted ammunition, and slipped both weapons into a large handbag.

As she left the bedroom and reached the top of the curving staircase that stretched down to the entrance hall, Pearl smelled the faint aroma of cakes she had baked early that morning. Everywhere she'd ever lived had borne that smell of baking, of cooking. It was a good smell, a smell that showed a house was a home.

The stairway loomed before her. She walked down carefully, the handbag containing the two loaded revolvers weighing heavily on her arm. The smell of cake caught in her nose again, and she deemed it propitious that she should be reminded of baking at a time like this. Baking . . . cooking . . . the preparation of fine food had always been Pearl's defense against stress. Only the problem that faced her now could not be solved while standing over pots and pans bubbling merrily on the stove.

It could be solved only with what she carried in the handbag.

Too bad, she decided sadly as she reached the bottom of the stairs. She would far rather have solved it by cooking.

BOOK ONE

Chapter One

Pearl's love of cooking was created in the womb. Her parents, Joseph and Sophie Resnick, owned a restaurant at the bottom of Second Avenue, and Pearl's introduction to the sizzle of roasting meat, the heady smell of freshly baked pastry, came filtering through amniotic fluid for her mother worked until the very day she gave birth.

Twice before, during her thirteen years of marriage to Joseph Resnick, Sophie had become pregnant. Both times she had lost the child. A miscarriage ended the first pregnancy; in the second, she went the full term only to deliver a stillborn boy. When she became pregnant for the third time, she reviewed her behavior during her first two pregnancies. Resnick had treated her like a piece of fragile china, allowing her to do nothing for herself. This time, Sophie put her foot down. She continued to cook in the restaurant's kitchen, resisting all her husband's efforts to make her rest. And when she gave birth, in the flat above the restaurant, to a healthy girl, she managed to wag a finger at Resnick, smile, and say: "So who was right this time, you or me?"

When Pearl was born, on a bitterly cold November night in 1905, Resnick's joy knew no bounds. He rushed downstairs to the restaurant he and Sophie had opened five years earlier, shortly after they had arrived in the country from Hungary, and hung a huge sign in the window. Written in large block capitals were the words: IT'S A GIRL! The following day, while Sophie nursed the baby, Resnick stood in the restaurant, beaming, inches added to his small frame as he passed out cigars to his regular customers and sent a complimentary slice of cake to each diner. He knew that his customers were as excited as he was. They had endured each day of Sophie's pregnancy with him, shared his anxiety and fear. Now they could share his happiness.

A week later, when Sophie finally allowed him to take the baby into the restaurant, Resnick went to every table and booth, and proudly introduced the warmly wrapped bundle he carried so gently in his arms. "This is my daughter, Pearl. Next week, she starts to work in the kitchen. Her mother's giving her lessons in cooking already." And then he'd laugh and move on to the next table.

Pearl's early world centered around the restaurant with its four booths, varnished wooden counter, and ten tables covered in cheerful red-and-white checkered cloths. She quickly became accustomed to the continual stream of hungry people who filled the restaurant during the day and early evening: businessmen in their suits, pushcart owners and peddlers in their scruffy, weatherbeaten clothes. When she was four, she invented her own game. A miniature of Sophie Resnick, with dark auburn hair, and light brown eyes dominating a heart-shaped face, Pearl would wander from table to table to ask, in mimicry of her mother, if everything was satisfactory. But the customers who good-naturedly patted her on the head were not enough to fill the needs of such a young girl. She needed company of her own age, and for that she was forced to look outside the restaurant. She did not have to look far, though, just to the bakery next door owned by Isidore and Helen Moscowitz, whose daughter, Annie, was only a few weeks older than Pearl.

From the moment Pearl discovered a girl of her own age, she made the bakery her second home, running in and out to play with Annie, a girl with wiry red hair and an impish sense of mischief. More than once, Annie's daredevil attitude led both girls into trouble. When they were six, Annie decided to leave home, but she wasn't prepared to go alone. She went into the restaurant where she quickly persuaded Pearl to accompany her. Feeling very adventurous, the two girls walked south to the corner of Second Avenue and Houston Street, turned right and kept on going. An hour later, they were completely lost. In the middle of Washington Square, surrounded by unfamiliar buildings, Pearl sat down on the curb and started to cry, while Annie, who refused to let such a splendid escapade end in tears, tried to pull her upright, exhorting her to carry on. Finally, a policeman approached the two small girls. Thirty minutes later, they were back on Second Avenue, trying to explain to their irate but anxious parents why they had strayed so far from home.

They started school together, always sitting next to one another. So close were they that at ten Pearl tried to emulate Annie by bleaching her own dark auburn hair a bright red. Between them, they concocted a mixture of household bleach and henna, which Annie applied in the kitchen of the Resnick flat. The result was like a patchwork quilt, splotchy reds, browns and pinks. When Sophie Resnick came up from the restaurant and saw what the girls had done, she threw her hands into the air and screamed.

"Your beautiful hair! What did you do to it?"

"I wanted to be like Annie, Mama." Pearl turned to her friend for support. She was just in time to see the red-haired girl running out of the flat and down the stairs.

"Joseph!" Sophie went to the head of the stairs and called down to the restaurant. "Come up here and see our glamorous daughter."

Resnick came upstairs and froze in astonishment when he saw Pearl's hair. His eyes opened wide and his mouth dropped. Then, very slowly, his entire body started to ripple with laughter. Pearl looked at her mother, relieved to see that she, too, was beginning to laugh.

"You're not angry?" Pearl asked her parents.

With tears in her eyes, Sophie Resnick shook her head. "No, darling, we're not angry. You haven't done anything to us. You're the one who's going to have to wear your hair like that until it grows out."

That evening, before going to bed, Pearl stared at her reflection in the mirror. She understood now what her mother meant—she'd be a laughingstock when she went to school the following day. It was then that she decided she would never again do anything to the color of her hair. Even if she turned white by the time she was twenty, she vowed, she would leave it alone.

Annie was waiting in the street when Pearl left for school the following morning. "It doesn't look that bad," Annie said, trying to comfort her friend. "There's a little patch there"—she touched a lock on the side of Pearl's head—"that's almost the same color as mine."

"It looks horrible. Everyone's going to laugh."

"I won't," Annie promised.

"You'd better not, not after the way you ran off last night."

"Did you get into trouble?"

Pearl shook her head. "My mother said that looking like this would be punishment enough."

"You're lucky. My parents would have killed me." Annie laughed and tugged at Pearl's arm. "Come on, we'd better hurry or we'll be late."

The moment they reached school, the other children started to make fun of Pearl. "Goldilocks!" they called out. "Are you going to break into the three bears' house while they're out?"

Aside from Annie, only one member of Pearl's class took her side, a short, skinny, studious boy named Lou Levitt, who had been at the school for two years after coming to the United States from Radomsk in Poland. When Levitt had started at the school, classmates had mocked the way he'd spoken. Pearl had taken his part, yelling at the others: "Did your mothers and fathers speak so well when they first

11

came to this country?" Now, Levitt supported Pearl.

"Don't listen to them when they laugh," he advised her in his heavily accented English. "People who mock you when you're different are only showing their ignorance."

Lou Levitt fascinated Pearl. He was by far the brightest pupil in the class, always coming in first on math tests, performing complicated multiplication and division with apparent ease. While other children scribbled furiously in their books, Levitt worked out the sums in his head. It seemed to Pearl that every question the teacher asked was always answered in that same accented voice.

"Why are you so good at arithmetic?" she once asked him.

Shrugging his narrow shoulders, he answered, "Figures are marvelous. You can do anything you want with them. Here, let me show you." From his pocket he pulled a book full of numbers and strange symbols that meant nothing to Pearl. "This is Pi," he said, pointing to that symbol. "You know what Pi is?"

"Something with apples in it?" Pearl asked hopefully, while Annie burst into a fit of giggles.

"Pi is the sixteenth letter of the Greek alphabet. It is also the mathematical symbol that equals twenty-two over seven. It's how you find the circumference of a circle, just by knowing its diameter. The circumference is always three and one seventh times the diameter."

Pearl took the book from Levitt and stared at the text. Was this how Levitt amused himself, by studying? What a strange boy, she could not help thinking.

Even stranger to Pearl was the friendship Levitt had with three older boys—Moses Caplan, whose widowed mother supported herself by doing sewing and alterations; Benny Minsky, the son of a peddler who sold pots and pans from a cart on Essex Street; and Jake Granitz, whose father was in the produce business, supplying shops and restaurants on the Lower East Side, including the restaurant owned by Joseph Resnick. Pearl always considered the four boys an odd combination. Levitt, so short and intense. Caplan, a chunky, muscular boy with unruly black hair. Minsky, so darkly complexioned with such tightly curled hair that other children had cruelly nicknamed him Nig. And Jake, tall and slim with wavy light brown hair that caught golden highlights when the sun shone.

"Just what is the connection between those four?" Pearl asked Annie one break time as she watched Levitt, Caplan, Jake, and Minsky walking quickly toward a shed that was used by the school's janitor to store supplies.

"Opposites attract," Annie answered. "Lou's small, so he hangs around with three big boys."

12

Pearl continued to watch as the four boys reached the shed, looked around furtively, and then pulled the door open. "What are they up to?"

"Only one way to find out," Annie answered with her customary impetuosity. Pulling Pearl's arm, she marched toward the shed.

By the time the girls got to it, all four boys were inside, the door tightly closed behind them. Nervously, Pearl gazed at the door and debated whether to pull it back. Annie was not so hesitant. She grabbed hold of the handle, and dragged the door open. Inside, squatting on the floor, were the boys, their eyes riveted on Levitt who was about to throw a pair of dice against the wall.

"Caught you red-handed!" Annie exclaimed.

Caplan leaped to his feet, pulled both girls inside the shed, and slammed the door. "Now we've caught you instead. What have you got to say about that?"

With the closing of the door, Annie's bravery deserted her. "Let us go," she pleaded. "We won't tell anyone what you're doing. I promise."

"Give me a kiss and we'll let you go." Caplan winked at Jake and Minsky, who were starting to laugh. Only Lou Levitt found nothing amusing in the situation. He slipped the dice into his pocket and glared at the girls, his bright blue eyes blazing.

"Why did you two come in here?" he demanded.

"We wanted to see what you were doing," Annie answered.

"Why? What business is it of yours what we do?"

Caplan stuck himself between Annie and Levitt. "Don't listen to him. Just give me a kiss and we'll let you both go."

Annie screwed up her face and kissed Caplan, half on the lips, half on the chin.

"What about me?" Minsky asked. "Have I got the plague?"

"Don't forget me," Jake said, looking at Pearl.

Pearl stared back at Jake and wondered what to do. She had never kissed a boy, but if she had to break the ice, Jake was the boy she would choose. He had a humor and warmth in his dark brown eyes that his friends lacked.

"Well?" Jake persisted.

Pearl took a deep breath, her mind all but made up. Just as she moved forward, the shed door flew back and the janitor loomed menacingly in the opening. "What the hell do you damned kids think you're doing in here? Get out, go play your stupid games somewhere else!"

All six hurriedly left. When they were twenty yards away, out of the janitor's hearing, Jake turned to Pearl. "Maybe your being nosy

13

just did us a favor. There'd have been hell to pay if he'd caught us shooting dice."

"And so there should be," Pearl replied primly, simultaneously grateful for and annoyed by the janitor's interruption. She still hadn't kissed a boy! "You're supposed to come to school to learn, not to play dice." Taking Annie's hand, she started to walk away. Jake ran after her, spun her around, and kissed her quickly on the lips.

"There, that's for the favor."

Pearl just stood there, uncertain, after all, whether or not she'd enjoyed being kissed by Jake.

All through the afternoon, she pondered the experience, and by the time she was ready to go home she'd reached a decision. She had enjoyed it. After school, she waited around with Annie, wanting to see Jake again. When she did spot him, though, he did not seem to notice her. With Moses Caplan and Benny Minsky, he was busily engaged in a conversation with a group of smaller boys.

"Will you just take a look at that?" Annie said. "Gambling's not enough for them. They're taking money from the young kids as well."

"Whatever for?"

"What do you think? For protection, of course. There," she said smugly as the three bigger boys accompanied the younger children away from the school. "They must walk them home, save them getting into trouble with the Irish kids."

Pearl watched, wishing she knew as much as her friend did. Annie always seemed so much more grown-up, so worldly; and Pearl was jealous. "Why isn't Lou with them?"

Annie laughed. "What good would that shrimp be if a gang of Irish bullies caught you down some dark street? He's too small to stand up to anyone. He'd have to beat them over the head with his books . . . that's if he could reach that high to begin with."

Pearl joined in the laughter. Arm-in-arm, the two girls walked toward home. "We're small as well," Pearl said, "but we don't need anyone to protect us, do we? We've got each other."

"Right," Annie answered. "God help the Irisher who tries anything with us. I'll turn his hair twenty different colors—"

"And then we'll leave him lost in Washington Square."

Doubled over, the two girls continued on their way home.

Chapter Two

During the school Christmas break that followed her twelfth birthday, Pearl started to work full-time in the restaurant, waiting on tables, washing up, and sweeping the floor. Working all day was a novel experience, enjoyable because she knew that she was returning something to her parents. More than anything, she loved to be in the kitchen, where she could watch her mother add ingredients to the bubbling pots and saucepans. Sophie Resnick never used a measuring cup. Her practiced eye was more accurate than any set of scales could ever be, and Pearl watched her, fascinated.

"You're like a witch making a magic potion," she told her mother one morning as Sophie prepared a large pot of mushroom and barley soup. "Will I ever be able to cook like you?"

"Of course you will," Sophie replied, laughing. "All you've got to remember is one little word . . . *shitenarein*. A little bit of this, and a little bit of that."

Pearl memorized the word by repeating it to herself. That lunchtime, when customers asked what the soup was, she proudly told them: *"Shitenarein* soup."

Of all the people who frequented the restaurant, Pearl disliked only two. Booth number four, at the rear of the premises, had a curtain that could be pulled across, and always boasted a handwritten Reserved sign, the only such sign ever seen in the Resnick restaurant. At precisely ten-thirty every morning, a balding, obese man in his middle forties, and a thinner, younger man with fair hair, a narrow face, and icy blue eyes would enter the restaurant and take that booth, remaining there until three-thirty in the afternoon, with the drape closed. Every so often, other men would visit the booth, remain behind the drawn curtain for a few minutes, then leave. Sometimes, the fat man would pull back the drape and snap his fingers at Pearl for service, ordering coffee, or something to eat for himself and his companion in curt, arrogant tones. Then the curtain would slide closed again, and the two men would return to their business.

Pearl hated these men. Especially the fat man. She didn't like his manners. She didn't like the way he smelled. Despite the expensive suits he always wore, the rings he flaunted, he smelled of stale cigars and fish. Pearl felt nauseous whenever she had to answer the finger-snapping summons. What galled her young sense of justice most of all, though, wasn't the smell of the fat man, or his arrogance; it was that the two men in booth number four never seemed to pay for what they consumed. When their business for the day was over, they would open the drape and simply walk out of the restaurant.

Could it be, Pearl asked herself as she stared at the closed drape, that these two men watched and waited for a moment each afternoon when her parents were busy, so that they could effect their escape without having to pay for what they'd eaten?

Within a couple of days, Pearl had decided to bring the matter to a head by herself. No one was going to cheat her parents and get away with it. The Resnicks worked too hard to merit this kind of treatment. She waited until a quiet period in the early afternoon, when the fat man drew back the drape and beckoned to her.

"Be a good girl and bring a couple of cups of coffee over here, and some of your mother's honey cake."

Pearl stared defiantly at the fat man. "Why should I bring anything for you when you always leave without paying?"

The fat man gazed calmly at Pearl. His younger companion shifted in the seat and bathed her with a chilling blast from his blue eyes. "For a little girl, you've got a big mouth," the younger man said. "Now quit standing there like a statue and get Mr. Fromberg what he asked for."

Pearl stood her ground. "Why should you be any different from anyone else? No one gives my parents anything for nothing—"

Suddenly, Joseph Resnick appeared at his daughter's side. His face was flushed, and his voice was harsh as he dragged her away from booth number four. "Come away from Mr. Fromberg and Mr. Landau at once."

The fat man named Fromberg held up a hand. "You've got a gutsy kid there, Resnick. She wants to know why Gus and me don't pay, so why don't you tell her?"

Resnick's grip on Pearl eased a fraction, but his voice remained angry. "Mr. Fromberg and Mr. Landau are friends of ours, Pearl."

"Then why don't they ever come upstairs like our other friends do?"

"Little girl . . ." Fromberg leaned forward and pinched Pearl's cheek between thumb and forefinger. "You see this booth with its curtain and its Reserved sign? This is my office. I work in this place, just like your parents do, and Mr. Landau works here as well. When your parents eat something here, they don't pay, do they? So why should we?"

"What work do you do here?" Pearl demanded. She hadn't seen either of them cook or sweep the floor or wash dishes.

Fromberg appeared to find her question funny. Laughing, he replied, "You wouldn't understand what I do, even if I told you, kid." Reaching into his jacket pocket, he pulled out a crumpled paper bag. "Here, take a piece of candy—it might sweeten you up."

"No, thank you," Pearl replied coldly before walking away. Behind, she heard Fromberg's throaty laughter and she knew he was laughing at her. It made her hate him all the more.

Minutes later, Resnick called his daughter into the kitchen, where Sophie was working, "Pearl, never let me hear you speak to Mr. Fromberg or Mr. Landau like you spoke to them just now."

"Don't worry," Pearl burst out, "I don't ever want to speak to either of them again. Especially not *him* . . . he's a fat horrible man and he smells of cigars and fish."

"You mean," Sophie Resnick cut in, "that he smells of our best lox."

The spontaneous remark drew a sharp, reproving glance from Resnick. Pearl noticed the moment of friction and stored it in her memory. It made her feel slightly better to know that her mother didn't like the fat man either.

Pearl was not to be denied one question. "Why don't they pay for what they eat?"

"That's none of your business. Now get back outside and see if anyone needs anything."

Resnick's tone, his continuing anger, frightened Pearl. The incident had made him act like a total stranger. He had never been this furious, not even when she'd run away with Annie; then he had done nothing more than send her to bed early, and the following morning he had laughed about it, told the story again and again to the restaurant's customers.

Annie! . . . Annie was the answer. Annie knew all there was to know about anything and everything. She'd know about the fat man in booth number four, and his cold-eyed companion. Pearl slipped next door to the bakery. Isidore Moscowitz, kneading dough, pointed through the back of the bakery to the flat where Annie's family lived. Pearl went through to find Annie helping her mother with laundry.

"Do you know the two men who always sit in our restaurant, in booth number four?" Pearl asked her friend. "Mr. Fromberg and Mr. Landau?"

Helen Moscowitz looked up from the sink. "Fromberg? Saul

17

Fromberg, the shylock? And Gus Landau, his bodyguard?"

"Shylock? What does that mean?"

"A man who lends money," Annie's mother answered.

"Like a bank?"

"No, darling, not like a bank. Like a thief is more like it. He lends money at rates that God would strike him dead for if there was any justice in this rotten world of ours."

Pearl was confused. "He says that his office is in our restaurant."

"That's right. All those people who come into the restaurant to see him, they all owe him money, or they're borrowing money. Same thing. He owns them, body and soul."

That evening, Pearl followed her mother down to the cavernous basement that ran beneath the restaurant and the shops on either side. While Sophie swept the broad expanse of stone floor, Pearl leaned against a pickle barrel, watching, wondering how to broach the subject without arousing the anger in her mother that her father had shown. Finally, she decided that the only course was to be completely open.

"Is Mr. Fromberg a shylock?"

Sophie Resnick swung around, dropping the broom in surprise. "Where did you ever learn that word?"

"I just heard it," Pearl replied, refusing to implicate Annie or her mother. "Is he? Do we owe him money?"

Sophie walked across the basement and put her arms around Pearl. "Darling, when your father and I came to this country from Hungary, we had no money. We had little but the clothes on our backs."

Pearl was amazed. She had always considered her parents wealthy. They had their own business, a thriving restaurant. "You borrowed money from him, just like those people who come to see him in booth number four?"

"We couldn't go to a bank. Banks are only for rich people. What bank would have lent us a cent when we had nothing to offer in return? We wanted to open the restaurant, we knew we could make it successful, so Papa had to go to Mr. Fromberg."

"And now"—Pearl spoke slowly, heart plummeting as her greatest fear was realized—"he owns us."

"No, darling, he doesn't own us. All Mr. Fromberg owns is a note on the restaurant."

"Still? After all these years?"

"It was a long-term loan."

"Why does he sit in booth number four all the time?"

"That's part of the agreement he made with Papa. Booth number four is kept solely for him, so he can carry on his moneylending business from there."

"His *shylocking* business," Pearl said, preferring that word; it sounded so much more ugly than moneylending, more in keeping with her opinion of the fat man. Moneylending was done by banks, respectable institutions made of marble, stone, and glass. Shylocking was done by people like Saul Fromberg, who smelled of cigars and fish. She remembered the spark that had flashed so briefly between her parents. "And while he and his friend sit there, they eat and drink for nothing. Is that also a part of the agreement he made with Papa?"

Sophie smiled wanly. "So what's a little lox and a bagel? We have the business—that's the important thing."

The lox and the bagel didn't concern Pearl. All that worried her was the hold this man Fromberg had on her parents. Despite her mother's words, aimed at reassuring her, Pearl could not get it out of her mind that Saul Fromberg did own them. All of them. Just like slaves were owned during the Civil War.

While she continued to work at the restaurant during the Christmas break, Pearl obeyed her father's order implicitly. Whenever Saul Fromberg pulled back the drape on booth number four and snapped his fingers, Pearl filled his order while speaking no more than was absolutely necessary. Both Fromberg and Gus Landau took enjoyment from her subdued behavior, knowing why she was so silent. When none of Fromberg's customers was present in the booth, the moneylender and his bodyguard would try to engage Pearl in conversation, playing a game to see if they could break through the wall she'd erected.

"Did your father tell you not to speak to us, little girl?" Fromberg asked as she brought coffee to the booth.

Pearl just set down the cups and started to walk away.

"You can talk to us if we ask you a question," Landau called out. "Your father won't mind that."

Pearl turned around. "I'm busy. Other customers are waiting."

"So let them wait," Landau said. "They're not as important as us."

"No one in this place is as important as we are," Fromberg added. "Just remember that, little girl." He reached out to squeeze Pearl's cheek. She stepped back; his touch was repulsive.

Just before one lunchtime rush, Pearl answered Fromberg's imperious summons once again. In front of the fat man were piles of bills and coins which he was busily counting. "Coffee, and give me a bagel and lox with it," Fromberg grunted.

Pearl stood staring at the money for a few seconds, until Fromberg lifted his eyes to look at her. "Didn't you hear what I said?"

She returned to the counter to prepare his order, all the while thinking about the money in front of him. What did he do to deserve such a fortune? Her parents sweated and slaved, and they didn't make a fraction of what Fromberg must have. There was—she recalled Helen Moscowitz's remarks about Fromberg—absolutely no justice in the world. If you wanted any, you had to create it for yourself.

When she returned to the booth, Fromberg was dividing money into neat piles of different denominations, writing figures in a small, dog-eared notebook. And on the table in front of Landau, half-hidden by a newspaper, Pearl saw the cold, metallic shape of a gun. Quickly, she put the coffee and bagel on the table and turned to go. Fromberg grabbed hold of her arm.

"When do you go back to school, little girl?"

"In another nine days."

"Be glad, will you? Or would you rather stay here and work with your parents?"

"I'll be glad. I like school." She stared at the table, eyes flicking from the money to the ugly snout of the gun that peeped out from beneath Landau's newspaper.

"That's good, school teaches you to be smart." Fromberg took a silver dollar from the table and held it out to Pearl. "You take this for looking after us. If I like the way you keep waiting on us, I'll give you another one before you go back."

Pearl gazed at the coin, uncertain whether to accept.

"Take it," Fromberg pressed. "You earned it with good service."

"Thank you." She dropped the coin into her apron pocket. She knew exactly what she was going to do with the money. Leaving booth number four, she went to the kitchen where her parents were preparing for lunchtime. Sophie Resnick was slicing bread while her husband was melting fat in a wide, deep saucepan. Set out on a tray next to him were potato pancakes ready to be fried.

"Mr. Fromberg just gave me this," Pearl said as she produced the silver dollar.

Resnick looked up from the saucepan full of fat. "A tip?"

Pearl nodded. "That's what he said, for good service. Put it toward what he owes us for all that food he and Mr. Landau eat."

"Who has the time to keep count of what they take?" Sophie asked.

"I do," Pearl answered. "Ever since *that* day, I've taken a note of everything they've eaten."

"He gave you the tip," Sophie told her daughter. "You keep it, spend it on something you want."

"I want to spend it on the restaurant." Pearl stuffed the coin into her mother's pocket and left the kitchen. At least, she'd got a dollar back on all the money Fromberg must have chiseled from her parents. It was only a drop in the ocean, but it was a start.

As the lunchtime crowd filled the restaurant, Pearl thought she could see a way to recover even more of the money. If Fromberg wanted to tip her for good service, she'd give him even better service . . . and better and better until it was coming out of his ears, and then he'd keep on tipping her. Or maybe she could even help herself to some of the money that littered the table of booth number four like so much debris. Would he miss it, a dollar or two each day? Could she find some way to distract him while she took the money?

Suddenly, a man's scream rose high above the hubbub of the crowded restaurant, an agonized bellow of pain that was lost in the thundering crash of metal on concrete. Knives and forks paused in midair, diners turned toward the kitchen from where the scream had come. Pearl raced toward the sounds, colliding with her mother who stood in the kitchen doorway, hands clasped to her mouth in horror. Writhing on the floor by the big stove was Joseph Resnick, arms flailing to beat out the flames which covered the upper half of his body. Next to him, rolling gently on its side, was the heavy saucepan which had held the bubbling fat.

Pearl threw herself on top of her father to smother the flames, beat at them with her bare hands. Resnick's hair was singed to the scalp, his face and clothing badly burned. Eyes that were dilated with agony flickered open and saw nothing. "Go next door!" Pearl screamed at the crowd of customers who had gathered in the doorway. "Go next door and fetch Mrs. Moscowitz! She knows first aid!" Turning back to her father, she tried to lift his head from the hard cement floor. Her efforts were rewarded with a low groan so wracked with pain that she stopped.

Helen Moscowitz came in with Annie and Isidore a minute later. While Isidore held Sophie Resnick, Helen squatted beside the injured man and sponged his face with a cold, damp cloth.

"We have to get him to the hospital, Pearl," Helen said urgently. "How did this happen?"

Sophie answered. "The fat caught fire and splashed on him. He was holding the saucepan . . . everything went up."

Helen looked up at the people jammed in the doorway and selected the two strongest men. "You two, get that board over there! Put Mr. Resnick on it. Gently . . . for God's sake, gently! You!" She pointed a finger at another man who sold secondhand clothing from a pushcart. "Clear those *shmattes* off your cart—we need it!"

Five minutes later, Resnick, covered by blankets, was lying on the

21

cart as it was wheeled toward the hospital. Pearl, her mother, and the Moscowitzes followed, a premature funeral cortège. Behind, they left a restaurant full of unwashed plates, food that was growing cold.

At the hospital, Resnick was lifted from the cart and taken into a treatment room. Pearl had her hands cleaned and bandaged. She and her mother had to wait three hours before they were allowed to see Resnick; and even then a doctor warned that there was little that could be done. The burns were too serious, the shock to his body too severe.

Pearl and Sophie stood by the bed, gazing down at the still figure swathed in bandages. Only the eyes and mouth showed. Slowly, those eyes opened, stared from one woman to the other before finally fixing themselves rigidly on Pearl. Sounds came from the split in the bandages over the mouth. Words, but so slurred, spoken so softly that Pearl could not understand them. Resnick's wrapped hand tugged at Pearl's wrist, dragged her down to the bed so that the mouth was only inches from her ear.

"You are daughter and son to us," the burned man whispered. "It is your . . . your responsibility to take care now . . . take care now of your mother."

"Papa . . ." Pearl's voice broke into a choked sob as she understood the finality of her father's words. He was passing on the mantle of family responsibility to her because he knew that he was dying.

Resnick's grip on her wrist turned into a painful vise. The agony such effort must have cost him squeezed tears from Pearl's eyes. "Don't talk . . . listen. Fromberg . . . gouged us all these years. Your mother . . . protect her from him. . . ."

"You'll be well again, Papa," Pearl declared frantically as tears burned their way down her cheeks. "Don't talk like this."

Weakly, Resnick shook his head. "Do as I tell you. Promise me."

"Papa . . ."

"Promise me."

"I promise, Papa."

The grip on her wrist relaxed. When Pearl looked into the slits in the bandages, she saw her father's eyes drop closed. The wrapped hand fell from her wrist and flopped onto the sheet. Whirling around, Pearl searched for a nurse, a doctor, anyone—but even as she looked, she knew it was too late. Her father was dead, killed by a freak accident, and on his deathbed he had made her promise to care for her mother. Pearl, a twelve-year-old schoolgirl, was now the head of the Resnick family.

*   *   *

Following the funeral, the mirrors in the flat above the kosher restaurant were covered with cloths as Pearl and Sophie Resnick commenced the week-long *shivah*, the ritual mourning period. They sat on low wooden chairs, their dark clothing displaying a rent to signify their bereavement. By the time the rabbi arrived to conduct the evening service, the flat was full with friends, and customers from the restaurant. Helen and Isidore Moscowitz stayed close to Sophie, while Pearl was protectively surrounded by her schoolmates—Annie, and the four boys the girls had caught shooting dice in the janitor's shed.

In the middle of the service, another visitor arrived—Saul Fromberg. Without his bodyguard for once, the shylock pushed his way through the people praying and stood near Sophie. Pearl stared angrily at him. What was he doing in the flat? He certainly wasn't a friend.

The service ended. Gradually, the visitors departed. The four boys from school, acting in a manner that belied their young age, took turns to shake hands with Pearl and Sophie, offering to do anything they could to help. When they left, all that remained were the Moscowitzes and Fromberg. The shylock stood around awkwardly, as if waiting for Annie and her family to leave. When they showed no sign of doing so, Fromberg's patience deserted him. He stood in front of Sophie and, bluntly, asked, "What are you going to do about the restaurant tomorrow?"

"It'll be closed. For a week. I'm in mourning for my husband. What do you expect me to do?"

"Where do I conduct my business?"

Sophie didn't answer, and Fromberg repeated the question. "Where do I conduct my business, Mrs. Resnick?"

Without getting up from her chair, Pearl said, "You'll have to find somewhere else for a week, won't you?"

Fromberg's face turned red, his chins trembled. "My business is run from downstairs, and I'm not about to move my office for a week. That restaurant had better be open when I come in tomorrow morning."

Pearl jumped up from the chair. "Don't you have any feelings at all? My father's just died."

Fromberg glared at her. "I don't need feelings. All I need is this." Like a magician, he plucked a piece of paper from his coat pocket. "This is a note stating what your family owes me. Your father's death doesn't cancel it out. It just means that you inherit it. You know what that means? You default on this note . . . I don't like the way you're running the restaurant . . . anything else that doesn't sit well

23

with me . . . and you're both out on the street. Get it? You and your mother are going to do exactly as I say, just like your father did."

Pearl tried to snatch the piece of paper away from Fromberg. He lifted it out of reach of her bandaged hands. "See you tomorrow, ten-thirty, booth number four. Just like always," he said. Slamming the door behind him, he left.

Pearl stood in the center of the floor, angry and frustrated. Slowly, she turned around to face her mother, forgetting about Annie and her parents. "Just how much money do we still owe him?"

Sophie stared at her daughter the same way she had stared at Fromberg. Her eyes were empty, no emotion showed on her face, her voice was a barely audible whisper. "More than we borrowed to begin with."

"How is that possible?"

"There were times when we couldn't afford to pay the weekly interest, times the restaurant didn't do so well. So the interest was added on to the original loan."

"Those rates I told you about, remember?" Helen Moscowitz said.

"All the years you've been paying him, and now you owe more than you borrowed?" Pearl whispered in disbelief. "How could you have had dealings with such a man? Because of him, we can't even do the right thing by Papa, otherwise we'll be thrown out on the street!"

"Pearl . . ." Annie stepped next to her friend, anxious to smooth out the situation. "You stay up here with your mother. School doesn't start until the *shivah*'s over. I can cook in the restaurant with my mother. We can get other help to wait tables, clean up. You'll see."

Pearl looked at Annie, then to Helen who slowly nodded. Finally, she looked at Annie's father. He gave her a soft smile. "One person can run a bakery," Isidore Moscowitz said.

Pearl felt overcome. Annie and her parents had saved her and Sophie from being thrown out on the street. The Moscowitzes had allowed them to show their respect for Joseph Resnick without having it cost them everything they owned.

She now understood perfectly the meaning of her father's last words, the exhortation to protect her mother, the promise he had made her take. As young as she was, Pearl understood the significance of a promise made to a dying person. She'd keep it. Somehow, some way, she'd keep it, she told herself. No matter what it cost.

When Saul Fromberg entered the restaurant the following morning, with Gus Landau, he made no comment on the absence of Pearl and Sophie. As long as the establishment was open, as long as he could conduct his business from booth number four, he was satisfied; whoever was working did not concern him unduly.

Pearl ventured down in the late afternoon, after watching through the flat window for Fromberg and Landau to leave. When she entered the restaurant, she halted in surprise. Annie and her mother were working in the kitchen, that Pearl knew about already. It was the help in the restaurant that caused her amazement. Behind the varnished counter, wearing one of her father's white aprons, stood Jake Granitz. Pushing a broom across the floor was Lou Levitt. Waiting on tables were Moses Caplan and Benny Minsky.

"What is this?" she asked in bewilderment.

Jake turned to her. "You're one of my father's best customers. You go out of business and he loses a good account."

"And the others? Lou, Moe, Benny?"

Jake nodded toward the street, where snow was falling. "Cold out there. This is the warmest place to be." He moved away to serve a customer. Pearl walked over to Levitt.

"Thanks for coming in, Lou. Thanks for your help."

He smiled, which surprised Pearl. She'd always thought of him as so serious and intense. "I thought it was time I learned about that other kind of pie, the one that made you and Annie laugh so much."

Remembering, Pearl also smiled. In turn, she went to Minsky and Caplan, thanking them. Then she walked into the kitchen. Annie was vigorously scrubbing out a large pot. Her mother was grating vegetables.

"I can't believe it," Pearl said, "the boys being out there."

"They wanted to help," Helen answered. "Annie went to see them last night, after that business with Fromberg."

"I went to Moe," Annie added. "He passed the word around."

Pearl nodded, comprehending. She knew that Annie hankered after Moses Caplan, ever since that day in the janitor's shed when he'd extracted a kiss in return for releasing her.

"How's your mother?" Helen Moscowitz asked.

"Sleeping."

"That's good. She'll need her strength for tonight when the people come again. Why don't you get some rest as well?"

Pearl shook her head. "I don't want to be by myself."

"Then stay down here with us," Annie said. "We won't let you

25

be alone."

Spontaneously, Pearl reached out to hug her friend tightly. Next, she threw her arms around Helen. Then she went outside, into the restaurant, to hug each of the boys in turn. In that moment, she forgot about her father, about the covered mirrors, the tear in her clothing. She felt like the richest person in the world.

Chapter Three

The moment school finished each day, Pearl rushed home to be with her mother, to offer whatever help she could. Her schoolwork suffered but, as always, Annie stood by her. When Pearl failed to complete homework because she was working in the restaurant, Annie offered her own to copy. It did not bother Pearl that Annie's work was poor—she was only concerned with turning in assignments—and the teachers, if they noticed any similarity of errors, never commented on it.

As it was bound to, Pearl's relationship with her friends suffered because she gave them less and less of herself. At first, they tolerated her brusqueness, the way she raced home each day without spending time with them. They understood the reason for such haste. Gradually, that understanding waned. It was Annie who brought up the subject one afternoon as she accompanied Pearl home.

"You can't keep going on like this," Annie complained. "You're working yourself into a breakdown."

Pearl stopped walking, turned to face Annie, and placed her hands on her hips. "You know that promise I made to my father."

"Sure I know it; it's all you ever talk about. Do you really think this is what he wanted from you—for you to wear yourself out like this?"

"It doesn't matter what I think." Pearl started to walk again, and Annie chased after her.

"You're mad, you know that? You made that promise to your father, all right, but a year's passed since then and you're taking it to ridiculous lengths. You don't have any kind of life anymore. When's the last time we did anything together other than walk to and from school or share homework?"

"I've forgotten," Pearl answered truthfully.

"That's right, you have. Because you're so obsessed with this promise."

"Wouldn't you have made the same promise if, God forbid, something had happened to your father and you had a man like Saul

27

Fromberg breathing down your neck?"

"Of course I would have, but I wouldn't take it to these extremes. You don't enjoy anything anymore. You know what you're becoming, Pearl? You're turning into one of those little old women you see all the time in the market, picking at the vegetables, prodding the chickens. Your mother doesn't want that of you, and I'm damned sure your father never meant it to happen when he asked you to make that promise."

"What do you know about what my father meant? Were you there?"

Annie was startled by the belligerence that had rushed into Pearl's voice. "I'm sorry. . . ."

Pearl was not listening. She was walking quicker than ever, soon leaving Annie behind. If Annie did not like the way she was honoring her father's final request . . . well, that was too damned bad!

Pearl left for school early the following morning, purposely avoiding Annie. During classes, the two girls sat next to each other without speaking. When the midmorning break came, Pearl remained alone while Annie talked with the four boys who had helped out in the restaurant during the week of mourning. From time to time, Pearl gazed angrily at the group. She knew that Annie still liked Moses Caplan. Now she had all four boys to herself and she was making the most of it. Little flirt, Pearl thought sourly.

After the break, as Pearl entered the classroom, Levitt approached her. "What's the matter between you and Annie? Yesterday you were the best of friends, and today you're enemies."

"I don't have the time to be the kind of friend Annie wants."

"But you and Annie were always so close. What happened?"

Pearl could swear that Levitt was almost as upset as she was about the rift. Maybe it was because he was younger than Jake, Caplan, and Minsky, but he seemed more sensitive, more easily disturbed. His vulnerability broke down Pearl's defenses. "Lou, everyone's day finishes the moment they leave here, but that's when my day really starts."

Levitt's sympathy disappeared. "You really think that's the case?" he asked. "You think I don't go home and work? You think Annie doesn't help out at home? You think Jake doesn't help his father with the vegetables? You think Benny and Moe put their feet up? We're all in the same boat, Pearl. Yours might be in a little rougher seas right now, but we're all there, pulling on the oars, just like you."

"What do you do—study your figures? And what do Jake, Benny, and Moe do?" Pearl asked before she could stop herself. "Take pennies from the little kids to walk them home?"

Levitt shook his head exasperatedly. "There's no point in talking to you, not the way you're acting now," he said before walking away.

That afternoon, books clutched under her arm, she left school alone, her mood dismal. Head down, she entered a long, narrow alleyway, staring at the cobblestones as she trudged along. Halfway down the alleyway, the sound of footsteps penetrated through her worries. She glanced up to see two teenaged boys walking slowly toward her. Fear gripped Pearl. The Irish boys, those same bullies who occasionally terrorized the younger children at school. Gripping her books more tightly, she turned around, ready to run. Another boy, who had quietly followed her into the alley, stood behind her, blocking escape.

"Let me past!" she snapped. Behind, she could hear the hammering of running feet as the other two boys raced to their friend's assistance. Hands grabbed her, pulled her to the ground. As one of the boys gripped her wrists, she lashed out wildly with her feet. A yell of pain rewarded her effort, then someone sat on her legs, pinning her securely to the ground. Another hand reached out to clamp itself across her mouth. A red, leering face, topped by shaggy blond hair, thrust itself into her vision.

"Don't fight," the boy said. "We only want to look."

For a moment, the hand across her mouth eased its pressure. "Look? Look at what?"

The boy with the red face and blond hair appeared very serious. "We want to see where your rabbi circumcised you. My dad says that your rabbis circumcise girls by cutting off the end of one of their tits."

Pearl closed her eyes. She felt the boy's hands press against her immature breasts. She heard his hurried breathing, hot against her face. And then a new sound intruded. A yell. The weight on her body subsided. She opened her eyes to see the red-faced boy kneeling on the ground beside her, hands clutching the top of his head, his blond hair stained with a patch of crimson. There was another shout, and Pearl saw Jake and Benny Minsky, lengths of wood held in their hands like baseball bats. The other two Irish boys jumped to their feet and started to run down the alleyway as though the devil himself were in pursuit. Slowly, the red-faced boy rose to his feet, watching Minsky carefully as he backed away. Minsky's swarthy face was expressionless as he feinted with the stick, and the Irish boy turned to chase after his friends.

"You all right?" Jake reached down and pulled Pearl to her feet. "Where did you two come from?"

"We saw those three hanging around near the school. We followed them. Lucky for you we did." He bent down to pick up the books she had dropped. "That's what happens when you go home on your own," he added sagely.

"Should I pay you instead, like the small kids do?"

Jake grinned. "I'd walk you home for nothing."

Remembering what she'd said to Lou Levitt earlier, the argument she had caused with Annie, Pearl felt an abrupt flood of guilt. She was turning her back on her friends, and still they refused to disassociate themselves from her. She didn't really deserve such friends. Standing on tiptoe, she kissed Jake on the cheek. "You did me the favor this time."

Jake seemed strangely embarrassed, as if scared that Minsky might make fun of him for allowing himself to be kissed by Pearl. "Why don't you go after those three?" he said to the dark-skinned boy. "Make sure they don't start with anyone else."

Minsky took off down the alleyway, the stick swinging menacingly from his hand. Carrying the books, Jake led the way toward the restaurant. They walked slowly, saying little. Every few seconds, Pearl would turn to look at him, each time noting a different feature—the wavy hair that shifted from brown to molten gold as the sun highlighted it, the humor in his eyes, the long, straight nose, the firm chin with the dimple in the center of it. By the time they reached the restaurant, she decided she was in love with him.

"Come in," she invited. "I'll get you something to eat."

"I've got to get home, give my father a hand. And you've got something to do as well, haven't you?"

"I do?"

"Annie," Jake said. "Don't you think you owe her an apology?" He handed her back the books, kissed her quickly on the cheek, and walked off down the street, turning once to wave. Pearl watched until he reached the end of the block. Light-headed, she entered the restaurant, not even noticing the handwritten Reserved sign on the table of booth number four. Suddenly, Fromberg and his henchman seemed very unimportant.

She stayed in the restaurant for ten minutes, gazing through the front window until she spotted Annie walking by. Rushing out into the street, she blurted, "Annie, I'm sorry about yesterday and today. I didn't mean it, any of it, honestly."

"I know." Annie smiled and hugged Pearl tightly. "Want to come by later on and copy my homework?"

The moment of antagonism was in the past, forgotten. They were the best of friends again.

*   *   *

Jake Granitz left school soon after the incident with the Irish boys, to work with his father in the produce business. Normally, customers came to the market to buy their goods, but Jake made an exception for the Resnicks' restaurant. In the evening, he would go to Second Avenue to take Sophie Resnick's order, and early the following morning—as soon as his father had stocked up for the day—he would deliver it on a pushcart. When Pearl was working at the restaurant during a school break, Jake would always take a little extra time, dallying over a drink and a piece of cake which she never failed to have ready for him.

Soon, Jake turned the restaurant into a regular hangout, coming in after he had finished work. He was usually accompanied by either Benny Minsky or Moses Caplan, both of whom had also left school, Caplan to become an apprentice mechanic, and Minsky to help his father on the pushcart in Essex Street. When Caplan came in, Annie would also join the group. After a while, they took chairs down into the basement, preferring to be away from the bustle of the restaurant.

Pearl could not wait to follow the example of the older boys and leave school. Like Annie, she found schoolwork tedious. Only Lou Levitt seemed to find any enjoyment in remaining at school. And even then, he worked three nights a week for a coat manufacturer, keeping tabs on the pieces that were sent to outworkers to be sewn and finished.

One evening, to Pearl's surprise, Levitt came into the restaurant with the three older boys. It was the first time he had been there since the week of Joseph Resnick's death; one of the few times that Pearl had ever seen him outside of school hours. She sensed that he had not come on the off-chance, brought along by Jake to waste a couple of hours. Levitt didn't believe in aimless wandering—everything he did seemed to be carefully planned. As usual, they all went down to the basement. Once there, Levitt walked around, inspecting every corner. Finally, he reached a heavy wooden door set in the wall.

"Where does this lead?" he asked Pearl.

"Stairs going up to the alleyway behind the restaurant."

"That's where deliveries are made," Jake said.

Levitt nodded, unlocked the door and peeked outside into the dark night. When he turned back, he nodded again, as though he had reached a decision. "How would you like to make some money, Pearl? You and your mother."

"Doing what?"

"Let us use this basement two or three nights a week, put on a dice game down here."

"No one would have to know," Jake added. "Not even that fat slug

31

who sits upstairs and robs you and your mother blind."

Pearl was impressed. The boys weren't frightened of Fromberg. Everyone else was. "What would my mother and I get?"

"You two would be the fifth partner," Levitt answered immediately. "Twenty percent of the take."

"That's a hell of a lot of dough," Minsky grumbled. "We're putting up the money to bankroll the game, we're taking all the chances. All they're giving us is the space."

Levitt allowed Minsky to finish, then, with ice in his voice, he replied, "Without this basement, we don't have a game. Eighty percent of something is a damned sight better than one hundred percent of nothing. Or didn't you learn anything at all at school?"

Minsky clenched his fists, and for a moment Pearl thought that he might strike the smaller boy. Simultaneously, she found the answer to a question she'd asked Annie long before . . . the connection between Levitt and the three older boys. They were big, they had the muscle— but Levitt had the brains. It was obvious that the whole idea of using the basement was his. One of the others must have mentioned how they used the basement as a meeting place, and Levitt had immediately imagined another, profitable use for it. That was his reason for coming tonight, to check it out. Looking at him now, it seemed so difficult for Pearl to believe he was only fourteen and still at school, the same as herself. Until she remembered that she shouldered just as much responsibility as he did. They were both mature for fourteen.

"What do you think your mother'll say?" Jake asked Pearl.

Pearl's mind was already racing far beyond that problem. How much would they make? How much would her twenty percent amount to? And how long would it take to put by enough money to pay off Fromberg? At last, she could see the faintest light at the end of the long, dark tunnel that signified their bondage to the shylock. "Don't worry about my mother. I'll speak to her."

"We still have not decided on Pearl's share," Levitt reminded the other boys. "Do we take a fifth partner, or not?"

"I'm with you," Jake answered. "Twenty percent of the take goes for the use of the basement."

Caplan nodded his agreement, leaving the dark-skinned Minsky as the only dissenter. "Well, Benny?" Levitt asked.

Minsky looked around, saw how outvoted he was. "I guess so."

"Good." Levitt opened the back door again and walked up the stairs to the alleyway. When he returned, he said, "We'll put a light out there. We don't want our customers falling down and breaking their necks before we have a chance to break their banks."

Only Jake laughed at the joke, but he had a far closer relationship with the little Pole than either Minsky or Caplan. It was Jake who had introduced Levitt into their circle, after he'd first encountered the younger boy. Levitt had been at the school for less than a year, and spoke English poorly, when Jake had offered to walk him home in return for money. Dressed in ill-fitting blue knickers and scuffed black boots, and weighed down by a heavy satchel, Levitt had tilted his head to look Jake squarely in the eye and snap back with some of the English he had learned.

"Fuck you!" He punctuated the words by launching himself at Jake, lashing out with such wild fury that the bigger, older boy had been forced to retreat. Eventually Jake had held him at arm's length, laughing, uncertain whether to hit Levitt or applaud his gutsiness.

"Okay. I'll give you a special deal because you're such a spunky kid. You can have my protection for nothing."

Levitt had looked at Jake and sneered. "You know where you can stick your protection, don't you?" he'd shouted in Yiddish, his English vocabulary nowhere near adequate enough to allow him to fully vent his anger. "Up your ass! I don't need no big, stupid *golem* like you to stand up for me!" Without warning, he swung the heavy satchel hard into Jake's stomach. Jake doubled over as the breath was slammed out of him. He saw the scuffed boot arcing toward his chin just in time to jump back. Levitt carried through with the kick, overbalanced; and Jake whipped out his own foot. The smaller boy toppled over and sprawled on the ground. Jake pounced on him, hands around his throat.

"Okay, bigshot, what have you got to say for yourself now?"

Levitt said nothing. He just spit into Jake's face. For an instant, Jake's fingers tightened around Levitt's throat. Those blue eyes began to bulge, but the blazing defiance never faded. Jake relaxed. Grinning, he pulled the younger boy to his feet. "You're all right, midget."

Levitt acknowledged the compliment with a sour expression before dusting himself down. Watching, Jake admitted to himself that Levitt was, pound for pound, the hardest kid he'd ever met. He was just as tough as Benny Minsky or Moses Caplan; tougher, probably, because he had brains to go with his guts. He didn't want any part of the protection racket at school, describing it as fit only for people without the intelligence or imagination to do any better. The only way to get on, he kept repeating, was to receive enough of an education so you knew more than anyone else. It was not an attitude that endeared him to Minsky, who had habitually finished at the bottom of his class.

When Jake had mentioned that he, Minsky, and Caplan were spending time in the restaurant, Levitt hadn't been in the least interested; such social time-wasting didn't appeal to him. Only when he learned of the basement did his curiosity rise. With the older boys providing security, Levitt had organized dice games before, using a deserted alley or an empty warehouse. Mention of the Resnick basement had sparked his interest. Now that he had seen it for himself, he knew it would be perfect.

"Will there be any trouble with the police?" Pearl asked in a moment of doubt. Despite the much-needed money, she didn't want problems from that direction.

Levitt shook his head. "We buy off the police. That comes out of our overheads."

When the boys left, Pearl confronted her mother. "Jake's going to give us twenty percent of his profits from a dice game if we let him use the basement." She didn't know why she'd used Jake's name, when it was so obvious that Levitt was in charge. Perhaps it was because her mother knew Jake so well, from his deliveries to the restaurant.

"A dice game? Surely that's illegal."

"Of course it is. But is it any worse than what Saul Fromberg does in the restaurant? And he"—she prepared to play her trump card—"won't get a single penny of it. We'll keep it all to ourselves."

Sophie Resnick remained unconvinced. She knew that her daughter was becoming a greater influence on the day-to-day operation of the restaurant, but this suggestion was far removed from that. "I don't know, Pearl. Breaking the law like this . . . I don't think we should let Jake go ahead with it."

"Why not? It's the only way we're ever going to get out of slavery to Fromberg."

Sophie shook her head. "Your father would never have approved."

"It was my father who put us into slavery in the first place. With you!" Pearl's mouth dropped as she realized what she'd said. Sophie stared at her incredulously, stunned by the anger in her daughter's words. It was the first time Pearl had ever raised her voice to either of her parents. Belatedly, Sophie recognized the fire and determination her daughter possessed.

Sophie's expression of shock and pain burned through Pearl like a blazing sword. She'd hurt her mother, the very last thing she'd intended to do. "I'll tell the boys," Pearl said, "that they'll have to find somewhere else."

"No, darling." Sophie's back became straighter; her expression was now composed. Belief in her daughter's dramatic course of action flowed through her. They had bent enough. Pearl was right—it was time to fight fire with fire. "Tell your friends they can use the basement. We'll make enough money to pay Fromberg off and get him

34

out of our lives forever."

Two days later, Moses Caplan rigged an outside light over the rear
door to the basement, and a week after that the four boys held their
first game. It started at nine o'clock and went through to midnight,
with the customers—apprised of the game by word of mouth—
announcing their arrival with a special code: two knocks on the door,
then one, then two. By nine-fifteen, the game was in full swing. One
corner of the vast basement was crowded. Smoke and a low buzz of
conversation filled the air as Lou Levitt ran the house operation,
working with a pile of bills, the origin of which Pearl did not even want
to guess. She watched avidly for half an hour, eyes flicking from the
parade of strange faces to the money on the floor. She tried to count
and gave up, bewitched and bemused by the speed with which Levitt
collected, paid out, collected again. He seemed like some fairy-tale
dwarf as he scrambled about on his knees, money flying this way and
that, amid a rattle of calls and orders which she didn't understand. All
she comprehended was that with each throw of the dice, Levitt's pile
changed, grew bigger, smaller, then bigger than before. She wondered
how much he'd won, how much her own twenty percent would be. He
had to win. The possibility of the house losing never entered her
mind. She just wanted to know whether her cut would be enough to
pay off Fromberg. She even thought of a name for the money. She'd
call it the Fromberg fund.

Tired of looking at Levitt, she walked around the basement. Benny
Minsky and Moses Caplan were at the door, listening for the coded
knock, checking out the new visitors. Jake was walking around, hands
clasped behind his back like the manager of the establishment.

"Is Lou winning?" she whispered.

"We're all winning," Jake answered with a quick grin. "The house
always wins, it's one of the rules." He pulled her away from the crowd
around the dice and the noise lessened. "You want to make some more
money for yourself?"

"How?"

"See if anyone wants refreshments."

"It's closed upstairs."

"Just coffee, cake, sandwiches. These people'll tip well."

Pearl went among the players. Orders were barked at her in gruff
tones by men whose attention was glued to the dice. She ran upstairs,
slipped into an apron, put on a large pot of coffee and began cutting
bread, slicing corned beef and brisket, setting out crockery.

When the coffee was ready, Jake came up. "Need some help?"

35

"Either that or another pair of hands," Pearl answered, looking at the two loaded trays. "Are gamblers always so hungry?"

Jake shrugged. "I'll tell you one thing—they aren't used to getting this type of service. Maybe you'll become fashionable. Just in case the others don't thank you . . ." Cupping her chin in his hands, he lifted her face and kissed her gently on the lips. "That's for letting us use the place."

Pearl felt she had to say something, but she wasn't sure what. "You're paying for the use of it."

"Then call this a bonus." He kissed her again, grinning when he saw the blush that spread across her face.

Pearl tried to remember how she'd felt that first time he'd kissed her, the quick brush of his lips across her own after they'd left the janitor's shed. More startled than anything else. This was different. Already excited by the game in the basement, Pearl felt lifted by Jake's kisses. Tender as they were, they sent a thrill right through her, making her stomach tremble, her legs weak. She wanted him to kiss her like that again, willed him to. His face came close to hers again, then the door leading from the basement slammed back.

"Where the hell's that coffee?" a man's voice yelled. The door slammed again, footsteps rattled down the stairs, and Jake let go of Pearl.

"You want tips, you'd better see to your customers," he said.

Pearl returned to the basement. Hands full of cups and plates, she went among the gamblers, remembering exactly who had ordered what. As she passed out food and drink, coins and paper money were returned, depending on the luck of each individual. Finished, she returned upstairs to the kitchen and added it up; the total came to seventeen dollars and thirty-five cents, which she earmarked immediately for the Fromberg fund.

At precisely midnight, the last gambler passed through the basement door. Moses Caplan slammed on the bolt, then they crowded around Levitt, who was kneeling in the center of the floor, pulling money from every pocket.

"We started the night with five hundred dollars," he said, checking a sheet of white, lined paper. "We finish up with"—he counted quickly, sorting the money into neat piles—"a grand total of eight hundred and fifty-two dollars. Take off twenty for the cops, that leaves us with a profit on the night of three hundred and thirty-two dollars. Split five ways"—he began to hand out the money—"that comes to sixty-six forty apiece." Pearl's cut was the last. He handed it to her and said, "We'll be here again this Saturday night. Thanks."

Pearl folded the money and dropped it into her apron pocket.

"Put a few chairs in here, maybe a couple of tables, and you could

36

urn this into a classy place," Levitt said. "Attract a richer type of sucker. Think about it." Waving a hand at Pearl, he ran up the stairs to the restaurant and went out the front door. A minute later, Minsky and Caplan followed, leaving Pearl alone with Jake.

"I'll help you with the cups and plates," Jake offered.

"That's okay, they won't take five minutes. Lou seems very confident about this game, like it's going to continue for quite a while."

"It will. It's managed properly. We pay off the cops, we don't get trouble."

"Where? . . ." She wondered whether she should be asking such a question. "Where did he get all that money to begin with?"

"It's ours, belongs to all of us. Lou's our banker."

He'd answered a question she hadn't asked, and Pearl let him get away with it. What he didn't want to tell her was his own business. She followed him up the stairs, through the restaurant to the door. As she held it open, he kissed her again. "Another bonus. See you early in the morning for your order."

"Coffee'll be waiting."

Standing in the doorway, she watched him walk toward Houston Street. When he was out of sight, she locked the door and stood with her back against it, gazing at the darkened restaurant. Sixty-six dollars and forty cents for the Fromberg fund. A few months like this and they would have paid off the shylock. She was so excited that she forgot all about the dirty crockery in the basement. She ran upstairs to the flat, woke her mother and thrust the money at her.

"This is what you give to Fromberg tomorrow! And this!" she added, remembering the other seventeen dollars and change she'd made from the tips. "We're going to be rid of him, Mama. Rid of him forever!"

Sophie gazed sleepily at the money, unable to believe that Pearl could be holding so much. Life began to sparkle in her eyes as she anticipated the following morning, when she handed it to Fromberg and proudly told him to put it against the principal of the loan. "Are Jake and his friends going to do it again?"

"This Saturday." Pearl sat down on the edge of her mother's bed. "And two or three times a week until we're all paid off. And then we can take that damned Reserved sign off booth number four and tear it into little pieces."

For the first time since just before her father had the accident that killed him, Pearl saw her mother smile.

For the next game, Pearl asked Annie Moscowitz to help her with

37

the refreshments, promising the red-haired girl twenty percent of the tips. Annie, needing money for a new dress, readily agreed; and Pearl was proud of the way she'd learned to negotiate from Lou Levitt.

Pearl's only regret was that she hadn't witnessed her mother handing over the money to Saul Fromberg, proudly telling him it was payment on the principal they owed. Sophie Resnick had described the scene for her daughter, though, the expression of amazement on the fat shylock's face, the grudging manner in which he'd written out a receipt for the money. Too bad, Pearl couldn't help thinking, that her father wasn't alive to see it. But somehow, she felt certain, he knew about it. He knew she was keeping her promise, even if it was in a manner he might never have envisaged.

The crowd for the second game was even larger, as news of the game had spread quickly. The coded knock on the rear door was like a machine gun, repeated, so it seemed to Pearl, every few seconds. Twice as many people crammed into the basement and Pearl wondered if she and Annie had prepared enough food. If the boys' game kept growing at this rate, it might be advisable to keep the restaurant open, let them play upstairs. What was it Levitt had said about putting in some tables and chairs, making it a really classy operation? Aspirations of grandeur began to flow through her mind as she watched the money being bet, the dice being rolled, and Levitt adding to his bankroll. Their bankroll!

When the game closed, Levitt quickly counted the winnings, took off the twenty dollars for police protection, and declared: "Four hundred and eighty dollars. Ninety-six bucks apiece. Everybody satisfied?"

Pearl looked at her share, added it to the thirty-three dollars that had been given to herself and Annie as tips. It seemed unfair that Annie would only collect less than seven dollars, so Pearl handed her half the tip money.

"When's the next game?" Pearl asked as the boys prepared to leave.

"Anxious?" Levitt asked, and laughed. "We'll let you know. Probably in three or four days."

Pearl nodded contentedly. More money for the Fromberg fund. Then she went upstairs to wake her mother and tell her of that night's takings.

The game continued, one or two nights a week, with Pearl and Annie going to school the following morning stifling yawns. Levitt never seemed to be affected by the late nights. He was just as sharp in

38

class as ever, running away with first place in any examinations. Pearl often wondered how he did it, until she remembered that, unlike herself and Annie, Levitt actually enjoyed school.

During class, there was never any mention of the game. Levitt acted as though he were two distinct people—the ambitious student by day, and by night the equally ambitious manager of a crap game. Pearl envied his ability to separate his life into such clear sections.

After a month, the Resnicks having repaid more than five hundred dollars to Saul Fromberg, disaster struck the crap game. The end came without warning one Sunday night. The basement was crowded. The boys, wearing suits they'd bought from their share of the take, were working their customary spots—Levitt handling the bets, Minsky and Caplan at the door, Jake walking around with his hands clasped behind his back in his best casino-manager manner. And Pearl and Annie were running up and down to the kitchen, filling orders. At eleven-thirty, as the night's losers started to realize they weren't going to stage a comeback, and those more fortunate wanted to push their streaks even further, the coded knock came again.

"Fresh blood," Moses Caplan murmured, and unlocked the door.

It burst from his hands like a live thing, knocking him off his feet. Four masked men charged through the opening. Three were holding guns, the other was wielding an iron bar.

A tremendous crash echoed through the basement as Annie dropped the tray of crockery she was holding. A scream of fear started from her throat, then died in a strangled gasp as the man with the iron bar swung around to glare at her.

"All your money, in here!" The man with the iron bar held out a paper bag to the closest players. "Make it quick, we haven't got all night."

Less than two minutes after smashing their way into the basement, the four men left. No one moved as the door slammed closed behind the raiding party. Another minute passed before the shock wore off, then they all turned on Levitt, whose own pockets were hanging out after he had turned over more than eight hundred dollars.

"You told us there was protection!" yelled one man as he advanced menacingly on the fourteen-year-old Polish boy. "Some protection. I just gave those guys more than fifty bucks."

"You never had fifty bucks to your name!" Levitt snapped back. His blue eyes were on fire, and for a moment Pearl thought he was going to attack the man who claimed to have lost fifty dollars. But Jake was there first, an arm around the man's neck, pulling him away from Levitt, whispering in his ear for him to calm down.

Levitt clapped his hands, the sound like gunshots over the hubbub

39

in the basement. "The game's closed! Go home!"

"You're damned right it's closed," someone muttered. "Next time I take my business where there is protection." An exodus began. In the basement, only the organizers remained, staring at each other with expressions of sorrow and anger.

"Take this, Lou." Pearl pulled out the money she'd been given for the food. It amounted to more than forty dollars, her best night yet. The four men who'd broken in hadn't bothered her or Annie; they'd only been interested in the men.

"You keep it," Levitt said. "You and Annie earned it."

Caplan came over to Annie and put an arm around her waist. "Next time we go out together, you'll have to pay," he said, attempting to make light of the robbery.

"Any ideas who those guys were?" Jake asked the group.

Levitt shook his head, stuffed his pockets back into his trousers. "What good would it do us if we knew? They had guns."

"So would we if you'd listened to me," Benny Minsky cut in. "I said we couldn't run this game for long if we couldn't back ourselves up."

"Guns are for fools," Levitt answered. "You want to play with guns, go join the army."

"Those guys didn't look so foolish just now, did they? A gun carries a lot more weight than all your genius brainwork."

Pearl shivered at Minsky's words. Had they actually discussed bringing guns into the basement? Had they argued among themselves over whether they should be armed, Minsky for and Levitt against? And what about Jake and Caplan? Where did they stand on the issue?

"The whole point is academic now," Levitt told Minsky, ending the argument as far as he was concerned. "All that matters is that we're out eight hundred bucks on the night, and the game's finished. No one's going to play with us again once word gets around." He turned to Pearl. The anger left his eyes, replaced by a gentleness she'd never seen before. "Pearl, I'm sorry about this. We know how much you needed the money. Maybe we'll be able to find some other way."

For an instant, Pearl could believe that Levitt had organized the game just for her benefit. It prompted in her a tremendous feeling of warmth and gratitude for her classmate, emotions she normally reserved for Jake.

Saul Fromberg and Gus Landau came into the restaurant the following morning half an hour earlier than their usual time. Immediately, Fromberg called Pearl over to the booth, told her to sit down and draw the curtain. Rather than sit next to the moneylender, she sat opposite, next to Landau.

"You take me for being deaf, dumb, blind, and stupid, little girl?" Fromberg hissed. "Your mother suddenly starts handing me bundles of money to pay off the principal, and you don't expect me to wonder where it all comes from?"

Pearl gasped. "Those were your men last night?"

"Of course they were my men. I hear about this big new game your pals are running, and I find I don't have a piece of it. That's not polite, so I take it all."

Pearl felt Gus Landau's thigh press against her own and she edged away. "That was me with the iron bar. Didn't recognize me, eh?"

Pearl glanced sideways and questioned how two pairs of blue eyes—Levitt's and Landau's—could be so different. Landau's eyes could never display the warmth that Levitt's had shown last night, she'd bet on that. She looked at Fromberg again, caught the smell of stale smoke and fish that his cologne failed to disguise. His face loomed large in her vision. She could see every pore of his skin, the hairs that grew out of his nose, the tufts that sprouted obscenely from his ears. Her self-control snapped in two. "How dare you! How dare you come uninvited into our basement and assault our guests?"

The outburst shocked Fromberg, but only for a second. Then he started to laugh. "Your guests, you call them? You invite guests to dinner, you don't clean them out like that little worm Lou Levitt does. I know all about him, the other games he's operated."

"What about that money we've given you?" She felt Landau's thigh press against hers again, and she moved right to the end of the seat.

"What about it?"

"That comes off what we owe you."

"*Half* of it comes off what you and your mother owe me. The other half I was entitled to as my cut of the game. And now none of it's going to count, you know why? Because you never asked my permission."

A third time Pearl felt the pressure of Landau's leg. She stood up, started to pull back the drape, and then swung around to slap Fromberg's bodyguard across the face. She didn't care anymore; what more could they do to her, what other humiliation could they create?

The imprint of Pearl's hand glowed instantly on Landau's cheek. His own hand flashed through the air, reaching out for her wrist, but Fromberg knocked it down, growled a warning at him. Smarting from the slap and the indignation, Landau watched Pearl walk away. She went straight to the kitchen where her mother was preparing the lunch menu. "All that money we gave him! And none of it counts! It was him last night, he sent those men!"

41

"I know."

"How did you know?"

"It had to be him," was all Sophie said in reply. She'd learned long ago that you couldn't win against men like Saul Fromberg. The Frombergs of the world were part of the system, the predators, and the Resnicks were another part, those preyed upon. Pearl hadn't learned that yet. Her fire and determination blinded her to it. But she'd learn soon enough. Sophie just hoped that the lesson wouldn't be too painful.

Chapter Four

At the end of 1921, as soon as she turned sixteen, Pearl left school and began working full-time. She took over the cooking, allowing Sophie Resnick to stand at the counter where she could oversee the operation of the restaurant. Working permanently in the kitchen suited Pearl. In the restaurant, she would have to encounter Fromberg, but back among the pots and pans full of nose-tickling, savory smells—she'd learned well from her mother—she could insulate herself from him.

As Pearl had grown older, the resemblance between mother and daughter became uncanny. Although Sophie's shoulder-length auburn hair now showed generous streaks of gray, both women had delicate builds, heart-shaped faces, and light brown eyes. Once Pearl had seen a photograph of her mother and Joseph Resnick, taken shortly after the couple had arrived in the United States. Looking at it, Pearl could have sworn she was staring into a mirror, so acute was the likeness. Except for one thing. Sophie Resnick's wide-spaced, gentle eyes reflected a sadness that never seemed to depart. Even when Pearl remembered her mother laughing, that trace of sadness had been present in her eyes, perhaps in some sixth-sense anticipation of the tragedy that was to come. Pearl knew that her own eyes were much more animated, more capable of showing fire. When she was angry or upset, they blazed with a light that turned them almost amber.

Sometimes, Pearl thought she understood her mother's attitude toward life. There had always been someone with her, another person to make the difficult decisions. The third daughter of a stonemason in Hungary, Sophie had married Joseph Resnick when she was just seventeen. It had been his decision to come to America, his decision to open the restaurant, and, ultimately, his decision to seek the money necessary to do so from Saul Fromberg. Over the years, she had become accustomed to such an existence, and after Resnick's death she had automatically accepted Fromberg as the dominant personality. The brief hope Pearl had given her with the boys' dice game in the basement had been dimmed by a certain knowledge that it couldn't really work. It wasn't meant to work. Making enough money to pay Fromberg back would upset the natural balance of things.

Sophie was not the only disappointment in Pearl's life at that time. The four boys who had organized the aborted dice game had stopped using the restaurant as a meeting place once they'd learned who had been behind the raid. When they'd so confidently organized the game, Pearl had been certain that they weren't afraid of Fromberg. She was wrong. They were just as terrified of the moneylender as everyone else seemed to be. She heard of Moses Caplan only through Annie, who went out with him once a week. A few times in the six months since she'd left school, Pearl had seen Caplan walk quickly past the restaurant on his way to see Annie. When he'd noticed Pearl, he'd waved hastily and hurried on. Lou Levitt, who had also left school, and Benny Minsky, Pearl didn't see at all. Only Jake, who came in every evening for the order, and made the delivery the following morning, never spending more time than was absolutely necessary. His manner was subdued, his former confidence, his light-hearted charm, had disappeared. Pearl could swear that he even looked about nervously before he entered the restaurant, just in case Fromberg was present. He didn't even stop for coffee anymore. Was she the only one who was unafraid of the moneylender? The only one who hated him with enough passion to banish fear?

She waited in the basement early one morning until she heard the sound of Jake's truck in the alleyway. As his feet clattered down the stairs, she opened the door. Straining under a sack of vegetables, Jake walked in.

"Coffee's fresh if you want some. And the bagels are hot, Annie's father just brought them in." She saw Jake hesitate, and she added, "Only the regular breakfast crowd's up there, Jake. It's safe for you to come up."

He dumped the sack on the floor and dusted his hands. "You trying to be funny, Pearl?"

"No. I just wonder why you don't stop by for coffee anymore, that's all. I miss you."

"Why do you think?"

"You are frightened of him, aren't you?"

"Hey, I don't need little Lou's mighty brain to tell me not to get into a cage with a mean-tempered lion, Pearl. I've got enough sense of my own to avoid doing that."

"No one's asking you to get into a cage with a lion, Jake. I just thought you and I were friends. All I ever see of you these days is hello, here's your order, thank you very much and goodbye. Friends don't act that way toward each other."

Jake spread his hands and gave her a disarming smile. "Business is brisk, what else can I say? I can't spare the time. What if I stopped off at every customer for—"

"No, Jake, that's not the reason and you know it. You're scared out of your wits that you might bump into him, aren't you?"

"Pearl, I don't want to talk about it now. I've got other deliveries to make."

"Then let's talk about it some other time. I can take an evening off. My mother can handle the kitchen."

"Are you asking me out?"

"Yes, I suppose I am," Pearl answered without giving it some thought.

"I always heard the man asked the woman."

"If I waited for you, Jake Granitz, I'd be an old woman."

"Dinner?" Jake offered.

"I see enough of restaurants. Pick me up at eight-thirty. We'll go for a ride in your truck. Now . . ." She became businesslike. "How much do I owe you?"

At promptly eight-thirty, Jake pulled the small, canvas-covered truck to a halt outside the restaurant. Pearl was waiting. She climbed in and Jake drove north, toward midtown. He was dressed up, wearing a double-breasted pinstripe suit, a striped shirt and a bright red tie. A white silk handkerchief peeked out from his breast pocket. Pearl asked where they were going, and he winked at her.

"You said you wanted to go for a ride. Okay, I'm giving you one." That was all he'd say for a few blocks as the truck rumbled along Second Avenue. As they neared Fourteenth Street, he nodded to the right. "See that place?"

Pearl looked uncertainly at a row of shops, all closed for the night.

"No, not the shops," Jake told her impatiently. "Where that light is." She looked again. Sandwiched between a hardware shop and a butcher's was a narrow doorway with a blue light over it. "That's the Bluebird," Jake said. "A speakeasy. Fromberg owns a piece of it."

Pearl stared as the truck rolled past. It seemed just like a door to her, innocent, innocuous; but even as she watched, it opened and two men came out into the night. Jake started speaking again. "This isn't going to be just a ride, Pearl. It's going to be an education. By the time we're finished, you'll know exactly why we're all running scared of that fat pig." He swung the truck onto Fourteenth Street, pointed to a restaurant. "There's a good-sized club below that place. Charlie's, it's called. Fromberg's got a piece of that one as well."

"All right, Jake, you've proved your point. There's no need to take me on the complete guided tour."

"You had to see for yourself, Pearl. You seem to think that Fromberg's just a fat, greasy shylock, and you're wondering why we steer clear of him. He's more than that. Since Prohibition came in, he's been laying money around this town like it's going out of style—"

"Our money," Pearl interrupted.

"Your money . . . the money he takes from you, the eight hundred bucks he stole off the rest of us that night. And a whole pile more besides. He's been buying his way into the liquor business. He's like some damned emperor now. Best thing to do is stay out of his way."

"It makes you wonder," Pearl said slowly, "why he even bothers with something as small as the restaurant."

Jake laughed. "Maybe he's just a big, sentimental softie at heart, the kind of guy who frames the first dime he ever made, so he can look at it and remember his humble beginnings."

"That's not the truth, and you know it. He's too cheap to part with even a cent."

Jake nodded. "Sure, he figures that if he doesn't look after the pennies, pretty soon the dollars'll be taking a hike." He shifted the truck into gear and moved off. Pearl asked where they were going. "You think I got all dressed up like this just to take you for a ride?" Jake responded. "We're going dancing."

"Dancing?" Pearl had never gone dancing in her life. She knew that Annie went with Moses Caplan, but she'd never had the time to go herself. Besides, no one had ever asked her. She wasn't even sure she knew how to dance. "Where?"

"You'll see." Jake turned north on Broadway and pressed his foot to the floor to pass a rattling streetcar. Pearl gazed avidly out of the window. They passed the Flatiron Building. Far ahead, gleaming like a mirage, Pearl saw the garish lights of Broadway proper, Times Square. The truck crossed over streetcar tracks, its rigid suspension jarring her in the seat. She barely felt the discomfort for her eyes remained fixed on the lights which were growing larger, more discernible. A massive sign for Wrigley's gum, a block long, or so it seemed to Pearl; on either side of the sign, three marionettes performed a manual of arms before throwing her a smart salute. Opposite, the White Rock maiden. And right ahead, in the short block that was Forty-seventh Street between Broadway and Seventh Avenue, a bright sign exhorted Pearl to use Squibb's dental cream. Instinctively, she ran the tip of her tongue across her teeth to check how well she'd brushed them before leaving home.

She bounced in the seat again as Jake drove the truck over the jumble of tracks where the Broadway and Seventh Avenue streetcars crossed. He went one block further north, before turning into Forty-eighth Street and stopping. As he helped Pearl from the truck, she stared in fascination at the group of people who paraded, in evening dress, in front of the tiny Belmont Theater while they waited for the next act to begin. Those people hadn't come by truck, she'd wager the restaurant on that. They'd come by taxi or limousine, and when they left the theater they wouldn't go home to sleep in a tiny flat.

"I don't want to go dancing, Jake," she suddenly decided. "I just want to walk around. I'm seeing things for the first time."

"Suit yourself." Jake took hold of her hand and they strolled back toward Broadway. Pearl stared at theater boards, peered into shop windows, and enjoying being caught up in the rush of pedestrians, listened excitedly to the clamor of streetcars, the horns of speeding automobiles.

"How often do you come up here, Jake?"

"Whenever I want to get away from down there."

"Who do you come with?"

"Sometimes Lou or Benny. Most times by myself, to walk around like you want to do. I want to keep reminding myself that there is more to life than there is where we live now. More to it than getting up at four-thirty each morning to help my father with the market—"

"Or work in a kitchen."

"Look at these people," Jake said as they passed a crowd outside the Gaiety. "You think they get out of bed when we do? You think they work as hard as we do? A bunch of fat cats living in luxury. They don't have to worry about where the next buck's coming from." He stopped walking and turned around to look back at the theatergoers. "I want to be like them. Damn it, I'm going to be like them."

"Was that the idea of the dice game?" Pearl asked.

"Sure it was. Any way to rake in money's okay. Or do you have principles that won't let you cut a few corners here and there? There's principles and there's principles," he added philosophically, before Pearl could comment. "Someone robs you, that's stealing. But if you rob a man like Fromberg, that's justice."

"Let's not talk about him," Pearl said. She removed Jake's hand from her own and guided his arm around her waist. There, that was better, her head resting against his shoulder as they walked along. It was almost like the time he'd walked her home after rescuing her from the Irish boys. That was the afternoon when she thought she'd fallen in love with him. She gazed at his profile, silhouetted against

47

the Wrigley's sign. He'd put on weight since that day, filled out. All except his face, which somehow seemed thinner, more ascetic. The dimple she'd noticed so long ago had enlarged, lengthened until it resembled a vertical gash in the center of his chin.

On Forty-second Street they passed a clock, and Pearl noticed that it was almost eleven. "You'd better take me home, Jake. Morning comes early for both of us."

Back on Second Avenue, he parked in front of the darkened restaurant, turned off the engine. Pearl was loath to leave him. Despite the bumpy ride, the inside of the truck—the hard seat, the canvas roof flapping over her head—suddenly seemed so comfortable, so much more secure than her own bed would feel. She was tired, but she felt she could quite happily fall asleep in the truck; as long as Jake was beside her.

"Are you going or staying?" Jake asked after she'd remained perfectly still for almost a minute.

Turning, she held out her hands. She'd learned more about him in this single evening than she had ever known before. He wanted desperately to get away from the old neighborhood—who didn't? But they were all tied to it, by family, by jobs, necessity. Jake would make it, though, Pearl was certain. He had the drive and ambition to carry him far from his father's produce business. Lou Levitt, too; the Lower East Side would never be able to restrict him. And what about the others? Moses Caplan and Benny Minsky? She didn't know them well enough to predict, but if they were linked with Jake, then they, also, would find a way out. Caplan would take Annie with him. And Jake? . . . Maybe . . . just maybe he'd take Pearl.

They kissed, a long, passionate meeting that swelled Pearl's heart and left her weak. She felt Jake's hands slide down her back until they rested on the curve of her buttocks. Her own hands dug into his neck, pressed his face harder to her. She closed her eyes, allowed her senses to be her sight. Jake's mouth was open, the tip of his tongue darting out. At first, her teeth blocked him. The illuminated advertisement for Squibb's dental cream flashed before her eyes. Did Jake's tongue find her teeth as smooth and clean as she had found them? She opened them to allow him inside, clamped gently to hold him there. It was a new sensation, strange at first, then just as natural as having his arms around her. She felt a warmth grow inside of her, spread through her limbs until her entire body seemed to be on fire. She didn't want to stop. She wanted the kiss to last forever, wanted to stay for all eternity in this truck with Jake.

It was he who broke the embrace. "What's wrong?" Pearl asked.

He nodded toward the sidewalk. Pearl looked. The front window of the flat above the restaurant was ablaze with light. A shadow passed across it. Her mother was still up? Waiting for Pearl because she was worried about the date with Jake?

"I'd better go," Pearl said breathlessly. She kissed him again, not with their earlier passion, just a quick touch of the lips. Jake watched until she was inside the building before driving away.

Pearl ran up the stairs, into the front room. Sophie Resnick stood in front of a mirror, holding a pale blue dress in front of her. On the chair next to her were two other dresses, one green, the other dark blue. Pearl recognized the dresses as having been purchased before her father had died. For the past five years, they'd sat in the closet, forgotten. Now Sophie had brought them out. Why?

"Have a nice time, darling?" Sophie greeted her daughter. There was a sparkle in her eyes that, like the dresses, Pearl hadn't seen for a long time.

"We walked around Broadway, that was all." She watched as her mother set down the light blue dress, exchanged it for the green one, then tried on the dark blue one.

"Which do you think is best, Pearl?"

"You'll look lovely in all of them," Pearl answered, still puzzled. "Why have you brought them out?"

There was an edge of triumph in Sophie's voice as she replied. "You're not the only one who gets asked out, you know. I have an admirer, too."

Pearl was delighted. "That's wonderful, Mama!" she exclaimed, truly happy. "Who is this man? Do I know him?"

"He came by the restaurant shortly after you left with Jake, asked me out for dinner tomorrow night, and then we're going to see some show or other at the Hippodrome. You'll have to look after the restaurant. I'll be busy."

"I'll take care of everything, Mama. You just have a good time. But you haven't told me who this man is. Do I know him?"

"Of course you know him. It's Saul, darling."

"Saul?" Pearl repeated uncertainly.

"That's right. Saul Fromberg. Imagine that, him asking me out."

Pearl's euphoria at her mother's good fortune was dashed. "You can't be serious. You can't possibly go out with *him*."

Sophie stiffened. "And why not, young lady?"

"Because . . ." Words dried up in Pearl's throat. How could she possibly explain what her mother must know already? "How can you ignore what he's done to us all these years? How he behaved on the night Papa was buried? Don't you remember? He threatened to throw us out on the street if the restaurant wasn't open the next day."

"That's just his manner of speaking. Sometimes he's a little demanding, but he's an important man."

Pearl wanted to scream at her mother, grab her by the shoulders and shake her vigorously. What had happened to her? What had Pearl missed by working in the kitchen and never venturing into the restaurant when the moneylender was there? "You want to know how important he is?" she burst out. "Tonight Jake showed me some of the speakeasies he owns. He's a criminal, a crook, a thief."

"That Jake, he's a fine one to show you such things. Him and his friends running that dice game in the basement was all within the law, wasn't it?" Sophie's voice became dangerously level. "Pearl, if Saul Fromberg shows enough interest in me to ask me out, and if I accept, that's all there is to it. What you think about him has nothing to do with it."

Pearl looked from her mother to the dresses she had been trying on and murmured, "Poor Papa, he must be turning in his grave at the thought of you with Fromberg."

So intent was she in looking at the dresses, trying to remember the last time her mother had worn them, she never saw the slap coming. Sophie's open hand cracked across her cheek and she reeled back, tears springing to her eyes. Sophie stood horror-struck the moment she realized what she'd done. Pearl turned and ran from the room, tears flowing unchecked down her face. Without knowing where she was going, she raced down the stairs and into the street. Habit made her turn toward the Moscowitz bakery. She banged on the door, and Isidor Moscowitz opened up, a coat thrown over his pajamas.

"What's the matter?"

Pearl rushed straight past him, seeking Annie. "He asked my mother out! For dinner and a show! And she said yes, can you believe that?"

"Hold on a minute!" Annie yelled back. "Who asked your mother out?"

"Who do you think? Fromberg!" She spat out the name.

"Your face?" Annie touched her friend's inflamed cheek. "What happened to it?"

For the first time, Pearl felt the sting of the slap. "We had an argument just now, my mother and me. She hit me." Only now was the truth sinking in. First, her father's uncharacteristic anger when she'd been rude to Fromberg five years earlier. Now her mother. The moneylender was destroying everyone she loved, everything she cared for.

"Sit down, Pearl," Helen Moscowitz said. "I'll make some tea. Then you can tell us all about it."

Sipping hot tea, Pearl related how she'd arrived home to find her mother trying on the dresses. They listened sympathetically. "I said my father would turn in his grave if he knew she'd agreed to have dinner with Fromberg, go to a show with him. That's when she hit me."

"Pearl, your mother hasn't had an easy time since your father passed on," Helen said. "Finally, a man's shown interest in her. Not only that, but he's a man who's very important in her life—your life as well. Your mother's not a young woman. When you grow older, you'll see that your attitudes change. Maybe all she's looking for is a little security. You can't deny her that opportunity."

Pearl shook her head angrily. "Fromberg's not interested in my mother for her sake. There's something else behind it. If he liked her, genuinely liked her as a woman, don't you think he would have said something before?"

"Maybe he thought he had to let enough time pass after your father's death," Isidore Moscowitz suggested. "A decent interval."

"Decent? Him?" Pearl shook her head again.

"Who's to know how his mind works?" Moscowitz persisted. "He's different from the rest of us."

"Sure, he's rich," Annie cut in. "That's a whole world of difference."

"Maybe that's what your mother sees," Helen said. "Can you blame her for wanting the chance of a little comfort in life?"

"But *him* . . ." Pearl thought of the people she'd seen in evening dress outside the theaters, the limousines that would take them home to their palatial mansions or their plush apartments. "There must be millions of other rich men."

"Of course there are," Isidore agreed. "All over the place. The only problem is, none of them has asked your mother out. Fromberg has."

"Go back home, Pearl," Helen urged. "If I know your mother, she's probably as upset as you are over this whole business. Try to see her side of it. And if he's got something up his sleeve, your mother will find it. She's no fool."

No, she's not, Pearl agreed silently. However, she knew Sophie was defenseless. She finished the tea and stood up, ready to leave.

"At least, your mother can get back some of the money you've given to him over the years," Annie said. "Tell her to order the most expensive dishes on the menu, make sure they get the best seats for the show."

A smile found its way onto Pearl's face. Annie had the right idea. Treat the situation with humor. And a prayer that Sophie wasn't as defenseless, as naïve, as she feared. She walked slowly back to her own home. Her mother was sitting in the front room, the dresses draped over the back of a chair. The sight of dried tears staining her cheeks almost made Pearl cry again, because she knew she'd been the cause of them.

"I'm sorry, Mama. I shouldn't have said what I did. Can you forgive me?"

"Of course I can." The sadness was back in her eyes, Pearl noticed; or had it been there all the time, as if Sophie, herself, really understood everything about the man who had asked her out to dinner?

Pearl didn't sleep that night. When she should have fallen off with warm memories of her time with Jake, she stayed awake with thoughts of Fromberg. Why did he want to take her mother out? What was behind his change of heart? There just had to be an ulterior motive.

Pearl's worries were not shared by her mother. Sophie wore the light blue dress for work the following morning—the dark blue one she'd save for her date with Fromberg that night. Pearl could never recall her mother dressing up for work before. The restaurant's popularity was in the food it served, not in the appearance of those who served it, or took money.

Fromberg, accompanied by Landau, came in at ten-thirty. Business was accomplished as usual, with the constant stream of people sitting behind closed curtains in booth number four, borrowing, repaying, having the sums noted in Fromberg's dog-eared notebook. At lunchtime, Sophie came back into the kitchen to collect two pastrami plates, with side orders of potato pancakes for booth number four. Fifteen minutes later, Fromberg, his napkin still tucked into his shirt collar, knocked on the kitchen door.

"My compliments to the chef," he said grandly. "The pastrami melted on my tongue."

Pearl stood, amazed at the visit, a ladle in one hand, a soup plate in the other. No one ever came back into the kitchen. "My mother taught me well," she managed to reply.

Fromberg closed the kitchen door and came right in. "You know, the sign of a good teacher is when the pupil becomes even better. One day you'll have a kid of your own to teach, you'll see for yourself."

Pearl wondered if that was Fromberg's only reason in coming back to the kitchen, to compliment her. She started to ladle soup into the plate she was holding.

"Pearl, I think your mother's a very special woman. That's why I asked her out tonight."

52

"It has nothing to do with me," Pearl answered in a high, strained voice. "My mother doesn't have to ask my permission before she does anything."

"It has everything to do with you. You can make your mother's life a misery if you choose to."

Obviously, Pearl decided, her mother had told Fromberg what had occurred the previous night. "And I suppose the way you've treated her all these years has made her feel like she's living in the middle of a bed of roses."

Fromberg considered Pearl's words. "I could have shut down this place any time I wanted to, your family owes me that much. I could have called in the loan, foreclosed, those times you couldn't pay. I didn't, did I?"

"Of course you didn't. You just added the missing interest to the original loan and charged interest on that as well. Besides, if you had foreclosed, you'd have had no place to run your own business."

Fromberg waved a pudgy hand in the direction of the street. "There's a million places out there that would have been just as convenient. The truth is, and I don't give a damn whether you believe it or not, I've always liked your mother. That's the reason I asked her out—that, and nothing else."

A slimy, grabbing Saul Fromberg Pearl could deal with. A sincere, conciliatory Fromberg gave her difficulty. Was he really telling the truth? Was there, deep down inside, hidden by layers of fat, a decent man? No, she kept telling herself; she couldn't have been that wrong about him. And her father couldn't have been so mistaken when, on his deathbed, he'd begged Pearl with his last breath to protect her mother from the shylock.

"You remember that time you hit Gus, slapped his face like he was some kid who'd gotten fresh with you?" Fromberg asked. "If I hadn't been there to stop him, he'd have knocked the hell out of you."

"Mr. Fromberg—"

The moneylender waved his hand again. "You don't have to call me that; it sounds so damned formal. We're going to be friends. Uncle Saul will do."

"Mr. Fromberg," Pearl repeated, "I told you before that if my mother wants to go out with you, it has nothing to do with me. But I'll tell you something else—you'd better treat her right."

"I'll treat her like the lady she is," Fromberg promised.

Fromberg collected Sophie at seven-thirty that evening, driving up grandly to the restaurant in a brand new yellow LaSalle. His first step in treating her like a lady was the gift of a dozen long-stemmed red roses. Pearl watched through the restaurant window as he helped her into the car before climbing in himself and driving away. She hoped that her mother would do as Annie suggested—sting the shylock by ordering the most expensive dishes on the menu—but she knew it wouldn't be so. Sophie had been forced to live frugally. She'd choose by price, the cheapest item there was. Ironically, such thriftiness would probably make Fromberg like her even more. Pity.

After closing up the restaurant, Pearl sat in the front room of the flat, the lights out as she gazed over Second Avenue. At eleven-thirty, the LaSalle coasted to a halt outside. Fromberg got out of the driver's side and helped Sophie down. Through the open window, Pearl heard her mother's laughter. They crossed the sidewalk. As footsteps came up the stairs, Pearl ran into her own room, closed the door, and dived into bed. Moments later, she heard them enter the flat. Her mother's words, asking Fromberg if he would like anything, filtered through to Pearl. He refused. More words were spoken, muted so that Pearl could not hear them. Then silence. Were they kissing? The idea horrified Pearl. The silence lasted for thirty seconds before she heard her mother's voice call out "Good night," as Fromberg descended the stairs. A minute later, the door to Pearl's room cracked open and Sophie looked in.

"Are you sleeping?"

Pearl stirred, opened her eyes and yawned. "What is it?"

Sophie came in and sat down on the edge of her daughter's bed. "Did you have a nice time?" Pearl noticed that her mother's lipstick was smudged. They *had* kissed!

"We had a lovely time. Was everything all right here?"

"Of course. Where did Fromberg take you?"

"Don't call him that, darling."

"I'm not going to call him Uncle Saul," Pearl objected.

"It's just . . . just how you say his name."

"It's how I've always thought of him."

Sophie let it pass. "We went out for dinner, and then we went to see the show. On the way home, we drove by his house."

"Where does he live?"

"On East Thirty-sixth Street. It's a beautiful house, large, like a mansion."

"Why does he need such a large house?"

"He likes a lot of space. He was married, you know. His wife died three years ago."

Any pity Pearl felt was reserved for the dead woman, not for the widower. "Do his children still live with him?"

"He has none. His wife couldn't have any."

Pearl sat up in the bed. "He told you all this, his entire life story, in just one evening?"

"We talked a lot over dinner."

"What did you eat?"

"Only a salad. I wasn't very hungry."

Pearl hid a smile. She'd been right—her mother must have selected the cheapest item on the menu. "Are you seeing him again?"

"Yes. Sometime this weekend, either Saturday or Sunday." She bent forward to kiss her daughter, then stood up and left the room. "Good night, Pearl." The door closed, cutting off the light.

Over the following two months, Fromberg took Sophie out twice a week, calling for her in the LaSalle, frequently bringing her a gift—flowers, chocolates, once a china figurine. On their tenth date, their anniversary as Fromberg termed it, he gave Sophie a small diamond brooch. She wore it that night when Fromberg took her out to dinner.

Pearl could not help noticing the change that was sweeping over her mother. Sophie's life, for once, did not revolve around the grind of the restaurant. She started to take pride in the way she dressed; she even went out and bought new clothes, something she would never have done under normal circumstances. Pearl suspected that Fromberg provided the money. He took with one hand and gave back with the other, a kind of benevolent dictator, an ambidextrous Robin Hood. Pearl wondered if that irony ever occurred to her mother, that Sophie was, in fact, paying for her own gifts. Probably not. She was too obviously smitten with Fromberg—the new Fromberg—to worry about where he got the money to buy her presents. Pearl didn't know what to make of it all. She discussed it with Annie, and the red-haired girl agreed with her. There had to be some underlying motive. For the life of them, though, neither girl could figure it out. Sophie wasn't a rich catch. She had no money of her own, only the restaurant. And that was in pawn to Fromberg anyway. Could it be that he'd told Pearl the truth that lunchtime when he'd come back to the kitchen? The truth being that Sophie was an attractive woman, and he wanted to be with her?

Once, Pearl even saw her mother and the moneylender out together. It was on a Saturday night, when the restaurant was closed and both mother and daughter could afford to be away. Pearl was on a double date with Jake, Annie, and Moses Caplan. The truck belonging to Jake's father was too small for the foursome, so Caplan had borrowed a Ford from the garage where he worked.

55

After parking the car, the four young people walked along Forty-second Street, debating which movie to see. Suddenly, Pearl pointed to the other side of the street. Traveling east was Fromberg's distinctive yellow LaSalle.

"Let's see where he's taking your mother," Jake suggested immediately. "Give you eight-to-five it's a cheap grease trough." Caplan's car was only fifty yards away. They sprinted back to it. Caplan swung the Ford around and gave chase to the LaSalle, which was now passing across Seventh Avenue.

"Hurry!" Jake urged Caplan. "You'll lose them."

Pearl craned forward from her seat in the back, watching the LaSalle continue east across Fifth Avenue. A worrying certainty began to grow in her heart. She knew exactly where the LaSalle was headed. "It's all right, Moe. Let them go."

Caplan wasn't listening. The thrill of the hunt caught in his nostrils and he wasn't going to stop until he'd found out exactly where Fromberg was taking Pearl's mother. Pearl sat back, sighing in resignation.

The LaSalle turned south on Park Avenue, then left onto East Thirty-sixth Street. Pearl watched with a sinking feeling in her stomach as it halted outside a three-story brownstone. The numb silence in the Ford was broken by Jake saying: "Keep going, Moe, otherwise we'll miss the beginning of the show."

The Ford passed the LaSalle as Fromberg helped Sophie out. Pearl resisted glancing back; she'd seen enough already. Wordlessly, Caplan drove back to Forty-second Street. As they walked into the theater, Pearl went to the ladies' room. Annie followed.

"Don't worry about your mother, Pearl," Annie said. "She probably went back to his place to see something. He's so rich he must have some gorgeous furniture, beautiful paintings."

"Shut up, Annie," Pearl hissed. She'd never felt so ashamed in her life, spying on her mother as Sophie went to a man's house—any man's, not necessarily Saul Fromberg's.

"Pearl . . ." Annie came closer, undeterred by her friend's angry words. "People your mother's age don't get up to anything like . . . well, you know what I mean. Will you stop worrying about it? She's old enough to take care of herself."

"My mother's not that old." At the moment, forty-seven seemed young to Pearl. Innocent, certainly.

She sat through the movie listlessly, seeing little that flickered on the screen in front of her. It must have been good, she supposed, because she heard Jake's laughter in between bouts of frantic playing by the pianist.

"What shall we do now?" Caplan asked as the movie ended. "The night's young and we've got a car."

"I don't want to go anywhere," Pearl said, cutting off Annie's request to go dancing. "Just take me home, please."

"You all right?" Jake asked.

"I just want to go home. Is there anything wrong with that?"

Jake shrugged and signaled to Caplan. The journey back to Second Avenue was completed in virtual silence as Pearl's mood touched the others; they felt embarrassed for her sake. Jake didn't expect a goodnight kiss, not that night, and Pearl didn't surprise him. She ran from the car to the door and up the stairs. In her own room, she threw herself onto the bed, face buried in her arms as she shed tears of shame and humiliation.

After a while, she composed herself. She left the bedroom and sat in the front room, waiting. Cars passed. Each time one slowed, Pearl's pulse quickened. Finally, at twelve-thirty, the LaSalle drew up outside. Sophie climbed out unassisted. As she entered the building, Fromberg drove away. The moment the door to the flat swung back, Pearl prepared to tell her mother exactly what she thought of her. Her mouth opened, but no sound came, not when she saw her mother's face. Sophie's eyes were red as if from crying. Her cheeks were puffed. Pearl's anger vanished, replaced by concern. "What happened to you?"

Sophie felt her way into a chair. "He just made a proposition to me, Pearl. He took me back to his big house, and there he made me a proposition."

"He proposed? He asked you to marry him?" What would Fromberg expect her to call him now? Papa? God forbid! And God forbid, too, that her mother had accepted!

"No, darling. A proposition, it's different from a proposal. You were right all along, and me . . . I was wrong. He wasn't courting me these past couple of months. He was courting our basement."

"Mama, what are you talking about?"

"Saul Fromberg, he wants to turn our big basement into a fancy night club." Sophie's voice became stronger, fired with the anger of a woman betrayed. "That's what it was all about, Pearl. Tonight, he took me back to his house. I wondered why . . . I had hoped . . ."

"Could you really see yourself marrying him if he'd asked you?"

Sophie gave a little shrug of the shoulders as if the matter were of little importance now. "We sat there for an hour, more, two hours, just talking. And then he put his proposition to me. He wants to decorate our basement, put in a stage, have a band there, a dance floor, lots of tables, a bar. King Saul, he wants to call the club. Can you

57

believe his nerve?"

"Are you really surprised?"

"I didn't say anything. I was too shocked, too amazed, to answer right away. He told me to think it over—there'd be something in it for me, he said—and he'd see me on Monday when he comes in."

"I can just imagine," Pearl remarked acidly, "what that something in it for you will amount to. He figures the few baubles he's given you already will pay for the basement and more. He'll have a nightclub that'll make lots of money, and you—you'll have a brooch and a few other bits and pieces."

Absently, Sophie fingered the diamond brooch on her dress. "Why are you up so late? Did you just get in?"

Pearl told her the truth. Sophie listened to the story of Moses Caplan following the LaSalle, and how Pearl had been ashamed to see her mother going into Saul Fromberg's house. Then Sophie said: "You thought that he and I? . . . A little? . . ."

Pearl nodded.

"Your friends as well? That's what they thought?"

Another nod. "All except Annie. She said people your age don't get up to anything like that." Belatedly, Pearl understood that this was the first time she had ever discussed sex, no matter how remotely, with her mother.

Sophie stared uncomprehendingly for a few seconds, then she started to laugh. "People of my age! I should slap that little red-haired minx in the head when I see her. You know why I'm laughing, Pearl? Not at your friend. I'm laughing at how stupid I've been, stupid because I didn't listen to you, stupid to believe that anything involving that man could ever lead somewhere decent."

Pearl's mind was racing. "It can lead somewhere, Mama. Somewhere very good, I think. Just leave it to me."

When Jake came into the basement the following morning with the delivery, Pearl said to him: "Look around you, Jake. Can you see a nightclub down here?"

Coffee sprayed from his mouth. "A nightclub?"

"That's what Fromberg wants to do, open a nightclub called King Saul down here. That'll be the entrance," she said, pointing to the door leading up to the alley. "That was the whole business with my mother last night. She thought he was taking her back to the house to propose to her. Instead, he tried to talk her into letting him open a nightclub down here. Dance floor, stage, the works."

Jake looked around, sized up the basement. "I guess it's big enough.

58

What did she tell him?"

"Nothing yet. He's expecting her approval tomorrow. That gives us just enough time to rehearse her for what she's got to tell him."

"The King Saul idea must mean a lot to him," Jake mused. "All the other places, he's just got a piece of them. This one would be all his own." He finished the coffee, handed the cup to Pearl. "I'll come back tonight with Lou. Between us, we'll work out a deal for your mother to put to him."

Pearl threw her arms around his neck and kissed him, compensating for her omission of the previous night.

Fifteen minutes after the restaurant closed that night, Jake came up to the flat with Lou Levitt. "Remember, Mrs. Resnick," Levitt said, "you've got to be hard tomorrow. Don't let him bully you, don't let him beat you down. He's going to come here expecting a pushover, and you're going to squeeze every last cent out of him. Now this"— Levitt drew a sheet of paper from his pocket, gave it to Sophie—"is what you're going to ask for. And you'll accept nothing less. He wants the nightclub, he's going to have to pay through the nose for it."

Pearl listened and watched with glee. As long as her mother did not fold tomorrow, Fromberg would learn that the brooch, the other presents he'd given to Sophie, were just the down payment on his King Saul nightclub. And a very small down payment at that.

Chapter Five

Heredity was foremost in Sophie Resnick's mind when she opened the restaurant on Monday morning. If parents really passed on genes to their children, Pearl should have developed into a meek, mild-mannered girl. She shouldn't have the strength, the determination she did possess, the iron will that seemingly bent for no one. Sophie understood that her own will was weak, too ready to bend before a stronger force. To a degree, her late husband had been the same way, preferring to seek compromise instead of confrontation. Not so Pearl. That morning, Sophie was hoping that heredity might work in reverse. More than anything she wanted Pearl's strength inside her own body, because she feared that her own character might betray her. She knew that Fromberg would not arrive at the restaurant until his regular time of ten-thirty; he was so supremely confident of her agreement that he wouldn't even change his habits on this day. He'd had his way so often in life that he would assume today would be no different. He'd wooed Sophie, charmed her, given her presents—how else would a weak, gullible woman react except to give him exactly what he wanted? Not today, mister, Sophie promised silently as she felt some of her daughter's strength. You're going to come in here today and you're going to get the shock of your life. Thanks to Pearl, I'm going to stand up to you.

"Nervous, Mama?" Pearl asked as ten o'clock passed. She had seen the way Sophie glanced nervously at the restaurant door each time it opened.

"A little," Sophie answered. "But a lot more angry."

"Good." Pearl kissed her mother on the cheek. "Just don't forget any of the points Lou told you to make."

"I won't. He wrote things down here I would never have thought of." She pulled Levitt's sheet of paper from a drawer in the counter, checked it again. "Is he going to be a lawyer, that one?"

"He'll be anything he wants to be." Pearl returned to the kitchen, leaving the door half-open so she could watch the restaurant while she worked.

Through the open door she saw Fromberg enter, with Gus Landau one pace behind. The bodyguard walked straight to booth number four and sat down. Fromberg, however, went to the counter where Sophie stood. Pearl remained where she was. This was Sophie's moment . . . and she prayed that her mother didn't wilt now.

"Thought over my proposal?" Fromberg greeted Sophie.

"Proposition," Sophie corrected him quite calmly. "You didn't propose to me—you offered me a proposition."

Fromberg inclined his head. "Proposal . . . proposition . . . what the hell's the big difference?"

Sophie turned away for a moment to take money from a customer. Watching, Pearl silently applauded her mother. Play on his nerves, that's it. Make the bastard wait a while. "Yes, I've thought about it," Sophie said when the customer had left. "You can have the basement—"

Fromberg did not allow her to complete the sentence. "I'll send around a few guys, get the basement cleared out, then the builders can start work this week." He started to move away, and for a moment Pearl thought that her mother had backed down. She'd told him yes without mentioning any of the conditions that Levitt had drawn up.

Then Sophie reached out a hand, tapped Fromberg on the shoulder. "Just a minute, Saul. You didn't let me finish."

Fromberg swung around slowly, an odd expression of curiosity and wariness forming on his face.

"I said you could have the basement, but I want something in return for it. A few dinners, some shows, a few cheap gifts . . . that only pays for having me listen to your idea. Now . . ." To Pearl's horror, Sophie produced the piece of paper, reading from it instead of saying the words she was supposed to have memorized. "Before you move a single thing out of that basement, before you paint one square inch of brick, this is what you're going to do."

Fromberg stood open-mouthed as Sophie read out Levitt's list. "First, you're going to cancel my debt. You and I will go to a lawyer and have him draw up an agreement voiding the debt. Secondly, that same lawyer will draw up a lease under which you will pay me rent of two hundred dollars a month for the use of the basement."

Drops of perspiration oozed out of Fromberg's scalp as Sophie calmly read out the conditions. It was then that Pearl realized why her mother had done it this way. By reading from the sheet of paper she had avoided looking into the moneylender's eyes. Whatever she saw there—anger, surprise, a threat—might have weakened her resolve. This way, all she saw were words that she could repeat parrotlike. In that moment, Pearl felt a tremendous admiration for her mother; she had found a way to conquer her fear of Fromberg by not looking at him.

"Is that all?" Fromberg finally managed to ask.

"No, it's not all." At last, Sophie was confident enough to raise her eyes from the sheet of paper. "There's one other condition. Your privilege at booth number four also ceases. I can make money from that booth. I don't need to waste it by letting you use it for nothing."

Fromberg snatched the sheet from Sophie's grasp, looked at Levitt's small, neat handwriting. "You have some goddamned accountant draw this thing up?" he snapped. "Only accountants write that small and neat." Without another word, he spun away from the counter and burst into the kitchen. "You're behind this, aren't you?" he accused Pearl.

"You must think my mother's a fool, trying to turn her head the way you did. She knew all the time that you wanted something, so she decided to play you along. We don't mind you having the basement, Mr. Fromberg—all we want for it is a fair price."

Fromberg shook his head. "No, kid, there's no way on earth that your mother could have worked all this out for herself. You put her up to it, didn't you?" He shoved the piece of paper in Pearl's face.

"That's not my handwriting, Mr. Fromberg."

"It's not your mother's, either. So whose is it?"

"Does it matter whose handwriting it is?" Pearl asked. "The only thing that does matter is what it says. You want the basement, fine—that's what you've got to give us to get it."

Fromberg let a mask slip over his face to hide his anger. And his panic. If he allowed that to show, God alone knew what this little vixen would add on to the price she wanted. Fromberg understood now that he'd made a mistake by believing that his faked interest in Sophie would sweep the woman clean off her feet. He'd been certain he'd get what he wanted and still be able to milk the restaurant. It had never occurred to him that anything would stand in his way. But Sophie's damned daughter had stuck in her two cents worth, and suddenly Fromberg found himself in a quandary. He was committed to using the basement for his club. He'd lined up builders, paid for the furniture. Above all, he'd made his contacts for the liquor the club would sell, ordered from suppliers who were convinced he was going places. He couldn't back out now. To do so would cost him more than money; it would cost him the reputation he was steadily building. Not that of a moneylender, but that of a big wheel who was going a long way in Prohibition America.

"So this is all you want?" he asked, keeping his voice level. "Your debt to me canceled—"

"It's been paid a hundred times over."

"Rent of two hundred a month," Fromberg said, reading down Levitt's list.

"Our own rent for the restaurant includes the basement," Pearl replied. "If you're using it, why should we pay for you?"

"Your rent doesn't come to no two hundred a month."

"True, but we're not operating a club either."

Fromberg gave Pearl a pasty smile, and she knew she was winning. Damn it, she'd won! "And you want me to give up using booth number four?"

"You can run your business just as well from the basement. Use one of the club's tables to fleece people."

"You're a cute kid, you know that? I've a damned good mind to let you stew in your own juice, open my club somewhere else, and let you and your mother get on with it."

"Go right ahead," Pearl invited. "We're not bothered about the basement the way it is now."

"What safeguards do I get that you won't throw me out once the lease expires?" Fromberg asked. For the first time in his dealings with the Resnick family, he felt vulnerable.

"You can have whatever safety clauses you want put into the lease. Besides," she added, knowing how to appeal to his greed, "do you think we'd be so quick to give up such a good rent?"

"Draw up your goddamned papers," he said angrily. "Who the hell needs the pennies you and your mother give me?"

Pearl could not resist one final jibe to make up for the years of misery. "Would you mind not spitting when you speak, Mr. Fromberg? Our food is tasty enough without any seasoning from you."

Fromberg's face turned as black as thunder. Lips stretched in a thin, straight line, teeth clenched so hard that his gums ached, he spun around, smashed back the kitchen door and stormed out. Moments later, both he and Landau left the restaurant. Pearl came through the kitchen door. Sophie was standing behind the varnished counter, staring at the front door as if unable to comprehend that the nightmare was finally over. Pearl walked to booth number four, picked up the handwritten Reserved sign and handed it to her mother.

"You can have the pleasure of tearing this up."

Sophie gripped it with both hands. As she was about to rip it into two pieces, she stopped. "Let's get it framed instead."

Pearl began to laugh. Other families might frame pictures but not the Resnicks. They'd frame a reserved sign which had served as a deed of slavery for all of Pearl's life. She felt a sudden surge of freedom. Shackles had been removed from her legs, as if struck by a bolt of lightning which had melted the metal and left her feeling uplifted.

"Where are you going?" Sophie asked as Pearl took paper and pen from the counter and walked toward the front of the restaurant.

"Just wait and see." Like her father had done almost seventeen years earlier, Pearl stuck the sheet of paper in the window. Instead of announcing It's a Girl! this piece read: "Resnick's Celebrates Independence Day! Free Food!" Then she returned to the kitchen to prepare more of everything. Today would be the busiest in the restaurant's history, and they wouldn't take in a penny. So what? This kind of independence came only once in a lifetime.

Sophie, Pearl, and Saul Fromberg met at a lawyer's office two days later. On the lawyer's desk was a deed revoking the Resnick debt. Grudgingly, Fromberg signed it, watched while it was witnessed. Next, the lawyer produced a lease he had drawn up.

"That's not necessary," Fromberg said.

The lawyer looked at Pearl and Sophie. "Why not?" Pearl asked. "You wanted safeguards."

"I thought a lot about you since Monday, kid. You've got a shrewd head on your shoulders, too shrewd to try and stiff me. All we need is a verbal agreement." He dug into his pocket. "Here's your first three months' rent. After that, I'll pay you first of the month." Sophie handed over the keys to the door leading from the basement to the alley. Fromberg took them, waved away the receipt for the six hundred dollars and stood up, ready to leave. As he reached the door, he looked back at Sophie. "She's no kid of yours, lady. You and your husband between you didn't have a tenth of the brains she's got."

Jake came around to the flat with Lou Levitt late that night to learn what had happened at the lawyer's office. They sat upstairs with Pearl and Sophie, listening as Pearl related the short meeting. When Pearl mentioned that Fromberg had decided to do without the lease, Levitt seemed thoughtful. She asked him what was wrong.

"Did he sign his name to *anything?*" Levitt asked in return.

Pearl looked to her mother. "Only the document about the money we owed him," Pearl said at last.

"He's a crafty one," Levitt said, half in disgust, half in admiration.

"What's so crafty about that?" Jake wanted to know.

Levitt looked scathingly at his friend. "Benny Minsky asks me to explain the obvious, that I can understand. I thought you had more brains. Fromberg doesn't put his name to anything, so who's to prove he's got any connection with the place?"

"He's calling it King Saul," Pearl protested. "How much more of a connection can you want than that?"

"Means nothing," Levitt said. "I can open a place and call it Louis the Fourteenth or something . . . doesn't mean to say it has anything to do with me."

"You know," Sophie said, "he seemed to make a point of not wanting the lease, as though he was afraid of signing—"

"Of signing anything that would tie him to the club," Levitt finished. "He's got more brains than I gave—" He broke off, cocked his head inquisitively. "What was that?"

"What was what?" Sophie asked, automatically assuming the same position as Levitt.

"That noise. There . . . there it is again."

This time they all heard it, a muffled crash from downstairs. Silence, then another noise, the sound of something being dragged across a floor. Pearl jumped up and gazed out of the kitchen window, which overlooked the alley. "There's a truck out there!"

Jake joined her at the window, glanced down, and then headed for the stairs. Pearl and Levitt followed. When Sophie stood up, slow to realize what was happening, Levitt told her to stay where she was.

They ran down the stairs and into the restaurant. The door leading to the basement was open. Jake darted to it, took the first two steps and then stopped abruptly. Coming up were two men, carrying a heavy pickle barrel between them. Jake stepped back as they brushed past him and dumped the barrel on the floor of the kitchen, next to the one they had brought up moments earlier.

"What's going on?" Pearl asked.

Jake took the stairs two at a time. At the bottom he saw that the door leading to the alley was wide open, held back by a wooden box. Fromberg stood in the center of the basement, shouting directions at men who were moving out the restaurant's supplies. Other men were setting up ladders and scaffolding, and even more men were manhandling building supplies down the stairs from the truck in the alley.

Fromberg turned around and saw Jake, Levitt, and Pearl. "Did I hand over six hundred bucks to you this morning?" he shouted at Pearl. "That means this is my place now. You come down here, you ask my permission first!"

"I just wondered what the noise was," Pearl answered lamely. "You should have told me you were starting work tonight."

"I don't have to tell you anything."

"Gangway!" a voice shouted from the door. Gus Landau appeared, walking backward, giving directions to two men following him. They were carrying a large, green-covered table, held sideways to clear the doorway. Numbers were marked on it in red and black, a grid twelve squares long and three squares wide. In the center of the table was a gaping hole. A third man followed them through, weighed down by a roulette wheel. Levitt pushed his way past Jake and Pearl to get a closer look at the wheel.

"Where do you think you're going, shrimp?" Landau reached out and grabbed Levitt by the collar of his jacket, swung him around.

"Let him go!" Fromberg ordered Landau. "If he wants to look, let him look." Beaming, he turned his attention to Pearl. "You think you got yourself some deal this morning, eh? I'll tell you what you got— you got nothing, you hear me? What I'm paying you is peanuts compared to what I'm going to clear down here. The shrimp there knows what I'm talking about. That roulette wheel, half a dozen slot machines—they're going to bring in more in a week than his penny-ante dice game would have made in a year. Look at it, Levitt . . . look at it and eat your heart out."

"You never mentioned gambling," Pearl said.

"You're my landlady," Fromberg answered. "You're not my mother. Come on! . . ." He clapped his hands at the men carrying the table. "Move it over there, out of the way!"

Followed by Jake and Levitt, Pearl returned upstairs. "It's Fromberg," she told her mother. "He's moving in already, setting up more than a club. He's having gambling down there as well."

Sophie looked worried. She'd had enough surprises recently. "Will that make any difference?"

Levitt answered. "Not if he runs a straight game, it won't."

"I'll get locks put on the door leading down to the basement," Pearl told her mother. "First thing tomorrow."

Sophie appeared satisfied. A perturbed expression remained on Pearl's face, though. Jake saw it, took her aside. "Thinking you didn't get such a bargain now?" he whispered.

Pearl thought carefully before answering. "We got Fromberg out of booth number four. In any language, that's a bargain."

Fromberg's builders worked feverishly, starting at seven in the morning and continuing through until eight or nine each night, seven days a week.

Each day that Jake came in, to collect the order or deliver, he asked

Pearl if she'd been downstairs to see how the club looked. Always she answered no. "I don't want anything to do with that place. Fromberg's paying for it, that's all I care about." She wasn't above walking along the alley behind the restaurant, though. Trucks were always parked there. The original door to the basement had been removed, brickwork knocked out to allow for a much larger, ornate door, made of heavily varnished oak with a gold crown in the center; just above the crown was a peephole.

After two weeks, the noise from downstairs lessened. That evening, curious, she walked along the alley. There were no trucks, not even a light peeping through the small, high window. Whatever work Fromberg had ordered had been completed.

Jake came by very early the following morning, at five-thirty, before the restaurant was open. Now that the basement was rented out, he parked the truck on Second Avenue. Pearl told him about the builders' trucks no longer being in the alley.

"Bet you're just dying for a look, aren't you?" Jake said.

Pearl recognized the challenge. Jake wanted to see the basement as much as she did. "Do you think we'll be able to get down?"

"Just because you put bolts on your side of the door doesn't mean Fromberg did as well. Knowing him, he's so cheap he wouldn't spend the money for his own locks." Taking her hand, he led the way toward the basement door. Pearl wondered whether to tell her mother, and decided against it. The older woman would only worry, and there was no need. The club would be empty; what harm could there possibly be in just looking?

Pearl's breathing quickened as Jake slipped the three bolts. She felt as she'd done that day at school with Annie, when they had spied on the four boys playing dice. Her stomach trembled and she knew she shouldn't go further. If Jake hadn't been with her, she wouldn't have. The feel of his dry hand inside her own lent her confidence.

The stairway was darker than Pearl remembered it, almost pitch-black. As light filtered down from the restaurant, she saw that a door had been erected at the bottom end. The adventure was over before it had really begun.

Jake went down ahead of her, pushed against the door. Thick, and padded for soundproofing, it swung back easily. Turning sideways, he bowed and swept his hand across his stomach in an invitation for her to precede him into the club. She felt the softness of carpet beneath her feet. Her hand found a light switch. She flipped it up. Light flooded into the basement. She heard Jake's whistle of surprise, her own sucking in of breath. "God almighty!" Jake whispered, awestruck. "And we thought he was cheap."

Pearl's eyes traveled down to the carpet, a rich floral pattern of reds and browns. It took her a few seconds to realize that the predominant motif was a crown, the same crown she had seen on the door. King Saul. She'd never seen such luxurious carpet in her life. Her head lifted, eyes focused on the heavy oak paneling that covered the brickwork she'd known. Crystal chandeliers hung gracefully from the ceiling. "I can't believe it," she whispered again and again. "He must have spent millions down here." It was how she'd always dreamed a palace would look.

Dazed, she walked toward the club's entrance, across a small dance floor, between tables covered with crisp white Irish linen. A cloakroom had been built close to the entrance, a place for coats; and Pearl noticed two doors, one marked Ladies and the other, Gentlemen. She turned around to survey the club, much as a guest would on entering. To her left, at the far end, was a small stage, half of which was taken up by a grand piano; next to the stage was a door on which the word *Office* was written in fine gold script. A gold velvet curtain hung from a ceiling track; when lowered it would conceal the office entrance. She counted the tables around the dance floor and in front of the stage. Twenty-four, pushed close together, each with four chairs. Across from her was a long, well-stocked bar. The only sign that work was still in progress was a small trestle table next to the bar; some carpentry tools rested on it.

A strange noise startled her, a sharp snap followed by a whirring sound. She turned quickly and saw Jake at the far right of the club. He was standing in front of half-a-dozen machines, holding the handle of one as three cylinders spun frantically behind a pane of glass. One by one, the cylinders clicked to a halt. Jake felt in his pocket, pulled out a coin, inserted it into the machine and pulled the handle again.

"What are they?" Pearl asked.

"Slots . . . slot machines, newest way to gamble. Fromberg must have real connections to get these babies."

"Don't give him any more of our money than he's got already," Pearl called out. Jake waved a hand at her, watching as the cylinders whirled around. Then he let out a joyous yell as three quarters were spit back at him. He thrust them into his pocket and turned around, a broad grin across his face. "Quit while you're ahead, that's the name of the game!"

As she walked the length of the club to join him, Pearl felt shabby. A woman should enter a place like this in an evening gown, furs, jewelry; not in worn-out shoes and a white apron, her hair pulled back in a functional bun. Then she laughed . . . she had no business

68

being down here anyway, so what difference did it make how she looked?

"Where did he put the roulette wheel?" she asked Jake.

"Probably in there." Jake pointed to another door, close to where they were standing. He pushed it back to reveal a large room. In here, the carpet was a rich green, the same color as the baize of the roulette and craps tables that shared the room. "A license to print money," Jake murmured in admiration. "That's what he's gone and done— he's given himself a license to print money. Now I can see what he meant about the two hundred a month he's giving you and your mother being peanuts. It is. You should have hit him for two thousand a month, and you'd still be undercharging him." Jake spun the roulette wheel idly, threw the set of dice that were sitting on the craps table. "Lou would have a ball if he could run a place like this."

"He likes to gamble, doesn't he?"

Jake shook his head. "No, he likes to see other people gamble, especially if it's his game. Don't you get it, Pearl? Gambling's numbers, that's all. Odds, angles . . . that's what Lou's brain's made of." Jake took a final look around, then said, "Let's go back upstairs. I'd better unload your order."

"You go on ahead," Pearl told him. "I want to stay down here for a while. I can't get used to the idea that this place—this . . . this luxury—used to be our basement."

"You sure?" Jake wasn't certain he liked the idea of leaving her alone. The basement didn't belong to Pearl and her mother anymore.

"What can happen, Jake? It's not even six o'clock yet."

Jake laughed. "Okay, here's a quarter—stick it in one of the slots."

"Are you encouraging me to gamble?"

"Maybe you'll hit the jackpot, break Fromberg before he even gets this joint opened up."

Pearl took the quarter and gave Jake a kiss in return. Maybe she'd play it, and maybe she wouldn't.

"Don't forget to turn off the fancy lights when you come up," Jake told her.

She watched him go, listened to his footsteps going up the stairs before she closed the padded door. Standing on the small stage, she tried to imagine what acts Fromberg would bring in. They'd have to be good acts to go down well in a classy place like this; the kind of people—Pearl pictured them in their evening finery—who'd patronize a club like this wouldn't stand for Broadway burlesque. She ran her fingers along the piano keyboard. Finally, she went into the office. It was decorated as lavishly as the rest of the club—thick carpet, heavy linen wallpaper instead of paneling, leather couch and chairs, and a large desk.

As she came out of the office, the six slot machines at the opposite end of the club drew her eyes like magnets. She had Jake's quarter. She just had to try her luck. Standing in front of the first machine in line, she inserted the coin, gripped the handle, closed her eyes, and pulled. The cylinders revolved. The first two clicked into place almost instantly; the third spun interminably, freewheeling almost silently until, at last, it snapped to a stop. What had she got? Before she had the opportunity to check the winning chart, a hail of quarters clattered into the metal cup at the base of the machine. Gleefully, she picked up the coins and continued to play, sinking one after another into the machine.

The rattle of each coin dropping, the clunk of the handle being pulled, the spinning of the cylinders and the final, jarring jolt of the symbols falling into line drowned out all other sound for Pearl. She never heard the car driving into the alleyway. She never heard the key being inserted into the door of King Saul, never noticed the door swing back.

The first Pearl knew she was no longer alone in the club was when a man's voice said: "I didn't realize we'd opened for business yet."

The quarters in her hand dropped softly onto the thick carpet as Pearl turned around, guilt spread across her face. Gus Landau stood just inside the door, a heavy carton gripped in both hands. He set the carton down on the floor, closed the door leading to the alley and slowly advanced on Pearl. She backed away. Landau stopped in front of the slot machine, picked up the quarters she'd dropped.

"Here . . ." He offered them to her. "Carry on playing. We'll take your money."

She stared at the silver he was offering her, then into his eyes. For the first time Pearl could remember, those blue eyes had an expression in them—amusement. It frightened her more than the coldness had ever done.

"Play," Landau repeated. "Maybe you'll get lucky."

Pearl opened her mouth to scream. No sound came. Her mouth and throat were dry, as brittle as old wood. Not that a scream would have helped; it would have been absorbed in the soundproofing Fromberg had installed.

Landau moved a step closer. Pearl retreated a step further. Another step and another, always matched exactly by Landau's advance. She had to reach the padded door. Once that was open she could scream and be heard. Jake would come down. He'd put Landau to flight just like he'd once sent the Irish boys running. He wouldn't need Benny Minsky this time, not for just one man.

70

Landau read Pearl's thoughts. He changed direction, moved to his right to cut off her retreat. The faint hope in Pearl's heart died. She took one more backward step, and felt something pressing into the base of her spine. The carpenter's trestle table, next to the bar. Smiling, Landau pocketed the quarters, reached out, and rested his hands gently on Pearl's shoulders.

"You're our first customer, Pearl. It wouldn't be right if I didn't give you a special welcome." His hands began to squeeze, fingers digging into the muscles of Pearl's shoulders. His face came closer, filled her vision. His lips pressed down on hers.

She opened her mouth a fraction. Landau's lips also opened. Then Pearl bit down savagely, teeth meeting through Landau's lower lip. He jumped back, roaring with pain and rage. Blood dripped from his mouth, dribbled down his chin. His blue eyes were glazed. Released from his hold, Pearl stumbled back against the trestle table. Tools! . . . There were carpentry tools on the table. She felt behind her, fingers scraping across the top of the table, desperately seeking a weapon.

"You goddamned little bitch!" Landau spit blood and saliva into Pearl's face. "I'm going to teach you a lesson you'll never forget!" He lunged at her, hands curled, aiming for her slender throat. Pearl's right hand touched a round piece of wood, gripped it. As Landau came close enough, she whipped the tool in front of her with all her strength.

The tool was a one-inch chisel. The blade drew a bright, shining arc in Pearl's hand. Landau jumped back, but not in time. The beveled edge of the blade slashed across his left cheek, gouging a wide but shallow cut from ear to chin, a vivid stripe from which blood sprang immediately. Pearl glimpsed the blade, the strip of skin that curled obscenely from the end. Landau's agonized yell was drowned out by Pearl's own scream of disgust as she realized what she'd done. As Landau clutched at his damaged cheek, Pearl ran toward the padded door, flinging it open and yelling for Jake. Landau gave chase, reaching the door when Pearl was halfway up the stairs. He threw himself at her feet, missed, and struck his chin on the cold stone steps. Pearl reached the top and burst into the restaurant. She saw her mother running out of the kitchen at the screams. And there was Jake, walking through the front door with a sack over his shoulder.

Still clutching the chisel, she shouted: "Jake . . . help me!"

Jake dropped the sack and rushed toward her. "What—?" The question died on his lips as Landau came charging through the basement door, his face disfigured, blood dripping from both his lip and the stripe along his cheek. Jake reached out for the closest weapon, an empty seltzer bottle that stood on the varnished counter. Gripping the neck, he smashed the end of the bottle against the counter's edge. Glass sprayed in all directions as he pointed the jagged edge in Landau's direction. In a cold, level tone, he said: "You don't belong up here, mister."

Landau's shoes skidded on the floor as he tried to stop himself from running into the broken bottle. Jake prodded with the weapon, forcing him back toward the doorway.

"You! . . ." Landau jabbed a finger at Pearl. "If it's the last thing I ever do, you little bitch! . . . And you!" The finger flew in Jake's direction. "The pair of you, so help me God!"

Pearl flinched at the threat. Not only for herself, but for Jake.

"Get out of my restaurant!" The order was shouted by Sophie Resnick. Only two weeks earlier, Pearl had driven Landau and Fromberg from the restaurant. Sophie was not about to let them back in. Any fear she might have had was overcome by anger. She wielded a heavy broom with such force that Landau was knocked back. Finger still pointing, he lost his footing and fell back down the stairs. Pearl leaped forward, slammed the door and shot all three bolts. Jake jammed a chair under the handle. Landau's fist hammered futilely from the other side of the door for a few seconds, then ceased.

"That's not the only door," Jake said needlessly. Pearl and Sophie had already realized that, and they looked anxiously at the door leading to the street. Not that a door would keep out a man like Landau for very long.

"I'll stay with you," Jake offered.

"Until when?"

"Until it's safe." He snapped his fingers. "Quick, run next door. Get Annie. She can go look for Lou and the others. Maybe she'll catch them before they go to work."

Pearl wasn't convinced that the boys would be protection enough. "Jake, Landau has a gun. I saw it once, on the table over there"— she pointed to booth number four—"when Fromberg was counting money. What good will Lou and Moe and Benny be against a gun?"

"Don't worry about it," Jake said, and hugged her comfortingly with his right arm. In his left hand he still clutched the broken bottle, while in Pearl's right hand was the chisel. The third combatant, Sophie, stood staring hostilely at the basement door, the broom gripped resolutely in her hands. "Landau's going to need help for his face first, before he bleeds to death. Now go next door and get Annie."

Pearl ran to the bakery. Moments later, she dragged Annie back with her. Jake filled her in on what had happened and gave her instructions. As the red-haired girl ran off down the street, Jake locked the front door, turned the sign to read Closed, and drew all the curtains; the restaurant would miss out on its early customers today.

When Annie returned, she had only Benny Minsky and Lou Levitt with her. "I couldn't get Moe!" she cried. "He'd already left for the garage."

"Never mind," Jake said. He looked at the two young men. "You know what's going on?"

Levitt nodded and made his way back to the kitchen. Minsky tugged at his jacket pocket, opening it just enough for Jake to peek inside; he saw the butt of a revolver. "We might need this, Jake."

"Don't let Pearl or the old lady see it, keep the damned thing out of sight." He heard Sophie yelling in the kitchen and forgot all about Minsky's gun. Was there an entrance back there, something he'd overlooked? Had Landau found a way in? "Keep an eye on the front," he ordered Minsky. He ran through the restaurant, scared of what he'd find as Sophie's voice continued its screaming tirade.

In the kitchen, Levitt was on his knees, head beneath the sink. Water gushed out onto the floor, spreading into a wide pool, seeping through cracks. And Sophie was standing over Levitt, hitting him on the back with the broomstick.

"What do you think you're doing?" she yelled furiously. "You're mad . . . you'll flood the whole place!"

Levitt pushed himself upright, his face red from exertion. "That's the idea, Mrs. Resnick." He took the broom from Sophie and threw it into a corner of the kitchen. "You and Pearl, Annie, get some mops. You had a flood up here—that's why Pearl went downstairs, to see if there was any damage."

Pearl and Annie brought mops, slopped the water across the floor. Jake slapped Levitt on the back. "You're a genius, you know that?"

"We'll see how much of a genius I am when Fromberg hears the story."

Half an hour later, the yellow LaSalle pulled up behind Jake's truck. Fromberg climbed out and banged on the locked restaurant door. Minsky peered out through a crack in the curtains. "It's Fromberg!"

"By himself?" Jake stood next to Minsky to look. The moneylender was alone. He unlocked the door, pulled Fromberg inside, and swiftly closed the door again. "What do you want?"

"What do you think I want?" Fromberg looked around the restaurant, saw the three young men eying him suspiciously, then strode into the kitchen. "What the hell happened down there this morning?" he shouted at Pearl. "What were you even doing down there?"

"Your trained ape attacked her; that's what happened," answered Jake, who had followed Fromberg through the restaurant.

"I just saw him at the hospital," Fromberg said, "having his face stitched up. If anyone did the attacking, it wasn't Gus." His glance fell on the chisel, which Pearl had dropped onto a table when she'd picked up a mop; the drying strip of skin still clung to its blade, like a thin sliver of shaved wood. "What I want to know now is what she was doing down there!"

Pearl pointed to the floor, spotted with a few small puddles of water. "We had a flood here this morning. I went downstairs to see if there was any damage."

"A flood?" Fromberg spun around, undid the three bolts on the basement door and ran heavily down the stairs. Pearl followed him. Jake went halfway and listened, motioning for the others to keep back. Fromberg turned on the lights, stared anxiously upward. A wet, circular stain, four feet wide, spread across the center of the ceiling. "Jesus Christ!" he muttered. Recovering, he swung around on Pearl again. "Okay, so you had a flood—what did that have to do with you playing the slots?"

"I saw them when I came down. I wanted to see how lucky I was."

Fromberg's attention switched from the damp stain to the slot machines and back to the stain. Relief washed over Pearl—he'd bought her story—gratitude followed, for Levitt's quick thinking.

"Why the hell didn't you say anything when Gus came in?" Fromberg demanded. "Why did you have to carve him up like a Christmas turkey?" He gazed in wonderment at Pearl, still unable to fully accept Landau's story of her attacking him with the chisel. A little kid like that, two puffs of wind would blow her clear across the East River into Brooklyn. Where did she come off getting the better of a man like Landau? And, more importantly, how was Fromberg going to keep Landau in check now? The bodyguard fancied himself as a ladies' man; he even operated a select prostitution service, offering young girls he'd lured into working for him. How successful would he be with that stripe down his face? Fromberg could not afford to let Landau seek revenge against the Resnicks. He had too much money tied up in the club to risk the bodyguard running amok.

"He never gave me a chance to say anything," Pearl answered. "He grabbed hold of me, tried to kiss me. . . ." Her voice trailed off when she realized that Fromberg was no longer listening. He was pulling a chair beneath the damp spot, standing on it while he prodded the ceiling with his finger. "I'll pay to get it painted," Pearl offered.

Fromberg climbed off the chair and glared at her. "I've got two versions of what happened down here, and I don't know which one to believe. Gus didn't mention any leak. All he said was that you were playing the slots, and when he came in you went for him with a chisel. You tell me another story completely. Now I'm going to tell you something. You stay out of my way. And the next time you have a flood, you call me, okay? You don't come down here for any reason."

Pearl retreated to the stairs, followed by Jake. Fromberg took a final look at the damp area and walked up after them. "You so scared of me that you had to bring your friends?" he asked Pearl when they reached the top.

"We come here for breakfast every morning," Levitt lied.

Fromberg studied the little Pole. He supposed Levitt knew all about the layout downstairs. He didn't believe for a moment that Pearl would have been satisfied with just trying the slot machines. While she was downstairs, she'd certainly taken the opportunity to nose around. Fromberg had little doubt that she'd told her friends about the club. "You, shrimp—write down your address for me."

"Why?" Levitt asked guardedly.

"I can use you downstairs."

Levitt wrote down his family's address on Broome Street. Fromberg took the piece of paper, recognized the tiny, immaculate writing. The shrimp could do more than run a dice game; he knew how to strike a tough bargain as well.

"You two, give me a place where I can reach you, too. I can find work for all of you." He had noticed how Minsky's hand had never strayed from his jacket pocket, and Jake had a truck at his disposal. Fromberg had seen this breed before—young, ambitious, an eye to the future. He'd seen them, employed them, and then cast them aside when he'd had no further use for them. The truck, especially, would come in handy. Jake and Minsky scribbled down their addresses. Fromberg pocketed them and left the restaurant.

"Is it safe to open up now?" Sophie asked.

Jake nodded. "He won't let Landau do anything—he can't afford to." He went to the front, drew back the curtains, turned the sign.

"Would you really work for him?" Pearl asked.

"Depends on what he offers," was Jake's reply.

"What about you?" Pearl asked Levitt. "And you?" She turned to Minsky.

"You and your mother take money from him, why shouldn't we?" was all Levitt said.

"That's not the same. He's paying us rent for using the basement, that's all. You'd have to work for him to earn his money."

"Money's money, no matter whether it's rent or wages," Levitt answered. "It all comes out of his pocket."

"It's not the same," Pearl stressed. She looked to Annie for help. If these three boys weren't opposed to working for Fromberg, Moses Caplan wouldn't be. Surely Annie must be as upset as she was at the prospect.

"Of course it's the same." This time it was Jake who argued. "His grubby hands touch it all. And if you think his rent money's any cleaner than the rest of it, you're just being a damned hypocrite."

Pearl was stunned by the sudden change in them, especially in Jake. They all had their reasons to despise Fromberg; one way or another, he'd robbed them all. What she was doing . . . what her mother was doing . . . was just getting some of that money back. But what Jake and his friends seemed bent on doing . . . A clear dividing line was plainly visible to her. She had to take a stand, even if it was against those she cared for. "Jake, if you go to work for Fromberg, then as far as I'm concerned you're no better than Gus Landau. And like him, you'll belong down there"—she jabbed a finger in the direction of the basement—"not up here!"

At first, Jake laughed at the threat. Then, as he realized how serious Pearl was, his face grew somber. "Are you blackmailing me, Pearl?"

"No. I'm giving you a choice. Lou as well. Benny, too. If you work for Fromberg, don't bother coming in here anymore. You won't be welcome."

A short silence followed, broken by Minsky saying, "I've got to get to work." He pulled back the door and walked out onto Second Avenue.

Levitt was next. He gave Pearl a long speculative look and followed Minsky. That left only Jake. "You're serious, aren't you?"

"I've never been more serious in my life."

"And you can't see a difference between taking his money or working for it? You're a strange girl, you know that? You can look at black and talk yourself into believing it's white if that's what you want it to be."

"Are you going to work for him?"

"You'd better find someone else to get your vegetables from in the future. I'll be busy . . . downstairs! Then see who comes to help you out the next time you get in a jam." Without another word, he walked out of the restaurant, climbed into the truck, and drove away. Pearl watched him go past, his jaw set like a piece of granite, never looking into the restaurant. She turned around slowly and faced her mother and Annie, who had remained so quiet during the

76

short but intense confrontation.

"What about you, Annie? What will you do if Moe goes to work for Fromberg as well?"

"I'll keep right on seeing him," Annie replied. "Working for Fromberg's no different from taking rent money from him. If you can't see that, you'd better get yourself some glasses. Sorry, Pearl," Annie added when she saw her friend blink back tears, "but in this case, you're wrong." She walked past Pearl to return to the bakery next door.

"And what about you?" Pearl asked her mother. "Are you going to tell me I'm wrong, too? Tell me I'm a hypocrite?"

"If I did, would you listen to me?" Sophie responded. "Would you believe me when you didn't believe your friends?"

Pearl thought about it. "I'd believe you, Mama."

"I'm not going to tell you anything, Pearl. The last time I told you that you were wrong, it turned out that you were right."

"About Fromberg and you?"

Sophie nodded. "This time I think it's best if you find out for yourself."

After leaving the restaurant, Saul Fromberg returned to the hospital to wait for Gus Landau. When the bodyguard came out, the left side of his face was covered by a huge dressing. He had two sutures in his bottom lip where Pearl had bitten him, but the doctor had been able to do little about the wide cut made by the chisel, except clean and cover it. It was too broad, too shallow, to stitch. It would be a long time before Landau could comfortably shave that side of his face.

"Did you see a leak when you went into the club?" Fromberg asked. "There was a big damp patch when I went down there just now. That's the reason the girl was there, so she says."

"No," Landau muttered. Talk was painful; he was trying to keep movements of his mouth to a minimum. "No leak. All I saw was her playing the slots."

"She said you tried to kiss her. Did you?"

Landau shook his head and regretted it immediately; that was even more painful than talking. "How can I remember what I did or didn't do? It all happened so damned fast. Maybe I grabbed her, shook her up a little."

"Yeah, and maybe you tried to put the make on her as well." Fromberg didn't approve of Landau's playing around, especially when it caused trouble like this. "I just told her to stay out of my hair, Gus, to keep her nose clean. The same goes for you. I've invested every dime I could beg, borrow, or steal in King Saul, and I don't want the place getting messed up because of you. Stay away from her. And stay clear of her pals. They might be doing some work for me in the future. And even if they don't"—Fromberg gripped Landau's arm tightly to be certain he had every ounce of the man's attention— "I don't need you crapping on my doorstep. Okay?"

"Sure . . . okay." Landau touched his face gingerly. Stay away? That meant forget. How was he supposed to forget what they'd done to him? A slip of a girl slashing his face with a chisel; a young punk jabbing a broken bottle at him; and an old woman pushing him down a flight of stairs with a broom. No man could forget that, unless he had no self-respect.

Maybe it would take ten years, but he'd get back at them. He'd make them pay, every single one of them.

Chapter Six

King Saul opened a week later. Pearl watched through the kitchen window of the flat, anxious to see how well attended the new club would be. Cars disgorged well-dressed men and women who walked along the alley to descend the stone steps leading to the door with the gold crown on it.

Pearl felt disappointed because of the steady flow of customers. She wanted the club to fail. She wanted Jake to see how wrong he'd been to throw in with Fromberg. Quite suddenly, the money Fromberg was paying Sophie Resnick for use of the basement seemed very unimportant. Pearl would happily go without it if only Jake would come back. She hadn't seen or heard from him for a week, not since she had given him the ultimatum.

At ten o'clock that night, an hour after the club had opened its doors, Sophie Resnick joined her daughter at the window. "Have you seen Jake yet?"

"I'm not looking for him," Pearl lied.

"Did I say you were? I just wondered if you'd seen him yet, seen him going to work at his new job."

"No."

"Look!" Sophie pointed down at the alley. "Isn't that Lou?"

Pearl stared down. A little figure was walking hurriedly, wearing a tuxedo, looking as elegant as any of the visitors to the club. Surely if Levitt was there, Jake couldn't be far behind, Pearl told herself. Levitt reached the top of the stairs and started down them, disappearing from Pearl's sight. Was he going to run Fromberg's dice game as he'd run his own? She imagined him scampering around like a little monkey, money flying this way and that as he paid out and collected; especially collected. A little monkey wearing a tuxedo . . .

At midnight, as people started to drift out of the club, Pearl and Sophie finally spotted Jake. Unlike Levitt, Jake was not wearing a tuxedo. He was dressed in rough working clothes, the same as Moses

79

Caplan and Benny Minsky who were with him. They drove up in a truck, parked close to the club's entrance, and began to unload wooden crates, stacking them neatly in the alley. Jake went to the door. Pearl heard him knock three times in rapid succession. Moments later, three waiters, attired smartly in black trousers and white jackets, came out to carry the crates into the club.

"Lou gets to wear a tuxedo," Sophie remarked, "and the other three carry boxes. Some bigshot Jake turned out to be. Fromberg won't even let him into the club."

Pearl tried not to laugh at her mother's sarcastic comment, but a smile managed to creep across her face.

"That's better," Sophie told her. "Why should you be so upset about losing a delivery boy?"

"Maybe I should have been fond of Lou instead. At least, he gets to wear a suit for work."

"Deliverymen?" Annie threw back her head and laughed the next morning when Pearl mentioned seeing the truck. "You thought they were three deliverymen?"

"What's so funny about that? That's what they looked like to me."

"You know what they were delivering, Pearl? Those crates were full of whiskey. Jake, Moe, and Benny help to bring it in from Canada, it's transported in relays, they bring it in the last fifty miles. Deliverymen for the stores should only get paid what they got paid for last night's work."

"That's dangerous. What if someone tries to steal it?"

"They have guards on the trucks." Annie lowered her voice conspiratorially. "You remember that time in the basement, when Benny said if they'd been armed they wouldn't have been robbed so easy?"

"Are they—?"

"Moe told me. They all carry guns."

Pearl trembled. Guns? Benny Minsky—him she could understand; he was the one who'd wanted guns in the basement. But Jake? And Moe? "Aren't you frightened, Annie?"

"I'd be a lot more frightened for Moe if he wasn't armed," was all Annie would say.

"So Lou's the clever one after all. He wears a nice tuxedo and he sits in comfort while he operates the dice game."

"Who told you that?" Annie asked. "He's a bookkeeper there, that's all. Fromberg pays him to keep the books. Maybe he wears the fancy suit because he thinks it makes him look bigger. Believe me,

Pearl, Lou gets paid far less than the others."

Pearl went back to her work. She'd been wrong about them all. Wrong . . . wrong . . . wrong! . . . She promised herself that she wouldn't even watch from the window anymore. She didn't want to know about them. Any of them.

Pearl kept to her word. She didn't watch from the window, but the nights that Jake, Caplan, and Minsky made deliveries she was always awakened by the sound of the truck in the alley. The other noises of the club never disturbed her, people coming and going at all hours of the night, car engines starting. Just the sound of the truck. It was as though she had attuned her mind to its rasping note, and was waiting for it; because she knew that if she heard it, Jake was all right.

Six months after the club opened, Pearl turned seventeen. It was a day like any other. She got up early, worked in the restaurant all day long, and looked forward to going to bed early. She wouldn't hear the truck that night. Jake had been in the alley the previous night, and his work had now developed its own rhythm, sometimes two deliveries a week, but never more than three.

In the afternoon, Annie popped into the restaurant to wish Pearl a happy birthday. The red-headed girl had turned seventeen a few weeks earlier, and she'd regaled Pearl with tales of how she'd celebrated her birthday. "Moe took me out in his new car for a fabulous meal. Then we went to a show. Afterward, he gave me this." She'd flashed a sparkling gold bracelet beneath Pearl's eyes. Today, Annie asked Pearl what she was doing for her own birthday.

"Bake myself the biggest cake you ever saw, cover it with icing, stick seventeen candles on it, and share it with my mother," Pearl answered. "You can come if you like."

Annie shook her head in desperation. "You're acting like you did in school that time, when you used to rush home by yourself and ignore the rest of us. Will you stop being so blind? You know you want to see Jake, and he wants to see you—"

"Who said he does?"

"He always asks about you."

"He knows what he has to do. Stop working down there."

"Sure. And you and your mother stop taking Fromberg's money. His rent's no cleaner than what he pays the boys."

"Yes, it is. We don't have to carry guns to earn it."

"Enjoy your birthday," Annie told her. "Save me a piece of cake. I'm going out with Moe tonight."

Caplan wasn't the only one who had a new car. Once Pearl saw Jake driving along Second Avenue as she swept the sidewalk outside the restaurant. He wasn't in the truck, he was in a brand new yellow LaSalle, just like the one Fromberg owned. In the passenger seat next to him was a girl with blond hair and a heavily made-up face. Standing in front of the restaurant, Pearl watched him drive slowly by. He didn't look in her direction at all, but the girl did. For an instant, her eyes met Pearl's; then the contact was broken as the LaSalle picked up speed. Pearl rested her chin on the broom handle and gazed after the car. So this was how Jake had turned out. The boy who'd delivered groceries now drove a big car and kept company with a fancy woman. Was that the kind of girl he really wanted for himself? A painted blonde? Such a girl wouldn't know how to make a barley soup that would keep out the cold on the most bitter winter day. Such a girl wouldn't know how to keep a home. A good-time girl with bleached hair and a paint store covering her face!

What could Jake possibly want with a girl like that? And then Pearl answered the question for herself. A girl who wouldn't tell him what he could or could not do, that's what. A girl who wouldn't give him an ultimatum.

Lou Levitt was the first to break with Fromberg, a year after the club had opened. At six o'clock on a Tuesday morning, just as Pearl and her mother opened the restaurant, he walked in the front door, bow tie undone, shirt collar open, face haggard. "Got a cup of coffee, Pearl?"

It took Pearl a few seconds to recover from her surprise. Then she pointed a finger at the door. "Out."

Levitt held up his hands in a gesture of peace. "All I want is a lousy cup of coffee."

"And I don't want your business. I told you a year ago, if you work downstairs you don't belong up here."

"I don't work there anymore." Levitt hoisted himself onto a stool at the counter. "I just quit."

"Why?"

"There's going to be trouble, that's why." He waited until Pearl poured coffee for him. "Fromberg's not satisfied with what he can steal legally. He had a mechanic down there last night, after we'd closed up. Rigged the roulette wheel so the croupier can stay clear of heavily backed numbers. He wants the odds even more in his favor. He'll get found out and then there'll be hell to pay." Levitt sipped from the cup, waiting for Pearl to say something.

"Did you tell him that?"

"No. If he's too dumb to see it for himself, why should I tell him?" Levitt shook his head sadly. "Stupid, a stupid man. He's got a gold mine down there—the house can't lose—but he's greedy. You any idea how much he made in the past year from that place?"

"I couldn't care less."

"He's got four or five clubs now," Levitt went on, unconcerned about Pearl's disinterest. He talked as though he wanted to hear himself speak, get it all off his chest to someone. "Those other clubs he had a piece of, now he owns them outright. He's bought real estate, bought into legitimate businesses. He's got a big fancy office now, just east of Third Avenue on Forty-second Street. Owns the building. All from money he's made downstairs. And now he's going to kill the goose that laid him the golden egg."

Pearl considered the information. She didn't care about Fromberg's other interests, only the club downstairs. If Levitt was right, King Saul would soon come to an end. She and Sophie wouldn't really miss the rent money. They hadn't spent any of it anyway. Every penny he'd given them had been saved, and with the restaurant now completely under their control, they had more than enough to live on comfortably. What would happen to Jake, though? Would she allow him back upstairs because he no longer worked downstairs? "Does Jake ever run into Landau?"

Levitt smiled at the question. "Jake doesn't come into the club except to get his orders. Him and Landau do a good job of staying out of each other's way. He doesn't give you any trouble, does he?"

"No, I've only seen him a couple of times. He looked straight through me." She thought back to those instances when she'd encountered Landau on the street. The stripe on his face was uncannily symmetrical, as though someone had used a ruler to create it. Stretching from just below his left ear to his chin, it had turned a pale purple in color, clashing with the unhealthy whiteness of his skin. He'd looked at Pearl, recognition—and something else—flashing in those cold blue eyes. Then he'd walked on.

"Fromberg keeps a tight leash on him. And"—Levitt paused like a man about to impart a secret—"Jake would kill him if he ever came near you, Pearl. So would I."

"Thanks, Lou." She reached out to touch his hand tenderly. "What about yourself, what are you going to do now?"

"Get a job as a bookkeeper where they don't load the dice. Work for a legitimate company for a while. It won't pay as much, but I won't be standing under the roof when it caves in." He finished the coffee, tossed a coin onto the counter and walked out into the early morning bustle of Second Avenue.

The roof caved in six months later, during the week of Pearl's eighteenth birthday. At two in the morning, the unique sound of the truck woke her. She lay in bed, listening to the crates of whisky being unloaded, the special knock, the waiters' footsteps as they came up from the club to carry the crates inside, and finally the noise of the truck driving away. Where was Jake going now? Back to his home, or to a late-night tryst with his painted blonde? Telling herself she didn't really care, Pearl closed her eyes again.

Five minutes later, lights flooded the alley. Doors slammed. Pearl heard the sound of feet pounding across the cobblestones. She climbed out of bed and ran into the kitchen. Sophie was already at the window, staring down intently.

"It's the police," she whispered.

Police? Thank God Jake left already, was Pearl's first thought. She joined her mother at the window in time to see eight police officers crowding down the stairs. The club's patrons poured out into the alley. At first, Pearl thought they were all being arrested, but there were no vans to take them away. They just drifted off toward their cars, talking excitedly about the raid as if it had been a part of the night's entertainment. Then Pearl saw two of the policemen carrying the roulette wheel between them. The slot machines followed. The police hadn't raided King Saul because it was selling liquor; they'd raided the club because it was cheating people. Because, just as Levitt had said, it was running a crooked game. As Pearl watched the wheel being loaded into one of the cars, she felt a surge of satisfaction. Fromberg was out of business downstairs . . . and in trouble with the police.

"I think our rent just stopped coming in," Pearl told her mother.

"Suits me. We can store food down there once again. And maybe you and your friends can use the basement like you used to."

"Maybe." Pearl returned to bed, but she was too excited to sleep. After half an hour, she got up again, dressed warmly, and went downstairs. The alley was deserted, the police cars gone. There was no sign of the club's patrons. Suddenly, the door with the crown opened and a shaft of light spilled out onto the stairs and the alley. Pearl looked around, spotted a doorway, and darted into it. She heard the club door close, footsteps, voices. Fromberg and Gus Landau walked by not five yards away, failing to see her huddled in the shadow of the doorway.

"I guess we can write that place off," Fromberg said. "Paid for itself, though, didn't it?"

Landau nodded. "Fixing the wheel gave us a nice extra edge. Who tumbled to it?"

"Who knows? Someone had to in the end. I said it would only last six months, but in that time we'd be able to clean up. It doesn't matter anyway. All the other joints are straight. This one was expendable."

"What about those kids? You going to keep them on?"

"Granitz, Caplan, and Minsky? If they want to stay I can always find them a place. You got any objections?"

"My objections can wait awhile."

Fromberg laughed and slapped Landau on the back. "After tomorrow they might not want to stay with me anyway. Depends how they feel about that kid and her mother being left holding the bag for all this."

Their voices trailed away as they reached the end of the alley. Pearl remained rooted in the doorway, replaying the conversation in her mind. What did Fromberg mean about the kid and her mother being left holding the bag? She had no doubt that the kid was herself, but the rest of the sentence made little sense, except that it was a threat of some kind. . . .

Pearl waited until she heard a car drive away, then left the doorway and returned to the flat.

Before the restaurant opened the following morning, Pearl went next door to pick up bagels—and tell Annie the news. "Did you hear about the club?"

"That it got raided?" Annie replied. "I'd have had to be deaf not to know about it. We watched it all happen."

"So did we," Pearl said. "What's Moe going to do now?"

"I don't know. I haven't seen him yet."

Isidore Moscowitz finished packing Pearl's order and handed two bags full of bagels to her. "What are you going to do now that you've lost your tenant?"

"Tenants like that we should all lose," Pearl answered gaily. She looked at the clock on the wall and realized she'd been gone for more than five minutes. The restaurant would be open soon; she'd have to get back.

"What if I see Jake?" Annie asked, as Pearl turned to leave. "Is there anything you want me to say to him?"

"You can tell him we found another supplier for produce. Very satisfactory. No . . . don't tell him anything. I've got to go; we have to work for our money now. 'Bye, Annie. 'Bye, Mr. Moscowitz." She pushed open the door and stepped outside . . . just in time to see three men escorting her mother from the restaurant to a waiting car. Pearl dropped both bags of bagels onto the ground and ran toward the group. "What's going on? Who are you? Where are you taking my mother?"

The leader of the three men turned around. "Your mother? We're taking her to jail."

"What?" Pearl stared at her mother. "What for?"

"Operating an illegal gaming house—"

Pearl cut him off before he could recite further charges. "My mother didn't run any gaming house!"

"It was operated on her premises. Her name's on the lease." He signaled to the other two men to put Sophie in the car. "That whole damned club was hers. You'd better see about getting your mother a smart lawyer, kid, not that it's going to do her much good."

Pearl threw herself at the car, trying to pull back the door as it closed on Sophie. One of the policemen held her back, despite her kicking and screaming. "You carry on and you're going right along with her. We've got room in the car for you." He pushed Pearl away and jumped into the front passenger seat. As the car moved off, Pearl picked up one of the bagels from the sidewalk and threw it as hard as she could. It bounced off the back window but the car didn't stop.

"What happened?"

Pearl turned to see Annie who'd come running from the bakery at the noise. "They've arrested my mother. They think the club was hers, the gambling, the crooked roulette game, everything."

"Come inside. My father knows a lawyer—"

"I don't want a lawyer. I want . . . I want Lou. Can you find him for me, Annie? Get Lou, he'll know what to do." She was desperate. Only moments earlier she'd been laughing about the club being closed, and now her mother had been arrested for running it. Fromberg! That slimy, cunning, conniving son of a bitch! The solution to a hundred unanswered questions flashed through her mind. The kid and her mother holding the bag . . . Fromberg's cash-only business, no receipts . . . his reluctance to sign a lease. He hadn't left his name anywhere. The only name that showed was that of Sophie Resnick, and she was going to be the one left holding the bag. Fromberg had made a fortune, and Pearl's mother was going to jail for it!

Annie ran off, and Pearl walked into the restaurant and sat down in booth number four. She imagined Fromberg sitting there, just like he'd done for so many years. She wanted to get her hands around his throat and squeeze until his eyes bulged like two balls. And then go right on squeezing, paying him back for every moment of misery he had caused her family.

The first customer of the day walked in and took a seat at the counter. "We're closed," Pearl told him.

"Closed? The door's open."

"We had a gas leak last night. We're closed until it's fixed." The man left. Pearl locked the door and turned the sign. The restaurant would remain closed until her mother returned. Whenever that might be.

Annie returned with Levitt half an hour later. Pearl started to tell him the story, but he held his hands out. "I heard already. Now you know why Fromberg never signed anything."

"I figured that out for myself already," Pearl replied impatiently. "What I want to know is how we get my mother out of jail."

"Slow down, will you? They won't put her in jail until she's tried and found guilty—"

"Can you see her being found not guilty?"

"No," Levitt answered quietly. "Fromberg stacked the deck against her. Those cops who picked her up are probably in his pay. He must have known this would happen from the moment he had that table fixed, from the moment he opened the club even. That two hundred a month he was paying—that wasn't rent, it was money for your mother to take the fall. Of course, it might not be a jail sentence. It might just be a fine."

"He's paid us thirty-six hundred dollars so far. We put it all away."

Levitt didn't have the heart to tell Pearl that the thirty-six hundred dollars might not be enough. "I'll get hold of a good lawyer, Pearl. He'll make sure your mother's released on bail. We can use Fromberg's money for that."

"Where's that bastard's fancy new office, Lou?"

Levitt shook his head. "No, Pearl, don't do that. It won't solve anything."

"Maybe not, but it'll make me feel a damned sight better. Where's his office? I'm going there the moment my mother gets back."

In eighteen months, Saul Fromberg had moved a long way from being a loanshark on the Lower East Side. Now he controlled a string of enterprises, from a tenth-floor suite of offices on East Forty-second Street between Second and Third Avenues. He delighted in parading himself as a successful businessman, a pillar of corporate respectability. He prided himself on his legitimate concerns, the real estate he owned, the theaters and restaurants in which he had an interest. And if those should fall upon difficult times, he could always rely on the money generated by the more profitable illegal activities which had enabled him to buy into legitimate businesses in the first place.

Pearl arrived at Fromberg's building in the middle of the afternoon, after her mother had returned to the restaurant following her arraignment and the posting of bond by a lawyer hired by Levitt. Pearl did not know what she would have done without Levitt that day. He had taken over completely—arranging details with the lawyer, appearing in court for the arraignment, and bringing Sophie back to the restaurant after bail had been granted. Pearl had been shocked by her mother's appearance. Sophie's face was white and gaunt, her bright eyes were lifeless, her hands trembled uncontrollably. Barely able to speak for sobbing, she told Pearl she was going upstairs to lie down, complaining of a headache. Pearl could never remember her mother being ill.

Reaching the tenth floor of the building, Pearl walked along the corridor until she found a door on which Saul Fromberg's name was written in gold script. She pushed it open and found herself in a reception area. Behind a desk facing the door sat a stern-faced elderly woman with tightly waved iron-gray hair.

"May I help you?"

"I want to see Mr. Fromberg, please."

"Do you have an appointment with Mr. Fromberg?" From the woman's tone, she obviously thought not.

Pearl shook her head timidly, overwhelmed by the office, the building, and the fearsome receptionist.

"I'm afraid Mr. Fromberg doesn't see anyone without an appointment. If you would like to leave your name . . ."

Pearl remembered her mother's state when she'd returned to the restaurant, and she remembered the promise she'd once made to her father. Timidity fled. "Mr. Fromberg will see me. I don't need an appointment."

The receptionist studied Pearl for several seconds as she tried to equate the young, sweet-faced girl with the voice of ice-cold anger.

"Are you just going to sit there staring at me, or are you going to tell Mr. Fromberg I'm here?" Pearl demanded. "My name's Pearl Resnick."

"Just a moment." Now it was the elderly woman who was uncertain. She left the desk and disappeared through a door. A minute later, she returned. "Mr. Fromberg *will* see you. Come with me, please."

Pearl followed her through a succession of small offices in which clerks and bookkeepers worked busily at desks, and she noticed men who, she would have sworn, had never sat behind a desk or pushed a pencil in their lives; they just stood and watched what went on, like lizards waiting for a fly to land near them. The elderly woman stopped in front of a heavy oak door, knocked, then ushered Pearl inside. Pearl entered a vast room with deep carpeting and rich oak paneling, just like the King Saul Club. Fromberg sat behind a leather-topped desk, a pair of heavy horn-rimmed glasses resting on the end of his nose as he scanned a set of figures. Slouched in an easy chair was Gus Landau.

As the receptionist closed the door behind Pearl, Fromberg looked up. "Come in, come in. What can I do for you?"

"What can you do for me?" Pearl almost choked on the words. "You can tell the damned truth to begin with! My mother was arrested this morning, she spent the day in court, all for that crooked game *you* were running in our basement!"

Fromberg's smile was beatific as he removed his glasses and set them carefully on the desk. "I don't know what you're talking about. You seem distressed about something, but you're not making yourself very clear."

"I think she means the game in the club," Landau interjected; the scar on his cheek twisted as his smile matched Fromberg's. "Did you hear about that club her mother had beneath the restaurant? There was a roulette game there, crooked. The police raided it this morning."

"That club had nothing to do with my mother!" Pearl shouted at Fromberg. "She never even went down there. She rented it out to you!"

Fromberg's smile disappeared; the little game was over. "If your mother had rented that basement to me, she'd have some document, wouldn't she? A lease or something. Show me my name—show me my signature on a lease."

Pearl moved toward the desk. Landau started from his seat but Fromberg waved him back. "Let me tell you the story as I know it," he said. "I wanted that basement. I wanted to put a club down there. I told your mother. But she was greedy, Pearl. She wanted it all for herself, all the money that could be made from it. And you can see what happened."

"No judge or jury will accept that story."

"Kid, you've got a lot to learn if you believe that. Your mother's worked hard all her life—now she's going to get a well-deserved vacation. Tell her, from me, she should enjoy it." He moved his hand again. "Gus, show her out."

Landau stood up. As he gripped Pearl's arm, she swung around a final time to Fromberg. "There are people who'll swear it was your club! Jake will. So will his friends!"

"You really think so? You think they're going to risk their necks to finger me? You think a judge is going to take the word of a bunch of punk kids over mine? He'll throw them in jail along with your mother once they mention their connection with the club—running booze in, carrying guns."

Desperately, Pearl sought another line of attack. She knew she'd lost . . . Levitt had been right . . . but she wanted one more chance to hurt Fromberg. "I'm going to sell off all that furniture you left in our basement, the piano, everything!"

To her dismay, Fromberg roared with laughter. "Go ahead and sell it. It doesn't belong to me. It belongs to your mother. Gus, get her out of here. She's giving me a headache with her whining!"

Landau's grip tightened painfully on Pearl's arm. He pulled her toward a door set in the side of the office, unlocked it, and swung it back. Pearl saw that three-inch steel lay beneath its oak paneling. When Landau dragged her through the doorway into the corridor, to come out opposite the elevator, she noticed that the wall of the office was also lined with steel. Fromberg had made sure that no one would take him by surprise; the only way in was through the reception area, where bodyguards waited along the route.

Landau pressed the button for the elevator. "Remember this?" He pointed to the livid scar on his cheek. "I told you I'd pay you back. You can think about this scar all the time your goddamned mother rots in jail." The elevator arrived. The moment the attendant opened the door, Landau shoved Pearl inside.

She didn't remember the journey back to Second Avenue. Like a robot, she alighted at her stop, walked to the restaurant. The sign still read Closed. She let herself in. Annie was inside, sitting in one of the booths with the four boys.

"Where's my mother?" Pearl asked.

"Still upstairs," Annie answered.

Ignoring the boys, Pearl ran up to her mother's bedroom. Sophie was lying on the bed with a cold, damp cloth pressed to her forehead. "I just saw Fromberg. He's sitting in his big office laughing at us, Mama." Pearl sat down on the edge of her mother's bed and began to cry.

Sophie clasped her daughter's hand. "We deserve to be laughed at, Pearl. Your friends were right. The money he paid us was just as dirty as the money he paid them."

"We'll use it to pay the fine."

"If there is a fine. Otherwise"—Sophie's voice broke and she joined Pearl in crying—"I'll be sent to jail."

"Of course you won't. No judge would send you to jail. You've never done anything wrong in your life."

"What will you do while I'm away, Pearl? What will happen to the restaurant, our home?"

"You're not going anywhere, Mama. That lawyer Lou got for us. He's smart, a top lawyer. He'll run rings around everyone, you wait and see." She left the room and returned downstairs, pausing only to dry her eyes. Annie and the boys were still sitting in the booth. Jake had a sour look on his face. Levitt seemed lost in thought, staring up at the ceiling. Minsky was nervously clasping and unclasping his fingers, and Caplan was holding Annie's hand on the table. They all looked as defeated as Pearl felt.

"Here's a bunch of strange faces," she said acidly. "Mourners come to grieve, have you?"

Caplan and Minsky looked away. Levitt continued to stare at the ceiling. Only Jake held Pearl's accusing gaze. "We're sorry, Pearl. We never thought anything like this would happen."

"Sorry doesn't solve anything!" she snapped back. The anger in her voice wasn't the result of their gloom, their seeming willingness to accept what had happened. It was the result of eighteen months without Jake, of not speaking to him for so long . . . of seeing him in his new car with that painted blonde!

Levitt finally took his eyes off the ceiling. "I saw what was wrong with the whole deal that day you got him out of here, when you told us he didn't want a lease. I said then, didn't I, that if he doesn't put his name to anything, who's to prove he has any connection with the club?"

"So why didn't you come up with what Fromberg was up to then, genius?" Minsky muttered sourly. "You're a great guy for hindsight."

"I remember," Pearl said. "While you were thinking about it, we heard that noise from downstairs."

"Fromberg's men moving stuff up from the basement," Jake added, recalling the night.

"And now Fromberg and his men have moved out," Annie said, "leaving Pearl's mother on the firing line."

"Jake, I want you to tell the truth at the trial. I want you and the others to stand up there and tell the judge who was running that club, who was responsible for cheating on the game."

"You're kidding!" Minsky burst out. "We'll all get the book

thrown at us."

"I don't care about you," Pearl answered. "All I know is that my mother is innocent and I will not let her go to jail for something she didn't do. Jake, what about it?"

He was saved from answering by Levitt. "Your mother might not have to go to jail. I spoke to the lawyer again. If she pleads guilty, he is convinced there'll just be a fine."

"Why should she plead guilty when she isn't?"

"Because the deck is stacked against her, can't you see that? She could have God and King Solomon testifying for her and it wouldn't help a bit."

"How much will the fine be?"

"It could be ten thousand dollars."

Pearl gasped. "We can't raise that much, it's impossible."

"Then it might be a jail sentence instead. Unless—"

"Unless what?"

"Unless someone else raises the money," Jake said. He looked to Minsky and Caplan for approval. "We'll put up the money for the fine, Pearl."

"*You* will?" Annie asked, turning to Caplan. "How?"

Caplan gripped her wrist. "You never asked where the money came from to buy that bracelet. Don't be so nosy now."

Annie fell quiet again, staring at the birthday gift Caplan had given to her the previous year. He was right. She didn't want to know how or where they would raise the money—just as long as they got it. They owed that to Pearl. The past eighteen months had seemed so strange, seeing Jake going out with different girls, girls Annie knew he didn't care for. Jake and Pearl had quarreled over a principle and neither would give way. Now they were together again, trying to avert a tragedy.

"I could get some of the money," Pearl said.

"How?" Jake asked.

"I could sell everything that's downstairs. It all belongs to my mother now. She owned the club, remember?"

"You'd get ten cents on the dollar for it," Levitt said. "Don't touch a stick of it. Leave it just as it is. When this is over, we're going to open that place again."

Pearl's mind reeled. So this was what they'd been leading up to, why they'd all turned up at the restaurant? They were ready to ease themselves into the gap left by Fromberg. They'd also offer Sophie an inducement, in this case the money for the fine. The club would be open for business again, under new management certainly, but with her mother's name on the dotted line, just like the last time. "Oh, you will, will you? I suppose that's the whole idea of you coming around today, to talk me and my mother into letting you have the basement. The hell you will!"

"You think we're a bunch of rogues like Fromberg?" Levitt snapped back.

Jake held up a hand, motioned for Levitt to keep quiet. "Pearl, we came here today because you and your mother are in trouble, and we're still your friends no matter what's happened. We came to offer help."

His sincerity sliced right through Pearl's anger. She didn't know about the others, didn't care. All she understood was that Jake spoke the truth.

Her friends left soon after, and Pearl went upstairs to see her mother, stayed with Sophie until she fell asleep. Then, hungry, she made herself a sandwich, took it to the front window, and sat watching the street below. As she ate, a yellow LaSalle drew up to the curb. Pearl's heart leaped. Fromberg! . . . What could he want now? What other misery did he have to add to her already heavy load? Suddenly she remembered that Jake, too, drove a yellow LaSalle, the one she'd seen him in when the blonde was with him. As he climbed out of the car, she ran downstairs.

"I had to come back and see you," he told her. "What I wanted to say to you couldn't be said in front of the others."

"Come inside." She led him into the empty restaurant, sat him down in one of the booths. "Can I get you something to eat, Jake? It won't take a minute."

"You always cook when you're upset or worried?"

"You know, I've never thought about that before but it's true. When I'm worried about something, I cook. It soothes me."

"Whoever marries you is going to wind up fat."

"Not if he doesn't give me anything to worry about."

"Sit down, Pearl."

She sat opposite him, her hands on the table. With Jake there again, she just knew that everything was going to be all right. "We've got eighteen months to catch up on."

"I know what's been happening with you. Annie told me."

"She told me about you as well," Pearl responded. "Jake, Annie told me once that you carried guns when you went to pick up Fromberg's liquor. He said the same thing this morning when I saw him—he said that was one of the reasons why you wouldn't dare testify on my mother's behalf."

"Not me," Jake said. "I didn't carry a gun. I just drove. Moe did, though. Benny, too. Benny wouldn't have taken the job without one,

no matter how much Fromberg was paying. He thinks they're toys."
He touched a finger to his head, made a face. "He's nuts that one,
bugs, *meshuggeh*."

"What about Moe?"

"He just does whatever he's told to do. Dependable, that's Moe."

"Annie likes him a lot."

"What do you expect? He's the first boy to ever kiss her."

"And you're the first boy who ever kissed me."

"Still remember, do you?"

Pearl nodded happily as she was transported back to that day. "A
quick peck, and you thanked me for doing you a favor."

"Wasn't much of a kiss, was it?"

"It was better than anything I've had in the last eighteen
months." She considered carefully what she wanted to say next.
Maybe Jake wanted her to be like Caplan, not say much and do
whatever she was told. But she didn't want, didn't intend, to be like
that. "Who was that girl I saw you with in your car?"

Jake seemed puzzled. "Which girl?"

"You mean there was more than one?"

"Hundreds," he replied with a quick grin. "I had to chain Lou to
an adding machine to keep track."

"The blond girl. You drove past here with her one day."

"Oh, her," Jake said, remembering. "Kathleen Monahan. I only
saw her a couple of times, that's all. Benny goes out with her now.
He's crazy about her. Chases her like a dog in heat, spends every
penny he's got on her."

"What does she do, this Kathleen?"

"Manicurist in a barber shop. Got hopes of being a singer. Takes
lessons, all that stuff, but she can't get a break."

"Too bad." Pearl dismissed Kathleen Monahan and Benny Minsky
from her mind. "These past eighteen months," she whispered, "I've
missed you, Jake."

Jake stood up and Pearl thought he was going to leave. Instead, he
walked toward the door leading down to the basement. "Why don't
we inspect the property? You and your mother own it outright now,
so what's the harm in looking?"

Pearl followed him down the stairs, uncertain what to expect.
Eighteen months again . . . that's how long it was since she had been
down there, that morning Landau had caught her playing with the
slot machines and Jake had come to her rescue. It seemed her entire
life had gone into an eclipse on that day eighteen months ago, and only
now was it coming back into the light.

"Left the place like a goddamned pigsty," she heard Jake mutter.

When she reached the bottom of the stairs, she saw what he meant. Chairs were overturned; tablecloths and glasses were scattered on the floor. The carpet was cleaner, newer looking, where the slot machines had stood. Pearl felt something beneath her shoe and looked down to see a crushed-out cigar butt which had burned a hole in the carpet. She bent down to pick it up and place it in an ashtray.

"Leave it," Jake said. "We'll get a crew in here, have the place looking new again in no time." He went to the bar and opened up a storage cupboard. "Nice windfall."

Pearl looked. Four cases of Canadian whisky were inside.

"You know how much this stuff's worth, uncut like this?" Jake asked. "Actual price is around twenty-seven bucks a case, but once it gets here you can get up to a hundred bucks a bottle for it. Good stuff, that is, not the home-brewed rotgut. Let's see what else Fromberg left us." Jake led the way into the gaming room. The roulette table was still there, a huge hole in its center where the wheel had been removed.

"Will there be gambling down here?" she asked Jake.

"Lou wants it. A clean, honest game, though. There won't be any trouble with the cops as long as the game's straight, and we'll still win plenty. We're the house, remember?" He led the way out of the room, through the club, and into what had been Fromberg's office. Here it was still neat. Obviously, the police hadn't come this far; they'd been satisfied with just removing the wheel and the slots. "Our new office," Jake said proudly.

"Is this where you'll work?" Somehow she didn't see Jake as the office type.

"Not me. This is going to be Lou's place . . . where he'll be adding and adding and adding all those gorgeous dollars." He sat behind the desk and swung his feet up. "Miss Resnick . . . take a memo, please."

Pearl sat on the edge of the desk, miming a secretary taking shorthand. "To whom, Mr. Granitz?"

"Yourself."

"And the address?"

He waved a hand airily. "Don't bother me with these small details. Are you ready?"

"Ready," Pearl replied, enjoying the game.

"Point number one, the name of the new club will be Four Aces and the Queen."

"How's that?"

"Me, Lou, Benny, and Moe—we're the four aces. You're the queen. But we'll call it Four Aces for short. Point two, shares in the Four Aces . . . and the Queen"—he prodded her in the rump with the toe of his shoe—"will be the same as they were for the dice game. You and your mother get twenty percent of the take between you. Point three, Lou and I will sign a lease with your mother for the basement for the token sum of one dollar a month."

"Thanks, Jake." The boys must have worked it out before, thrown in that condition to steer Pearl and Sophie clear of any trouble in the future.

Jake stood up, walked around the office and then dropped heavily onto the leather couch. "What are you still doing sitting on the desk? A secretary's supposed to sit on her boss's lap. What kind of secretarial school did you go to?"

"I didn't." Pearl slipped off the desk and sat on Jake's knees. "How's that, better?"

"Much better." Jake put his arms around her, rested his chin on her shoulder, and buried his nose in her long auburn hair. "Point four . . . will you marry me?"

She slid off his knees onto the couch beside him. His arms were still around her. "Are you being serious?"

"Never more serious in my life, Pearl. I've thought about it for ages; that's how much I've missed you. And when you think about something for a long time, you generally come to the right conclusion."

She felt his arms squeeze tighter around her body and she responded automatically. She didn't know how to answer. One voice inside her head screamed yes, get on with it, you fool; tell him yes before he changes his mind. Another voice, quieter but just as insistent, urged caution: Take your time, don't let anything happen too quickly.

"Well?"

She listened to the second voice. "I need to think about it, Jake."

"What's to think about? Or don't you like being the one who gets asked?" He gave a dry laugh, and Pearl asked what he found so amusing. "Just remembering that first time we went out together, when we drove in the truck to Times Square. You asked me then, told me if I waited until I asked you, you'd be an old woman."

"That has nothing to do with it, Jake. I've just turned eighteen, you're only twenty-one. My mother was married at eighteen—"

"So? She set you a good example."

"Maybe it's a good example if you're living in nineteenth-century Europe, Jake, but we're living in twentieth-century America. Besides, the decision isn't mine alone. I've got my mother to think about. She's been through hell, she needs me."

Jake nodded soberly. "I can wait. Someone once told me patience is a virtue, and someone else told me anything worth having is worth waiting for."

"They were right."

Despite his apparent lightness, Jake felt utterly deflated. He'd been sure she'd say yes. If she'd missed him only a tenth as much as he'd missed her, she would have flung herself at him. But then again, he could understand her argument. Her mother was a widow who had been through hell these past six years. She couldn't be left alone. And maybe Pearl was right about their being too young. In Europe, everyone had married young, even Jake's own parents who'd come to America from the Pale in the 1890s. They'd met on the boat coming to the new world; two people in their late teens, they'd fallen in love on the boat and married soon after landing. What else had they had to do with their lives? A struggle shared was easier than two struggles faced alone.

Yes, he decided, Pearl was right. He could wait. He could wait until he'd made himself into something by picking up the pieces Saul Fromberg had left scattered around. "Will you still go out with me? I mean . . . will you go out with me again?"

"You just try to stop me after eighteen months."

Chapter Seven

Until Jake had mentioned that Pearl sought refuge in cooking when she was upset, she'd never given it much thought. If it was true, though, the following morning she was given ample evidence of where she'd inherited the trait. When Sophie came down from the flat, she went straight into the kitchen and shooed her daughter away from the stove, saying she would cook that day. Pearl knew better than to argue. If her mother wanted to bury her fears this way, she wouldn't try to stop her.

Sophie ran the kitchen for two weeks, but cooking did not completely ease her anxiety. While she prepared food for others, she ate barely anything herself, and Pearl swore that she could see worry etching itself, like acid, across her mother's face.

"Mama, in a few days it'll be all over. The fine will be paid by Jake and his friends. You've got nothing to worry about." She did not know how the young men were going to raise the money; they hadn't confided in her. It was enough that Jake had said they would. "The trial will be a formality, over before you know what's happened."

"Will it also be a formality when my name is in the newspapers? What will our friends think then?"

"Any friend who matters knows the truth already, that you were railroaded by Fromberg. Other people . . . who cares what they think?"

Sophie remained unconvinced. "I still believe it would be better if I tried to tell the truth in court."

"And plead not guilty? No, Mama. In Hungary, it might work, but here in America, it's different. You have to deal with the system, otherwise you'll end up in jail. And then where would I be, without you?"

Sophie sliced onions, dropped them into a large skillet of sizzling fat. "In all my life, I never so much as picked up a playing card. Now I have to go into a court of law and say I'm guilty of cheating at roulette. How, in God's name, do you play roulette? I don't even know."

Pearl was uncertain whether her mother's tears were caused by the pain such public humiliation would bring, or just the onions frying in the skillet.

When Pearl entered the courtroom with Sophie, they were not alone. The Moscowitzes were there, having closed the bakery for the morning. Isidore and Helen wore their best clothes, those they normally reserved for going to the temple on the High Holy Days. Annie, who sat next to Moses Caplan, wore a dark dress in deference to the court's somber décor.

Pearl took a seat behind her mother and the lawyer, sharing the bench with Jake, Levitt, and Minsky. All the boys wore suits in the latest style—striped with wide, padded shoulders—except Levitt who was dressed in a conservative, dark gray three-piece suit, with the gold chain of a watch stretched across his narrow stomach. With a wry smile, Pearl decided that Levitt looked more like a lawyer than the lawyer did.

The judge entered the courtroom and took his seat. The proceedings began. Pearl kept her gaze on her mother as the charges were read, the guilty pleas entered. In that moment, Pearl thought Sophie could pass for her grandmother. She had aged tremendously in the past two weeks. Her face was gaunt, her eyes sunken. She had lost ten pounds, and the clothes she wore hung shapelessly on her. The amount of gray in her hair appeared to have doubled; barely any of the rich auburn color remained.

Clearing his throat, the judge launched into a vitriolic condemnation of Sophie. "Not only did you encourage the people of this city to gamble, but you then proceeded to cheat them, to remove by sophisticated mechanical means even the remotest possibility of chance working in their favor. You are a vile and cunning woman. I have no hesitation whatsoever in imposing a harsh sentence . . . one year in jail or payment of a ten-thousand-dollar fine."

Pearl saw her mother flinch at the severity of the sentence. Then she felt Jake stir beside her. He took four bulky envelopes from his jacket pocket. "Give these to the lawyer, there's twenty-five hundred bucks in each envelope."

Pearl accepted the envelopes, weighing them in her hand. Levitt had talked about the possibility of such a large fine, and Jake had assured her the money would be raised. But to actually hold it! . . . She opened one of the envelopes and peeked inside. "Where did you get it?"

Jake's voice took on a harsh edge. "Just do as I say, will you? Give it to the lawyer and let's get this damned business over!"

Pearl looked past him and saw that the Moscowitzes and Caplan were standing up, ready to leave. So was Minsky. The case was over. All that remained was to pay the fine. She leaned forward and passed the envelopes to the lawyer, patted her mother encouragingly on the shoulder. "We'll be going home soon, Mama."

Sophie reached up to place her hand over Pearl's. "Thank God your father isn't alive to see this terrible day," was all she said.

Pearl and Sophie left the court half an hour later with Jake and Levitt, after the fine had been paid and the paperwork completed. Sophie was more composed now, finally accepting that the worst was over. She had survived; that was the important thing. Now she must put her life back together, continue on as if nothing had happened. Pearl foresaw her mother being in the kitchen for a long time.

As they neared the courthouse exit, Pearl noticed a small crowd. Suddenly a voice yelled out: "There she is—there's the roulette restaurateur!" A blinding flash exploded as a photographer darted forward to snap a picture of the two women. Pearl heard Jake's roar of anger, saw a blur as he leaped at the photographer. The heavy camera and flashpan smashed to the floor as Jake's fist pounded into the man's face, sending him staggering back into two more photographers. Another flash went off, a third, a fourth. The air was full of the acrid smell of burned powder. A reporter jumped in front of Pearl and Sophie, rattling questions. Pearl only heard "Are you going back into business again, Mrs. Resnick, or are you going to stick to slinging hash?" before a sharp backhanded slap from Levitt knocked the man's pad and pencil sideways.

"Get out of our way!" Levitt demanded. Another reporter took the place of the first. Before the man could open his mouth, Levitt hit him with a sharp jab to the stomach. The reporter folded over, gasping for breath, and the little Pole's knee came up to crack him in the jaw.

Jake grabbed hold of Pearl's arm and hustled her toward the door. Levitt followed, dragging Sophie with his left hand, using his right hand to clear a path. Then they were outside, running down the courthouse steps. Jake raced on ahead to open the doors of the LaSalle. He bundled Pearl and her mother into the back. Then he and Levitt jumped into the front and the car sped away from the courthouse, leaving behind the photographers and reporters who had waited for Sophie.

"Everyone all right?" Jake asked breathlessly.

"Photographers," Sophie murmured. "Why did they want pictures of me?"

"You're a famous lady," Jake answered. "Right, little man?" he asked Levitt, who sat quietly. "Tell Pearl's ma that she's the most famous lady in New York right now."

"That's right, Mrs. Resnick. If you'd have spent that ten grand buying advertisements in newspapers, you wouldn't be any more famous than you are now."

They reached the bottom of Second Avenue. The restaurant was in darkness, the blinds drawn, when Pearl unlocked the door. She stood uneasily in the doorway, senses telling her that something was wrong. She felt Jake pushing from behind but she didn't move. It was nothing she could see, nothing she could smell or hear. Just intuition. She was certain—it was the strangest feeling—that people were in the restaurant, waiting for her. But it couldn't be; the door had been locked.

"What's the matter?" Jake asked.

"I don't know."

Before Pearl could stop him, Jake pushed past, leading Sophie into the restaurant. Lights flared on. Pearl gasped. Then she laughed. Her senses had been right, only they hadn't been cautioning her against danger. Instead, they had been warning her of a surprise party.

Three tables had been pushed together in the center of the floor, covered with linen cloths, sparkling silverware, and dishes. Pearl recognized the silverware immediately. It belonged to Annie's parents, a wedding gift which they always kept on show on the sideboard and used only on special occasions. The five people who had left the court the instant the judge had pronounced sentence were in the restaurant—Annie and her parents, Caplan and Minsky. Above the long table was a banner which read Welcome Home. And in the center of the table stood a cake that Isidore Moscowitz had painstakingly prepared the previous night. Rectangular in shape, it was covered with green icing, and in the center was a meticulously sculpted roulette wheel.

"Today," Helen Moscowitz said, "you don't cook. Neither of you. Annie and I did it all before we left for that place this morning; then we rushed back to bring it in."

Pearl could see that Sophie was overwhelmed as Isidore held out a chair for her at the top of the table. "Sit down, sit down. We've been waiting half an hour for our guest of honor to show up." He motioned for the others to sit. Sophie leaned forward and touched the green icing with her finger. "What are you looking for?" Isidore asked.

"Those sophisticated mechanical means which I used to cheat people." She looked up at Jake and Levitt. "How did Fromberg do that?"

"A pedal beneath the table, Mrs. Resnick," Levitt answered. "The

101

croupier could speed up the wheel or slow it down, do it so finely that you wouldn't even notice, just enough to keep the ball away from numbers that would have broken the house."

"Someone noticed," Pearl said.

"Someone had to in the end. That's the law of averages."

"Lou, show me how to play this game," Sophie said.

Levitt began to explain. Helen and Annie cut off the lesson by serving an appetizer of herring salad. "Forget the roulette," Helen said. "It's caused enough trouble for today."

As they ate, Pearl glanced occasionally at her mother. Sophie was digging into the food with as much enthusiasm as she normally showed when cooking. A miraculous transformation had taken place. She seemed a totally different woman from the one who had fretted away the past two weeks, flinched when the judge pronounced sentence, shied away in terror from the reporters and photographers outside the court. What had brought about the change? The knowledge that the ordeal was over? Or was there more to it, like finding out the loyalty of the friends who surrounded her?

Pearl wondered how strong her mother really was. How long would it be before she could tell her that the basement would once again be used as a club? In the two weeks since its closure—since she had gone down there with Jake—no one had set foot in the club. Debris still littered the floor. The boys would be impatient, though, she knew. Especially Jake and Levitt—those two didn't like grass to grow beneath their feet. They had to find some way of recouping the ten thousand dollars they'd laid out today to ensure Sophie's freedom. That prompted another thought. . . .

"Jake, I want to speak to you," Pearl said when the meal was over, the table cleared. She undid the bolts on the basement door and led the way downstairs, through the club to the office. "First, I want to thank you for everything you and the others did today. I also want to know where that money came from."

"Be satisfied that it was there to pay your mother's fine."

Pearl shook her head. "Once before I asked you where money came from, the stake that Lou had for the first dice game. You avoided answering me then by saying that Lou was your banker, he took care of all money matters. This time I want a proper answer because that ten thousand dollars directly concerns me. It changed my life, don't you see that? Without it, my mother would be in jail right now."

Jake looked deeply into Pearl's light brown eyes. "Are you giving me another ultimatum?" he finally said.

"If you want to call it that."

"It's really important to you, eh?"

102

"Yes, it is. Where did you get that money, Jake? Did you steal it?"

He made up his mind to tell the truth. "Yes."

She stared right back, uncertain whether to be shocked or not. "From where?"

"Where do you think? From Fromberg, of course."

Saul Fromberg had started out as a partner in a Fourteenth Street speakeasy called Charlie's, which Jake had pointed out to Pearl on the night he'd taken her to Times Square in the truck. With the money he later made from King Saul he bought out his partner—as he did in four other clubs—and took control for himself. Charlie's was now one of Fromberg's most successful clubs, catering to a wealthy, spoiled clientele which considered it exciting to wander from uptown to Fourteenth Street to slum it in the evening.

A week after the closure of King Saul, Charlie's was visited by four young men for whom a visit to Fourteenth Street was a trip *uptown*. Jake and Levitt rode in a truck that Caplan had stolen an hour earlier from outside a warehouse on the East River. Caplan and Minsky followed in a car. Jake drove the truck to the entrance of Charlie's which, like King Saul, was in an alley. With a flat cap dragged low over his forehead to hide his face, the collar of his reefer pulled up to his mouth, Jake went down the steps and knocked on the door. A spyhole the size of a hand opened.

"Delivery for-a Charlie's," Jake said, stamping his feet from the cold as he pointed to the truck behind him. He hoped the noise of his feet on the ground would muffle the Italian accent he'd adopted.

"We're not expecting anything."

"Now-a you are." He stepped aside and Benny Minsky—cap low, collar high—shoved the barrel of a shotgun through the spyhole into the man's face. The door swung back. Jake led the way in, a revolver in his hand. Levitt, Minsky, and Caplan followed, each holding a sawed-off shotgun. The club was full, its tables jammed with well-dressed men and with women who had jewelry dripping from their ears, necks, and hands. On a stage, a girl was singing while a man played piano. Minsky put a stop to that by firing his shotgun at the chandelier in the center of the room. Glass and plaster showered over those below. A woman's scream rang out, was silenced when Caplan waved his weapon menacingly.

"We're-a coming around with-a the hat!" Jake yelled across the suddenly silent club. "Be-a generous, Christmas is-a coming." He distorted his voice, making it deeper as well as altering the accent. While Caplan, Levitt, and Minsky covered the club's patrons with shotguns, Jake went quickly from table to table, holding out a sack. "Cash-a only, no checks," he said, brandishing the gun for emphasis. "Thank-a you very much, merry Christmas." There were at least a hundred people in the club. A hundred dollars from each of them—they had to have that much on them when they dressed this well—would make a round ten thousand. Anything over would go into the bank Levitt held.

The raid was over in five minutes, and was as efficient as the one Landau had staged in the basement on Second Avenue. "Thank-a you, thank-a you, you're-a all-a wonderful people." Jake turned to his three friends who formed a semicircle, their backs to the door. *"Avanti, presto!"* He went first, through the door and into the truck. As the other three came out and ran toward the car, Jake gunned the truck's engine and drove it straight toward the steps leading down to the club. As the front tipped forward, he jumped out. The truck dropped down to block the club's exit and prevent pursuit. Clutching the sack full of money, Jake ran to the car, jumped in, and slammed the door. Caplan sped away.

"Hey-a, Giuseppe James, how-a much-a did-a we-a get?" Minsky called out from the back seat. "You sounded as Italian as my old man when he yells from the cart on Essex Street!"

"Those crumbs in there were too drunk to worry about things like that," Jake answered.

"Never mind that," Levitt said. "How much?"

"More than enough." Jake had seen heavy wads of money being tossed into the sack, some of it held by thick gold clips. The clips didn't interest him, only the money. These people wouldn't miss it anyway. They'd probably write the whole experience off as part of their night out. "Guess what, darling," he could hear them saying to friends over lunch at some fancy restaurant the following day. "It was just marvelous. We went downtown and got robbed at gunpoint. Gunpoint! You should try it sometime. You just haven't lived until you've been stuck up by four Wops holding guns." The thought made him roar with laughter.

Caplan drove to the residential hotel on lower Fifth Avenue where Jake now lived. He had taken a small suite there, leaving his family's home, once he had begun working for Fromberg. In the living room, Jake emptied the sack onto a table, leaving it for Levitt to count. The little Pole immediately discarded the money clips into a pile. "These get thrown out, along with the clothes we wore tonight."

"What the hell for?" Minsky demanded, angry at such waste. He picked up one of the clips, studied the engraved initials. "Gold doesn't grow on trees, you know."

"Learn that at school, did you?" Levitt asked sarcastically. "The money's untraceable—those clips aren't."

"We could get the clips melted down, make nice rings." Minsky placed the clip on the back of his fingers, admiring it as though it were already a ring. Levitt reached out and snatched the clip away, pushed the whole pile across to Jake. "You take care of these, will you?"

Jake dropped the clips into the sack while Levitt continued counting, dividing notes into different denominations. "Twenty-three thousand, four hundred and eighty-one dollars," Levitt said at last. "Not a bad night's work. On top of what Pearl needs, we show a handsome profit. Got any envelopes, Jake? Four?"

Jake found the envelopes in a drawer. Levitt counted again and inserted twenty-five hundred dollars into each envelope. "Give these to Pearl when you find out how much her mother's fine is. Give her however many envelopes she needs."

Jake set the envelopes aside. "Let me have your coats and caps," he told the others. They undressed, changed into their everyday clothing which had been left in Jake's suite. Later that night, Jake went for a ride and dumped the clothes they'd worn for the robbery and the money clips from the center of the Brooklyn Bridge into the East River. . . .

Pearl listened to the story of the robbery. The Italian accent, the use of Italian words—that was clever. So was the entire operation, right up to the point of blocking the club's doorway with the truck. Only one aspect of the robbery bothered her. "You carried a gun, Jake?"

"You think people are going to hand over money just because I ask nicely? Wish them a merry Christmas maybe?"

"You told me you never carried a gun. You just drove, you once said, remember?"

"I didn't want you worrying."

"I worry more when you tell me lies, Jake. Do you think a gun's a toy like Benny does?" She remembered that Minsky had been the one to shove the shotgun through the spyhole, and that he had then let loose with it to bring down the chandelier. Minsky was dangerous. She wished Jake wasn't so friendly with him, but you didn't discard, like a piece of junk, someone with whom you'd been close since schooldays.

"No, I don't. And I never carry one unless it's absolutely necessary."

"Promise me you won't carry one at all."

"I can't promise you that, Pearl. Any other promise I can

make . . . but not that. Not unless you want me to break it."

She thought hard. What promise did she want from him in its place? At last, she decided. "All right, promise that you'll never lie to me again."

"No matter how much the truth hurts?" He tried to make it sound like a joke, suddenly feeling awkward because of the intensity he heard in Pearl's voice.

"Truth always hurts less than a lie, even if it's only in the long run."

"I'll make that promise only if you promise not to give me any more ultimatums."

"All right, I promise."

"Then I promise to tell you the truth in future."

"Tell me something true now."

"That's easy. I love you."

"Are you sure that's the truth?"

Laughing loudly, he hugged her. "I'd be as crazy as Benny to lie about that, wouldn't I?"

When the following day's newspapers referred to Sophie Resnick as Roulette Restaurateur—the title bestowed on her outside the court— she showed no sign of anxiety or regret. It was like having a tooth pulled, she told Pearl. For two weeks it hurt like crazy, with the terror of the impending visit to the dentist compounding the pain. Then, when it was finally over, you felt such relief that you could even look back with a little fondness on the pain.

A week after the trial, when Jake mentioned it was time to start thinking about the new club, Pearl passed on the news to her mother. She began by talking of the lease Jake and Levitt would sign, the token payment of a dollar a month. Sophie waved away the idea.

"I'd trust those two without a lease more than I would trust Saul Fromberg with one."

"You don't have to worry about him anymore, Mama. You don't even have to mention him again."

"Maybe you should call this new club Sophie's Place," Sophie suggested. "Four Aces and the Queen sounds nice, I know, but I'm the famous one, isn't that what your friends said?"

Pearl had a vision of her mother working as a hostess in the club. She knew the thought should have appalled her, but somehow it didn't. The trial had been an education, awakening in the older woman an interest in such things. Sophie now wanted to find out all about gambling, and the sin against decency for which she'd been punished. "I think your place is up here, Mama. Mine certainly is, and yours should be with me."

"You're right. Tell your friends I'll sign their lease."

Under its new name, the club reopened for business on New Year's Day 1924, looking much the same as when Fromberg had operated it. The main differences were the installation of new carpet and a roulette wheel that spun freely, without assistance from the croupier.

The opening of the club afforded Pearl an opportunity to meet a girl she'd heard about from Jake and had seen once in his yellow LaSalle— Kathleen Monahan. On Benny Minsky's insistence, Kathleen was hired as the hatcheck girl.

"I saw you once, when you were sweeping the sidewalk outside the restaurant," Kathleen said when Pearl was introduced to her. She had a deep, rough voice, and Pearl, recalling Jake's saying Kathleen wanted a singing career, silently questioned how beneficial such a voice would be to those particular aspirations. "I was riding in Jake's big yellow car at the time."

"Were you?" Pearl responded sweetly. "And now I've seen you taking coats. Since I'm a partner in his club, I guess that just about makes us even."

The barb flew right past Kathleen. "I should make a lot of tips here; that's what Benny told me. Even more than I got as a manicurist. And Benny said he could get me up there"—she nodded toward the stage—"get me a chance to sing."

Pearl walked away, thinking that Kathleen Monahan was the perfect match for Minsky. They were both lacking in brains.

Jake and Caplan said nothing about Kathleen working in the cloakroom, but Levitt wasn't reticent about voicing an opinion that coincided with Pearl's. "Like attracts like, eh?" he said to Pearl one evening, shortly after the restaurant had closed and the Four Aces had opened for the night. Jake and Caplan were walking around, showing customers to tables, helping to operate the club, while Minsky was standing by the cloakroom, talking to Kathleen. "Benny's supposed to be a partner in this place, but he's spending so much time over there we don't even need a damned hatcheck girl. Benny could do it in her place for all the use he is elsewhere."

"He's in love with her," Pearl said, feeling she had to stand up for Minsky in this one instance. Love was always excusable.

"He'd better be in love with her," Levitt said. "He's spending every penny he's got on her, what with the presents he buys her, the singing lessons."

Pearl looked toward the cloakroom again. Kathleen was wearing a diamond pendant around her neck, rings on four fingers, and a gold bracelet. No hatcheck girl ever flashed that amount of jewelry.

Levitt kept on talking. "Jake finds himself a nice girl—"

"Thank you."

"Moe finds himself a nice girl, too. And what does that jerk Benny find for himself? A *shikse*—"

"A *shikse* with bleached hair and a paint store covering her face," Pearl thought aloud. She blushed when she realized what she'd said, and then sought to change the subject. "What about you, Lou? When are you going to find someone for yourself?"

"Me?" He seemed surprised that she should even ask. "I've got plenty of time yet. But when I do start looking, maybe I'll look for"— he ran his eyes up and down Pearl's trim figure—"maybe I'll look for someone like you. At least, you're my size."

Pearl didn't share Levitt's laugh. Something about the way he'd spoken bothered her. She'd known him for a long time, since his first days at school in America. She'd supported him when the other children had mocked the way he spoke. Had that moment of kindness triggered some emotion within Levitt that was only now beginning to surface? Pearl had never thought of him as being like anyone else, a person with feelings. He had always seemed so aloof. Even when he'd helped to escort her and Sophie from the court, joined in the melee with the press, his punches had not been thrown with fury like Jake's. They'd been cold, clinical, just as damaging but accompanied by no visible exhibition of anger. Now she was forced to reappraise him. Were his feelings actually as strong as Jake's, but so heavily disguised that they didn't show?

"I'd better get back upstairs, Lou. My mother can't do all the clearing up by herself."

"Come back down when you've finished. You lift the tone of the place," Levitt answered.

Pearl promised that she would. As she climbed the stairs, she turned her head for a final time toward the cloakroom. Minsky was holding Kathleen's hand in both of his own, caressing it with his lips while the blonde just gazed off into space.

After the Four Aces had been open for a month, Levitt chaired a meeting of the partners in the club's office. Spread across the desk in front of him were two ledgers, one for expenses, the other for income. As he began to speak, however, he ignored the ledgers in front of him, discussing topics unrelated to the club's profit and loss picture.

"Item one on the agenda," Levitt said. "We have to consider jobs, cover for ourselves. We'll be taking a certain amount of money out of this place and we're going to have to show where some of it came from. Pearl, you're already set up with the restaurant. Moe, why don't you look into the possibility of starting something with Benny? Give it some thought, all right?"

"What about you and Jake?" Caplan asked.

"We're buying a taxicab company. With your background, why don't you think about buying a garage, you and Benny owning it between you?"

While Caplan and Minsky thought it over, Levitt continued speaking. "Item two. We need to discuss the formation of a special fund which, for want of a better term, we'll refer to as the grease account. I move that ten percent of our profits each month be put into this account with a view to buying protection and influence."

"We already pay off the police," Caplan pointed out.

"I'm painting a much broader picture, Moe, one that includes politicians and judges. The larger this grease account becomes, the more influence we'll be able to buy."

Minsky rapped his knuckles on the desk. "You talk about taking money out of this place, and then you talk about ten percent of the profits going into this grease account. For Christ's sake . . . let's talk about the damned profits! How much did we make?"

Levitt gave a thin smile. "That's what I like about you, Benny . . . never mind the apéritif, what's for the main course?"

"That's what we're in business for, right?"

"Right." Levitt let his smile travel from Minsky to Jake, then Caplan and finally to Pearl. "That's what we're all in business for." The smile faded as Levitt glanced down at the ledgers in front of him. "In the past month we cleared just over forty-two thousand dollars, of which thirty thousand came from the back room."

Pearl did some speedy mental arithmetic. "A thousand dollars a night from the tables?"

"From straight tables," Levitt corrected her. "If nothing else, that shows how stupid our predecessor was in killing the goose that laid the golden egg." He reached into a desk drawer and pulled out five separate stacks of currency. He handed one stack to each of his partners.

"There's only two thousand dollars here," Minsky exclaimed. "Where's the rest?"

"The rest is working capital, Benny," Levitt explained slowly. "Just because we take in forty-two thousand dollars, that doesn't mean we share it. In our business we pay for our supplies cash-on-delivery. We don't get thirty days."

Minsky was not interested in the finer points of managing a business. He tossed the money back onto the desk. "I've got expenses. This chicken feed isn't going to cover it."

"We're all getting fed up with your expenses," Levitt answered. "We see her every night, standing there like some model in a shop window while you whisper sweet nothings in her ear. She's taking you for a ride, Benny, and you're too dumb to see it."

"No woman takes Benny Minsky for a ride! Anyone who says otherwise is a damned liar!" Minsky's face glowed a dark crimson. He started to rise from the chair, but Caplan laid a steadying hand on his arm.

"Sit down and shut up, Benny," Caplan whispered.

Minsky shook off Caplan's hand. "Another thing—when Kathleen was hired to run the hat check, we promised her that she'd get a break here, a chance to sing."

"*We* didn't promise her anything," Jake cut in. "*You* made that promise all on your own."

"Benny, we need established singers who'll draw a good crowd," Caplan tried to explain. "We can't insult the customers with amateur talent."

"She's no amateur! I've heard her. You guys have got to listen to me." Minsky sought out Pearl as if she were the only partner who would back him up. "She's got a voice that'll melt your eyeballs."

Pearl never got the chance to say anything, for Levitt sneered and then declared, "You've heard her . . . all you've heard from her is a groan when you're lying on top of her. And she's even faking that for you."

Minsky's eyes flashed dangerously at Levitt. "One of these days you're going to say the wrong thing once too often, midget!"

"Sure, Benny," Levitt answered. He knew how to handle their dark-skinned partner—just let him wear himself out. "And maybe one of these days you'll say the *right* thing." He glanced at Pearl as if to say See how well I control everything? Pearl looked away, disturbed. She was uncertain whether to feel proud of Levitt's skill at managing both the business and his partners, or sorry for Benny Minsky, crazy though he was! Minsky seemed to be getting it from everyone—from his girlfriend and from his partners.

Sorry for Benny Minsky? Pearl almost had to pinch herself to believe it. Minsky was the one who had wanted to bring guns into the restaurant basement when Levitt had run the crap game. Minsky was the one, according to Jake, who would not have taken Fromberg's job unless he was allowed to carry a gun. And Pearl was feeling sorry

110

for him?

She drove any trace of sympathy from her mind. A man like Benny Minsky, who allowed himself to become so involved with a dumb blonde, was not deserving of her sympathy. *I was riding in Jake's big yellow car at the time*, Kathleen had said to Pearl. Indeed! Well, she wouldn't ride in it again, that was certain. The only woman who would ride in Jake's car in the future would be Pearl herself . . .

. . . Even if she wasn't prepared to marry him just yet.

BOOK TWO

Chapter One

Pearl's first impression of Kathleen Monahan was wrong. Benny Minsky's girlfriend was not the dumb blonde Pearl had imagined her to be. What Kathleen lacked in education, she made up for with burning ambition—she wanted to be a singer, and everything she did was planned to forward that aspiration. Kathleen knew her voice was unusual. When she spoke it was deep, almost like a man's, hoarse as if she were suffering from a cold. But when she sang, the roughness metamorphosed into a breathless huskiness, sexy enough to send a shiver down a man's spine when it was directed at him.

It was Kathleen's voice that had first attracted Benny Minsky. Lying back in a barber's chair, feeling the razor skim lightly across his face, he'd heard that deep voice say: "Would you like a manicure today, sir?" Despite the razor poised perilously close to his throat, he'd sat bolt upright. Kathleen was new at the barber shop. Minsky had never seen her before. He didn't even take that much notice of her looks, just enough to see the bleached yellow hair cut in a bob, the green eyes and heavy make-up. It was her voice that captivated him, making him tingle more than the hot towels had done.

Minsky had never had a manicure in his life; he felt doing that was foolish, something a queer would do. Nonetheless, he held out his hand. "Sure I'd like a manicure." He lay back again, allowing the barber to continue. Kathleen's fingers went to work on his nails, filing, massaging, pushing back his cuticles. All new sensations, all pleasurable. It did not take much imagination on Minsky's part to feel her hands moving all over his body. Every time she spoke, every time she asked if he were comfortable, he wanted to reach out and hold her, make love to her while listening to that voice. It drove him wild.

When she finished, he gave her a five-dollar tip and expected her to fall all over him. She didn't. She just thanked him politely before moving on to her next customer.

Undeterred by the apparent snub, Minsky could not wait to tell Jake about Kathleen. "You want to see this doll who did my nails! She'll knock your eyes out!"

Working for Fromberg at the time, and angry with Pearl over the ultimatum she had given him, Jake went to the barber to see for himself. He was not as smitten as Minsky was, liking neither the bleached hair nor the made-up face. He preferred the natural attractiveness of Pearl, who never wore make-up or played with the color of her hair. Nonetheless, he asked Kathleen out. Two dates were enough. The first time, they went to a show; the second time, for dinner and a ride, during which a moment of bloodymindedness had made him drive past the restaurant so Pearl could see him. Jake found Kathleen to be too interested in herself. She spoke only of the singing career she wanted, the big break for which she was waiting. Jake sensed she was looking for someone to bankroll her, and he decided, charitably, to leave that to Minsky.

"I've got a pal who likes you a lot," Jake told her before saying good night on their second date. "You do his nails—Benny Minsky."

"Him?" Kathleen's mouth curled in distaste. "That nigger?"

Jake began to laugh as school memories came flooding back. Other children had nicknamed Minsky Nig in those days. Minsky had hated the sobriquet, had fought violently with anyone who'd dared to use it. Yet Jake could swear that Minsky's skin had grown darker, his hair even more tightly curled as the years had passed. "Benny's no *shvartse*. He's just suntanned."

"No suntan's that dark."

"His folks came over from Russia thirty years ago. You ever hear of a Russian coon?"

"Are you giving it to me straight?" Kathleen asked. The five-dollar tip was the largest she'd ever had. Any man that generous wasn't to be rejected without a second look at his credentials.

"You think I'd hang around with a *shvartse*?"

The next time Minsky gave a five-dollar tip for his manicure, Kathleen was more receptive. Confident, he asked her out. She accepted. On their first date, he agreed to pay for her singing lessons. On their second date, he bought her a diamond pendant. On every successive date he showered her with gifts, but he was unable to fulfill her greatest wish—an opportunity to sing.

Then King Saul was raided. As soon as the decision was made to reopen it as the Four Aces, Minsky told Kathleen he could get her the big break she wanted. He found her a job in the club. After that, he kept telling her, it would be only a matter of time before his influence got her onto the stage.

Kathleen was patient at first. Her boyfriend was a partner in the Four Aces . . . he'd use his power on her behalf. That knowledge, and the gifts with which he plied her, brought comfort as she took coats and listened to other singers perform from the club's stage. Gradually, as Minsky tried—unsuccessfully—again and again to coerce his partners into giving Kathleen a chance, her patience eroded. Great songs were being written by fantastic new composers—Berlin, Gershwin—and no one was asking Kathleen to sing them.

The final indignity came one snowy Saturday night, thirteen months after the Four Aces had opened. A featured singer on her way to the club was involved in a taxicab accident on the icy streets. When Kathleen witnessed the ensuing panic—a full club and no entertainment—she pushed Minsky to do something.

"You keep telling me about the influence you've got here, that you're one of the partners. Now use your influence, Benny, and get me on that stage." She watched him walk quickly away, chase after Jake who had gone into the office to use the telephone. Two minutes later, Minsky returned to the cloakroom, shaking his head sadly.

"Sorry, baby, they've already got someone lined up."

Kathleen spotted Jake emerging from the office, shrugging himself into a topcoat. Leaving Minsky, she marched across the club. "Jake, I want to speak to—"

He cut her off with a wave of the hand. "Some other time, Kathleen. I've got to go out in this lousy weather and find a replacement act, otherwise we don't have anyone tonight." He hurried past her to the door.

Open-mouthed, Kathleen watched him leave the club. Slowly, she swung around to glare at Minsky who had remained by the cloakroom. "You son of a bitch!" she hissed. "You never even asked him, did you?"

"Honey—"

"Don't you honey me!" She turned her head away, refused to look at him. Minsky shrugged his shoulders and walked away. In his pocket was a new gift for her, a gold brooch in the shape of a dog with tiny diamonds for its eyes. Kathleen loved dogs. She kept two borzois, named Verity and Leila. By the time the night was over, she'd be eating out of his hand again, just like a dog.

Minsky was due for a surprise. When he gave her the brooch that night in her bedroom, she flung it back at him. "What the hell's the matter with you?" he yelled. "Suddenly gold's not good enough for you?"

"I don't want your fucking presents, Benny! I want what you promised me . . . a chance to sing!"

Kathleen's swearing never failed to excite Minsky. When she was mad she had the vocabulary of a dockside laborer, and screamed

114

obscenities in that husky, grating voice. It was always worth continuing an argument just to hear her; the longer the argument went, the more heightened his anticipation became, and the sweeter was the reconciliation when that voice turned to whispering terms of endearment. "Kathleen, you've got to be patient! We've got established singers, top-of-the-line performers, just busting down the doors to sing at our joint!" he yelled back, subconsciously using the argument Levitt gave him every time he rejected the idea of Kathleen singing. "You've got to wait your turn." From outside the bedroom he heard one of the borzois barking nervously at the raised voices.

"And I've got established cocksmen busting down the doors to get in here!" Kathleen shouted, pointing between her legs. "Maybe it's about time you waited your goddamned turn as well! You didn't even ask Jake, did you? You and your equal partner bullshit. Benny, you're an errand boy there, that's all you are. You might get a share of the money, but you don't get to make any of the decisions!"

That stung Minsky because he knew it was true. "Hey, come on, give me a break, baby."

"Benny . . ." Kathleen touched the top of her bleached hair. "I've had it up to here with you and your goddamned empty promises, you . . . you . . . you fucking half-caste!"

The instant the words left her mouth, Kathleen knew she had irrevocably overstepped the mark. Minsky backhanded her savagely across the face, knocking her back onto the bed. "Don't you ever call me that!" he yelled. His face was purple, veins popped in his temples. "You ever say that again and I'll break your fucking face wide open!"

Both borzois were barking frantically now. Minsky swung around to leave, no longer interested in staying the night. At that moment, he hated Kathleen. She had brought back memories of school; the taunting of other children had only ceased when his strength and violence had made them eat their insults. No one had made fun of his dark coloring from then on. No one had dared to mention it. Until now.

Kathleen began to cry. The sound of her tears stopped Minsky. He sat down on the bed, cradled her head in his lap. "Honey, I didn't mean to hurt you, you know that." He gazed down into her face. Her right cheek was beginning to redden and swell. Why had he hit her? She was too beautiful to hit, too beautiful to be working as a hatcheck girl. Hadn't he promised her a break, a place on the stage? That was where she should be, so Minsky could sit back and let everyone envy him because she was his girl.

"You keep promising me, Benny," she said, contrite now. "And all I keep getting is more coats to check. I can't keep waiting forever."

115

"I know, baby, I know." He lifted her head and kissed her. Slowly, she started to respond, arms snaking around his back, fingernails digging into him. The fight, the name-calling were forgotten as Minsky worked at the fastening of her dress. He felt her fingers tugging at his shirt, pulling it free from his trousers.

"I love you, Benny."

The husky voice did more for him than her questing fingers. He pressed down on her lips, a crushing, bruising kiss that left them both breathless. He couldn't lose this. He couldn't let her walk away from him. But he knew he would lose her if he didn't come through with his promise.

Minsky was supposed to work the following day, driving with Jake and Moses Caplan to Newburgh in upstate New York to collect a shipment of Canadian whiskey. When he awoke in Kathleen's bed shortly after nine o'clock, he telephoned Jake and complained of feeling unwell. Jake told him not to worry; he and Caplan would handle the pickup.

At noon, Minsky walked into the Resnick restaurant. He sat at the counter, waiting for Sophie to come to him. "I'm looking for Pearl, Mrs. Resnick. She around?"

"In the back. Can I get you something?"

"Maybe later, thanks." He swung himself off the stool and went into the kitchen. Pearl was not alone. Annie was with her. Both girls seemed surprised to see Minsky. "Jake said you weren't feeling well," Pearl said. "He was in here for breakfast with Moe before they went up to Newburgh."

"Did he also mention what happened last night at the club?"

"About having to find a substitute singer?"

"That's right," Minsky answered. "He went running out in the middle of a snowstorm to find someone, and he had Kathleen just sitting there, checking coats. Why the hell couldn't she fill in?"

Pearl gave a silent groan. "Benny, you know what the situation is downstairs. We've got customers who spend a lot of money because they expect the best. The club can't afford to take a chance on Kathleen."

"She can sing a damned sight better—"

"Benny, we've got your word that she can sing, but what if she can't? What if she's given a chance and then goes up on the stage and blows it? Who's coming back the next night?"

"Pearl, if I don't get her a break"—the words flew out in a rush before Minsky could stop them, before he could even think about

116

what he was saying—"she's going to leave me."

This doesn't sound like Benny Minsky, Pearl thought; it doesn't sound like him one little bit. "You want me to have a word with Jake, is that it?"

Minsky nodded. "And you," he said to Annie, "maybe you could lean on Moe a little bit. If Moe and Jake are willing to give her a chance, maybe that little midget won't get his way for once."

Pearl took offense at that. "Benny, Lou gets stuck with making the decisions because he's the most qualified. If Lou thinks Kathleen doesn't belong up there on that stage—"

"He's going to think that no matter what. If she had a voice like one of these fat broads from the Met, he wouldn't want to know. Don't you understand, Pearl? If it was anyone else, he'd give them a shot at it. But because it's Kathleen, and she's my girl . . ."

Pearl understood perfectly. The antagonism between Levitt and Minsky went back to their schooldays. Even working closely together hadn't bridged it. Levitt just thought of Minsky as a piece of meat, his only value to the Four Aces being his strength and fearlessness. Minsky, in turn, believed that Levitt's guile, his cleverness, were overrated. Neither man considered that the other carried his fair share of the load.

Half a minute passed while Pearl pondered Minsky's request. She could not believe that Kathleen could sing well enough to entertain the Four Aces' patrons; she felt the girl's speaking voice could not possibly lend itself to music. Yet she was loath to turn Minsky down out of hand. She had never seen him like this, crawling. She could not help but take pity on him.

It was Annie who finally spoke up. "Benny, we can't push for Kathleen if she's got a voice like a truck—it wouldn't be right to ask us to do that. Let's hear her sing. If we think she's good enough, we'll do whatever we can."

Minsky looked horrified at the prospect. What would Kathleen think of him, of his influence, if she was forced to audition for Pearl and Annie first?

"We can use the club," Annie said. "Moe and Jake are away until early this evening, and Lou won't be coming in until much later."

Minsky realized that he had no choice. If he turned down Annie's suggestion, neither young woman would go to bat for him. Somehow he would have to find a way to make it seem more acceptable to Kathleen.

By the time he picked her up half an hour later, he had his excuse all worked out. "We've been getting complaints about the way voices travel in the club," he told her.

117

"Acoustics?"

"That's the word. Some of the customers are complaining that they can't hear the singers. While it's empty, come down and sing a few numbers, then we can judge better for ourselves."

"Judge whether voices carry well, or judge if I can sing?" Kathleen asked, seeing through his lie immediately. "Come off it, Benny, I wasn't born yesterday. What are you doing, trying me out? Are you scared that I can't sing worth a damn?"

Minsky became angry at being found out so easily. "Okay, you want to hear the truth?" he demanded belligerently. "I don't know—that's right, me!—whether you can sing in front of other people or not. For all I know you can only sing when you're locked away in the can and there's no one to hear you! How do you like that?"

Kathleen jumped at the bait. "I'm not scared of singing anywhere!"

"Good. Now you've got the chance to show you can sing as big as you talk." He braked violently to a halt in the alley behind the restaurant. Entering the club, he found Pearl and Annie waiting. Kathleen came in and Minsky pointed to the stage. "Help yourself."

Kathleen looked at the empty piano stool. "Don't I even rate an accompanist?" She glared scathingly at Minsky and then climbed up onto the stage. "Don't worry about it, Benny; I don't need anyone to help *me* sing." From the raised vantage point of the stage, Kathleen watched Minsky sit down with Pearl and Annie at a table fifteen feet away. Some damned audience this was. An audition, and not even to the club's main partners . . . her Benny's *equal* partners. Just to their girlfriends. What was Minsky trying to do, use the girls to twist their boyfriends' arms? Sure Pearl was one of the partners . . . big deal! She only owned a piece of the club in lieu of rent for the premises; she was as unimportant to the success of the Four Aces as Minsky was. The only two partners who carried any weight at all were Jake Granitz and Lou Levitt; all the others were just ballast.

"What are you waiting for?" Minsky called out.

Kathleen's anger left her. She was where she wanted to be, on a stage, singing to an audience. So what if that audience was only three people? So what if she had no accompanist? She was going to give it her best shot.

Snapping her fingers softly, tapping out a beat with her foot, she launched into "Tea for Two."

Sitting a comfortable distance from the stage, Pearl was instantly struck by the same excitement that Minsky had experienced as he'd sat in the barber's chair. Kathleen's voice was as voluptuous when she sang as it was husky when she spoke. She'd been right about not needing a pianist; any other sound would have interfered with that

118

voice which had a tone all of its own, simultaneously brazen and seductive.

"Okay, Benny," Pearl whispered. "I'll talk to Jake. More than that I can't promise."

Minsky's swarthy face split into a grin. If Pearl could lean on Jake like Kathleen could lean on him, he was in. Damn it, he did have influence in the club after all, even if he had to channel it through devious routes.

Jake and Moses Caplan came into the restaurant later that afternoon after returning from Newburgh. They sat in a booth with Annie. After bringing over coffee and sandwiches, Pearl joined them. She didn't waste any time.

"You've got to give Kathleen a chance to sing, Jake. Annie and I heard her earlier today. She's terrific."

The coffee cup paused halfway to Jake's mouth. "Pearl, I'm tired, it was a lousy trip, and I'm not in the mood to listen to this. Lou says no, and that's good enough for me."

"He says no because he hasn't heard her," Pearl argued.

"And because she's Benny's girl," Annie added for good measure.

"You as well?" Caplan asked. "What is this, be-nice-to-Benny Minsky day?"

"No, it's do-something-sensible day. Jake went out in the middle of a blizzard last night to find a singer when he had one right in front of his nose."

"If she sings like she talks, she'll empty the place quicker than a police raid," Jake said.

"That's what I thought as well, until today," Pearl replied. "The singers you bring down here—pay fortunes for—they can't hold a candle to her."

Jake set down his coffee cup. "If I promise to talk to Lou about it, will you quit nagging me?"

Pearl's eyes met Annie's; an expression of triumph passed between the two friends. "I promise."

At seven o'clock that evening, two hours before the club opened, Levitt came into the restaurant. Dressed in his tuxedo, he sat in a booth and ordered dinner. When Pearl served him, he clutched her wrist. "Jake told me about what you and Annie want. The answer's no."

"Just like that? Why don't you give her a chance?"

"Because she's obviously not the caliber of singer we need. If Benny didn't have his brains down here"—Levitt nodded toward his crotch—"he'd know that as well."

"Okay, Lou, whatever you say." Pearl walked away, leaving him to eat. Nagging hadn't worked after all. It was time to take a more direct approach.

Half an hour after the club opened, Pearl and Annie went downstairs. Jake was in the office with Caplan, the door ajar. It was too early yet for the club to be busy. A few couples occupied the dance floor, smooching while a slow number was played on the piano. A third of the tables were in use. The only real activity was in the back room, where Lou Levitt ruled his kingdom of odds and numbers. Followed by Annie, Pearl walked to the cloakroom where Minsky, as usual, was standing with Kathleen.

"Name two songs you'd like to sing," Pearl told Kathleen.

"'Tea for Two' and 'Fascinating Rhythm.'"

Pearl waited for the pianist to finish the piece he was playing before she went up onto the stage, spoke to him. Then she turned to face the customers. Levitt wouldn't be able to hear what she said, not with the door to the back room closed. Jake and Caplan would be able to hear, though. "Ladies and gentlemen, we've got a special surprise for you tonight—a new voice that's going to sing its way right into your hearts."

The office door swung wide open. Jake appeared, staring in disbelief at the petite figure on the stage. Before he could interrupt, Pearl went right on. "You've seen Kathleen Monahan plenty of times. You've handed her your coats. Tonight, you're going to lend her your ears." She signaled to Kathleen, who walked away from the cloakroom while Annie stepped in to take her place behind the counter.

"What the hell do you think you're doing?" Jake muttered when Pearl joined him by the office door.

"Shut up, Jake," Pearl said angrily. "Just shut up and listen instead of talking all the damned time."

Kathleen climbed onto the stage, then whispered something to the pianist, who began a soft introduction to "Tea for Two." Kathleen felt her way into the song, growing stronger as she became accustomed to the pianist's tempo. Every head in the Four Aces turned toward the stage. And at the back of the club, as Kathleen's deep voice reached right into the gambling room, the door opened. A man looked out, snapped his fingers urgently at those inside. Soon, a crowd had gathered in the doorway. It parted only when Levitt pushed his way through. Hands on his hips, he looked around the club to find out what had disturbed the games. When he saw Kathleen, his lips stretched into a thin red line and his blue eyes blazed. But he kept quiet, too much the businessman to interrupt his customers' enjoyment.

"Well?" Pearl asked smugly as Kathleen finished the first song, and applause echoed through the club.

"Not bad," Jake answered grudgingly.

The applause died slowly. As it tailed off, the pianist began to play a quicker tempo and Kathleen launched into Gershwin's "Fascinating Rhythm." The husky voice rang out across the Four Aces. Customers began to clap their hands in time with the beat, and Pearl realized her own foot was tapping on the floor.

"Not bad, is that all you've got to say?"

"She's great." The compliment came from Caplan who had joined them by the office door.

"Thank you," Pearl said graciously, as though Kathleen were her own discovery. But her euphoria lasted only as long as it took her to spot Lou Levitt walking quickly along the side of the club. He strode straight past the small group by the door and headed into the office. Just inside the doorway, he swung around.

"Just who gave her the okay to get up there and sing?"

"I did," Pearl answered. "I'm a partner in this place as well, remember?"

Taken aback by Pearl's forthrightness, Levitt was momentarily speechless. Pearl gained strength. "You were wrong, Lou, now admit it. Just listen to that voice, look at your precious customers. Benny was right all along."

"Screw Benny," Levitt murmured.

"No—not screw Benny. For once he's right, can't you even acknowledge that?"

Levitt didn't answer. He pushed past Pearl and stood outside, watching and listening. His eyes swept over the customers, taking in their enjoyment. For the moment his dislike of Minsky was tempered by his appreciation of salable merchandise. At last, his eyes rested on Benny, who had left the cloakroom area and was walking toward the group by the office door. Levitt knew his purpose. Minsky was coming to gloat.

Suddenly, a burly, black-haired man at a stage-side table leaped to his feet and shouted at Kathleen. "Baby, you're the cat's pajamas!" He followed the compliment by blowing Kathleen a kiss and lurching drunkenly toward her.

"Get that bum out of here!" Levitt hissed at Jake and Caplan. Before either of them could move, Minsky darted between the tables and threw himself at the man. One arm around his throat, he dragged

121

him from the foot of the stage. Looking down on the violent drama taking place right in front of her, Kathleen kept on singing, never missing a word or a beat.

"You keep your filthy hands off my girl!" Minsky yelled as he pulled the drunk down and started hammering his head against the carpeted floor. "I catch you looking at her again, I'll kill you!"

Caplan grabbed Minsky from behind and pulled him away. Then Jake jerked the drunk upright and hustled him toward the exit. "Don't bother coming back, mister," he warned before throwing the man out of the club. When he turned around, he saw that Caplan and Levitt were pushing Minsky toward the office. When Jake got there, he closed the door.

"Okay, Benny, your girl's got a great voice," Levitt was saying. "We were wrong and for the first time in your life you were right. But she's not going to sing here if you start beating up any customer who looks twice at her."

Minsky shook himself free of Levitt and Caplan, shrugged his shoulders to straighten the jacket of his tuxedo. Suddenly his fury departed and a happy smile covered his face. "She can sing, can't she? Didn't I tell you she could sing?"

"Yes, Benny, she can sing." The agreement came stintingly from Levitt. He'd noticed the reaction of the customers, the way the gamblers had even left the tables to listen to this new voice. Kathleen was dynamite. A nightingale mixed up with a frog, Levitt thought, and somehow it all came together to make one of the sexiest sounds he'd ever heard. No wonder that drunken jerk had jumped up from his table. Kathleen's voice, with her brassy good looks, caused that kind of reaction. Only Minsky's response bothered Levitt. The Four Aces couldn't afford to have him assault a customer whose applause was a little too enthusiastic.

"Are we going to give her a job?" Minsky asked.

"On one condition. You don't lay a hand on anyone unless Kathleen's life's in danger, okay?"

"Sure, okay." Minsky threw back the office door. Kathleen was still on the stage, singing a reprise of "Fascinating Rhythm," for the crowd had refused to let her go. For ten seconds he stood watching her; then he sought out Pearl. "You did it for me!" He gave her a hug and a kiss. "No more working in the cloakroom for Kathleen. From now on, it's going to be up there; Lou told me," he said, pointing to the stage. In that moment he could even feel some warmth for Levitt.

Excitement bubbled through Minsky as Kathleen neared the end of the song. He couldn't wait to relay the news to her. She wouldn't leave him now, not when he'd gotten her this break. "You helped me out on this one, Pearl," he whispered. "I'll find a way to pay you back."

"You and the others have paid me back plenty, Benny." She felt happy for Minsky. She'd rarely seen him like this. Usually his dark face was like a glowering thundercloud waiting to burst.

"I've paid you back nothing. You just wait, one day I'll do something as big for you as you've just done for me." He turned back to the stage as Kathleen finished, reaching out his arms for her to jump into. "You've got it, honey! You've got it! You're on your way now!"

Kathleen kissed Minsky hard on the mouth. Watching, Pearl didn't feel in the least embarrassed at being a witness. She shared in their happiness, delighted that she had helped to bring it about.

"Remember, Pearl . . ." Minsky said as he guided Kathleen toward the nearest empty table. He snapped a hand at one of the waiters and called out loudly for champagne. "Just remember, one day I'll do something just as big for you."

Pearl nodded, smiled. Like Minsky, she had no idea that it was a promise he would be unable to fulfill for more than forty years.

Kathleen's debut, engineered by Pearl and Annie, and grudgingly recognized by Lou Levitt, coincided with the start of an expansion era. During the next eighteen months, the young partners opened three more clubs, all with names derived from gambling—the Full House, on Fifty-second Street and Broadway; the King High, on Seventh Avenue and Fifty-fifth Street; and the Straight Flush, across the Hudson on the Jersey Palisades.

Although each new club was based on the Four Aces—lavish décor, top entertainment, and a small casino in the back that was run by men handpicked and trained by Levitt—Pearl had no financial interest. Her sole involvement remained in the Four Aces. When the new clubs were being planned, she was offered the opportunity to invest but she declined. As it was, she and Sophie Resnick found it impossible to spend the money they earned from the Four Aces. Sophie's background, the years of struggle, of being in bondage to Saul Fromberg, had left an indelible mark. No matter how much came in, she treated every penny as if it were her last, always looking for new places in which to squirrel away money. When Pearl decided to completely remodel the restaurant and the flat, Sophie argued heatedly that they could not afford such an expense. Pearl went to one of the hiding places, drew out a thousand dollars, and waved it under her mother's nose. "What do you mean we can't afford it? We've got money coming out of our ears, and we're not spending any of it."

"Don't touch that. I put that by for a rainy day."

"Mama, the rainy season's over, can't you understand that? From now on, the sun shines every day."

Sophie remained less than convinced. She demanded that Pearl get at least half-a-dozen estimates; they would choose by price. Knowing that Sophie had been through too many hard times to change now, Pearl found the builder and furniture maker she wanted, and then she bribed others to tender deliberately high estimates. Sophie looked them over, complained at how expensive everything was becoming, and then told Pearl to use the merchants she had already decided upon. Triumphant, Pearl had the work done; she knew how to get around her mother.

But Benny Minsky had no problem in finding ways to spend his money. He continued to buy gifts for Kathleen, and as his income increased, so did the value of the presents. He installed her in an apartment on Riverside Drive and, in one four-week period during the winter of 1925–26, he bought her two full-length fur coats—one wolf, the other Persian lamb—and topped that off by giving her a Packard Sport Phaeton.

By July 1926, when the last new club was opened, Kathleen was a regular at all four of them. Wherever she sang, Minsky would be on hand. Despite giving her a car, he would drive her to the club, watch the show, and then take her home again. He refused to let her out of his sight, his dark face beaming with pleasure as he heard the applause, then scowling with barely repressed fury when he thought a man might be taking too much of an interest. Pearl was amused by Minsky's continuing infatuation with the blond singer. She even used it to tease Jake. During a dinner date shortly after Minsky had bought the fur coats and the Packard, Pearl told Jake that she thought such generosity was romantic. Grinning to herself, she waited for his retort.

"Romantic, hell!" he snorted. "It's blackmail, that's all. He's spending all his dough on her because he's scared that she'll up and leave him if he doesn't."

"That's not the truth," Pearl answered, although the boys seemed to believe it was. Pearl was convinced that money alone could not hold a woman to a man. There had to be more to Minsky's relationship with Kathleen. The blonde must feel something for the dark-skinned young man, even if Minsky himself was convinced that once he stopped giving she would leave him. He had even tried to persuade his partners to back a musical that would have Kathleen in the lead role. Levitt had turned thumbs down on it, and justly so; the musical had lasted two nights. "Benny spends his money on Kathleen because he loves her," Pearl said, "and I think that's romantic."

"Are you telling me you want a wardrobe full of furs and a car you wouldn't even know how to drive?"

The following day, Jake made a grand show of giving Pearl a toy car. Delighted with it, she placed it on her dressing table next to a photograph of herself and Jake, taken when they had gone to Coney Island during the previous summer. Pearl didn't need expensive gifts to know that Jake loved her. Hadn't he already asked her to marry him, that night after King Saul had been raided and they had made up their quarrel? She had told him then that she needed time to think, to grow. Although more than two years had passed, Jake had not mentioned the subject again. Neither had Pearl, because she understood that Jake also needed time. He wanted to get firmly on his feet. The clubs were only a beginning, stepping stones to larger enterprises. Yet Pearl knew that Jake's feeling for her had strengthened, just as her feeling for him had. Time either nourished or destroyed, and when she married Jake, as she was certain she would, she would have no doubts about the depth of their love.

Sophie Resnick, though, did not share her daughter's patience. As Pearl approached twenty-one, Sophie's questions about Jake became more insistent. She would mention the names of girls with whom Pearl had gone to school, all married now, with families. And then she would ask: "Pearl, what are you waiting for?"

"I'm waiting for the same thing as Annie, Mama—the right time." Pearl was grateful that her red-haired friend had not yet married Moses, although it was obvious that she would. Annie and Caplan had an understanding similar to that of Pearl and Jake. The boys wanted to get settled first; before marriage there was work to be done. Aside from the clubs, Jake and Levitt had started a taxicab company called Jalo Cabs. It operated a hundred vehicles from a West Side garage, and Minsky and Caplan had joined together to buy the service station which maintained the Jalo fleet. There was also something much bigger in the wind. Jake had hinted at it to tantalize Pearl's curiosity, but he had been unwilling to divulge the exact nature of the scheme.

"You'll both keep on waiting then," Sophie said sagely. "You'll wait so long that before you know where you are Jake and Moe'll find other girls. If you want Jake, grab him now, before he gets the chance to run away."

"Is that what you did with Papa? Did you grab him before he could run away?"

"I didn't have to grab your father. He was wise enough to know what he wanted the moment he saw me. That Jake, maybe he's not so smart."

"Jake asked me to marry him more than two years ago."

Sophie was visibly shaken. "He asked you? And you told him no?"

"I told him I needed time."

"Two years is a lot of time. Or are you, perhaps, worried that he isn't the one for you after all?"

"I'm not worried at all," Pearl replied, but the question gave her a moment of unease. It made her think of little Lou Levitt and his statement that when he was ready to marry he would look for someone exactly like Pearl. His words had bothered her at the time; they perturbed her even now. Since the expansion of the business, Pearl seemed to see Levitt more than the others. Jake, Caplan, and Minsky were away more and more frequently, supervising the increasing liquor deliveries and splitting their time between the other clubs, while Levitt worked every night in the back room of the Four Aces. And when he wasn't overseeing the gambling, he was sitting in the office, going over the books, administering the business. Often he came up to the restaurant during the day for a cup of coffee or something to eat; just as frequently, during a quiet spell, Pearl would venture downstairs to talk to him. To a degree, Levitt fascinated her. Every time she held a large sum of money in her hands she felt nervous, as though such wealth were dangerous, but Levitt handled huge amounts of cash with such impersonality—disinterest even— that the bills might just as well have been wads of colored paper. He had no fear of money, treated it with the contempt born of familiarity. He knew it represented power, but he was unafraid of it.

"Just grab that Jake if you're really sure you want him," Sophie advised her daughter. "And tell Annie to do the same with Moe. If you stand around waiting, they'll get away."

Pearl laughed. She could just imagine how Jake would react if she told him they were going to get married now, or else! Obviously, Kathleen's approach worked with Minsky; she snapped her fingers and he jumped to her tune. But Jake was not Minsky, and Pearl certainly was not Kathleen. Jake wouldn't jump, and she wouldn't expect him to. As she had told Sophie, she would just have to wait until the time was right.

And when the time was right . . . That particular thought sent a delicious warmth coursing right through her body.

Chapter Two

A week later, Lou Levitt asked Pearl out. It happened one morning when she went down to the club's office to take him a fresh cup of coffee. He was sitting behind the desk, a fountain pen gripped in his right hand as he totaled a column of figures in a ledger. To his left were white envelopes, open, with the edges of bills peeping out. On the envelopes were names, some of which Pearl recognized—policemen and city politicians, all recipients of payoffs from Levitt's grease account.

"I thought you might like some coffee."

"Thanks. Busy upstairs?"

"Not now." She set the cup down on the desk before sitting on the leather couch. "Lou, what's this big new scheme you're planning?"

Levitt capped his fountain pen, replaced it in his jacket pocket. "Who told you we were planning anything?"

"Jake. But he didn't mention what it was," she added quickly, fearful that she had breached a confidence.

"You'll know in good time, Pearl. But I'll tell you this—when it comes off we're going to be the biggest thing to ever hit this town."

"You're worse than Jake. You give me a morsel and then leave me hungrier than ever."

Levitt's blue eyes turned mischievous. "Come out for dinner with me one night; then I'll tell you everything."

She was uncertain whether he was joking or serious. "I can't do that, Lou. What would Jake say?"

"He wouldn't have to know. Just dinner one evening, before the club opens, that's all. Two friends having dinner—two business partners."

He *was* serious. Pearl tried to refuse again, but her resolve weakened. The mischief, the amusement in Levitt's eyes were hypnotic, drawing her in, cutting off her denial. All she managed was, "Lou, I—"

"This Saturday evening, early. Jake'll be away with Moe. Have dinner with me and I'll fill you in on everything."

"Just dinner, Lou."

"Of course. I have to be here before nine o'clock."

Pearl left the office and returned to the restaurant. What, in God's name, had possessed her to agree? She had never been out with anyone but Jake. Now, only a week after telling her mother that she would wait until Jake was ready, she had accepted a dinner invitation from Lou Levitt.

Pearl didn't mention the date with Levitt to her mother. She did not tell anyone. Somehow, if she shared the secret, she knew that word of what she was doing would get back to Jake. She didn't want that to happen. Jake wouldn't look on them as two friends—two business partners—having dinner together. It would cause trouble, not only between her and Jake but between Levitt and Jake. Pearl didn't want that either.

As she dressed on Saturday evening, she again questioned why she had agreed to go out with Levitt. Just to learn what this new scheme was all about? No, she was honest enough with herself to know that was not the real reason. Sooner or later she would have found out. The truth was Levitt intrigued her. He always had, ever since those early days at school. He was so different from the others, intellectually superior. Levitt didn't belong in the company of a Benny Minsky or a Moses Caplan. Or even . . . or even a Jake Granitz. With his brain he could buy and sell them all.

For fear of being seen locally with Levitt, Pearl arranged to meet him at a restaurant close to Central Park. After eating an early dinner they went for a walk and ended up sitting by the lake, talking.

"Lou, how is it that you and Jake have been such good friends for so long?"

Levitt's narrow face twisted into a smile. "Physics."

"Pardon?"

"Opposites attract, surely you learned that at school, Pearl. What Jake lacks, I have. And vice versa."

"What does Jake lack?" Offhand, Pearl could think of nothing.

Levitt tapped his forehead. "Sometimes he lacks *sechel*, good common sense. He acts before he thinks. Everything with Jake comes straight from the heart."

"And what do you lack, Lou?"

"When I first met Jake, I lacked size. I used to think it was important to be big and strong, like him and Moe and that crazy Benny. Now I know it doesn't matter so much." Crouched forward on the bench, he looked across the lake toward the buildings on Central Park West, eyes half-closed. "I found out for myself that I was as

128

tough as any of them, and I had twice as much brains as the three of them put together. That's because"—he turned to Pearl and his face split into a wide grin—"Benny gives them a minus factor in the brains department."

"Why do you dislike him so much?"

"Benny? Because he's a fool. And not only is he a fool, he's arrogantly proud of the fact. Look at him, Pearl, he throws himself away on some cheap *shikse*, humiliates himself over her. He runs amok."

"He's in love with her." Pearl's simple rationalization of Minsky's behavior sounded less convincing to her ears every time she used it.

"How can he be in love with a *shikse?*" Levitt's grin disappeared; his voice became low and earnest. "You, Moe, Jake . . . all of you . . . you were born in this country. Your parents came here many years ago, and they've forgotten the things that happened in the old country. They've forgotten because they wanted to forget. But not me. I was born over there, Pearl. I remember the stories of pogroms, of priests riling everyone up, of *goyim* getting drunk and then coming to look for us. I remember those things—that's why I only feel comfortable around other Jews."

"Like Saul Fromberg and Gus Landau? How could you feel comfortable being around people like that? They're the worst scum in the world, worse than any *goyim* in Poland or Russia could ever have been."

Levitt allowed her to finish. "Pearl, no matter what Saul Fromberg and Gus Landau do, they're not going to turn around and call me a goddamned kike. But sure as hell, that's what Kathleen's going to wind up calling Benny one of these days, and he's too dumb to see it." He switched his gaze back to the apartment buildings on Central Park West. When he spoke again, his voice was so soft that Pearl had difficulty in hearing his words, but they struck her with the force of a thunderbolt.

"Pearl, you coming down to the office every day like you do . . . it's driving me nuts. I'm in love with you. I think I've been in love with you ever since we were kids at school."

Pearl's heart started to pound uncontrollably; blood rang in her ears. "Lou, don't say that."

Levitt ignored her plea. "Remember that day you stood up for me, when the other kids poked fun at the way I spoke? I guess I never forgot that. You were the first person at that school to show me any decency, any kindness. And what were you then, eight, nine?"

She tugged at his arm until he faced her. She could swear that his eyes had altered color, turned a deeper, softer blue. Her own face was burning. Damn, she wished she'd never accepted his dinner invitation; she'd known it was wrong to do so. And simultaneously she knew that she'd wanted to hear those words from Lou; they were the very reason she had agreed to have dinner with him. Some perverse instinct had carried her along; yet she had to deny him. "Lou, you don't mean it, you know you don't. I'm in love with Jake."

Levitt bathed her with a sour, lopsided grin. "Lucky Jake. Annie's in love with Moe, Kathleen's in love with the money Benny blows on her, and you're in love with Jake. I guess that leaves me doing the damned books and picking up after everyone else." His voice was bitter, and Pearl felt an enormous wave of sympathy for him. No matter how he boasted of no longer being bothered by his diminutive stature, she knew it hurt. Levitt felt he'd been cheated by nature. A massive brain was squeezed into his tiny body while all around him lesser intellects were blessed with strength.

"Lou, remember what you told me once—that when you went looking you'd find someone like me because I was your size? That's not important. You don't have to worry about how tall or how small a girl is—"

Whatever reassurance Pearl was about to offer, Levitt did not want to hear it. His eyes hardened and he silenced her with a wave of the hand. "I promised to tell you what this big deal was all about, didn't I? This is it." He withdrew a bulky brown envelope from his pocket. "Take a look inside."

Confused by his abrupt change in attitude, Pearl took the envelope. Inside were steamship tickets for the SS *Leviathan*, leaving New York in seven days' time. "You're going to England?"

"Scotland. We're going into a new business, importing our own stuff, the best stuff. The distilleries over there don't give a damn about our Volstead Act. They'll sell us the goods, ship them to us, as long as we take delivery outside the three-mile limit and bring them in the rest of the way."

"You're going to all this trouble for just four clubs?"

Levitt had changed completely. His angry disappointment at Pearl's rejection had been replaced by a driving, positive attitude; he was all business again. "That's just *our* four clubs, Pearl. What about all the other joints in New York, in Jersey, all over this area? What about the Garment Center where the manufacturers have got to show the buyers a good time before they'll place an order? We're going to supply everyone with the finest Scotch. That's what Jake and the others have been so busy doing these past months, making the arrangements. We've got our own distillery in Philadelphia, that's where Jake is today. We'll bring the stuff in on the south Jersey shore, move it to Philly, cut it there with grain alcohol, and then rebottle the excess in identical bottles to the original. We're going to own the whole of the East Coast, Pearl."

She handed him back the tickets, not as interested in the scope of the operation as in the fact that Levitt would be away. "How long will you be gone?"

"Six weeks." He checked his watch, saw that it was almost eight. "I've got to get to the Four Aces. Do you want a ride?"

Pearl shook her head. "I'll take a taxi." As Levitt stood up, she caught hold of his arm. "Lou, I'm sorry."

"It's okay, Pearl. I should have known."

Staying on the bench, she watched him walk toward the park exit and his car. She felt wretched because she'd brought Levitt pain. She understood why he'd so suddenly switched subjects, brought out the tickets for the *Leviathan*—to mask that pain. And he'd done it with such aplomb that Pearl could even believe he was accustomed to rejection and was prepared for it.

For almost an hour she remained on the bench, watching courting couples stroll by the lake. Some of the women glanced at the lonely figure on the bench, as if pitying her for her solitary state. If only they knew the truth, Pearl thought. I don't have one man in love with me—I have two. And maybe, just maybe, I'm not in love with one man, but with two. A spark *did* exist within her for Levitt, a spark that had been nurtured just enough to keep it alive—during her trips down to the office to see him, to speak to him. Tonight, it had burst into life, fanned by traits that were so peculiar to Levitt—his seriousness and intensity, characteristics that were lacking in Jake.

On the journey home in a taxi—ironically a Jalo cab owned by Jake and Levitt—Pearl was confused and frightened. She had wanted to meet Levitt far from home so that no one would see them together; she had desperately wanted to keep their tryst a secret. Now she needed to share that secret with another person. Annie was the obvious choice, but if she told her then Caplan would soon know and so would Jake. It had to be her mother. She entered the flat, guessing that Sophie would be in bed already. The older woman always retired early in preparation for opening the restaurant the following morning. The restaurant was her entire life, a solid connection to Joseph Resnick. Only illness or, God forbid, death would ever drag her from it.

"Can I speak to you?" Pearl asked on entering her mother's bedroom.

Sophie sat up, patting the bed beside her. "Of course. What is it?"

Pearl sat down and leaned back against the headboard. "I may have waited too long, Mama."

"For Jake?"

"No. Lou. I had dinner with him just now." She heard her mother's shocked gasp. "He asked me out a few days ago, a dinner between friends, between business partners, he said. We went to Central Park afterward, sat by the lake. We started talking. And then he told me . . ." She turned to look into her mother's eyes. "Mama, he told me that he loved me."

"Do you love him?"

"What kind of a question is that?"

"The right question, Pearl. If you had no feelings for Lou, you wouldn't even be bothered."

Pearl took her mother's hand. "I like him, Mama. I always have, because he's so different from Jake, from the others."

"You told him you like him?"

"No. I just said that he shouldn't say any more, that I was in love with Jake. Then he pulled steamship tickets out of his pocket to show me he's going to Scotland next Saturday."

"How long will he be gone?"

"Six weeks."

"And are you sure you love Jake?"

"Yes."

"Then use those six weeks to marry him. Put yourself out of bounds to Lou, and that will take care of it."

Pearl had never witnessed such revelry as that which accompanied the Saturday-afternoon sailing of the *Leviathan*. She went to the dock with Jake, Moses Caplan, Annie, Benny Minsky, and Kathleen. Together, they stood on the quay, looking up at the massive steel wall of the ship. Behind them, a brass band belted out a Sousa march. Above their heads, paper streamers rocketed through the air.

"There he is!" Jake yelled. He pointed up. Leaning over a rail, scanning the crowd below, was Levitt. He appeared totally out of place, his dark blue suit standing out against the light summery colors of other passengers's clothing like an ink blot on pristine white paper.

"Hey, Lou!" Caplan bellowed, hands cupped to his mouth. "You make damned sure those Scots don't pull the wool over your eyes!"

"Fat chance of that," Jake said, laughing. "You ever know a Scot to get the better of a Jew?"

Levitt yelled down something in reply, but his words were lost in the general clamor as a blast of the *Leviathan*'s horn bade farewell to New York. Barges nudged the massive liner toward the center of the

Hudson. The band continued to play, and the liner responded with more blares from its horn as it began the journey down the Hudson to the bay.

"Makes you wonder, doesn't it?" Jake mused. "Lou came here twelve, thirteen years ago, the same way our parents did, on some stinking little tub that probably made him throw up every five minutes. And now look at him, not turned twenty-one yet, first-class passage, living it up like some damned lord."

"Look at all of us," Minsky cut in, not wanting all the credit to go to Levitt. "Any one of us could be on that boat. Hell, in a year's time we'll be able to buy one just like it. Hey, what an idea . . . let's do it, moor it outside the territorial limit and turn it into a gigantic floating nightclub." He reached out to clasp Kathleen around the waist. "You want to sing on a boat, baby? You want a boat named after you?"

Caplan waited for Minsky to stop fooling around, but he couldn't find fault with his partner's exuberant behavior. They were all keyed up. The moment the *Leviathan* had weighed anchor, they had taken the first step on a journey that would make them millionaires. "How about we all go out tonight and celebrate?" he suggested. "Let's be customers at one of our joints for a change."

Annie seconded the idea enthusiastically. Business had been too brisk to allow time for pleasure, and the opportunity for a big outing was too tempting to pass up.

"How about you?" Jake asked Pearl.

"Why not?" Pearl forced a smile onto her face as she watched the liner move gracefully down the river. Levitt was out of her life for six weeks. Her mother was correct—she had to use those six weeks to make certain that he stayed out of her life. The few hours she had spent with him the previous Saturday had opened up a need in her for him. She had to cauterize the opening as soon as possible.

That evening, the three couples went to the Full House on Fifty-second Street. Jake ordered a bottle of champagne, poured it into six glasses, and then raised his own. "To little Lou. Let's hope he's having the time of his life on board that tub."

"He's probably found himself some dame already," Minsky said. "I can just see him, dancing with her cheek to chest." He burst out laughing at his own humor. "Get it, cheek to chest?"

"You're not funny, Benny," Pearl said. "Lou might be short but he stands a mile taller than a lot of other people."

"If I know Lou he's got a card game going already," Caplan broke in. "He's trying to finance the entire trip from the suckers on the boat. He wouldn't let an opportunity like that go to waste."

"What do you think he's doing?" Jake asked Pearl; he was surprised at the way she'd sprung to Levitt's defense.

"I think he's in bed by now. He's on a business trip, right? Lou takes business very seriously."

"Boy, what a waste," Minsky grumbled. "A trip of a lifetime and he's already in bed. And by himself!" Laughing again, he grabbed hold of Kathleen's hand and pulled her onto the dance floor. Annie and Caplan followed, leaving Jake and Pearl alone at the table.

"Why did Lou go to Scotland?" Pearl asked. "Why not you?"

"Lou can negotiate the best deal. We're talking about millions here, and Lou's the only guy I know who doesn't break out into a cold sweat when that kind of dough's on the table. All that learning he did is finally paying dividends."

Pearl recognized a tremendous warmth in Jake's voice just then. Was it for the little man himself, or just for his ability to handle money? "You're really fond of him, aren't you?"

"I love him like a brother. If it wasn't for Lou, none of us would be where we are today." While Pearl considered how true that really was, Jake turned to look at the dancing couples. "Are we going to sit here talking or are we going to dance?"

On the floor, he held her tightly, swaying gently in time with the slow beat of the music. "I haven't seen very much of you lately," Pearl said.

"We were busy. I'm sorry."

"Setting up your own distillery and bottling plants in Philadelphia so you can cut and rebottle the Scotch once it's landed?"

Jake's body stiffened. Amazement imprinted itself across his face. "How the hell—?"

"Lou told me."

"That doesn't sound like Lou at all. He plays his cards too close to his chest. How did you make him cough up that information?"

Pearl had wanted to surprise Jake with her knowledge. Now she feared she'd said too much. "When I took him coffee I slipped something into it."

Before Jake could pursue the topic, the dance ended. They returned to the table, and Jake ordered another bottle of champagne. When the waiter brought it, he whispered something in Minsky's ear. Minsky nodded and turned to Kathleen, who stood up and walked onto the stage. Minsky lifted his chair and carried it down to the edge of the platform, where, unobstructed, he could gaze up at her.

Jake called the waiter over. "The customers recognize Miss Monahan," the man explained. "They want to hear her sing."

"Maybe we should have gone to someone else's club," Annie said. "Kathleen's too well known here for us to have a private party."

"She wouldn't have it any other way," Caplan replied. "Neither would Benny. Look at him, will you? He thinks the sun shines out of her rear end. He wasn't kidding about buying the damned boat. Once we start making the big dough, you know what he's going to do? Investing in a show won't be enough for him. He'll buy her the whole theater, the orchestra, the works."

Kathleen started to sing "Always," letting that husky voice explore every note of the song and give it new meaning. It was easy to understand where her appeal lay. Other vocalists used maximum power, driving home each word like the thump of a steam hammer. Monahan just let the music drift, confident that her unusual sound would arrest every ear.

"Are we allowed to dance while Kathleen sings?" Annie wanted to know. "Or will Benny get mad?"

Caplan stood up and pulled back Annie's chair. "He only gets riled up about other men applauding too loudly." They went onto the floor, leaving Pearl with Jake.

"Tell me what you slipped into Lou's coffee," Jake whispered.

"Oh, Jake, I was only joking. He just told me everything during the course of a conversation."

"What else did he talk about?"

"He talked about her," Pearl answered, gesturing with her head toward the stage. "And Benny. He seemed genuinely upset that Benny would get so involved with a *shikse*." She heard the last notes of "Always"; then the club's patrons began calling for Kathleen to sing "Fascinating Rhythm." Like "Always" it was no longer a new song, but the voluptuous treatment she gave it kept it a favorite.

"And? . . ."

"And what?" She knew he was probing, still uncertain why Levitt had chosen to confide in her. "He also told me that he only feels comfortable around other Jews, because even men like Fromberg and Landau won't turn around and call him a kike."

"All of this while you took him a cup of coffee?"

"That's right. He was doing the books."

"Pearl, none of us can get the time of day out of Lou when he's going over his damned books. He's incommunicado. How did you work the miracle?"

Finally Pearl realized how jealous Jake was. She had spoken to Levitt, gleaned information from him that no one else had been willing to divulge. Jake was accusing her. "All right," she answered, as a slow anger began to build in her, "if you want to know the truth, I

135

had dinner with him last Saturday, before he opened the Four Aces."

"What the hell did you have dinner with *him* for?" There was no warmth in Jake's voice now as he spoke of Levitt.

"Because I was tired of waiting for you. You were never there, Jake."

"I've been working, in Philly."

"I know, and I'm getting fed up with hanging around while you work. At least Lou's downstairs. He's someone I can talk to. With you, I have to make an appointment that'll fit in with your travels."

"He *asked* you out for dinner?"

"That's right. He probably gets fed up as well, with no one to talk to down there."

"Is this a private argument," a woman's voice asked, "or can anyone join in?"

Startled, Pearl looked up to see Annie and Caplan. Kathleen had finished singing "Fascinating Rhythm" and requests were now being called out from the tables. Minsky continued to sit by the stage, eying each man who shouted out the name of a song.

"It's open to the public," Jake replied. "That's why we're having it here."

Caplan appeared hesitant about sitting down, becoming part of an argument that didn't concern him. Annie, as usual, had no such qualms. She dropped into a seat and gazed expectantly at Pearl and Jake. "Okay, put me in the picture. What's it all about?"

"Something you should be able to sympathize with," Pearl told her, guessing Annie would take her side. "I got fed up waiting for Jake to be around, so last Saturday night I had dinner with Lou."

"How exciting!" From Annie's tone it was evident that she did not really think so. "How many times did he add up the check to make sure it was totaled right?"

For a second there was pure silence; then Annie's sarcasm broke the tension. Pearl began to laugh. Jake joined in. "If you complain about me being away now," he said, "how much more are you going to nag if I'm working nights once we're married?"

"I think he just proposed to you," Annie said.

No one got an opportunity to say more because a worried-looking waiter appeared at the table. "Mr. Granitz, Mr. Caplan, come quickly, please. It's Mr. Minsky. There's trouble with Mr. Minsky."

Jake stood up, motioned to Caplan. The two young men followed the waiter to a table near the stage. Pearl also rose and saw Minsky arguing quietly with a tall, fair-haired man. On the stage, Kathleen was doing her best to ignore the situation.

"I catch you giving my girl the eye again, mister, and I'm going to break both your legs," Minsky growled at the man, who had done nothing more than throw a rose, which Kathleen had caught, onto the stage. "You keep your filthy hands off her."

"Okay, Benny." Jake grabbed hold of his partner's arm and pulled him away. Caplan smiled at everyone at the table, apologized for the misunderstanding, and told the waiter to supply them with free drinks for the remainder of the evening. As Jake hustled Minsky back to the table, Kathleen began to sing again. "How many times have we got to tell you to leave the customers alone?" Jake snapped as he shoved Minsky into a chair. "You and your damned jealousy are going to run us clean out of business."

"He was making eyes at Kathleen."

"He threw her a goddamned rose," Caplan muttered. "Since when is that making eyes? For Christ's sake, Benny, will you grow up?"

Minsky glared at the man he'd accosted. Despite the offer of free drinks, the entire table was getting up to leave.

"Benny, when Kathleen finishes that song, get her off the stage and out of here," Jake said. "And so help me, if you ever pull a dumb stunt like that again, I'm going to make damned certain that she doesn't sing here anymore!"

For five seconds, Minsky sat brooding in the chair. Then, saying "I'm not even waiting that long," he jumped up, walked quickly to the stage, and, in midverse, pulled Kathleen off it. Her song changed to a shriek of protest as Minsky dragged her toward the exit. Once outside the club, he shoved her into his heavy Chrysler Imperial and drove wildly toward Riverside Drive.

"What the hell do you think you're doing, you mad bastard?" Kathleen yelled at him as she recovered from the shock of being hauled out of the club.

"Shut up!" One hand on the wheel, he turned and slapped her across the face with the other. "I saw the way you looked at that guy! You encouraged him, you slut!"

"You're crazy, Benny. Your friends are right about you. You're nuts."

"Shut up, I told you!" He slapped her again and she cowered back in the seat. "I pay for you, I pay for everything. I own you, just remember that!"

"You don't own shit, you creep. Stop this car, I'm getting out!" As Minsky slowed for an intersection, Kathleen pulled back the door handle. The door swung open and Minsky jammed his foot down on the gas pedal. Kathleen screamed in terror as she almost fell from the moving car. Both her hands frenziedly gripped the swinging door, one foot was hooked under the seat, and her body swayed only inches from the road surface before she managed to clamber back inside. Minsky reached across and grabbed hold of her bleached hair.

"You want to get out, do you?" Gripping her hair, he shoved against her head. She screamed again.

"Benny, don't!"

Minsky roared with laughter and pulled her by the hair back inside the car. Still shrieking with terror, she slumped back in the seat. He reached across her to pull the door closed. As he did so, he momentarily lost control of the car, and the swinging door slammed into the rear of a parked truck. It crashed shut, a deep dent in the side.

"Now look what you've gone and done, you dizzy bitch! I've a damned good mind to take back that Packard I gave you!"

"Take it back, Benny," Kathleen answered, clutching the rose which, somehow, she had managed to hold onto despite the wild ride. "Take it back and see if I care. I don't want the fucking car or you!"

"Yeah? And what about all those singing spots?"

"What about them? Singing at your joints isn't the be-all and end-all of my life, buster. I've got bigger ideas than that."

He reached the block on Riverside Drive where Kathleen lived. The Packard was parked at the curb. Minsky's lips drew into a tight line as he aimed the Chrysler at the rear of the smaller car. Kathleen stiffened in the seat. "Watch what you're doing, you lunatic! That's my fucking car!"

At the very last moment, he slammed on the brakes. The Chrysler pulled up inches short of the Packard. "Take it back, eh? See if you care, eh?"

"You're crazy, Benny. Certifiably crazy, you know that?" She glared at him. The son of a bitch was still laughing, a kid who'd just done something his parents had always told him was dangerous. Done it and gotten away with it.

"Made you wet your drawers just now, didn't I?"

Kathleen couldn't help herself. She began to laugh as well. Minsky's madness was contagious, a wild, wonderful ride on an out-of-control roller coaster. Exhilarating . . . and downright terrifying. A dangerous thrill, that was Benny Minsky. Life with him was like a profit and loss column. His generosity was balanced by his jealousy; his charm by his madness; the exciting aura of danger that surrounded him by the chilling knowledge that he could turn violently against her.

Even without Minsky's help, Kathleen knew she would have gotten the breaks. Maybe it would have taken a few years longer, but her talent would have won through in the end. If she had found some other way to get on, though, she would have missed the charge of seeing Minsky sitting by the stage for every song, going crazy because some man threw her a rose, and then dragging her from the stage and hauling her bodily out of the club. Minsky was excitement. His irrational jealousy and wild temper aroused something deep within Kathleen; he brought forth the instincts, the appetite, of an animal. Simultaneously, he terrified her because she knew it was always possible that he would overreach himself, be unable to pull back. A glutton for punishment, that's what I am, Kathleen decided. I indulge myself with him, but I pray that he remembers this is only a game.

Still holding the rose, she stepped down from the Chrysler. Minsky ran around the car and inspected the dent in the door. "Goddamned stupid bitch, look what you did!"

"You should have stopped. Who told you to drive like a maniac?"

"I don't drive like a maniac. Who told you to open the door?"

"Who told you to start beating up on me?"

Minsky looked at the rose in her hand and he began to laugh again. "A flower, for Christ's sake! Some cheapskate that guy must be. Any man wants you, he's got to give you fur coats, a car, keep you in a fancy joint like this. More than just a goddamned flower!" He tried to snatch it from her hand, and she drew back.

"I'm going to put it in a vase," she said defiantly.

"One lousy flower in a vase, it'll die of loneliness. Go ahead, stick it in a vase, pour water on it, make it soaking wet like the drip who threw it at you."

Still quarreling, they reached her apartment. The moment they were inside, the borzois rushed forward. Minsky shoved them away and then drew back his hand to slap Kathleen as hard as he could across her buttocks. "That's for what you did to my car!"

The rose flew out of Kathleen's hand to land on the floor. She swung around and lashed out with her own hand. Minsky blocked the blow and caught hold of her wrist, bending her arm back until he forced her onto her knees.

"Say you're sorry about what you did to my car."

It was still a game to Minsky, but suddenly the fun had departed for Kathleen. This time, she was certain, he really intended to hurt her. His eyes had narrowed to tiny slits; the blood rushing to his face turned it a deep scarlet. She looked to the two borzois for help; they were both cowering in a corner, whimpering.

"Benny, you're hurting me."

"Say you're sorry."

"I'm sorry! Now will you let go?"

He did. His fury turned to passion as he lifted her from the floor and kissed her. She wrapped her arms tightly around him, a boxer holding an opponent in a clinch. While she held on, Minsky couldn't hurt her. Mistaking the strength of her embrace for responsive ardor, Minsky crushed his lips down on hers. His trousers became constricting. He wriggled his hips, ground himself into Kathleen's flat belly. It was too much. Already aroused beyond restraint, he climaxed in his trousers.

Kathleen felt him soften, spotted the expression of disgust that flitted so quickly across his eyes. Risking another beating, she said, "You crud, you can't even hold yourself in, can you?"

No beating came. Minsky stepped back, face still red, but now with shame, not rage. He sucked in his stomach, tried to draw himself away from his sticky pants.

"Little boy want to take a bath?" Kathleen taunted. All the slaps were worth this, to see Minsky so humiliated. "Had a wet dream, did you?"

Minsky didn't say a word. He just spun around and walked out of the apartment, slamming the door. Kathleen ran to the door, turned the lock and threw the bolt. She didn't want him back tonight, certainly not in the mood he was in. Tomorrow would be another day, she could handle him then. Looking out of the window, she saw him walk awkwardly out of the building and get into his car. He didn't even glance up before driving away.

With Minsky gone, the two borzois padded over to offer Kathleen whatever comfort they could. Stroking them absently, she sat down, only to jump up again as pain tore through her. That son of a bitch had hit her really hard. She went into the bathroom, undressed and stood before a full-length mirror. Her face was slightly swollen from the two slaps in the car, but when she turned her body to view her buttocks, she gasped. The imprint of Minsky's hand stood out like a red flag on her white flesh. She dabbed the area with a cold, wet washcloth. It didn't help. Throwing on a robe, she returned to the living room where she spotted the rose lying on the carpet where she'd dropped it. All this over a damned rose! She picked it up, noticing for the first time the strip of white that showed over the tightly budded petals. Curious, she pulled back the petals. A tiny scrap of paper fell out. Written on it was a name and telephone number.

David Hay . . . so that was the name of the bastard who'd started all this. Angry, she started to roll the piece of paper into a ball. Then she stopped. Minsky had beaten her up without cause. Now, she thought, as she remembered the tall, fair-haired man throwing her the rose, she'd give him cause aplenty.

At the Full House, no one said a word for fully five minutes after

Minsky's dramatic departure. Pearl, Jake, Annie, and Caplan sat staring awkwardly at each other, aware that the club's customers were also looking at them. Kathleen being dragged off the stage and hauled from the club by Minsky had created a vacuum. Even a troupe of vivacious dancers failed to fill it.

"Let's get out of here," Jake finally said. He knew that once they left, and took with them the memory of Minsky, the club might return to normal. Right now, everyone was too frightened to move. No drinks were being sold. Word of what had happened had even reached the tables in the small casino and business had dropped off. It was just as well that Levitt was on the boat. He would have a fit if he knew what Minsky had done.

Pearl, alone, was loath to leave. If she went now would she ever hear the end of what Jake had to say . . . about how she would feel about him working nights when they were married? Or had he really said that? There had been such commotion, so much pandemonium, that she was no longer certain of anything.

"Are you coming or not?" Jake asked. Caplan and Annie were already standing. "We'll go somewhere else, get a bite to eat maybe."

"Come back to Second Avenue," Pearl invited. "I'll make something to eat there." The restaurant would be closed, her mother in bed. She did not want to go anywhere else, though. Like Lou Levitt who felt comfortable only among other Jews, Pearl felt most at home while cooking.

Jake agreed. "Moe and I can drop down to the Four Aces while we're there, check if we're doing enough to make up for what we're losing here."

On Second Avenue, Pearl turned on the kitchen lights. While Jake and Caplan went downstairs, she and Annie busied themselves by making coffee and sandwiches. "Did I imagine it?" Annie asked her friend, "or did Jake really ask you to marry him?"

"He's asked me before."

"He has? When?"

"A couple of years ago. I told him I needed time."

"He's given you time, for God's sake! How much more do you want?"

Pearl regarded Annie oddly. "Why are you so desperate to see me married?"

"Why do you think? If my Moe sees Jake married, then maybe he'll get his finger out and ask me." Annie gazed dreamily at the ceiling. "Don't get me wrong, Moe's a wonderful guy, but he has to be led, shown the way sometimes. And he's sure not going to be shown anything by Lou or Benny. Lou won't get married until he finds a girl who looks like a dollar-bill sign, and that Benny . . . he's a fine example altogether."

"I'm not getting married just to help you out."

"Then marry him because you love him. You do love him, don't you?"

"Of course I love him! Do you seriously think I would have hung around all this time if I didn't? Annie, I'm almost twenty-one—"

"So am I. And I'm getting just as many hints from my parents as you're getting from your mother."

"Remember Rachel the humpback?" Pearl said, mimicking Sophie Resnick. "Two hundred children she's got already . . . what's the matter with you?"

"Shh." Annie raised a warning finger to her lips. "They're coming back up."

Pearl heard heavy footsteps on the stairs leading from the club. She returned to making sandwiches, determined to say nothing. She'd leave it all to Jake. He had broached the subject before Minsky had suffered one of his bouts of envy; it was up to him to continue it.

"It's packed down there, thank God," Jake said as he entered the kitchen. "Might make up for what we lost tonight at the Full House. Damn that lunatic Benny!"

"Never mind Benny," Annie said. "Has anyone given a thought to Kathleen? Maybe we should call her, see if she's all right."

"What, and disturb their making up?" Caplan joked. "Their rows don't last that long—they're just inconvenient to other people."

"Annie's right," Pearl said. "I think we should call her." She walked past the two men, down the stairs to the club, and let herself into the office. When she put through a call to Kathleen's apartment, the line was busy.

"They probably disconnected the telephone," Caplan said when Pearl returned upstairs. "Didn't want to be disturbed."

The comment made Pearl laugh. Benny Minsky and his tantrums. They were over as quickly as they started. Levitt knew how to handle him all right, just let him burn himself out. Kathleen obviously knew the same thing. Now if only Pearl knew as much about Jake.

The telephone in the apartment on Riverside Drive wasn't disconnected. Kathleen was using it, hoping that David Hay, the man who had thrown her the rose, had returned to his home after leaving the Full House. More than an hour had passed, he might have. Gently massaging her sore bottom, she listened to the telephone in David Hay's home ring on unanswered. Perhaps she'd reached the wrong

142

number. She tried again. What would she say if he answered? Hello, this is Kathleen Monahan, you threw me the rose tonight at the Full House and you got the hell beaten out of you in the process? No, that wasn't the right approach. Something more straightforward. Hay was interested in her, wasn't he? Otherwise why had he thrown her the rose?

She almost dropped the telephone in fright when a fist hammered on the apartment door. The two borzois began to howl. Who the hell was that? As she turned around to face the door, the hammering came again. The howling of the dogs increased. Simultaneously, a man's voice spoke in her ear. "Mr. Hay's residence."

"Kathleen!" Minsky roared from the hall. "Open this door!"

"Mr. Hay's residence," came the voice again, a plum-in-the-mouth English accent. "Is anyone there?"

Kathleen dropped the phone and ran across to the door. Minsky stood outside. "Now what do you want?" she demanded. She held the door with one hand, ready to slam it in his face the moment he tried to step inside. She wasn't having any more of him, not now anyway.

Whatever anger he might have exhibited when he'd banged on the door and yelled her name wasn't showing now. His mouth drooped, his shoulders sagged; he looked totally contrite. "I'm sorry, honey, really I am. I shouldn't have gone off the deep end like I did. It was only a rose that some creep threw you. It wasn't your fault."

Kathleen let go of the door. Minsky looked as though he might burst into tears at any moment. She saw that his curly hair was damp, his suit and shirt different from those he'd worn earlier. He'd gone home to change his soiled clothes, to bathe. The entire picture touched her. "Come in," she said resignedly. She stepped back, closing the door after Minsky had entered the apartment. He stood sheepishly, gazing around as if uncertain what he was even doing there.

In that moment, Kathleen felt like a boxer who'd just stunned an opponent with a crushing blow; all that remained now was the final punch. She may have let him in, but she wasn't going to forgive him that easily. While he was down she was going to kick him but good. Maybe he'd stay down—that way he'd be easier to live with.

"You see what you did to me, you son of a bitch!" She hoisted her robe and exposed her flaming bottom. "I can't even sit down."

At the sight of her naked flesh, some of Minsky's gloom departed. He stared, fascinated, at the handprint on her bottom. "Looks like a Japanese flag. Did I really do that?"

"No, someone else did. Who the hell do you think did it?" She continued to hold her robe up. Minsky got down on his hands and

143

knees like a dog. "What do you think you're doing now?" she asked.

"I'm going to kiss it better."

"The hell you will." She kept the robe up, though, as Minsky's lips caressed the sore spot. "You really are nuts, you know that, Benny?"

"Would you have me any other way?" He kissed her again and could feel himself growing hard. Without warning, he wrapped his arms around her legs and dragged her down onto the carpet. As he pulled the robe wide open, kissed her breasts, a hot, wet tongue slurped across his ear. He snapped around and the long snout of one of the borzois stuck itself in his eye.

"These fucking dogs! One day—"

Kathleen silenced him by dragging his face down to her breasts again, filling his mouth with flesh. He lashed out with his foot and the borzoi backed away, but Minsky knew the respite would be only temporary. The moment he dropped his trousers, they'd both be back, sniffing around him like he was some bitch in heat. In this apartment there was only one bitch in heat, and if anyone was going to do any sniffing, it would be him, not the damned skinny, hairy dogs.

Lifting Kathleen up in his arms, he carried her into the bedroom, slamming the door in the faces of the two borzois. They could stay out there and whine all they wanted to. He'd already wasted one good orgasm tonight; he wasn't going to let two neurotic mutts stop him from achieving another.

"You're a real bastard, Benny. You beat me black and blue, and then you come back here expecting to crawl straight into my pants. What the hell gives you that right?"

"My charm," he answered, struggling out of his trousers. "If I didn't have such charm, you wouldn't have opened the door."

"Sure, you've got charm. Like an alligator's got charm." She lay back, arms and legs open to receive him. The rest of his body was as dark as his face. A mat of thick curly black hair covered his chest, arms, and legs. A bush grew from his groin. And standing up straight from that bush, like a royal palm soaring above a clump of palmetto . . . Kathleen shivered in anticipation.

But as she clasped him to her, raked her nails across his muscular back as he drove into her, it wasn't Benny Minsky she was thinking about. It was the man named David Hay, who had thrown her the rose.

Chapter Three

To Pearl's disappointment and annoyance, Jake never said another word about marriage. It was as if the scene in the Full House between Minsky, Kathleen, and the fair-haired customer had driven it completely from his mind. Had it not been for Annie swearing that she'd heard Jake mention marriage, Pearl would have been certain that she'd dreamed the entire episode. To make matters worse, she saw even less of Jake during the following weeks. He seemed to spend most of his time down in Philadelphia, taking Caplan and Minsky with him to put the finishing touches on the distillery. Additionally, they had purchased a trucking company to handle distribution of the cargo Levitt was busily arranging in Scotland; that took up even more of Jake's time.

When the sixth and final week of Levitt's absence began, Pearl reached a decision. "Annie," she said to her red-haired friend, "if he doesn't say anything to me before Lou gets back, that's it."

"Stop being so proud," Annie answered. "If he doesn't bring it up, then it's up to you."

Pearl shook her head adamantly. "It's not leap year. February the twenty-ninth's a long way off. And if you've got any brains, you'll do the same thing with Moe. They're both taking advantage of us."

Annie gave a slight grin. "I can just see you telling Jake where to go."

"I wasn't afraid to do it once before."

"But you took him back."

"That was then—this is now. I'm getting fed up with being taken for a ride."

Annie's grin grew even wider. "You're enjoying the scenery too much to end the ride."

"No, I mean it," Pearl said, becoming angry with her friend for not supporting her. "I'm not joking, Annie; I'm deadly serious. If, by the time Lou's ship docks, he hasn't said anything, then that's the end. I really mean it."

Listening to herself, she could even believe she did.

The *Leviathan* was due to dock in New York on a Thursday morning. On the night before, Jake had dinner in the restaurant; then he invited Pearl for a drive in his car. He seemed to wander aimlessly around Manhattan, up the East Side, west on 125th Street, and then south along the West Side. When Pearl asked where he was going, he didn't answer. Finally, she figured out their eventual destination for herself.

Ninety minutes after leaving the restaurant, Jake stopped the car by the dock where the *Leviathan* would unload its passengers the following morning. The dock was empty now, ghostlike; scraps of paper fluttered in the river breeze to provide the only movement. Far beyond the dock, lights glimmered on the Jersey side of the river.

"Through that gate tomorrow walks our fortune," Jake murmured. "Little Lou with a head full of prices, shipping schedules, and delivery times. When he left here six weeks ago, it seemed like a dream—if I pinched myself I'd wake up. Now it's coming true. Nothing'll ever be the same again, Pearl. We'll make so much money that even Benny won't have the time to spend all of his on Kathleen."

"I'm not interested in Kathleen," Pearl answered. "All I care about is where I stand." There! Despite telling Annie that she would not be the one to broach the subject, she'd done it. And now that she had taken that first difficult step, nothing was going to stand in her way. "Jake, how much patience am I supposed to have? You and the boys want to get on, that's fine by me. Go ahead and do it. But somewhere, sometime, you've got to think about other things in your life. Me, for example!"

"You were the one who wanted time," he answered levelly. "I gave it to you."

"When I said time I didn't mean eternity. Six weeks ago, just before Benny started that fight, you were talking about once we were married as though just mentioning it would keep me happy. Well, it doesn't!"

Jake started to chuckle, and Pearl glared angrily at him. "What's so damned funny? I don't see any joke."

"You're funny." While Pearl had been speaking, Jake had slipped his hand into his jacket pocket. Now he held out a small box. "I wanted to wait until tonight before giving you this. Lou's last night out, and all that, everything changing from tomorrow on. But you never gave me a chance." He lifted the lid from the box and allowed Pearl to gaze upon the diamond ring inside. "Should I put this on your finger, Mrs. Granitz-to-be . . . or should I put it on your tongue to stop your God-awful nagging?"

Pearl felt her face begin to burn. "Jake, I'm sorry. I . . . I must have sounded like an idiot."

He lifted the ring from the box and slipped it onto her finger. "Just don't go wearing it when you're working. I don't want it dropping into a bowl of soup and some pushcart peddler getting more than he bargained for." He sat watching as Pearl admired the ring, turning her hand this way and that to catch the light from the streetlamps.

"Where was your grand speech leading to?" Jake asked. "What would you have done if I hadn't given you that ring tonight? Would you have left me?" He slipped an arm around her tiny waist and squeezed, pulling her closer.

"I kept telling Annie I would. I told her I wasn't going to put up with being left to wait around until you found the time to get to me."

"I know. She told me."

Pearl wasn't surprised. "She's frightened. She thinks Moe won't do anything until you do. How does it feel to be a trend setter?"

"This is one trend I don't mind setting."

Pearl rested her head against Jake's shoulder. She was almost twenty-one years old, and she'd known Jake for more than half her life. Now she was going to share the rest of it with him. Had such a fate been decreed that day when she and Annie had broken up the dice game in the janitor's shed at school? That would be something to tell their children—and their grandchildren. How did we meet? Over a dice game. Strange that, dice games had played a large part in her relationship with Jake. And with Levitt, she couldn't help thinking as she looked at the empty dock and imagined the *Leviathan* being nudged into its berth the following day.

Six weeks Levitt had been away. In that time, Pearl had achieved what she'd set out to do; she'd used those six weeks to make herself inaccessible. But what would Levitt feel when he disembarked the following day? She recalled him walking away from her in Central Park, his words of acceptance and defeat: *It's okay, I should have known.*

Had those six weeks helped him over his disappointment as well? Desperately, Pearl hoped so.

Despite Jake's jesting warning, Pearl could not resist wearing the ring in the restaurant the following morning. All the customers who came in remarked upon it, and each time Pearl glanced at her mother she saw Sophie smiling happily.

Just after midday, a taxi pulled up outside the restaurant. Out of it climbed Lou Levitt, carrying a leather suitcase. He marched straight to the counter where Pearl stood.

"Welcome home, Lou!" Without thinking, Pearl leaned across the counter and kissed him on the cheek. "How was your trip? How

147

was Scotland?"

"Cold, damp, and windy. No wonder they make such good Scotch over there—they have to drink it to stay warm." He hoisted the suitcase onto the counter and snapped open the locks. A roll of tartan cloth spilled out, vivid reds and blues and greens. "Here's something else the Scots make well. It was this or a set of bagpipes, and I figured you wouldn't know what to do with the pipes."

"I'm not sure I know what to do with this."

"Make anything you like with it." He pulled the cloth right out of the case, spilled it across the counter. "Feel how soft it is, like butter. Did you ever feel such cloth?"

Pearl reached out to the cloth with both hands. Instantly, Levitt's eyes caught the flash of her ring. "What's that, Pearl? On your finger?"

"This?" She brought her hand to her mouth. "Jake gave it to me last night."

"You getting married?" Levitt's blue eyes had turned into chips of ice-covered rock.

"Yes. I think he's going to ask you to be best man."

Slowly, Levitt's eyes regained their normal luster. He reached out for Pearl's hand, brought the ring close to his face. "Nice ring. *Mazel tov.* Maybe you can find someone to make a wedding dress out of this tartan cloth."

"I think I'd prefer white."

"I guess I'd better go see Jake, Moe, and Benny. We've got business to discuss. I'll tell you one thing, though, Pearl—you're not going to be seeing much of Jake over the next week. Our first shipment's due in a couple of days, and I've got dibs on him. You might have him for the future, but I've got him for the present." He snapped the case shut and walked out of the restaurant.

Pearl turned around to see her mother standing in the doorway leading to the kitchen. "There goes a very unhappy young man," Sophie said.

"What did he expect, Mama? I told him a long time ago that I loved Jake."

"Maybe you shouldn't have gone out for dinner with him that time. Who knows what he read into that one date?"

"It wasn't a date."

"That's obviously not how he feels about it. Ah," Sophie waved a hand toward the front door through which Levitt had just passed. "Give him time, he'll get over it."

*　　　*　　　*

The first shipment arrived on Saturday night, two days after Levitt's return. Jake, Minsky, Levitt, and Caplan drove down together to the Jersey shore to meet it. Just before one o'clock in the morning, they reached a dock south of Ocean City. A dozen light trucks were already parked there, lights out, engines off. Groups of men stood around, talking quietly, smoking. Jake climbed out of the car, eager to stretch his legs after the lengthy journey. He muttered something about being glad the city was going to open the Holland Tunnel; that would cut a lot of time off the journey.

Levitt walked over to the edge of the dock and stared down at the water. Half a dozen large speedboats were moored there. They could swiftly make the run to the three-mile limit where a British freighter would be waiting, then load up and return.

Levitt looked out to sea. In his hands was a signal lamp. He flashed it three times, paused, flashed three times again. From far out to sea came a coded response. Levitt felt excitement boil within him as he gave the countersign. This was like the first time he'd organized a dice game, or operated a casino, or added up a column of figures and reached the correct answer. A first was always thrilling because it signified another peak conquered. He raised two fingers to his mouth and gave a short, sharp whistle. Below him, the powerful engines of the speedboats roared into life. Wake spilled out as they headed into open water.

Within thirty minutes the first boat was back, its cargo space piled high with cases of Scotch. Men formed a human chain to unload the contraband and bring it up to the trucks. More boats returned, unloaded, headed out to sea again. For five hours, until the first traces of gray speared the black of night on the eastern horizon, the frenzied activity continued. The moment trucks were loaded, they left in pairs for Philadelphia, escorted by cars carrying armed men.

As the last two trucks prepared to pull out, the four partners stood on the dock and gazed east a final time. Three miles out, the British freighter was only a hazy shadow on the horizon. Smoke spilled from its stacks as, empty of contraband, it began the journey north to dock in New York where it would unload legitimate cargo for other customers.

"Gentlemen," Levitt intoned solemnly, "we are witnessing a historic moment."

"Never mind that," Jake said. "How many cases did we bring in?"

"Twelve hundred." Levitt closed his eyes and the adding machine inside his head started to tally the night's work. Each case cost twenty-seven dollars from the distillers in Scotland. Add to that shipping costs, the payments from the grease account to ensure safe passage from the dock to Philadelphia, distribution, the other intangibles. After cutting the Scotch, adding coloring, rebottling it in duplicate bottles, they would wind up with more than three thousand cases and get up to five hundred dollars a case. Even more for a few cases they would leave uncut, genuine off-the-boat Scotch. Levitt smiled. Another shipment was due in two days' time. And after that? . . . However much the market would bear, and he was certain it would bear plenty. In the few hours it had taken to unload the consignment, the four clubs had become chicken feed.

The four partners accompanied the final two trucks west along the narrow New Jersey roads that led to Philadelphia. When they reached the distillery, the other trucks were already unloaded. Whisky was being emptied into huge vats to be cut precisely with grain alcohol. Soon, the diluted Scotch would be on its way to thirsty customers. Levitt shut himself away in the distillery's office to check on the amount of grain alcohol, the coloring, and the bottles being used. He needed a precise rundown of every penny that was spent; he wanted to see where he could cut costs in the future. As he sat down, he looked through the window at his three partners. They were standing around, unable to assist in the specialized cutting process. He knew they all wished they were back in New York—Jake with Pearl, Caplan with Annie, and Minsky with his goddamned blond *shikse*. Instead, they had to hang around the distillery, and then return to the dock for the next shipment. Too bad, Levitt thought. He didn't have a woman in New York to rush back to, so why should he allow them to go home? His love was his work. It was more faithful to him than any woman could ever be. Pearl had shown him that with painful clarity. He'd thought all those times she'd come down to his office to see him had really meant something. She'd led him on, and then when he'd finally plucked up the courage to tell her how he really felt, she'd cut him off at the knees by explaining how ridiculous his feeling for her was. She was in love with Jake. Coldly, cleanly, clinically—she'd turned his emotions inside out and left them to dry in the sun.

Yes, he'd learned his lesson well. Only work—ambition—were faithful mistresses. His partners would do well to learn that lesson, too.

While Jake and Caplan were away, Pearl and Annie had each other for company. Kathleen Monahan was not so fortunate. Once she finished singing for the night, she had no one. She even had to drive herself home in the Packard which Minsky had given to her. Past three in the morning, while Minsky and his partners watched the unloading of their first shipment, Kathleen sat in the living room of her apartment with just the two borzois for company. The dogs weren't enough to satisfy her. She missed Minsky . . . damn it, she really did! Half the time she was with that crazy bastard, she loved him; during the other half, she hated him with enough passion to commit murder. But when she was without him, a yearning, a hiatus, existed which nothing else, no one else, could fill.

When Minsky was away for just one night, that was bad enough. Now he would be away for three or four nights—or however long that little taskmaster Levitt kept them running between Philadelphia and Ocean City—and that was unbearable. Kathleen felt odd without Minsky sitting by the stage when she was singing. What did it matter if customers made eyes at her when Minsky wasn't there? She recalled a question she'd once heard, about a tree falling in the forest—if no one was there to hear it, did it really make a noise? She hadn't understood the meaning of the question at the time, but now she thought she did. Without Minsky's jealousy to spur her on, some of the bounce went out of her singing.

At four o'clock, she finally went to bed. After sleeping for six hours, her mind refreshed, she thought she knew of a way to bring some excitement into her life while Minsky was away. She searched through a bureau for the tiny, folded scrap of paper. Holding her breath, she dialed the number of David Hay.

The same English accent answered. "Mr. Hay's residence."

"Is Mr. Hay there, please?" By now, Kathleen had decided that the English accent belonged to a butler. She didn't know anyone who employed a butler; that Hay would have one boded well.

"May I ask who's calling, madam?"

Madam? Kathleen liked that, too. No one ever called her madam. "Just tell him the lady he threw a rose to six weeks ago. I thought it was about time I thanked him for it."

David Hay came on the line. "I would have thought after that scene you'd never call me, or ever want to see or hear from me again. Your boyfriend—that was your boyfriend, wasn't it?—didn't take very kindly to my interest. In fact he specifically threatened to break both my legs if I even so much as looked at you again."

That sounded like Minsky. "I wouldn't exactly call him my boyfriend."

"No? What would you call him then?"

"He's just a man who has my interests at heart. He's one of the owners of the Full House, and he thinks it's his responsibility to ward off unwanted attention."

"Was mine unwanted?"

"No, not at all. But I didn't get the opportunity to tell him that."
David Hay seemed to know enough about her, Kathleen decided; it
was time she learned something about him. "Was your wife with you
that night, David?"

"I'm not married. Do you think a wife would allow me to throw
roses at a pretty girl like you?"

Kathleen appreciated the flattery. It was a lot different from what
she was accustomed to receiving from Minsky.

"Do you think your swarthy friend would mind if I took you out to
dinner one night?" Hay asked.

"I don't think he'd mind at all," Kathleen answered, silently
adding, just as long as he doesn't know. "We'd have to work it around
my schedule. I'm singing four nights a week."

Hay sounded disappointed. "How about lunch instead? Today?"
Kathleen agreed instantly; with Minsky away, what could be better?
"Give me your address and I'll send my chauffeur for you at one
o'clock."

The call ended, Kathleen sat back and patted the two dogs. It wasn't
that she was so interested in this David Hay; she viewed him only as a
means of avenging herself on Minsky. Even if he would not be aware
of her perfidy—and she'd make damned sure he wouldn't find out—
for her it would be sweet revenge.

At one o'clock, Kathleen waited in the lobby of the building. A
Marmon cabriolet town car pulled up, and a smartly liveried
chauffeur jumped out from the open driving compartment. "Miss
Monahan?" He held open the rear door as she stepped inside. When
the chauffeur drove away from the building, Kathleen pulled back the
screen and asked where they were going.

"Mr. Hay's estate, ma'am. He said to tell you that he thought you'd
enjoy lunch there."

Estate indeed. It was a long way from Benny Minsky to Mr. Hay's
estate. Kathleen leaned back against the opulent upholstery, enjoying
the ride.

David Hay's estate was near Manhasset, out on Long Island. As the
Marmon passed between stone pillars, Kathleen pressed her face
against the window, almost unable to believe what she saw. Surely no
man lived like this. The damned place was bigger than Central Park,
and that was the largest expanse of green she'd ever seen.

The Marmon coasted to a stop beneath a stone archway that led to
the front door of the largest house Kathleen had ever seen. She wasn't
even certain that *house* was the proper word to describe the building.
Castle was more like it, or palace. Mansion at the very least. It must
have a hundred rooms, like a hotel. David Hay—Kathleen's heart

warmed toward him—had to be lousy with money, crawling with it like a mongrel crawled with fleas. Suddenly Benny Minsky and his interest in the clubs, the liquor-smuggling racket, seemed very paltry.

A butler—Kathleen felt elated at being right—opened the door. "Please wait in the drawing room, madam. Mr. Hay will be with you directly."

Kathleen had barely sat down when David Hay entered the room. "Miss Monahan, I trust you enjoyed the ride. As it's such a beautiful day, I thought we would eat out on the terrace."

"That sounds delightful." Kathleen studied her host. She'd barely had a chance to see him that night before Minsky, once the rose had been thrown, had charged at his table like an angry bull. Hay was tall, over six feet, and languidly elegant with his white cotton trousers and cream jacket. His fair hair was long, combed back and held with just a trace of oil, and his eyes were gray. Kathleen finished her inspection by staring at his hands. He had the longest, slimmest fingers she had ever seen, she noted with professional interest. His nails were perfectly shaped, the half-moons of his cuticules showing evenly. She'd bet every penny that Minsky had ever spent on her that this David Hay had not done an honest day's work in his entire life.

They lunched on the terrace, overlooking a large swimming pool. Between courses, Kathleen managed to extract all the information she needed about Hay. He was thirty years old, the only child of a successful stockbroker who, with his wife, had died three years earlier in an automobile accident. With more money than he could ever spend, he made enjoyment his life's work. "My own pleasure is my priority in life," he explained quite easily to Kathleen. "And my greatest pleasure is beautiful women."

Kathleen had never met anyone quite like Hay. That was because she had never known anyone who had been born into wealth. Those men she knew with a few dollars behind them had struggled to make money. They respected their wealth, flaunted it. Hay acted as though he didn't give a damn about it.

"Would you like to go swimming?" he asked, nodding toward the pool. "It'll be cool but invigorating."

"I didn't bring a bathing costume with me. I had no idea that we would be lunching in such a beautiful setting." When the occasion required, Kathleen was not above laying on flattery herself.

"It is rather beautiful, isn't it?" Hay responded, pleased with Kathleen's observation. "It belonged to my parents. And I don't remember asking whether or not you'd brought bathing attire with you, only if you wanted to go swimming. My servants are very discreet, if that's what's bothering you."

The idea appealed to Kathleen, swimming in the nude with a man she hardly knew. That would really send Minsky over the edge. Like two children unashamed of their bodies, they undressed. Kathleen jumped into the water first and swam a length with an easy breast stroke while Hay stood watching at the side of the pool. Then she looked up at him, drew the comparison with Minsky. Hay's chest was almost hairless, his body slender and lightly muscled, his frame that of an artist instead of Minsky's fighter's bulk. Her eyes moved down for the final comparison, and there Minsky won out easily. Kathleen felt disappointed.

Hay dived into the water, barely making a ripple. He swam two complete lengths with a fast, effortless crawl which Kathleen watched appreciatively. His slim build was deceptive. It hid an athlete's wiry strength. Maybe the same was true of him elsewhere. Treading water at the deep end, Kathleen watched as Hay took a deep breath and somersaulted beneath the surface. She saw the blur of his shape as he moved toward her; then his arms wrapped themselves around her legs. She squealed as he dragged her under, felt the warmth of his body pressing against her in the chill of the water. It was an odd mixture of sensations, hot and cold, sweet and sour. Together they bobbed to the surface. He gripped her hand, pressed it down toward his groin. He grew firm in her grip and she rubbed herself against him. Could you . . . the question tantalized her . . . screw underwater?

It was not her destiny to find out. Continuing to let her hold him, Hay stroked his way to the side of the pool. Kathleen saw that large white fluffy towels had been laid out on the terrace. Who had done that, the butler? One of the other servants? Those discreet servants of whom Hay was so proud. And were they even now watching from one of the multitude of windows? The thought of being spied upon sent a thrilling shiver clean through Kathleen's body. They wanted to watch? Okay, she'd give them something worth watching. She was in show business, wasn't she? She'd put on a show they'd never forget, and Hay would be the lucky recipient of her endeavors.

Letting go of him, she climbed out of the pool and briskly dried herself on one of the towels. Hay hauled himself out of the water, picked up a towel. They stood facing each other, his erection bobbing up and down as he pulled the towel back and forth across his shoulders. The sun beat down on Kathleen, heightening her feeling of warmth and well-being. She let the towel fall to the ground and dropped onto her knees in front of Hay. His own towel fell away as she took him in both hands, massaging gently. And then she took him in her mouth. Minsky had always wanted this, and Kathleen had always refused. For a bizarre moment, she wished that Minsky was part of that audience inside the big house. He'd explode with envy, just as David Hay would soon explode inside her own mouth. Too bad, Benny, Kathleen thought; eat your fucking heart out.

Hay stood there, knees trembling as Kathleen's lips and tongue drew him ever onward toward an incredible, onrushing orgasm. Never for an instant did he realize that Kathleen was simply doing what she did best. Playing to an audience.

There wasn't one wedding, but two. Two couples stood beneath the *chuppah*, the traditional wedding canopy, on a Sunday in early October, Pearl with Jake, and Annie with Moses Caplan. The two girls had been inseparable nearly all their lives; their weddings would not split them now. Not only were they sharing the ceremony, they would honeymoon together in Atlantic City, and when they returned to New York they would live in the same building. Each couple would move into a three-bedroom apartment on the same floor of a luxurious apartment house on lower Fifth Avenue, close to Washington Square.

Unaccustomed to performing dual ceremonies, the rabbi paused when he came to the rings. He looked first at Lou Levitt, who was acting as best man for Jake, then at Benny Minsky, who was performing the same office for Caplan. Finally the rabbi held out both hands, one for each ring, making certain not to mix them up.

After the ceremony, a dinner dance was held at the Four Aces, which was closed for regular business that night. A catering staff crowded into the restaurant's kitchen to prepare the dinner to be served downstairs. The slot machines were covered, the doors to the office and the back room locked. Only the bar was open, and Pearl could not help but notice how Levitt's eyes continually followed the waiters as they moved swiftly from table to table to refill empty glasses. She had known Jake and Levitt for the same amount of time, and it still amazed her that two young men who were so close could be so different. Jake was open, predictable, always willing to share whatever he had. Levitt was a maze of contradictions, simultaneously generous and stingy. For wedding gifts, he had presented each couple with a gold-rimmed, bone-china dinner service for twelve. Additionally, he had proposed that the Four Aces be closed for one night and used for the wedding party. Now, Pearl was certain, he was mentally adding up how much liquor was being consumed.

Following dinner, the two wedding couples opened the dancing. After the first few steps, the guests joined in. Minsky brushed past Pearl, in his arms Kathleen, who wore a long black dress and a glittering sapphire necklace that Pearl had never seen before. Another

155

gift from Minsky, she supposed; his generosity was as great as ever. Settled comfortably in Jake's arms, she looked around the dance floor to see whether Levitt would find a partner. She spotted him leading her mother onto the floor, and she felt grateful toward him for ensuring that Sophie Resnick was not made to feel left out.

As the first dance ended, Pearl and Jake found themselves standing next to Levitt and Sophie. "May I?" Levitt asked. With a movement as deft as any of his throws of the dice, he handed Sophie over to her new son-in-law and then took Pearl in his own arms.

"Enjoying yourself?" Pearl asked.

"Sure. This party appeals to my sense of economy—two for the price of one."

Pearl was surprised that Levitt was such a good dancer, well balanced, light on his feet. She'd never considered him a man who placed any importance on such social attributes. Surely he'd think of dancing as frivolous?

"Are you happy?" he asked her, then answered his own question. "Of course you are. What bride isn't happy?"

"I know I'd be a lot happier if I could see more of Jake, and I'm sure Annie feels the same way about Moe."

"Busy times, Pearl. Any new venture has to be gotten off the ground. Be grateful that I'm letting Jake take a couple of weeks off for his honeymoon."

She was uncertain whether he was joking or serious. "You'd have got a mouthful from me if you hadn't."

"You I can handle. You're my size, remember?" Levitt dropped his voice to a whisper. "Pearl . . . what happened before I went away, I behaved like an idiot. I kept making myself see something that wasn't there, something that was never there. If I made you uncomfortable, I'm sorry."

"That's all right, Lou." She gave him an affectionate kiss on the cheek, relieved that any animosity he might have harbored toward her was finished. Whatever his feelings had been, they hadn't been totally his own fault. She'd encouraged them to a degree by constantly going down to the office to see him, by accepting that one invitation to dinner. It wasn't love that had drawn her to him. She'd just been fascinated, intrigued, because he was so different.

"Your mother's keeping the restaurant open?"

"I'll help her for a while, until Jake and I . . ."

"Until you start a family? A bunch of kids running around," Levitt mused. "Pearl, it doesn't seem that long ago that we were kids ourselves."

"Sometimes I think we still are. You and me. Lou . . . you're barely twenty-one, and I've still got another few weeks to wait."

Levitt turned philosophical. "I don't think I was ever really a kid. While the others were playing, throwing a ball around, I was working, studying. I wanted to be a grownup from the moment I could walk. From the first time I saw a shopkeeper take money for an item, I wanted to be a businessman."

"You've got your wish. You head a big business." Pearl made no attempt to pretend that Levitt's other partners had equal charge of the operation. All the planning was Levitt's. The others just did as he told them, even Jake.

"Not big enough, Pearl, not big enough by far. All this—the clubs, the booze—that's peanuts compared with what's really out there. You and Annie just married a couple of guys who are going to be very, very rich. You'll never have to worry about being able to afford to send your kids to college—you'll be able to buy a damned college for each one of them. Now that's what you really call power."

"Lou, there's more to life than money, the power it brings. Don't forget, while you're making all these millions, to give yourself a little happiness as well. You can learn something there from Jake and Moe."

"Sure, Pearl. I'll do it when I'm ready."

Pearl wondered if he really meant it.

Annie and Caplan were the first to leave, at nine-thirty. They were driving straight through to Atlantic City to spend their wedding night there, while Pearl and Jake would begin their honeymoon in a suite at the Waldorf-Astoria before driving south the following day.

"Make sure you don't drive to the dock by mistake," Jake told Caplan. "There's nothing waiting for us tonight."

"He's not going anywhere near a dock," Annie assured Jake. "The only water he's going to see tonight is in the bathtub." She pulled Pearl aside. "We're two old married women now; life's all over."

"Are you nervous?" Pearl asked.

"Only about driving down to Atlantic City in the dark. How about you?"

"I wish I knew. One moment, I'm so happy—the next, I want to run away."

Annie kissed Pearl on the cheek, hugged her warmly. "That's called being in love. It's when you don't feel anything that you've got to worry."

They waved farewell to the guests and disappeared through the door leading to the alleyway. An hour later, Pearl and Jake followed suit. It seemed so strange to her to leave the club through the exit to the alleyway where Jake's car was parked; every other time she'd gone up the stairs to the restaurant, and then up another flight to the flat above. A whole existence had ended when the ring had been placed on her finger, when Jake had smashed his foot down on the glass. Pearl sought out her mother who was sitting at a table, talking with Annie's parents. "Mama, Jake and I are leaving now. Will you be all right?"

Sophie dabbed at her eyes with a lace handkerchief. "Go. Don't worry about me. How far do I have to walk before I'm home? And Lou assured me that if I need anything while you're away, all I have to do is go downstairs and tell him."

Pearl looked around for Levitt. He was standing by the bar, sipping a drink. She had considered asking him to keep an eye on her mother while she was on her honeymoon, but he had offered to do it without being asked. He really seemed to be going out of his way to make up for any bitterness he'd shown when he'd learned of her engagement. Holding the long train of her wedding dress, she went over to him. "Thanks for offering to look after my mother."

"If something happens to her, who cooks dinner for me?" he answered with a smile. Pearl kissed him and then looked around for Jake, finally spotted him talking to Minsky and Kathleen. "Maybe Benny's thinking of asking the *shikse* to marry him and he's getting information from Jake on how to go about popping the question."

"Lou, Benny's not that slow."

"Don't bet your last dime on it," Levitt said before turning away.

After saying goodbye to everyone, Pearl and Jake left the club, climbing up the stairs to the alleyway. "In all this time I never came out of that door," Pearl said. "Can you believe that?"

"That's because it's the customers' entrance, and you were one of the partners." He took her by the arm and hurried her toward his car which was parked at the end of the alleyway.

Pearl's feet slipped on the cobblestones. "Jake, I can't run, not in this dress, not in these shoes."

"Then I'll carry you." Laughing, he reached down and lifted her into the air. She squealed in fright and then joined him in laughter, wrapping her arms around his neck as they kissed. "Put me down. What are my neighbors going to say?"

"Your neighbors?"

"My mother's neighbors, then."

"Let them say whatever they like."

A car's headlights flickered on. Pale yellow beams caught Pearl and Jake in stark relief against the buildings. Jake froze, and Pearl's cry of fear was stifled in her throat as a car door opened. She could just discern a bulky, familiar figure.

"Is it too late to give the happy couple a present?" Saul Fromberg asked.

"What the hell do you want?" Jake demanded. He squinted in the light and saw another figure behind the steering wheel; he knew it had to be Gus Landau.

"I was disappointed not to get invited to your wedding," Fromberg said, "but that rudeness doesn't stop me from wanting to wish you good luck or from giving you a present. Here, take it."

Jake set Pearl down and advanced toward Fromberg. The moneylender held out a box.

"Take it, it's a gift."

Jake eyed the box warily, wondering what kind of trick Fromberg had up his sleeve. The moneylender didn't know it had been Jake and his friends who had robbed his club to raise the money for Sophie Resnick's fine; he might have guessed but he couldn't be certain. He had to be sore, though, because of the success the four young men had made of the club he had sacrificed.

Pearl remembered telling Levitt that this was one day on which she could forgive anyone for anything, but she found there were still exceptions. "We don't want any gifts or good wishes from you."

"Listen to that." Landau's voice came from the car. "The little girl's still got a big mouth on her." He opened the door and stepped out, uncoiling from the seat like a king cobra. As he stepped into the glare of the lights, Pearl saw the broad stripe she'd put across his face. The sight of it still made her gasp.

"Such a happy occasion should be a time for letting bygones be bygones," Fromberg said amiably. "I want to give you a pair of silver candlesticks, that's all. This is a sentimental occasion for me, the little girl with all the questions getting married. Even if you didn't see fit to invite me, I still feel I've got to give you a gift. Besides, your new husband and his partners, they're worthwhile competition to me now. I've got to show a little respect. After all, who knows when we might be able to do each other a favor, eh?"

Pearl tore her eyes away from the stripe on Landau's cheek and looked at the box in Fromberg's hands. "Save your candlesticks for a wedding that you *do* get invited to." Taking Jake's arm, she walked on. Neither Fromberg nor Landau made any attempt to stop them.

"Maybe we should have taken the damned candlesticks," Jake said, once he'd started the engine of his own car. "What harm would it have done?"

"We don't need anything from the likes of him. He only robbed you and the others once, but he robbed my family for years. And he tried

159

to put my mother in jail. Can you believe the nerve of the man? Turns up at my wedding, all sore because he wasn't invited."

When they reached the Waldorf-Astoria, arm in arm, they entered the lobby. A clerk on duty showered rice on them as they hurried past, Pearl laughing delightedly. "Did you pay him to do that?"

"Pay him?" Jake made a face. "How often does he see such a beautiful bride passing through here? He paid me."

"Tell me the truth."

"Okay, I may have slipped him a bottle of the good stuff."

"Thanks, Jake." She squeezed his hand. "You think of everything."

When they reached their suite, Jake swung back the door, lifted Pearl in his arms, and carried her across the threshold. "Home at last, Mrs. Granitz."

"Temporary, but home nonetheless."

Still holding Pearl, Jake kicked the door closed. "See how smart we were? Moe and Annie are somewhere in the back of beyond—most probably broken down—and we're snug for the night. They must have been crazy."

Suddenly, Pearl felt nervous. Jake's strength, the hardness of his body threatened to overwhelm her. She clung tightly to him as he carried her through the suite to the bedroom. On a table was a vase full of fresh, bloodred roses. Next to it was a silver bucket containing a bottle of champagne. So much for Prohibition, Pearl thought, and she began to feel less tense. The government passed a law and her Jake got rich by breaking it . . . he became popular by making thousands of people happy. Some law it must be when everyone was only too willing to break it, even the desk clerk who'd thrown the rice.

Very gently, Jake set Pearl down on the edge of the bed. His eyes were liquid soft as he looked at her, like those of a child anticipating a treasured gift. Were her own eyes that soft now? Of course they were. Wasn't Jake the gift she'd wanted all these years? She watched him walk to the table, ease the cork out of the bottle of champagne, and fill two glasses. When he offered one to her, she took just the tiniest sip before setting it down on the bedside table. It wasn't champagne she wanted.

Jake sat next to her, hands resting on her shoulders as he began a gentle massage. There was such strength in his hands, and he used that strength with such tenderness. Such strength . . . such tenderness . . . The words repeated themselves in Pearl's brain, over and over again. It seemed impossible that two such attributes could be so complementary, yet they were. Jake's long, blunt fingers traced across her like those of an artist, simultaneously soothing and arousing as they moved from her shoulders to glide across her body, reaching places that no one had ever touched before, building in her a fire the like of which she had never experienced.

Kathleen! . . . The picture of Kathleen Monahan riding in Jake's car leaped unbidden from Pearl's memory. Why? What reason could she have for remembering that day now, the day when Jake and Kathleen had driven by while she was sweeping the sidewalk? Was it because of seeing Fromberg and Landau, because Jake had been working for the fat moneylender then and Pearl had forbidden him to come into the restaurant? Jake had said he'd only been out with Kathleen a couple of times before turning her over to Minsky. Had he been telling the truth, or had Jake been like this with Kathleen? Was it with Kathleen that Jake had learned such gentleness? Such skill?

The blaze within her grew brighter, fiercer, and Pearl did not care about Kathleen anymore. All that mattered now was that she had Jake. Whoever had come before, Jake would not have meant as much to her as he did to Pearl, nor had any other woman meant as much to him as she did. Now was important, what was past was forgotten. The blaze burned everything in its path until all that remained was her need for Jake.

Deep within her a moan began, low and throaty at first, then moving upward a register, quickening, soaring. It burst from her lips in a torrent as she clawed at Jake. It dimmed, then changed into a long, breathless sigh and finally into a bitter cry as, above her joy, another image imprinted itself on her inner eye . . . Lou Levitt standing in the restaurant after his return from Scotland, the bleakness of his stare, the pain and anguish on his face as he saw her ring and understood its meaning.

The party broke up shortly after the departure of Pearl and Jake. Levitt escorted Sophie Resnick to the flat above the restaurant and then returned to the club just long enough to have one more drink before leaving. As he walked toward his car, Gus Landau materialized from a shadowy doorway.

"Hey, shrimp! Mr. Fromberg wants to talk to you."

Levitt wasn't the least surprised. Ever since the first shipment from Scotland, he'd expected an approach. "Where is he?"

"Over here." Landau led Levitt to the car, opened the rear door for him. Inside, wreathed in cigar smoke, sat Fromberg. The box containing the gift he'd tried to give to Pearl and Jake lay on the seat beside him.

"Your two friends aren't very hospitable," Fromberg greeted

Levitt. "First they don't invite me to their wedding—second, they refuse my present. Maybe you want to give it to them for me?"

Levitt glanced down at the box, disinterested. "If they refused it, they probably had their reasons."

Fromberg let it pass. "They're not the only ones who need congratulating. I hear you're doing pretty good for yourself these days."

"Can't complain." Levitt watched Landau settle into the driver's seat and wondered if he was going to be taken for a ride. Landau did not start the engine, though; he simply sat there, half-turned so he could watch as well as listen.

"That's good booze you're supplying," Fromberg said. "Lot of people are looking at your operation with greedy eyes, saying it's too big for a bunch of kids like you and your pals to handle all by themselves."

"We're all old enough to vote."

"Barely." Fromberg removed the chewed cigar from his mouth and laughed. "But I've got nothing against youth. I was young myself once. There's one thing I always remember from those days—I needed someone older, wiser, to look after me."

"What are you offering?"

"A deal. You and me, we go into business together. I've got the muscle to make sure no one else takes too much of an interest."

"It's not for me to give an answer," Levitt said. "I'd have to put it to my partners, get a vote on it."

"Your partners don't mean nothing, little man. You're the brains in that outfit. What you say becomes law."

Levitt knew it was true, but he was not about to allow Fromberg to flatter him. "Like I said, I've got partners to consider. When Jake Granitz and Moe Caplan get back from their honeymoons, I'll talk to them about it; then I'll let you know."

"Yeah, you do that. But just remember, there are a lot of sharks swimming out there who'd be only too happy to gobble up a little minnow like you."

"Thanks for the warning." Levitt opened the door and stepped out. "I'll bear it in mind." As he walked toward his own car, he replayed the conversation in his mind. It was obvious to him what a partnership with Fromberg would mean. They'd lose their power. Eventually they'd lose all their business. Right now, they were competition for Fromberg; he saw them as a threat. If they agreed to work with him, he'd be able to control them until he could find a way to dispose of them. Levitt knew that was one of the dangers of becoming successful—you attracted the attention of predators. One

162

of the ways to fight back was to become bigger and tougher than anyone else. A better way by far was to become smarter—use brains instead of brawn. Being smart always won out in the long run.

Driving home, he considered the options open to Fromberg once his offer was refused. Violence? Fromberg sitting in his plush office, giving the orders to Landau who carried them out? Levitt didn't think so. Fromberg couldn't afford a fight. Not only would it be costly to both sides, it would draw the attention of the police. No, Fromberg had to choose some other route. The whole thing was like a chess game. It was Fromberg's move; they could do nothing but wait and hope that he hadn't spotted a weakness in their defense, an unprotected piece whose capture could lead to a speedy mate.

By the time Minsky and Kathleen left, Fromberg and Landau were no longer in the alleyway. Not that Minsky would have noticed them. He had eyes only for the sapphire necklace Kathleen was wearing. He didn't recall giving it to her. He couldn't remember every single gift he'd bought for her, there had been so many—clothing, furs, jewelry. But a sapphire necklace? Minsky had bought her diamonds because everyone bought diamonds, rubies because he liked their fire, emeralds because they matched the green of Kathleen's eyes. But sapphires? . . . No, he was sure of it.

"Where did you get that necklace?" he asked as they drove toward Riverside Drive and Kathleen's apartment.

"This?" Kathleen raised a hand to it. "It was my mother's."

"How come you've never worn it before?"

"I always wanted to wear what you gave me, but"—her voice turned coy—"you haven't given me anything lately."

"When we get back to your place," Minsky promised, "I'll give you something."

Kathleen was glad to let the subject drop. The sapphire necklace had not belonged to her mother. It was a present from David Hay, given on her last trip out to his estate on Long Island the previous Sunday when Minsky had been with his partners ferrying more liquor from Ocean City to Philadelphia. Since that first time when she and Hay had gone swimming in the nude and then had made love on the fleecy towels by the side of his pool, his chauffeur had come to call for Kathleen at least once a week. For once she was grateful to Levitt for working his partners so hard. Minsky was away much of the time, leaving Kathleen with plenty of opportunities to see Hay.

She knew she shouldn't have worn the necklace that night, but some perverse instinct had forced her to, just to see if Minsky would recognize it as not being a present he'd given her. He had, and she was instantly ready with a lie about its origin. Had he believed her? Or was his insane jealousy working overtime? Asking who . . . where . . . when? There was no way he could catch her out, she'd been too discreet for that. As much as she'd love to flaunt David Hay and all his old wealth and elegance in Minsky's face, she would not dare to do so. She had to keep both men entirely separate in order to enjoy what each had to give her.

The moment they were inside the apartment, Minsky exploded, cutting loose the temper he'd been holding back during the entire ride. He dragged Kathleen into the bedroom, slammed the door on the two dogs and yelled: "Your mother never had two cents to her name! She never owned a piece of ice like that!" He reached out to snatch the necklace from Kathleen's pale throat, breaking the clasp. "Who the hell gave it to you?"

Kathleen was so stunned by the abruptness of the assault that she stood transfixed in the center of the room.

"Who gave this to you?"

"I told you—my mother!"

"And I'm telling you that you're a goddamned liar!"

"Where are you going?" Kathleen screamed as she watched Minsky march toward the window. He threw it open. "What are you doing?"

Minsky never answered. When Kathleen finally regained the use of her limbs and threw herself at his back, he tossed the sapphire necklace out into the night. It fell five stories to the sidewalk.

"You lunatic bastard!" She let go of him and raced toward the bedroom door, wanting to be downstairs to pick up the necklace before someone else did. Minsky flung himself at her, caught her around the waist in a football tackle. She crashed to the carpet with him on top of her.

"You're seeing some guy, aren't you? Tell me the truth or I'll beat the living daylights out of you!"

"I'm not seeing anyone!" She writhed around until she was on her back. Her fingernails arced toward his face, clawed across his cheek.

"You fucking bitch!"

Kathleen closed her eyes, tensed, waited for the blow. It never came. Minsky's weight on her body lessened. She opened her eyes to see him dragging back the doors to her closet. Before she could move, a sable coat he'd given her followed the necklace out of the window. "When your closets and drawers are empty, your dogs are going out!" he yelled, rushing back from the window. "And then you'll be next unless you tell me the damned truth!"

"Benny, I'm telling you the truth. There is no one!" She watched, horror-stricken, as he threw her Persian lamb coat out of the window. It sailed through the air like a gigantic, misshapen bat. "You son of a bitch! Why don't you listen to me?"

He returned to the closet yet again, buried himself in it. When he backed out, his arms were filled with a mink and half-a-dozen dresses. "Next it's the dogs, then you!"

She jumped onto his back. Arms holding her clothing, he tried to shake her off. She pulled back his jacket, saw a leather strap biting into his shoulder. Kathleen's toes clawed into the carpet as she was dragged toward the window. She clung onto his neck with one hand and used the other to wrest Minsky's automatic out of its shoulder holster. Minsky felt the gun being tugged clear. He swung around, eyes wide in apprehension. Kathleen was pointing the automatic at his chest, her knuckles white around the trigger.

"Put it down, baby."

"You put my clothes down."

"And give you a clear shot?" He clutched the clothing tighter to his chest. If she squeezed the trigger, she'd blow a hole through her precious clothes before she blew a hole through him. "Put the damned gun down before it goes off. I believe you about your mother giving you that necklace."

"It's a bit late now, isn't it?"

"We'll go down and get it. And if it's not there, I'll buy you another one." He saw that the gun was beginning to waver in her grasp. Another few seconds, that was all he needed. "I'll buy you new furs, whatever you want." The barrel of the gun continued to move, swaying back and forth. Minsky straightened his arms with all the force he could muster. The clothes flew through the air at Kathleen. She raised her hands instinctively. Flame belched from the muzzle of the gun, a roar reverberated through the room. Minsky never felt the wind of the bullet as it passed three inches from his head and smashed into the wall. He jumped forward, snatched the gun from Kathleen's hand, and flipped it onto the bed. Grabbing her by the arm, he dragged her across the carpet to the window, lifted her up, and balanced her on the sill.

"Want your goddamned necklace? Go get it yourself!" He gave her a vicious two-handed shove.

Kathleen shrieked in terror as she began to fall. At the last moment, Minsky's hands, like two vises, closed over her wrists. She jerked to a halt, legs waving wildly in space, feet kicking against the wall.

"Please, Benny . . ." She looked up at him, eyes begging. "Pull me in. Please."

"When you tell me the truth."

"I told you the truth already." As terrified as she was, she knew that continuing to lie was the only hope she had. If she told him the truth, the real truth—about David Hay, about the stolen days out on Long Island—she knew Minsky would not hesitate to open his hands. "Benny, please pull me up!"

He stared down at her dispassionately, a scientist studying the results of an experiment. "Do you think I'd lie to you now?" Kathleen cried out.

"No, I don't think you would." A strange grin stole across his face, twisting his mouth, narrowing his eyes. He hauled her back inside and she collapsed onto the floor. Tears spilled from her eyes, her chest heaved. The necklace, the fur coats, they were all forgotten now. She was just grateful to be alive. Each time Minsky came a fraction closer to overstepping that mark. In another week, another month . . . who knew when he'd open his hands and let her go?

"You shouldn't have pointed that gun at me, baby," he whispered soothingly as he knelt down beside her and ran his fingers through her blond hair. "You shouldn't have tried to shoot me."

The change was coming over him again, madness to regret. Like a Catholic going to confessional . . . everything could be forgiven as long as you got it out of your system by telling it all to the priest and accepting his punishment. Only Kathleen didn't have any fit punishment to administer to Minsky, no Hail Marys for him to recite. All she could do to chastise him was continue to cheat on him.

But she knew she'd have to be more careful in future. Minsky's regular absences had made her overconfident, careless. She wouldn't be able to accept any more gifts from David Hay . . . or if she did, she'd have to make certain they were gifts that would not arouse Minsky's suspicions.

Chapter Four

To Sophie Resnick, the flat seemed empty with her daughter gone. She had always known that one day Pearl would grow up, get married, have a family of her own; but she'd never been able to bring herself to dwell on it. Aware that the wrench would be painful enough when it occurred, she had not anticipated the break. Only now it had happened. Her only daughter, her only child—a miniature copy of herself—had left home. When Pearl returned she would move into her own home with her own husband. Sophie wondered if the Moscowitzes next door were experiencing such bittersweet feelings. No, the loss of their daughter would not affect them so severely. They still had each other, while she had no one.

The two weeks Pearl was away passed with excruciating slowness for Sophie. True to his word, Lou Levitt kept in constant contact with her, coming into the restaurant every day to eat before going down to the Four Aces, never neglecting to ask if she needed anything. He was such a considerate young man that occasionally Sophie even wondered whether Pearl might have made a better choice by marrying him. He was certainly interested in her, always wanting to know if Sophie had heard from her daughter. Sophie would smile and answer that Pearl was too busy to write or telephone home. Home? . . . No, not home. Her mother's home. Pearl had her own home now, Sophie had to remember that. It wasn't easy, though. There were too many memories in the flat.

When Pearl came back from her honeymoon and returned to the restaurant, Sophie could easily make herself believe that nothing had really changed. Her daughter still looked the same in her white apron, her dark auburn hair tied up in a bun, light brown eyes fixed in steely concentration as she worked in the kitchen. It was only in the evening that the difference manifested itself. Pearl no longer went upstairs with her mother. She went home to the apartment on lower Fifth Avenue to prepare dinner for her husband before he went to work.

"Why can't he eat here like he always used to?" Sophie asked her daughter.

"Single men eat their dinner in a restaurant," Pearl answered. "Lonely men. Happily married men have wives who cook for them. Annie cooks each night for Moe. I cook for Jake."

"What about Lou? He still eats here. So does Benny sometimes."

"I'm not concerning myself with them, Mama. Only with Jake. He works hard all week long, and it's my responsibility to see that he eats properly."

Sophie remembered when her husband was alive. Every night, after the restaurant was closed, she would prepare dinner for him upstairs. She'd been no different, and she shouldn't expect her daughter to be. She should just be grateful that Pearl had found someone who loved her as much as Jake did, who could provide for her so handsomely. There was no need for her to continue working. There had never been any need. She cooked in the restaurant because she enjoyed it, and when she went home in the evening, she enjoyed cooking again. Cooking was always a pleasure when the results were appreciated. Sophie remembered that from her own marriage.

Pearl's first Friday in the new apartment coincided with her twenty-first birthday. She celebrated by inviting her mother and the Caplans for Friday-night dinner. Sophie wanted to help in the kitchen. Politely but firmly, Pearl told her to remain at the table with Jake, Annie, and Moses Caplan. This was her home. Only she would cook and serve here.

Shortly after the meal was finished, Jake and Caplan excused themselves. They had to go to work—the clubs and the liquor business did not recognize God's day of rest.

"May I at least help you to clean up?" Sophie asked as she watched Pearl and Annie take plates into the kitchen.

"Sit, Mama. Relax. You've worked all week."

"I don't know how to sit and relax." Sophie collected cutlery from the table and followed the two young women into the kitchen. "Besides, in a few months, please God, you'll be wanting me to help, when your hands are full of diapers."

Pearl and Annie looked at each other before bursting into laughter. "You think we're going to have babies nine months after we're married? We're in no hurry."

"You might not be," Sophie told Pearl, "but I am. I'm fifty-two. How long am I supposed to wait before I'm blessed with grandchildren?"

Pearl had never thought of her mother as being old. Now she realized that she was. Annie's parents were ten years younger and had been through little of the hardship Sophie Resnick had endured. Even the last few years of comparative luxury could not compensate for the earlier struggles; nothing could make her mother younger. When Pearl had told Jake that she would continue working with her mother until they had children, they had both looked on that event as something in the distant future. Suddenly, children became important to Pearl, not so much for herself, but for her mother's sake—and for the children's sake. If Pearl wanted her children to know a grandmother's love, she'd better start a family soon.

"You won't have to wait long, Mama," she promised.

Annie, as if connected telepathically to Pearl through their years of friendship, caught on immediately. "Haven't you heard, Mrs. Resnick? Pearl and I have a bet between us on who has a child first."

"Please God you both have daughters like yourselves," Sophie replied. "They'll leave home when they're six, they'll color their hair with household bleach. And maybe"—her voice trembled—"maybe they'll bring as much happiness as you two have."

"Go sit down, Mama," Pearl said as she choked back tears. "This might be a large apartment, but the kitchen's only big enough for two."

The marriages of Jake to Pearl and of Moses Caplan to Annie, and the couples' subsequent moves into adjacent apartments on Fifth Avenue, prompted the other two partners to change their ways. As long as none of them had left the old area, they'd been content to remain there, Levitt in a residential hotel way down on First Avenue, and Minsky in a small furnished apartment on Fourth Street. By the end of 1926, however, within eight weeks of the double wedding, both young men had moved. Levitt had leased an apartment on Central Park West, overlooking the lake. Minsky had moved farther uptown, to West End Avenue. He'd considered moving in with Kathleen on Riverside Drive, but she had raised so many objections that he'd decided not to. He didn't like her dogs, she told him, and there were neighbors to think about—as if neighbors who'd heard their regular arguments would raise an eyebrow at seeing Kathleen living with a man to whom she was not married; she was in show business, a strange mode of life was to be expected. Most of all—and this argument she kept to herself—if Minsky lived with her it would seriously curtail her time with David Hay. Sneaking those secret dates with Hay was no problem when Minsky was away on business *and* living somewhere else. It would be far more difficult if he were sharing the apartment and might conceivably come home unexpectedly. All hell would break loose when he demanded to know where she was in the middle of the night, if not at home?

Levitt commemorated his move with a housewarming party in the new apartment. It took place on a Sunday afternoon. The only guests were Levitt's partners, their wives, and Kathleen. He had no friends outside his business circle, no one else to whom he felt close. After caterers had served luncheon, Levitt invited Pearl, Annie, and Kathleen to look around the large apartment. Once they had left the dining room, he called his partners close.

"When I left the Four Aces on the night of the weddings, someone was waiting for me—Fromberg."

"He was waiting for us as well," Jake said. "He wanted to give us a wedding present. Silver candlesticks, I think it was."

"I know. He asked if I'd pass them on to you."

"Where are they then? Don't tell me you hocked them? Nice friend you are, hock a friend's wedding present."

Levitt laughed. "I told him you and Pearl must have had your own reasons for not accepting them." He paused for a few seconds, as if to generate tension. "He had a gift to offer me as well. A partnership with him, for all of us. We'd share what we have—the booze, the clubs, the book we're planning," Levitt said, referring to a bookmaking operation that would be conducted through more than one hundred small shops in Lower and Midtown Manhattan. Each shop would act as a collection point for betting money, telephoning in business to a central office. "In return, Fromberg said he'd give us his protection, guard us against the bigger sharks."

"What did you tell him?" Minsky asked.

"I told him that I couldn't give him an answer, that I'd have to speak with my partners first."

"How come you waited two months before mentioning anything to us?" Caplan wanted to know.

"I didn't think it was worth mentioning, that's why. Obviously, we're going to say no. We throw in with him and we put ourselves at his mercy."

"So why bring it up now?"

"Because he got back to me a couple of days ago, wanted to know if I'd discussed it with my partners."

"Tell him yeah, you spoke to us," Minsky muttered. "And your partners all agreed that the fat pig should go fuck himself."

Levitt's voice took on a contrived note of patience. "I intend to do just that, Benny. With a little more tact, though. There's no point in making waves unless you can sink someone, and we can't sink Fromberg. Not yet, anyway. So I suggest we send him a case of our best Scotch—"

"A case?" Minsky gasped. "That's worth—"

"I know exactly what it's worth. Call it a premium on an insurance policy. We'll send it to him tomorrow with a respectful note telling him that at the moment we prefer to carry on by ourselves. But if in the future we should feel that a partnership is advantageous to us, he's the man we'd go to." He broke off as the three young women returned from their tour of the apartment. "How do you like it?"

"Very nice, Lou," Annie answered. "You've decorated it with a lot of taste."

"I paid someone to decorate it with a lot of taste."

Pearl left Annie and Kathleen and walked slowly to the window where she looked out over the park. Skaters were gliding across the frozen lake, long scarves trailing in the wind of their passage. Her eyes moved from the skaters to the benches by the lake, settled on the one she had shared with Levitt that Saturday evening before he had sailed for England. Another young couple occupied it now, braced against the winter cold in bright woolen hats and heavy coats. They were bending down to tie the laces on their skates.

Jake left the table and joined her at the window. "Is that where you expect me to take our kids?"

"Would you?"

"Only if I didn't have to teach them how to skate."

"Coward."

Levitt made a third at the window and asked what was so fascinating. Jake explained that Pearl was already insisting that he teach their children how to skate. Levitt smiled and looked at her. "Is that why you're so interested in the park, the lake?"

Pearl turned away, certain that Levitt understood why she had been looking. He had an ability to make her feel uncomfortable. It had been easy to forget him for the six weeks he was away, and for the two weeks she'd been on her honeymoon. Now that their regular routine had resumed—Levitt in the Four Aces all the time, Pearl in the restaurant above—she saw too much of him to make forgetting easy. It was another reason to have children quickly, to break the routine completely .

"Ooh, skating!" Kathleen exclaimed as she crowded into the group at the window. "I love ice skating." She swung around on Minsky. "Why don't we go one day?"

Minsky regarded her as though she were mad. "I like my face pointing in the same direction as my feet," was his reply. "If God meant us to skate—"

"He'd have given us blades on our feet instead of soles and heels!" Angrily, Kathleen finished Minsky's statement. "If you won't take

171

me, I'll find someone else."

Minsky began to laugh. "No one's crazy enough to take two risks for you—having me to answer to, and breaking his bones into the bargain. Forget it."

Kathleen flounced off. If Minsky wouldn't go skating with her, she knew who would. There was a small lake on David Hay's estate out on Long Island. That would also be frozen. While Minsky was away on his next trip, she'd go skating with Hay.

Lou Levitt's carefully worded letter and a case of Scotch were delivered the following morning to Saul Fromberg's office on East Forty-second Street. Fromberg read the letter twice before screwing it up into a tight ball and flinging it furiously against the oak-paneled wall.

"That scumbag!" he yelled at Gus Landau who sat calmly in a chair opposite Fromberg's desk. "That dirty little Polack scumbag! He writes me a flowery letter like some goddamned diplomat, sends me a case of Scotch as a peace offering, and what he's really telling me to do is go jump out of a window!"

"That's what you get for playing nice with little creeps like that," Landau answered sagely. "You shouldn't have tried to sweet-talk him. You should have hit him and his pals right away."

"No." Fromberg shook his head. He understood how much Landau wanted to move against the four young men he had once employed—and against the pipsqueak of a girl who'd put that stripe down his face with a chisel. Fromberg could not afford it. He wanted to settle this—take over the complete operation for himself—another way. Landau would go in there with a crew and blood would flow. Fromberg would inherit nothing but ruins. He wanted more. He wanted everything in working order when he took over: the clubs, the liquor business, the new bookmaking scheme he'd started to hear about. Also, he wanted the expertise the four partners could provide. Especially Levitt's expertise. That little Polack had a brain that was too good to waste—much too smart to put a bullet through.

"Always remember that there's more than one way to skin a cat, Gus." Fromberg walked to the window and looked down ten floors to Forty-second Street. "Right now, we're going to be patient. We'll wait for the right moment—until they've got this new book running properly—and then we'll demonstrate to them what real power is. At the same time, we might even be able to score a few points with the Feds."

Landau was unimpressed. He tapped the gun he wore in a holster beneath his jacket. "Real power comes from here."

"No. It comes from here." Fromberg touched his temple with his index finger. "What you're calling power's just desperation, because you've got nothing else to go with." He sat down at the desk, pulled a sheet of paper from a drawer, and began to write. "I want you to deliver a letter for me. Go to the Four Aces and give it to Levitt."

"Whatever you say."

The letter Fromberg wrote was as diplomatic as the one he had received. He thanked Levitt and his partners for their most gracious gift, assured them that he understood and fully respected their wish to remain independent. He ended the letter on a solicitous note, expressing his gratitude that Levitt and his partners would look to him should they ever need an alliance. The letter was warm, full of thank yous, assurances. It was oil on troubled water. And Saul Fromberg, when he signed his name to the bottom of it, didn't mean a single damned word.

Kathleen got her opportunity to go ice-skating in the middle of the week. Minsky was away in Philadelphia and she had a night off. She contacted David Hay who sent his chauffeur for her. Wrapped up warmly in a fur coat, a wolfskin blanket across her knees, Kathleen watched the frozen city glide by. The comfort of the car, the crispness of the air, calmed her, gave her mind room to wander. She knew it was time to think seriously about her situation, where she stood with Benny Minsky and David Hay. If she had any brains at all, she told herself, she'd dump Minsky completely. Who the hell needed to be held out of a window five floors above the ground? Hay was a perfect gentleman . . . a perfect, rich gentleman, a thousand classes above the likes of Minsky and his racketeering cronies. There was never an angry word out of Hay, no threat of violence. Never even a raised voice, let alone a raised hand.

And that, Kathleen thought disconsolately, might just be the trouble with Hay. Seeing him provided a wonderful counterpoint to her hectic life with Minsky. Being with him permanently might just bore the hell out of her. How much niceness could she take and remain sane? It might be more acceptable if she had been raised in that style of life, men holding chairs for women, opening doors, walking on the outside to shield them from mud thrown up by passing vehicles. If she came from that kind of background, she might expect it. But she didn't. She came from a working-class family where her father, a boisterous Irish dockworker, always sat first at the table, held open a door for no one but himself, and walked on the outside only if doing so put him closer to the nearest bar.

Perhaps it was better after all, she decided, to leave things the way they were, to enjoy both men for what they could give her—Hay, gentility; Minsky, excitement—yet keep them distinctly apart.

They skated on the frozen lake for half an hour, the ice illuminated by the headlights of the car. Kathleen could not remember the last time she had put on skates. She fell over half a dozen times before the skill returned. Hay didn't fall at all. He just glided across the lake, hands held nonchalantly behind his back as if skating were the most natural action in the world. Kathleen tried to picture Minsky in a similar situation. He wasn't the outdoor type at all. He'd probably fall over a few times, lose his temper, pull out his gun, and blow holes in the ice.

When Kathleen and Hay returned to the big house, a fire was blazing in the drawing-room hearth. The butler carried in a silver tray bearing hot toddies and toasted sandwiches. After asking if Hay needed anything else, the servant discreetly withdrew, closing the double doors behind him.

Hay stood with his back to the fire, gazing at Kathleen who sat on a leather chesterfield while she sipped her drink. Finally, he said, "There's something for you on the table."

Kathleen saw a flat, velvet-covered box on the table beside the chesterfield. Putting down the drink, she opened the box to find a diamond tiara. "David, it's beautiful."

"It was my mother's. She always wore it once a year, for opening night at the Met when she sat with her friends in the Diamond Horseshoe. I think she would have liked your kind of singing, too."

"I can't possibly take this."

"Whyever not?"

"It belonged to your mother. You should keep it." Regretfully, Kathleen replaced the tiara in its box. She could just see Minsky tossing it out of the window. After their last argument, when they'd gone downstairs, they hadn't found the sapphire necklace or the furs. They wouldn't find this either. She wondered if scavengers deliberately camped beneath her windows now, waiting to see what other tasty baubles came flying out into the night?

"My mother would have wanted you to have it. She would have liked you, Kathleen."

"Really? An Irish Catholic girl who sings torch songs in speakeasies?"

"My mother wasn't above taking a drink herself. She considered the Volstead Act a law of fools . . . legislated by fools to pacify fools. I think the night she and Father died they'd been drinking." He seemed

174

lost in thought for several seconds, melancholy. Then he snapped out of it, a smile appearing on his pale face. "Believe me, if Mother were still here she'd be drinking that whiskey your friends supply. Like me, she would only tolerate the best."

"I still can't take it."

"But I want you to have it. Damn it, Kathleen, I'm in love with you."

That was more than Minsky had ever told her. For a moment, Kathleen let herself imagine life out here on the Island. Old money, so much cleaner than the kind Minsky brought in; society functions; a leisurely, relaxed existence. It almost appealed to her. She looked at the tiara again, saw it on her head. Princess Kathleen. Too bad there was no royalty in America. She might have married a goddamned prince!

"Kathleen . . ." Hay was speaking again, his voice low and earnest. "I'm tired of being able to see you only once a week, twice if the gods are smiling on me. I want to see you, be with you, all the time."

"You want to marry me?"

"In a word, yes."

Slowly Kathleen shook her head. "I can't marry you, David."

He seemed stunned by her instant refusal. "That dark-skinned man at the club that night . . . he's your boyfriend, isn't he?"

"He pays for my apartment. He thinks he owns me, but he doesn't. He helped to get me into the clubs, got me my start singing."

Hay came away from the fireplace and sat next to Kathleen. "Why didn't you tell me this when I first met you?"

"Who wants to talk about Benny Minsky? There are better topics of conversation."

"Leave him. Live here with me, marry me, and you'll never have to worry about him again."

"You're kidding yourself, David. If he knew about you, this whole country wouldn't be big enough for you to hide in. Or me."

"Are you that scared of him that you won't leave him?"

"I keep asking myself the same question. I hate him, David, but I think I love him as well."

"And what about me?"

"I just love you."

"Then give him the heave-ho. I'm not frightened of that hooligan, that . . . that hoodlum."

To hear such a word coming from Hay was more than Kathleen could bear. She leaned back, rocking with laughter. The word *hoodlum* was a natural for a Benny Minsky, but David Hay made it sound as though he were speaking a foreign language. "David," she finally

175

managed to say, "why can't we just carry on as we're doing now?"

"Because I don't want to share you with anyone. All my life I've had the money to buy whatever I need. Now that I've found what I want more than anything, I learn that you're not for sale. Not to me, anyway," he added bitterly.

"Not to anyone."

He drew closer to her, lifting his toddy which had now become cool. "To carrying on as we are now. And to you changing your mind."

"To carrying on as we are now," Kathleen responded.

Hay emptied his glass and set it down. He slid an arm around Kathleen's waist and pulled her onto him. "How did this Minsky get you a break?"

Kathleen told a slightly altered version of the truth, leaving out how Minsky had been forced to go through Pearl and Annie. "He told his partners to give me a shot and they did."

"I see. You know, I'm quite frequently approached to back Broadway shows. When I put up the money, I suppose I'm entitled to certain privileges. I've never used them yet, I've just been content to take whatever profit accrues. However, I'm sure I could stipulate that a certain torch singer be given favorable consideration for a lead role."

A curtain swung back in front of Kathleen's eyes, new vistas opened up. The big break, the leap from clubs to the Broadway stage. For a chance like that she'd even risk Minsky's wrath. "I'd like that, David. I'd like that very much."

"I thought you would." He leaned back against the arm of the chesterfield as Kathleen's fingers traced across his thighs, picked at his trouser buttons. In the glow of the fire he watched her run her tongue across her gleaming lips, and he shivered in delightful anticipation.

Each time she made love with Jake, Pearl wondered if that miracle of nature had occurred. Had she conceived? Knowing had become very important to her, ever since she'd realized how much her mother wanted to become a grandmother. Sophie deserved happiness—who knew how many years were left to her?—and if something as simple as grandchildren would constitute that joy, Pearl would not deny her.

She became impatient, wanting to know ways of telling whether or not each act of lovemaking had achieved the desired result. She knew the obvious sign, the missing of a period. That was little help, though, as her own menstrual cycle had never been regular to begin with. Besides, she did not have the tolerance to wait until that time each month. She wanted to know immediately. Faced with this dilemma, she went where she had always gone for an answer—next door to see Annie.

"Someone told me that your breasts feel tender the morning after you conceive," Annie advised. "Does that help?"

Each morning, Pearl prodded her own breasts. It didn't help at all. "Are you sure there are no other signs?"

Annie chewed her bottom lip thoughtfully. "I once heard that if you carry high it'll be a girl, and if you carry low it'll be a boy. Or was it the other way around?"

"By the time I know whether I'm carrying high, low, or in between, I'll also know I'm pregnant. I don't care if I have a boy or a girl, I just want a baby."

Annie grimaced, as though offended that her advice was unwanted. "Try harder."

For two months, Pearl did try harder. Jake was, at first, surprised, and then gradually pleased when Pearl frequently assumed the role of instigator in bed. He understood how much she wanted a child and he happily obliged. And when he witnessed Pearl's disappointment each time her period started, he did his best to cheer her up.

"It's like everything else, Pearl, the time's got to be just right. There's no point in getting upset." He took her in his arms, comforted her. "If you like, I'll go see a doctor. Who knows, maybe there's something I can take, a pep pill or whatever. Hey, maybe there's even something wrong with me. I'll get a checkup, find out what it is, and have it put straight."

"Or there might be something wrong with me," Pearl answered quietly. That possibility haunted her. What would she do then, adopt a child? Perhaps she would be able to give an adopted child as much love as a natural child, but what about her mother? Whoever heard of an adopted grandchild?

"There's nothing wrong with you," Jake assured her.

"Since when are you a doctor?"

"I could have been," he answered, pretending offense. "I know how to put a plaster on my face when I cut myself shaving. What else does a doctor need to know?" He felt happy at seeing her start to smile. "Do you think it could be something wrong with the pair of us? Like we're going about it the wrong way?"

Pearl's smile broadened, yielded to a burst of laughter. "If this is the wrong way, let's keep doing it wrong. It's too enjoyable to stop."

Despite the laughter, Pearl's disappointment continued. In the middle of February, when she was two weeks late, and certain that this time she was pregnant, her period finally came to shatter her delusion.

Jake found her in the kitchen when he returned from work at three in the morning. In front of her, still hot from the oven, were two freshly baked honey cakes.

"What are you still doing up?" he wanted to know.

"Try some." Pearl cut a slice and handed it to him.

"Delicious. Now what problem has you baking at three o'clock in the morning?"

"We did something wrong again."

"Pearl, it's not the end of the world."

She held up a hand to him. "Jake, perhaps you're right. Maybe we should go see a doctor, the pair of us. At least, that way we'll know what's what."

He finished off the piece of cake, licked crumbs from his lips. "One more time," he told her. "We'll try it one more time, one more month. Then we'll see a doctor. We don't want to deprive ourselves of the fun of trying, do we?" He gave her a big, irrepressible smile.

"All right, one more month. But after that, we go to a doctor."

"Okay. The next time I come home at three in the morning, I don't want to see you in the kitchen."

"I won't be. I'll be in there"—she nodded toward the master bedroom—"waiting for you."

Pearl was true to her word. No matter what time Jake returned from work, whether at the clubs or on a liquor run, she was waiting for him in bed. Their lovemaking became frenzied, as if the fate of the entire world depended on its successful outcome. Exhausted, they would fall asleep in each other's arms, to awaken the following morning and make love again before Pearl left the apartment to go to the restaurant. If she was not pregnant yet, she reasoned, it certainly wasn't for the want of trying! Often, she found herself dozing off in the restaurant during the day, and she knew that Jake had difficulty in staying awake during the long hours he put in at work. Thank God his partners thought it was just fatigue. They had all been working extra shifts after rejecting Fromberg's offer of an alliance, fearing that his conciliatory letter delivered by Gus Landau was just a ruse to make them complacent. If they knew the real reason for Jake's tiredness . . . she could just imagine the jokes that would be made!

Two weeks later, at the end of February, the strain caught up with Jake. On a Saturday evening, as he set out for Ocean City with Benny Minsky, he fell asleep at the wheel of his car. Before Minsky could react, the car mounted the sidewalk and slammed nose first into a shop window. Minsky's head cracked into the windshield. Jake crashed against the steering wheel. A sharp pain seared his chest, he felt something snap in his left arm, then he blacked out. Clutching his injured head with one hand, Minsky pulled Jake back from the wheel. Blood poured from his nose; a long gash scored his forehead.

Minsky jumped from the car. "Get an ambulance!" he yelled at pedestrians who stood gawking at the wreck. He dragged Jake out of the driver's seat, fearful that the car would catch fire. Lastly, while he waited for the ambulance to arrive, he telephoned Lou Levitt at the Four Aces.

"How badly's Jake hurt?" Levitt demanded.

"How the hell do I know? He's bleeding and he's groaning like he's fit to die."

"Stay with him until the ambulance gets there. Then come here. Are you all right?" he asked as an afterthought.

"Couple of bruises. Thanks for asking."

"Sorry. Go in the ambulance with Jake. I'll meet you at the hospital."

Minsky rode the ambulance to St. Vincent's Hospital. While Jake was being admitted for treatment, his head wound was checked. By the time Levitt arrived, Minsky had been given a clean bill of health; he had a splitting headache, nothing more.

"Where's Jake?"

Minsky shrugged. "They took him through on a stretcher—last I saw of him."

Levitt found a doctor who told him that Jake had suffered three broken ribs, a fractured arm, and a possible concussion. He was being kept in. Levitt returned to Minsky.

"What the hell happened?"

"He fell asleep at the goddamned wheel. We hadn't even gone a mile before he passed out on me."

Silently, Levitt fumed. Of the three men supposed to be in Ocean City that night to supervise the latest load, two were incapacitated. There was no point in telling Minsky to go down there. He didn't look fit to drive five miles, let alone one hundred and fifty; even as Levitt looked, he could see a wide bruise darkening Minsky's already swarthy forehead. "You go home, get some sleep. I'll get word to Moe in Jersey that he's on his own tonight."

"What about him?" Minsky jerked a thumb toward a door. "Pearl should be told."

"I'll do it," Levitt answered. "You just worry about yourself."

Once Minsky was discharged, Levitt drove him home to West End Avenue before returning to the Four Aces. Entering the club, he wondered if he should inform Sophie Resnick as well as Pearl. No, there was no point in having the old lady all upset; she'd find out soon enough. He picked up the telephone to call Pearl, changed his mind.

You didn't give someone bad news over the phone, but face to face. Especially when that someone was as close to Levitt as Pearl. She didn't deserve to be left alone in the apartment after being told such news. As Jake's friend—as Pearl's friend—Levitt should be there to assist in any way he could. For a few hours, the club could look after itself; that was what the managers were paid for.

By the time Minsky entered his apartment on West End Avenue, his head felt like an overripe melon, ready to burst. He poured himself a large drink and lay down. Sleep eluded him for an hour, at which point he gave up trying. His body wasn't used to being in bed by midnight. He never went to sleep before three or four in the morning. He was a night owl—what the hell was he doing trying to change the habits of a lifetime just because of a crack on the head?

He picked up the telephone and called Kathleen's apartment. The phone rang unanswered for fully a minute before Minsky remembered that she was singing tonight at the King High on Seventh Avenue and Fifty-fifth Street. He'd go down there, catch her act. That'd surprise her, to see him when she thought he was in South Jersey. The bruise across his forehead—he stood in front of a mirror to admire it—would provide an even greater surprise. Kathleen would take him back to Riverside Drive, pamper him, give him even more affection than she gave those goddamned skinny, hairy dogs of hers.

He replaced the earpiece. The pain in his head eased slightly as he contemplated the expression on Kathleen's face when he walked into the King High. He drove to the club only to learn that he had missed her. Having finished her act twenty minutes earlier, she'd already left. Minsky stayed long enough to have a couple of drinks before driving over to Riverside Drive.

"Kathleen!" He yelled her name as he banged on the apartment door. "Kathleen, open up, you've got an invalid out here!"

The only sound to greet his summons was the howling of the two borzois. Minsky hammered on the door again, impatient and annoyed at being kept waiting. She couldn't be sleeping—no one could with that racket going on. And if she wasn't sleeping, if she wasn't opening the door, where was she?

With the howling of the dogs echoing in his ears, Minsky returned to the street and looked along it. Kathleen's Packard Sport Phaeton was parked at the curb. He walked to it, rested a hand on the hood. A trace of warmth told of recent use, the drive home from the King High. Minsky didn't like it. Kathleen's car was here, and she wasn't. He returned to his Chrysler, parked twenty yards from the building entrance, and settled himself in the driver's seat. It was bitterly cold. He covered himself with the wool blanket he kept on the back seat for those long trips to the Jersey shore. His head was starting to throb again. He'd catch pneumonia as well, waiting out in the cold for Kathleen. Where was she? She had no business being out. So help him, he'd kill her when she got home . . . if his headache and the cold didn't kill him first.

Levitt left the Four Aces and drove to Pearl's apartment building on lower Fifth Avenue. He had to knock twice before she opened the door, a robe thrown over her nightgown. When Pearl saw Levitt, her face reflected concern. "Lou . . ."

Levitt reached out to hold her by the shoulders. "Pearl, listen to me. Don't get upset, it could have been much worse."

"*What* could have been much worse?"

"Jake's in the hospital. He was in an automobile accident."

Pearl's face turned ashen, her legs trembled. If it were not for Levitt holding her, she would have fallen.

"Pearl, believe me, it's nothing serious. A busted arm, some cracked ribs, maybe a concussion. They're just keeping him in for observation."

"Who was driving? Benny?"

"Jake. It happened in his own car. Benny got away with just a crack on the head—it might even smarten him up a bit."

Pearl regained her composure. She shook herself free of Levitt's grip and retreated into the apartment. Levitt followed. "What hospital is he in?"

"St. Vincent's."

"Will you take me there?" She was already heading for the bedroom to change.

"It's late. They won't let visitors in now."

As Pearl spun around, her robe swung open. Levitt caught a glimpse of her white gown, creased from her lying in bed. She walked right up to him and he felt . . . smelled . . . the warmth of her body. A lump formed in his throat, a churning began in his loins.

"Lou, I don't give a damn what time it is. Jake's in a hospital and I'm going to see him." Her light brown eyes blazed amber as she dared him to contradict her. "Are you going to take me, or do I call a cab? Jake does own half a cab company, you know."

"I know. I own the other half. Get yourself dressed; I'll take you." Hypnotized by the brightness of her eyes, he had to force himself to look away. He sat down while Pearl returned to the master bedroom.

181

He heard her moving around, imagined her actions. He pictured the robe coming off, tossed onto the bed in her hurry. He moved his legs, trying to make himself more comfortable as he envisioned the nightgown following it. To think he'd laughed at Minsky, mocked him for making a fool out of himself over Kathleen . . . In that moment, as Levitt imagined Pearl walking around the bedroom naked, her long auburn hair cascading down onto her white shoulders, he realized that he had been an even bigger fool. Minsky's folly was in proclaiming his love. Levitt had been the jerk of all time for hiding his, burying his feelings in ledgers, in planning. It was in his nature to be retiring, to let others enjoy the limelight. This once, by letting Jake make a virtually uncontested play for Pearl, Levitt had made a terrible mistake. That one time he had pushed himself to the forefront, asked Pearl out, it was already too late. She was committed to Jake, and Levitt had lost.

Pearl emerged from the bedroom, hair pinned up at the back, a fur coat thrown haphazardly over a dress. She hurried downstairs, climbed into Levitt's car and perched herself nervously on the edge of the seat. Levitt started the engine and drove toward St. Vincent's. Every few seconds he flicked his eyes to his right, taking in Pearl's rigid expression, the tight set of her lips. She doesn't even know I'm in the car with her, he thought.

At the hospital, Levitt's request that Pearl be allowed to see her husband was politely rejected. He turned to her, about to say I told you so, when Pearl pushed her way past him to confront the nurse at the desk.

"I haven't come out in the middle of a freezing cold night to be told that I cannot see my husband. If he's awake, I want to see him, and if he's sleeping, I'll damned well wait here until he wakes up."

The nurse appeared startled. "Just a moment." She left the desk to return a minute later with a young, fresh-faced doctor. Pearl repeated her demand.

"He's resting, Mrs. Granitz. I don't think he should be disturbed. It's not just a hospital regulation, it's for your husband's welfare."

"I think I know what's best for my husband's welfare," Pearl fired back. "If he's awake, seeing me will do him more good than all the mumbo jumbo you can do."

The doctor looked at Levitt, who just shrugged his shoulders. "I'll check on him. If he's awake, you can see him, but only for a minute."

Jake was awake, moving listlessly on the bed, his head bandaged, chest strapped to protect the broken ribs, his left arm in a cast. The doctor ushered Pearl into the small private room, leaving Levitt to wait outside in the hall. Pearl came out of the room two minutes later, her face even whiter. Levitt fell into step beside her as she walked toward the exit.

"How was he?"

Pearl didn't answer. She said nothing for the entire journey home. Only when they reached the apartment building did she speak, and then it wasn't about Jake. She looked at Levitt and said, "You must be starving, Lou. Come in. I'll make you something to eat."

Levitt followed her into the apartment, threw his coat over the back of a chair in the living room, and joined her in the kitchen. Already she had a frying pan on the burner, eggs on the draining board. She was placing slices of corned beef on a plate. Levitt watched her prepare an omelet. He wasn't particularly hungry but he knew, as Jake did, that when Pearl was miserable she lost herself in cooking. If that worked, he was content to help her.

They sat at the dining-room table. Levitt ate. Pearl didn't touch the food in front of her; she simply stared at her plate. She had only wanted to cook; she didn't want to eat. Suddenly she looked across the table at Levitt. "You didn't say anything about Jake falling asleep at the wheel."

Levitt had purposely refrained from imparting that information. "Pearl, we've all been putting in extra shifts. If Jake felt tired, he should have said something." He felt his answer wasn't sufficient. Obviously, Pearl blamed him. He'd overworked his partners and now one of them was in the hospital. "Look, perhaps I have been pushing too hard. Maybe it was my fault."

Pearl's response stunned Levitt. "No, Lou, it wasn't you. It was me. I'm the one who's been pushing Jake too hard."

"What?" Levitt stared, amazed, as tears began to trickle from Pearl's eyes. "What are you talking about?"

The words began to pour forth in an unstoppable torrent. Pearl forgot all about how worried she had been that Jake's partners would learn the real reason for his tiredness. Jokes didn't matter anymore. She desperately needed to share her sorrow, her pain, with someone. "I wanted a baby more than anything in the world. I wanted a grandchild for my mother. We've tried and tried and tried, and nothing happens, so we try even harder." She wondered if Levitt understood what she was saying. He sat there so quietly, just watching her. "Did you think it was your working Jake hard that made him come in tired every day? Didn't you ever notice me at the restaurant? I could barely keep my eyes open most of the time. And now look what's happened. He could have killed himself. He could have killed Benny."

Levitt felt himself perspiring. He should have been relieved that she

183

wasn't blaming him. Instead, he felt embarrassed at being privy to this strange confession. He reached across the table and rested his hand on Pearl's. "You're being irrational. You can't blame yourself for what happened."

She shook off his comforting gesture and stood up, walking away from the table. "I put him in that hospital, Lou." Pearl's voice came from the living room. "My selfishness put him there."

"Stop beating yourself over the head. Jake wants a kid just as much as you do." He stood up, the meal forgotten, and walked into the living room to join her. She was standing by a couch, looking down at a framed photograph taken outside the synagogue after her marriage to Jake. Both couples were in the picture, the Granitzes and the Caplans. Levitt spotted himself standing off to the side, a black silk top hat perched precariously on his head. He'd been a reluctant best man then, holding the ring for the man in whose place he should have stood. Best man in name only, he'd been. Jake had been the real best man, and that day Levitt had loathed him for it. His best friend, and he'd hated him passionately as he stood beneath the *chuppah* with Pearl.

He plucked a freshly laundered handkerchief from his breast pocket and held it out to Pearl. "Here, clean your face up. When you go see Jake tomorrow, you don't want to look like a wreck, do you?"

She dabbed at her eyes with the handkerchief, blew her nose. Levitt walked to the chair where he'd left his coat. "I'd better get back to the Four Aces. You need anything, just holler."

He slipped into his coat and walked toward the door. As he was about to unfasten the lock, Pearl called after him. "Lou, please don't go. Don't leave me here by myself."

His hand fell to his side. Slowly, he turned around. She was standing, staring at him. The damp handkerchief drooped limply from her hand. Her eyes were misty with tears; her skin was drawn across her high cheekbones. Somehow, the pins at the back of her head had fallen loose, and auburn hair waved softly down onto her shoulders.

"Don't leave me by myself." Before it had been a statement. Now it was a heart-wrenching plea. Levitt walked toward her, raised his arms as he drew near. She moved forward into his embrace, her face pressed against his. He felt tears dribble down his cheek, warm like a summer rain. She clung to him, seeking comfort. He drew her closer, held her tighter. His lips brushed against her hair, across the soft skin of her cheek. Before his mouth pressed against hers, he murmured, "Pearl, I still love you. I always will."

"I know."

Levitt possessed none of Jake's gentleness, none of his skill. The quest of his tongue inside her mouth was a desperate lunge, not a gentle probe. The movements of his hands were disjointed, not smooth and lulling. Everything was wrong, and yet it all seemed so right to Pearl. He loved her, he'd loved her all these years but had been too reticent, too shy, to proclaim that love. It made no difference. All that mattered now was that he did love her, and his love could bring solace.

Holding his hand, she led him toward the bedroom. At the last moment she listened to some inner voice, but only enough to choose the second bedroom instead of the one she normally shared with Jake. "Love me," she whispered as she fell back onto the bed. "Love me."

Levitt's breathing grew harsh and ragged; his chest and head pounded. In the dim light filtering in from the hallway, Pearl's eyes appeared to be two pools, whirlpools that sucked him, unresisting, onward. Struggling out of his clothes, he never gave a thought to his original reason for coming here, Jake's being in the hospital. The act of love drowned out all else.

Pearl felt Levitt inside her. She clasped his small, compact body tightly to her own, terrified that even now he might return to his senses and run from the apartment. Her pelvis began to move, a slow, gentle tempo as she tried to stabilize Levitt's own rapid, jerky rhythm. Was she—the question popped in and out of her mind—the first woman he'd ever made love to? The notion didn't seem at all odd. Levitt wasn't like the others, certainly not like Benny Minsky who, before Kathleen, had chased every girl he saw. A man like Levitt would need a special mental rapport with a woman. Did he find such a rapport with her? She heard him groan and clutched him even tighter. And then, like a burst paper bag, he collapsed on top of her, spent. His heart, fluttering like a butterfly inside his rib cage, beat a rapid tattoo against her right breast.

For five minutes Pearl remained with Levitt, feeling him soft within her. Staring at the ceiling, she tried to gather her thoughts, rationalize what she had just done. Under the guise of seeking comfort, she had made love to her husband's best friend while her husband lay alone in a hospital bed. Gradually, the full import of her action became clear. She shuddered, tried to slide away from beneath Levitt's dead weight.

He moaned softly, a wheezing rush of breath. She realized that he was asleep. She grabbed his biceps and shook him. "Lou, wake up. You've got to leave here at once."

His eyes opened, blank, unfocused. Suddenly his head snapped up as he recognized her, remembered what had happened only five minutes earlier. "Pearl—"

"Don't say a word. Just go."

185

He needed no second bidding. Averting his eyes from her, he slid off the bed, gathered his clothing from the floor and hurried into the hallway to dress. Pearl picked up her own clothes, slipped into them. When she came out of the bedroom, Levitt was fastening his bow tie. She walked past him and stood by the front door.

"I'll drop by the hospital tomorrow sometime . . . today, I mean," Levitt added, when he realized how late it was. "Maybe I'll see you there."

"Perhaps." The moment he was through the doorway she closed the door and leaned against it. How could she possibly face Levitt again and not betray herself? How could she face Jake? How could either of them face Jake? God, what had she done in the name of seeking comfort?

She returned to the bedroom where she savagely ripped the sheets and blankets from the bed, threw them into a pile on the floor. Later they would go into the incinerator. She went to the bathroom, filled the tub with hot water. Her clothes joined the bedding, destined for destruction. Steam filled the bathroom as she lay in the tub, trying to cleanse herself from the experience. No matter how much soap she used, how hot the water, she'd never be clean. Even if Jake never found out, she would always know; that would be punishment enough. The remainder of her life would be haunted by this one night, this single moment of weakness.

They hadn't even taken any precautions! A shriek of alarm tore right through her. She quelled it with the simple logic that if she had not conceived during all the times she had made love—real love— with Jake, there was no chance of doing so from a hurried, fumbling coupling with Lou Levitt. It was a small consolation, but a consolation nonetheless.

As Lou Levitt drove back to the Four Aces from the Granitz apartment, Benny Minsky was still sitting in his Chrysler twenty yards from the door of Kathleen Monahan's Riverside Drive apartment. Only the pain in his head kept him awake. Without it, he would have fallen asleep in the car.

At six-thirty, a Marmon pulled to a halt in front of the building. Minsky leaned forward in the seat. A uniformed chauffeur jumped out, walked around to open the rear door. There she was . . . Kathleen, all wrapped up in a fucking sable coat he'd bought for her! Minsky grabbed at the door handle, ready to jump out and face Kathleen in the street. A savage stab of pain ripped through his head, and he sagged back against the seat. Tears sprang to his eyes. By the time the crash of hammers on anvils had diminished, Kathleen was inside the building and the chauffeur was climbing back into the Marmon.

The pain gave Minsky time to think, to get a better grasp of the situation. Kathleen had been somewhere, seen someone. She'd expected him to be in Ocean City that night—while the cat was away, the mouse went out to play. If he went to the apartment now, she'd lie to him. He could beat her black and blue, and still not be certain that he'd learned the truth. What he needed was the identity of the man she'd seen. He started the Chrysler's engine, followed the Marmon as it drove away. Of course, there was an alternative to following the limousine. Minsky could go to the police—he and his partners owned enough of them, didn't they? He could pass on the license number of the Marmon, then let one of their paid blue-uniformed stooges check through records. By going about it that way, though, Minsky would associate himself with the Marmon and its owner. That was the last thing he wanted, because he was going to kill whoever had been seeing Kathleen while he was away.

Inside the building, the two borzois leaped forward to welcome Kathleen as she entered the apartment. In its mouth, one carried a leash. That made Kathleen feel guilty. On these stolen nights with David Hay, she neglected the dogs. She'd make it up to them now. They would enjoy a brisk walk in the crisp, early morning air. So would she; it would help her to think.

Dawn slowly lit up Riverside Drive, revealing a cloudy gray sky with more than a hint of impending snow. Kathleen shivered luxuriously inside the sable coat. The borzois stopped to inspect trees and hydrants, and Kathleen waited until they were satisfied. Being a dog couldn't be so bad, she decided. All they had to do was be affectionate to earn their keep. Unlike people, they had no major decisions to make. Unlike people! . . . Unlike herself! She was faced with a decision now, one that should be so easy. But because of Minsky—his irrationality, his incredibly insane jealousy—it was the most difficult decision she'd ever faced.

"Leave Minsky," David Hay had said earlier that night as he and Kathleen lay naked on a sheepskin rug in front of the drawing-room fire. "Leave him and marry me."

"I told you, David, I can't."

"I don't like playing second fiddle. I'm not used to it. I'm not happy having you only when that hoodlum's away." He said the word with more conviction this time, Kathleen thought, as though he'd been standing in front of a mirror practicing it. "Where is he tonight, anyway?"

"South Jersey."

"Another shipment?"

Kathleen nodded.

"He's not the kind of man for you, Kathleen. You deserve much better." He shifted his position on the rug, rested upon an elbow so he could look down at her. "Some friends and I have been approached to put together the backing for a new show, a musical. It's based on a novel about the Mississippi. Helen Morgan's name is being batted around for one of the roles, and I'm sure I can swing enough weight to get you into it. If . . ."

"If what?"

"If you leave that hoodlum and marry me."

"I don't appreciate ultimatums, David."

"And I don't like playing second fiddle," he repeated. "Kathleen, I've been seeing you for almost six months, grabbing a few hours whenever your boyfriend's away. I thought you'd be able to make the right choice all by yourself, but I was wrong. You need a push. Okay, I'm giving you one. Leave him, and I promise you I'll put up the lion's share of the backing for this show and I'll make sure you get a damned good role, with a couple of numbers written especially for you. Your name'll be in lights the following day—there'll be a thousand silver stars on your dressing room door."

"And if I don't leave him?" Kathleen's voice had become brittle.

"Then there'll be no show, no part for you."

If Hay thought the threat would intimidate Kathleen, he was wrong. It stung her to fury. "Who the hell are you to tell me what I can and cannot do? You might be stinking rich, buster, but that doesn't give you any rights!" She stood up and glared at the figure of Hay. "I thought you were a gentleman. You sure as hell treated me like one at first, swept me right off my damned feet."

"Kathleen, your voice and your language are grating on my ears—especially your voice."

That was the one insult guaranteed to get to her. "My voice never grated on your stinking rich ears before, did it? Your mother would have liked my kind of singing, remember what you said? Take a look at yourself, you sap, lying down on a sheepskin rug like some fucking hotshot Arab prince!" She saw him flinch at her profanity and enjoyed it. "With all your damned money you're not fit to wipe Benny Minsky's ass!"

"I assure you that I wouldn't want to." He stood up and advanced lazily toward Kathleen. Her eyes dropped from his face to his crotch.

"And look at that!" She pointed to his penis. "Benny's got a pinky finger bigger than that shriveled up toothpick."

If he'd hit her then, she told herself, she might have regained some respect for him, if he'd pushed her around, held her out of a window like Minsky had done. Instead, he did nothing except let his shoulders sag, his head drop.

"You're a gutless wonder, you know that, David? You think your old money buys it all, makes everyone jump to your tune. Let me tell you something, buster, it doesn't do shit for me! That's right, pal, you heard me. Your fucking old money doesn't do shit for me. Neither does your fucking."

"I'll call the chauffeur. He'll take you home."

Silently she dressed, and then left the house. Hay stood rigidly by the front door, face expressionless. As Kathleen passed by him, he said, "I'm quite prepared to forget this little scene if you should come to your senses."

"And marry you? Not a chance, buster."

"Good night, Kathleen." As she walked out into the night, he called after her, "Kathleen, if you don't turn around this instant, you'll never see or hear from me again."

Unable to resist one parting shot, she yelled back: "And even that will be too soon!" She shoved her way past the chauffeur as he held open the door of the Marmon and sat down. Who the hell did that pompous son of a bitch think he was? What was he trying to do, make her into a respectable woman? She was more than respectable enough already! . . .

The two borzois stopped to sniff another tree. Cold now, Kathleen tugged at the leashes, eager to return home. She had to work that evening and needed sleep. The previous night had given her none, a show followed by a trip out to Long Island for a late dinner and lovemaking with David Hay. After that, he'd given her his ultimatum, dangled the offer of a Broadway role beneath her nose as if he were baiting a donkey with a carrot. She could still take it, she knew that. If she deserted Minsky, went crawling back to Hay, everything would be all right. She'd get the role, her name would go up in lights, stars would adorn her door. If she went crawling back . . .

Damn him! She wasn't going to crawl to him. There were plenty of other men around, there was plenty of money. Old money, new money—what was the difference? It was all money; it all bought the same goods. And with Minsky's money came excitement. David Hay could go stew. There, she'd reached her decision. Like she'd told Hay, if she never saw him again, if he never called her, it would be too damned soon!

*   *   *

Pearl took a taxi to St. Vincent's Hospital the following afternoon to see Jake. She was grateful that her mother and Annie were with her. They would lend moral support in case she came face to face with Levitt at the hospital. She had little doubt that he'd be there. He was still Jake's business partner, and his friend.

"How are you feeling?" Pearl asked her husband. She knew her voice sounded stiff; perhaps Jake would believe it was because she was not alone.

"Okay. They said they'd let me out in a couple of days. Guess it was a pretty stupid thing I did, eh? You don't look too hot yourself. What's the matter?"

"I didn't sleep, worried about you."

"I'm sorry. I still don't know what happened. One minute I was driving down Houston Street. Next thing I know, Benny's screaming like a maniac. How is he? I don't even know."

"He banged his head, that was all."

"Who told you that, Lou?"

Pearl nodded. "Lou brought me here last night to see you and took me home again."

Jake remembered. "You're going to be stuck with me around the apartment for a week or more, until this lot begins to knit together again. Want to look after a cripple?"

"You just try and stop me."

The three women stayed in the room for half an hour, until Jake's head began to nod. As they left, Jake tugged at Pearl's hand. "Looks like we tried too hard, eh? I'm supposed to fall asleep in bed, like I'm doing now, not at the wheel of a car."

Pearl squeezed his hand, kissed him and left the room without a word. Outside, her stomach trembled when she saw her mother and Annie talking with Lou Levitt who had just arrived. Pearl drew a deep breath and steeled herself. Levitt nodded to her casually, asked how Jake was. Sophie and Annie walked on toward the exit.

"He should be home in a day or two," Pearl answered.

"That's good." Levitt looked up and down the corridor to ensure that no one was within hearing. He grabbed Pearl by the wrist. "About last night—"

"I don't want to talk about last night. Ever!"

"I just wanted to apologize—"

Again she cut him off. "If you've come to see Jake, you'd better go ahead before he falls asleep."

Levitt accepted the rebuff. "Sure, Pearl, whatever you say. But just remember," he said to her back as she started to follow her mother and Annie, "I'm still your friend. You ever need anything, any help, you come to me."

She walked away quickly, catching the other two women. An adjustment would have to be made. Levitt inhabited the same world she did. If she avoided him, Jake would want to know why. She'd have to be a consummate actress to pass this test. And she would pray that memories of the previous night would recede enough to allow her to resume a normal life.

Except . . .

In the guise of buttoning her coat before venturing out into the cold, she touched the underside of her breasts. Annie and her crazy old wives' tales. What had she said . . . the day after you conceive the underside of your breasts feel tender?

They felt tender now.

Chapter Five

David Hay! Benny Minsky's head echoed with the name of the man who'd been seeing Kathleen while he was away, the man who'd obviously given her that sapphire necklace she had claimed came from her mother. Kathleen's family had never had the money to pay for the clasp, let alone the whole necklace! David Hay, some rich son-of-a-bitching playboy who thought, because his money came from a business more acceptable than bootlegging, he was better than anyone else.

After seeing Kathleen leave the chauffeured Marmon early on Sunday morning, Minsky had followed the car. The chauffeur must have been blind or half-asleep not to notice the Chrysler tailing him all the way out to the Long Island estate. Minsky did not even need to investigate deeply to learn the identity of the man who lived there. The name David Hay was posted in big bronze letters on the stone pillars between which the Marmon passed. Minsky kept on going for half a mile before pulling the Chrysler off the road and debating what to do next. He decided to wait, driving past the stone pillars every half-hour to see if he could spot anyone moving around in the grounds. On his third pass he was rewarded. As he neared the stone pillars, a horse and rider cantered out onto the road. The horseman stared straight ahead. Minsky slowed the car and looked up into the face of David Hay. Recognition was instantaneous and shocking. That fancy bastard from the Full House on Fifty-second Street, the one who'd thrown Kathleen a rose on the night Levitt had set sail for Scotland. Minsky's promise to break both of his legs obviously hadn't ended his interest. Nor had threats intimidated Kathleen. They'd both thumbed their noses at him. No one did that, not to Benny Minsky.

Fuming, Minsky drove back to Manhattan, entered his apartment, and locked the door. He had to decide what to do. No, he knew that already; he knew exactly what to do. He had to figure out how to go about it.

He telephoned Levitt, said that he still felt sick and would not be in for a few days. Levitt, sounding sympathetic, told him not to hurry back; he and Caplan were managing everything.

That evening, Kathleen telephoned. "I just heard from Lou about the accident. Are you all right?"

"I'm fine. A few bruises and a headache that won't quit."

"You sound terrible."

Minsky coughed to clear his throat. "I was in bed when you called."

There was a pause from Kathleen's end of the line, then, "Didn't you go to Ocean City last night?"

"How could I? Jake smashed us up on Houston Street."

"What did you do?"

Minsky smiled bleakly. He knew exactly why she'd called, what was going through her mind. "I went to the hospital with Jake. Later on I popped into the King High to catch your act. I missed you, though. So then—"

"So then?" Kathleen brushed away perspiration that had sprung from her forehead. Had he come to the apartment, found that she wasn't there?

"I went home to lie down. I felt like a truck had backed over me."

"Oh, poor Benny." Thinking she hadn't been found out, Kathleen turned genuinely solicitous. She'd almost fainted when Levitt had mentioned the accident, the fact that Minsky hadn't gone south for the weekend. "I'll come over, Benny. I'll look after you."

"Stay where you are," Minsky answered roughly. "Right now I want to be left alone." Her concern angered him. She'd called to be sure he hadn't found her out, and now that she believed he was still in the dark, she had the gall to sound so damned anxious.

"I'll come by tomorrow."

"Don't bother. When I want to see anyone, I'll let you know. Right now, all I want is to be by myself." He broke the connection and went back to bed. Although still angry, he was touched by her worry. It seemed so genuine. She was the only woman in the world who gave a damn about him, and he was still hopelessly stuck on her. They loved each other, they hated each other. Most importantly, they couldn't do without each other. A realist, Minsky knew that the money he spent bought some of her loyalty, her love; but there was more to it than that. Kathleen was the type of woman who'd never be satisfied with a mundane, nine-to-five man. She wanted someone strong, independent, a man not ruled by the laws that governed others. She wanted someone like him.

And then he cursed her. Double-crossing, contrary bitch! She worried about him, and she two-timed him. Women! . . . Who the hell ever knew how their minds worked?

More than anything he had wanted to say yes, come around, make me feel better. He wanted to feel her arms around him, hear that husky voice croon in his ears. But he was still so bitter that he might let something slip, admit that he was aware of her infidelity with Hay. He didn't want to do that. First, he wanted to settle accounts with Hay, put him where he belonged—in the ground. That would be Hay's punishment for crossing Minsky. Kathleen's would be much more subtle. She'd never hear from Hay again. Minsky would make him disappear so completely that Kathleen would be left to wonder what had happened to him, where he'd gone.

Minsky liked that. Subtlety. A really subtle punishment for Kathleen. Levitt wasn't the only guy in the outfit with brains.

Jake was discharged from the hospital after two days. Left arm strapped across his chest, ribs taped, head bandaged, he was helped to a car by Lou Levitt who drove him to the apartment building on lower Fifth Avenue. At each bump in the road, Levitt apologized for any discomfort. The fourth time he did it, Jake said, "Knock it off, will you? I'm not some piece of fragile china marked Handle with Care. If I didn't wipe myself out driving into a shopfront, this isn't going to hurt."

"Can't jar those ribs," Levitt said. "Might puncture a lung."

"Okay, just quit being so damned apologetic." Jake watched as Levitt slowed to navigate another pothole left by the snow and ice. "How's Benny, you seen him?"

"Not since I told him to go home on Saturday night. He called in to say he was staying put for a couple of days."

"I'll give him a call later today. Does Kathleen know?"

Levitt nodded. "She spoke to him and he told her not to come around. Says he just wants to be left alone." Levitt glanced nervously at Jake, wondered what he knew. Had Pearl slipped up somewhere, given Jake a hint about what had taken place? No, Jake wasn't a good actor. He wouldn't appear so calm if he knew the truth. Levitt knew him too well, understood how he reacted to situations. If Jake even thought that Levitt had made love to his wife . . . Levitt shivered—he didn't want to think about it. Jake's rage was as wild as Minsky's. Just because he was far more adept at controlling it didn't mean the earth wouldn't shake should he ever lose control. Pearl had kept her mouth shut, Levitt decided; she had as much to lose as he did.

When they reached the building, Levitt assisted Jake up to the apartment. He knocked on the door, stepped back as Pearl answered. "I brought you a present. You can play nurse for a while."

Pearl forced a smile onto her face. She had been dreading this moment. It had been relatively simple to keep the truth from Jake while he lay in a hospital bed. Now she would face a more stringent test. Her every word, every action, might be revealing.

"Welcome home. I missed having you around." She moved to hug her husband and he took a step back. Pearl stood awkwardly, arms outstretched, face confused. Why this act of rejection? Did he know? What had Levitt said during the trip from the hospital?

"Easy," Jake cautioned. "You want to undo all the good work the doctors did?"

Levitt, guessing the reason for Pearl's frozen attitude, jumped in quickly. "Don't you see that he's got a label pasted across his chest— Do Not Touch, Ribs Mending."

Pearl gave a brittle laugh of relief. "I forgot."

"How could you forget?" Jake asked. "I almost kill myself and you've forgotten already. It's okay to give me a kiss, though."

She did. Taking over from Levitt, she held Jake gently by his good right arm and helped him into the apartment. Levitt followed for a few steps before saying, "I'd better get down to the office. Someone's got to do some work around here."

"Stay awhile," Jake protested. "Even in the hospital I was allowed to have visitors. Tell him to stay, Pearl."

"Why don't you?" Pearl said, but there was no conviction whatsoever in her voice. Her tongue invited Levitt to stay; her eyes begged him to leave.

"Two's company, three's a crowd," Levitt responded as he backed toward the door. "You haven't been alone with each other for a few days. And if I'm here"—his blue eyes twinkled—"Pearl won't be able to give you hell for driving the way you did." He retreated out of the apartment and closed the door.

"Welcome home again," Pearl said. With the departure of Levitt, her confidence rose a fraction.

"That's better." Jake placed his good arm around her waist and squeezed. "You sounded like you meant it that time."

"How did it sound before?"

"Like you weren't too sure. Like you were mad at me for getting myself banged up."

She relaxed a little more. Jake wasn't the least suspicious. So open himself, he couldn't see deceit in the people he loved. In herself or in Levitt. Their betrayal would remain their secret. Only one hurdle remained to be cleared. For once, Pearl could not wait for her period to commence. It would prove that Annie's fable about tender breasts was just that—a fable. She'd have her period just like always. Only this time it would not catapult her into a fit of depression. It would be a cause for rejoicing because it would mean that God had forgiven her moment of deceit with Levitt.

Minsky stayed home all of Monday and Tuesday, only venturing out when his stomach shrieked with hunger.

When the telephone rang at four-thirty on Tuesday afternoon, he thought it was Kathleen calling again. He answered it gruffly. The caller was Jake.

"I just got out of the hospital, thought I should find out how you were."

"I'm never getting in a car with you again, you lunatic, that's how I am."

"I'm sorry. I don't know how it happened."

"You fell asleep, damned near killed us both."

"Why don't you come over here for dinner tonight?"

"Who else'll be there?"

"Just Pearl and me."

"Okay, I'll see you later." Someone else who's worried about me, Minsky thought.

It wasn't Jake who was worried about Minsky, though. The invitation had been Pearl's idea, prompted when Jake had said he should find out how Minsky was feeling. Despite her earlier boost in confidence, she was finding it difficult to be alone with Jake. Before she uttered a single word, she had to think carefully. Each time he looked at her, no matter how innocently, she tried to determine if there was something peculiar in his stare . . . a hint of wonder, an outright accusation. But how, in God's name, could he possibly know anything? Still, her own guilt plagued her. Punishment for a sin isn't being found out. It is living with the knowledge that you have sinned.

Minsky arrived just before seven. For once, Pearl was genuinely pleased to see him. She sat him down in the living room with Jake, made a weak joke about the two invalids keeping each other company, and then set about getting the food on the table.

"Has Kathleen been to see you?" she asked Minsky over dinner.

"No. I told her not to come."

"Why not?"

Minsky pointed to his bruise. "I don't want her pitying me. She'll start petting me like one of her damned dogs."

"That's because she's worried about you."

"I don't need anyone to worry over me. I can take care of myself."

"That's what I thought as well," Jake said as he leaned back in the chair so that Pearl could cut the roast beef on his plate. "Saturday night changed my mind. Look at this, will you? I can't even cut my own food."

"Go see Kathleen," Pearl urged Minsky. "Let her see you're all right. She must think she's done something wrong because you won't let her visit you."

"What did she do wrong?" Minsky asked immediately. Did everyone know about Kathleen's infidelity? Everyone but him? "She didn't do anything wrong."

"Then see her." Pearl warmed up to the conversation. It was so easy to forget one's own problems while trying to help others; it was almost as good for her as cooking.

Minsky looked to Jake for help. "I don't know what's worse, a woman who pities you or one who nags. Okay, I'll go down to the Four Aces from here. I'll see her there."

When Pearl served tea with lemon after the meal, she handed Jake a bottle of pills. He took one, washing it down with the tea. Minsky eyed the bottle curiously. "What are those?"

"Sleeping pills. I take one now, and in half an hour or so I feel drowsy. The doctor gave them to me."

As Minsky continued to stare at the bottle, an idea began to form. He knew exactly what he had to do . . . the problem was how. His eyes remained riveted on the small brown bottle sitting in the middle of the table; he thought he knew.

After thirty-five minutes, Jake put a hand in front of his mouth to stifle a yawn. "Bedtime for you, mister," Pearl said. Holding Jake's right arm, she helped him away from the table. The moment they were out of the room, Minsky scooped up the brown bottle. He guessed it held twenty of the white tablets. Three wouldn't be missed. He dropped them into his pocket and replaced the bottle seconds before Pearl returned.

"I'm leaving," he told her. "Thanks for dinner."

"Thanks for coming around. Jake appreciated the company."

There was a jaunty spring in Minsky's step as he walked toward his car. He'd let Kathleen pet and pity him. He'd let her see just how important she was in his life. And while he was doing that, he'd let her become his unshakable alibi.

He arrived at the Four Aces as Kathleen was approaching the end of her first stint. She would sing for twenty minutes, take a break, and begin her second turn at eleven-thirty. Her eyes followed Minsky as he walked from the entrance toward the stage. He waved at her before heading on toward the office. Moses Caplan was sitting in a chair, reading a newspaper. Levitt was behind the desk.

"Thought you guys might need some help."

Caplan dropped the newspaper. "For Christ's sake, look who's here."

Levitt looked up. "Thought we were going to have to pension you off. How's the head?"

"Still attached. I look a damned sight better than Jake. I just left him."

"Did you see Pearl while you were there?" Levitt had worried about her for two days. Knowing that she did not want to see him, he had deliberately refrained from telephoning the apartment or visiting Jake. "How was she?"

"She's mothering him," Minsky answered, dismissing both Pearl and Jake from his thoughts. "Anything need doing here?"

Levitt shook his head. "Not for a while. We've got a run coming in on Friday, we'll need you for that, otherwise why don't you just take it easy? Sit outside. Listen to your songbird."

Minsky returned to the club, pulled a chair up to the stage and sat down. Kathleen was singing an old favorite, "Nobody Wants Me." When she looked down at Minsky, in his regular position, she closed one eye in a sly wink. Someone did want her after all. Maybe not David Hay, from whom she hadn't heard since Saturday night. But certainly Minsky. He'd come back to her, ignorant of the way she'd two-timed him. That settled it for Kathleen. She wouldn't contact Hay, not for all the starring roles in all the musicals. Not for all the lights on the Great White Way. She didn't want to hear from him again.

When the song was finished, she waved to the audience before jumping into Minsky's arms. "Benny, why didn't you let me come around?"

"I'm rotten company when I'm ill."

She fingered the bruise, pulled his head down so she could kiss it. "You can be rotten company when you're well."

"Would you have me any other way?"

"I guess not."

He swatted her affectionately across the bottom. "I just didn't want you fussing over me, driving me nuts." Guiding her to one of the tables, he snapped his fingers at a waiter. "Bring over a bottle of champagne."

While he continually filled Kathleen's glass, Minsky was careful not to drink too much himself. Tonight he wanted to remain sober. When Kathleen did her second performance, he remained at the table. At one-thirty in the morning, they left the club together. In Kathleen's apartment, Minsky poured more drinks. Into one of the glasses, he tipped the ground-up powder from one of Jake's sleeping

198

pills, stirring until it dissolved.

"Tastes bitter," Kathleen complained, studying the glass.

"All that champagne you drank before, it ruined your taste buds."

"Either that or it's a bad batch of Scotch."

"Off the boat," Minsky protested. "Since when is that so bad?"

Kathleen shrugged her shoulders and emptied the glass. Half an hour later, she was asleep with Minsky beside her. Snuggled up to the heat of her body, he listened contentedly to her regular breathing. No two ways about it, he'd missed her while he'd been cooped up in the apartment, missed her too much to allow her to double-cross him again. When he went south this Friday night, he wouldn't have to worry about her seeing someone else. That was his final thought before he drifted off to sleep.

At five-thirty, he awoke. Climbing out of bed carefully to avoid disturbing Kathleen, he dressed and prepared to leave. The dogs were waiting outside the bedroom door. He shooed them away quietly and let himself out of the apartment. By seven o'clock, he was driving along the narrow road that led to David Hay's estate. He passed the stone pillars, continued for another half-mile, found a space to swing the car around, and headed back in the opposite direction. He continued this tactic for almost an hour until he saw the horseman cantering out of the gate. Satisfied, he returned to Manhattan. Two more sleeping pills . . . two more days.

When he entered Kathleen's bedroom, she was still fast asleep, an arm thrown across the top of the sheet. He undressed and slid in beside her. His hands began to glide across her body, and he felt himself growing hard as he pressed into her. Slowly, she awoke, rubbing herself against his hard body.

"What time is it?"

"Nine-thirty. Time to get laid."

"I should take the dogs out." She yawned loudly. "Christ, let the damned dogs take themselves out. I'm going back to sleep."

Minsky pressed himself against her again. He had an erection to beat all erections, a red-hot iron rod. What was he supposed to do with it if Kathleen fell asleep again? He took her hand, held it to himself.

"If you've got so much energy," she murmured, "you can take the dogs for a walk." And then she fell asleep again, not to wake until eleven-thirty.

That night, Kathleen sang at the Full House, where she'd first met David Hay. Minsky took her home afterward and ground another sleeping pill into her nightcap. At six o'clock the following morning, he drove out to Long Island again, this time in Kathleen's Packard. At precisely eight o'clock, David Hay appeared on his horse. Minsky arrived back at the apartment just before ten to find Kathleen still sleeping.

On Thursday night, Kathleen was booked to sing at the King High on Seventh Avenue and Fifty-fifth. Minsky picked her up, sat through both shows, and then took her home. Wanting to keep her up as late as possible, he suggested that they take the dogs for a walk. Afterward, he powdered the final sleeping pill and dropped it into a glass of brandy. Kathleen drank the brandy and fell asleep almost immediately, even before the drug had time to work. Minsky lay beside her until five o'clock, when he rose and put on the tuxedo he'd worn to the King High that night. Before he left, he gazed at her, sleeping so peacefully. "Sweet dreams," he whispered, stooping to kiss her on the cheek. She never moved a muscle.

He drove his Chrysler back to his West End Avenue apartment. There, he changed from the tuxedo into a pair of rough trousers, a roll-neck sweater, and a heavy coat. The final object he took from the apartment was an automatic, onto which he screwed a silencer. It was the same gun Kathleen had snatched from his shoulder holster when she'd fired past his ear. He deemed it fitting that he should use this particular weapon for the work he had to do.

At seven-thirty, he parked the Chrysler a hundred yards from the gate leading to David Hay's home. Getting out, he propped up the hood and stared at the engine, assuming the role of a man perplexed by machinery. He hoped that no one would come along during the next thirty minutes. Not that he expected anyone to. During his previous visits to this spot, he had seen no other motorists, no one at all except David Hay.

He remained bent over the engine, the automatic resting within easy reach. At eight o'clock, he heard the sound of hoofbeats. Without moving his body, he looked along the road. Wearing the boots, breeches, and thick sheepskin coat he had worn every day was Hay. Minsky bent further over the engine, his face completely out of sight.

The hoofbeats drew closer, slowed, stopped.

"What's the problem?" It was Hay's voice.

Minsky grunted something about the fuel line. Hay dismounted. Holding the reins, he walked closer to the car. "I've got a telephone in the house you can use to call a mechanic, if that's any help."

Minsky straightened up, the gun in his hand, the silenced barrel pointing directly at Hay's chest. "Maybe you should use it to call an undertaker for yourself."

Hay looked into the swarthy face, the gleaming black eyes. The

200

blood fled from his own face, leaving it like yellowed parchment. "You! . . ."

Minsky relished the shocked expression. "Make a fool of me, will you? Have your fucking fancy chauffeur pick up my girl so you could screw the living daylights out of her and then drive her home before I got there? What do you think I am, Hay, dumb?"

Hay's eyes dropped from Minsky's face to the gun. The weapon was held rock-steady. Reason with the man, Hay thought. Don't do anything that might throw him over the edge. Reason—calm, deliberate reason. "You don't have to worry about it anymore, Mr. Minsky. Whatever existed between Kathleen and me is finished, I assure you."

"You're damned right it's finished," Minsky answered, and squeezed the trigger. Hay's eyes went blank in disbelief as flame speared from the weapon and a bullet pierced his sheepskin coat before smashing into his chest. He dropped the reins and pitched forward. Minsky caught him, dragged him toward the back of the Chrysler. Opening the trunk, he stuffed the corpse inside. The horse remained by the car. Minsky slapped it hard across the rump and watched it gallop away in the opposite direction from the gate. After slamming the hood shut, he drove west toward Manhattan. He glanced at the dashboard clock; five minutes after eight, it read. Perfect. By nine-thirty at the latest he'd be back at Kathleen's apartment. Hay's disappearance wouldn't be discovered for a long time yet. Even if the horse returned to its master's home without its rider, it would be assumed that Hay had been thrown, had suffered an accident. A search would be started. It might be nighttime before anyone realized that something more sinister had occurred. By then, Hay would be where no one would ever find him.

He drove first to West End Avenue. Before going into the apartment to change back into the tuxedo, he checked that the trunk was locked. Finally, he returned to Riverside Drive. Smiling in satisfaction, he saw that Kathleen still slept. He cuddled up to her, confident of his alibi should he need one. Now he could sleep. Later in the day, he'd figure out a way to dispose of Hay's body.

Jake proved to be a difficult patient. Bored with remaining at home while his bones healed, he turned Pearl's life upside-down by demanding constant attention. Furthermore, he complained about his partners. With the exception of Caplan who lived next door, he'd seen little of them during this time. Minsky had come that one night for dinner, and Levitt hadn't visited him at all.

"What kind of friend does Lou call himself?" Jake demanded of Pearl. "Three days I've been home and he hasn't even called to see how the hell I am."

Pearl was grateful for that. She still wasn't certain how well she could carry on the charade with Levitt. It was much easier for her when she didn't see him. By now she was certain that Jake had no inkling of what had happened. The only way he'd learn of it would be through a mistake on her part, or on Levitt's. The longer Levitt stayed away, the less chance there was of that occurring.

"I'm going down to the Four Aces tonight," Jake suddenly decided. "If Moe, Benny, and Lou are going to Jersey, there should be someone at the club."

"What will you do there?"

"I can keep an eye on things. That's not too much of a strain, is it, nurse?"

Pearl surrendered. She supposed it wouldn't do any harm. "How will you get back? You can't drive."

"Oh, for Christ's sake, I can call a cab." For the first time he noticed the petulance in his own voice. "Lousy patient, that's me," he declared.

"A lousy patient," Pearl agreed. "But that doesn't stop you from being a wonderful husband. Just don't get home late."

"Midnight," he promised.

"Ten o'clock," she told him.

"Eleven o'clock and you can come with me."

"I don't want to go. My mother's coming for dinner tonight."

Jake made a face at her. "Since you got married, you're no fun at all."

She kissed him. "That's because I'm a respectable woman now."

With Pearl's assistance, Jake put on his tuxedo that evening and left for the Four Aces with Caplan. Pearl was relieved to get him out of her hair, and Jake was glad to be out of the apartment. The confinement drove him wild. He knew he'd be alone at the club once his three partners left. That didn't bother him. He'd still be able to wander around, talk to people, watch the gambling action in the back room. He'd be able to get into the swing of things again.

Levitt was surprised to see Jake turn up with Caplan. "Thought you were convalescing for a week."

"And I thought my pals might drop around from time to time, see if I was dead or alive."

"We're running a business here, not a society for visiting the homebound. Next time drive more carefully."

202

"You can say that again," muttered Minsky, who was standing in the office with his coat on. "I still haven't sent you my medical bill."

"Send it to him," Jake answered, pointing at Levitt. "He handles the money."

Levitt gazed oddly at Minsky, noticing the coat for the first time. "You cold?"

"No. I'm ready to go."

"Tide's not due until four in the morning. It's not even nine o'clock now. What's the big rush?"

"Weather's bad. One of us should get an early start. There might be trouble on the road."

"You're going to miss out on watching Kathleen?" Caplan asked.

Minsky seemed flustered. "What's the big interrogation for? I heard a report of bad weather, a load of snow coming out of the west. One of us should leave early, make sure there's someone on the dock to give orders when the shipment comes in."

Caplan laughed and pointed a quivering finger at Minsky. "You make a resolution to be conscientious or something? Normally we've got to beat you over the head to get you away from here when Kathleen's singing."

"Shut up, Moe," Levitt said. "Maybe he's right. If bad weather's due, it won't do any harm for one of us to get an early start. Go on, Benny, take off. We'll see you down there."

"See you guys later." Minsky left the office, walked through the still-empty club and up to the alleyway. He couldn't care less about snow. He needed the extra time to dispose of David Hay. He'd had no difficulty in shooting the man, but all day long his mind had been plagued by the problem of getting rid of the body. It hadn't been as simple as he'd thought.

Instead of heading toward Jersey, he drove across the East River to Queens. In Flushing Meadow, he pulled the car off the road, turned off the lights, and drove slowly over snow-covered ground. When he cut the engine he was in virtual blackness. A quarter of a mile away, he could barely make out the lights of cars on the road he had just left. He opened the trunk. Next to the body of Hay was a broad-bladed shovel. Using it, Minsky attacked the ground. He cursed when the shovel quivered in his hands. The ground was like rock, frozen solid. Damn the cold! How was he supposed to bury a body when he couldn't even dig a damned hole for the grave? He changed tactics. Picking up the shovel in both hands like an axe, he swung the edge of the blade mightily at the ground. The force of the blow almost tore his hands off as the shovel cannoned back, then flew from his grasp. He hopped around, clutching his hands beneath his armpits.

"Burying treasure, Benny?"

Minsky swung around, a hand automatically snaking toward the gun in his shoulder holster. Before he could draw it, a figure materialized from the gloom.

"Don't pull a gun on me, Benny," Levitt said. He stooped to pick up the shovel, offered it to Minsky. "Here, carry on with what you're doing. I'm interested."

Minsky ignored the shovel. "What are you doing here? Why did you follow me?"

"Because I wanted to know why you were so damned eager to leave before." Still holding the shovel, Levitt walked around the car. He stopped by the open trunk. "Anyone I know, Benny?"

"No. And it's none of your business either."

"I think it is." Very sure of himself, Levitt pulled back the blood-stained sheepskin coat and felt through the pockets. He found no identification at all, no money, nothing. "Okay, Benny. Who is he, and what's he doing in your trunk?"

"Fuck yourself, you midget. It's none of your fucking business."

Levitt swung the shovel with an economy of effort, a short arc that Minsky barely saw in the gloom. The flat of the blade caught him on the side of his left leg and sent him sprawling onto the ground. Before he could move, Levitt had the pointed edge pressed against his throat. "Wrong, Benny. It is my business, and I'm going to tell you exactly why. I'm running a big operation, and I don't want it put at risk by your leaving corpses lying around. You get nailed for murder—I don't give a damn if you fry. But I'm not going to let you bring heat on the rest of us. Now, Benny, tell me who he is, otherwise the cops"—he pressed harder on the shovel, cutting off Minsky's breathing—"are going to find two stiffs out here tomorrow."

Minsky gasped as the blade bit into his throat. "Guy who was . . . who was making it with Kathleen."

The pressure on his throat eased slightly. "What's his name?"

"David Hay."

"Where did you kill him? When?" He lifted the shovel clear of Minsky's throat, leaving it hanging six inches above like a sword of Damocles.

Minsky blurted out the story. "Some stinking rich guy who lives out on a big estate?" Levitt asked in disbelief. "How did you think you were going to get away with something like that?"

"They'll think he got thrown from his horse."

"And when they figure he didn't, you're going to be the first person Kathleen points a finger at. What have you got for brains—rocks?"

"Kathleen's my alibi. I was sleeping with her when he disappeared,

204

when he died." He told Levitt about the sleeping pills, how he had made dry runs on the previous nights. Levitt listened, admitting grudgingly that maybe Minsky had more sense than he'd ever given him credit for. It was a neat little plan he'd worked out, except for getting rid of the evidence. "I was going to bury him," Minsky said. "Just make him disappear into thin air."

"Bury him? You'd be here all night and not make a decent hole. Even if you could have put him in the ground, dogs would come sniffing around. They'd scratch a hole in no time once they caught the scent." Dropping the shovel to the earth, he reached down and pulled Minsky to his feet. "Lock your trunk. We'll find a place where no one'll ever stumble over him."

"Where?" His anger at being followed—at being found out—had disappeared. Minsky's own plan had been frustrated at the last hurdle, by nature. Now he was dependent on Levitt.

"We've got a dock, we've got boats. We drop him overboard outside the three-mile limit and he'll be an international worry, not ours. By the time the fish have finished feeding on him, he'll be unrecognizable."

Minsky rubbed his neck where the shovel's blade had bitten. He peered through the gloom as Levitt returned to his own car which he'd left a hundred yards away. God, how he hated Levitt, hated him and needed him. The little man could see right through him, as though he were made of glass. He'd tumbled to why Minsky had wanted to get an early start. Followed him and discovered what Minsky had done. And now he was offering to help him, putting Minsky forever in his debt by helping him avoid a date with the electric chair. Why? "How come you're doing this for me?"

Levitt's answer drifted back through the chill air. "I'm doing nothing for you, Benny. I'm doing it for the rest of us. If you go down, you might drag us all with you. You're a lunatic. You always were. But for better or worse we're stuck with you."

Minsky's hand strayed toward his automatic. He could kill Levitt now, lock him in the trunk with David Hay, perform two burials at sea. And just like Hay, no one would ever know what had happened to Levitt. He'd disappear into thin air. The fish would get a double feast, not that there was much to nibble on Levitt's bones. He didn't draw the gun, though, because he knew he needed Levitt. How could it be otherwise, when he'd pored over maps and overlooked the simplest burial spot of all—the ocean? Minsky, Caplan, Jake—they contributed strength and daring to the business. Levitt's insight, his quick, incisive thinking, welded them together. Without him, they were lost. And because of that, Minsky hated the little man even more.

One day, he prayed, the situation would be different. He'd have enough power of his own to get rid of Levitt once and for all. That day could not come soon enough.

They reached the dock just after midnight. Although the ship was not due for another four hours, trucks were already parked there, men waited. Brusquely, while Minsky backed his car right up to the edge of the dock, Levitt ordered the men to take a walk. Minsky hoisted Hay's body over his shoulder and carried it down to a speedboat. Moments later, Levitt joined him, carrying two heavy lengths of chain which he had found in a shed on the dock. Once the chain was wrapped around Hay's legs and body, Minsky guided the boat out to deep water. When the shore lights were nothing more than pinpricks, he cut the motor.

"Push him over," Levitt ordered.

Minsky grunted under the weight. The boat swayed as he lifted Hay's body up to the gunwale and pushed it overboard. It sank immediately. Minsky steered the boat back to shore.

"Don't bother thanking me," Levitt said.

"You want me to lick your boots for you as well?"

"No. In the future, just think before you let your prick rule your head." Levitt disembarked and clambered up the wooden steps to the dock, glad that he'd suspected something was wrong when Minsky had seemed so impatient to leave the club. Thank God, he'd followed him. Minsky was the only member of the outfit whom he distrusted totally. Now Levitt had something on him. He had Minsky on a leash which he could jerk this way and that. If Minsky ever stepped out of line, he'd be gambling with his own life—because Levitt's testimony could send him straight to the electric chair.

There was no mention of David Hay in Saturday's newspapers. Only on Sunday did word of his disappearance reach the press. Kathleen noticed it as she read the Sunday edition of the *Daily News*. On page four was a photograph of Hay, under a headline which read "Millionaire Disappears on Horseback Ride."

She stared in shock at the picture before reading the complete story. After Hay had not returned from his regular morning ride, the butler had summoned the police. The horse had been found two hours later, grazing peacefully in a field four miles from the point where Hay had been killed. At first, the police assumed that Hay had been thrown and was lying injured somewhere. A daylong search on Saturday revealed nothing. After twenty-four hours, Hay was listed as a missing person. A subsequent police statement to the press hinted ominously at foul play.

The newspaper was still open at page four when Minsky returned from Philadelphia after seeing the latest consignment through to the distillery. He glanced quickly at the story, taking in the pertinent details. "Did you see this?" he asked Kathleen. "Some guy faking his own disappearance so his wife can collect on the insurance dough."

"Don't you recognize him?"

Minsky made a show of studying the photograph. "Should I?"

"He's the man who threw me the rose that night."

"What night?"

"That night you went crazy and dragged me out of the Full House."

"Baby, that was six months ago. How am I supposed to recognize him after that long?" His eyes narrowed suspiciously. "How come you remember him so well. Is that"—he took a menacing step toward her, jealousy gleaming in his eyes—"the guy you've been seeing?" He snapped his fingers; with Hay feeding the fish he was confident enough to carry through the act. "The guy who gave you that necklace you swore your mother gave you?"

"Don't be stupid," Kathleen answered quickly. "I just remember him, that's all. You threatened to break his legs that night. If anyone remembers, that might make you a suspect."

"A suspect in what?" He laughed abruptly. "Anyway, I don't hold a grudge for six months. If I was going to bust his legs, I'd have done it there and then."

Kathleen joined in the laughter. "That's right, you would have, you crazy bastard." She threw her arms around his neck, pulled down his head so she could kiss the fading bruise. "You couldn't have done it anyway. He disappeared Friday morning, according to his butler, and you were here with me. Snug as two bugs in a rug we were."

"Maybe he threw a rose at someone else's girl, and that guy wasn't so forgiving."

"Or he wasn't in such a warm, comfortable place on Friday morning." She drew him toward the bedroom. "What were you thinking of all the time you were driving back from Philadelphia?"

"Cuddling up to you."

"I kept the bed warm for you." She pushed open the door, drew him toward the bed. There were no choices left now. No Broadway roles; not for the time being, anyway. She didn't even feel sorry about David Hay. She felt nothing at all. One way or the other, he was out of her life forever.

Jake returned to work, performing light duties around the clubs. Simultaneously, Pearl went back to the restaurant to help her mother.

The first day back, Lou Levitt came up from the Four Aces for lunch. He saw Pearl standing behind the varnished counter and nodded casually to her as though he had seen her only a few minutes earlier.

"What's good today?"

"The cabbage borscht'll stick to your ribs."

"Give me a bowl, and a roast beef sandwich on rye."

"Are you eating at the counter?"

"Booth."

A minute later, Pearl brought his lunch to the booth. Levitt took a sip of the cabbage borscht. "You make this?"

"Can you tell the difference?"

"Your mother doesn't cook with so much spice."

"If it's no good I'll take it back."

"It's fine. Different, that's all." He took another sip. "Everything all right at home?"

"A lot better since Jake started working again."

"You know what I mean. With you. How are you managing?"

"What's there to manage?" She slipped into the booth opposite him. "Lou, nothing happened that night. You took me to the hospital, you brought me home again. That's all."

"You're right, Pearl. That's all that took place."

A customer took a seat at the counter. Pearl left the booth to serve him. Levitt remained for a further fifteen minutes, reading a newspaper while he finished his lunch. Whenever he looked toward the counter, it seemed that Pearl was staring at him. She could think, say, whatever she liked. Levitt knew it wasn't over for her—or for himself. Maniac Benny Minsky killed for a woman. Levitt could not imagine himself doing that, but it did not make him love Pearl any the less. Perhaps, he told himself, he should be grateful that there had been that one time. A single instance when her emotions had been wracked, her defenses down. She'd loved him for a few minutes with a passion that equaled his own. If that memory was all he had to keep him warm, it would suffice. For the present anyway, he decided, as he returned downstairs to the club's office.

From that day, Pearl erected a wall between herself and Levitt. She wasn't frightened of him as much as she was scared of herself. She was terrified that those feelings she'd shown for him might surface again, trouble her during another unguarded moment. She fought against the possibility by ignoring Levitt. Each time they met she greeted him with aloofness, nothing outright that might cause Jake to take notice, just a cool civility. Even when Levitt visited the apartment to see Jake, Pearl treated him like a casual acquaintance, not a friend . . . or a lover.

Two months passed. Jake's ribs and arm healed. A narrow scar across his forehead was the only visible memento of the automobile accident. He resumed working full-time, traveling between New York, Ocean City and Philadelphia. When Pearl was left alone, she sought the company of her mother and Annie, using it as a barrier against Levitt. He understood, and wisely kept his distance.

Then, at the beginning of May, Pearl's world turned upside-down. Irregular or not, she had missed two periods. She was pregnant. Jake was overjoyed. He threw a party at the apartment, invited all his friends. "This is nothing," he went around telling everyone. "Wait until you see the big bash we have when the kid's born."

Sophie Resnick joined in the happiness. She handed out advice to Pearl on how to behave, what to eat, what she would need.

Only Pearl failed to join wholeheartedly in the mood of celebration. She faced the future with a chilling numbness. For in her heart of hearts, she could not be certain whether the father of the child she carried was Jake or Levitt.

BOOK THREE

Chapter One

As she commenced her ninth month, Pearl was swollen grotesquely. Each time she surveyed herself in the mirror, she became more critical of her appearance. It seemed impossible that she could go any longer—become any bigger—without bursting. She felt like she was carrying an elephant inside of her, an elephant that was as active as a kitten, one that could kick with all the ferocious strength of a kangaroo. The simplest chores were difficult now. Even sitting down was a strain. She needed more and more help from her mother to get through the day.

To exacerbate matters, Pearl could not even go next door to Annie for help. Two months after Pearl had discovered she was pregnant, Annie had burst into the apartment, a wide grin covering her face. "Guess what?" she'd demanded of Pearl.

"I give up. Tell me."

Annie rolled her eyes and patted her stomach. "You're not the only one who's going to be busy washing diapers."

"You?" Pearl ran to her friend and hugged her.

"Me. I told you that Moe had to be shown the way, didn't I? Jake proposed to you, so Moe proposed to me. Jake's going to be a father, so what does Moe do? He follows suit again."

"It's a coincidence, that's all."

"Coincidence, hell," Annie said, laughing. "I'm still waiting for the day that the big klutz drives his car into a shopfront, just like Jake did."

In November of 1927, when Pearl was two weeks short of her full term, the Holland Tunnel was finally opened. Jake was eager to use it. The tunnel would cut an hour off each of his trips to the Jersey shore. But when his first opportunity to try it arose, on a Saturday evening toward the end of November, he had second thoughts about going. The reason was Pearl. The previous night she had been unable to sleep, constantly complaining about being unable to get into a comfortable position. Saturday evening, as he sat down to a dinner of

210

cholent, a thick, rich stew which Sophie Resnick had slow-cooked for twenty-four hours, he studied Pearl carefully. He didn't like the idea of leaving her.

"I don't think I'll go tonight," he said finally. He turned to Moses Caplan who, with Annie, was having dinner at the Granitz apartment before driving south. "You figure you and Benny can handle everything tonight?"

"No problem. If we haven't got it cut and dried by now, we might as well pack up shop and go home."

"You go," Pearl told her husband. "Nothing's supposed to happen here for another couple of weeks."

"Are you sure?"

"My mother's staying over. Annie's next door. What's there to be sure about? And just supposing something did happen?" She looked to Annie for support. "What good would a man be?"

"They just get you into trouble," Annie responded. "That's all they're good for."

After dinner, Jake left the table and went to the bedroom. Caplan followed, while Annie helped Sophie to clear the table. "What time's the boat due?" Jake asked as he dressed in a thick roll-neck sweater, heavy trousers, and fur-lined boots.

"Last report we had was for sometime after midnight." Caplan watched, fascinated, as Jake withdrew a pair of ivory-handled revolvers from a bureau, checked the loads, and fitted the weapons into a double shoulder holster. "You look like some kosher Billy the Kid."

Jake laughed. "Thank God I've never had to use these damned things. I don't even know if they work." The matching guns were a gift from Benny Minsky on Jake's last birthday, his twenty-fifth. Only that lunatic would give such a present, Jake had thought at the time. Everyone else gave me a tie, a pair of gloves, or a set of cuff links; and Benny gives me a pair of ivory-handled revolvers. He chuckled at the memory of the words on the card that had accompanied the unusual gift. "If you need protection," Minsky had written, "then protect yourself with style." Jake knew that Levitt disliked Minsky, looked down on him, but Jake could not repress a certain fondness for the dark-skinned man. He was as close to Jake as Levitt was, and even Minsky's frequently irrational behavior failed to dampen Jake's affection.

Minsky had done a lot of settling down in the last six months. He'd moved into Kathleen's Riverside Drive apartment, and he now exhibited less of the jealousy he'd shown earlier. Jake guessed that he felt more secure, more certain that Kathleen's feeling for him was

211

genuine and not simply the result of the money he spent on her. Not that money meant much to Kathleen anymore. She was the highest-paid of any of the singers who appeared at the clubs owned by the four partners, and frequently sang at other establishments that Jake and his friends supplied with liquor.

Still chuckling about the card that had accompanied the guns, Jake returned to the clothes rack and selected a navy blue reefer jacket and a pair of thick woolen gloves. The weather forecast was for bitter cold, with the probability of snow.

Dressed, Jake returned to the living room where Pearl was sitting in a straight-backed chair while she listened to the radio. She stood up, hugged him tightly, and, in a muted whisper, urged him to be careful. His last act before leaving the apartment was to say goodbye to his mother-in-law. He found her in the kitchen, washing dishes while Annie dried.

"If something should happen, the number of the distillery's underneath the telephone. Otherwise, get ahold of Lou. He'll be at the Four Aces until the early hours. Failing that, you'll catch him at home."

"You just make sure nothing happens to you," Sophie told him. "I'm too old to help bring up a child."

"It's okay. Moe's driving, not me."

"You know what I mean, Jake."

Quite unashamedly, Jake clasped his mother-in-law around the shoulders and kissed her. "Your trouble, old lady," he told her in mock seriousness, "is that you believe all these stories you read in the newspapers." He blew a kiss to Annie and left.

Pearl felt the first stab of pain a few minutes after the departure of Jake and Caplan. It came like a knife thrust, skewering through her belly. She gasped and clutched at the arm of the chair, steadying herself as the pain ripped through her. Gradually, it receded. She straightened up, probing her abdomen gently with her fingertips. Could it be? The doctor wasn't God Almighty; he was fallible like any other man. He could have misjudged by two weeks. He wouldn't be the first or the last doctor to commit such an error.

She looked at the watch on her swollen wrist, eying the second hand as it swept around the face. Perhaps it wasn't a contraction after all, just a healthier than normal kick from the monster she carried inside her, a reminder that she was not alone.

Five minutes passed and she became easier in her mind. It was a kick after all. She stood up and walked slowly to the window, looked out. It was time to think about Jake, not herself. He was in for a lousy drive to the Jersey shore that night, even if the Holland Tunnel was open. Snowflakes drifted lazily by the window, heralding an early winter storm. Silently, she offered up a prayer for Jake's safety.

Finished with the dishes, Sophie entered the living room. "Annie's making you a cup of tea. Sit down and drink it, you shouldn't be standing up like that. Give your legs a rest."

"I'll take it in the bedroom. Maybe I'll go to sleep."

"Are you feeling all right?"

"My guest just gave me a kick to end all kicks. I guess he's impatient to get out."

"Don't worry, in a couple of weeks you'll be able to serve eviction papers on him."

When Annie came in with the tea, Pearl checked her watch again. Ten minutes since that stab of pain. It was a kick after all. Holding the tea, she kissed her mother and Annie good night and walked into the bedroom.

And then, eleven and a half minutes after the first pain, another spear of fire ripped through her. The cup and saucer dropped onto the night table and shattered into a hundred pieces. Alerted by the noise, Sophie and Annie rushed into the bedroom to find Pearl leaning against the wall, her face white and sweaty, hands clasped to her belly.

"Get the doctor," she gasped. "My guest has decided it's time to check out."

Jake and Caplan drove from Ocean City to Philadelphia with the first convoy of trucks, leaving Benny Minsky to supervise the stragglers. The operation had been simple, the British freighter on time, the run out in the speedboats uneventful; although bitterly cold, the sea was calm.

"You still worried about Pearl?" Caplan asked as he drove ahead of the lead truck across the flat, snow-covered Jersey road.

"If it was Annie, wouldn't you be worried?"

"If Annie insisted she was okay, I'd listen to her. She knows better than me about those things. Put your mind at ease; call Pearl the moment we reach Philly."

"I was going to do just that."

They reached Philadelphia just after eight in the morning. The city was deserted as they drove through the outskirts. "Only bootleggers have got to be out on mornings like this," Jake muttered. "People who drink the stuff get to stay in bed."

"Quit complaining," Caplan told him. "You're getting rich, aren't you? Buy yourself a fur coat. Otherwise be like Lou; have brains and stay in the club where it's warm."

"Yeah, brains pay, don't they? He gives the orders, we get to go out in the cold." He removed his hands from his pockets, rubbed them together, stamped his feet on the floor. "Jesus, you got a heater in this thing?"

"It's on."

"You think Benny's going to marry the *goyishe* nightingale?"

"Why does your mind jump around so much?"

"It's got to, to stay warm. Well, do you?"

"How the hell do I know?"

"He moved in with her."

"Saves on rent."

"That's the kind of logic I'd expect from Lou, not from Benny." They both laughed.

Caplan swung the car into the distillery's loading area. Huge doors were swung open to allow entrance to the trucks. Jake watched approvingly. The whole operation was down to a fine art now. The distillery was located in an industrial area; no nosy neighbors to worry about. The local police were paid off handsomely from Levitt's grease account, and no inquiries were ever made about the steady movement of trucks in and out of the building. Guided by Levitt, the outfit had put together an impressive operation—importation, distilling, bottling plants, labeling, transportation, and distribution, Jake sometimes wondered how well they would have done if they'd put their brains and energy into a straight business. Who knew? Who even cared? It was more fun this way. A little extra edge because it was illegal, a restricted market. A little excitement, a little danger.

"Jake . . . Jake Granitz!"

His name was yelled the moment he entered the distillery. He looked around, spotted a bookkeeper waving at him from the office. Had something happened to the second stage of the convoy? "What is it?"

"Your mother-in-law called last night around nine o'clock. Your wife got taken to the hospital."

Jake raced to the office, picked up the telephone, and dialed the operator. In an infuriatingly calm voice, she informed him that no calls could be made to New York. Snow and ice had disrupted the service. Jake slammed down the earpiece and looked around for Caplan.

"Drive me to the station. I'll catch the next train back to New York." He hoped the trains were running.

Caplan flipped his keys to Jake. "Take my car. I'll catch a ride back with Benny this evening."

Jake didn't argue. He reversed Caplan's car out of the loading zone

214

and headed north toward New York. The journey took an impossibly long five hours. Hunched over the wheel, Jake cursed and fretted as he watched the car's tiny wipers try to cope with the snow that had started to fall moments after he'd begun the journey. The road, barely visible, was littered with stalled vehicles. On the clearest stretches, he dared not drive faster than thirty miles an hour.

At last he entered the Holland Tunnel, speeding along the dry surface as though he could make up all the time in this one short stretch. One-thirty in the afternoon. More than eighteen hours since he had left home. God, how much could happen in eighteen hours? He prayed like he had never prayed before that Pearl was all right.

He parked outside the building entrance, threw open the door, and ran upstairs. He hammered on the apartment door and thrust his key into the lock at the same time, bursting into the hallway like a tornado. "Is anyone here?"

Sophie appeared from the living room. "Wish me *mazel tov*," she said grandly. "In fact, wish me a double *mazel tov*. My daughter has twin sons."

"Twins?" Jake gasped. "When?"

"Just after midnight. We tried to reach you in Philadelphia again to leave another message, but we couldn't get through."

"The snow, the ice, wrecked the lines," Jake answered. "I tried to call you this morning." Twins? He couldn't accept that news so easily. "How come the doctor didn't know it was going to be twins?"

Sophie shrugged. "Why question? Instead, why don't you give your favorite mother-in-law a kiss?"

Jake did. He held tightly onto Sophie, needing her support. Twins! Not one son, but two. How in God's name could a tiny girl like Pearl give birth to twins? Where was there room? No wonder she'd grown so big. Twins!

"*Mazel tov*, Jake," a man's voice said. Jake let go of Sophie and spun around to see Levitt standing in the living room with Annie.

"Thanks." He shook Levitt's hand. "What are you doing here?"

"I've been here since early morning. Annie called me at home when you couldn't be reached in Philadelphia."

In a daze, Jake saw Annie come close, felt her lips on his cheek. Coupled with the long, perilous drive north, the lack of sleep made him groggy. Yet nothing could stop him from seeing Pearl and his twin sons. "I'm going to the hospital."

"They won't let you visit her," Annie warned. "They had to cut her open, do a Caesarean. Tomorrow, maybe."

"Tomorrow? I can't wait that long."

"Maybe tonight," Sophie told him. "Go to the hospital this

evening. Perhaps they'll let you see her then."

"In the meantime," Levitt suggested, "why don't you get some sleep?"

Jake slept for five hours, waking at seven. Levitt was still in the apartment, reading the Sunday newspaper. Annie had returned to her own place, and Sophie was in the kitchen, preparing dinner. When Jake walked into the living room, Levitt set the newspaper on the table. "You going to the hospital now?"

Jake nodded. "How come you're still here?"

"I thought that you or your mother-in-law might need some help."

"It's okay, we'll manage. You can go open the club."

Levitt seemed hurt by Jake's rejection, as though his staying there all day had earned him more. "If you want anything, you know where to reach me." He opened the front door, started to go through and then turned around. "When you see Pearl, ask if I can visit her."

Finding nothing odd in the request, Jake promised he would. After Levitt left, Jake took Sophie to St. Vincent's Hospital. Pearl was in a private room, and when Jake opened the door Sophie held back.

"You go in first," she insisted. "Pearl might be my daughter, but she's your wife."

The moment Jake saw Pearl lying in the bed, his excitement disappeared. In its place was guilt for being responsible for putting her through an experience that had left her looking the way she did. Her face was ashen, cheekbones pushed hard against skin, eyes sunken and lifeless. He sat by the bed, holding her hand. "I should never have listened to you. You told me to go to Philadelphia, but I shouldn't have listened. I should have stayed with you."

"You're here now, so what does it matter?" she asked weakly. "Jake, believe me, I look a lot worse than I feel. Tomorrow I'll be much better. I need time, that's all. No woman's going to win a beauty contest in a maternity ward."

Jake's guilt turned into anger at the medical staff. "How come that doctor didn't know anything about twins when he examined you?"

"He's a doctor, not God. Have you seen them yet?"

"No. I came to see you first."

"Go look at them. They're beautiful, like two dolls."

"What are we going to call them?"

"The older one we'll call Joseph, after my father. The younger one . . ." She looked into Jake's eyes. "When you see him, Jake, he's got a tuft of hair down the back of his neck, like a lion's mane. How about Leo?"

"Leo the lion? That sounds like a cartoon character. Or maybe he'll grow up strong and ferocious."

216

"Like his father?" She squeezed his hand. "Ask the nurse if you can see them."

He rose to leave. "Your mother's waiting outside. Feel up to seeing her?"

"She won't leave until I do."

Jake brought in Sophie, who sat by the side of the bed. Pearl's eyelids were already drooping. He knew it wouldn't be long before she fell asleep. He sought out a nurse, who led him to his sons. A mask over his face, Jake gazed down at the twins, pride yielding to confusion. He'd always thought of twins as identical. These were not. Joseph's body was longer, thinner than Leo's. And Leo had that odd little tuft of hair on the back of his neck. The nurse explained that identical twins rarely looked alike at birth; similarities asserted themselves as they grew older. Jake listened, but nothing, he knew, could alter the color of his sons' eyes. Joseph's were a deep, moist brown. Leo's were totally different, an undefinable shade that seemed to drift through a spectrum of colors, hazel in one light, almost a toneless gray in another.

"Do they meet your expectations, sir?" Pearl asked when Jake returned.

"And if they don't?"

"Too bad. You can't send them back for an exchange."

"They go beyond my expectations. By the way, Lou asked if it was all right to pop up and say hi?"

"When did you see him?"

"Just now. He's been at the apartment all day. Annie called him this morning."

A mask slipped over Pearl's face. "I don't think so, not now. When I get home we'll have everyone around." Levitt was the last person she wanted to see. Despite the way he'd performed his role whenever they had come into contact with each other, she had always known that once the baby—babies—came, he'd ponder the possibility that he was the father. Levitt's strength was in figures, in planning. How much knowledge of figures did it require to go back nine months and remember what had happened on that day?

"Okay, I'll tell him. He'll understand."

Pearl fell asleep soon after. Jake kissed her gently on the forehead and left the hospital with Sophie. He asked his mother-in-law whether she wanted to return to her own flat or go home with him. "I'd better come back with you," Sophie answered instantly. "You look too shaken up to be left alone with just a pregnant woman next door in case you need anything."

When they reached the apartment, the telephone was ringing. The caller was Levitt, wanting to know about Pearl and the twins. Jake felt a spontaneous warmth for the little man. "You sound anxious enough to be the father yourself," Jake jested.

"You want some company?"

"My mother-in-law's staying the night."

"I'll drop by later on for an hour or so, maybe you'll want someone to talk to then."

"Probably will." Jake appreciated the offer. He could see himself walking the apartment all night long. He'd never get to sleep now, not when he'd seen his twin sons—Joseph and Leo the lion!

Levitt came over at midnight, an hour after Sophie had gone to bed. The tuxedo he wore reminded Jake that he had left work for a social call; how uncharacteristic an act that was.

"Did you get to see the twins?" Levitt asked.

"For a few seconds, that was all."

"What did they look like?"

"What are one-day-old babies supposed to look like? Funny thing, they're not identical. Their eyes are different colors."

"That's good," Levitt pronounced sagely. "You ever know any identical twins? They're peculiar, two bodies controlled by a single mind. Weird. Did you"—Levitt dropped his voice—"did you ask Pearl about me visiting her?"

Jake felt awkward. "She said no. She's too tired to see anyone right now. When she gets out we'll have a big bash."

Levitt took the refusal stoically. "I understand." He cocked his head inquisitively as a rapid knocking sounded on the front door. "You expecting visitors?"

"No." Jake walked quickly toward the door, suddenly afraid. His first thought was of Pearl—something had happened to her, to the twins.

"It's not the hospital," Levitt called out as he followed Jake along the hall. "They'd have telephoned."

Jake threw open the door. Moses Caplan and Benny Minsky stood outside. "What are you two doing here?"

Caplan pushed past Jake into the apartment. "We couldn't find Lou at the club, that's what we're doing here."

"What's wrong?" Levitt asked. Agitation and worry were now his lot.

"The distillery got raided."

"Police?" Levitt asked in disbelief.

"No. Feds."

Levitt seemed stricken. "That means we've lost the whole damned load."

218

"How did you two get away?" Jake asked.

"We bolted out the back way, jumped into my car," Benny Minsky answered. "A few other guys made it out as well."

"How the hell did the Feds know about that place?" Levitt demanded.

"Maybe they looked into a crystal ball."

"A whole shipment," Levitt muttered disgustedly. It was the biggest setback since they'd started importing their own liquor.

"Don't forget the distillery," Minsky reminded him. "They'll wreck the place, take axes to everything. We'll have to set up a new operation."

Levitt shot Minsky a sour look. "Thanks for not letting me forget it."

Jake looked from one man to the other. "Who gives a shit about it?" he asked. "There'll be other shipments, other distilleries."

His three partners regarded him with amazement.

"Pearl's in the hospital right now because she's just given birth to the two greatest kids you ever laid eyes on."

"Twins?" Caplan asked. He'd forgotten all about Pearl, the telephone message that had dragged Jake back to New York. "She had twins? God forbid that Annie does the same!" He grabbed Jake's hand and shook it repeatedly, only letting go when Minsky pushed him aside.

"Congratulations, you son of a gun," Minsky said. "Twins, eh?"

"That's right, twins. So what the hell are we all doing here with these long faces? Damn the booze . . . damn the trucks . . . damn the whole distillery. Let's celebrate. Let's drink to my sons' health!"

The day after Pearl returned from the hospital with the twins, Jake held a party in the apartment. Lou Levitt arrived, arms weighed down with boxes. The twins may not have been identical, but he had brought identical gifts for them—complete outfits of clothing that they would not be big enough to wear for at least a year, their first pairs of shoes, and giant stuffed bears, one blue, the other green.

It was the first time Pearl had seen him since going into the hospital. At her request, he hadn't visited. Now, unable to behave in any other way in front of guests, she welcomed him warmly, thanked him for the presents with a kiss on the cheek. "Lou, you're going to spoil them rotten. It's bad enough I'll have Jake doing it. I don't need to fight you as well."

Levitt walked into the third bedroom which had been converted to a nursery. "How else am I supposed to treat them?" he asked as Pearl followed him. "I'm their godfather."

Pearl glanced around nervously, made certain that no one else was in earshot. "Just remember that," she warned. "*God*father only."

Levitt gave her a sly smile. "Pearl, I can count. Give me credit for that."

"If you can count so well, it was only eight and a half months between their birth and . . . and . . . and . . ." She couldn't bring herself to say it.

Levitt helped her out. "And the night of Jake's accident?"

"That's right, the night of Jake's accident."

"I know. But don't forget that you were two weeks ahead of schedule." He walked away from her to stare at the twins lying in their cribs. Both babies were fast asleep, curled up peacefully. Watching Levitt, Pearl hated him at that moment. He was convinced that he was the father. How long would it take before Jake realized that, before her life, her family, were ruined?

As if reading her mind, Levitt turned from the cribs to face her. "Don't worry. I won't open my mouth."

"Jake would kill you if he knew—"

"He probably would."

"—if I didn't kill you first."

Levitt regarded her coolly. "I really think you mean that."

"Make no mistake about it, Lou. I do."

They were interrupted when Benny Minsky and Kathleen entered the nursery. Arm around her waist, Minsky dragged the singer over to the cribs. "You ever see a nicer sight?"

Kathleen's expression made it obvious to Pearl that she had seen many preferable sights. "Tell her, Pearl," Minsky urged. "Tell her how wonderful it is to have kids."

"If you really want children, it's wonderful."

"I don't," Kathleen said firmly.

"Do you?" Pearl asked Minsky, grateful for the intrusion. Levitt had taken advantage of the opportunity to rejoin the party, as if objecting to being in the same room with Minsky.

Minsky nodded and grinned. "If I should die tomorrow, what's going to happen to all my dough? I've got to leave it to someone. Even Kathleen can't find ways to spend it all."

"You surprise me," Pearl admitted. "I never had you pegged as the fatherly type."

"I need some roots. Everyone does. Even him." He gestured toward the doorway through which Levitt had just passed.

"You want roots, go find yourself an oak tree," Kathleen told him. "I've got a career that comes first. It's okay for you to talk about

220

kids—all it means to you is a few minutes of exercise. I'd have to do the real work."

"It's not so much work," Pearl said, standing up for Minsky. As crazy as he was, he often displayed traits that pleasantly surprised her. "Look at Annie, she's due in a couple of months and she's running around like there's nothing the matter with her."

"She doesn't sing for a living."

"Hey, if you're so worried about your voice and your career," Minsky said, "take a look at those fat broads over at the Met. I read somewhere that their voices get better once they've had a kid."

"You never read anything but the racing results in your entire life," Kathleen retorted.

Minsky winked at Pearl. He'd get the better of Kathleen. He always did. Hadn't he found out who her boyfriend was and taken care of him, without Kathleen even knowing about it? David Hay's body had never surfaced, nor would it, not with the chains he and Levitt had wrapped around the corpse before dropping it overboard three miles out to sea. Levitt had only mentioned the incident once. That was after he had written a detailed report of the event and had left it in the safekeeping of a lawyer. He'd told Minsky what he'd done. "Just so you don't get any ideas, Benny. Call it an insurance policy, if you like."

"I should have thrown you overboard as well," Minsky had told him in return.

"You wouldn't have had the brains to get back to shore by yourself."

"What's this insurance policy for?"

"Just so you don't get any bright notions about doing something on your own. Remember, Benny, I can send you straight to the chair."

"And make yourself an accessory."

"Perhaps. But you wouldn't be around to gloat, would you?"

Minsky had been unable to argue with that. "How many other people do you carry these insurance policies on?"

"None. I don't need to. You're the only weak link in this outfit."

Perversely, Minsky had taken that as a compliment, the only one he'd ever received from Levitt. . . .

Kathleen looked at the two cribs again. "If I ever got pregnant, I'd have an abortion."

Pearl sucked in her breath, and Minsky's mouth dropped.

"How could you destroy life so callously?" Pearl wanted to know.

"What's life? It's not alive until it's born, and I wouldn't let it get that far. Despite what Benny says about those singers at the Met, my voice is fine the way it is."

221

"Wait until you get pregnant," Pearl said. "You'll think differently then."

"You wait," Kathleen answered as she left the nursery. "Just don't hold your breath for too long."

Following the party, the men went to work at the Four Aces. There were no shipments due that night, no convoys to guard. Only Levitt worked, shut away in his domain at the back of the club. The other three partners took it easy.

Shortly after midnight, when Jake and Caplan were sitting in the office, playing a hand of gin rummy, Minsky burst in. Pointing a quivering finger through the doorway, he hissed: "Guess who just walked in like he owns the damned place, sat down and ordered a drink—Saul Fromberg, that's who!"

"By himself?" Jake asked.

Minsky shook his head. "Landau's with him."

"Of course," Caplan murmured. "Does the Pope ever travel without his retinue?" He looked at Jake. "Shall we see what he wants?"

"Why not? It'll be our pleasure to throw that fat scumbag out." He glanced at Minsky. "Go get Lou, he won't want to miss this either."

Minsky left hurriedly to fetch Levitt from the club's casino. Jake and Caplan waited for half a minute before leaving the office. Skirting the dance floor, they approached the table where Fromberg sat with Gus Landau. Their timing was perfect; they arrived at the table just as Minsky appeared with Levitt.

"Gentlemen . . ." Fromberg rose and greeted the four young men in a courtly manner. Landau stood also, but there was nothing welcoming about his demeanor. His cold eyes swept over the partners, leaving little doubt in their minds that if they wanted to harm Fromberg, they'd have to go through Landau first.

"An unexpected visit," Jake said. "Is there a purpose, or is it just a social call?"

"I might have brought a gift for your two sons, but after the manner in which my wedding gift was rejected, I didn't think that would be very prudent. Yes, there is a reason for this visit. Sit down, so that we may discuss it like civilized men."

"What reason?" None of the partners made a move to sit.

"I have information for you."

"What kind of information?" Levitt asked.

"About your little mishap in Philadelphia the other day."

Levitt pulled out a chair and sat down, his dislike of Fromberg outweighed by his need to know how the Feds had learned of the distillery. "What do you know about it?"

222

Fromberg waited for the other three men to take chairs. Then, in a quiet, almost jovial voice—like a man extremely pleased with himself—he said, "I was responsible."

"You?" Minsky was furious. "You tipped off the Feds and now you've got the gall to come in here and brag about it? Don't you place any value on your life?"

"I place much value on my life. I also place value on a possible cooperation between us. I offered it before and you rejected me. I had to make you see that it would be wise to change your minds."

"You wiped out a distillery of ours," Levitt said evenly. "How can we talk about cooperation, partnership, when you're that far ahead of us?"

Fromberg's eyes twinkled as though he found the situation vastly amusing. "Are you telling me that you and your friends did not rob a club of mine to raise the money for Sophie Resnick's fine?" He was guessing about the robbery, but the shocked expressions on the faces of Jake, Minsky, and Caplan told him he was right. Levitt was the only partner to keep a perfectly straight face, not that Fromberg had expected anything less from the little man. He was like a good poker player—his face remained exactly the same whether he was holding four aces or a busted flush.

"What about the time you robbed us?" Caplan asked. "Sent your goons into this basement to break up our game and clean us out."

Fromberg sighed exaggeratedly. "When warring nations sit down to talk peace, the delegates do not consult a list of casualties and say: 'We lost more than you did.' They just make peace and forget about the past for the good of all."

"Is that what this is?" Levitt asked. "A peace conference?"

"Peace and more. I am proposing a partnership again, because only that will ensure us of continuing prosperity. On my side, I would offer strength, protection."

"And on our side?"

"What do you think would be fair?" Fromberg decided to leave the first move to Levitt and his partners. He wanted to see what would be forthcoming voluntarily.

"What's the alternative to a partnership?" Jake asked.

Landau answered. It was the first time he had spoken. "A war of attrition. We fight over territories, we wear each other down. Then someone who's done nothing to deserve such good fortune steps in to pick up the pieces."

"Give us five minutes," Levitt said. He gestured for the others to join him in the office. When they were all assembled, he looked from one man to the other. "Well, what do we do?"

"To hell with him," Minsky said. "He's sitting out there, fat and helpless. Him and that scar-faced goon Landau. Let's get them now."

"You think he hasn't got an army sitting outside to make sure he comes out safe and sound?" Levitt asked scathingly. He looked at Jake, hoping for a more sensible course of action.

"A week or two ago, I wouldn't have given him the drippings off the end of my nose," Jake said quietly. "That's all changed now. I've got a couple of kids to worry about."

Levitt nodded, satisfied. Next, he looked at Caplan. "You? What have you got to say?"

"Same as Jake. Annie's going to have a kid in a few weeks. I can understand how Jake feels. Peace would be nice."

"Benny, you're outvoted," Levitt said coldly. "My vote goes with Jake and Moe . . . but there's a rider. We go into a partnership with Fromberg. We offer him half the take on the book and accept the protection he has to offer us—"

"Half the book?" Minsky protested. "That's twenty grand a week."

"At the very least. But it's cheaper than having our clubs raided, our shipments lost, and our distilleries wrecked. It's only a temporary payoff, though. We'll be partners with him until we can topple him."

They returned to Fromberg's table. "We may have a partnership," Levitt said. "But get this straight—we're not giving you a dime's worth of our booze business. We worked too hard to set that up to share it with anyone."

"What are you offering me then?"

Levitt noticed Fromberg's disappointment, despite the effort to conceal it. "Half the take from our book. That'll be twenty grand a week in your pocket further down the road when we open more places. For that, you give us your protection and you keep your people away from our interests. And"—Levitt stared hard at Fromberg and Landau, his blue eyes like two marbles—"you don't buy your booze from anyone else in the future. Your clubs'll sell only our merchandise."

"You drive a hard bargain," Fromberg admitted. "But from you I never expected anything else."

"Do we have a deal?"

"Yes, little man, we have a deal."

Jake was uncertain how Pearl would accept news of the partnership with Fromberg. He found out when he arrived home that night. Pearl was awake, having just fed the children. When he told her what had happened, she angrily denounced the pact.

"You agreed to join up with a slug like that? Jake, that man

224

hounded my parents. He's responsible for my father's death."

"Aren't you overreacting a bit, Pearl?"

"No, I'm damned well not! My father was so overworked trying to make payments to Fromberg that he got careless. That's why he died. Do you seriously think Fromberg's any different now? Look at the way he courted my mother, just to get the use of the basement. He'll cut your throat the moment you offer it to him, and he thinks he can get away with it. He's not going to be satisfied with twenty thousand a week. Whatever you give him, he'll only want more." She stood staring at Jake, wondering if she were getting through to him. "What did the others have to say?"

"They agreed."

"Even Lou?" Levitt's name popped into her mouth. As hard as she'd tried to ignore his existence—the danger he posed to her, to her marriage—she failed.

"Him too. Except he stressed that it was a temporary arrangement."

"Temporary is right, until Fromberg double-crosses you like he double-crosses everyone else."

"Lou sees it the other way—until we carve Fromberg up. Pearl, this arrangement is only going to last for as long as it's beneficial to us. Once we become stronger than Fromberg, we've got no more use for him."

Pearl bit her lip and shook her head anxiously. "For God's sake, Jake, be careful. I don't want to be a young widow with two kids to raise. If that happened, so help me God, I'd kill myself."

"What are you saying?" Jake demanded. "I promise you, Pearl, nothing's going to happen to any of us."

"Jake, you're lying to yourself, you're lying to me. You're in a big-money business, an illegal business. Do you think I don't know the risks you take?"

"There are no risks. We're too careful."

"So I saw with the distillery. If Fromberg's made himself powerful enough to have sway with Federal agents, do you really believe you can stand up to him, be an equal partner with him?"

"Pearl, just wait. Lou knows what he's doing. Fromberg might think he's smart, but Lou can buy and sell him before he knows what day of the week it is."

"Sure," Pearl said dejectedly. "Good old Lou, the brains of the gang." Wherever she looked, Levitt was there. Whatever she touched already bore the marks of his fingers.

Two months later, Annie gave birth to a baby daughter named Judy.

Despite being busy with the twins, Pearl repaid her friend for the help she had given her. She was constantly in and out of the Caplans' apartment, offering advice to Annie on everything from bathing the baby to the position of the crib in the nursery.

"What makes you such an expert?" Annie asked.

"I've been a mother longer than you."

"Sure, ten weeks longer. Big deal."

"Ten weeks of being a mother to twin boys is equal to a lifetime of anything else," Pearl answered.

As winter turned to spring, the two young women began to wheel their baby carriages to Washington Square, enjoying the compliments paid by people who stopped to look at the sleeping tots. By the time the twins were six months old, the differences that Jake had noticed soon after birth were even more evident. Leo, who had long since lost the tuft of neck hair which had given rise to his name, was a good two inches shorter than the older twin, yet he weighed almost a pound more, being short and chubby while Joseph continued to be taller and thinner. Looking at them, Pearl could never be certain whom they resembled. Joseph's deep brown eyes could be Jake's, but Leo's eyes, and that odd alteration of shade, bemused her.

Pearl learned to use those eyes as a barometer of Leo's feelings. When he was content, his eyes were a dreamy hazel. When he wanted something that was not immediately forthcoming, the gray color crept into them, growing stronger as his babyish temper heightened. Unlike Joseph, who was the most easygoing child Pearl had ever seen, Leo could be a tyrant. If his demands were ignored, his eyes would undergo that peculiar transformation and he would begin to scream, grabbing hold of whatever was within reach and throwing it as far as his tiny hands could manage.

There was never any doubt as to whom Judy took after. From birth, the Caplans' infant had a headful of bright red hair that matched Annie's for brilliance and thickness. Pearl particularly enjoyed seeing Moses Caplan go as soft over his daughter as Jake did over the twins. Moe would hold Judy carefully in his arms and carry on a long, one-sided conversation, as though she could understand what he was saying, and then he'd lapse into strange sounds and make even stranger faces, refusing to put her down even when she began to cry and wave her arms and legs in terror. Pearl knew that if she and Annie weren't careful, all three children would grow up to be spoiled brats.

The person who spoiled the infants most, however, wasn't even a father. To Pearl's surprise it was Benny Minsky, who used every opportunity to visit the two apartments on lower Fifth Avenue, never failing to bring some gift. On sunny days, when Pearl and Annie sat in the park with the baby carriages, Minsky would often wander by and spend a few minutes with them.

"He doesn't give a damn about us," Pearl told Annie once. "It's these monsters he wants to see."

"Benny's the last person I'd expect to have a soft spot for babies—any kind of a soft spot except for Kathleen."

Pearl told her of the conversation that had taken place in the twins' nursery between herself, Kathleen, and Minsky. "He said he was making so much money that he'd have no one to leave it to if he died."

"That's no reason to have children," Annie said. "You have them because . . . because"—she shrugged helplessly—"because you want them, not because you need beneficiaries."

"Benny's just a big softie, that's all," Pearl said. Deep down, she really thought he was; such sentimentality would be a perfect counterpoint to his irrational moods. "But if he wants to have a child with Kathleen, he'd better come up with some pretty persuasive arguments."

Annie dropped her voice, made it raspy in a reasonable imitation of the blond singer. "My career comes first and a baby would interfere with it. I guess we decided to make careers out of being mothers."

"I can think of worse things." And worse times, Pearl thought. Right now was a perfect time to be a mother. Despite her own misgivings, the deal with Saul Fromberg was working well. The four partners gave him half the take from the book operated through small shops. In return, Fromberg let them carry on their liquor business, while letting it be known that any other organization with ambitious eyes would have to reckon with him. A new distillery had been opened in Philadelphia, and there had been no trouble with Federal agents. Nonetheless, Pearl dreaded the time when the other shoe would drop.

An elderly woman stopped by Pearl's double baby carriage. "Lovely children. Which is older?"

"Twins," Pearl answered. "Fraternal twins, that's why they don't look alike," she added, noticing the woman's air of confusion. Like Jake, she'd always thought that twins came in identical pairs. Now that she knew better, she liked to share her knowledge.

The woman walked away. "Lou's full of surprises as well," Annie remarked. "Who'd have thought he'd have a sentimental bone in his body? Yet he spoils your twins like crazy, though he hardly ever asks about Judy."

"That's because he's the twins' godfather." Pearl felt she had to say more, find some stronger reason for Levitt's attachment to the twins. "I think he was always closer to Jake than he was to Moe or Benny."

"Certainly to Benny," Annie said and laughed. "It's a wonder those

227

two haven't come to blows yet."

"It was Jake who befriended Lou at school, introduced him to the others. Maybe he thinks he owes Jake."

"Whatever he owes, he's paid back. I sometimes ask myself how well we'd all be doing if it weren't for Lou."

"Me, too," Pearl said, but her thoughts were quite different. Perhaps they wouldn't be so wealthy, but she'd know for certain who the twins' father was. Or would there be no twins at all? That made her wonder. After all, there had been nothing physically wrong with her. The fault, if fault there was, had been Jake's. Was he sterile? Able to make love but incapable of producing offspring? Supposing he was, would he ever learn of the problem? And if he did? . . .

Despite the warmth of the spring sun as she sat with Annie in Washington Square, she shivered.

Lou Levitt had no doubt that the twins were his. He knew it the same way he knew when a gambler's lucky streak was about to break, when a customer was going to throw snake's eyes instead of a natural seven. Levitt's instincts had been honed to razor sharpness by constant observation of gamblers, the hopeless cases trying to strike it rich, the winners stretching their streaks to breaking points because greed made them want one more lucky roll. He'd watched people play the games he operated, watched them dispassionately while learning to call the shots. To Levitt, human nature —life itself—was a turn of a card, the roll of dice, the click of a ball bouncing over numbered slots. Instinct told him what was going to happen, while cold, clear logic guided him to take advantage of every gamble. Both instinct and logic told him that the twins were his.

For a man still in his early twenties, Levitt knew he had come far. Thirteen years earlier, he had arrived in the United States with his family, unable to speak English, a foreigner in a strange land. Now he was the mover behind a million-dollar business, controlling men and equipment and an organization that, because of the Volstead Act, had mushroomed with such speed it made Henry Ford seem to be standing still. For that Levitt was pleased with himself, but not as proud as he was to know he was the father of Pearl's twins.

It wasn't just the date, the coincidence of the timing between their births and that night he had made love to Pearl. Levitt didn't base such important decisions on mere coincidence. He knew Pearl and Jake had been trying hard for a family. Jake had tried and failed. Levitt had succeeded.

228

But his pride was tempered by regret. He wanted to tell the world, shout it from the rooftops, that the twins were his. A man who habitually remained in the background while others attracted attention, Levitt yearned to make an exception in this particular instance. But for his own sake as well as Pearl's, he dare not. Closest friend or not, Jake would go crazy. His eruption would destroy everything Levitt had labored to build, and so the little man had to be content with assuming his customary role, staying out of the limelight while others reveled in the glory of what he had wrought.

In his role of godfather, he could still spoil the twins. He did it tactfully, never visiting the apartment when Pearl was alone. He always waited for Jake to invite him, and then he would tour shops, load up with gifts for the twins. When Pearl protested, Levitt knew her complaints were not because he might spoil the children—they were aimed at him, chiding him because he dared to believe that the twins were his.

Like any father with two children—or any man who believed he had fathered two children—Levitt had a favorite among the twins. Leo. Even in the boys' first year, their physical dissimilarities were complemented by differences in personality. Joseph, the older of the twins, was quieter, more thoughtful. Leo was not only a daredevil, crawling everywhere, into everything, but he began to demonstrate a knack for manipulating his brother. This behavior of his intrigued Levitt. He first saw an example of Leo's hold over Joseph when the twins were eleven months old. Invited by Jake for dinner one Saturday evening before both men went to work, Levitt asked if he could see the twins.

"They're asleep," Pearl answered. "I don't want to disturb them."

"Oh, come on," Jake complained. "What's a little peek going to do?"

Unable to fight both Jake and Levitt, Pearl acceded. She pushed open the door to the nursery. The twins slept in separate cribs, pushed close together. Tonight, Joseph's crib was empty. Both twins were snuggled up in Leo's crib.

"What is this?" Levitt asked. "Are you saving one of the cribs for another child?"

"This has been happening every night for the past couple of weeks," Jake whispered, "ever since they started to stand. Pearl puts them down in their own cribs, and when she looks in later they're together."

"How?"

Jake shrugged. Levitt looked at Pearl, who said, "I don't know. I guess Joseph just climbs over."

"Some climb, the railing's almost as high as he is." He watched as Pearl lifted Joseph from his sleeping twin and placed him back in his own crib.

"Not that it's going to help," Pearl said. "In half an hour, they'll be back together again."

A tiny cry interrupted her whispered sentence. All three adults stared down at Leo. His eyes were open, his face turning red as he gathered air for a lustier cry. This time it was a shriek that ripped around the nursery as he realized his twin had been taken from him. Pearl and Jake started to leave. Levitt pulled them back. "Wait. Let's see what happens."

"He'll never get back to sleep if we're here."

Levitt shook his head. "He doesn't even know about us. Look."

Pearl and Jake stared at Leo. It was true. His eyes had turned that odd steely gray and he was gazing intently, not at them but at his twin brother who was still asleep. As they watched, Leo squirmed over to the side of the crib, stuck his arm through both sets of guard rails and punched his brother's shoulder.

Joseph whimpered and woke up. Like his younger twin, he did not seem to notice the three adult visitors. Slowly, he turned toward Leo as another tiny punch landed on his shoulder.

"Jesus Christ, will you look at that?" Jake murmured. Like a man in a trance, Joseph staggered to his feet, clasped the bars of the crib and began to draw himself up. All the while, Leo lay watching, waving his chubby arms and legs in encouragement. Grunting with the effort, Joseph hauled himself onto the top of the two guard rails. He balanced for an instant before toppling over to land on his twin. Leo wrapped his arms around Joseph, as if congratulating him. His eyes closed. Within a minute, both boys were fast asleep again, as if they hadn't even awakened.

"Can you believe that?" Pearl asked.

"I wouldn't if I hadn't seen it with my own eyes," Jake answered. "And I'm still not sure I do." He turned to Levitt. "What can you say about that?"

"Twins," Levitt answered. "Identical or fraternal, there's some odd bond between them." He walked out of the room, beckoned for the others to follow. He wanted his twins to sleep undisturbed.

230

Chapter Two

Initially, Benny Minsky did not take much notice of the gray-haired man. He was like many of the other customers who came to the Four Aces, sitting quietly at a table near the stage, drinking moderately. Minsky found nothing strange in the fact that the man came alone. Some men liked to drink by themselves, he reasoned; get away from their wives for a few hours, go out and enjoy themselves. Even when the man leaned forward in his chair the moment Kathleen appeared onstage, Minsky wasn't troubled. The man had to be sixty years old. With all the money in the world, no old guy like that had a chance of turning Kathleen's head.

A week later, it was a different story. No matter which club Kathleen sang at, the man was there. Minsky became suspicious. It was a month less than two years since the murder of David Hay. In that time, Kathleen hadn't looked at another man, nor had any man taken undue interest in her. Minsky was such a regular fixture wherever she performed that he had become a walking deterrent. Until now.

"Anyone know who that old geezer is out there?" Minsky asked Jake and Caplan one night when the gray-haired man made his usual appearance.

"Beats the hell out of me," Caplan answered.

"New customer," Jake said. "Only started coming in recently."

"I know. I just don't like the way he ogles Kathleen. The moment she finishes her turn, he gets up and leaves."

Minsky started to walk away and Jake grabbed his arm. "Don't go starting anything with him, Benny."

"I'm going to talk with him, that's all. Talk. I just want to find out what the score is." He shook himself free of Jake's grasp and returned to the club. In the middle of a song, he walked in front of the stage and sat down next to the gray-haired man. "Hey, pal, you got a name?"

"Shh." The man raised a finger to his lips. "Have some respect for Miss Monahan."

Minsky gaped. No one told him to shut up, no matter how deferentially it was accomplished. "I've got all the respect in the world for her, buster. I'm Benny Minsky, the guy she lives with."

If he thought that revelation would cause a tremble, he was mistaken. The man gave him a patient smile and said, "Congratulations. I hope you're both very happy. But I'm the *guy* who can put her voice where it belongs. On the Broadway stage, not in some tawdry joint like this. I'm Irwin Kuczinski."

"Irwin Kuczinski the producer?" Minsky dropped his belligerent attitude and came as close to fawning as he had ever done. During the past six years, Kuczinski had produced three hit Broadway musicals. If he was checking out Kathleen, that meant the big time was just around the corner.

"Irwin Kuczinski the producer." He handed Minsky a gold-embossed card.

"What do you think of her, Mr. Kuczinski? The cat's pajamas, eh?"

Kuczinski nodded his head in approval. Now that he had the respect he felt he deserved, he was no longer so reticent about talking. "I'm convinced that Miss Monahan is exactly what I've been looking for."

"For what?"

"For my next show, of course."

"What kind of show?"

"A musical called *Broadway Nell.*" Kuczinski became quite expansive as he talked of his project. "It's about an Irish girl named Nell, who sings in a place like this on Broadway. For the past three months, I've been looking for my Nell."

"She gets to sing?"

"Of course, that's what singers normally do in musicals."

Minsky ignored the sarcasm. "How many songs?"

"There are six written into the score for Nell."

Minsky clapped the producer on the shoulder with such vigor that the older man winced. "You've found your Nell, Mr. Kuczinski. When she finishes her act, I'll bring her over, introduce her to you."

"That won't be necessary."

"Don't worry about a thing. Just leave it with me, Mr. Kuczinski, just leave it with me." Minsky got up from the table, called over a waiter, and instructed the man to pay special attention to the producer. Everything was on the house.

Kathleen sang two more numbers before ending her turn. Minsky was on hand to help her as she stepped from the stage. "Baby, I've got someone I want you to meet. A friend of mine, a very important friend."

"Not now, Benny. Let me get a drink first."

"Forget the drink." Pulling her by the arm, he guided her to Kuczinski's table, sat her down, and took a chair for himself. "Baby, this is my very good friend, Mr. Irwin Kuczinski. I told him all about you, and now he wants to put you on Broadway."

"Thank you, Benny," Kuczinski said, playing up to Minsky's game. It was no skin off his nose if Minsky wanted to lie, if Kathleen believed him. The producer's only concern was getting the singer he wanted. "I've been watching you and listening to you for quite a while, young lady—"

"He wants you to sing in this musical he's putting together," Minsky cut in.

"You've got a good stage presence and an excellent singing style."

Again Minsky interrupted. "The musical's you, baby, about an Irish nightclub singer named Nell."

At last Kuczinski decided to take full control. He held up a hand for Minsky to be quiet; he didn't need any help from a nightclub goon, even if the man did live with the singer Kuczinski wanted for his lead role. "Would you be interested in a Broadway production, Miss Monahan?"

"Would I? Just tell me what I've got to do."

"Sing exactly like you sing here. Does that sound difficult?"

"Hell, no," Kathleen answered. And she swung around to give Minsky the biggest, warmest, wettest kiss he'd ever had.

Broadway Nell was due to open in April 1929, three months in the future. Kathleen continued to sing at the clubs, but during the day she studied the score of the show. At Kuczinski's suggestion, she even took acting lessons. To Minsky's vast amusement, whenever they were alone she would practice Nell's accent, a broad Irish brogue that rolled off her tongue like molasses.

"With your voice and that accent, you sound like some Irish dockworker," he told her one night as they lay in bed. "The last thing you sound like is a nightclub singer."

"You think a club with a deep-voiced Mick is any worse than a club with four Hebes like you, Lou, Moe, and Jake?"

Minsky did not object to her mocking his background—it was the price he had to pay to be able to make fun of her own—just as long as she never said anything about his complexion. Even now, his darkness was still a sore point. Only recently, he'd told Jake that if he ever got to meet his maker, he'd demand to ask one question before being consigned to either heaven or hell. That question would be: "Why the hell did You have to make me so dark? If You wanted me to be a *shvartse,* You should have made me one, a proper one with thick lips and gleaming teeth—not a Jew who looks like his mother strayed into the wrong part of town one night." Jake had laughed uproariously, but Minsky hadn't meant it as a joke.

"Of course, you realize that my singing fee's going up for you guys once my name goes up in lights," Kathleen said.

"We'll take care of it," Minsky assured her. The night after Irwin Kuczinski had identified himself and made his interest known, Minsky had jokingly suggested to his partners that they open another club, name it after Kathleen and cash in on any name she might make for herself. He'd expected the idea to be laughed at. Instead, Lou Levitt turned very serious.

"Not a bad idea, Benny. How many Broadway stars have got a joint of their own? It bears looking into. But first we'll see how well Kathleen does in this *Broadway Nell* show."

Minsky knew that such a club—he even had a name for it: Kathleen Monahan's Hideaway—wouldn't be a major moneymaker for the outfit. It would bring in peanuts compared to the liquor smuggling and the book. That didn't matter. He was just elated that one of his ideas had finally gone across well. It would be another feather in his cap as far as Kathleen was concerned. How many other guys had nightclubs named after their girlfriends?

"Hey, baby." He cuddled up to her, spoon-in-spoon. "I've done plenty for you, right? How about doing something for me?"

"What?" Did he want her to go down on him? Forget it.

"Marry me."

She squirmed around to face him in the darkness. "You serious?"

"No, I'm making a big joke, you idiot. Can't you see the grin on my face? Of course I'm goddamned serious. I'm always serious in bed."

"Just a minute, buster. Do you want to marry me because you love me, or just because I'm going to be a big Broadway star?"

"Because you're going to be a big Broadway star. I want good tickets for nothing."

"Can't you ever say anything romantic, you creep?" Kathleen asked angrily. "In all these years, I don't think I've ever heard you say once that you love me."

"I put up with you and those two skinny, hairy excuses for dogs. If that isn't love, what is?"

"Just once, Benny. Just once, say something nice."

He put a hand to her face, surprised to feel the wet warmth of tears. Now what had upset her? The marriage proposal or the fact that he didn't tell her he loved her every five minutes. "Okay, I love you."

"Do you really mean it?"

"What is this, interrogation time at the precinct house? If I told you I love you, it's because I love you. Now will you marry me?"

"Yes, Benny. I'll marry you, you crud."

Minsky's wedding to Kathleen three weeks later was the first marriage ceremony Pearl had ever attended that did not take place in a synagogue. It was a Saturday-afternoon civil service followed by a party at the Four Aces. Somehow, it did not seem to her that the bride and groom were really married. Some justice of the peace reciting well-worn English words did not carry the same solemn weight as Hebrew vows taken beneath a *chuppah*.

Whatever opinions Jake might have harbored about the oddness of a civil ceremony were kept to himself. Even when Pearl tried to draw him out while they were dancing at the club, he just shook his head and said, "A wedding's a wedding. As long as there's a bride, a groom, and a ring, who the hell cares where it takes place?"

Pearl cared. Brought up a certain way, she felt peculiar when she had to step outside its strictures.

Midway through the evening, Levitt approached the table where Pearl sat with Jake and the Caplans. Very properly, he asked Jake's permission to dance with Pearl. Pearl considered claiming that her feet hurt, but she decided she had no choice but to accept.

The dance was a waltz. Levitt held Pearl very correctly. His hands were light on her, and he kept several inches of daylight between their bodies. "Who's looking after the twins?" he asked.

"My mother. She's doing double duty tonight. Judy's sleeping in the apartment as well." She hoped Levitt wouldn't talk anymore about the twins.

He didn't. He switched subjects completely. "So Benny finally got married to his *shikse*, eh?"

"It had to happen eventually."

"Sure, with a jerk like Benny it had to happen. Sure is some happy occasion when the groom's parents don't even turn up."

Pearl could barely recall Minsky's parents. She might have seen his mother a couple of times, his father a little more frequently than that. Old man Minsky still peddled his pots and pans. He refused offers of money from his son because he knew its sources and despised it. The old man had come to America more than thirty years earlier to better himself by making an honest, if hard, living. He respected the laws of his adopted country and would not accept money—even from his son—that came from breaking those laws. "I can understand Benny's father not wanting financial help," Pearl said to Levitt, "but you would have thought he'd have come to his son's wedding."

"If he'd married properly, the old man would have come. Instead he married a *shikse*. If one of your sons marries a *shikse*, what would you do?"

"It's a bit early to think about that, isn't it, Lou?"

"Never too early. You make sure you bring those boys up right, Pearl."

At the end of the waltz, Kathleen climbed up onto the stage. "There's a man here tonight who's very special to me. In fact, he's changed my life."

Levitt returned Pearl to her seat. "Some change," he muttered sourly, thinking Kathleen was referring to Minsky; who else would be special to a bride on her wedding day if not the groom?

Kathleen pointed down to a table where Irwin Kuczinski sat. The producer had been at the very top of her guest list for the wedding party. "Mr. Kuczinski's had half a dozen great songs written just for me. You'll hear them all in a couple of months when Mr. Kuczinski's latest musical, *Broadway Nell*, opens at the New Amsterdam." She waved a hand for the producer to take a bow. Modestly, he stood up and inclined his head as the guests applauded. "But tonight, ladies and gentlemen—I'm sorry, I mean treasured guests. Guess I forgot I wasn't working. Tonight, we've got a special treat for you. A preview of *Broadway Nell*, one of the songs. Mr. Kuczinski, why don't you come up here and introduce it?"

Another round of applause broke out as Kuczinski climbed onto the stage. Pearl glanced toward Benny Minsky who, even on this day of all days, was occupying his customary position at the foot of the stage. She wondered in that moment if he was jealous of the producer's professional closeness to Kathleen. One never knew with Minsky.

"First, let me tell you all about Nell," Kuczinski began. "She's a girl pretty much like Kathleen, an Irish girl with a big voice and a big heart, so big that she's the softest touch on Broadway. . . ."

"Sounds like Benny could have walked into that part," Annie whispered across the table. "He's a soft touch where Kathleen's concerned."

". . . And she sings in a place like this. Or should I say a joint like this?" Kuczinski asked with a smile.

From the foot of the stage, Minsky objected loudly. "This place ain't no joint, Mr. Kuczinski. Joints are for the riffraff, not for classy guys like you!"

"Then what the hell's Benny doing here?" Caplan asked softly, and grinned when the remark was met with chuckles from the rest of the table.

"Our Nell's a busy, busy lady," Kuczinski continued. "And she's also a very lonely lady. That's why she introduces herself in the first act with this particular song, 'Lonely, Lonely Me.'"

As Kuczinski stepped down to resume his seat, the small band moved into a slow, plaintive introduction. "This isn't an off-the-cuff performance," Pearl said. "She's had the band rehearsing this."

"It's her wedding," Annie countered. "She's entitled to do anything she likes today. Besides, if we hear her now, we won't have to pay to see the show."

"That'll be the day. Any one of us is missing from the first night, and Benny'll come looking." Pearl turned her attention to the stage as Kathleen started to sing.

"I sing for the customers all night long.
I never get a moment just for me.
And I'm sure they don't see me on the stage,
While they're sipping Scotch from cups that should hold tea.
As I sing of romance I'm so lonely,
As lonely as a lonely girl can be.
All I want from life is a man who'll love me,
Love me for all eternity."

At Pearl's table, Moses Caplan sat with his chin propped on his hands, staring, almost hypnotized, at the stage. "Hey, that's not bad," he murmured.

"Not bad. It's damned good," Jake countered.

"Only an Irish girl would wear a bridal gown while she sings about being lonely," Levitt commented. Nonetheless, he listened with the same rapt attention as the others at the table.

The applause that greeted the end of the song was deafening. Leading it was Irwin Kuczinski. He was beaming at Kathleen's performance and the reception given to the song. The producer had a hit two months before the curtain rose, and he couldn't be happier.

Kathleen climbed down from the stage to be instantly mobbed by well-wishers. For once, Minsky didn't try to fight them off. He was content to just sit there, gloating. The first night her name went up in lights, he'd stand outside the theater admiring the marquee. And God help anyone he saw walk past the theater without buying a ticket.

Minsky did just that. As workmen put the title of the show on the marquee of the New Amsterdam, Minsky stood below, his chest expanding a little more as each letter of Kathleen's name was placed

237

into position. When the complete name was up, he stopped the first person passing the theater, a man in his sixties.

"Hey, you . . . you see that show?"

"What about it?" asked the man as he squinted up at the title.

"You be there when it opens. Take your wife, your kids, your friends. But be there—it's the musical experience of a lifetime."

The man regarded Minsky as though he were totally insane. "Mister, I've got better things to do with my money."

Minsky's face clouded over, his eyes narrowed. "You be there. I'll be looking out for you, and God help you if I don't see your face."

"Sure, mister, whatever you say." The man averted his eyes from Minsky's, frightened by the threat of violence he saw in them, and hurried on.

Clapping his hands together, Minsky turned back to the marquee. The hell with ticket agencies, advertisements in the newspapers. The theater should hire him to sell tickets. He'd guarantee them a full house for the next five years.

On opening night, Minsky made sure that his partners and their wives attended by buying them tickets and treating them to dinner after the show. Kathleen's melancholy rendition of "Lonely, Lonely Me" in the first act brought the house down. Her remaining five songs also brought forth instantaneous applause; but they were almost anticlimactic, following the rousing success of the first song.

Levitt excused himself after the show, saying he had to return to the Four Aces. Minsky, feeling warm toward Levitt for once—he loved everyone on this particular night—thanked him for attending and even went so far as to pat him on the shoulder.

At Sardi's, Kathleen turned to the adjoining table where Irwin Kuczinski sat with his own party. "When will the reviews be out, Irwin?" she asked.

"We should get copies in about an hour. In the meantime, why don't you enjoy yourself? Celebrate. You've earned it, my dear."

A waiter brought over copies of the *Times* and the *Tribune* as they were finishing dinner. Ceremoniously, he placed them in front of Kathleen on a silver tray. Nervously, she picked up the *Times*. Before opening it, she glanced at Kuczinski's table again. When the producer gave a little bow from the waist, it became obvious to Kathleen that he had either seen the reviews or had been told about them, and they were good.

"Well?" Pearl asked. "Tell us the worst. None of us have ever had our names in the newspapers."

"I seem to remember that your mother got her name in the papers once. Sophie Resnick, the roulette restaurateur," Jake quipped, and

238

Pearl kicked him under the table.

"Who's this Brooks Atkinson?" Kathleen asked.

"The critic for the *Times*." The answer came from Kuczinski who had left his own party to stand behind Kathleen, where he could read over her shoulder. "Tell your husband and your friends what Mr. Atkinson has to say."

Kathleen coughed to clear her throat. "'A new star shines over Broadway, a lusty voice that can tug at the heartstrings and wring tears from the eyes.'"

"You wrung a few tears from my eyes as well," Minsky said. "All those gifts I bought cost me a fortune."

"Shut up, Benny," Annie called across the table. "Kathleen can buy and sell you now."

"Read the *Trib*," Kuczinski suggested.

Kathleen dropped the *Times* onto the table, picked up the other paper the waiter had brought. "Percy Hammond?"

"The *Trib*'s top critic," Kuczinski explained.

"He says"—Kathleen paused, drew breath—"'after hearing Miss Monahan sing "Lonely, Lonely Me," any man in the audience who doesn't want to rush onstage and cradle her in his arms must have a heart made of stone.'"

"They'd have had feet made of cement the moment they'd tried it," Minsky muttered darkly.

"Benny, Kathleen belongs to the world now," Kuczinski told Minsky. "She's not just your Kathleen anymore. You have to share her willingly."

Even as the producer spoke, two men approached the table and asked Kathleen to sign their playbills. Minsky watched it all from beneath half-lowered eyelids. He knew he had to make a choice. Treat Kathleen's admirers as he had always treated them—with violence— or accept them. Magnanimously, he decided on the latter. "Some star, eh, buster?" he called out to one of the autograph seekers. "Some voice?"

The man nodded automatically and paid absolutely no attention to Minsky. Kathleen was the only celebrity at the table. Minsky watched as more people came up, men and women, to congratulate Kathleen, to shake her by the hand. For the first time in his life, Minsky felt totally in awe of another person. He had money, a fancy apartment, a new car whenever he wanted one, any material comfort. But the world had never revolved around him, not like it was spinning around Kathleen at that moment. Onstage, she had been the star in *Broadway Nell*. And now, in real life, she was the center of attention in Sardi's. Minsky felt like pinching himself to be certain it was really happening.

A manicurist with a sexy voice to whom he'd given a five-dollar tip. A hatcheck girl at the Four Aces who couldn't get a break because Lou Levitt kept repeating that the club's clientele shouldn't be insulted by amateur talent. And now look at her! Signing autographs, for Christ's sake! Some amateur talent. And what have you got to say for yourself now, little man? No wonder Levitt had passed up the dinner; he didn't want to be shamed by having his bad judgment rammed down his throat!

During the journey home to Riverside Drive, with awe still in his voice, Minsky spilled out those thoughts. Kathleen listened patiently until he'd finished. Then she said, "Why the hell do you sound so surprised, Benny? Didn't you have any faith in me when I started at the Four Aces?"

"Of course I did. I had all the faith in the world."

"All the faith, but no influence." She saw his hands tighten on the steering wheel and she regretted reminding him that he'd had to seek support from Pearl and Annie. The whole deal couldn't have worked out any better if Minsky had owned the Four Aces outright. All the waiting around, all the checking hats was worth this single moment, to see her name lauded on the pages of the *Times* and the *Tribune*.

As they opened the apartment door, one of the borzois bounded forward with a leash in its mouth. "Benny, make some drinks. I'll take the dogs for a walk."

"Nothing doing, star. Broadway legends don't take dogs for a walk. I'll take them. You make the drinks. C'mon, mutts, give the star some privacy." He took the borzois a hundred yards along Riverside Drive, just far enough for them to do whatever they had to do, before dragging them back. Kathleen was opening a bottle of champagne, and she poured two glasses. She and Minsky drank those; she poured more. Soon, they were midway through a second bottle.

"To fame," Kathleen said, raising her glass.

"To fame," Minsky responded. "And to success, money, and everything else that comes with it."

"Taxes come with it." That was a sobering thought.

"What's taxes?"

"Where the Alamo is." Kathleen giggled and realized she was quite drunk. Hell, why shouldn't she be? If you couldn't get pie-eyed on your Broadway debut, when was the proper time?

They finally staggered into bed at five o'clock. Minsky fell asleep immediately, mouth hanging open as he snored loudly. Kathleen tossed and turned, unable to find a comfortable position. It was after seven when she eventually drifted off, warm memories of her triumphant Broadway debut mixing with a queasy feeling in the pit of her stomach. Debut or not, she'd eaten and drunk too damned much.

When she awoke at nine-thirty, Minsky was still asleep and still snoring. She barely gave him a glance as she jumped out of the bed and rushed into the bathroom. All of Sardi's came up. Simultaneously hot and cold, face icy with sweat and forehead burning, she knelt on the floor, head hanging over the bowl.

She threw up again, flushed the toilet, and watched the discolored water swirling down the bowl. She had to pull herself together. She had a show to do that night. And the following night, and the night after that. She couldn't let herself slip back now, let herself be remembered as a one-show singer, a nightclub torch singer who'd made it all the way to Broadway—but for one performance only. They were depending on her. Irwin Kuczinski. Her whole public. Her entire future! No booze tonight, she decided as she made her way back to bed.

The second performance of *Broadway Nell* was a flatter experience for Kathleen. Minsky wasn't out front this time; he was away on a run down to Ocean City to meet another of those interminable shipments. As she stood listening to the applause that followed "Lonely, Lonely Me," she couldn't help smiling. All those super-respectable people out front should only know that my husband and his crew do for real what they're seeing here in a show, she thought. These people would look with horror down their long snobbish noses at Benny and his pals, and while they were looking down their noses, they'd drink their booze. Hypocrites, she decided . . . the whole goddamned lot!

Irwin Kuczinski escorted her home and saw her as far as the lobby of the building. She considered asking him in for a drink, but decided against it when she recalled her resolution. No booze. She stayed up long enough to walk the borzois and was in bed before one o'clock.

The following morning, she woke at seven, made the same urgent rush to the bathroom. Kneeling on the floor, watching the familiar swirl of water in the bowl, the worst possibility of all slammed into her.

Goddamn it! She'd gotten herself pregnant!

No . . . wait a minute. She leaned back against the bath, wiped the sweat from her face. She hadn't done it! Minsky had! That son of a bitch and his wanting kids. Dragging her to see the Granitz twins. Forcing her to look at the Caplans' kid, Judy. He'd wanted kids all along. And now, just when she'd finally clawed her way to the summit, that bastard had made her pregnant! How? A faulty contraceptive? Was she cursing Minsky when the blame should lie with the contraceptive manufacturer? A grim smile etched itself across her face. She wouldn't put it past that dark-skinned shitheel to have gotten busy with a pin.

Damn him! He'd wrecked her life for her. First he'd helped her to get this big break, and then, when she had her hands firmly on the ladder, he'd kicked it from beneath her. That was just the kind of stunt that would appeal to his perverse nature.

Well, two could play at that game. She'd wait a few weeks, just to be certain. By then, she would have sung herself into the hearts of all New York, and she would be able to step down for a few days because of illness. Only it wouldn't be a genuine illness. It would be a manufactured one, a miscarriage. She'd do every damned thing possible to promote a miscarriage. Pearl and Annie had looked after themselves, avoided taking any risks that might endanger the growth of the children they were carrying. That was fine for them because they wanted the kids. Kathleen was determined to travel in the opposite direction. She'd subject her own body to such abuse that the child within her wouldn't stand a chance. The damned thing would be glad to end its pitiful existence in a gush of blood and tissue.

Minsky suspected nothing. Kathleen kept her bouts of morning sickness a secret, only returning from the bathroom when she was in control of herself. Every night she appeared at the New Amsterdam, singing to continuing full houses.

A doctor's appointment served to confirm Kathleen's worst fears. She was carrying another Minsky, God help her. And God forgive her for what she was about to do. Although she never attended church, some of her Catholic upbringing remained firmly embedded in her psyche. She was planning to commit a sin. She consoled herself with the odd thought that it was a lesser sin than bringing Minsky's child into the world.

After a month of singing *Broadway Nell*, she requested time off. Influenza, she told Irwin Kuczinski. Regretfully, he replaced her temporarily with an understudy. Instead of singing at the New Amsterdam that night, Kathleen put her plan into operation. She drank a full bottle of brandy, gritted her teeth, and followed it with a bottle of castor oil. Then she ran a bath so hot she could hardly sit in it. After half an hour, she stood in a freezing cold shower for ten minutes, until her teeth chattered. Five minutes later, she was sitting in another scalding bath.

At four o'clock in the morning, Minsky arrived home from work to find Kathleen lying naked on the living room floor, unconscious. Her face rested in a pool of vomit. Next to her, whining pitifully, were the two borzois. Half an hour later, she was in a hospital bed.

Minsky stayed around until nine o'clock, kicking his heels in the waiting room. At last, a doctor came. "Your wife will be all right, Mr. Minsky. She was very lucky you came home and found her when you did. Any further delay and"—he shrugged his shoulders expressively—"she would probably have lost the baby."

"Baby? What baby?"

"Your wife's pregnant, Mr. Minsky. Didn't you know?"

"I had no idea."

The doctor dropped his voice to a conspiratorial whisper. "From what you told me about the way you found her—the brandy bottle, the castor oil—it's my belief she may well have been trying to abort the pregnancy. It would be perfectly understandable in her position. A hit show, the possibility of a long run."

Minsky barely heard the doctor's words. "When can I see her?"

"Tonight should be all right. Just let her get some rest."

Minsky left the hospital, unsure where he was going? Pregnant? He was numb with shock. Kathleen was pregnant and she hadn't told him. Not only that, but she'd tried to kill the kid, just as she'd always promised she would. He drove around aimlessly. He didn't want to go back to the apartment, not until it was cleaned up. Go to Second Avenue for breakfast? No, he wasn't hungry. What he needed wasn't food, it was a sympathetic ear. He needed help.

Without even thinking, he found himself parking in front of the apartment building on lower Fifth Avenue. He stared at the building uncertainly. Why had he come here? To seek assistance from Pearl because she'd helped him once before with Kathleen? Why not?

He entered the building and banged on her door. Pearl opened it, surprised to see him. "Benny, what are you doing here? Jake's still sleeping." She took a closer look at him, saw the circles beneath his eyes, the haggard face. "You look awful, what's happened?"

"It's not Jake I want to see. It's you. May I come in?"

"Of course you can." She led him into the kitchen, poured him a cup of coffee. "Is it Kathleen?" she asked, thinking of no other reason why Minsky would want to see her.

He nodded, hand shaking as he held the cup of coffee. "I just came from the hospital. She swallowed a bottle of brandy and a bottle of castor oil because she wanted to get rid of the baby she's carrying."

Pearl's shock was as great as Minsky's had been. "Kathleen's pregnant?"

"I didn't know it either."

"Did she lose the baby?"

"No. The doctor claims it's some kind of a miracle that she didn't. What am I going to do, Pearl?"

"You think she'll try again?"

"Of course she will. You were there in the nursery with us when she said she'd get an abortion if she ever got pregnant."

"Do you want me to come with you to see her?" Why else, Pearl asked herself, had Minsky come to her?

"Would you?"

"If you think it'll do any good."

"It's got to be better than anything I can do." He finished the coffee and left. On the way out, he stopped in at the nursery to watch the twins playing on the carpeted floor. Sadly, he shook his head. How in God's name could Kathleen not want that?

Kathleen's attitude was hostile when she received her visitors that evening. Before Minsky could even say a word, she demanded, "Did the doctor tell you what I did?"

"He told me."

"I didn't succeed this time, Benny, but there'll be another time. And another time after that, if necessary. I won't always be so unlucky." She looked at Pearl. "What's she doing here? Did you bring her for support?"

"Kathleen, why did you do it?" Pearl asked. "You could have killed yourself."

"Killed myself?" Kathleen gave a harsh laugh which started her coughing. "I might just as well kill myself if I have to give up that role in Kuczinski's show because of some goddamned kid. It'll be the end of my career."

"No, it won't. Plenty of other singers take time off to have a family."

"Not when they've just got their first big break, they don't. What kind of a life will I have if I'm stuck at home washing shitty diapers all day long?"

Pearl ignored the obscenity. She didn't like to hear such language, especially from another woman, but now was not the time to object. "No one'll forget you if you're out of the public eye for a year or two. You're too big a hit to be forgotten so easily."

"Says you. Hey, you're fine; all you ever wanted out of a life is a couple of screaming brats. That's being a woman for you. I want more. I don't want to sit around like you and Annie while your men feed and clothe you. I've got a voice and I want to use it to make my own way in the world."

When Minsky spoke, his voice was so calm, his attitude so reasonable, that Pearl was surprised. "Kathleen, whatever belongs to you—you can do whatever you like with it. But that child you're carrying is half mine. You can't get rid of something I own fifty percent of and say you're being fair."

"You own fifty percent? Then why the hell is it me who throws up in the morning? Why don't you do it half the time instead of lying in bed snoring your head off? Why don't you carry this thing for four and a half months so I can get back to the show? Why don't you get as big and fat and ugly as I'm going to get if I keep the kid? Your fifty percent, buster, amounts to sticking your prick in and getting your rocks off!"

"Kathleen, you're upset—" Pearl began.

"Damn right I'm upset. Upset because he got me pregnant, and double upset because I failed to get rid of it. This time anyway." She rolled over to face the wall, ignoring her two visitors completely.

Pearl touched Minsky's arm, motioned for them to leave. When they were outside the hospital, she said, "Do you think it would do any good to get ahold of the show's producer? Maybe he can make her see some sense."

"I was thinking about that."

"Leave it until she comes home. Stay with her all the time to make sure she doesn't try anything again. And Benny . . ." Pearl held his hands, almost fearfully. "You just make sure you don't do anything silly either."

"Like what?"

Pearl shrugged and smiled at him.

"Don't worry, Pearl. I'll be a loving, caring husband."

"I know. But don't do anything silly all the same."

Kathleen was discharged from the hospital two days later. Minsky drove her home. When they arrived, Irwin Kuczinski was sitting in the living room, absently patting the two borzois.

"Lovely dogs you have, Kathleen," he greeted her.

"What are you doing here?"

"Is that a nice way to say hello to your favorite producer? I came to see how my star was recovering from her bout of influenza."

"Recovering just fine, thank you. And she'll be back at work as soon as she's—"

"As soon as she's managed to miscarry?" Kuczinski finished for her. "Don't you think you're being a little bit drastic? Kathleen, my dear, in your condition you can continue to sing for another three or four months."

"I can just see a pregnant woman singing 'Lonely, Lonely Me.' Can't you? You'll have to change the name of the show to *Broadway Virgin Mary*."

"We have wardrobe mistresses who can work wonders."

Kathleen swung around on Minsky. "Did you bring Irwin up here, get him to join you to make me have this thing?"

"I came up because you're my star," Kuczinski answered for Minsky. "My star's welfare is always closest to my heart."

"And I'll be your star again, Irwin, once I get rid of my unwanted visitor."

Kuczinski sighed. Minsky had sought his help, and he was sympathetic toward the young man; but this was not going to be easy. "Let me put it to you another way, Kathleen. In a few short weeks, you have absolutely captivated the public. They're yours. But my experience tells me that they are going to turn on you overnight once they learn that you did away with your unborn child so that you could carry on with singing. They would think much more highly of you if you had the baby, took a year off, and then returned. You could come back triumphantly in a new show, to ever greater acclaim. There's nothing Broadway loves more than mush and sentiment, and a star with a child ranks top in both categories."

Kathleen stared at the producer. Finally, he had struck home, explained it all in a way that she could understand. But was he right? A year out of the limelight she had yearned for so desperately—could she come back from that long a hiatus? "Why would the public have to know if I got rid of the kid?"

"My dear, for a Broadway star, you're incredibly naïve. Don't you ever read the newspapers? Journalists make a living out of feeding information about people like you to the public. Writers like Winchell have teams of investigators sniffing around for stories such as a big star putting career before family. He'd make hay with it. Some folks might sympathize with you," Kuczinski said condescendingly, "but I'd bet that a lot more would hate you for it. And that hate translates into poor ticket sales. Think about that."

Kathleen promised Kuczinski that she would. Satisfied that he had done his best, the producer left. For a minute, Minsky and Kathleen stared at each other. If there was to be a reconciliation, it would have to come now.

Minsky spoke first. "Baby, you've heard Irwin, you've heard Pearl. Now listen to me. I want that kid you're carrying more than anything else in the world. Please, I'm begging you, don't do anything stupid again. You'll not only hurt the kid, you'll hurt yourself, don't you see that? You could have died with all that crap you poured into yourself the other night. Irwin says you won't lose anything by going through with it, and he should know what he's talking about. And even if you did lose out, I'd make it up to you. I'd buy you a goddamned theater.

I'd kidnap Gershwin, Hammerstein, Kern; and make them write stuff just for you."

"I don't need your help, Benny. I got where I am on my own, and I'm going even further, exactly the same way."

Minsky's hope died. None of the allies he'd thrown against Kathleen had swung the battle in his favor. He made up his mind to give it one last shot on his own. "Kathleen, can I ever leave you alone again? Can I go about my business and know you won't be doing some other crazy thing to make yourself miscarry?"

"Benny, brandy and castor oil, hot and cold baths, they didn't work. But I promise you this," Kathleen spat out viciously, "the moment you walk out of that door, I'll try something else. I'm not having your kid or anyone else's goddamned kid. Do you understand that? You can bring the whole world up here to plead with me, and it's not going to change a single fucking thing!"

Minsky's eyes turned damp. His dark face contorted itself into a mask of misery. Kathleen watched as he walked into the bedroom and slammed the door. She'd never seen him like this before, so cowed, so close to tears. What she was carrying made her all-powerful.

She heard the bedroom door open. When she turned around she saw that tears were coursing freely down Minsky's face—he was blubbering like a little kid—and gripped firmly in his right hand was a heavy revolver.

"Kathleen . . ." He grabbed her by the hair, slammed her into a chair and forced her head back. She gasped in pain, and gasped again when the muzzle of the revolver was jammed into her ear. "I'm telling you just once, and you'd better listen. You promise me, you swear to have that kid, or else I'm going to blow your fucking brains all over the fucking carpet, right here and now!"

Despite the pain she felt as her hair was almost tugged from its roots, the coldness of the gun stuck in her ear, Kathleen managed one last barb. "That's right, Benny. You stick your prick in one end of me, and your gun in the other. Your answer to everything, you fucking maniac!"

The click as Minsky thumbed back the hammer was the most deafening noise Kathleen had ever heard. "Kathleen, let me hear you're going to keep that kid."

He meant it! The crazy son of a bitch really meant it! He had finally flipped over the edge of whatever precipice he'd been dangling on all his life! With a chilling certainty, Kathleen knew that the next words out of her mouth could be her death sentence. She had thought he was trying to beat her down, just like always. He'd tried reason, thrown other people into the battle. Then he'd tried tears. None of these approaches had worked, so he had resorted to what he knew best. Violence . . . the threat of a gun. Only this time it wasn't a threat. The maniac meant it. Even now his knuckles were whitening with stress as he slowly squeezed the trigger toward the point of no return. She could imagine the hammer falling, hear the tremendous explosion, feel the searing pain of the bullet ploughing through her skull and pulverizing her brain, see blood and tissue all over the floor. A gush of blood and tissue! Just the way she'd envisaged the end of Minsky's kid. Not her kid! She didn't want the damned thing. Minsky's kid!

"Okay!" she cried out. "Okay, Benny!"

"Let me hear you say it, swear on your life that you'll keep the kid, see this thing through." The muzzle of the gun remained fixed firmly in her ear.

"I swear it, Benny! On my life, I swear it!"

At last the pressure eased. "You lie to me, Kathleen, and I'll kill you. I promise you that. Anything happens to that kid, I don't care what, and you die right along with it. It doesn't matter where you run, where you hide. I'll find you, and when I do I'll kill you."

She turned her head to see the gun hanging limply in his hand, muzzle pointing down at the floor. His face was streaked with tears, dried tracks acting as conduits for the fresh deluge. She had never been so terrified of him, of anyone or anything, in her entire life. Even the time he'd pushed her from the window, some instinct deep within her had known that he would grab her, wouldn't let her fall. But not this time. She'd come a split second—a half-pound of finger pressure, a single word—away from death.

"I won't run anywhere, Benny. You won't have to come looking for me."

Kathleen remained in *Broadway Nell* until July, when she was six months pregnant and even the wardrobe mistress was unable to conceal her condition. Not that the crowds who continued to flock to the show were unaware. Walter Winchell's column had carried a teasing little question that went: "Guess which Lonely, Lonely girl on Broadway isn't quite so lonely after all?"

Despite her promise to Minsky, she was uncertain whether he trusted her completely. As she neared full term, he found reasons to stay at home for more and more of the time, wriggling his way out of convoy duty with the shipments from Ocean City to Philadelphia. Not that he was needed on it. There had been no trouble of any kind since the deal with Saul Fromberg was struck. Did Minsky still mistrust her, or was he just worried like any prospective father—any husband—

would be? She couldn't help thinking that his behavior was almost motherly; he brought her breakfast in bed each morning, walked the dogs, did chores around the apartment. He even decorated the spare bedroom himself, turning it into a nursery.

"Do you love me, Benny?" she asked once, as she watched him taking out the garbage.

"More than anything else in the world, baby."

"I really think you mean it."

"I do." He hoisted the garbage bag up to his chest, looked at her over the top. "Don't you know that by now?"

"Would you have fired that gun?"

"Don't make me answer that."

"You would have fired it, you son of a bitch." There was no anger in her voice, just certainty.

Kathleen knew that the answer shouldn't make sense, but somehow it did. The biggest madness seemed to make sense around Benny Minsky, she thought as she ran a hand across her swollen belly. Here she was, in a condition she'd sworn she'd never be in . . . and that made sense as well. Maybe the picture wasn't as bleak as she had once painted it. She might not be carrying another Benny Minsky. She might be carrying another Kathleen Monahan.

She decided that was just as bad. She didn't need the competition.

In the middle of October, Kathleen gave birth to a seven-pound boy. In memory of her only brother, who had died in the trenches at Ypres during the First World War, the baby was named William. At Kathleen's insistence, although she had no religious feeling whatever, the boy was baptized into the Catholic faith. It was the first time she had been inside a church since her childhood.

Minsky felt even stranger, standing in the church while his son was baptized. He thought back to his youth, the Saturdays his parents had made him attend the tiny temple on Broome Street, his bar mitzvah there. And here he was, watching his son being baptized. The mother was Roman Catholic, therefore the kid was also Catholic. What did it really matter anyway? Knowing Kathleen, this would probably be the first and last time the kid would ever see the inside of a church. He glanced sideways at his friends who had come to the baptism. The Granitzes and the Caplans hadn't made any comment when he'd informed them of the baptism. They had just attended because they were his friends, because it was expected of them. Levitt hadn't come, though. Minsky had invited him as well, but Levitt had looked at him as though he were insane.

"You're having your son baptized into the faith of the mobs who slaughtered your ancestors, Benny, that's what you're doing. Your grandparents must be spinning in their graves."

"That was over there," Minsky had pointed out. "What happened over there stays over there, gone and forgotten."

"Maybe by you, but not by me. I lived through it before I came over here. You want your kid to be a *goy*, go ahead. Just don't expect me to be there applauding from the front row."

"Suit yourself," Minsky had said as Levitt turned away. Who the hell wanted that midget with his sour puss anyway? He'd make the kid scream with fright.

The day after William Minsky's baptism, the stock market crashed. While Wall Street reeled in the following weeks, Lou Levitt called a meeting of this three partners in the office of the Four Aces.

"We're embarking on a new business venture," he stated flatly.

"A new business?" Jake laughed. "Bankers are throwing themselves out of windows, and you're talking about a new business. What?"

"Same as the guys who are busy throwing themselves out of windows. We've got millions in cash. We generate more each day. We're going to put it to work for us, out on the street earning interest."

"Loansharking?" Caplan asked. "What's the big deal about that?"

"Not loansharking, Moe. Banking. You mark my words, this whole country is undergoing a complete financial purge. Guys with stocks find they're worthless because the companies go bust. Real estate will drop like crazy. Precious stones aren't going to be precious anymore. The only thing that'll have value will be hard cash, because everyone's going to be screaming for it. So we're going to offer money at reasonable rates. We're not doing it for a profit—"

"Since when is profit a dirty word in your vocabulary?" Minsky wanted to know.

"It isn't, but sometimes it pays to use a little forethought. Think about all the business we do in the Garment Center with our booze. For a manufacturer to sell a line during the past few years, he's had to entertain the buyer. These manufacturers are in a hand-to-mouth business, always running to banks for quick loans so they can put out another season's line. The banks'll stop lending money. That's where we come in. We take a piece of a company as collateral. All nice and legal."

"Supposing they go broke?" Jake asked. "That leaves us nice and legally in the hole. Who are we to loan money when banks won't?"

Levitt emitted a silent groan. Sometimes he wondered if he was the only partner with any foresight whatever. "If loans go bad, the banks pick up whatever the collateral was. That's why they won't lend out money, because a clothing company, a transportation company, isn't any good to them. Banks are in the money business—all they want is money. We're not so fussy because our objectives are different. If our loans go bad, we'll take whatever we can get—companies in the *shmatte* business, transportation companies, you name it."

"What do we need them for?" Minsky asked.

This time, Levitt's groan was audible. "Look . . ." He leaned forward on the desk, very earnest. "This Prohibition racket isn't going to last forever. Sooner or later it'll be repealed. If we carry on like we're doing now, we'll be left with the book, a few nightclubs, some other bits and pieces. Now's our chance to buy utter respectability, buy our way into legitimate companies for the price of a loan that can't be repaid. You three should be all for it. Just think . . . you want your kids to inherit nightclubs or to walk into respectable businesses?"

Put that way, it made sense to Levitt's listeners.

That night, when Jake walked into the twins' bedroom to kiss them good night, he picked them up in his arms and carried them to the window which looked north along Fifth Avenue. "You see up there?" he asked, not caring whether they understood him or not. "You two are going to own all of that. You'll have companies that'll make your suits for you, other companies that'll make the dresses and coats your wives are going to wear. And the trucks that carry the cloth from the mills to the manufacturers will also be owned by you—even the guys who make the needles they put in the sewing machines."

Pearl watched as Jake explained the future to the twins. "You're painting a very impressive canvas for them, Jake. From what I hear, most kids'll just be glad to be able to afford a secondhand suit in the next few years."

"That's because most kids don't have Lou for a godfather. Sometimes I wonder if that little Polack is human. He never makes a damned mistake."

"Is that good or bad?"

Still cradling the twins, Jake swung around. "What's that supposed to mean?"

"I don't know. Maybe his always being right might lead you to being careless. If he were wrong once in a while, you'd all be more cautious."

"It's the cautious guys who are jumping out of windows right now, Pearl."

"I hope you're right, Jake." Leaving him to put the twins to bed, she went next door to see Annie. All these dreams of expansion worried her. The bigger Jake and his partners became, the more of a target they represented for other ambitious men. They were going into lending money to legitimate businesses, buying their way to respectability because Levitt was convinced that with the ultimate repeal of Prohibition they would lose a large source of income. Wouldn't other bootleggers be feeling the same pinch, be looking for the same opportunities? Wouldn't they watch with envy Jake's success? Sometimes, Pearl wished that she still operated the restaurant on Second Avenue with her mother. It had been hard work, a struggle to make ends meet most times. But she'd been more at peace with herself in those days, never having to constantly fear for the safety of those dear to her.

"Are you worried about what they're doing, how big they're becoming?" Pearl asked Annie.

"Worried? For God's sake, why? Pearl, don't you understand what's happening now?" Annie grabbed her friend by the shoulders and shook her. "Wake up! You're not living in fear of a man like Fromberg anymore. Moe and Jake are going to be more powerful than that fat pig ever dreamed he could be. We're rich already, right? Now we're going to be respectable. People'll look up to us like they look up to the Vanderbilts and the Whitneys. Those four boys we caught throwing dice in the janitor's shed are going to build an empire that'll be the toast of Wall Street."

"That's not much of a toast these days."

"You know what I mean. They'll own this city, and if you own New York, Pearl, you own the entire world."

"I suppose so." But there was no conviction in Pearl's voice. Whatever success Jake achieved, she knew that Levitt's hand would be ultimately responsible for it. Perhaps she'd feel happier if it were someone else who pulled the strings.

Chapter Three

Lou Levitt's dream of buying respectability through loaning money to companies with cash-flow problems turned quickly into reality. By the beginning of 1932, when the Depression was biting hard across the country, prudent loans had given Levitt and his partners interests in companies as diverse as meat-packing and clothing, restaurants and bakeries. In a time of breadlines and soup kitchens, they were experiencing an era of plenty.

Wealth rolled in as the liquor shipments came through in a steady flow. The clubs continued to cater to well-heeled patrons. The book, operated from the small shops, continued to take in huge sums from people even more desperate to hit that big winner. Additionally, they had embarked on another gambling venture, the numbers racket. People could play for pennies, and pray for a six-hundred-to-one payout. Policy slips covered the poor areas of Manhattan, offering a chance at a miracle.

Secure in the Fifth Avenue apartment, Pearl found it difficult to believe that the country could be in such straits. For her, nothing seemed to have changed. She read about bank and business failures, riches-to-rags nightmares, in the newspapers, but only rarely did she see any evidence of this turmoil. That was when she took the twins to Second Avenue to visit their grandmother. There, men and women walked the streets with their shoulders bent, their faces twisted into permanent lines of grief and anxiety. Pearl wished that her mother would close the restaurant after all these years, move away from the area. Sophie Resnick was fifty-seven now. She'd worked long enough, she deserved some comfort. But when Pearl suggested such a move during an afternoon visit with the twins, Sophie scorned the idea.

"If I close down, who's going to feed all these people?" she asked, indicating the dozen customers in the restaurant.

Pearl was surprised that business was so good. The afternoon had always been a slack period, or had time played games with her memory? "Someone else will buy the restaurant, Mama. It'll still be here."

"Aha! But will that someone else charge the same good prices that I do?"

Uncertain what her mother meant, Pearl looked in the cash drawer. It was empty. "What have you done with the money?"

"What money? People pay me what they can. And if they can't pay, so who cares anyway?"

"How long have you been running the restaurant like this?" No wonder the afternoon business was so brisk, if her mother was serving customers for nothing.

"Who counts days?" Sophie asked.

Pearl smiled fondly at her mother. "All that money you were always putting by for the rainy day you were certain was coming—what happened to it?"

"I used it for the rainy day. Only it was their rainy day"—Sophie gestured toward the customers—"not mine."

Pearl let her gaze sweep over the restaurant. She recognized familiar faces, peddlers she'd seen come into the shop when she was young, and more prosperous businessmen, shopkeepers. Only now they all looked alike, downtrodden. They were men who had surrendered to life's hardships. "When's the last time anyone paid the price written on the menu?"

"Your friend, Lou . . . he always pays. He's the only one of the old crowd who still comes in regularly."

He would pay, Pearl thought. Proper to the end, in debt to no one. Pearl noticed the twins standing by the counter, gazing up at the glass cover over the tray of cakes. They stood motionless for several seconds, then Leo nudged Joseph's arm, murmured something, and pointed to an empty stool. Obediently, Joseph hauled his tiny body up onto the stool, balanced precariously on it while he gazed down at the cakes.

"You've got a couple more customers for handouts," Pearl told her mother. "Better see to them before they start helping themselves."

"They're my favorite customers of all. I'd even pay them to eat here." Sophie lifted Leo so that he, too, could look down on the cakes. "What do you want?"

Joseph indicated a piece of apple strudel. "And you, darling?" Sophie asked the younger twin. "You want a jelly roll like always?"

Leo's head bobbed up and down in anticipation. Pearl could swear that the first words he'd ever learned had been *jelly roll*. From the moment she'd brought him into the restaurant, he'd been fascinated by the thick coating of confectioner's sugar on the sticky treats. By the time he was finished eating one, sugar and jelly were spread all over his hands, face, and clothing. Joseph was a more fastidious child who chose less messy cakes and ate carefully with a fork and a plate.

"Mama, if things get better, if people don't need the handouts from your kitchen anymore, would you consider selling the restaurant then?"

Sophie considered the question. "Pearl, this is my home. What am I going to do if I leave it? Sit in some fancy apartment where I don't know anyone? Talk to the walls? This money that Jake and his friends earn, it's made a big difference to you and to Annie because you're both young enough to appreciate what it can buy. But it can't do anything for me."

Pearl nodded in resignation. "That's exactly what I thought you'd say."

"What else would you expect from me? When my time comes, they'll have to carry me out of here."

"Not for a hundred and twenty years," Pearl said automatically, but she knew her mother was right. Trying to think of another, more comfortable subject, she looked at the twins who had finished their cakes. Leo's face was a red-and-white mask as he walked along the counter, spinning the empty stools. Joseph, perfectly clean after eating the piece of strudel, was helping himself to a glass of water to wash it down. They aren't like twins at all, Pearl thought. At four years old, Joseph was a good three inches taller than his brother, yet Leo weighed more because of his stocky build. The only similarity Pearl could discern was the color of their hair, a brown so dark it was almost black. Everything else was different. Joseph's face was thin, brown eyes wide within it. Leo's face was almost square, and his eyes still retained that odd ability to shift color according to his mood. Now, as he happily spun the stools like giant tops, they were a clear hazel. But Pearl knew that the moment she told him to stop, that he was annoying the restaurant's customers, his eyes would slowly turn to that steely gray.

Four years old already. It didn't really seem possible. Only a few months had passed, surely, since the night she'd assured Jake that she was all right as he'd prepared to set off for Ocean City. She knew that Annie felt the same way. Once you had a child, your own youth, your own childhood, were over. No matter how young you felt, a child was always a mirror to your growing older.

Pearl saw almost as much of Annie's daughter, Judy, as she did of the twins. The little girl was always running in and out of the Granitz apartment, up and down the hallway, playing with the boys. Just as Pearl and Annie had done. Joseph was Judy's favorite, but he had time for her, while Leo frequently did not want to be bothered. Leo only wanted his twin brother as a playmate; anyone else was an intruder. Only a few weeks earlier, Pearl remembered, the twins had even fought over Judy. Bright red hair tied in braids, she had wandered into the apartment to play with the twins, who were pushing toy cars around the floor of their bedroom. While Joseph had wanted to allow Judy to join in, Leo had been dead set against it. An argument had started. By the time Pearl had heard the raised voices and come from the kitchen to investigate, the twins had been rolling on the floor, punching, pulling hair, and kicking; Judy had stood against the wall, fingers to her mouth, entranced at her first experience of being fought over.

Leaving the twins to continue their battle, Pearl had returned Judy to the Caplan apartment. "Your daughter's a troublemaker," she'd jokingly told Annie. "She's got the boys fighting over her."

"What can I tell you? They've both got good taste in girls."

"You mean your daughter's got good taste in boys."

Annie had burst out laughing. "Did you ever think we'd quarrel over our kids? Come in, I'll make you a cup of coffee."

"Who's got the time to drink coffee? I've still got a fight to break up."

Pearl had returned to her own apartment to separate Joseph and Leo. Holding them apart, like a referee between two boxers, she'd said, "That's it, now shake hands and be friends."

Joseph had offered his right hand. Leo had glared at it. "Promise to play with me and not with Judy."

Promise him, Pearl had said silently. Promise him anything, but just shake hands.

"Judy's my friend," Joseph had answered.

"I'm your twin brother, that means more," Leo had said stubbornly. He'd stared at Joseph until the older twin had averted his gaze.

"All right, I promise."

The boys had shaken hands, Pearl had breathed a sigh of relief. It was the first time she'd noticed that odd little streak of jealousy in Leo. She and Jake had told the boys they were twins, how special their relationship was, but she hadn't realized that Leo would attach such significance to it. Young as he was, he seemed to view it as a bond of loyalty that could not be broken for any reason.

Pearl decided that Annie didn't know how fortunate she was with only one child to worry about. Kathleen, as well. One child was simple compared to the mayhem twins could cause. But Pearl didn't really want to have it any other way.

Kathleen seldom worried about her only child, William. She hadn't wanted him in the first place. She hadn't asked for him. She'd gone through with the pregnancy only out of fear. Consequently, she'd be damned if she'd give the boy the love a mother usually bestowed on her child.

On the day William turned one, Kathleen resumed her career by rehearsing for a new musical that Irwin Kuczinski was producing, and she considered that her maternal responsibilities were at an end. The family moved to a larger apartment in the same Riverside Drive block, and Kathleen hired a housekeeper to care for William. After that, she left her son totally in that woman's care.

As the child grew older, he could have been forgiven for believing that his parents were Benny Minsky and the housekeeper, a kindly, middle-aged woman named Florence Wickham. The woman whom he knew as his real mother was nothing more than a heavily made-up blonde who passed by him infrequently in the apartment on her way to work or to a rehearsal for the new show.

Unfortunately for Kathleen, the next Kuczinski show proved to be an expensive flop. The producer had gambled everything on the venture, a glittering spectacular called *Fever*, based on the California Gold Rush. Kuczinski had planned the show as methodically as he'd planned earlier, successful musicals. He used the same team of songwriters who had concocted the score for *Broadway Nell*. He had the same star. How could it go wrong? Only during his planning, Kuczinski had not reckoned with the grinding poverty that was sweeping the land. Ticket sales were minimal. Despite the half-dozen numbers written especially for Kathleen, there were no hit songs. After a week, the show closed, leaving Kuczinski bankrupt and Kathleen seeking a scapegoat for her misfortune. She found one quickly, in her son, William.

"That damned kid!" she raged at Minsky one evening as they sat in the living room. "He kept me out of the public eye. It's because of him that *Fever* flopped."

"It's not because of William and you damned well know it! Your precious Irwin Kuczinski didn't read the times properly," Minsky told her. "He produced an extravaganza which no one could afford to go and see. Anyway, what the hell are you worried about? It's not as though you're broke. We've got more money than we'll ever need, plus there's Kathleen Monahan's Hideaway."

"Kathleen Monahan's Hideaway!" She snorted. The club had opened on West Fifty-seventh Street, in the short stretch between Seventh Avenue and Broadway, soon after Kathleen had opened in *Broadway Nell*. Even when she'd become too big to sing in the show, she'd performed there. But having a club named after her was no longer enough. Not after she'd tasted success on the legitimate stage. And failure! "Big deal, Kathleen Monahan's Hideaway! You and your pals get all the loot from that joint."

"Like you don't see a single penny! You've got a piece of the action there. You're what makes the place tick, Kathleen. People go there to hear you, not to drink."

"I don't want to go back to being just another nightclub singer. There's more, much more than that."

"Maybe you're not cut out to be anything bigger, you ever stop to consider that?" Minsky asked. "Just be grateful they want to hear you at the Hideaway and shut the hell up!"

The living-room door opened and the housekeeper looked in. She was accustomed to arguments between Kathleen and Minsky. Show business folk always led such emotional lives. Normally she didn't let their disputes worry her, as long as they didn't affect her little charge. "Do you think you could keep your voices down?" she asked softly. "William's just gone to sleep."

Minsky raised a hand. "Sorry, we'll tone it down."

Miss Wickham's grateful smile was cut short by Kathleen's next outburst. *"You'll* tone it down, but not me. I've still got things to say. That kid has ruined my life. You've ruined my life. I've a goddamned good mind to leave the pair of you."

Minsky dug his hand into his trouser pocket, pulled out a gold moneyclip full of bills and flung it in Kathleen's face. "How much do you need to leave? Take it, take it all. You can have Kathleen Monahan's Hideaway as well, whatever you damned well want. Just leave. For all the goddamned good you are as a mother to our son, you might just as well not even be here. Miss Wickham and I can manage pretty well by ourselves. Right, Miss Wickham?"

The housekeeper stood uncertainly in the doorway. Of the two, she preferred Minsky. Despite his odd working hours—she wasn't even sure what he did, just that he was also in the entertainment business—he spent much more time with his son than Kathleen did. When he was at home, he would proudly take the child for a walk, the two borzois tied to the handle of the push-chair which he wheeled along Riverside Drive. He'd even gone so far as to take an interest in bathing and changing the baby. All unmanly acts, according to Miss Wickham, but definitely signs of a father's love for his child.

258

Kathleen stared at the money on the floor. She'd reached a crisis and she was uncertain how to react. Minsky's tactics—throwing the money in her face, telling her to get out—had confused her. Two years ago, just threatening to leave would have sent Minsky into a fury, into screaming and swearing at her; it would have brought on the jealous rage that signified how much he really needed her. The kid had changed all that. Minsky doted on the child to the exclusion of Kathleen. When she wasn't there, the bastard didn't even miss her. He had the damned kid to play with, to shower his affection on. By going through with the pregnancy, she'd created a rival, given Minsky a substitute that had moved upward into first place. The threat of leaving him was no longer so traumatic.

"Pick up the money, Kathleen," Minsky said. "Pick it up and get the hell out of here. See who else you can find to support you."

"I don't need anyone to support me. My voice can do it better than any creep like you."

"Yeah, so I saw in the reviews for *Fever*. Face it, Kathleen, you hit the big time at the wrong time. Broadway couldn't cope with you *and* the Depression. Kuczinski went broke finding that out. You're luckier—at least you've got me."

Resignedly Kathleen turned away. She couldn't leave, not yet, not while this goddamned Depression had the country in its icy grip. The only businesses that seemed to be doing well were the kind Minsky was involved in. He and his cronies had cash to lay around everywhere, unlike the people who had flocked to see her when she'd sung in *Broadway Nell*. That kind of a glittering audience was just a memory now. Minsky was right—she'd hit the big time at the wrong time. Just like she'd had the kid at the wrong time. Everything she ever damned well did was at the wrong time.

In comparison to what was taking place across the country, Kathleen's career was a minor casualty of the Depression. Rich men had become poor overnight, and poor men had become destitute.

In his oak-paneled office on East Forty-second Street, Saul Fromberg considered himself to be one of the major casualties. The legitimate enterprises he had labored to build up now lay in ruins around him. Real-estate values had dropped. He couldn't sell his buildings to raise cash even if he wanted to; no one had the money to buy. His restaurants and theater interests, once such prestigious assets, were now liabilities. Few people had the money to eat out and see shows as they had done in the days before the crash.

Only his illegal activities generated cash, but not enough to rescue him from the financial chaos of his other dealings. If it were not for the money he received regularly from Lou Levitt—half of the bookmaking operation which now amounted to more than thirty thousand dollars a week from some two hundred small shop outlets—Fromberg knew he would be out of business altogether. Even then, the bookmaking money did not constitute profit. It was living expenses, the payroll for his men. Once he ran out of payroll money, his men would desert him in favor of a boss who could afford to pay them in these difficult times. They'd go, caps in hands, to Lou Levitt and his crew, looking for work. And Levitt, once he had Fromberg's men on his own payroll, would have no reason to continue the payments, no need for the arrangement.

Fromberg was sixty now, an age at which he'd thought he would be able to sit back and enjoy life. Instead, he was working harder than ever just to remain where he was. Nine years had passed since he'd opened his first major club, the King Saul, in the basement of the Resnick restaurant on Second Avenue. By the time he'd bailed out, leaving Sophie to face the music, he'd amassed what he'd deemed enough to build an empire that would last for all time. He'd been wrong. Like Irwin Kuczinski and many others, Fromberg had not taken the Depression into account. Now, his entire existence depended on Levitt's messenger with his envelope full of money.

The messenger came promptly at ten o'clock every Monday morning, taking the elevator up to the tenth floor and being escorted to Fromberg's office through the maze of anterooms occupied by clerical staff and bodyguards. After Fromberg had counted the money, ensured that it tallied with the slip of paper that detailed, in Levitt's tiny handwriting, the take for the week, he would write out a receipt. The messenger was then escorted through the office's side door to come out opposite the elevator for the downward journey.

"Look at this," Fromberg said to Gus Landau after the messenger had left one Monday morning. He tossed the envelope full of money onto the leather-topped desk. "I'm reduced to being a beggar, a charity case who lives off handouts from that little Polack. And he used to work for me."

Landau was unsympathetic. "You should have seen the writing on the wall that day he sent you the case of Scotch. Now look at what's happened. We're living on the droppings from their table, and they're coining it in like they own the damned United States Mint. I hear on the street that their numbers racket is making ten times what the book's pulling in."

"Tell me about it, Gus," Fromberg said sarcastically. "Levitt's got more runners on the streets of New York than New York's got cockroaches!" He gazed pensively at his lieutenant. Landau was the one man Fromberg didn't have to worry about. Even if the bookmaking money stopped coming in, and everyone else went over to Levitt, Landau would stand by him. The scar on his cheek was testimony to his loyalty. Landau wouldn't go crawling, begging, to the people who'd put that scar there. "Tell me all about the businesses they're buying into, Gus. Tell me about how they're jacking up the price of the booze they're selling to me, and I can't go anywhere else because Levitt'll claim our agreement's void. He gives with one hand"—he picked up the bulky envelope, dropped it again—"and he takes with the other."

Landau drew his chair closer to Fromberg's desk. His icy blue eyes gleamed. "You made a mistake when you stopped me from going after them, didn't you? Saul, let's do it now while we've still got the men who can take over Levitt's operations. Let's do what we should have done years ago—wipe those bastards off the map."

Fromberg drew in a deep breath, expelled it in a long, painful sigh. He had never wanted a war. He'd thought he could win it all without firing a shot. But he'd been outsmarted, paid off to keep the peace while those doing the paying had been making themselves omnipotent. Before he lost all power, all respect, he had to fight back. It was time to turn the reins over to Landau, time to let violence have its way. "Kill Levitt," he said in an ominously quiet voice.

"Granitz as well," Landau replied. By sheer will power, he managed to keep the jubilation out of his voice. At last Fromberg had recognized the truth. Landau could take over—could get revenge. He fingered his cheek, remembering the chisel slashing across skin, the difficulty and pain of shaving which had been his heritage since that day. A long time had passed since that incident in the King Saul. Not only did Landau want his revenge, he wanted it with nine years interest, compounded daily.

"What's the big deal with Granitz?" Fromberg wanted to know. "Levitt's the head of the snake. Take him out and the others will collapse. We'll be able to pick them up whenever we want to. Or do you want Granitz because of his wife? What she did to you?"

Landau ignored the insinuation. "Other than Levitt, Granitz is the only guy there with any brains."

Fromberg felt an involuntary moment of sadness. Killing Levitt seemed such a waste, and like any good businessman Fromberg abhorred waste. He didn't care about the other three men. None of them had Levitt's abilities, not even Jake Granitz. Despite Landau's claim that Jake was dangerous, Fromberg knew that his lieutenant only wanted to pay Pearl Granitz back for disfiguring him. And what better vengeance was there than killing her husband?

"Well?" Landau prompted, impatient for an answer. While Fromberg just sat there thinking, time was running away. Too much had been wasted already.

Finally, Fromberg nodded. "All right, Levitt and Granitz."

For most of the day, Fromberg and Landau remained in the oak-paneled office. They discussed tactics, the men to use for the work, alibis for themselves. Landau's mind was especially keen that day. Long ago, he had told Fromberg that power came from the muzzle of a gun, and Fromberg had tapped his temple and replied that real power came from there—the brain. Now, Fromberg had finally come around to seeing it Landau's way. And Landau wanted to be sure there were no mistakes.

Slowly, the two men formulated their scheme. They would seek executioners outside New York. Outsiders would have a better chance of getting close to the quarry. Not only outsiders, but men from a different ethnic group entirely. If Levitt and Granitz suspected Fromberg of any duplicity, they would be on the lookout for Fromberg's men, for fellow Jews. They would not be looking for red-faced, boisterous Irishmen.

At six o'clock that evening, Fromberg placed a telephone call to Boston. Fifteen minutes later, Landau was making arrangements to take a train to that New England city to discuss a business deal with an Irish bootlegger named Patrick Joseph Rourke.

Unlike Saul Fromberg, and Lou Levitt and his three partners, Patrick Joseph Rourke kept his illegal interests concerned solely with the importation and distribution of alcohol. He had never been involved in what he considered run-of-the-mill criminal enterprises such as gambling, loansharking, and prostitution. Rourke viewed such activities with contempt; they were beneath his dignity. Even his entry into bootlegging had not occurred because he possessed a criminal mentality. It had been simply a natural progression.

Rourke's family had been brewers in New England since emigrating from Dublin in the 1870s. The moment Prohibition had come into force, their two breweries in the Boston area had been boarded up. After that, beer had been made behind closed doors. Rourke himself, far more ambitious than the rest of his family, had taken three of the brewery's trucks and made the short trip north to Canada, returning with a load of Canadian whiskey for which he'd had no trouble finding customers. Later, as Levitt had done, Rourke had crossed the Atlantic. He had gone to his ancestral home, Ireland, not to look up uncles, aunts, and cousins he'd only heard about, but to approach distillers of Irish whiskey and to arrange for its shipment to the New England shore. Being Irish, if only by ancestry, Rourke deemed it right and proper that he should have a corner on the Irish whiskey market. He also had an interest in everything that moved through New England. Other gangs that used his territory to bring liquor down from Canada paid a premium for safe passage.

Rourke's refusal to enter wholeheartedly into the underworld was not a decision based on his own saintliness. It was prompted by concern for his three sons. He did not want them branded as the sons of a criminal. There was no such stigma attached to bootlegging. Men who quenched the nation's thirst would eventually go down in history as folk heroes. A relationship to a folk hero would not harm his sons' futures, and Patrick Joseph Rourke was very anxious about those futures. He had grandiose ambitions for his three sons.

A short man in his early forties, with thinning, sandy hair and sharp blue eyes that sparkled behind wire-rimmed glasses, Rourke resembled the popular conception of a small-town schoolteacher, a clerk, or even a country doctor. He controlled his entire operation from behind a respectable front, a rental car company which, in keeping with his Irish heritage, was called Shamrock Cars.

A Shamrock car was waiting at the station when Gus Landau stepped off the train from New York. The red-haired driver chauffeured Landau to the Shamrock depot in the center of Boston. Landau followed the man through a large service area to an untidy office, where Rourke sat waiting behind a scratched metal desk that was cluttered with repair authorizations and dispatch sheets. The only item on the desk of a personal nature was a small framed photograph of Rourke's three sons. As Landau sat down, he glanced at the photograph of the three boys. Ranging in age from ten to seventeen, they all looked alike, bushy fair hair and freckled faces. Irish kids, Landau thought disparagingly. Faces like spotty raw potatoes. There was no character, no color, no life, in such faces.

"You've made a long trip from New York," Rourke greeted his visitor. "What is it I have that you can't find in your own back yard?"

"An accommodation. We'd like you to recommend reliable men to solve a problem we have in New York."

"Why the hell can't you Jews fight your own damned battles?" Rourke smiled inwardly as he watched Landau stiffen in the chair. The Hebe wouldn't dare do a thing, not here, not in Boston. All Rourke had to do was snap his fingers and half-a-dozen mechanics from the repair shop would be in the office immediately.

Remembering where he was—what his mission was—Landau bit

back his anger. "Our own men are too well known to be able to get close."

"Close to whom?"

"Lou Levitt and his pal, Jake Granitz."

"Levitt and Granitz? I've got no quarrel with them. We do business together. They like my Irish whiskey in their clubs." Leaving Landau to ponder that, Rourke picked up the framed photograph and gazed at it as a gypsy might peer into a crystal ball. He could also tell fortunes. He knew what the lot of his three sons would be, just as he could prophesy the fortunes of the sons of men like the one sitting opposite him now. While the children of the Jews continued in the criminal empires their fathers had created, Rourke's sons would grow up to be respected pillars of the establishment. Doors that would swing wide open for them would never crack ajar for the sons of Jews.

"When Levitt and Granitz are gone," Landau said, "we'll take over their enterprises. You'll do even more business with us."

Rourke replaced the picture on the desk. He didn't care who took his whiskey, just as long as he was paid in cash on the barrel head. "Say I do agree to help you find the men who can solve your . . . your problem, what do I get out of it?"

"I'm authorized to offer you fifty thousand dollars." Getting that much out of Fromberg had been like smashing concrete with bare hands. Such a sum left Fromberg virtually helpless.

Fifty thousand dollars, Rourke mused, was the offer of a desperate man. A competent killer could be hired for five hundred dollars, a thousand tops. Human life was cheap with money so damned scarce. "That's a lot of money—" he began.

"Then we're agreed?"

"—but it's not enough by half. For me to arrange what you want—taking care of a couple of my good customers—I want a hundred thousand."

"You're a thief!" Landau hissed.

"I'm a thief?" Rourke rocked back in the chair and roared with laughter. "Then what the hell are you? A hundred thousand's the price, that's if you agree right now. Take more than a minute to think about it, and the price goes up by fifty thousand. Take five minutes to think about it, and I'll get on the horn to Lou Levitt and let him know there's a price on his head."

Landau did not know whether Rourke was making an idle threat or a sincere promise, nor could he afford to find out. He hoisted the overnight bag he'd brought from New York onto Rourke's desk, sending documents fluttering to the floor. "There's fifty thousand dollars in there, small bills. Consider it a down payment on your services. You'll get the balance when you've completed the work to our satisfaction."

Rourke's face flared a dangerous red. "Who the hell do you think you're talking to? I'm not your goddamned servant!" He glared at Landau until the scar-faced man averted his gaze. Removing the money from the bag, Rourke counted it closely. Every so often, he lifted his eyes to Landau who sat seething in the chair.

"Tell your boss he's got a deal," Rourke said at last. He turned toward the open door that led to the repair shop and yelled out a name. The red-haired driver who had brought Landau from the station entered the office. "Mr. Landau's leaving. Take him back to the station and put him on the train."

As Landau was escorted out, Rourke rose from his chair, went to a wall safe, and deposited the money. A hundred thousand dollars. Talk about grand larceny. No one was worth that much. Rourke would be able to put together the operation—make it a first-class, luxury affair with all the trimmings—for five thousand dollars at the very most. For ten thousand he was certain he could arrange a team that would be able to reach right into the White House and murder the President. And Landau's boss would be giving him ten times that much just to arrange the murder of a couple of troublesome Hebes.

Reach into the White House and murder the President . . . Rourke decided that was in bad taste. He shouldn't think of murdering presidents. One day—he returned to his desk and picked up the photograph of the three boys again—one of his sons might just fill that honorable position.

Not the son of a Jew, but the son of an Irishman. Which son would it be? he wondered as he studied the three similar faces in the picture. Would it be Patrick Junior, the oldest? Would it be Joseph? Or John, the youngest?

Rourke delegated the job to his nephew, John McMichael, the red-haired man who had collected Landau at the train station. The only son of Rourke's older sister, McMichael was accustomed to performing violent, dangerous work for his Uncle Patrick. Tall and strong, with an Irish love of adventure and excitement, he had, for the past five years, organized the security crews that protected Rourke's convoys of Irish whiskey. He had also led raiding parties to hijack convoys which passed through New England without the courtesy of first paying protection to his uncle. Rourke had no hesitation about using his sister's son to commit murder. Only his own sons concerned him. They were never to dirty their hands.

Two days after Landau's visit, McMichael and three other men he had hand-picked from the convoy crews traveled down to New York and took up residence in a vacant apartment on the East Side of Manhattan. Landau became their guide. He drove them around the city, pointing out Jake's home and Levitt's, showing both men's business concerns. After three days, McMichael and his henchmen were able to follow their targets unassisted. Half-a-dozen times they could have killed either Jake or Levitt, but they held their fire. Through Landau, Fromberg had stressed one condition: the killings were to take place on the following Thursday, between two and four in the afternoon, when both Fromberg and Landau would have unimpeachable alibis. At that time, both men would be in the company of an Internal Revenue inspector who would be auditing the books of Fromberg's legal businesses.

McMichael split his squad into two units. He and a man named Richard Keith made Levitt their target. The other two men, Henry Fallon and Gerald Kenney, stayed close to Jake. On Thursday, the day selected for the murders, the four men left their East Side apartment at eight o'clock in the morning. By eight-thirty, they were all in position—McMichael and Keith stationed opposite Levitt's apartment on Central Park West, and Fallon and Kenney pulled in close to the entrance of the apartment building on lower Fifth Avenue. Wherever their targets went that day, the two teams would follow. And between two and four that afternoon, they would kill them.

At eleven o'clock, McMichael and Keith saw Levitt come out of his apartment building, bundled up against the brisk February wind. He walked south along Central Park West and then entered a restaurant. Half an hour later, after eating a late breakfast, he returned to his apartment. The two Irishmen settled down again to continue their vigil.

Just after midday, Fallon and Kenney got their first glimpse of Jake. He came out of his building, climbed into a silver Cadillac and headed north. His would-be assassins followed him to Herald Square, where he parked the car and entered a store. Ten minutes later he came out, carrying four cartons the size of shoe boxes. Getting back into the Cadillac, he returned home. Fallon and Kenney took up their previous position and resumed their watch.

As it drew nearer to two o'clock, both sets of Boston killers began to ponder the possibility of having to kill their targets inside their homes. That prospect did not daunt McMichael and Keith. Levitt lived alone. They'd get into his apartment, use silenced guns to shoot him down. Fallon and Kenney were more concerned. According to their information, Jake Granitz's apartment was a zoo; a whole tribe lived up there, a wife and two kids. Not only that, but one of his partners, Moses Caplan, lived next door with his wife and daughter. It would be a slaughter. Fallon and Kenney sat in their car and prayed that Jake would show himself on the street again by four o'clock, the latest time appointed for his death. The two Irishmen had no personal interest in this killing. They didn't want to harm his family. Nor did they want to kill four or more people for the price of one. That wasn't good business.

"What's in the boxes?" Pearl asked when Jake returned from his shopping expedition.

"You'll see." He placed the boxes on the floor and, followed by Pearl, went into the twins' room. "You two guys want to go ice-skating over in Central Park this afternoon?"

Joseph and Leo dropped what they were doing and rushed excitedly over to their father, clinging to his legs. "You bought them ice skates?" Pearl asked. "Why four boxes?"

"There's a pair for me. And"—he gave her a wide grin—"there's a pair for you."

"Not on your life," Pearl said. "Besides, I'm not sure taking them over to Central Park's such a good idea. Leo's coming down with a cold, I think. His nose is running and his forehead's hot."

"So wrap him up warmly. He'll throw a fit if you tell him he can't go after I've said he could."

Pearl saw the wisdom of that. As long as Leo was dressed up well, what harm could it do? "I'll make lunch for us all first, good hot soup to keep us warm."

"Maybe I'll call Lou, tell him to watch out for us from his window," Jake said.

For once, Pearl forgot her fear of Levitt. "Tell him he can have the fourth pair of skates."

At one fifty-five, Fromberg was sitting in his office with Gus Landau. There was a knock on the door and the secretary ushered in the tax inspector. Fromberg had the books for his legitimate companies set out on the desk. He greeted the inspector warmly, introduced Landau, and then offered his visitor a cup of coffee which was graciously accepted. Fromberg had nothing to fear from a tax inspector. These books were immaculate. The men he feared did not work for the government, and they took him for far more than the revenuers. But not for much longer.

As he sat down, he glanced at the telephone and wondered when it would ring. When Rourke's men would call to say that they had fully earned the exorbitant sum he was paying them.

The two Irishmen parked at the base of Fifth Avenue were chewing sandwiches when Jake and his family finally emerged from the apartment building at two-thirty. Gerald Kenney jammed his half-eaten sandwich into a paper bag, grabbed a pair of field glasses, and focused on the group. "Christ Almighty! The whole mob's going ice-skating!"

Henry Fallon took the glasses. This wasn't supposed to happen. They were to wait, hope that they could get Jake alone during the allotted time; otherwise, if push came to shove, they were to break into the apartment, kill him in front of his family. Who the hell would have thought they'd all go out ice-skating? "Follow them!"

Kenney started the engine. "We don't even know where they're going. It could be a rink. It could be a park. There might be a thousand people there."

Fallon came to a decision. He reached into the back of the car and withdrew a Thompson submachine gun from beneath a blanket on the floor. "We'll hit him in the car."

"With his wife and kids?"

"Them, too." Fallon snapped in the drum magazine and chambered a round. "Whoever gets in the way."

Kenney pulled away from the curb as Jake's silver Cadillac began to head north along Fifth Avenue. In the seat beside him, Fallon flicked off the Thompson's safety.

Fifty yards ahead, Jake glanced in the rearview mirror at the twins sitting in the back seat. They were so wrapped up he could barely see their faces for woolen hats and long woolen scarves. With their thick coats and leggings, it didn't matter how many times they fell over. Like rubber balls, they'd bounce right up and carry on. "Tell your mother she's got to go skating with us."

Leo clapped his hands, but his thick woolen mittens deadened all sound. "You come with us, Mummy! You hold our hands."

"See?" Jake said. "They don't want me to hold their hands."

"They don't trust you," Pearl answered. She reached into the back of the car to wipe Leo's wet nose.

Jake laughed and again looked in the mirror at the twins. Quite abruptly, his laughter died. "Kids, stop jumping up and down for a minute, will you?"

"What's the matter?" Pearl asked, puzzled by the change in Jake's demeanor.

"Take a look behind, that black Chevy. It's been sitting on our tail since we left home. And now that I think of it, the same car followed me earlier, when I went to the store to buy the skates. Followed me there and back."

Pearl felt ice run down her back as she swung around in the seat. Thirty yards behind and slowly gaining was the black Chevrolet containing Henry Fallon and Gerald Kenney. "Two men are in it."

Jake pressed down on the gas pedal, increased his speed by five miles an hour. The Chevrolet also picked up pace, held steady for a few seconds, and then started to close the gap even more. Twenty-five yards ahead, at Twenty-third Street, was a traffic signal. Jake pressed down harder on the gas pedal, pleading with God to let the signal remain in his favor.

God never heard his prayer. The signal changed almost instantly, when Jake was still twenty yards away and moving at thirty miles an hour. He lifted his foot from the gas pedal, hesitated over the brake, jammed it back on the gas. Pearl twisted around in the seat, tried to reach the twins in the back of the Cadillac. Jake stared fixedly ahead, hands gripping the steering wheel like vises, arms locked rigid.

The Cadillac reached the intersection fifteen yards ahead of the black Chevrolet. A van crossing with the signal began to pull out. Simultaneously, a young boy ran off the sidewalk to cross the road. Jake blasted the horn, swung the heavy car right and left to whip past the boy and the van. As he cleared the intersection and neared the point where Broadway slanted across Fifth Avenue, he heard a screech of tires from behind, followed by a high-pitched scream that was suddenly cut off.

"They hit that boy!" Pearl yelled.

"Did it stop them?" Jake hated himself for such callousness—he had two young sons of his own—but right now, they and Pearl were all that mattered to him. He flashed a look at the mirror but could make out little due to the confusion at the Twenty-third Street intersection.

"They're still coming!" Pearl shouted as the Chevrolet broke free of the other traffic. The headlight on the passenger side was missing, ripped off in the collision with the boy.

"Look after the twins!" Jake snapped.

Pearl scrambled over her seat into the back of the Cadillac, threw the boys to the floor. Her last words before covering the twins with her own body were: "Jake, watch out!"

Engine racing, the Chevrolet roared up alongside. Jake glanced left, caught the vivid glimpse of a red face, the ugly snout of the Thompson poking through an open window. Without even thinking, he braked hard and threw the steering wheel to the left.

The red face of Henry Fallon opened wide in dumb surprise at

269

Jake's maneuver. The front end of the Cadillac whipped around, smashed into the Chevrolet's passenger door. Fallon felt the Thompson whisked from his grasp. The index finger of his right hand, hooked around the trigger guard, was torn clean off. Before he could cry out, could even realize that he had lost both the gun and a finger, he was sent flying across the car. Gerald Kenney's hands came off the steering wheel as he sagged under the weight of Fallon's body. The Chevrolet skidded across the width of Fifth Avenue, mounted the sidewalk on the opposite side and plowed into the front of a furniture shop. Glass shattered as the car crashed through a window. The rear end of the Chevrolet rose up, slammed down again. A booming explosion echoed across Fifth Avenue as the car's gas tank erupted. A plume of flame, a searing blast of heat, tore out from the center of the furniture display. Fallon and Kenney were incinerated in their seats.

Jake stood on the brakes. The Cadillac slewed to a halt. People came running from all directions. Jake jumped out, yanked open the back door, and looked inside. Pearl was on her knees, face white as she clutched Joseph to her. Leo was struggling on the floor. His nose was bleeding and his eyes were a steely gray, fixed open, terrified. Jake lifted him out of the car and cuddled him. "It's okay, everything's okay."

"Bad men . . . bad men . . ." Leo kept murmuring.

"They're gone now. Everything's all right."

Still holding Joseph, Pearl climbed unsteadily to her feet. She looked across the street at the Chevrolet blazing in the furniture store. "Who was it, Jake?"

"I don't know, and that's the God's honest truth. And I don't know why." He gritted his teeth to try to stop his body from shaking. His twins . . . Pearl . . . they'd almost been killed. They would be dead if he had not reacted so quickly. But why him? Who was after him? "Hold Leo for a moment," he told Pearl. He ran into a candy store, spotted a telephone in the back, dropped in a nickel, and dialed Levitt's home.

"Lou . . . get a hold of Moe and Benny right away."

"What's going on?"

"Two guys just tried to hit me in the middle of Fifth Avenue."

"On your way to the lake? Were Pearl and the twins with you?"

"Yes, we were on our way to go skating."

"Are they okay?"

"They're fine. Contact Moe and Benny, get them to take their families out of town right away. We've got friends across the river in Jersey. Tell them to take everyone there. You as well."

"Who was it, Jake?"

270

"How the hell do I know? Whoever it was, they're fried to a crisp."
He quickly explained the chase, the accident.

"We've got to learn who was behind it," Levitt said.

"Just get out of town. We can sort things out later on."

"I'll get word to the others," Levitt said, "but I'm staying."

"Why?"

"If they went after you, they'll come after me as well." Levitt was certain it would be so. If this was a move against the outfit, he would be the main target. "I'll be waiting for them."

"You're crazy, little man."

"Like a fox," Levitt said. "I'll see you in Jersey."

Before Jake could say anything else, a gloved finger pressed down the hook. He swung around to see a police sergeant standing next to him.

"I'd like to get a statement from you," the sergeant said.

At three-thirty, John McMichael and Richard Keith decided it was time to take the bull by the horns and murder Lou Levitt in his apartment. Since Levitt had returned from eating breakfast, the only movements they'd seen occurred during his two appearances at the living-room window, at two forty-five to close the drapes and ten minutes later to open them again. Framed by the living-room lights, Levitt had stood in the window for an instant, wearing a bright red silk robe.

"He's not coming out," McMichael said resignedly. "Doesn't want to make it easy for us. Okay, if the mountain doesn't want to come to Mohammed . . ." He walked from the car toward the building. Keith followed five yards behind. Instead of using the elevator, they ran up three flights of stairs to Levitt's floor. The long hallway was empty. Thick carpet muffled their steps. Outside Levitt's apartment they hesitated. McMichael pressed his ear to the door and caught the faintest strains of music. It reassured him. The radio would drown out any sounds he might make with the lockpick. Easing the pick into the lock, he jiggled it gently.

The door swung back on well-oiled hinges. The music became louder. Gripping silenced automatics, the two Irishmen entered the apartment, following the sound of music to the living room. A high-backed chair faced the window. Next to it was a table and a reading lamp. On the table was a book, pages open. In a large crystal ashtray, a cigarette had burned down to a long, white string of ash. The music Keith and McMichael had heard was coming from a highly polished radio set against the wall. From where they stood, all they could see of

271

Levitt was his left elbow resting on the arm of the chair. The remainder of his body was hidden by the chair's high back. Dressed in the same red robe they'd seen him wearing earlier at the window, Levitt was fast asleep.

McMichael could not repress a savage grin. Taking him in the apartment was the easiest way after all. Treading softly on the carpet, the two men walked to within ten feet of the high-backed chair, leveled their weapons and opened fire. Shreds of fabric flew into the air as a hail of bullets ripped through the upholstery. The elbow jumped. Like a Chinese dragon at New Year, sweeping red silk flowed from the chair. It was nothing more than an empty robe with the left sleeve stuffed to give the appearance of an arm inside.

"Put those guns down! Very slowly."

McMichael and Keith turned slowly to their left. Standing in the doorway to a bedroom was Levitt, a short, brutal-looking sawed-off shotgun gripped tightly in both hands. Its twin barrels pointed unwaveringly at a spot midway between the two Irishmen.

"Put the guns down, I said. Your two pals, who tried to kill Jake Granitz, are already dead. Burned alive in their car. Whether you join them in the next few seconds is up to you."

Two automatics dropped to the carpet. Levitt ordered the men to move back to the wall, drop down onto their knees, and clasp their hands behind their heads. Holding the shotgun in one hand, he picked up the pistols and ejected the magazines. One was completely empty; the other contained one live round. His would-be assassins had shot an empty chair and a red silk robe more than a dozen times.

"Who sent you?"

Licking his lips, McMichael gazed uneasily at the shotgun.

"I'm not going to kill you. I just want to know who sent you, and then I'm going to use you to take a message back to him." The last thing Levitt wanted was blood shed in his own home. The silenced shots his two assailants had fired would not have been heard outside the apartment. Any damage could be easily repaired. Levitt's neighbors considered him a respectable businessman. He wanted nothing to happen that might change those opinions.

"Scar-faced guy," McMichael eventually answered. It was no skin off his nose what the Jews did to each other. "Scar-faced guy, name of Landau."

"That's what I figured. You and your pals had orders to hit me and Jake Granitz on the same day, right?"

"Between two o'clock and four o'clock."

"Why that time spread?"

"So Landau and his boss would have an alibi. They're with a tax

272

inspector, being audited."

Levitt smiled grimly. Nice alibi. "What deal did you work with Landau? How were you going to let him know you'd done the job?"

"We were to call him. I've got the number here on a piece of paper." He nodded toward his coat pocket. Levitt told him to take it out with two fingers. McMichael dropped a scrap of paper onto the floor and Levitt stepped forward to look at the number. He recognized it—Fromberg's place on Forty-second Street.

"Call him now. Call Landau and tell him you've done your job. Tell him everything went off okay, you understand me?"

"What if he asks about the others?"

"Your pals who fried? Them, too. They did what they were supposed to do. They got Jake Granitz."

While Keith remained kneeling on the floor with his hands clasped behind his head, McMichael made the telephone call to Fromberg's office. Levitt watched like a hawk while the Irishman waited for the telephone to be answered. . . .

Saul Fromberg resisted an impulse to snatch the earpiece from its hook the moment he heard the first ring. The tax inspector was still in the office, studying the accounts of a restaurant Fromberg owned on Seventh Avenue. Fromberg wanted to do nothing that might lodge in the man's memory—like show he was waiting for a certain call.

After the third ring, Fromberg said to the inspector, "Would you excuse me for a moment?" He answered the call, listened for a few seconds. "Gus, it's for you." Handing the set to Landau, Fromberg returned to the inspector's side. His eyes were on the accounts, but every nerve of his body was straining to hear what Landau said.

"This is Landau . . . good to hear from you! What's that? You've completed the assignment, and well within the contract time! Great! And your associates?" Fromberg felt himself starting to sweat. He could only guess what was being said by Landau's reactions. Had the Irishmen got them both?

"Marvelous!" Landau exclaimed, and Fromberg heaved a sigh of relief. "Give them my congratulations, and rest assured that the remainder of the payment will be forthcoming. Be speaking to you . . ." Landau replaced the earpiece on the hook and turned to Fromberg. There was no need for words. Landau's icy smile spoke volumes. . . .

As McMichael completed the call, Levitt stepped back and

motioned for the red-haired man to join his colleague against the wall. Levitt knew who was behind the plot. Now he wanted to learn who had been allied with Fromberg and Landau. "Throw your wallets on the floor."

McMichael and Keith did as they were ordered. Levitt picked up the wallets, scattered the contents onto the carpet. He spotted train tickets. Boston. Satisfied, he kicked the wallets back toward their owners. "Beat it, the pair of you. If I see either of you again in New York, I'll kill you."

The two men grabbed their wallets and ran toward the apartment door. Levitt watched them race along the hallway, down the stairs. Less than a minute later, through the living-room window, he saw them crossing the street. After noting the license number of the car they jumped into, he telephoned the closest precinct house and as a concerned citizen reported that he had just witnessed two men break into an automobile and steal it. That would keep those two busy for a while, stop them from double-crossing him by calling up Gus Landau with a true report.

Before that happened, Levitt wanted to be certain that his partners were all right. Not just Jake, but Caplan and Minsky as well. Yes, even Minsky. He'd contacted Caplan and Minsky earlier, immediately after Jake's urgent call, and had told them to take their families over to New Jersey. Levitt didn't want to leave anyone exposed to Fromberg's wrath when he learned that he'd been duped. The four partners might argue among themselves, but when faced with an outside threat they closed ranks. United, they could not be defeated.

He telephoned Jake's home. There was no answer. Nodding in satisfaction, he dialed Caplan's number. Again, the telephone rang on. He tried Minsky. A woman answered, identified herself as Miss Wickham the housekeeper. She told Levitt that Minsky had taken Kathleen and William from the apartment, and she did not know when they would return. Lastly, Levitt dialed the number of the Resnick restaurant. He caught Jake there.

"I'm just picking up my mother-in-law," Jake said. "We're leaving for Jersey in a few seconds."

"Why are you still there?" Levitt asked angrily. By putting himself at risk, Jake was also placing Pearl and the twins in danger. "You called me almost an hour ago."

"I had to get rid of the cops. They were swarming all over that accident like flies on shit. They wanted a statement."

"Okay, okay. Just get everyone out of the city."

"Wait . . . did anything happen with you?"

"They tried for me as well. Two of Rourke's Boston Irishmen."

Quickly, Levitt explained what had happened, the attempt on his life, McMichael's telephone call to Gus Landau. "All I can figure is that Fromberg's in a bad way, desperate enough to want us knocked off."

"So he can grab our businesses?"

"Has to be." Levitt glanced at his watch. "We'll talk about it when we get to Jersey. Just get Pearl and the twins over there now, that's the important thing."

"Okay, see you there."

Levitt hung up, looked around the apartment to see what he would need during his enforced absence. Five minutes later, lugging a hastily packed suitcase, he left the building. The crisis he had always wanted to avoid was now upon him. By paying Fromberg off, Levitt had hoped to neutralize him, buy enough time to topple the man.

For some reason, time had run out.

The tax inspector finally left Fromberg's office at four-fifteen. The moment he had gone, Fromberg opened his desk drawer, brought out a bottle of whiskey, and poured generous measures for himself and Landau.

"To Rourke," Fromberg said, raising his glass. "A fine Irishman."

"A fine, expensive Irishman," Landau rejoined.

"Maybe, but worth every damned cent. Once we move into Levitt's places, take over his book and his numbers racket, pick up his booze business, that hundred grand'll seem like peanuts."

Landau ran a finger across his scar. The debt was paid. The little girl who'd given him that was now a widow.

The telephone rang. Landau reached out for it. The caller was John McMichael again. Police had pulled him and Richard Keith over within three minutes of Levitt's stolen-car report. It had taken the police a further twenty minutes to determine that the call had been a hoax, that they were holding innocent men. Now the two Irishmen were at the railroad station, ready to board a train home to Boston. Before they left, McMichael told Landau the truth.

Landau's face turned a sickly shade of gray as he listened to McMichael's words. "What's the matter with you?" Fromberg demanded as he watched the glass of whiskey fall from Landau's fingers onto the floor.

Landau gestured toward the telephone. "They didn't do a damned thing. The guy who called earlier made the call because Levitt had a shotgun jammed in his ear. The two guys who tried to kill Granitz were burned to death in an automobile accident."

Fromberg clutched at the corner of the desk, his legs weak, heart hammering. "Find them!" he yelled at Landau. "Find them all! Levitt! Granitz! Caplan! Minsky! Find them and kill them! Do what those stupid Irish bastards couldn't do!"

Landau fled from the office, took three men, and went to Jake's home. They kicked in the door to find the apartment empty. The adjacent apartment belonging to the Caplans was also unoccupied. Simultaneously, other men stormed the homes of Levitt and Minsky. Only at Riverside Drive did they find anyone. When they smashed their way in there, Florence Wickham stood her ground.

"What do you think you're doing?"

They bound and gagged her, then searched the apartment. After they'd gone, the housekeeper wriggled free and called the police.

Landau's final raid was mounted on the restaurant on Second Avenue. Pasted across the door was a notice: Closed until further notice. There was no one in the restaurant or the flat upstairs. Like all the other places, it bore the signs of a hurried departure.

When Landau returned to Fromberg's office, the two men knew that their roles were in transition. Their quarries had escaped. Now they would have to take precautions, or else the hunters might become the hunted.

Chapter Four

While Gus Landau's crews were kicking down the doors of empty apartments, the men they sought were already on the other side of the Hudson River, assembled with their families in a heavily guarded house in Fort Lee. Situated at the bottom of a cul-de-sac, and surrounded by tall hedges, the house was owned by a businessman named Harry Saltzman whose enterprises included a string of gambling clubs and roadhouses along the Jersey Palisades, all supplied with liquor by Lou Levitt and his partners.

Jake and Pearl, with the twins and Sophie Resnick, were the last to arrive. As they reached the end of the cul-de-sac, their way was blocked by a large, wrought-iron gate. A man appeared, inspected the inside of the car and swung the gate back. He didn't quite manage to hide the shotgun behind his back.

"That man's got a gun!" Joseph called out excitedly from the back seat. He turned to his twin brother and pointed out of the window. "Look, that man's got a gun!"

Leo, sitting on Sophie's lap, seemed disinterested. The nosebleed he'd suffered during the incident on Fifth Avenue had stopped, but his face was flushed, his breathing heavy. The cold that Pearl had worried about was becoming worse by the minute.

"He's got a gun because he's a policeman," Jake said as he drove through the gate, along a wide, circular driveway, and pulled to a halt behind Levitt's car.

"Some policeman," Pearl murmured. Jake gave her a sharp glance. He didn't want the twins to know what was happening, that they were all fleeing because someone wanted their father dead. That would give the boys nightmares. Right now they thought they were going on a special trip, a vacation. It was bad enough that Sophie Resnick knew the truth. Jake had been forced to tell her after he'd turned up at the restaurant with Pearl and the twins, and had brusquely ordered all the customers to leave.

"What do you think you're doing?" Sophie had demanded angrily after Jake had locked the door behind the last surprised diner.

"Throw some clothes in a suitcase. You're taking a break."

"Why?"

"Don't ask questions," Pearl said sharply. "We'll tell you everything in the car."

Sophie had never seen her daughter so agitated. She was holding the twins tightly by the hand, and when Joseph started edging toward the counter where the cakes were on display, she pulled him back roughly and slapped him. He squealed, half in pain, half in shock at the rough treatment. It was then that Sophie realized this was an emergency, so she just did whatever Jake told her to do.

In the car, Pearl told her mother about the attempt on Jake's life—on all their lives—as they had driven toward Central Park. Instead of speaking English which the twins would understand, she spoke in Yiddish.

"It's that pig Fromberg?" Sophie asked.

"No one else. Him and that animal who always followed him around."

Sophie shivered. "That time you hit him with the chisel, you should have stuck it in his throat, not in his face."

"Too late for that now," Pearl said.

"There'll be a second chance," Jake muttered grimly.

"How long will this last?" Pearl asked Jake as he opened the car door.

"As long as it takes us to get to Fromberg." There was no point in pretending it could be any other way. "It could be a day, it could be a week. Why? Are you in a hurry to go somewhere?"

Pearl flicked her eyes toward the back of the car. "I don't like the look of Leo."

"He's coming down with a cold, that's all—cook him some chicken soup, that'll keep you busy." He grinned at her and she smiled back.

Pearl was the first to enter the house. As she walked through the door, Annie rushed forward and kissed her. "This is even better than being neighbors!"

"Until we get fed up with being in each other's pockets."

Annie shook her head. "This place is more than big enough for all of us. There are four bedrooms upstairs, and there's a beautifully finished basement. Moe and I were the first ones here so I worked everything out." To Pearl's amusement, Annie produced a sheet of paper on which she'd written a breakdown of sleeping accommodations. "You, Jake, and the twins can have the basement. Moe and I'll take one of the bedrooms with Judy. Benny, Kathleen, and William can take another. Lou can have the third, and your mother can have the fourth room. How's that?"

"And where's the man who lives here going to sleep? In a tent on the front lawn?"

"Harry lives in New York," Jake answered. "Got a fancy apartment in the Waldorf Towers."

"Then why does he own this house?"

"He owns a lot of houses. He dabbles in real estate."

Pearl knew she had to be satisfied with that. Taking the list from Annie, she perused it quickly. "This is all a big game to you, isn't it, Annie?"

Annie nodded excitedly. "It's like a big party, all of us together."

"It's no party, Annie. We're not here for a vacation. We're here because Saul Fromberg just tried to kill Jake and Lou. Your Moe would have been the next one on the list." She was gratified to see some of the thrill disappear from Annie's eyes. "You remember me telling you I was worried that the boys were getting too big? Now you know why I was so worried."

She took the twins down to the basement, making her own plans as she looked around. She found a room with two single beds that the twins could use. On the floor of another room—a den, she supposed—was a large, brand-new mattress, with pillows, sheets, and blankets piled neatly on top. There was even a full bathroom and a narrow kitchen in the basement. It occurred to Pearl that this Harry Saltzman owned the house for the very reason they now needed it—it was a hideout for friends on the run.

By early evening, walls separated the occupants of the house. The four men—Jake, Levitt, Minsky, and Caplan—stayed clustered in the front downstairs room. The women were shut off completely. Pearl and Sophie busied themselves preparing a makeshift dinner for everyone—there was a fully stocked larder and icebox—and after that they sat with Kathleen and Annie. Even the children remained in a group, playing together in one of the bedrooms; all except Leo who, by the time evening set in, was in bed after complaining about a sore throat and headache.

The children were fed first and sent to bed soon after. Rather than place Joseph in the same room with Leo and risk the older twin's catching the cold, Pearl sent him upstairs to sleep in Sophie's bed. The older woman didn't mind such company. Leo would have to be kept away from the others until his cold improved. Poor kid, Pearl thought as she went down to the basement to see him. He was fast asleep, breathing heavily through his mouth.

At eight o'clock, the men emerged from their meeting and the adults sat down to dinner. It was a haphazard affair, everyone lining up in the kitchen to be served, some sitting at the dining-room table, others balancing plates on the arms of chairs or on their knees.

"You and your mother are performing miracles," Jake told Pearl after she'd filled his plate with sausages, fried onions, and mashed potatoes.

"This is slipshod. Wait until tomorrow, when we have the time to prepare a proper meal."

Sophie served herself last. As she carried her own plate to an armchair, she asked cheerfully, "Everyone happy? No complaints?"

"Not if you don't mind eating pig swill," Kathleen answered. "My dogs get better food than this."

Sophie ignored the comment, but Minsky didn't. "Be glad you're over here right now. Otherwise you'd be dog's meat yourself."

"Why should I be over here?" she shot back. "I've done nothing to be frightened of. Seems to me that if *you people* want to kill each other, why should it make my life a misery?"

Lou Levitt glanced up sharply from his plate. "Why don't you shut the hell up, Kathleen?"

The blond woman lowered her head. She had just heard more menace in Levitt's voice than she'd ever detected in Minsky's, even in the instances when he'd threatened to kill her. Pearl glanced at Levitt. His face was pale, his bright blue eyes, now tiny luminous buttons, were fixed on Kathleen. She saw loathing in them, and she remembered all the comments Levitt had made about Minsky's *shikse*. He really did hate the singer. It seemed as if he had been waiting all along for this one reference to their being Jewish and her being different.

Annie piped up. "I found some cards when I was looking around before. Why don't we play afterward?"

"We're busy," Caplan muttered, and Annie's forced, happy grin dropped from her face.

"My mother and I'll play," Pearl said, "after we get through cleaning up."

"Why don't you help them?" Minsky asked Kathleen. "You're sitting on your ass eating the food they make. The least you can do is give them a hand cleaning up."

"We can manage," Pearl said quickly, eager to gloss over the awkward moment. "Didn't you ever hear the story about too many cooks spoiling the broth?"

"She'll spoil it all right," Minsky replied. "She cooks like she's a first cousin to the Borgias."

Kathleen pushed aside her plate and stood up. "Go to hell, Benny! It's bad enough I've got to be in this zoo without putting up with your crap!" She stormed out of the room and slammed the door behind her. Jake caught Pearl's eye and inclined his head in the direction Kathleen had taken, so she followed Minsky's wife into the front room which the men had used for their meeting.

"What do you want?" Kathleen snapped. "Can't you see I want to be alone?"

Faced with Kathleen's sharpness, Pearl lost her own temper. "Kathleen, instead of moaning about why you're here, why don't you realize how damned lucky you are?"

"Lucky? How?"

"Lucky that Benny cared enough about you to take you out of danger. Lucky that you're not still a hatcheck girl, or even a manicurist in some barbershop, cleaning some guy's fingers that he's been sticking up his nose! You've been nothing but a pain in the neck from the moment Benny dragged you into the Four Aces. Why don't you show a little gratitude for a change? Be thankful that Benny cares enough about you to bring you here!"

"He doesn't care a damn about me! All he cares about is that"— Kathleen pointed up at the ceiling—"that kid up there."

"Don't you?" Even as she asked the question, Pearl knew what the answer would be.

"Sure I do," Kathleen replied sarcastically. "He took me off the stage in the middle of a hit show. I care about him, all right. The only reason I went through with that pregnancy was because Benny stuck a gun to my head and swore he'd blow my brains out if I didn't. Did Jake do that to you when you were pregnant with the twins? Did Moe do it to Annie?"

Pearl knew she should have been shocked, but she wasn't. Nothing Minsky did surprised her. Remembering Kathleen's stay in the hospital after she'd tried to miscarry, Pearl could even feel some sympathy for him. "Kathleen, you've taken everything Benny and the rest of us have given to you. That's right . . . *us people,* what we've given to you! How about giving something back once in a while?"

"You've given me nothing. I could have gotten on without any help. . . ." Kathleen's voice trailed away. There was no longer any conviction in her claim. Tears brimmed in her eyes. "Pearl, he doesn't give a damn about me. I could leave and he wouldn't even notice that there was an empty space where I'd been standing. When I had William, I gave Benny someone else to love and he forgot all about me."

"That's because you're so selfish. You only think about yourself and no one else. No matter how much he loved you, that would wear thin eventually. Just think about that for a while." Pearl left Kathleen alone in the room and went back to the others.

Kathleen returned five minutes later, her face dry and composed. Without saying a word, she went from place to place and collected the dirty plates. Minsky and Levitt watched her expressionlessly, while Jake gave Pearl a tiny, congratulatory smile. Maybe under that self-centered exterior was a warm, loving woman after all.

Harry Saltzman, the owner of the house, arrived at eleven o'clock that night, and the men locked themselves away in the front room again.

"Word's out on the street already that you four guys have taken it on the lam," Saltzman said in a slow bass voice. "You leave it that way for a couple of weeks, and the word's going to be gospel. You'll lose everything."

"We've got men guarding the businesses," Levitt pointed out.

"Means nothing. Fromberg won't have to attack your joints. He'll just sit back and let you destroy yourselves by staying hidden. Every day you stay here, Fromberg gets stronger. He's hanging out a sign that reads business as usual, and you are in hiding. Word'll get around that you're scared to show yourselves."

"We know what we've got to do," Caplan said. "The tricky part is how. How do we get rid of him and Landau?"

"Storm their offices on East Forty-second Street." Saltzman made it sound like the simplest thing in the world.

"You got a couple of howitzers we can use, Harry?" Jake asked with a smile. "Because that's what we'd need to get into that place. A dozen bodyguards on one side, steel walls on the other. No one storms that office. No one gets in without an appointment."

Saltzman tilted back his chair and left the method of operation to the others. A man who was fully aware of his limitations, he understood that intricate planning wasn't his strong suit. Brute force was. Tall and muscular, Saltzman was not a man to be easily forgotten. Dark brown eyes smoldered in a square, swarthy face, and black hair, parted low on the left side, dropped down across his forehead to disguise an abnormally low hairline. That low hairline had been the bane of Saltzman's childhood in Jersey City. A poor scholar, he'd been the butt of jokes made by teachers and pupils alike. Simian Saltzman, they'd called him—the missing link. When he'd been fifteen, one teacher too many had used the hated nickname. Saltzman had responded by beating the teacher senseless in front of a class too terrified to intervene.

For the assault, Saltzman had been sentenced to eighteen months in the reformatory. On his release, he'd joined a Jersey City mob, the Hudson Street Gang, which operated around the docks. By the time he'd turned twenty, he was heading it, using a sly cunning that had not served him well at school. It was appropriate for the tough dock areas of Jersey City. He guided the gang from warehouse robberies and extortion into the more lucrative business of loansharking—moving money around the docks, often trading repayments for information on valuable cargoes that could be rifled. Profits were invested in roadhouses along the Jersey Palisades. Simultaneously, Saltzman became intrigued by the power he could wield through control of unions. Using money and muscle, he rigged elections on both sides of the Hudson. Now, nearing thirty, he was in a position to call the downing of tools at a butcher's local, a strike at the docks in Jersey City, or a walkout that would paralyze half the garment district in New York. . . .

While Jake, Caplan, and Minsky batted around suggestions on how to reach Fromberg, Levitt sat quietly, eyes half-closed. He heard what was going on around him, but he paid little attention. He didn't expect his partners to come up with the solution. It would be left to him to provide the master stroke, just as it always was. Suddenly, he clapped his hands together. "Harry's right," he pronounced. "We do get Fromberg in his office."

Jake turned to stare incredulously. "Didn't you hear what I said? A dozen bodyguards—"

"Yes, I heard you. And that's why it's the last place Fromberg would expect trouble. Listen . . . those Irishmen today, they had to do their work between two and four this afternoon. You know why? Because between two and four, Fromberg and Landau were meeting with a tax inspector, having the books audited. So we send up tax inspectors again, and they'll do a spot check like it's never been done before." Without waiting for his partners' approval, Levitt turned to Saltzman. "Harry, find me three guys, and they've got to look like the biggest *goyim* you ever laid eyes on. I want archetypal gentiles."

Saltzman straightened his chair. "No problem."

"Make them smart guys as well, a little brains, okay?" Levitt said, tapping his head. "Uncle Sam doesn't hire idiots to collect his taxes, remember that."

When the meeting finished ten minutes later, Jake went down to the basement to find Pearl already asleep on the mattress on the floor. He undressed and snuggled in beside her. She awoke at his movement.

"What happened upstairs?"

"It's all been taken care of. A week at the very most and we'll be out of here. How's Leo?"

"He woke up before. I gave him a glass of warm milk and he went back to sleep. He had difficulty swallowing, though."

He put his arms around her, needing the familiar feel of her body to compensate for the strangeness of the house. "What did you tell Kathleen before?"

"That she was a selfish bitch, and that if it wasn't for Benny and the rest of us, she'd still be clipping nails."

"Good for you. No wonder she came back and did the dishes. I never knew you were such a diplomat. Maybe we should turn you loose on Fromberg. You could talk him into retiring, moving down to Miami."

Jake was joking, but when Pearl answered, her voice was deadly serious. "With that man the time for talking's long past. I told you he couldn't be dealt with like any other man. You should have killed him before—for what he did to my father, to my mother, and for what he tried to do to you, to all of us today." She paused. "Anyone who hurts my family, Jake, I want to see him dead."

Jake held her even tighter. He had no desire for sex; he just wanted the warmth of her closeness. "You know something? I look at Kathleen and I look at Annie—one's selfish, and the other one's a scatterbrain who thinks this is all a big adventure—and I realize that I married the only normal one."

"Would you ever have been interested in Annie?"

"No. She was too forward that day in the janitor's shed. She stuck her face out too quickly to be kissed."

"And I ran away."

"Running's the wisest course sometimes," Jake told her. As long as you don't keep on running, he added silently. He fell asleep thinking of Levitt's idea. Tax inspectors, Jersey boys who looked like *goyim*. Fromberg was out of his league when he pitted his wits against Levitt's. . . .

The sound of Leo's crying woke both Pearl and Jake at seven-thirty the following morning. Pearl ran into Leo's room. "What's the matter?"

"It hurts. It hurts." The child pointed to his head and then to his throat. "It hurts, Mummy." His voice was so hoarse that Pearl could barely understand him. Tears were spilling down his cheeks, and his hand was shaking. Pearl placed the flat of her hand on his forehead; it was burning.

"Jake, he's worse. I don't think it's just a cold."

"What do you mean?" Jake rushed forward to feel Leo's forehead.

Above, he could hear the sound of running feet as the other children got an early start on the day's games. "Christ, he's on fire. I'm going to find him a doctor." He took the basement stairs two at a time and exploded out into the hallway, almost tripping over Joseph who was playing tag with Judy Caplan. He ran through the house looking for Levitt, eventually finding him in the kitchen, pouring coffee from a pot Sophie had made.

"Lou, I've got to go out, find a doctor for Leo."

Levitt put down the cup. "What's the matter with him?"

"He's sick, burning up with fever."

"You stay where you are. You can't go out."

"What do you mean I can't go out? That's my son down there."

"You think Fromberg hasn't got men looking for you and me this side of the Hudson?" Levitt asked. "He knows we've got friends over here, he'll be looking. You step out into the open and you'll come back full of holes."

"What am I supposed to do then—let Leo lie there getting sicker by the minute?"

"Let me see him." Followed by Jake, Levitt ran down to the basement. Pearl was still bent over Leo, bathing his forehead with a cool, damp cloth. "What do you think it is?" he asked.

"Just a cold, I thought. But now—maybe influenza."

"Lou's trying to tell me I can't go for a doctor," Jake said.

Levitt raised his hands in exasperation. "Use your brains. Harry'll be here in half an hour. He'll find a doctor. He must know someone locally. That'll be quicker than you running around panic-stricken in a strange town. You think I don't want help for Leo? Just remember, that's my godson lying there."

Saltzman arrived just after eight o'clock to find Jake and Levitt waiting outside the house. He mistook their presence for enthusiasm. "Your three tax inspectors'll be along in a couple of hours."

"Never mind that now," Levitt answered. "One of Pearl's kids needs a doctor in a hurry."

"What's the matter with him?"

"Sick, running a temperature, headache, sore throat."

"Let me see him." Saltzman headed downstairs, went to Pearl who was sitting by Leo's bed. With a gentleness that seemed contradictory in such a big, violent man, he rested a hand on Leo's head. Pearl noticed that his fingernails were tiny, embedded in flesh and highly lacquered. Saltzman whistled softly. "I'll be back with a doctor in half an hour. Don't let anyone else down here. We don't want whatever the kid's got being passed around."

Jake and Levitt watched through a window as Saltzman beckoned to one of the men guarding the house. The man climbed into a car with him and it headed down the circular drive toward the wrought-iron gate. Twenty-five minutes later they were back. A third man was in the car, a scarf wrapped around his eyes. Saltzman guided him into the house, removed the blindfold, and handed him a black bag. "Here's your doctor."

The doctor, a man in his late fifties with stringy gray hair, stood blinking in the sudden onslaught of light. Jake gripped his arm and led him down to the basement. Levitt followed, closing the basement door to cut off any noise from the rest of the house.

Leo was lying in the same position he'd been in when Jake had last seen him. Only now his breathing was much worse. It was forced and strained, each breath wheezing in and out of his lungs as if he were an old man. The doctor sat on the edge of the bed. While Pearl, Jake, and Levitt watched anxiously, he took Leo's temperature, peered into his open mouth.

After a minute, the doctor swung around from his patient and glared at the three observers. "What is this child doing here? He needs to be in a hospital. He's suffering from diphtheria."

"Diphtheria?" Pearl repeated numbly.

"Yes. He should be in a hospital for treatment, and to keep him away from the other children I saw in this house. Otherwise they'll catch it from him. Show me to a telephone. I'll make the necessary arrangements."

Levitt forced words from his mouth. "He can't go into a hospital. He can't leave here."

Pearl exploded, all her worry about Leo turned into fury at Levitt. "Didn't you just hear what the doctor said? Leo's got diphtheria!"

Levitt stood his ground, his face composed like a chunk of granite. "He's not leaving this house, Pearl. None of us is."

"I don't believe this!" Pearl burst out. "What the hell is more important—Leo's health, or you hiding out from Saul Fromberg?"

"Pearl!" Jake grabbed hold of her with one hand, used the other to gesture excitedly at the doctor. "Why don't you give him our names as well? Give him Fromberg's telephone number so he can call him the moment he leaves here?"

Stunned, they all turned to gaze at the doctor. For the moment, Leo was completely forgotten. "I don't know who you are," said the doctor, "and I couldn't care less what you're all doing in this house. I don't even know where this house is. Your heavyset friend upstairs walked into my home in Washington Heights with a hundred dollars in one hand and a gun in the other. I decided it would be prudent to accept the hundred dollars. I was blindfolded the moment I climbed into his car." He looked from one to the other. "Your business isn't my concern. All I care about is this child."

Jake's face burned with shame. Didn't *he* care about his own son? Of course a hospital was the best place for Leo, but he knew that he also had to balance Leo's welfare against the good of everyone, and that included Pearl and Joseph. Fromberg was not without contacts. If he somehow learned that Leo was in a hospital, he might get a lead on everyone. Jake loathed himself for what he had to say next, but he had little choice. "Doc, could my son be cared for in this house?"

The doctor considered the question carefully. "It would depend on the severity of the illness. I could supply drugs, a serum to fight the infection. He would have to be quarantined, kept down here. Someone would have to remain with him for the entire time— someone who would not mix with the other people in this house."

"Pearl . . ." Jake looked expectantly at his wife. She stared back at him, torn between worry over the younger twin's welfare and loyalty to her husband.

"Pearl"—it was Levitt's turn—"you can do as much for Leo as any hospital can."

She glanced at Leo lying on the bed, face flushed, breathing tortuous. And she thought about Joseph playing upstairs with the other children. Thank God she'd had the foresight to separate the twins the night before. If it wasn't too late already! . . . "Could I care for him?" she asked the doctor.

"You're the child's mother, aren't you? If your husband and his . . . his companion are so set against the boy being admitted to a hospital, a mother is probably the best substitute. But I must warn you—if his condition worsens, he could die without an operation. There is a membrane—skin—partially covering his throat. If it grows, the boy will need a tracheotomy to allow him to breathe. That could not be performed here."

"But if his condition doesn't worsen?"

"Then, with my advice, you might be able to care for him."

Pearl straightened her back; her chin jutted out a fraction of an inch. "I'll look after him down here. This basement will become a quarantine area. I can cook—"

"I doubt very much if the boy will be able to eat or drink for quite a while. He'll have tremendous difficulty in swallowing." Gradually, the doctor felt a sense of admiration building in him for the tiny woman who seemed so determined to care for her child. He didn't even begin to understand the situation that had caused all these people to be locked away in this house; he didn't want to understand it. His only concern was the child. "The next forty-eight to seventy-two hours will be the most critical. Either the fever will break in that time, or we'll know for certain that he has to be admitted to a hospital."

"If we need you, you'll come?" Jake asked quietly.

"I'll come. The men who brought me here just now—when they return me to Washington Heights, I'll send back the serum with them. Will you be able to handle a syringe?" he asked Pearl.

"I'll manage."

"You can give the boy aspirin as well, if he can manage to swallow it."

Levitt dug into his pocket, pulled out a roll of bills, and counted off two hundred and fifty dollars. "Take this as a retainer—and to keep your mouth shut."

The doctor accepted the money. While Jake and Levitt took him upstairs to be blindfolded for the trip back across the George Washington Bridge, Pearl remained with Leo. She sat on the bed, cradling her son in her arms, rocking him gently. At first, he cried, as though the easy movement put more strain on his body, but slowly his tears ceased. He closed his eyes and fell asleep. Pearl looked down and smiled tenderly. She'd been furious with Levitt—and with Jake—for not allowing hospital treatment, but now she started to see their refusal in a different light. What could any hospital, any impersonal medical staff do, that a loving mother could not?

Holding Leo in her arms, she considered the other people in the house, made plans for them. Joseph would have to continue sleeping upstairs with his grandmother. He would not be allowed into the basement; none of the children would, nor could the adults come down. Not even Jake.

Diphtheria! Pearl shuddered. Why, on top of everything else that was happening, did Leo have to contract such a terrible sickness? Then, as a warm, comforting thought enveloped her, she smiled weakly. Was it such a terrible sickness? or was it something else entirely—an example of God moving in strange and mysterious ways? Was this God's way of protecting her from the shock of all that was happening? The attack on Fifth Avenue, the hiding out. Was He giving her so much work that she would forget how close she, Jake, and the twins had come to death?

Viewed that way, Leo's illness was not so terrible.

Shortly after the doctor left for the return trip to New York, Jake and Levitt sat down with Joseph. "Your twin brother has a bad illness that you might catch if you go near him," Jake said. "You can't see him or play with him. You've got to stay up here until he's better."

"What about Mummy?"

"She's staying downstairs with Leo. She has to look after him all the time."

"She won't be with me?"

"She can't be with you, Joseph. She has to be with Leo."

Levitt touched Jake's arm, indicated that he wanted to say something. He had noticed Joseph's brown eyes cloud over at the dreadful possibility that his mother cared for Leo more than she cared for him. "Your mother loves you every bit as much as she loves Leo," Levitt said. "That's why she doesn't want you to go downstairs until Leo's better. She doesn't want you to be ill as well."

Joseph pursed his lips in childish thought. At last, he nodded somberly. "She doesn't want me to be sick like Leo?"

"That's right, because she loves you." Levitt patted the boy on the head.

Leaving Joseph with Levitt, Jake went to the top of the basement stairs and called Pearl's name softly. She came to the bottom and looked up. "Lou and I just told Joseph that he wouldn't be able to see you or Leo for a while. He took it well."

"Good." That was one problem out of the way. "When Harry gets back with the medicine from the doctor, let me have it straightaway."

"Of course."

Saltzman returned an hour later with a package from the doctor. It contained two syringes, serum, and detailed instructions. Jake waited at the top of the stairs while Pearl administered the serum.

"Everything go all right?" he asked when she reappeared.

"I followed the instructions. Maybe this'll put me in good standing if I ever decide to become a nurse." The humor she was trying so desperately to project was strained.

Jake squatted on the top step. "What about you? Will you be able to make it?"

"I'll have to, won't I?"

"Pearl, if Leo—God forbid—gets worse . . . Damn Lou, damn everyone! We'll take him straight to a hospital."

"He won't get worse," Pearl said.

Jake hoped he could believe her. "Is there anything else you need? I can leave it on the stairs for you."

"I've got everything I need for the time being. What about you? Where will you sleep?"

"On a couch in the living room."

"Poor Jake, it's much too small for you."

Jake was touched by the concern in her voice. "I'll manage."

Hearing footsteps, he turned around. Levitt stood behind him.

"Harry's three tax inspectors have just arrived. Let's go do some work."

Pearl watched the basement door close. She walked into the room where Leo lay, stood over the bed for five minutes staring down at her son. His breathing was rough, his lungs were laboring, his forehead still burned. Very gently, so as not to wake him, Pearl laid a damp towel across his brow. Simultaneously, she offered up a silent prayer for his recovery.

The three men chosen by Harry Saltzman were all in their late thirties. The leader was a man named Jerry Greenblatt, who was one of the original members of Saltzman's Hudson Street Gang. All three men lacked stereotypical Semitic features. Greenblatt had blond hair, light blue eyes, and a short, straight nose. His two companions, on looks alone, would have been admitted to the most exclusive country clubs. Levitt looked them over with grim satisfaction.

"*Goyim*," he said approvingly. "Three bigger *goyim* I never saw in my entire life." His tone turned sharp and he indicated the striped suit and wide, flamboyant tie that Greenblatt wore. "First thing, those clothes'll have to go. Federal employees don't dress like movie hoodlums. You're all going to have to wear plain suits, cheap suits. You'll have to look the part, you'll have to sound the part. That's what you're going to spend the next few days doing. I don't give a damn if you can't add up two and two right now, if you don't know the difference between net and gross. That's all going to change. You're going to become superb actors. When you walk through the door of Fromberg's office, you won't be three of Harry's strong-arm guys. You'll be three Internal Revenue men."

Greenblatt and the other two men were installed in another empty house Saltzman owned, in Edgewater, less than a mile from the house in Fort Lee. For the remainder of that day, and for the next two days—Saturday and Sunday—the three men were drilled incessantly, from early morning until late at night. Levitt honed the fine edges in dress and mannerisms. He pounded the basics of an accountancy education into their skulls. He explained the layout of Fromberg's office, how many people would be there. "You're only interested in two people—Saul Fromberg and Gus Landau. Landau sticks to Fromberg like glue. They're a pair of Siamese twins, never apart. Send them both to hell together."

Jake was grateful for the diversion created by the training of Saltzman's men. It took his mind, temporarily, off the torment Pearl was going through over Leo. He knew that three times a day Pearl got Sophie to telephone the doctor in Washington Heights to give him the details of Leo's condition—his temperature, how he looked and felt. The report never varied. Leo could barely swallow any liquid; eating the smallest morsel of solid food was impossible. The doctor offered more advice, prescribed more medication which one of Saltzman's men would cross the Hudson to collect.

Each night after returning from the other house, Jake would sit at the top of the basement stairs and talk to his wife for an hour or so. He would describe how Saltzman's three-man team was progressing, he'd try to make her laugh by imitating Levitt when he yelled at the fake inspectors for making a mistake. "If we ever give up this business, Lou can get a job at some university teaching accountancy or math," he joked.

"Professor Levitt, handing out diplomas he's printed himself. And what would you turn your hand to, Jake?"

"A business that wouldn't require you and the twins to be in this position. A business where we wouldn't be too frightened to go to a hospital if we were ill."

Kathleen appeared behind Jake, carrying a tray with coffee and cake. "I thought you might like this," she said, leaving it next to him on the top step.

"Thanks." Jake set a cup and a piece of cake midway down the stairs. When he had retreated, Pearl ascended to collect it. "See what you did?" Jake said to Pearl when Kathleen left. "She's as good as gold now."

"My mother was telling me that she actually helped her and Annie cook dinner this evening. Can you believe that?"

Jake tried to remember how it had tasted.

"I think she finally reached a decision after our little talk," Pearl continued. "Unless she changes, Benny is going to kick her out. If that happens, she's not sure what she'll do. She needs him."

"Until she gets another big break," Jake said. "Then see how much she needs him."

"You're beginning to sound like Lou."

"Maybe that's because he was right all along about her. Oil and water don't mix too well."

On Sunday night, following the third day of drilling Saltzman's team, Jake lay on the living-room couch, squirming uncomfortably as he tried to fall asleep. He was too excited, too pent-up to relax. This had been the last day of rehearsal. Levitt was finally satisfied that his pupils could pull off the masquerade. Tomorrow the curtain would go up on the real show.

He lifted the drapes so moonlight showed through and then checked his watch. Ten after two. The remainder of the house was quiet. He threw back the blanket and got up. Opening the basement door, he called Pearl's name, softly at first, then louder until she answered. Huddled warmly in a woolen dressing gown, she came to the bottom of the stairs and looked up.

"What is it?" she asked. "What's the matter?"

"Is Leo all right? Are you?"

"He's sleeping. So was I."

"I'm coming down."

"No." Pearl held up a hand. "You can't come down, Jake. This is supposed to be a quarantine area. You might carry something back upstairs."

"I'm coming down," Jake repeated. Almost three days had passed since he'd seen his younger son, since he'd been close to Pearl. An eternity. Damn the quarantine! Damn the diphtheria! He moved cautiously down the stairs. Pearl backed away, her hand still held out toward him, a protest on her lips. It died, pushed aside as her own feelings—her own need for Jake—rushed to the surface. Too long she'd been shut off in the basement, locked away like a leper while she cared for Leo. If anyone deserved comfort, she told herself, she did. Surely an act of pure love would not be punished by the spread of the infection.

She drew Jake toward the mattress on the floor, the bed that she was to have shared with him. He was not supposed to sleep awkwardly on a couch. Nights were meant to be spent together.

"Jake, I've missed you. Me at the bottom of the stairs and you at the top isn't good enough."

"Shh." He pressed a finger against her lips. They'd talked too much during the past few days, indulged in long-distance communication without intimacy. He removed his clothes, let them fall to the floor. Pearl was already in bed, her dressing gown lying in a heap on the floor. He climbed beneath the covers. She clung fiercely to him, a last vestige of sanity in a world that had suddenly forsaken normality for utter madness.

A loud cry split echoed through the basement. Pearl sat up rigid as the cry was repeated, followed by a scream of "Mummy! I want my Mummy!"

"God, it's Leo!" She leaped out of the bed, stumbled on the woolen dressing gown and dragged it around herself. Jake was only a pace behind, wrapping a blanket around his body as Pearl rushed into Leo's room. She turned on the light. Leo's face was white, bathed in a sheen of perspiration as he sat up in the bed, his tiny hands gripping the top of the sheet. Pearl rushed to him, panic-stricken because of his screaming. In the past three days she had become accustomed to his being so quiet, making no sounds other than muted whimperings. She lifted him from the bed and whispered soothing words. Jake held the blanket to himself with one hand and rested the other on Leo's forehead. He snatched it back immediately.

"What's the matter?" Pearl demanded.

"Feel his forehead!" Jake almost shouted the words. "Feel it for yourself, go on!"

Pearl raised a hand to Leo's forehead. She let it remain there, eyes opening wide as she understood the reason for Jake's excitement. "Cool." She whispered the single word in wonderment.

"That's right. Cool. What did the doctor say about the first forty-eight or seventy-two hours being the critical time? His fever's broken, Pearl, and you did it! We'll call the doctor now, tell him what's happened."

"It's three o'clock in the morning." Still the truth had not fully penetrated Pearl's senses.

"So what? Doctors don't keep office hours. I'll hold him and you call the doctor." He reached out both hands to take the boy. The blanket fell away and Jake stood naked. He didn't care. Leo's body pressed against his own was the most marvelous sensation he'd ever felt. "What's all the screaming about?" Jake asked. "How come you wake your mother and me in the middle of the night?"

Leo gazed solemnly at his father. "I'm hungry. I'm thirsty."

"Did you hear that?" Jake yelled after Pearl. "Tell that doctor my son's hungry and thirsty!" Putting Leo back on the bed, Jake covered himself with the blanket again and followed Pearl.

Fingers trembling as she held the telephone, she made the call to Washington Heights. The doctor answered, sleep distorting his voice, and Pearl gave him the news.

"Tell him we're sending someone to pick him up," Jake told Pearl. "I want Leo examined *now*."

Pearl relayed the message. The moment she finished, Jake rushed through the house, the blanket flapping behind him like a train. The first door he reached led into the room in which Minsky slept with Kathleen. Jake burst inside, threw on the light, and yelled: "Leo's fever's broken!"

Minsky snapped awake and clawed at the revolver that rested on the bedside table. When he saw Jake standing with the blanket wrapped around him, he stared in blank astonishment before bursting into laughter. Kathleen sat up in bed, clutching the covers to her. From a mattress in the corner of the room, their son, William, screamed in terrified protest at the intrusion.

Clutching the blanket, Jake ran through the house. He hammered on Levitt's door, repeated the performance on Moses and Annie's. Lastly, he smashed his fist on the door to Sophie Resnick's room, yelling, "He's better! Leo's better!"

Within a minute, the entire house was awake. The occupants assembled downstairs, anxiously awaiting the return of the two guards who had driven across the bridge into Manhattan. When the doctor arrived, he was blindfolded, wearing an overcoat over his pajamas. Jake guessed that Saltzman's men had not even allowed him time to dress properly. Jake followed the doctor down to the basement, leaving the door at the top of the stairs open so that the others could watch and listen. Pearl sat with Leo on her lap, holding a glass of warm milk to his mouth.

The doctor examined the child carefully. When he replaced his instruments in his bag, he was smiling. "His temperature's dropped, the membrane covering his throat is disappearing."

"It's over, thank God," Pearl murmured with relief.

The doctor's smile faded. "I should explain that diphtheria is a particularly debilitating disease. The fever may have broken but the child will remain weak for a considerable time. Right now, he's dehydrated because of his inability to swallow during the last few days. That can be corrected by an ample supply of fluids. But diphtheria"—he closed his black bag with a loud snap—"can have serious aftereffects."

"Such as?" Jake asked fearfully.

"The infection may have caused damage to the heart, the kidneys, the nerves. It spreads a toxin throughout his body, the effects of which might not be apparent immediately. When the child grows up, he could conceivably be stricken with heart or kidney problems. He could suffer from nervous disorders. All stemming from this attack of diphtheria." He saw the glum expressions on the faces of the child's parents, and quickly added, "I'm not saying this will happen, but it remains a possibility."

A pall of gloom descended over Pearl and Jake as they looked at each other. It reached right up the basement stairs to those gathered in the doorway. Despite Pearl's work, despite their prayers, it was not completely over. It might never be over. Leo seemed like a different child now, temperature down, able to swallow a little liquid. But what would the future hold for him?

Only the children returned to bed. The adults stayed up once the doctor left. Too much was happening to allow sleep. On top of Leo's fever breaking, there was the knowledge that when the sun rose that day, it would rise for the final time on Saul Fromberg and his icy-eyed lieutenant. Dawn would also signify the end of their confinement.

The men played cards. Pearl remained downstairs with Leo, watching him while he slept. The sound of his breathing was the sweetest music she had ever heard. Each breath he took seemed to come easier than the one before it.

Shortly after five o'clock, to Pearl's surprise, Kathleen came to join her. "That was wonderful news about Leo, well worth being woken up for," Kathleen said. "You did one hell of a job with him."

"Thank you." Kathleen was the last person Pearl would expect to be concerned.

"Pearl, I've been wanting to speak to you since the other night, but I couldn't because of . . . because of . . ." She nodded toward the slumbering child.

"What about?"

"What you said. It hurt."

"Because it was the truth?" When Kathleen didn't answer immediately, Pearl asked: "Did Benny really stick a gun to your head and swear he'd kill you if you lost the baby?"

Kathleen nodded. "He also held me out of the window once, five floors up. That was before we were married and he thought I was seeing another man."

"Were you?"

"No," Kathleen lied. "It's just Benny; he's so jealous that he's mad."

"You don't have to tell me . . . I've seen him in action."

Kathleen smiled at that. "Yes, you have. He and I, we've had some great rows." Kathleen recalled the time she'd almost shot him, and her smile grew wider.

"You say that almost affectionately."

"That's it. He's as mad as they come, and I can't think what life without him would be like. The way he chased me—I thought that no matter what I did, he'd continue to do it. And then along came William, and it all changed."

"You've got to give as well, Kathleen. You're not the only game in town anymore." It was the same message she'd given to the blond before, only now there was warmth in Pearl's voice, not anger.

"I will. I'll concentrate more on being a mother, and not so much on being a singer. You know, I lied the other night. I've been lying to myself all along. I didn't get so far on my own. It was Benny. And you."

"I lied as well," Pearl admitted. "You wouldn't still be working as a hatcheck girl or a manicurist."

Chapter Five

The three bogus tax inspectors arrived at the house in Fort Lee at exactly seven-thirty for a final briefing and inspection by Lou Levitt. Each man wore an inexpensive dark gray suit, a narrow-brimmed hat, plain coat, highly shined shoes. They all carried well-worn leather briefcases. If they were surprised to see so much activity in the house so early in the morning, they said nothing. They merely accepted the cups of coffee offered to them by Sophie Resnick before they followed Lou Levitt into the front room.

Levitt produced three small leather wallets. "Identification," he said, passing one to each man. "Good Anglo-Saxon names to go with your *goyishe* good looks."

Jerry Greenblatt and his two colleagues inspected the fake credentials. His own wallet identified him as Howard Hutton. He liked that name; it had a good, respectable ring to it.

"Fromberg's an early bird, he's in his office every day by nine-thirty. Be there ten minutes later."

Greenblatt drove his team into Manhattan in an inconspicuous black Ford. They crossed the George Washington Bridge and headed south along Broadway until they reached Times Square. A freezing wind whipped across the intersection of Broadway and Seventh Avenue, whistling through the car, making the occupants shiver. The Ford passed a long Salvation Army bread line, and Greenblatt said: "Look at those poor bastards. Aren't you glad you've got good-paying, honest jobs with Uncle Sam?" He laughed at his own joke and swung the car to the left, onto Forty-second Street.

At nine-thirty-five, Greenblatt parked the Ford in the street behind Fromberg's building, and the three men entered the rear entrance. An elevator whisked them up to the tenth floor. Their footsteps echoed along the corridor as they passed the steel door to Fromberg's own office and approached the door on which the name of Saul Fromberg was written in gold script. At precisely nine-forty, Greenblatt pushed open the door, whipped out the identification Levitt had provided and thrust it in the face of the woman sitting behind the reception desk.

"Mr. Fromberg, please."

The other two men produced their own credentials, flashed them for an instant before replacing them. The woman rang through to Fromberg's office.

Fromberg answered the telephone and listened to the announcement of his official visitors. It was a nuisance, nothing more. He had nothing to fear from the taxmen. His legitimate accounts were always impeccable. "I'll be out in a minute," he told the receptionist. After replacing the earpiece, he looked at Gus Landau who sat on the other side of the desk. "Internal Revenue agents. A surprise inspection of the books, I suppose. Trying to catch me napping after the audit."

"You want me to sit in?"

"What the hell for? We don't need an alibi this time."

"We didn't need one last time either, the way things turned out."

"Instead of making wisecracks, why don't you find out where they've all gone to? All those guys and their families can't just disappear into thin air like that!"

"Christ knows where they're hiding out. If you gave me the go-ahead to start hitting their businesses—the books and numbers drops, the clubs and convoys—we could flush them out that way."

Fromberg shook his head. "We want those businesses—we don't want wreckage—and we can't afford that kind of violence. It draws attention to us. All I want from you is to find Levitt, Granitz, and the rest of them, and kill them. Quietly and efficiently." He pointed to the steel door that led from the office to the corridor. "Leave me alone while I deal with these jerks from the tax office."

Landau rose from the chair, opened the door, and stepped out into the corridor. He turned left and walked to the washrooms at the end of the corridor. Leaning against the wall, he lit a cigarette and waited. Taxmen! If Fromberg waited much longer, there wouldn't be any money to avoid taxes on!

Inside the office, Fromberg cleared his desk and stood up. He walked into the next room and snapped his fingers at the bookkeeper who worked there. "Have the books in my office ready for inspection by Internal Revenue agents." Then he proceeded through the labyrinth of small offices to the main reception area.

"Good morning, gentlemen. How can I help you?"

Greenblatt was a credit to Levitt's training, all business, an efficient bureaucrat. He pulled out the leather wallet again. "Mr. Fromberg, I'm Howard Hutton. We're here to inspect your company's books."

"Certainly, Mr. Hutton." Fromberg smiled effusively. "I always believe in cooperating with my government. Please follow me."

As they walked toward Fromberg's office, Greenblatt checked the face of everyone they passed, seeking the cold-eyed, scar-faced man he'd been told was Gus Landau. There was no sign of him. When they reached the office, the bookkeeper was setting the books out on the desk. Fromberg waved a hand in a gesture of dismissal; he had been through this routine so many times that he could answer any questions that might arise.

"Help yourselves, gentlemen."

Greenblatt found himself in a major quandary. His orders had been explicit: Kill both Fromberg and Landau. He had been told that the two men were inseparable. Yet now that he was in Fromberg's office, where the killings were to take place, there was no sign of the scar-faced man. Greenblatt was uncertain what to do.

He waited until he heard the door close behind the bookkeeper, then he bent over the set of books. While he ran an index finger down a column of figures, he weighed his options. Should he wait, stretch out the mock inspection in the hope that Landau showed up? Or should he get on with it, take whatever he could and get out? He lifted his head and looked around the office. Fromberg was standing by the desk, watching. A second member of the team was inspecting another ledger. The third man stood off to one side, holding his briefcase in both hands and looking very official.

Greenblatt lowered his eyes to the accounts again. To linger would be to invite danger. The ruse of pretending to be tax inspectors had worked so far, had gained them access to Fromberg's office. But how long would it continue to work? How much time would pass before Fromberg became suspicious and called for help from the men who sat outside?

Slowly, as he turned a page and started to check the next set of figures, he arrived at his decision. "There's something here I don't quite understand, Mr. Fromberg." Greenblatt pressed the tip of his finger against the page. "Could you explain this to me?"

"What?" Fromberg joined Greenblatt, peered at the entry alongside his finger. "What's so difficult to understand?"

"This expense here."

The man who had been holding the briefcase in both hands withdrew a blackjack from it and stepped behind Fromberg. Lifting the weapon high in the air, he crashed it down on the back of Fromberg's skull. Fromberg gave a short, surprised grunt. His head slammed into the desk top and his large body slowly collapsed onto the floor. Greenblatt walked across the office to the window, swung it wide open and looked out. The freezing wind seared his eyes as he stared down at Forty-second Street a hundred feet below. Half-a-dozen cars were parked at the curb, a few figures struggled along the sidewalk in the face of the wind. Greenblatt went to the door leading to the next office and securely jammed a chair beneath the handle. Returning to the window, he beckoned with his finger. The other two men dragged the unconscious figure of Saul Fromberg to the window. Greenblatt looked down again. The moment the sidewalk was clear of pedestrians, he gave the order.

"Shove him out."

Fighting against the dead weight, the men hoisted Fromberg's body to window height and pushed. The moment the center of balance was passed, they stepped back, retrieved their briefcases and walked quickly to the steel door leading to the corridor. They never saw Fromberg's body plummet through the air like a sack of coal to smash against the sidewalk. By the time his blood spattered the concrete, they were passing through the doorway.

From the end of the corridor, Gus Landau saw the first tax agent walk out through the private door. Quickly, he pushed back the washroom door and slipped inside, holding it open just enough to allow a narrow view. Landau didn't like it, not one little bit. Such spot inspections usually took anywhere from fifteen minutes to a couple of hours—they weren't over in less than two minutes—and tax agents were not shown out of Fromberg's office through the private door. They came out through the company's reception area, just like every other legitimate business caller.

The elevator arrived. Landau had no idea what had happened in Fromberg's office in so short a time. He only knew what instinct told him—that something was terribly wrong. He watched the three men enter the elevator. The instant the door closed behind them, and the elevator began its downward journey, Landau emerged from his hiding place and ran along the corridor. He used a key to open the steel door, pushed it back and stepped into the office. A frigid blast of air from the open window slammed into him. Why the hell was the window open? Large strides took him across the office, but even before he looked out he knew the answer.

Ten floors below, a handful of people were clustered around Fromberg's shattered body. A woman looked up, pointed at the open window. Landau stepped back, leaned against the desk, and tried to collect his wildly scattered thoughts.

Tax agents! Those bastards Levitt and Granitz! He fingered the scar on his cheek as fury and fear struggled within him for supremacy. A minute passed, two. Landau heard a commotion from the book-keeper's office. A man's voice yelled Fromberg's name. The door handle turned. The door shook but refused to yield. Landau saw the chair jammed beneath the handle but he made no attempt to remove it. His body, his brain, were frozen with shock, unable to function.

"Mr. Fromberg! . . . Are you all right?" A shoe crashed against the door and the wood around the handle splintered. The noise galvanized Landau into action. In three strides he was at the steel door. He ran through into the corridor. He didn't wait for the elevator. He raced down the stairs, all nine flights, to the building's lobby. The crowd around Fromberg's body was larger when Landau burst out onto the street. He didn't stop. He walked quickly to where he had left his car, jumped in, and drove away.

Landau knew now that he had to get to Levitt and Granitz before they got to him. He might not be so fortunate the next time.

The three bogus tax inspectors drove straight back to Fort Lee. When Levitt learned that only Fromberg had been killed, he flew into a fury, yelling so loudly that his voice could be heard through the entire house.

"What do you mean Landau wasn't there?" he shouted at Greenblatt. "You can bet your bottom dollar he was somewhere around! You were told that he stuck to Fromberg like glue. Why the hell didn't you wait around, take them both together like you were supposed to do? What was your big hurry?"

"The joint was crawling with guns," Greenblatt tried to explain. "God knows how long our cover could have stood up. I couldn't stand there with my finger in Fromberg's fucking books forever. He would have figured out something wasn't kosher. So we just took him. I thought we'd get Landau later on."

Levitt's expression was one of dumb amazement as he turned to look at Jake, Minsky, and Caplan. "Did you hear that? He thought . . . that's what he did." The amazement changed to a snarl as he swung back on the unfortunate Greenblatt. "Who the hell told you to think anything? I'm the only one around here who's got the ability to think. And a fat lot of good it does when imbeciles like you screw things up."

"Lou . . ." Jake stepped in between Levitt and Greenblatt. "Cool down, for Christ's sake; they can hear you in Paterson. Fromberg's out of the way, that's the important thing. His people'll come over to us. We only have to worry about Landau now, and he's just one man."

"He's not just one man! He's a wild animal! And he's cornered, so that makes him even more dangerous." Levitt continued to seethe. He shoved Jake aside and confronted Greenblatt again. "You were rehearsed until you were faultless. I told you what to look for in Fromberg's books so you could stall him. You should have been able

300

to talk intelligently for hours about his company's accounts. Now, because of your ineptitude, we cannot leave this house yet."

"What's that?" Jake asked.

"You heard me. We can't leave here while Landau's still on the loose."

Caplan pushed in front of Jake. "You'd better tell Annie that. She's going crazy being locked up in this place."

"Never mind Annie," Jake said. "What about Pearl and the twins?"

"What about them?" Levitt asked.

"Leo's been ill. Pearl wants to get him home, to our own doctor."

For a moment, Levitt appeared ready to yield. Then his eyes turned hard. "No one leaves here until we've found Landau."

"What do you think the guy's going to do?" Minsky wanted to know. "Start a one-man war against all of us?"

"Yes, that's exactly what I think," Levitt answered. "He can't come over to us—he knows that. So what alternative does he have? He's got nothing to bargain with, so he'll try to go out in a blaze of glory."

Jake headed toward the door. "I'm going to tell Pearl that she can't leave. Better hide yourself, Lou."

"What's all the shouting about?" Pearl asked when Jake came down to the basement.

"Lou. Those three guys messed up the job. They didn't get Landau. Fromberg's gone, but Landau didn't accompany him like he was supposed to."

"Oh, God." Pearl's face paled. Landau was the more dangerous of the two men. Fromberg had never used violence—he'd got others to use it for him.

"Lou says that none of us can leave this place until he's found."

Her fear at learning Landau was still alive disappeared. "Jake, I don't care if we have to have guards sitting in our apartment, if my mother has to have men sitting in the restaurant. I'm not staying here with the twins any longer. Stuck here, Leo's going to take a year to recover. He needs to be home where he can be cared for properly. Where is Lou now?"

"In the front room."

Pearl ran up the basement stairs. Instead of going immediately to the front room, she rounded up her mother, Annie, and Kathleen. Then, in a posse, they confronted Levitt.

"What is this, a delegation?" Levitt asked when the four women burst into the front room. "Women already got the vote."

"A delegation is exactly what it is, Lou," Pearl replied. "Three of us

301

have children to worry about, and one child has been very sick. Keeping them crammed together in this place is harming them."

"Pearl, it's your welfare I'm concerned about. Landau's still out there, and now he's a bigger threat than ever because he's desperate."

"So am I! I want to get back home. We all do. Just because you haven't got a family to worry about"—she spaced the words out, knowing they would hurt Levitt, wanting them to—"doesn't mean that we feel the same way."

Levitt's small body sagged as though he'd been struck. Before he could recover his poise, Sophie added her voice to the battle. "There're a lot of people on Second Avenue who haven't eaten a decent meal since Jake came into my place last Thursday and put the closed sign on the door. If I don't get back, they'll starve because they can't afford to eat elsewhere."

"And what about you two?" Levitt said icily to Annie and Kathleen. He had a revolution on his hands. He could handle his partners when they kicked about his orders, persuade them to see things his way, because they were conditioned to believing he was right. Women were another matter entirely.

"My Judy's fed up with being cooped up here," Annie said.

"And I'd like to get back to Kathleen Monahan's Hideaway before the paying customers forget who the hell Kathleen Monahan is," Kathleen added.

"All right! You all want to go home? You don't want to listen to me? Go home then! See if I give a damn if you walk into a bullet!" Levitt stormed out of the room and went upstairs, cursing his partners, their wives, their children, their entire families. In the whole load, not one of them possessed a single ounce of brains. Sophie worrying about the poor people she fed for nothing as though she were some kind of saint! Even Pearl, concerned with Leo. The worst was over with the kid, wasn't it? The fever had broken; he was on the mend. And that shot Pearl had taken at him—just because he didn't have a family . . .

Some minutes later, there was a knock on the door to Levitt's room. "Come in!" he called out.

Jake stood in the doorway. "We're all ready to head out."

"You sure you know what you're doing?"

"I think so." Jake entered the room and closed the door. "Lou, we've been friends a long time. I know you've made a lot of decisions that have benefited all of us, but this time you're acting like some hard-done-by parent whose kids don't obey him anymore. Is that how you look on all of us, like we're your kids and you're our father?"

"Don't be so ridiculous. We work together and that's it. I just don't think we should leave this place. Fromberg's gone. Our businesses

302

aren't in danger; they can run themselves. So why should we risk our necks by putting ourselves in plain view for Landau to take a shot at us?"

"You know something, Lou?" Jake said. "Maybe Pearl was right about what she said before. Outside of yourself, you've got no responsibilities. Well, I do. I want to get Leo to a proper doctor, not one we have to kidnap every time we need him." Jake opened the door to leave. "When you decide to come out of exile, give me a call. In the meantime, we'll look after your share."

Minutes later, Levitt heard the sounds of car engines starting, the slamming of doors. Soon, there was nothing but silence. He went to the window and looked out. All he saw were the guards patrolling the grounds; they wouldn't leave until everyone was gone.

For half an hour he remained in the room, thinking. Scared? Him? He wasn't scared of anything. He simply had enough sense to know when to tread warily. What was it about fools rushing in? . . . The improbable crossed his mind. Could the fool in this instance be himself? Was he wrong? For once, were his partners and their families ahead of him? It was common sense to be wary of a man like Landau, but wasn't it also common sense to question what just one man could do? One man who knew that if he showed his face anywhere, he'd be put down out of hand, like the wild dog he was?

At last, Levitt made up his mind. He packed the suitcase he'd brought with him from Central Park West and left the house. On the way out, he told one of the guards that their tour of duty was at an end.

Sophie had the restaurant open for business again the following day. As grateful customers filled the booths and tables, none of them paid any attention to the two men who occupied a table close to the door, casting their eyes over everyone who entered. Jake was taking no chances on his mother-in-law's safety. . . .

When Kathleen returned the following night to Kathleen Monahan's Hideaway, she barely noticed the men who stood close to the club's entrance, men more interested in the patrons who visited the club than in her singing. She was too happy to be back to worry about the bodyguards Minsky had ordered to watch her every move.

Before she'd left for the club that evening, Kathleen had surprised the housekeeper by taking over one of the woman's duties—reading William a bedtime story. At first, the child had been confused at seeing the strange blond woman come into his room. Mrs. Wickham always told him a story, kissed him good night, and tucked him into bed. This woman had just floated in and out of his life without giving him any sign of affection. Kathleen read the story of "Little Red Riding Hood," making all the necessary ferocious faces and growling when appropriate, a dedication she normally reserved for the stage. The child was entranced. After Kathleen kissed him, she turned around to see Minsky standing just outside the room. He had watched and had listened to the entire story.

"Kid's suddenly realized he's got a mother," Minsky said. "Carry on like that and you'll put Miss Wickham on the breadline."

"Fat chance. I cook like the Borgias, remember?"

"You can learn." He held her face in his hands and kissed her. Kathleen could never recall him being so gentle. "Corned beef and cabbage, with potato latkes."

Now, Kathleen looked down at Minsky sitting by the side of the stage. As she finished singing, she blew him a kiss. Those few days of hiding out had been the best thing to happen during their topsy-turvy marriage. That, and her no-nonsense talk with Pearl. She was going to give this marriage everything she had, and she was convinced that Minsky would, too. . . .

Pearl's first act on returning home to the Fifth Avenue apartment was to summon the family doctor. He examined Leo thoroughly, then checked Joseph just as carefully.

"Leo's over the worst, and Joseph shows no sign of having picked up the infection," the doctor told Pearl. "Tell me, why didn't you have Leo admitted to a hospital when he came down with diphtheria?"

"We were away at the time. I didn't know what to do."

"So you took it upon yourself to treat him?"

"With the help of a local doctor."

"You're very lucky. Leo's a strong child. That could have been what saw him through it, or it might have been your caring, your love. In the same situation, most mothers would have had to bury their children."

Once the doctor had gone, Pearl made arrangements for Annie to take Joseph during the day while she fussed over Leo. The younger twin, still terribly weak from his ordeal, spent much more time in bed than on his feet. Even a short walk rapidly tired him, and he was very dependent on his mother, constantly calling out for her.

"Is Leo getting better?" Joseph asked one morning before he went next door to play with Judy.

"Every day he gets a little better," Pearl answered, pleased that Joseph was taking such an interest.

"But when will he be really better?"

"The doctor says it might take a few months."

"I want him to be better soon," Joseph said determinedly. "I want you to spend some time with me as well."

"Judy is expecting you," Pearl said sharply. Was she just imagining it, or had the worst just happened? How jealous was Joseph of his twin brother, and of the time she spent with him?

For two months, Leo steadily regained strength, and the day came when Pearl knew his recovery was almost complete. "Where's Joseph?" he demanded as she fed him lunch one day. "Where's my brother? I want to play with him."

"He's next door, with Judy." It was the first time Leo had asked for Joseph since he'd been taken ill.

Leo screwed up his face in displeasure. "What's he doing with her? He's my twin; he should be here with me. Why's he playing with a girl?"

Pearl waited and watched. Sure enough, within a few seconds Leo's eyes underwent that odd transformation. "You stay here. I'll get him." Leaving Leo at the table, she went next door. Joseph and Judy were playing on the floor with a doll's house, rearranging the furniture in the miniature rooms.

"Something the matter?" Annie asked.

"No. It's just that Leo's asking for Joseph. He wants to play with him."

"Hey, good news. He must be better." She looked past Pearl at the open door. "And here he is."

Pearl swung around. "Who said you could leave the table, young man?"

Leo paid her no attention. His eyes were riveted on his twin brother. "Why are you playing with her? You should be playing with me!"

Running past Pearl, he leaped with both feet onto the doll's house, smashing it into fragments. Judy burst into tears. Joseph jumped to his feet and squared up to his brother. Pearl and Annie, shocked by the abrupt outburst, just stood by and watched the twins argue.

"What did you do that for?" Joseph shouted.

"Why are you with her?"

"I can be with anyone I like!"

"No, you can't! You belong with me. We're twins!"

At last, as she saw Leo clench his fist and raise his arm, Pearl stepped forward. She caught hold of Leo just as Annie dragged Joseph away. Judy, sitting in the middle of the floor among the wreckage of her doll's house, crying, was ignored.

"Stop it this instant!" Pearl told Leo. "You apologize and go back inside and finish your lunch!" When she let go of him, he started to walk toward the door. Suddenly he swung around and hit Joseph, who was still being held by Annie.

"That's for making Mummy shout at me!" He ran from the apartment.

Letting go of Joseph so he could run to his mother, Annie lifted Judy from the floor and comforted her. "I think you might have made a rod for your own back, Pearl. Ill or not, Leo expects his every whim to be indulged. You can see what happens when he doesn't get his own way."

Pearl cuddled Joseph to her. "I thought . . ." Just what had she thought? That months of pampering Leo to the exclusion of Joseph would have no lasting effect? "I thought that once Leo got better, everything would be normal again."

"You can't give him something and then take it away without upsetting him."

"But he was ill, that's why I pampered him so much."

"He doesn't understand that, Pearl. He's four and a half years old, too young to be able to differentiate between—"

"Being his mother's favorite, or being favored only because he's recovering from a serious illness?"

"That's it, Pearl. Now it's up to you to figure out a way to put him straight. Otherwise you're going to have murders in that apartment of yours."

Pearl looked down at Joseph. "Going to?" she asked Annie. "Didn't you just see what happened? I've got them already."

An extensive search during the following two months brought forth no news of Gus Landau. Gradually, even Levitt came to believe that the danger was over. Landau had simply disappeared, been swallowed up by the earth. He'd used the little brains he had to dig himself a deep hole and he was remaining in it. The guards on the clubs and the books were withdrawn. The state of siege which had prevailed since Fromberg's death was replaced by normality.

Almost . . .

There was one debt remaining from Fromberg's attempt to kill Jake and Levitt.

At the end of April, Levitt summoned a special meeting of his partners. Included was Harry Saltzman, who had provided such stalwart assistance during the battle. The meeting took place in the early afternoon at the Four Aces, and Levitt came directly to the point.

"Unfinished business is on the agenda. Patrick Joseph Rourke up in Boston thinks he got away with helping Fromberg. Now that Fromberg's been gone for two months, Rourke's hoping we've forgotten his involvement. But we can't afford to be so charitable. We've got to teach him a lesson, see that he stays up in Boston with the rest of the Irishmen in the future. So we're branching out. We're going into the business of distributing Irish whiskey . . . Patrick Joseph Rourke's Irish whiskey. He's got a big shipment due in a couple of days, and we're going to relieve him of it."

Jake lifted a finger. "I'm going to be in charge of that raid."

"Why put yourself at risk? Harry'll lend us a couple of dozen guys; that's why he's here. Maybe Greenblatt and those other two jerks can get back in our good books."

"I've got a personal stake in this," Jake argued. "It wasn't Harry's men who were almost killed by Rourke's boys. It was me, Pearl, and the twins."

"You want it that badly? Okay, you can have it. But just remember, all we want is the whiskey. We don't want a wholesale slaughter just because you're itching to try out those guns Benny gave you for your birthday a few years back."

"I know the score," Jake answered. "Get them to lay down their arms and then put them to sleep. When they wake up, they've got no trucks."

"Be sure that's the way it goes."

Jake debated whether to tell Pearl the reason for the journey. He was away so frequently that she was accustomed to his absences, but this trip was different. She, too, had a personal stake in it.

"We're taking one of Rourke's convoys, up in Massachusetts," he said conversationally over dinner that evening.

Jake's casual tone lulled Pearl for a moment. He might just as well have been discussing the weather. Then her eyes became sharp. "Because he helped Fromberg?"

"Can you think of a better reason?"

"Why are you going?"

"Because Rourke's men tried to kill us."

"Did Lou *appoint* you to go?"

"No. He was against it. Going was my idea."

"He was right." Pearl set down her fork, and stared at Jake across the table. "I don't want you to go. I've got enough on my hands now with Leo and Joseph. I haven't got the time to worry about you as well."

"You won't have to. This'll be straightforward."

"A straightforward armed robbery? Is there such a thing? And

307

since when do you go in for stealing other men's shipments? What was it Lou said when he had that idea about lending money—that you could buy into respectable businesses that way? Become respectable, so all of our kids would have legitimate companies to inherit, not clubs and bookmaking joints? Just where does this fit in?"

"This fits in under *R* for revenge, Pearl, that's where. Paying Rourke back for what he tried to do to us. Think how close Leo came to dying because we couldn't take him to a hospital like normal people."

"Forget revenge, Jake. If you've got to get even with Rourke, let someone else go. Even better, forget the whole damned thing. Let him stay up there."

Jake got up from the dinner table, unable to continue to meet his wife's reproachful gaze. Why couldn't she see what he did? If you let a man like Rourke get away with something like this, what might he try the next time? The Irishman had to be taught a lesson. And Jake had to be the one to teach him because it was his family that had been attacked. Never mind about no one being hurt. The knowledge that someone had tried to harm his family was reason enough.

He left for Massachusetts the following afternoon, traveling in a car with Jerry Greenblatt. Pearl watched through the window as he drove away, and she wondered whether she would ever see him again, just as she did each time he went to Ocean City to meet an incoming shipment. With the exception of the raid on the distillery, nothing had ever happened. But this time was different. Jake was going to steal a valuable cargo that belonged to another man.

She walked into the twins' room. For once, they were playing peacefully. No arguments, no fights, just two small boys sitting on the floor with a large-piece jigsaw puzzle in front of them. Would they ever be like normal children, able to see their father every morning and evening, spend weekends with him and be taken to the park or the zoo, share the many activities other fathers shared with their children? God damn Lou Levitt and his grandiose schemes to make everyone respectable! Why hadn't they worked yet? Interests in wildly diverse businesses did not compensate for the danger Jake was placing himself in now. Damn Jake for his stupidity in going after revenge! And damn herself for allowing him to do it. . . .

Jake returned early the following afternoon. She heard the front door open and breathed a long sigh of relief. He didn't call her name. He just walked into the kitchen, where Pearl was washing vegetables for dinner that night. His face looked ghastly, drawn and pale. Lines were etched around his mouth and eyes.

"What's wrong?"

"Everything," he answered. "Those stupid Irish bastards—"

"Jake, what is it?"

"Can you believe what those stupid Irish bastards did? They were outnumbered two to one and . . ." He leaned back against the wall. "Two to one. And, oh God, they tried to make a fight of it."

At one o'clock in the morning, a tree was felled across a narrow, rarely used coastal road some twenty-five miles south of Boston, at a spot three miles from the docking area where Patrick Joseph Rourke brought ashore his cargoes of contraband Irish whiskey.

For two and a half hours, the two dozen men from New York waited silently. Just before three-thirty, the roar of trucks in low gear carried through the narrow-trunked trees. Jake snapped out orders in a quiet, authoritative tone. The men doused their cigarettes and took up concealed positions from which they could command the road.

A minute later, a car came into view. Behind it, at ten-yard intervals, were four large trucks, another car, four more trucks, and at the rear a third car. Each car carried four men. The lead car stopped as it reached the fallen tree. Two men climbed out. They walked forward warily to inspect the obstacle. Had Levitt been on the scene, he would have recognized the two men as those who had burst into his apartment on Central Park West—Richard Keith, and John McMichael, Rourke's nephew.

"Raise your arms in the air!" Jake called from behind the cover of a tree.

Keith and McMichael spun around. Simultaneously, the doors of all three cars were flung open. Men rolled out clutching weapons. The crash of gunfire echoed along the coastal road. Bullets zipped harmlessly into branches.

Before Jake could yell again for surrender, a single shot rang out from the trees. The other New York men took it as a signal to open fire. Jake stood helplessly by as all three escort cars were riddled with bullets and shotgun pellets. Those of Rourke's men fortunate enough to have jumped from the cars did not enjoy their luck for long. Caught in a withering crossfire, they were shot down on the road.

"Hold your fire!" Jake roared above the sounds of the guns. "Hold your goddamned fire, do you hear me!"

One by one the guns fell quiet. In the crisp silence that followed, a pall of smoke drifted lazily across the carnage. Not one of the trucks was even scratched, but all twelve guards lay dead. As Jake grimly surveyed the stretch of road, a door on the point car swung open; a body dropped halfway out, head trailing on the ground.

"You in the trucks! Come out with your hands where we can see them!"

Eight truck doors opened simultaneously. Terrified, the drivers stepped down. They were bound and gagged, left to lie at the side of the road. The three shot-up cars were pushed aside. Half-a-dozen men struggled to move the tree out of the way.

Ten minutes later, with Jake's men behind the steering wheels, the trucks moved off, their destination no longer Boston but New York. As Jake climbed into the car with Jerry Greenblatt, he bestowed a final glance on the stretch of road. He shuddered to rid himself of the image of the slaughter. It refused to fade. Perversely, he blamed the victims. Stupid Irish bastards! What the hell had they been thinking of? Didn't they know they were supposed to roll over if they were so outnumbered?

Pearl listened in horror as Jake related the events. "You killed twelve men—"

"I didn't fire a single shot!"

"It doesn't matter whether you did or not! You were in charge! You wanted to be in charge! Is this the kind of respectable occupation our children are supposed to inherit? An ambush—a massacre?"

"Who told them to open fire on us? What did they think, that they could beat two-to-one odds?" First he'd been mad at the Irishmen, seeing them as responsible for causing their own slaughter. Now he was becoming angry at Pearl for being so unsympathetic toward him.

"What did Lou say?"

"He doesn't know yet."

At six o'clock, after the twins had been fed, Jake took the family over to Second Avenue. Although busy with the dinner rush, Sophie Resnick left the kitchen and came out to welcome her favorite customers. They ran toward the cake display, and Leo began shouting: "Jelly roll! I want a jelly roll!" Sophie looked at Pearl for permission.

"That's why I brought them here. I gave them dinner, you can feed them dessert."

Jake stayed in the restaurant only long enough to kiss his mother-in-law. Then he went downstairs, pushed open the office door, and sat down opposite Levitt. Slowly, he explained everything that had taken place the previous night.

A glint of anger shone in Levitt's blue eyes. "I warned you not to get personally involved. If it had just been Harry's men, who would have cared? Stupid Irish bastards, just like you said. But because you were there, you're now a part of it. If Rourke gets wind of that, it could mean trouble down the road, not just for you but for all of us." Levitt leaned across the desk, closing the distance between himself and Jake. "Pearl doesn't know about any of this, I hope."

Jake nodded glumly. "She guessed something was wrong."

"So you told her? For God's sake, where are your brains?"

"Lou, would you speak to her? She's upstairs now, with her mother."

"What do you expect me to say? That there's nothing to worry about because twelve men died?"

"You'll think of something," Jake said angrily. Like Pearl, Levitt was giving him no sympathy. "You keep telling us you're the one with all the smarts."

Levitt knew that Jake was right. He had to think of something to tell Pearl. The raid on Rourke's convoy had been his idea. That it had grown to such murderous proportions reflected on him. He accompanied Jake upstairs to the restaurant. Pearl and the twins sat at the counter. In front of each boy was an empty plate. Joseph's face was clean, while his brother's was covered by a sticky mess of sugar and jam which Pearl was trying to clean with a napkin.

"Leo looks like he's feeling better," Levitt said to Pearl. "That's one hell of an appetite."

"Did Jake tell you what happened?" Pearl asked.

"A regrettable accident—"

"Accident?"

Levitt held up a hand. "Let me finish. Nothing can ever be connected to us. The affair's over. Besides, what kind of men were they? They were armed. They opened fire. Pearl, Irish killers died, that's all. The same kind of men who tried to kill you and your family on Fifth Avenue. What loss are they?"

"To their families they're a loss."

"It should be their families who suffer the loss, not our own." He dropped the subject as Sophie came along the counter with another jelly roll for Leo.

Levitt watched Leo take the first bite; then he nudged Jake's arm and nodded toward the door. The two men left the restaurant to stand on the sidewalk outside. "Jake, you're a fool. First you involve yourself in something you should have left to others, and then you compound your stupidity by telling Pearl. Next time, maybe you'll listen to me. What I tell you's for your own good."

Jake wasn't listening. He was watching a truck rolling slowly toward them. It brought to mind the previous night, the eight trucks so miraculously unscathed, the three cars pitted like colanders. He'd never forget that sight. The truck drew level, its grumbling engine noise punctuated by a sharp shriek of metal as the driver missed the change. As it passed, Jake's eyes stayed fixed on the apartment building opposite. In a darkened window on the second floor, a tiny orange light flickered rapidly. Jake felt a tug on his sleeve. Behind him, the glass window of the restaurant shattered into a thousand pieces.

"Get down!" he yelled. He lunged sideways, and with both hands shoved Levitt to the sidewalk.

The flickering orange light died. An echo of machine-gun fire drifted across Second Avenue as the truck rumbled on. The second-floor window was now completely dark. Jake rose unsteadily to his feet. His head was ringing. His trousers were torn, his knees skinned from the fall. "Lou . . . are you all right?"

Levitt lifted his head. "I'm okay. Inside! See about inside!"

Jake spun around and rushed into the restaurant. The first thing he heard was screaming. Customers, who only moments earlier had been sitting at tables, were now lying on the floor. Some held their hands over their heads for protection. One man lay among the wreckage of a chair, groaning as he stared at his blood-soaked leg.

Pearl! . . . Where was she? At last he spotted her, cowering in a booth with the twins, shielding them with her body. The counter, where they had been sitting, was chewed up, like a million termites had been feasting on the wood for a century. Behind the counter, the wall was pitted with large holes.

"I'm all right!" Pearl screamed. "Behind the counter! See about my mother, she was standing there!"

Jake vaulted over the counter. He barely felt the pain as his hand pressed into splintered wood. All his senses were concentrated on what he would discover on the other side. Sophie Resnick lay on the floor, eyes fixed open but unseeing. The front of her white apron was stained a vivid red. "Get an ambulance!" he yelled at Levitt.

Levitt ran through to the kitchen to use the telephone. With the twins clinging to her legs, Pearl ventured over to the counter. "Stay away," Jake growled at her. "Stay the hell away from here!"

"My mother, is she? . . ."

"I don't know. Let's just get her to the hospital."

A patrolman rushed into the restaurant. "Over there!" Jake yelled. "Building across the street, second floor. The shots came from the second floor!"

Levitt came out of the kitchen. "There's an ambulance on the way." Walking behind the counter, he knelt down beside Sophie's prostrate form. When he looked up at Jake, he shook his head.

Jake stood there, numb. Somehow, he forced himself to turn

toward Pearl who had remained on the other side of the counter. "It was meant for us," he murmured, as if that could make it more acceptable. "Me and Lou, it was meant for us."

Tears choked Pearl's voice. "Who was it, Jake? That man Rourke in Boston, paying with my mother's life for what you did last night?"

None of them noticed Leo. Still clutching a half-eaten jelly roll, he came around the counter. As he stood next to Levitt, an expression of wonder crossed his face. "Look," he said, pointing first to the cake in his hand, then to the blood staining Sophie's white coverall. "Jelly roll. Jelly roll."

"Leo!" Pearl shrieked. She rushed around the counter to drag him away. Levitt was quicker. He picked up the child and carried him to the other side of the restaurant, talking softly as if to soothe him. Only Jake remained behind the counter, his stomach heaving as he stared down at his mother-in-law.

Jelly roll. Jelly roll. He couldn't stop the words from ringing in his ears, couldn't dismiss the memory of Leo standing by the body of his grandmother and making the bizarre comparison. Finally, Jake turned away and threw up on the floor.

Police checked the apartment opposite the restaurant. A man calling himself Joey Goldfarb had leased it the previous week, paying two months rent in advance. The description the landlord gave of Joey Goldfarb fitted Gus Landau. Abandoned in the living room, police found a heavy-caliber, water-cooled machine gun, set up just inside the window where it had a clear field of fire across Second Avenue. They surmised that Landau had fired just the one burst before fleeing, confident that he had hit both his targets. Instead, he had killed a fifty-eight-year-old grandmother.

There was still no sign of Landau two days later when Sophie was buried in a plot beside Joseph Resnick. Following the funeral, Pearl began the week-long mourning period. She sat on a low wooden chair, a rip in her clothing signifying her bereavement. The mirrors were covered. Jake did his best to explain the situation to the twins, but he was glad when night came and he could leave them in Annie's care.

At least once an hour, Pearl asked Jake if Landau had been found. Each time his answer was the same. "We've got two hundred men combing the city for him. If he's here, they'll find him."

"Maybe we should all have listened to Lou," she said.

"And stayed in that house forever?"

"My mother would still be alive." She gazed off dreamily into

313

space, musing aloud. "Perhaps I'm the reason this all happened, Jake. I put that stripe across his face. That's why he hated us so much. He wanted to kill you to hurt me." She took a deep breath. Her eyes became hard, her voice toneless. "Jake, I want you to find him. Find him and make him suffer like he's made my family suffer."

"I will, Pearl. I promise you I will." If only he knew where to begin the search.

Pearl was not the only person to mourn a loss. In the Boston office of Shamrock Cars, Patrick Joseph Rourke sat like a piece of stone behind his scarred metal desk. Emotions suffocated him. Shock, grief, fury washed over him in ever-increasing torrents.

Twelve men dead, including his sister's son. A quarter of a million dollars in Irish whiskey stolen from him. Rourke didn't know which hideous aspect of the hijacking to concentrate on first.

The telephone on his desk rang. He answered it automatically. The caller was the wife of one of the men who had been killed. She wanted to know how she was supposed to feed and clothe her three children now? Rourke listened sympathetically, offered his condolences, and promised he would help. He expected other such calls. The families of the dead men would come to him for help. Their breadwinners had died while working for him; now it was his duty to see that they did not starve.

Rourke understood the reason for the hijacking. The men he had contracted to kill for Fromberg were behind it. Fromberg was dead, a suicide apparently, one of many distraught businessmen leaping from a window after a final, bitter glance at the books. Rourke knew better. Levitt and Granitz had gotten to him. And now they had struck back at the instrument Fromberg had used. They had come into the very heart of Massachusetts, where Rourke was strongest, and hurt him grievously. Rourke's own spies in New York were bringing in reports of Irish whiskey suddenly flooding the market down there, but there was little the Irishman could do about it. The Jews were too powerful for him to tackle alone; they had just demonstrated that. He knew from talking to the convoy drivers that his own men had initiated the battle, had ignored the order to surrender. That made no difference to Rourke. What did it matter who'd fired first? His only concern was his own loss.

The telephone rang again, jarring Rourke. Another widow seeking help for her family. Once more Rourke gave the assurance that his hand would always be open. As he hung up, he considered the financial cost of the hijacking. The quarter of a million dollars he'd lost in whiskey. The trucks. At least another hundred thousand to square the accounts of the men who had died. The loss of his nephew, his strong right hand. Rourke knew he couldn't fight back. Not now. Perhaps not ever.

He reached out to the photograph on the desk, the picture of his three sons. Patrick Jr., Joseph, and John. One day, they would carry on the fight for him. He would instill into them his hatred for the scum who had cost him so much. His sons would wage a holy war for him. Not with guns and ambushes, like the Jews had done. His sons would not be gangsters. They would wage their war from the heights of respectability.

Let the Jews pass on the hateful legacy of the gangster to their sons. Patrick Joseph Rourke would pass on real power.

Pearl used her week of mourning to come to terms with her own life. Many notions flitted through her mind as she sat on the low wooden chair. What she could have done; what should she have done? Even an idea that had never surfaced before came to her. What if she had never allowed Jake back into the restaurant after he had gone to work with Fromberg? That was the most difficult of all the questions to answer. If she had stuck to her principles, allowed none of the boys to come back, would she be mourning her mother now?

She dwelt on the idea for most of one day, until she finally reached her decision. An ironic decision. If she hadn't allowed Jake back into her life, she would not be sitting *shivah* for her mother now. She would have sat *shivah* for Sophie Resnick much earlier. Her mother would have worked herself to death in the damned restaurant, trying to pay off what she owed Fromberg, or she would have gone to jail on that trumped-up charge because Jake and Levitt and the others would not have been on hand to steal the ten thousand dollars for the fine. Because of Jake, the restaurant had become a joy to Sophie, not a labor. The final years of her life had been filled with more happiness than she had ever known before. She had even become—despite her own pain, Pearl could not help but smile—a philanthropist, turning the restaurant into a soup kitchen for those stricken by the hard times.

No, Pearl would change nothing. She had no regrets. Except, of course, one. The night of Jake's accident. She'd alter that. She would make herself stronger, force herself not to lean on Lou Levitt for support. But if she could change that, would she have the twins? Had Levitt's single act of lovemaking achieved what Jake had failed to do?

As the week wore on, Pearl stopped considering the ifs and buts.

315

Nothing could be altered; what was done was done. Her mind shifted to the future, the respectable future that Jake talked about. She would rather die than see her sons go through the same troubles she had known. Joseph or Leo must never experience the horror and shame that Jake had exhibited after returning from Boston. Her own parents who had come from Hungary had worked hard to make her life better. She, in turn, would continue the tradition. She would work to see that her children fared better than she had. They would not make nocturnal trips to pick up shipments of illegal wares. They would be businessmen, upstanding, honorable.

As the mourning period drew to its close, Pearl's resolve hardened. She mentioned nothing to Jake, or to Annie. Her friendship with the red-haired woman was as firm as it had always been, but over the years Pearl had realized that she was made of stronger mettle than Annie. Annie had never suffered as she had; her character had not been tempered in such a blazing fire. Annie would not stand up for herself the way Pearl would. Besides, her responsibilities were nowhere near as great as Pearl's. She had one daughter to worry about, while Pearl had two sons.

Sons who would not follow in their father's footsteps . . .

BOOK FOUR

Chapter One

Despite knowing that Leo had fully recovered from the bout of diphtheria, and that he was as physically healthy as his twin brother, Pearl could not bring herself to treat the boys equally. Some subconscious instinct always reminded her of how ill Leo had been, how close to death, and she was unable to stop leaning toward him. If both twins should fall and hurt themselves, Leo would unfailingly receive an extra kiss, a special degree of pampering. In return, he became completely dependent on his mother, even to the point of using her in any argument with Joseph.

Once the twins began attending school, it became clear that Joseph was far brighter. He shone through the first four grades while Leo labored to keep up. One child was as gifted as the other was slow. Joseph learned to read and write, to add, subtract, multiply, and divide before anyone else in the class. Leo was among the last to master such basics. Pearl found excuses for Leo's poor scholastic performance in his illness. Hadn't the doctor said there might be aftereffects? But even the attention she paid to him at home failed to soothe the discomfort he felt at school, where Joseph was obviously more appreciated than he was. In the classroom, there was no Pearl to take Leo's side. He was permanently in his brother's shadow. And Joseph, after playing second fiddle to Leo at home, relished his superiority, especially when he could show off for Judy Caplan who was in the twins' class. The little red-haired girl would sit chewing her braids, eyes wide with adoration as Joseph reeled off answers to questions that confused the rest of the class.

Gradually, Leo's frustration at being unable to complete academically with Joseph turned to envy of everything his twin brother did, and he began to devise his own crafty methods of squaring accounts.

The twins homeroom teacher, a heavy, bustling woman named Mrs. Roberts, opened class each morning by having the children take turns in reading aloud from that day's *New York Times*, which she brought

317

in with her. This exercise gave her students an opportunity to improve their reading skills and, through a short discussion period afterward, to gain a grasp on what was occurring in the nation and the world. On the Friday morning before the twins' tenth birthday, Mrs. Roberts asked Joseph to read first, an article on the front page of the *Times* concerning international reactions to President Roosevelt's speech three days earlier in Chicago, in which he had called for a quarantine against Germany, Italy, and Spain, countries he had described as aggressor nations.

Joseph had not read more than a paragraph, enunciating clearly in a high, sharp voice, when Leo, sitting next to him, pushed a stack of three books onto the floor with a loud crash. As heads swung around toward the disturbance, Joseph faltered and then stopped.

"Sorry, Mrs. Roberts," Leo mumbled. "The books were too close to the edge of my desk."

"Then I suggest you place them in the center," Mrs. Roberts replied primly.

She indicated that Joseph should continue, and he resumed reading the article. A sentence later, there was another crash. Leo, in the middle of retrieving books from the floor, suddenly coughed. The books dropped again.

Joseph swung around on his twin, eyes blazing. "You did that on purpose!"

"No, I didn't."

"I say you did!" Joseph rolled up the newspaper, lifted it as if to strike his brother. Mrs. Roberts stepped between the two boys and removed the newspaper from Joseph's grasp. Leo, apparently unconcerned, resumed the task of picking up his books. The moment the teacher's back was turned, he stuck out his tongue at Joseph and grinned maliciously. "Teacher's pet," he whispered. "Little goody-goody, that's what you are."

Joseph flung himself on his twin brother, knocking him out of his chair, and the two boys rolled in the aisle, pummeling each other until Mrs. Roberts managed to drag them apart. To prevent any further disturbance, she made them sit on opposite sides of the room.

For the remainder of the morning, Joseph avoided eye contact with Leo; during break time he played with other boys, leaving Leo alone to sulk. When they walked home for lunch, Joseph strode along with his head held high, talking to Judy and ignoring his twin brother completely. Fifty yards from the apartment building, Leo raced past them so he could reach home first. He burst into the apartment and rushed to Pearl, tears streaming from his eyes as he clung to her.

"Joseph wouldn't play with me at school! He wouldn't talk to me!

He got the other boys to hate me!"

Pearl did her best to comfort him. She wiped the tears from his eyes and whispered soothing words. "Where's Joseph now?"

"He's coming in with Judy."

"You sit down and start your lunch. I'll speak with Joseph." Leaving Leo at the table, Pearl walked slowly toward the front door. She harbored little doubt that Leo had, in some way, been responsible for whatever had happened. Joseph wasn't a spiteful child who would deliberately snub his twin. Yet, she felt that she had to speak to Joseph about his behavior. As she did, he had to bend for Leo. Through the door, Pearl heard Joseph and Judy say goodbye.

When Joseph entered the apartment, he did not seem in the least surprised to see his mother waiting. He'd seen Leo run on ahead, and he'd guessed it was to promote his own version of that morning's events.

"Why wouldn't you play with Leo at school this morning?" Pearl asked.

"Because he tried to make me look like a fool in class. I was the first one Mrs. Roberts asked to read the newspaper, and he kept interrupting. He dropped his books onto the floor and made a lot of noise."

"Oh, Joseph, he didn't do it on purpose."

"Of course he did!"

Pearl's voice assumed a sharp note. "Don't speak to me in that tone, young man," she warned.

"Leo didn't drop his books once—he dropped them twice. He did it because I was asked to read first, because I can read better than he can. I'm cleverer than he is. He's jealous of me."

Pearl understood the truth of Joseph's claims. In school, he was far more able than his twin, and because of that Leo *was* envious. Pearl found it odd that twins, even if they were fraternal and not identical, should be so different, not only in appearance, but in personality and aptitude. The only common interest they had was sports. Jake had taken them to several baseball and football games, but the spectacle they loved above all else was boxing. A month did not pass without Jake taking them to the fights at Madison Square Garden, and for their ninth birthday the previous year, he had even bought them overstuffed boxing gloves. The twins' favorite pastime was turning their room into a boxing ring and sparring with each other, usually with Jake acting as referee. Pearl had been afraid they'd get hurt the first time she had seen them wade into each other. Her pleas for them to stop had been overruled by Jake. "What do you want them to be when they grow up?" he asked her. "A couple of sissies or two kids who can stand up for themselves? Boxing's good for them, it's healthy, builds character." Eventually, Pearl had agreed. With the overstuffed gloves, no real harm was done. And when the twins boxed, it seemed to her that was the only time they ever acted with the togetherness twins were supposed to have.

Jake's involvement with the boys had become much stronger since the end of Prohibition four years earlier. Now he was like a normal father, keeping regular hours. There were no more overnight trips to meet convoys, no more late nights at the clubs. All the clubs had been shut down, including the Four Aces which had had a symbolic closure on the very night Prohibition had been repealed. A band had played "Auld Lang Syne," and legal champagne had been given away free to all the regular patrons. Only the casino in the back of the Four Aces had taken in money that night. Pearl had not been there to see any of it. Since her mother's death, she had ventured into none of the clubs; she had cut herself off from that part of Jake's business dealings entirely. She could accept the gambling that still flourished, but the liquor business, which had launched their success, was anathema to her. Only on the bootlegging convoys had Jake worn those ivory-handled revolvers Benny Minsky had given him. Still unfired, they now lay in their walnut presentation box at the bottom of a locked bureau. With no liquor business, Jake no longer had any use for the weapons. Pearl hoped that one day he would forget about them completely, and then she would throw them into the river. . . .

"Joseph, you have to realize something. You're lucky to be so clever, to do so well at school." She held her older son's hands and looked deeply into his eyes. She knew he was more open to reason than Leo, more understanding. "Not everyone is so lucky, though. Leo isn't as good at school as you are. It has something to do with the illness he had. You shouldn't keep reminding him that he isn't as smart as you because it hurts him. That's why he interrupted you today."

"I don't remind him," Joseph protested. "Mrs. Roberts just asked me to read first. Is that my fault?"

"No, it's not. But don't you think you should let someone else read first in the future? If you like, I'll speak to Mrs. Roberts about it. I'm sure she'll understand."

Joseph fought back tears. It was unjust. He was better at school than Leo. Instead of being rewarded for it, he was being punished.

Pearl believed that Joseph's silence signified his approval of her suggestion. "Now come inside and shake hands with Leo."

Wordlessly, Joseph followed his mother into the dining room where Leo was sitting at the table, humming contentedly as he ate his lunch. "Leo, your brother wants to shake hands with you," Pearl said. "It's time for you to be friends again."

Leo hesitated. A triumphant smirk flashed across his face, but he was in no hurry to heal the rift—not when he knew he was winning.

Pearl put her foot down. "If you don't shake hands, I'll cancel your birthday party this Sunday."

The threat was enough. Leo set down his knife and fork, and reached out a hand. Slowly, Joseph shook it. "That's better," Pearl told them. "Always remember that you're twins . . . that's something very special." She went to the kitchen to bring out Joseph's lunch. By the time she returned, the boys were talking to each other. She smiled. Whatever differences they had were quickly forgotten. Soon they'd be the best of friends again, just as twins should be on their birthday.

Only a small birthday party was planned for the twins. Initially, Joseph wanted to invite schoolfriends, but Leo, who had no one at school he could call a friend, fought against the idea. Pearl, as always, found reason to support him, explaining to the disappointed Joseph that since Leo had no one from school to invite it was only fair that neither twin should ask schoolfriends. So invitations were sent out only to Jake's close business associates and their children—the people who had hidden out in the house in Fort Lee six years earlier.

Before Joseph could protest this latest unfair treatment, his father took his side. "Why should Joseph be punished because he makes friends easier than Leo?" Jake demanded of Pearl. "That's not the right way to treat the boy."

"If Joseph's friends come, they'll all play together and ignore Leo completely," Pearl answered. "And that's not the right way for Leo to have a birthday party, sitting alone in a corner while Joseph enjoys himself."

"What are they supposed to do when they grow up, Pearl? Stick like glue to each other? Is Joseph supposed to go through life always putting Leo first? It's about time you realized that Leo's recovered . . . he's been better for years. You can stop treating him like he's made of china." Jake understood that this was the first time he'd ever challenged Pearl on the way she was bringing up the twins. He'd allowed her to favor Leo because he'd always thought she knew best; but now he was beginning to wonder. "There's nothing wrong with Leo, so quit treating him like he's some invalid the whole world's got to revolve around."

"Physically there's nothing wrong with him," Pearl concurred. "But don't you ever notice how moody he gets, how depressed?"

"Sure, when he doesn't get what he wants. You've made him that way, Pearl. If you'd let him stand on his own two feet, he wouldn't be like that. Look at him when he and Joseph put on the gloves . . . he can stand up for himself then."

Pearl waved aside Jake's arguments. "I was the one who stayed in that basement with him while he was ill. I nursed him back to health. I'm closer to him than anyone. Believe me, Jake, I know what's best for him."

"Fine, but do you know what's best for Joseph? Carry on like this, always saying yes to Leo, and Joseph's going to wind up hating his brother's guts."

"Jake, for the first six years of their lives, you left me to raise those children on my own while you were running around, quenching the thirst of half this country. Don't start telling me now what I should or should not do."

Jake gave up. There was no way to argue against that kind of reasoning. He knew Pearl was right about those first six years. He hadn't been any kind of father to the boys, but he was determined to make up for that.

Next door, in the Caplans' apartment, the twins' birthday party also aroused strong feelings. Judy Caplan hated Leo. She loathed him for the tantrums he threw each time Joseph wanted to play with her, but most of all she hated him for the time he had jumped onto her doll's house. Her hatred of him was as strong as her liking for Joseph, and when she prepared to go to the party that Sunday, she wanted to take only one gift.

"Why should I take anything for Leo?" she asked her mother and father. "I don't want to go to his half of the party. I only want to go to Joseph's half."

"Don't be silly," Annie told her daughter. "You can't just go to one-half of a birthday party. Both boys invited you, so you have to take them both a gift."

"I could have said no to one of them . . . to Leo."

"Moe, will you speak to her?" After much deliberation, Annie had bought painting kits for the boys; now she had visions of Judy purposely leaving Leo's gift behind.

"What do you expect me to say?" Moses Caplan asked. "I should tell her that she's got to give a present to the boy she hates as well as to the boy she likes?"

"Thanks, you're a lot of help." Annie turned back to Judy. "These gifts aren't just from you—they're from us as well. We're also invited,

322

and we want to give a present to Leo. Okay?"

Judy clutched Joseph's present to her chest as though it were the most precious thing in the world. "Then *you* give Leo his present. *I'll* give this to Joseph."

The Caplans were the first to arrive at the Granitzes. Judy rushed into the apartment, eager to present Joseph with his gift. She ignored Leo completely, leaving him to receive his painting set and birthday greetings from her parents. The scene was not lost on Pearl. She drew Judy aside. "Don't you think you should wish Leo a happy birthday as well?"

"Leo doesn't like me," Judy stated defiantly. "And I don't like him."

"You know that's not really true."

"It is. He says I interfere—he says I come between him and his twin brother."

Pearl sighed. "Judy, please make this one day an exception. Go up and wish him a happy birthday."

Reluctantly, Judy approached the younger twin. "Happy birthday, Leo."

Leo smiled condescendingly. "Thank you, Judy. I hope you enjoy the party." He knew exactly why Judy had come to him. His mother had ordered her to. Whenever something needed doing, his mother was always there to ensure that it was done for him.

Benny Minsky and Kathleen were the next guests to arrive, with their son, William. Now aged eight, William didn't resemble his father at all. He had fair skin, hazel eyes and light brown hair without the slightest trace of a curl. Minsky was grateful for that; there was no chance his son would endure the torture he had gone through as a child, having his dark complexion mocked. Kathleen, too, was glad. If her son was not taunted unmercifully as Minsky had been, perhaps he would not grow up with his father's violent streak. Not that Benny's perverse behavior was so prevalent anymore. During the past few years, Kathleen had noticed that Minsky had mellowed. He even seemed—dare she use such a word where Minsky was concerned?—content.

Kathleen knew the reason why. For the first time in his life, Minsky had a stable home life. Following repeal and the end of the bootlegging operation, Minsky could, like Jake and Moses Caplan, spend more time with his family. The pell-mell attitude that had characterized their lives before repeal was gone. Minsky worked reasonable hours, splitting his time between the bookmaking and numbers operations based above the Jalo Cab garage on the West Side and the downtown headquarters of a trucking company he owned. Called B.M. Transportation, the fleet was comprised of trucks which had been used for the bootlegging business. Minsky had converted them, fitted them with rails; and they were now used to haul dresses and coats for Garment-District manufacturers in whose businesses he and his partners owned interests. Jake and Levitt still ran the taxi company, and Caplan's concerns included restaurants and a small construction business. The money generated by these legitimate enterprises was modest compared with the gambling profits, but it gave the four men what they wanted most—a veneer of respectability.

The closing of the clubs, especially Kathleen Monahan's Hideaway, had affected Kathleen. Deprived of that unique platform she had been forced to search out her own singing spots. She soon learned that it was a very competitive world. She'd had two small roles in Broadway productions, and recently she had made several New York appearances with Tommy Dorsey. Singing with a band, on a radio show or in a dance hall, was not for Kathleen. It paid little, and she had no desire to travel around the country in a bus. So she quit Dorsey and waited for something more to her liking.

In her early thirties, Kathleen exhibited far more patience than she had ten years earlier. She watched other female vocalists, and she realized how difficult it would be for them to reach the top. She had been there already. She had experienced the thrills that, in all probability, these other women would never know. She knew she should be thankful for that. Slowly, she had come to terms with the havoc wrought by the depression. Now, as it began to recede, she found herself being happy just to be Benny Minsky's wife and William Minsky's mother. For the time being . . .

Lou Levitt was the last of the guests to arrive. He shook hands with Jake, kissed the cheek that Pearl offered to him, and nodded to the other adults. Finally he turned to the twins. "Who wants to go down to my car and bring up a birthday present?"

"I do!" Joseph answered instantly.

"Don't you even want to know what the present is?" Levitt winked at Pearl and Jake, as though they were a part of his game.

"I'll find out when I get down there," Joseph answered. If his Uncle Lou had brought a gift, it had to be something special. Levitt never disappointed the boys.

"What about you, Leo?" Levitt asked. "Aren't you interested in seeing what I've got for you?" He tossed car keys to the younger twin. "Go with your brother. It's for both of you."

The twins raced excitedly from the apartment. "What did you get them?" Jake asked.

"What every boy should have—a dog."

"Lou, you should have asked first," Pearl said reproachfully. "Leo's always been terrified of dogs. On the street, if he sees one he'll find a way to walk around it."

"What about Joseph?"

"The opposite. Goes up to every stray and pats it. But Leo—"

"It's an irrational fear. A boy shouldn't be frightened of a dog. It's not natural. Boys and dogs go together. You know, maybe getting a dog was a good thing."

Both Pearl and Jake appeared undecided. Kathleen spoke up. "Lou's right, dogs and kids go together. When my two borzois died, William was so broken-hearted that we had to get another dog." She looked at Levitt. "What kind of a dog did you get for them?"

"A German shepherd pup, couple of months old."

"A German shepherd?" The incredulous question came from Minsky. "That's a guard dog, for Christ's sake, not the dog you give to a couple of kids as a pet."

Levitt gave Minsky an icy stare. "You think a couple of borzois and whatever mongrel you've got now make you such an expert?"

"No. But I wouldn't let William near one of those things. They'll take your damned leg off as soon as look at you."

Levitt did not bother answering. What was the point when Minsky tried to compare his son with the twins? The twins were lively, aggressive kids. Minsky's son was quiet, retiring, a shy boy who seemed so scared of his own shadow that Levitt doubted he would ever amount to anything. In a gesture of dismissal, Levitt glanced out of the window to where his car was parked. The twins were running toward it, and Levitt tried to imagine their pleasure when they learned the nature of the gift. Never mind Pearl's concerns . . . what kid didn't like a dog?

Leo was back first. He rushed into the apartment, threw his arms around his mother and screamed: "It's a dog! Uncle Lou got us a dog! I hate dogs!"

"It's a little puppy," Levitt said, taken aback by the outburst. "How can you hate a puppy?"

Joseph returned to the apartment two minutes later, the German shepherd puppy cradled tenderly in his arms. The leash around the dog's neck dangled to the floor, and Joseph's face was bent forward so that the dog could lick it. "See what Uncle Lou brought for us," Joseph said delightedly. "It's just what I wanted."

Levitt turned triumphantly to Pearl and Jake. "Well?"

Leo risked a nervous peek at the dog. He was balanced on his toes,

325

ready to flee should Joseph bring it too close. Instead, Joseph took it to Judy, a warrior presenting his beloved with a trophy. "Here, let him lick your face."

Obediently, Judy put her face forward to be licked. Next, Joseph went to William, who reached out tentatively to stroke the puppy. "He's beautiful, Uncle Lou," Joseph said. "Thank you very much."

"Joseph, put him down. Hold the leash and let your brother stroke him," Levitt suggested. It wasn't right for the boy to be so frightened of a puppy. Levitt wanted to cure that fear immediately.

Joseph set the dog down carefully. Holding the leash, he advanced slowly toward Leo. "Go on," Levitt encouraged. "Stroke him, he won't hurt you."

Very gingerly, Leo held out a trembling hand. The puppy came closer, sniffed the hand. Its tail wagged, and suddenly it gave a short, sharp bark. Leo jumped back into his mother's arms.

"He knows you're afraid," Levitt said. "Look, this is what you do." He knelt beside the dog and rubbed its head. The dog's tail lashed back and forth in frenzied movements. "Don't be frightened of him, he only wants to be your friend."

"I don't want him to be my friend. I don't want him in this apartment. Take him away, Uncle Lou."

"Well, I do want him here," Joseph said stubbornly. "He's going to sleep on my bed. I'll look after him. You won't have to touch him."

Leo sought assistance where he had always sought it. "Mummy, I don't want the dog. Make him go away."

For an instant it seemed that Pearl would adopt her normal stance. She caught Jake's stare, recognized the accusation in his eyes, and remembered what he had said. Did she always side with Leo? Was her attitude toward him overly protective, damaging to both Leo and Joseph? "Leo, come with me. I want to talk to you." Leaving the others in the living room, she led Leo into the bedroom. "Listen to me, Leo . . . there's nothing to be afraid of in a dog."

"He barked at me. He wanted to bite me."

"He was playing, that's all. When dogs bark it's their way of speaking. Do you want everyone else to think a big boy like you is frightened of a tiny dog?"

"I'm not frightened."

"Well, that's what they're going to think."

Leo considered that. "Joseph thinks I'm frightened as well?"

"They all do, Joseph, William, Judy. Is that what you want? They weren't scared to stroke the dog, and neither should you be."

"I'm not frightened," Leo repeated. "If Joseph isn't frightened of the dog, then neither am I."

"That's better. Now go back inside and show them all."

Leo returned to the living room. Joseph had found a ball which he was rolling across the floor for the puppy to chase. "Bring it back! Bring it back!" he cried excitedly. "This is the best birthday present I ever had, Uncle Lou! The very best!" The dog retrieved the ball, dropped it at Joseph's feet and barked for it to be thrown again. Joseph rolled the ball toward the far wall. Before the dog could reach it, Leo stepped on the ball. The puppy skidded to a halt and gazed questioningly into Leo's face.

"Take your foot off that ball!" Joseph yelled at his brother.

"I want to throw it." Summoning up all his courage, Leo waved a hand at the puppy to retreat. He picked up the ball and rolled it along the hallway. The puppy gave chase.

"That's better," Jake said. "He's a friendly dog, you see?"

The puppy came back and gazed uncertainly at the twins before dropping the ball at Leo's feet. Leo picked it up, forced himself to pat the puppy's head.

"Throw it again," Levitt said. "Let him get used to you."

Leo rolled the ball along the hallway again, but this time with all the force he could muster. The ball slammed into the door. As it bounced back, the dog skidded into the door with a loud crash. Inwardly, Leo smiled. He hoped the dog had hurt itself. He hated it, and he *was* frightened of it. For no reason at all, the puppy had barked at him. Just like all dogs did, as if they could sense his fear. Why did Uncle Lou bring him a dog as a birthday present? A dog Joseph loved as much as Leo hated it. And why hadn't his mother supported him?

"I want to take the dog for a walk," Leo announced solemnly.

Pearl smiled. "Of course you can."

Levitt passed the leash to Leo. "See how easy it is? Just walk him slowly around the block, let him get used to you."

Holding the leash, Leo looked at the other three children. Joseph's eyes were the last he met. "I'm not afraid of a dog."

"You just be careful with him," Joseph warned. "He's my dog as well as yours."

"Of course I'll be careful." Leo jerked the leash toward the door. Tail wagging, the puppy walked alongside the boy. The moment Leo had gone, Joseph rushed over to the window and looked down, waiting for his brother and the puppy to appear. When Leo came out of the building, Joseph slid open the window, leaned out and shouted: "Don't cross the street with him! You take care of him!"

Pearl rested a hand on Joseph's shoulder. "He's not going to let anything happen to the puppy. Stop worrying."

"But he doesn't like dogs," Joseph replied. "He's only taking the puppy for a walk to show us all he's not scared. But he is."

"By taking the dog out, Leo's teaching himself not to be frightened," Levitt said. He glanced out of the window, just in time to see Leo turning into an alleyway that ran behind the building. "A beautiful picture, eh? A boy and his dog."

Leo returned ten minutes later, huge tears dribbling from his eyes. There was no sign of the puppy or the leash.

"Where is he?" Joseph yelled at the forlorn figure of his twin.

"He ran away."

"What do you mean, he ran away?" Joseph clenched his fists. His eyes blazed. Quickly, Jake stepped between the two boys.

"Just that," Leo answered. "He saw another dog and"—he threw his arms wide open—"he jerked the leash out of my hand and ran. I tried to catch him, but I couldn't."

"Which way did he go?"

"Toward Washington Square."

Joseph darted toward the door. Jake grabbed hold of him and swung him around. "Hold on! There's no point in you chasing all over the place looking for him."

"We'll all look," Levitt said quickly. Not for a moment did he believe that the German shepherd puppy had jerked itself free. The puppy was the gentlest dog Levitt could find in the pet shop; especially good with children, the salesman had said. It would not just run away. Levitt turned to the other people in the room. "Let's split up into groups. Moe, you take Judy. Benny, you and William look for the dog together. Jake, you go with Joseph, and I'll take Leo."

"What about us?" Pearl asked, indicating Annie and Kathleen.

"You stay here. The dog might find its way home." Turning back to the search parties, he said, "At four-thirty, in half an hour from now, we'll meet back here. Okay?"

Joseph was already tugging at Jake's hand. Levitt and Leo were the last to leave. "Show me exactly where you took the dog," Levitt said.

Leo pointed south along Fifth Avenue. "I went straight down there."

"Okay, let's see what we can find." As they began to walk south, Levitt lifted his head toward the window of the apartment from which Joseph had shouted his warning to be careful, and from which Levitt himself had seen Leo turn down the alleyway.

Leo led the way, walking two yards ahead of Levitt. When the boy reached the mouth of the alleyway, he looked straight ahead and kept on walking. Levitt slowed, and Leo turned around. "Come on, Uncle Lou. We went further than this. Much further."

Levitt picked up his pace. He knew for certain now that they would never find the puppy. None of the search parties would. With Leo, he walked the few blocks south to Washington Square, looking along each street they crossed, peering into doorways. "He's not here," Leo kept repeating each time they stopped. "He must have run a long way."

"We'll find him."

"Will we, Uncle Lou?" Optimism appeared on Leo's face. "I do hope we find him. I was frightened of him at first, but I got to like him. I wasn't scared of him when I took him out, was I?"

"No, Leo, you weren't. You were a very brave boy."

After twenty minutes, they began to walk back toward the apartment building. Again, Leo led Levitt right past the entrance to the alleyway. As they reached the building entrance, they met Jake and Joseph, who had looked north along Fifth Avenue. Joseph's face was wet with tears, and Jake wore a mask of gloom.

"Not a sign of the damned dog," Jake muttered.

"Same here. Maybe Benny or Moe had more luck." Levitt gazed down at Joseph who was making an attempt to check his tears. "We'll find him, Joseph. And if we don't, I'll buy you another dog just as nice as that one."

"I don't want another dog. I want that dog." Joseph glared at his twin. "You lost him. You let him go after I told you to look after him."

"It was an accident," Leo answered. "I wouldn't lose him on purpose."

"You lost him because you were scared of him."

"I was not." Leo peered up at Levitt. "Tell Joseph I wasn't scared of the dog, Uncle Lou."

"No, you weren't scared. If you had been, you would never have taken him for a walk."

Within five minutes, Minsky and Caplan returned. Their long faces made an oral report unnecessary. The dog had disappeared completely. Jake tried to console Joseph, continually telling the boy that he could have another dog, but Joseph was heartbroken. Tears streamed down his cheeks, his body shook from sobbing. Even Judy's forced cheerful assurances that the puppy would return failed to stem the flood.

Levitt held back as they entered the building. "While I'm down here, let me get a pack of cigarettes. I'll be up in a few minutes." He handed Leo over to Jake and walked away. Leo looked back, eyes suddenly hard and gray as he watched Levitt. He knew where Levitt was going. Leo had fooled the others—even his brother—but he had not fooled his Uncle Lou. Levitt wasn't going to buy cigarettes. He was going—Leo stretched his neck, trying to keep Levitt in sight as

Jake pulled him into the building—to see what was down the alleyway.

Entering the narrow alleyway, Levitt looked up at the buildings that hemmed him in. He wasn't even certain what he was seeking. He was going on instinct alone. He had seen Leo take the dog into the alleyway, but later Leo had deliberately led him past it, not once, but twice.

Levitt flicked his eyes around, took in the neat rows of garbage cans awaiting the following day's collection. Ten yards into the alleyway, he saw men removing furniture from a truck. Levitt approached a heavy, balding man who appeared to be the foreman of the moving crew. "You see a young boy come along here with a dog?"

"Kid with a dog? Yeah, about half an hour ago. He went right to the end." The man pointed to where the alleyway swung around in a sharp turn before rejoining Fifth Avenue on the northern side of the apartment building. "Running like he had the devil after him. Damned dog could barely keep up."

"Thanks." Levitt walked on. He passed the bend in the alleyway and saw Fifth Avenue twenty yards ahead. The moving truck was now out of sight. Levitt knew that whatever he was seeking lay in the twenty yards ahead of him. He looked in doorways, but found nothing. Finally, he began to lift the lids of garbage cans. In the seventh one he tried, he discovered the body of the puppy. The leash was pulled tightly around its neck, and its head was smashed to a pulp. Levitt closed the garbage can and swept the immediate area with his eyes. On the building wall he spotted a patch of dried blood and matted hair. Breathing deeply, he walked on.

What kind of a kid killed a dog like that, swung it on its leash like a hammer thrower and slammed its head into a brick wall? A terrified kid? Or a vindictive, sick kid? Levitt didn't know. Nor did he know what to do. Should he tell Pearl and Jake what he'd found or keep the information to himself, let the animal's corpse be collected with the trash the following day, let it be abandoned on the city dump?

When he returned to the apartment, Levitt noticed that Leo watched him carefully. Levitt could read volumes in the boy's eyes, not just the subtle change of color as Leo's mood altered; he could see fear in them. He tore his gaze away from the boy, still uncertain what to do.

The disappearance of the dog killed the party atmosphere. Joseph sat with a mournful face while he watched Judy and William play with the clockwork truck the Minskys had brought. And Leo simply stood, eyes boring into Levitt as he tried to guess what the man had found.

Pearl appeared with two birthday cakes, each studded with ten candles. She set the cakes on the dining-room table and clapped her hands. "Come on, birthday twins . . . time to blow out your candles and make a wish."

"You can wish that your dog finds its way home," Jake told Joseph.

"He's not coming home," Joseph answered with despondent certainty. He lifted his eyes to skewer his brother with an angry glare. "Leo lost him on purpose. He didn't like the puppy, so he went out and lost him."

"Don't be so silly," Pearl said. "Of course Leo liked the dog. Come on, blow your candles out now."

Leo went to the table first and extinguished all ten candles on his cake with a single breath. Joseph followed, but with little enthusiasm. He blew on his candles. Half of them flickered and died; the other five remained alight.

"Your wish won't come true," Levitt told him.

"It won't come true anyway. He'll never come back. He'll just run around the streets until . . . until he gets run over by a car. That's what Leo wanted!" Joseph burst into a fresh flood of tears and then ran to his bedroom, slamming the door. When Levitt looked at Leo, the younger twin wore the faintest trace of a smile, as if his wish had already come true. Levitt supposed that it had. The boy had hated the dog and now it was dead.

Soon after the lighting of the candles, the Minskys and the Caplans left. Levitt stayed for a further fifteen minutes, trying to decide what course of action to take. He knocked on the door of the twins' room and entered to find Joseph sitting disconsolately on the bed. "Here's twenty dollars," Levitt said. "Buy yourself whatever you like for your birthday."

"I don't want to buy anything, Uncle Lou. I want that dog. You bought him for me, and I want him back."

"Joseph, you've got to understand something—he might not come back. Did you ever hear the expression about crying over spilled milk?"

"I didn't spill the milk."

"So Leo spilled it; what difference does it make? Either way, there's no point in crying over it. You've got to move on."

Joseph stared at the twenty dollars in his hand, crumpled it into a ball and threw it at the wall. "I want my dog, not twenty dollars."

"Suit yourself," Levitt said. If the boy was not open to reason, he'd leave him alone. Returning to the living room, he said goodbye to Pearl and Jake. Then he crooked a finger at Leo. "Why don't you walk to my car with me, Leo? I'll give you something in place of the puppy."

Leo followed Levitt out of the apartment. Together, they took the

331

elevator down to the ground floor. "I found the dog," Levitt said conversationally.

Leo's head jerked up. "Where? Where did you find him, Uncle Lou?"

"Where do you think I found him? Where you left him, Leo. Stuck in a garbage can with his head bashed in. Why did you do it?"

"Do what?" Leo's eyes were open wide, soft hazel, beguiling.

"Why did you kill the dog? I know exactly what you did. You swung him on the leash and you smashed his head against the wall. The moving men saw you do it. They told me."

"No, they didn't. I made sure they didn't see me!" Leo burst out. The instant he realized what he'd said, he turned his face away.

Reaching the street, they walked toward Levitt's car. "Sit down and talk to me for a few minutes, Leo." Levitt opened the passenger door and Leo hopped inside. "I'm not going to tell anyone. It's better that they think the dog just ran away. All I want to know is why you did it."

"Because I hated that dog." A wide appealing smile crossed Leo's face. "Why did you get me a dog when I hate dogs, Uncle Lou?"

"Had I known that, Leo, I would have got you something else." There was a lot he didn't know about the twins, he decided ruefully. He could not visit the apartment as often as he wanted to. Pearl continued to maintain an icy coolness toward him, as if she were terrified that he would give the game away. Levitt's invitations had to come from Jake; they never came from Pearl. Frequently, those invitations were for dinner, when he would only get to see the boys for half an hour or so before they went to bed. "Tell me something, Leo. If you hate dogs so much, why did you want to take him for a walk?"

"To show Joseph I wasn't scared. If he wasn't frightened, I had to show him that I wasn't frightened either." Leo made it sound so logical, Jake thought. Sibling rivalry taken to gruesome extremes. "Did someone see me?" Leo asked.

"No. No one saw you."

"I was clever, wasn't I?"

Levitt shook his head, and the smile that had been growing on Leo's face fell away. "You weren't clever at all, Leo. I saw you go down that alleyway with the dog. I was watching through the window. And when we all went out to look, you deliberately led me past the alleyway. You showed your hand."

"You won't tell anyone, Uncle Lou?"

"No, Leo, I won't tell anyone." He gave the boy twenty dollars, the same amount he had given his twin. "Buy yourself another birthday gift with this."

"Thanks, Uncle Lou." Leo threw his arms around Levitt and kissed him on the cheek. "You're the greatest uncle in the whole wide world."

"Sure," Levitt said. "Now go back upstairs and be nice to your brother. What you did upset him. It's up to you to make it up to him, you hear me?"

Leo nodded soberly. "I'll be the best brother in the world to him."

"You just remember to be, because I'll be keeping my eyes on you." He watched the boy leave the car and run back to the apartment building. Two brothers, twins, and not the slightest similarity. One was a sensitive kid, reduced to tears because his new puppy disappeared. And the other? Terrified of a dog, so he killed it to prove he wasn't really frightened. And not only did he kill it, but he made certain that no one saw him commit the act. At ten, Leo had used more brains than an adult Benny Minsky when he'd murdered Kathleen's boyfriend. Bad luck had caught Leo out, Levitt's choosing that particular moment to glance out of the window and see the boy taking the dog down the alleyway. As with Minsky, though, Levitt now knew one of Leo's secrets. Not a secret with which he could control the boy, but a secret nonetheless. It was always good to know such things about people, even a boy as young as Leo.

Sitting in the car, Levitt compared the twins again. Joseph was bright, good at school, but Leo possessed a sly smartness. Which trait, Levitt wondered, would serve the twins best as they grew older? Brains or cunning?

The bout of diphtheria . . . where did that fit in? Levitt recalled the day Sophie Resnick had died, Leo's words that shocked them all. "Jelly roll . . . jelly roll." And now this, killing the dog. Did both incidents have something to do with the illness six years earlier? Those aftereffects the doctor had mentioned. Nervous disorders. Was nervous disorder another name for a mental illness so severe it caused such savagery in a ten-year-old boy?

It was a question that even Levitt, with his cold, analytical mind, could not answer.

Chapter Two

During the summer of 1939, as the Granitz twins approached their twelfth birthdays, the world was in a contradictory state. Americans, buoyed by a rebuilding economy, were finally throwing off the shackles of the Depression decade. They seemed blissfully unaware of what was taking place on the other side of the Atlantic Ocean, where international tensions mounted toward an inescapable and shattering climax. In late August, when Germany signed its doom-laden nonaggression pact with the Soviet Union, the New York World's Fair was doing a record business. Few of the fair's two million visitors paused to consider why the Czechoslovakian exhibit had failed to open, a casualty of Hitler's recarving of the face of Europe.

The big movie hit was *The Wizard of Oz*. Pearl and Jake took the twins to see it at the end of August. Leo and Joseph were still talking excitedly about the film two days later, when Neville Chamberlain solemnly declared that his country was at war with Germany. That Europe should be embroiled once again in war mattered little to most New Yorkers. They had more pressing concerns—a fierce heat wave that continued to scorch the East Coast, and a milk strike that had the city in an iron grip. In Europe, after a respite of only twenty-one years, men were learning once more to kill each other. In New York, people were learning to drink their coffee black.

In Jake and Pearl's circle, only Lou Levitt seemed totally absorbed in the dramatic events in Europe. He read newspapers from cover to cover, listened avidly to news broadcasts. He even moved a shortwave radio into the office he shared with Jake on the floor above the Jalo Cab Company garage.

Behind this office the four partners' gambling empire was centered. A door led from it to the vast room which occupied the remainder of the floor. To this room, in which there was the continual clatter of adding machines, the crisp crackle and jingle of bills and coins being tallied, came the numbers runners and handbook collection agents. Eight men operated telephones. Counting, checking, and settling bets and numbers payoffs was a team of a dozen bookkeepers, all handpicked and trained by Levitt. He watched them like a hawk. Not for theft; they were too well paid to be tempted. He looked for mistakes, accidental miscounting because two bills were stuck together, overlooking a winning ticket. Levitt prided himself on being scrupulously honest in his gambling dealings. The odds were heavily in favor of the house, so when a player won, Levitt wanted to be certain that the ticket was paid off in full. It was the finest form of advertising. No matter how many times a man lost, he would always tell his friends when he won—and, more important, where he had won.

In those first few days of the war in Europe, however, as the news became gloomier, Levitt's interest in gambling began to wane. He spent more and more time in the office, fiddling with the dial of the radio as he tried to pick up yet another news broadcast.

"That's my country those bastards are doing their goosestep all over," he kept saying. "I come from there. That's my country."

"What the hell do you care about Poland?" Jake asked him. "You're an American. You're naturalized."

"If there weren't three and a half million Jews over there," Levitt answered grimly, "I'd say the country could go burn in hell. Those Jews are the reason I care."

Jake fell silent. He had never considered that Levitt might still have family in Poland. The little man had never spoken of cousins, aunts, uncles. He was probably the least family-oriented man Jake had ever known.

In October, as reports became even bleaker—Poland was incorporated into the Reich, Polish Jews were deported for resettlement in the Lublin Reserve, and finally one of the Royal Navy's proudest ships, the *Ark Royal*, was sunk in Scapa Flow—Levitt's mood plummeted. "Those bastards are going to walk right over everyone," he muttered after one Friday-night dinner at the Granitz apartment. The twins were already in bed, and Levitt sat with Pearl and Jake in the living room. "They're going to walk over everyone because no one made any preparations to stop them."

"Lou, you're going to make yourself sick," Jake told him. "You can't change a damned thing by worrying."

"Don't you worry? Don't you care what happens over there? Sure, let the *goyim* go ahead and kill each other, they enjoy fighting. But why should the Jews be murdered by this madman?" He began to pace around the room, switching subjects so abruptly that Pearl and Jake were thrown completely off balance. "In just over a year, the twins'll be thirteen. What arrangements have you made for their bar

335

mitzvahs?"

"We hadn't even thought about it yet," Jake answered.

"Maybe you should start thinking about it," Levitt said. "A year's not such a long time."

Pearl regarded Levitt quizzically. He had always been the only member of the group to place any real importance on being a Jew. He had criticized Benny Minsky for marrying Kathleen; he had even found a redeeming feature in Saul Fromberg, a man who would cheat and rob, even organize murder, but who would not turn around and call you a dirty Kike. Since the trouble in Europe, though, Levitt's Jewishness had become an obsession with him. "Why the sudden concern about the twins being bar mitzvahed?" Pearl asked him.

"Because it's time to stand up and be counted, that's why. These past few years have demonstrated that. The German-American Bund, Gerald L. K. Smith, Father Coughlin, all that scum. If you don't stand up, if you don't make a commitment, you might as well forget the whole thing because it means those bastards have won." The fire in his voice died, and he gave Pearl and Jake a little lopsided grin, as though embarrassed at his vehement outburst. "Remember, I'm the twins' godfather—their spiritual upbringing is supposed to be my responsibility. I don't want to see them deprived of anything. Out of all the kids, Joseph and Leo are the only ones who'll get the thrill of being bar mitzvahed. Judy won't; she's a girl. And as for Benny's boy, William. Pah! . . . Baptized, a Catholic, another soldier for Christ!"

Levitt's words turned Pearl introspective. "I wonder," she mused aloud, "if Benny ever misses a Jewish home life. You know what I mean—just the idea of candles being lit on a Friday night, that kind of thing."

Levitt ridiculed the notion. "Of course he doesn't. He's still so besotted with his Irish thrush that he doesn't know what day of the week it is. He doesn't know what's happening in Europe; he couldn't give a damn. Anyway, who the hell cares about Benny or his kid? The twins are all that matters. Hire a teacher for them, so when their bar mitzvah comes they can stand up and look as though they know what they're doing. More importantly, so they can stand up and show the world that they're not ashamed to be Jews."

Listening to Levitt, Pearl stared at the candles she had lit that evening when the sun had gone down. They were nothing more than guttering stumps now, smoking grayly as flame tried to burn through the build-up of wax. Levitt's concern about the twins' bar mitzvahs began to make sense . . . the stand-up-and-be-counted speech, the talk of pride. Levitt, the only one of the four partners to take any active interest in Judaism, wanted to be sure that the twins were bar mitzvahed because he wanted his sons brought up that way. He still believed that Joseph and Leo were his. He would never believe otherwise.

To her own surprise, Pearl found herself agreeing with him. Jake had never cared for religion. Levitt did. Now Pearl realized that she, too, cared. The token gesture of lighting candles on a Friday evening was no longer enough. Pearl followed that tradition because her mother had taught her to do so, but there was more to it than that, more than just blind imitation.

She and Jake hired a private tutor, an elderly man named Isaac Cohen, to teach the twins the portions of the Old Testament they would read for their bar mitzvahs. Cohen came to the apartment once a week, for three hours every Sunday morning. Sometimes, while the old man was giving the twins their lesson, Levitt visited the apartment to eavesdrop. As the twins practiced, Levitt would look at Pearl and Jake with pride on his face.

"You ever think Benny's going to get this kind of pleasure from his son?" Levitt asked, before answering the question himself. "No, he'll get no joy from his Catholic kid and his *shikse* wife. Trouble's all he'll get from them, tears and aggravation. Which is all that crazy animal deserves out of life."

Through the end of 1939 and the beginning of 1940, as Benny Minsky saw the Granitz twins preparing for their bar mitzvahs, he began to feel remorse because his own son would never follow their example. Ten years earlier, when William had been born, Minsky had not been unduly worried because Kathleen had wanted the boy baptized into the religion of his mother. Minsky had just been grateful for the safe birth of his son, for Kathleen's having gone through with it. Then, as Kathleen's singing career had stagnated and she had settled down to being a mother and a wife, Minsky had been so lulled by their comfortable routine that he had paid scant attention to his son's religion. But now, when he heard about the Granitz twins, something reached deep within him, a poignant memory of religion and tradition.

Minsky's own parents had brought their religion with them from Russia, and they had made sure that their son followed it, forcing him to attend the synagogue and Hebrew classes, which he had hated passionately. Once he had been bar mitzvahed, he had cut himself off from religion. His parents hadn't complained—at that time, their son's lack of belief and commitment had been the smallest of their worries; they had been far more concerned about the friends he'd

337

made, the trouble they could see him getting into.

Minsky had not missed religion at all. Openly shunning it was part of his rebellion against established convention. Nonetheless, he could not help but feel a tug of sentiment when Jake told him about the twins, and that tug grew in strength with each passing week. Minsky even made excuses to visit the Granitz home on Sunday mornings when the tutor would be there. With Jake and Levitt—and sometimes Moses Caplan, who was drawn from the adjacent apartment by the same sentimentality—Minsky would listen to the twins rehearse. Levitt never questioned Minsky's presence in the apartment on those Sunday mornings. He knew exactly why the dark-skinned man was there. All these years after marrying Kathleen, Minsky was questioning the heritage he had forsaken. Levitt felt vindicated, because he knew that of all the battles Kathleen and Minsky had fought, the most explosive was still to come.

And it would come for the very reason that Levitt had always said it would.

In March 1940, eight months before the twins were due to be bar mitzvahed, Kathleen's journey in the wilderness came to an end. Hollywood was planning a movie version of *Broadway Nell*, the musical in which Kathleen had shot to fame eleven years earlier, and she was asked to play the role.

The summons came out of the blue. Hal Brookman, the producer of the movie, was in New York. On a Sunday morning, while Minsky was at the Granitz home and William was out playing with friends, Brookman turned up at Riverside Drive and banged on the door. Kathleen didn't know him from Adam, and he didn't bother to identify himself. All he said was: "How would you like to come out to California and do a screen test for the movie role of *Broadway Nell?*"

Kathleen's ambition, which had lain dormant for so many years, soared like an eagle. "Who do I have to fuck?"

Brookman grinned. Like Irwin Kuczinski before him, Brookman was already certain that he had found his Nell. "No one . . . unless you want to. All you've got to do is sing in that crazy, throaty voice of yours."

"Come inside and tell me all about it. And while you're doing that, you can tell me who the hell you are as well."

"Hal Brookman. I'm producing the movie, and your name was the first that popped into my head. Kuczinski had a hell of a hit with you in the stage production, and I'm damned sure I can do even better with you in the movie."

338

"I'm eleven years older."

"So? Who said Nell had to be a young virgin? Older, more worldly women are coming into vogue." Brookman followed her into the living room and sat down. "I hear that you're a family woman now with a son. Is that going to affect your coming out West?"

Kathleen shook her head. "I had a housekeeper before, to look after William, and I can get one again."

"And what about your husband?" Brookman knew all about Benny Minsky's pedigree. Anyone who was aware of Kathleen's history—the clubs, her short reign at the top before the baby—was also aware of the role Minsky had played in her career.

"Benny?" Kathleen thought about him. Would he go crazy if she suddenly upped and took off for the West Coast for the screen test? Even more important, what would he do if she were away for six or eight weeks to shoot the movie? "I don't know. I'd have to talk to him first."

"Where is he now?"

"At the home of some friends." Kathleen didn't know the reason for Minsky's regular visits to the Granitz home on Sunday mornings; she just assumed he went there for business meetings. It would never have entered her mind that Minsky could be interested in anything even remotely connected with religion. "He'll be back in an hour or so. How about a cup of coffee while we talk?"

"Why not?" Brookman followed her into the kitchen, watching as she prepared the coffee. "You still remember all the songs from *Broadway Nell?*"

"Remember them? They're engraved on my memory." She sang the first lines of "Lonely, Lonely Me." "How does that sound to you?"

"Better than when you did it eleven years ago. Time's been kind to you."

Kathleen rewarded him with a bright smile. "Are you stroking me, or are you telling the truth?"

"Used-car salesmen lie, not movie producers. Your voice is warmer than it used to be. I saw you in *Broadway Nell*—must be four times."

Kathleen felt herself being drawn toward Hal Brookman, and she wasn't certain why. In his mid-forties, he was handsome enough, tall and lean, with dark hair turning gray at the temples. He had the tanned good looks Kathleen had seen on many men from the West Coast, as if he spent a lot of time on the beach or by a pool. It wasn't his appearance which attracted her, though. She had seen more handsome men than Brookman, and none of them had turned her head. The attraction was his offer of a trip back to the bright lights—

he'd awakened in her a yearning which she had thought was dead and buried.

"If you're interested in trying for a comeback, I've got the bucks and the role," Brookman said. "Your voice is even better now, you're a more rounded person. I'll bet if Kuczinski was putting on *Broadway Nell* for the first time right now, you'd be an even bigger sensation. You've got more personality, more warmth. You've grown as a person; that'll come across in your portrayal of Nell. We can even change the story line a little. Instead of having Nell as a single girl, we'll make her a widow with a kid. That'd fit right in, make you a more sympathetic character."

Kathleen took the coffee into the living room, her mind exploring the possibilities that Brookman was opening up. She could see Nell as a young widow with a child—the audience would lap it up. For half an hour, she and Brookman discussed the role; then Kathleen heard the sound of Minsky's key in the front door. She jumped up and ran to meet him in the hallway. She didn't want him walking into the living room and seeing her sitting there with a strange man. God alone knew how he would react. Now that opportunity had come knocking after all this time, Kathleen didn't want Minsky blowing her big chance by pulling a crazy jealous fit.

"We've got a visitor," she greeted him, "who's come all the way from Hollywood to see us."

"Oh?" To Kathleen's surprise, Minsky didn't seem particularly interested.

"A movie producer, Hal Brookman. He's putting together a movie version of *Broadway Nell.*"

"Sounds good. Does he want you for the lead?"

"So he says. Come inside and say hello to him. You wouldn't mind me going away, out to Hollywood, would you?" she added as she drew him toward the living room.

"Will it make you happy?"

"What do you think, Benny?"

Brookman rose as Minsky entered the room. Kathleen made the introductions. Instead of displaying the irrational anger she'd feared, Minsky was charming. "You must be like a ray of sunshine to Kathleen," he told Brookman. "I know how much she's missed singing these past years."

Brookman was lulled by Minsky's manner, struck by the difference between the man's reputation and the man himself. "Sometimes you've got to wait for the right thing to come along, Mr. Minsky."

"I've had plenty of other attractions to fill my time," Kathleen added, sliding an arm around Minsky's waist. Christ, had Benny ever changed! Seeing her with a strange man would have sent him into a screaming fury a few years ago, and the possibility of her leaving him for a couple of months would have had the same effect. But now he seemed happy for her sake.

"When does this thing start?" Minsky asked Brookman.

"First there's a screen test, but I'm sure that's going to be just a formality—"

"Then start shooting the movie as quickly as possible," Minsky interrupted. "Kathleen's the girl for the role. Don't keep your big star waiting."

Kathleen regarded Minsky with undisguised amazement. "Are you sure? I could be away for a couple of months, Benny."

"Of course I'm sure. You want to get back into the swing of things, don't you? Here's your chance. Go out to Hollywood, do your screen test, get the role, and then shoot the damned movie and make a name for yourself again. You deserve it." He waved a breezy farewell to Brookman as he headed into the bedroom he shared with Kathleen. Behind, he left two absolutely stunned people who had feared anger and had found, instead, heartfelt good wishes.

Lying on the bed, fully clothed, with even his shoes on, Minsky gazed up at the ceiling. Thoughts flashed across his mind, but they weren't concerned with Kathleen's news. He was engrossed in the time he had just spent at Jake and Pearl's home, and what he had learned there.

That morning, an agonizing truth had sunk home to Minsky. He would never see his only son bar mitzvahed. And that little sawed-off bastard Levitt had been the one to rub it in. . . .

After the twins' lesson that morning, their tutor, Isaac Cohen, had joined Pearl, Jake, Levitt, and Minsky for a cup of coffee and a piece of cake. Cohen had been full of the twins. "When you gave me the job of teaching them," he told Pearl and Jake, "never for a moment did I dream they would be so attentive, learn so quickly. There is competition between them, to see who can learn the best and the fastest, and the one who benefits is me. They make my job easy."

While Pearl and Jake smiled at the tutor's words, Levitt turned to give Minsky a sympathetic look. "I've got to feel really sorry for you, Benny. Jake and Pearl are going to get all this pleasure from the twins, and what are you going to have?"

"Lou!" Pearl's voice snapped across the room like a whip. "You've got no call to speak to Benny like that!"

Levitt feigned injured innocence. "What did I say? Just that Benny's not going to have the pleasure you're going to get, that's all. What the hell's wrong with that?" He turned toward Minsky again.

"Did I say anything wrong, Benny?"

"You don't have a son to be bar-mitzvahed?" Isaac Cohen asked Minsky, failing to understand the flare-up.

"I've got a son, all right," Minsky replied softly. His eyes burned with a dark hatred as he stared at Levitt. "Only his mother's a Catholic. My son was baptized into the Catholic faith."

"I see." Cohen stared down at his cup, and Minsky's hatred for Levitt grew even blacker. The sword Levitt held over his head for the murder of David Hay was nothing compared with the anguish he had just inflicted on Minsky—the reminder that Benny had cut himself off from his heritage, and there was no way back.

Or was there? Minsky switched his gaze from Levitt to Cohen. "You're a man who knows about religion. Could my son, with his Catholic mother, be bar mitzvahed?"

Cohen forced himself to lift his eyes and meet Minsky's brooding gaze. "I can speak only for Orthodox Jewish law, and the answer is no. The mother of the child must be Jewish."

"What about unorthodox Jewish law?" Minsky noticed Levitt stand up and walk to the window, his back to the others. Minsky was sure the little man was smiling.

"Are you really serious about this, Benny?" Pearl asked.

"Of course I am. Why do you think I've been coming up here on Sundays?"

"We never thought you cared. When you married Kathleen, you let her have William baptized."

Jake shared his friend's anguish. Turning to the tutor, he said, "What about a reform synagogue, Mr. Cohen? Would they be able to help Benny?"

"Perhaps." From the tone of his answer, it was obvious that Cohen did not wish to discuss it further.

Levitt swung around from his position at the window. "Yeah, why don't you try a reform synagogue, Benny? That's almost like a church. You and William should feel right at home there."

"You little son of a bitch!" Minsky jumped up from the chair. Levitt never batted an eyelid as the dark-skinned man lunged at him. At the last moment, Jake threw himself at Minsky and pinned his arms.

"Take it easy!" Jake hissed. "What's the matter with you, Benny? And you, Lou? What the hell's so terrible about Benny wanting to see his kid bar mitzvahed. He made a mistake and now he wants to rectify it."

"You made your bed, Benny," Levitt said. "Now enjoy lying on it."

Minsky shook himself free of Jake's grip and left the apartment.

During the drive home he fought back tears. The sentiment triggered by listening to the twins had turned into a drowning gush of self-pity. He would give anything to be able to see his own son going through the same experience that the twins were enjoying. Once, he hadn't cared. Now he knew differently. Like Esau in the Bible, he'd sold his birthright for a mess of pottage.

When Kathleen came rushing to meet him at the door, he was so deeply concerned with his own particular problem that he barely noticed her excited mention of a visitor. Only when she identified the man as Hal Brookman, a Hollywood producer who wanted to make a movie of *Broadway Nell*, did Minsky's interest awaken. And then his thoughts catapulted ahead, for he perceived an answer to his worries. Kathleen wanted to go to Hollywood? Good, let her go, he thought as he lay on the bed and stared up at the ceiling. She wanted to be away for a couple of months while she made the film? Let her. Three months, four, a damned year! Then he would be alone with his son so he could try to erase the mistake he'd made ten years earlier when he'd allowed Kathleen to have William baptized.

Goddamn that son-of-a-bitch Levitt! That little bastard had known all along that this would happen, that Minsky would see the Granitz twins getting ready for their bar mitzvahs and he'd feel left out. Levitt and his infernal ability to plot and plan, to prepare for the future. He had mocked Minsky all along because he could see the heartbreak that was in store for him. And now that Minsky had found it out for himself, Levitt was sitting back and laughing. Screw him! He wouldn't laugh for long. When William turned thirteen, he'd have a bar mitzvah as good as any other kid's. Minsky would get William interested in having one, just like Jake had got the twins interested. He'd use the time Kathleen was away to steal William back from Catholicism, coax him back from Kathleen. He'd get the boy all to himself. Kathleen hadn't wanted him anyway. For God's sake, look how hard she'd tried to get rid of him! She wouldn't miss him. She'd have her career again. She wouldn't know, wouldn't even care what went on outside of that career. . . .

Minsky lay on the bed until he heard the front door close. When he returned to the living room, Kathleen was looking at her reflection in the wall mirror while she hummed the tune of "Lonely, Lonely Me."

"Well, what did you and your producer decide?" Minsky asked.

"He's not even going to bother with a screen test," Kathleen replied. "He just offered me the part, straight-out. I'm going out West and we'll start filming as soon as possible." She hesitated, still uncertain about Minsky, the way he was reacting. "Is that okay with you?"

"Kathleen . . ." Minsky gave her a broad smile and rested both hands on her shoulders. "Whatever you want is okay by me, don't you know that, baby?"

She lifted her face to kiss him. "I've been married to you for eleven years and I still can't make you out. When I think you're going to hit the roof, you surprise me by being the greatest guy in the world."

"Why should I hit the roof? I only want what's best for you. Take what this guy offers and make a new name for yourself. Show the world that Kathleen Monahan's still alive and kicking."

Kathleen left for California a week later, after hiring a housekeeper to look after William. As soon as Minsky had seen her off, he visited the Granitz home. Pearl, sitting in the living room with Annie, was surprised when Minsky turned up unannounced. She had not seen him since the Sunday he'd left the apartment after the argument with Levitt.

"Something wrong?" she asked.

Minsky shook his head. "I think everything's just turning very right, but I'm going to need one favor from you."

Pearl glanced at Annie. "Is it Kathleen again?" she asked fatalistically.

"No. For once it's not Kathleen. It's my son."

"William?" Annie asked. "What's the matter with him?"

"You remember the other Sunday—"

"When you and Lou? . . ." Pearl hesitated. "He was way out of line that day, Benny. He had no business saying what he did."

"He was out of line all right, but maybe he wasn't so wrong. I've been a real fool where that kid's concerned. While Kathleen's away shooting this movie, I want to make everything right. I want to start taking William to a synagogue on Saturday mornings."

"A reform synagogue?"

"I guess—who else would have him now? But even a reform synagogue is better than nothing. There's more, though. You light the candles every Friday night, you have a *Shabbas* dinner. Pearl, the favor I'm asking . . . would you invite us around, me and William?"

"I'd be delighted to," Pearl declared. "That's no favor, Benny. That's a good deed. But"—she paused—"you know, Lou sometimes comes around on a Friday night, Jake invites him."

Minsky's face soured. He could handle Levitt's wisecracks, but how would his son feel upon seeing his father put down, hearing his mother denigrated?

Pearl noticed the change of expression. Minsky wanted help

344

because he was vitally concerned about his son's future. She wouldn't deny him. "Leave it to me, Benny. I'll have a word with Lou." She looked at Annie. "You, Moe, and Judy come as well. From now on, we'll have a big party every Friday night."

Pearl told Jake about Minsky's visit, her plans for a big Friday-night dinner. Jake sympathized with Minsky; how could he feel otherwise? The man had a son whom he felt he had betrayed. Now he wanted to make it up to the boy. Jake's friendship for Minsky urged him to help, but he could not ignore Levitt's animosity.

"Pearl, you know what's Lou's like. When I bring him here on Friday night and he sees Benny with his son, he won't be able to resist saying something. Benny's like a red rag to a bull as far as Lou's concerned."

"Then how come they work together? How come Lou lets Benny be an equal partner in the business?"

"Because there are a lot of bucks involved. Half the guys working above the taxi garage—the bookkeepers, the runners—they're all on the books of B.M. Transportation, Benny's trucking outfit, so they can show a legal source of income, pay taxes on it. Lou's dead straight in business. He knows Benny's a partner and he accepts it. But he doesn't want to see him socially." He gazed in exasperation at Pearl; she was looking at him with a gleam in her light brown eyes, as though she had not heard a single word he'd said. "You're just asking for trouble with this idea, Pearl. Drop it."

"You just watch how much trouble it is," Pearl went to the telephone and dialed the number of Levitt's apartment on Central Park West. "Lou, this coming Friday, Benny's bringing his son here for dinner. He wants William to see candles lit—he wants him to learn what it's all about."

"It's a bit late for all that now, isn't it?" Levitt asked. "He should have thought of that before he threw himself away on Kathleen."

"Listen to me, Lou. If you say one word that's out of place, you won't be welcome in my home. Do you understand me?"

"Are you serious? You're really going to have that jerk around?"

"You heard me. He's all broken up about William. He sees Leo and Joseph, and he feels he's deprived his son of something. What right do you have to question what he wants to do?"

"Pearl, he should have considered all this long ago."

"Lou, you're the one who's always going on about the importance of remembering you're a Jew, about how necessary it is to stand up. Now Benny wants to do just that. Either you promise me you'll behave decently while he's here with William, or you don't have to bother coming here on Friday night."

"Okay, I'll be as good as gold. But you're making a mistake in helping him. He wrecked his own life—he deserves whatever he gets."

"Lou, you're a real swine, you know that?"

Levitt laughed and broke the connection.

Kathleen telephoned Minsky on Friday evening, just before he left the apartment with William for dinner at the Granitz home. He didn't mention the dinner or his plan to take William to a reform synagogue on West End Avenue the following morning. He still wasn't certain he could believe it himself. Everything had happened so quickly—the realization of what he was missing, the decision to win back the boy. When Kathleen mentioned that due to some union difficulties the filming might go on for three months, until August, he made sympathetic noises, while in reality he was delighted. By the time Kathleen returned to New York, William would have absorbed enough knowledge and tradition to make a relapse impossible.

Minsky and William were the first guests to arrive. The boy was puzzled by the table setting, the silver wine goblets, the plaited loaves of bread, the candles waiting to be lit. Minsky had not explained the purpose of the dinner to his son; he had been uncertain of how to go about it. He wasn't even sure of how to explain why they were attending synagogue services the following morning.

"Is it someone's birthday?" William asked when he saw the candles. "We didn't bring a present."

Minsky laughed. "Did you hear that? He wants to know if it's someone's birthday," he said to Pearl and Jake. "No, it's not a birthday, it's *Shabbas.*"

"It's what?" William asked.

"The Sabbath," Jake explained. Despite any misgivings, he was throwing himself wholeheartedly into the scheme. "Those candles are lit at sundown, a few minutes from now, when the Sabbath begins."

"The Sabbath's Sunday."

"For Christian people it is," Pearl told the boy. "For us"—she looked uncertainly at Minsky—"for Jewish people, the Sabbath begins on Friday night and ends when the sun sets on Saturday."

William's face reflected confusion. "Are we Jewish people?"

Pearl let Minsky answer that question. "Of course we are," the dark-skinned man told his son. "That's why we're here." He called over Joseph and Leo. "You know the twins; you've been to their birthday parties. Their next birthday's their thirteenth. . . ."

Slowly, he started to explain the significance of a boy's thirteenth birthday.

"That's when we become men," Joseph said proudly. "When you're thirteen you'll become a man as well." With Leo, Joseph had been primed by Pearl to make William feel welcome, to help to describe the significance of the Friday-night meal. Pearl reasoned that if anyone could get the message across it would be the twins; they had an infectious enthusiasm about their impending bar mitzvahs, and she was certain they would communicate it to William.

Everything was new to William, and like any child, he was curious. When the Caplans arrived, Jake made a big show of passing out skull caps to the men and boys. William held the black silk headcovering in his hand, uncertain what to do with it. Leo took it from him and set it firmly on his head.

As the sun went down, Pearl gazed pensively at the unlit candles. "Shall I light them, or do we wait for Lou?"

"Give him a few more minutes," Jake replied. "He's never been late before." He wondered if Levitt was coming. Had Lou decided to skip the Friday-night meal because of Minsky's presence?

Even as Jake debated the reason for Levitt's tardiness, there was a knock on the front door. Levitt entered, barely able to walk beneath the weight of the massive parcel he carried. "For the twins," he said grandly, before Jake or Pearl could even ask him.

The dinner, the lighting of the candles were forgotten as Joseph and Leo clustered around Levitt. "What did you bring for us, Uncle Lou?" Leo asked.

"Presents for my two favorite boys." Levitt took his time unwrapping the parcel, glorying in the cries of excitement as the twins spotted the expensive train set he'd bought for them that afternoon. "There you go—engines, coaches, miles and miles of track, stations, bridges, points, shunting yards. Do whatever you like with them; make your own railroad."

Pearl glanced at William Minsky. The boy's eyes were wide with jealousy and pain; the twins had received a present and he had been given nothing. Judy, too, had an injured expression on her face, but Pearl knew that Levitt had never considered the girl's feelings when he'd purchased the train set. He hadn't even really been thinking of the twins. He was merely using them to hurt William and, through William, Benny Minsky.

Pearl refused to let him get away with such behavior in her home. She clapped her hands loudly, and when she spoke her voice was sharp. "Leave that train set alone!" she ordered the twins. "This is Friday night. I want to light the candles and serve dinner. Now is not the time to be playing with toy trains!"

"But—" Joseph began.

"You heard me. Come to the table at once."

Joseph obeyed, taking the seat next to Judy. Leo was slower. He remained with Levitt and the train set, uncertain whether to listen to his mother or explore the treasure further. His mother couldn't really be angry with *him*. . . . Pearl made the decision for him. She walked the few feet to where he stood, grabbed his hand, and pulled him roughly toward the table. Then she picked up the train set, carried it from the room and dumped it unceremoniously in the hallway.

"Tomorrow afternoon you can play with it to your heart's content," she told the twins. "But right now it's dinner time and we have guests." Her eyes sought out Levitt, dared him to challenge her. He held her gaze only for a moment before looking down at the carpet. Pearl was as determined to support Minsky and his son as Levitt was to make them miserable, and she had won this round.

Levitt left the apartment immediately after dinner. He had barely spoken a word during the entire meal, as though, robbed of mocking Minsky, he had no other topics of conversation. The moment he had gone, Pearl told the twins they could play with the train set, just as long as they invited William to play with them. Judy joined the boys as they set up the track in their bedroom, leaving the adults in the living room. Annie let out a long, appreciative whistle and then gave Pearl a broad grin. "Boy, you sure took good care of Lou. You cut him right down before he had a chance."

"He didn't buy that train set for the twins," Pearl said. "He bought it to embarrass Benny, to make Benny's boy feel left out."

"He's a clever devil, all right," Moses Caplan said grudgingly.

Annie corrected him. "Devious is the word you're looking for. There are a lot of clever men out there who aren't so successful. Only the devious ones make it to the top." She turned to look at Minsky. "You're taking William to services tomorrow morning?"

Minsky nodded. "The old guy Jake got to teach the twins—he's orthodox, thinks like Lou, didn't want to know about helping me. Maybe I'll get more joy out of a reform rabbi." He paused to consider the task that lay ahead. "Some job I've set myself, eh? Trying to get my own son converted."

"What do you think Kathleen'll do when she finds out?" Caplan asked.

"I guess she'll blow her stack, but I'm hoping she'll be so involved with this movie deal that she won't really care."

"And if you're wrong?" Pearl asked.

"I'll worry about it when it happens."

"You've got some pluck, Benny," Jake acknowledged. "But then you were never lacking in that department."

Minsky appeared to be embarrassed by such praise, especially so when Pearl gave him a warm smile. The same kind of pluck which had once made him chase Irish bullies was now serving a far different purpose. Perhaps a far more important purpose . . .

On the journey back to Riverside Drive, Minsky had a long talk with his son. He asked William if he'd enjoyed the dinner, and listened to the boy try to explain his confusion at the strangeness of the tradition. Then Minsky told William that the following morning they were going to the synagogue. "You see, William, when your mother and I got married, I was so crazy about her that I let myself forget how important other things were—like dinner with the candles tonight, going to the synagogue tomorrow, bar mitzvahs."

"Like Joseph and Leo are going to have?" William still wasn't sure what it was all about, but he sensed that it mattered a lot.

"That's right. It's only when you got to be this big that I remembered you should be bar mitzvahed as well when you turn thirteen. I want you to be, but first there are some details to iron out."

"Is Mummy Jewish as well?"

"No. That's one of the details." Remembering that he was talking to a ten-year-old boy, Minsky kept his explanation as simple as possible. He talked about the differences in religions, how William had been baptized into Catholicism, how he wanted the boy to be Jewish like himself. Minsky realized that it was probably the first time he had ever talked this deeply with his son, but William was a serious, studious boy and Minsky guessed that he would understand better than most other kids of his age. What Minsky was banking on was his son's memory. He hoped the boy remembered who had shown him the most love. Minsky had loved his son from the moment William had been born; even before. To Kathleen, maternal affection had come later, when her singing career had been temporarily thwarted, and even then her feeling for the boy had never rivaled Minsky's.

When they got out of the car in front of their apartment building, William held onto his father's hand. "Pa, if you want me to be Jewish, that's what I want to be," he said.

Minsky picked up the boy and kissed him. Then he carried him all the way up to the apartment.

During the next two months, Minsky and William became regular fixtures at the reform synagogue on West End Avenue. From the rabbi, Minsky received a sympathetic audience; the boy with a Jewish father wanted to be Jewish himself, and the rabbi said that such a change was possible. But first, the boy would have to be instructed in Judaism. Minsky enrolled William in Hebrew classes. It was the boy's first real immersion into religious training and he accepted it for two reasons, because his father wanted him to learn these things and because he found them genuinely interesting. To a boy who'd had an overly religious upbringing, atheism might seem an attractive proposition. In William's case, the reverse was true. Having been deprived of religious training, he welcomed this opportunity to learn about Judaism.

Then, in July, Kathleen returned unexpectedly to New York. Plagued by industrial strife, the shooting of *Broadway Nell* had been halted. Hal Brookman had told his cast to take two weeks off while he tried to reach agreements with the unions involved. Kathleen elected to spend that time in New York. To surprise Minsky, she did not bother to tell him in advance that she was coming.

The surprise was hers when she arrived home on a Saturday morning to find only the housekeeper in the apartment. Kathleen felt deflated because there was no one to greet her. It didn't matter that she hadn't called ahead. She was a Hollywood star now, wasn't she? People adapted themselves to her, not the other way around. Brookman had waited on her in California. He had made her feel like the most important person in the world. He'd put her up in his luxurious house, surrounded her with servants and a chauffeur, taken her out to dinner regularly. Kathleen's only disappointment was that he had not tried to bed her, but there was plenty of time for that yet. Brookman was divorced and available, and with Kathleen's return to show business, she had found that she was interested in other men, not just Minsky. Besides, with three thousand miles between them, there was little chance of him finding out.

"Where're Mr. Minsky and William?" Kathleen asked the housekeeper.

"They went out," the woman answered.

"Oh? Where?"

"Where they go every Saturday—to the synagogue on West End Avenue."

"They went where?" Kathleen was unsure that she'd heard correctly. Minsky going to a synagogue? What would he do there— steal whatever valuables weren't nailed down? And why the hell had he taken the kid? "Did you say they go there every Saturday?"

"That's right."

"And when did these little outings start?" She looked around, saw silver candlesticks on the table. They had not been there when she'd left for California."

"Right after you went away, Mrs. Minsky."

"Oh?" Kathleen would see about that. Waving aside the housekeeper's offer of a cup of coffee, she sat down to wait. She might be married to a Jew, but she wasn't going to allow any kid of hers to be raised as one.

Father and son returned home at twelve-thirty. By the time Minsky's mind registered that Kathleen was back from California, she was screaming furiously at him. "What the hell do you think you're doing—taking my son to a goddamned synagogue?"

"I'm giving him what he should have had years ago, pride in himself, pride in being a Jew. What are you doing here anyway? You're not due back for another month."

"The studio's been struck. We stopped shooting for a couple of weeks, so I came back here. And that's just as well from what I hear about what's going on in this place. You've got no damned right to take my son to a synagogue. He's no Jew. He's a Catholic . . . just like me!"

"Some Catholic you are." Minsky sneered. "If you went to confession, you'd tie up the priest for a week." He pushed William toward his mother. "He doesn't want that. He wants to be like me. Ask him yourself."

"I don't want to ask him!" Kathleen yelled across the top of her son's head. "He's too young to know what the hell he wants. All that matters is what I want, and I don't want my kid raised as a Hebe!"

"What you want isn't important anymore," Minsky pulled the boy to him and whispered something in his ear. Then William went to his bedroom and closed the door, leaving his parents to fight it out in front of the housekeeper. "You don't really give a damn about how William grows up," Minsky said in a quiet, level voice. "Well, I've got some news for you. I do care. So I've decided to do something about it. That boy goes with me to the synagogue every Saturday morning. He attends Hebrew classes, and when he turns thirteen in less than three years, I'm going to watch him be bar mitzvahed."

Kathleen missed all the danger signs. Minsky hadn't raised his voice at all; that should have told her something. He hadn't threatened her, hadn't lifted a hand to her; that should have told her even more. Instead, she missed everything. Placing her hands on her hips, she burst into harsh laughter. "You want him to become some kind of rabbi as well, maybe? Grow a scruffy beard and wear a dirty coat and hat like those old men we used to see on the Lower East Side? Get the fuck out of here, Benny. So long as I'm that kid's mother, he's

351

not getting any Hebe mumbo jumbo drilled into his head. If you want a kid that grows up Jewish, go find yourself some Jewish broad to marry. That's if you can find one who'll marry a lunatic with a nigger face like you!"

Minsky backhanded her across the face, grabbed her and hit her again. There was no sign of the raging fury he'd once displayed during their fights. The beating he gave her was calm and methodical. He knocked her head from one side to the other with the flat of his hand, and by the time the housekeeper managed to force herself between them, Kathleen's eyes were almost closed, her lips were split, and her nose bleeding copiously. Minsky didn't even look at her as she lay sobbing on the couch. He went to William's room and took the boy from the apartment without giving him the chance to see what had happened to his mother. They went to the Granitz home, where Minsky calmly explained what had occurred. That night, Minsky and William stayed in a hotel. The following morning, Minsky sent the boy, as usual, to Hebrew classes. In the afternoon, he telephoned his own apartment. The housekeeper told him that Kathleen had been treated by a doctor, and was preparing to return to California.

Two days later, Minsky returned with his son to the apartment on Riverside Drive. Kathleen had left. Her closets and drawers were empty; every trace of her was gone. Over the next three weeks, Minsky received two letters. One was from a lawyer representing Hal Brookman: The studio was suing Minsky for delaying the shooting of *Broadway Nell* even more by incapacitating its star. The second letter was from a lawyer hired by Kathleen: She was suing for divorce.

Minsky wasn't the least perturbed. If anything, he was relieved. He had more than enough money to pay Brookman for the extra production costs. And as to Kathleen wanting a divorce, it was the best thing that could happen. Now Minsky would have his son all to himself.

If he was angry at anyone, it was at Lou Levitt because the little man had been right all along—just like he always seemed to be.

Chapter Three

After Pearl's support of Benny Minsky and his son, Lou Levitt cut down on his visits to the Granitz apartment. He never came at all on Friday nights, when Minsky and William would be there. Instead, he occasionally had dinner with the family on a weekday, after an invitation had been extended by Jake. The few times Pearl saw Levitt, he offered no reason for the decrease in his visits.

Like Levitt, Jake never spoke of the evening when Levitt had brought the trains, as if he were embarrassed at the rift which had sprung up between his wife and his friend. Only Annie, who was rarely loath to express an opinion, spoke out, and she agreed wholeheartedly with Pearl.

"You saw what Lou was like that time we were all hiding out from Saul Fromberg. We rebelled against him by wanting to go home, and he didn't like it one little bit. He felt we were questioning his damned conceited assumption that only he knows what's right."

"He was right that time, Annie," Pearl reminded her friend.

Annie bit her tongue. How could she have forgotten what had happened because they hadn't listened to Levitt in that particular instance? "Well, he's not right to go on so about Benny," she finally said, "but don't give yourself any gray hairs worrying about it. The closer it gets to the twins' bar mitzvahs, the way Lou idolizes those boys of yours, the more friendly he'll become . . . just as long as you stop inviting Benny and William around on a Friday night."

Pearl shook her head determinedly. "Not on your life. That's one thing I won't stop. I've gotten to like those Friday nights with you and Moe and Judy and Benny and William. Besides, since Kathleen left, I've never seen Benny look so happy."

"You can say that again," Annie responded. Everyone had noticed, even the kids. Each week that passed seemed to soften Minsky's character even more, as if he had rid himself of his hostility in that final break-up with Kathleen, the beating he'd given her. Through Minsky, Annie and Pearl had heard that Kathleen had finished the movie and was staying out West. He wasn't contesting the divorce, just as long as Kathleen didn't fight him for custody of William, and Minsky doubted that she'd do that. She had moved in with Hal Brookman, the producer of the movie version of *Broadway Nell*. Brookman had no children of his own, and Minsky guessed that Kathleen would not want William to interfere with her new career and her new man. Minsky saw the irony of the situation, all right, only he wasn't about to share his perspective with anyone: Many years earlier, he'd murdered a lover of Kathleen's, David Hay, shot him down in cold blood; and now, he was wishing her latest lover a long and healthy life!

"I've got to hand it to Benny," Annie said. "I, for one, never thought he'd stick it out. I thought he'd be a five-minute wonder, but he's not. Every Saturday he's taking William to services, every Sunday he takes him to Hebrew classes. Who'd have believed such behavior was possible for Benny Minsky?"

"Not me," Pearl said. "Not for the old Benny Minsky anyway. It's children who make you change. What was unimportant when you were free and single can suddenly seem the most urgent thing in the world when you've got a child to consider." She gave Annie a wistful smile. "I've got to send out invitations for the bar mitzvahs soon, and I'm wondering if Lou will even turn up. After all, Benny'll be there with William."

"Of course he'll turn up. Joseph and Leo are his godsons, remember. Nothing will keep him away from his godsons' bar mitzvahs."

Isn't that the truth? Pearl thought. Especially when Levitt considered them to be his sons in flesh and blood!

The following week, Pearl mailed invitations that included the synagogue service, a catered luncheon back at the apartment, and then a dinner dance on the Sunday after the ceremony. Levitt was among the first to respond. Unlike other guests who mailed in their replies, Levitt made his in person, turning up at the apartment one afternoon when Pearl was alone.

"You're coming then?" Pearl asked after looking at the reply card Levitt handed to her. "Benny's going to be there with William."

"You think I'd let that keep me away?"

"Annie and I were wondering."

"What does Annie have to do with it?"

"We talked it over, the way you don't come around here anymore on Friday nights."

"Oh? And what conclusion did the pair of you reach?"

Pearl ignored the sarcasm. "We decided that you were being damned stupid, Lou."

To Pearl's amazement, Levitt nodded. "You're right. Annie, too. I was the one who kept getting on Benny's back for marrying Kathleen. Now he's finally gone and done the decent thing and I'm still giving him a rough time. I don't change easily, Pearl. It's a fault, I suppose, but then again, sometimes I wonder if it's not a blessing instead."

Pearl understood perfectly. Levitt did not blow hot and cold on an issue. He just took a stand and remained with it forever, right or wrong. "Are you going to make an exception this time? Are you going to change?"

"And be nice to Benny?"

"No one's asking you to be nice. Civilized. Benny needs all the support he can get for what he's doing, Lou. He made one hell of an about-face to go through with this."

Levitt chewed his bottom lip thoughtfully, and then his narrow face creased into a smile. "Little Pearl, the patron saint of waifs and strays. You're always worrying about the downtrodden. Okay, I'll show some appreciation for what Benny's doing."

Levitt's promise to normalize his relationship with Minsky removed the sole cloud from Pearl's horizon. She had been frightened that the twins' bar mitzvahs would be marred by a public squabble between the two men. With that possibility out of the way, she could look forward to the big occasion with an easy mind.

Instead, the squabble erupted between the twins. For the first time in their lives they would be the undisputed center of attention. Because of that, Pearl wanted to be certain that neither boy had more than the other. Each had two new suits for the occasion, one for the Saturday synagogue service and the luncheon that followed, and one for the dinner and dance the following evening. Each boy had learned a speech that would be delivered during the dinner. Annie and Pearl between them had taught the twins how to waltz. And therein lay the problem. Traditionally, the first dance of the evening was between the bar-mitzvah boy and his mother. Only here there were two bar-mitzvah boys. Who would partner Pearl for the first dance?

Joseph had no doubt about the answer. "I'm the oldest," he stated logically. "I get to dance first with Ma."

Immediately, Leo began to sulk about the prospect of being second to his brother. "Why should it be you? We're both being bar-mitzvahed. Why not me?"

"Because I'm older than you are," Joseph answered. He saw no problem at all. He was the first twin to be born, and that was it. Finished.

"Being older's got nothing to do with it!" Leo argued.

"Wait a minute." Pearl stepped in quickly. "I've got an idea. How about Leo having the first dance with me?"

Joseph's face collapsed. "Why should Leo have the first dance with you? I'm the older twin."

"Let me finish," Pearl said. "Leo has the first dance with me, while Joseph has the first dance with Judy?" She congratulated herself when Joseph's expression brightened. Score one for maternal tact, the ability to avoid a fight with some quick thinking.

As the twins grew older she still found herself siding with Leo, but now she did it in a manner that would not upset the older twin. To have denied Leo the first dance with his mother would have been to invite mayhem. She could even imagine him running from the hall in a fit of temper. She understood that Joseph could be negotiated with; he'd trade off a dance with his mother for a dance with Judy. But not Leo. Never Leo. With Leo it was all or nothing.

Whoever said that twins were a double blessing? They could also be double trouble, constantly forcing their mother to scale undreamed heights of ingenuity to keep the boat from rocking too violently. In all, it wasn't too different from dealing with Lou Levitt and Benny Minsky.

Pearl felt doubly pleased with herself.

Jake awoke early on the day. It was still pitch black outside when Pearl felt him move in the bed beside her. He walked to the bathroom, and Pearl lay quite still, waiting for him to return. Only after she heard the shower running did she realize that he wasn't coming back to bed. She turned on the bedside lamp, checked the alarm clock. It wasn't even six o'clock yet.

Jake returned to the bedroom twenty minutes later, smelling of soap and shaving cream. He began to dress in the new suit he'd had tailored for the synagogue ceremony. Pearl watched, and was amused when he turned around and asked her how he looked.

"Very handsome." She meant it. The lines that had come with age had added character to his face. The cleft in his chin was more noticeable. His face seemed thinner, sharper; yet the warmth of his brown eyes quashed any trace of coldness. "You'd better be careful you don't take anything away from the twins today."

Jake smiled. "I think I should get them up."

"For God's sake, let them sleep," Pearl protested. "They don't have to be up for another hour yet. And neither do you." She patted the bed. "Come and sit down. Talk to me."

Jake sat with his back to Pearl. She wrapped her arms around his waist and rested her chin on his shoulder. His breathing was heavy and his heart was beating with unusual force, hammering right through his chest. "What's the matter with you?" And then, before Jake could give her an answer, she understood. "You're nervous, aren't you? Jake Granitz, you're more nervous about today than your sons are. And it's not only today . . . you've been like this for weeks. Couldn't sleep, tense. You're worrying over nothing, Jake. They'll be perfect today."

He rested his hands on hers. "I'm their father. I'm entitled to worry, right?"

Pearl started to laugh. "You're like the father of some homely girl who's getting married. All during the weeks leading up to the wedding, he's frightened that the groom'll change his mind. Why don't you take off that nice suit and come back to bed?"

Jake undressed, set the alarm clock for seven, and slipped into bed beside Pearl. She ran a hand over his face. "Smooth . . . you never shave before you go to bed at night."

"I never knew you wanted me to."

She placed a finger on his lips. "Don't waste time talking. That alarm'll start ringing before we know it."

The alarm clock rang at exactly seven o'clock. While Pearl went into the shower, Jake dressed and knocked on the door of the room the twins shared. Sticking his head inside, he said, "Time to get up. Today's the day you're going to knock them all dead."

Leo jumped out of bed, tugging at his pajama trousers as they slid down. He walked the few steps to Joseph's bed. His twin was still asleep. Shaking him by the shoulder, Leo yelled: "Get up!"

Joseph woke slowly. Only when the importance of the day penetrated through the fog of sleepiness did he become alert. "Nervous?" Jake asked.

"A little," Joseph answered truthfully.

"How about you, champ?" Jake asked Leo.

"Me?" Leo scoffed at the notion. "I'm not at all nervous."

"That's the spirit!" Jake laughed and swung a gentle, looping right toward Leo's head. The boy jumped back and countered with his own punch. The kid's full of beans, Jake thought, just raring to go. Not at all like Joseph who has to work up his confidence. Jake wondered which was better: too much confidence, or too little?

Once the twins were dressed in new navy blue suits, Pearl inspected them critically. They would be on show today. Any faults in their appearance would reflect on her. At last, she was satisfied. Today, her twins would make her proud.

The bar mitzvah was to be held at the Lower East Side synagogue where Pearl and Jake, and Moses Caplan and Annie, had been married. Fittingly, both families traveled together to the synagogue, parking their cars a respectful distance away and completing the Sabbath journey as it was supposed to be done: on foot. Jake walked arm-in-arm with Pearl, Caplan with Annie, and Joseph walked alongside Judy. Only Leo walked alone, striding ahead of the group in his brand new suit, wanting the whole world to see him. He might be the younger twin, Pearl thought as she watched him forge ahead, but he appeared older, more impressive. Although shorter than Joseph, Leo had the first dark, wispy traces of a mustache, and his squat, solid body showed the promise of manly strength. Joseph was slim, frail-looking next to Leo. The comparison was deceptive, though, Pearl knew. In the boys' sparring sessions with the boxing gloves, Joseph gave as good as he got, countering Leo's advantage in strength with guile and speed.

When the group reached the synagogue, Pearl, Annie, and Judy went into the women's section. Jake, Caplan, and the twins took front-row seats in the men's section. Lou Levitt was already there, sitting next to the tutor, Isaac Cohen, who had come to see his pupils perform. Also there was Harry Saltzman, his muscular bulk squeezed into the seat on the other side of Levitt. Pearl guessed it was the first time that Saltzman had seen the inside of a synagogue since his own bar mitzvah almost twenty-five years earlier.

A few minutes later, Benny Minsky and his son entered the synagogue. Pearl watched Levitt shake hands with the dark-skinned man. A few words passed between them. She felt relieved that Levitt was honoring his promise.

As each section of the service—each prayer, each psalm—passed, Pearl felt herself become more anxious. She wiped perspiration from her forehead with a dainty lace handkerchief. Her stomach twisted itself into tighter and tighter knots. Needing support, she reached out to hold Annie's hand. "What's the matter?" Annie whispered.

"I'm terrified."

"Don't be so silly. They're going to put on a show like they've been starring on Broadway for ten years."

"I hope you're right. If you think I'm nervous," she whispered to Annie, "you should have seen Jake this morning. You'd have thought he was the bar-mitzvah boy."

"There's one who's got no nerves." Annie gestured toward Levitt who was leaving his seat to ascend the raised dais in the center of the synagogue; from this dais, the service was conducted. The Torah scroll had been removed from the ark, and each member of the bar-mitzvah party was being called to read from it. The last would be the twins. "He hasn't got blood in his veins like normal people—he's got ice water."

Levitt glanced just once toward the women's section before climbing the two steps to the dais. He gave Pearl a quick smile but the warmth failed to reach his eyes. They stayed a hard, glassy blue—the eyes of a man with a serious mission to accomplish.

"We're lucky being women," Annie added. "All we have to do is sit and watch. We don't have to perform."

Jake followed Levitt onto the dais, then Caplan, and finally Minsky. Each man had a subsidiary role to play in that day's production. At last, the twins were called, by their Hebrew names.

Leo went first, singing in a clear rich voice the words that were written on the Torah set out in front of him. Once, as he successfully negotiated a tricky section, he turned to smirk at his brother. Joseph recognized the challenge and was determined to be even better. When Leo finished, he stepped back to be patted on the shoulder by his father. Joseph took his brother's place. In the women's section, Pearl leaned forward with even greater concentration. Was it her imagination, or was Joseph's voice thinner, lacking the rick strength of Leo's? Joseph was the only one of the twins who had confessed to nerves. Were they beginning to show through?

"Was Leo clearer than this?" Pearl asked Annie, as Joseph completed his portion and commenced the closing blessing.

"You're imagining things—they're the same," Annie replied without even bothering to compare. She thought that Pearl was choosing Leo's performance over Joseph's strictly out of habit, just as Judy, to Annie's left, would undoubtedly think that Joseph's voice was better. "You know, you were talking about Jake being nervous, I think Moe was a bit funny about this as well. He's been kind of withdrawn lately, now I think of it. I just figured he was going through some kind of mood. Maybe he was worried for the twins as well."

"You live next door," Pearl pointed out, relieved that she and Jake weren't the only ones to be so concerned. "Tension travels through a wall."

The service ended an hour later, and both twins rushed toward their mother as she left the women's section. Leo reached her first and threw his arms around her. "Did you hear me? Did you hear me?"

"I heard you, Leo, and you sounded marvelous." Pearl managed to break Leo's tight grip long enough to allow her to hug Joseph. "You as well. You both sounded better than any boys I've ever heard."

"Who was the best?" Leo demanded.

"You were equally good."

"No! No!" Leo cried out. "One of us had to be the best!"

"To me you sounded as good as each other. Different, but just as good."

Leo's face sagged a little as some of his enjoyment evaporated. He had expected his mother to say he'd been the best. She always stood up for him. Why was this time different? Before he could ponder the riddle more, Judy ran toward Joseph and hugged him. "I thought you were the best, Joseph! The very best!"

Leo swung around furiously. "What does a stupid girl know about a bar mitzvah?"

Any possibility of a bigger scene was quelled by Pearl who took each boy by the arm and walked them toward the waiting group of men. Isaac Cohen was standing next to Jake. When he saw Pearl and the twins approaching, the elderly man regarded them with a fond smile.

"What do you think of your handsome sons now, Mrs. Granitz? Did they make you proud?"

"Prouder than they've ever made me, Mr. Cohen. You did a wonderful job with them."

Cohen shrugged modestly. "You handed me a length of fine cloth, and I made a beautiful suit for you." He turned to beam at Jake, sharing in the family's happiness.

Jake took Pearl's arm and walked her toward the exit. Noticing that he still seemed tense, Pearl attributed that to the excitement of the occasion. She decided that she did not really know Jake as well as she thought she did. She'd always considered him a man who could confront any situation. Yet today had made him shaky; it had been more of an ordeal for him than it had been for the twins.

"Glad it's over?" she asked as they waited outside the synagogue for the others to follow. A chill wind gusted along the street and Pearl shivered inside her coat.

"Is it over?" Jake asked. "Or are we going to have those two at each other's throats for the next six months over who did a better job?"

"Who do you think sang best?"

"Leo," Jake answered instantly. "But I'm not going to tell him that."

"Same here. I told them they were equally good." Pearl swung around as Harry Saltzman and Benny Minsky came from the synagogue. Minsky was holding his son by the hand. "Looking forward to your turn, William?" Pearl asked.

The boy nodded somberly. He had been awed by the significance of the service. He had two years in which to prepare, two years in which to learn about the religion his father had so abruptly decided he should follow. Pearl sympathized with the boy, thinking he must be really confused, having to cope with his father's turnabout, his mother's disappearance. No child should have to confront such turmoil.

With a twin on either side of him, Jake led the way toward where the cars were parked. Levitt, who was walking ten yards behind, called out the boys' names. "Leo! Joseph! Come here a minute. See what you get as a reward for doing such a good job!" Levitt held out two slim boxes. The twins looked at Jake, who nodded his consent for them to accept the presents.

"What is it, Uncle Lou?" asked Leo, who was the first to reach Levitt.

"Open it, you'll see. You as well, Joseph." Levitt smiled happily as the twins undid the boxes. Inside each was a gold wristwatch.

"Lou, those are beautiful gifts," Pearl said. "Thank you." On this occasion she knew that Levitt had no ulterior motive in giving the presents.

The twins wasted no time in strapping the watches to their wrists and proudly showing them off. Even Minsky, who had a gift of money in his pocket for them, was impressed.

Isaac Cohen walked from a group of people toward Jake, who had remained where he was. "If that's what they get for singing so well, what should I get? Doesn't the teacher receive a prize as well?" He laughed and raised his hand dismissively, just in case Jake took him seriously. "My payment was the pleasure of listening to them."

"Jake!" Pearl called. "Come over here and see what Lou's given to the twins!"

As Jake began to walk toward them, his name was called again, only this time it was a man's voice that yelled out: "Jake! Jake Granitz!"

Jake stopped in the middle of the sidewalk and glanced around, uncertain where the second summons had come from.

"Over here, Jake!" The voice had a hearty ring to it, with just a note of impatience. "Over here, in the car!"

A black Chevrolet was rolling slowly along the side of the curb, its front windows open. Puzzled, Jake stepped toward the car. Three yards away, he stopped. Simultaneously, the blunt snout of a shotgun poked through an open window. An explosion rocked the street, a shattering roar that dovetailed into the racing of the Chevrolet's engines, the spinning of tires as the car sped away. Pearl's horrified shriek punctuated the sound, as she saw Jake flung back across the sidewalk like a sack of rags to crash into Isaac Cohen's arms.

"Jake! . . ." Pearl rushed from the group around her to her husband. Hard on her heels were Levitt, Saltzman, and Caplan. Annie grabbed hold of the twins before they could follow, while Minsky held

361

tightly onto his own son and Judy, trying to pull them further away from the scene.

Under Jake's weight, Isaac Cohen staggered backward until his retreat was halted by a wall. Pearl reached him as he let Jake slip down to the concrete sidewalk. Levitt tugged at Pearl's arm, tried to swing her around before she could see the damage caused by the shotgun blast. He was too late. Pearl glimpsed the huge red patch that covered Jake's chest, the expression of dumb surprise that was etched for all eternity upon his face. Before she could cry out, Levitt thrust a hand behind her head and buried her face in his shoulder.

Caplan and Saltzman ground to a halt beside them. They looked down at Jake; then Caplan lifted his head to stare along the street, squinting in the crisp wind. The black Chevrolet from which the single shot had been fired was already forty yards away, speeding unimpeded down the block.

"Forget it," Saltzman growled, assuming that Caplan was trying to read the license plate. "Whoever did this didn't use a plate we could trace."

Levitt passed Pearl to Saltzman. "Harry, make yourself useful and get her the hell out of here! Moe, find a phone, get the cops and an ambulance!" He knelt down beside Jake, felt for his pulse. There was nothing, not even the faintest irregular tremor of life. Realistically, Levitt had not expected it to be any different. No man with a wound like that would still be alive. Jake's chest, which had taken the entire load of buckshot, seemed to have exploded. Blood and bone and flesh and cloth were all ripped up and reformed into a red, soggy, indefinable goulash.

Isaac Cohen spoke. Leaning against the wall, ashen-faced, hands stained with Jake's blood, the elderly man murmured: "Such a scar. In all my life I never saw such a scar before on a man's face."

His voice was just loud enough to reach Pearl. *Such a scar* . . . After nine years Gus Landau had come back to claim his revenge.

There was no bar-mitzvah luncheon, no dinner the following evening, no opportunity for the twins to open the dance with Pearl and Judy. There was only a funeral, followed by a week-long *shivah* in the apartment which had witnessed such excitement on that Saturday morning when the twins had departed as boys and had anticipated returning as men.

Among the visitors who thronged the apartment during the mourning period were police seeking information on the man who had murdered Jake Granitz. All Pearl could tell them—all anyone could

362

offer—was what Isaac Cohen had seen. A man with a stripe of a scar on his left cheek. After a nine-year hiatus since creating his last piece of havoc, Gus Landau had returned to snatch the joy from Pearl's mouth and replace it with an unpalatable bitterness. He had paid her back with interest for the time she had disfigured him.

During this *shivah*, the twins did not leave the apartment to be looked after by Annie next door as they had nine years earlier. Now they were men. They joined their mother on the low wooden chairs reserved for the bereaved, accepted the condolences of their father's friends, and mourned his sudden passing with a feeling of hollow emptiness. Of the twins, only Leo had caught a good look at Jake lying on the sidewalk. When an ambulance had arrived five minutes after the shooting, Leo had ripped himself free of Annie's grasp and had run forward. Levitt had shoved him back, yelling furiously at Annie to keep the boy under control. But Leo had seen. The vision stayed imprinted on his mind. He tried to talk about it with Joseph, but the older twin refused to listen. Joseph just wanted to blot out the entire scene, as he had erased an earlier, similar scene, when his grandmother had been killed in the restaurant by bullets intended for his father and his Uncle Lou. So Leo dwelt on the picture alone, comparing it with the earlier scene which, unlike Joseph, he recalled in graphic detail. Blood was so red. Such a deep, rich shade. Leo decided that red was his favorite color. Its magnetism drew his eyes whenever he saw something of that color—a dress worn by a woman who came to the apartment to visit the bereaved, a tie worn by a man. But he was especially drawn to blood. It had a unique redness, a glistening texture all of its own.

Lou Levitt remained in the apartment for every waking moment of the mourning period, arriving early each morning and leaving after the other mourners each night. He maintained a position next to Pearl, standing by her like a sentry at his post. Often he would hold her hand. "Be strong," he kept advising her. "Pearl, now is the time when you must show more strength than you've ever shown before. You owe it to the twins."

"How can I be strong, Lou? All of us, we stood there and let it happen."

"We had no chance." He patted her hand. "Pearl, you know I'll do everything in my power for you and the boys, but you have to show them the way. For their sake you must be strong."

His quiet voice imbued her with a fragile confidence. Hadn't she displayed strength before when it was necessary? She was not unaccustomed to standing on her own two feet. But this time . . .

when the shock was still so great? She was glad of Levitt's constant company, his exhortation for her to be strong. No one else had the power to reach her. No one else meant as much to her as he did. Not now—not with Jake gone. Somehow she couldn't even remember how he had once endangered her relationship with Jake. She no longer thought it so important that Levitt believed he was the father of the twins. None of that carried any weight anymore. All that mattered was that he was next to her, supporting her, seeing her through this terrible time in her life.

After a few days of sitting on the low wooden chairs, Pearl's thoughts switched to the man responsible for her occupying the chair again. Late one night, as Levitt prepared to leave, and the twins were in bed, she asked, "Did you have any idea that Landau had come back, Lou?"

The little man nodded. "We picked up a rumor about three or four weeks ago. We heard he'd been hiding out in Canada, in Toronto; that he'd left there to come back here. Once we heard, we started looking for him."

"But you didn't find him." Pearl recalled Jake's anxiety, the tension which she had ascribed to the impending bar mitzvah. "Was that why Jake was so worried?"

Levitt nodded again. "We were all worried. He just showed it more than I did."

"Why didn't you tell me anything? I had a right to know."

"We talked it over between us, about telling you. We decided not to because of the bar mitzvah. We didn't want to spoil things for you or the twins. It might have just been a rumor, nothing more."

But it wasn't, Pearl reflected. It had been the absolute truth. "Have the police found him yet?"

"No. We've got men looking for him as well. It's better that we find him—we'll know how to deal with it."

"You didn't find him the last time. What makes you think you'll find him now?"

Levitt had no answer for that.

The mourning period ended. Once more Pearl removed the cloths that covered the mirrors, arranged for the low wooden chairs to be taken away, and tried to put her life back together. Twice she had been robbed of family members—first her mother and now her husband. Her father, too, if she counted his accident as a part of the ill-fated violence that seemed to dog her.

Pearl made her life revolve around her sons. Each evening, she prepared a special meal for them as if by showing her love through cooking she could soften their feeling of loss. Joseph was more deeply affected than Leo. He withdrew into himself, barely spoke. Pearl asked Judy what he was like at school. The young girl replied that Joseph had changed completely. He was no longer so active in class, so determined to prove that he was the smartest. Now he did his work silently, and virtually shunned the boys with whom he had been friendly. Pearl asked about Leo. Judy said he was the complete opposite. The twins were the center of attention at school since the story of Jake's murder had been in the newspapers. Everyone wanted to know what had happened. While Joseph ignored his classmates' excited questions, Leo reveled in describing in gripping detail the scene outside the synagogue. Judy had even heard him tell his classmates that his father's murder would not go unavenged for long. "The police won't find the man who did it," Leo had said. "My father's friends will. And God help him then."

For Pearl, the worst time was in the evening, after the twins had completed their homework and gone to bed. Then she would sit alone in the apartment. On the fourth evening after the mourning period had ended, Pearl reached the bottom of the pit. Caring for the twins during the day drained her for the night when she was alone and apt to dwell on her every worry, on her grief. This night was the worst. When she went to bed at eleven o'clock, she lay there for an hour, just staring at the ceiling, eyes following the faint beams of light that flicked across as cars passed below. The longer she lay there, the more awake she seemed to become, the more despondent. All too easily she could imagine Jake lying next to her, feel his arms around her, the hardness of his body. She turned over to bury her face in the pillow on which his head had rested. She could swear that the pillow retained the scent of his hair cream. It soothed her but only for a moment, that instant it took her to realize that he would never be coming back. Fourteen years of marriage to Jake—and all she had was a pillow that smelled like hair cream.

She climbed out of the bed, wrapped a dressing gown around herself and began to prowl through the apartment. Peeping into the twins' room, she saw that they slept soundly. Then she sat in the kitchen for fifteen minutes, nursing a cup of tea until it turned cold. Leaving the cup and saucer in the sink, she returned to her bedroom where she turned on the light and looked around. Jake's clothes still filled his closet. She would have to do something about them, donate them to a charity. What good did they do anyone sitting there? She opened the closet door and went through his suits. At the very end of the rod was the new tuxedo he had ordered for the bar-mitzvah party. Pearl started to weep as she took it out and felt the cloth. A tuxedo had been Jake's habitual style of dress once; in the days of the clubs, of Prohibition, it had almost been a uniform. Since repeal, he'd hardly worn one at all. He'd dressed in business suits, like any other businessman. But for the twins' bar mitzvah, he'd had a new tuxedo made. And he'd been robbed of the opportunity to wear it.

Replacing the tuxedo in the closet, Pearl turned to study the bureau where Jake kept his personal papers and valuables. Her eyes were drawn to the locked bottom drawer. The key was kept in the bedside table. She fetched it and opened the drawer. Inside were documents which Jake had refused to keep in a safety deposit box at the bank. She leafed through them—their wedding license, the twins' birth certificates. That brought a fresh flood of tears to her eyes. She dabbed them away with the sleeve of the dressing gown.

Beneath the documents lay a polished walnut presentation box. Pearl's heart jumped when she recognized it. She had forgotten all about the birthday present Benny Minsky had given Jake when he'd turned twenty-five. Opening the box, she saw the card Minsky had written. She picked it up, read the scrawly handwriting: "If you need protection, then protect yourself with style." There, beneath the card, were the two ivory-handled revolvers, a cleaning kit, and twelve rounds of ammunition.

Pearl remembered Jake saying that he did not even know if the two revolvers worked. He had always carried them, but he had never fired them, not even on the night when twelve of Patrick Joseph Rourke's men had died along a narrow coastal road in Massachusetts. Jake had worn the guns as good-luck tokens, nothing more. Pearl lifted one of the weapons from the case. She knew nothing about firearms, but it did not take her long to discover how to swing out the cylinder and drop the shells into the chambers. She snapped the cylinder shut and weighed the gun speculatively in her hand. It would be so easy, she thought as she sat down on the edge of the bed. Lift the gun to my head. Pull back the hammer. Gently squeeze the trigger. All my problems, all my sorrow, would be over then.

She lifted the revolver to her head. Thumbed back the hammer. The muzzle felt cold against her burning temple while the trigger blazed like molten iron against her index finger. How much pressure? How many pounds of it before the diabolical mechanism that rested inside the gun slammed the hammer forward, exploded the shell, and sent the bullet searing along the barrel to smash into her head and end her grief forever?

A loud bang echoed through the apartment. Pearl dropped the revolver to her lap, fearful that it had already gone off. No, the hammer was still raised. She stared stupidly at the weapon. The noise came again. The door . . . the front door! Someone was knocking on the front door, a savior sent to interrupt her before she could push herself completely over the edge. She gently thumbed down the hammer, put the still-loaded revolver back in its presentation box and locked the bureau drawer again. Dropping the key into the pocket of her dressing gown, she ran along the hall toward the front door.

"Lou . . . Benny!" she gasped when she swung back the door. She threw her arms around them, never so glad to see anyone in her life. "What are you doing here?" She was so grateful to see them it never occurred to her that she should be surprised to find them together.

Levitt kissed her perfunctorily on the cheek and stepped into the apartment. Minsky followed. "We found Landau."

"Where?"

Instead of replying, Levitt walked to the twins' bedroom and peeked inside. Pearl looked to Minsky, but his dark face gave nothing away. By some miracle the twins had not been disturbed by the knocking. They still slept soundly. Levitt closed the door and then led Pearl into the kitchen. "Landau was holed up in some apartment in the Bronx, off Fordham Road. He's dead, Pearl."

She heard the words and tried to make herself believe the news would lift some of the despair that had almost forced her to take her own life just moments earlier. She failed. "Lou, it doesn't make me feel any better. I don't feel anything at all."

Levitt took her in his arms and she burst into tears; these past days, tears sprang too readily to her eyes. For a minute he stood there, arms around her as she continued to sob. Only when her tears began to ebb did he speak again. "Pearl, look at me. This is very important, and I want you to listen carefully."

His tone alarmed her. His expression frightened her even more. His face was a mask of hopelessness, eyes bleak and hollow, skin pallid. Sweat beaded his upper lip and forehead. The calmness, the shrewdness, she had always associated with Lou Levitt were conspicuously absent.

"I didn't come here to make you feel better, Pearl. I came because I need your help."

"What is it?"

Levitt dropped his arms and leaned back against the sink. He looked as though he didn't have an ounce of strength in his body. If the sink were removed, she felt he would collapse onto the floor. His blue eyes left Pearl, traveled to Minsky as if pleading with him for help.

"It was Moe who found him, Pearl," Minsky said softly. "We had a tip that Landau was hiding out in that apartment. Moe went in after him, all by himself."

"Maybe he wanted to pay him back real bad for what he did to Jake," Levitt added. "Who the hell knows why he did it on his own?"

Pearl said nothing, asked no questions. If the two men wanted to take a roundabout way she would not hurry them. For she was certain that whatever they had to say only meant more sorrow.

"We don't know all the details yet," Levitt said. "Just what our friends in the police precinct up there have told us. It looks like Moe surprised Landau—burst into the apartment and shot him—from the way the police found Landau when they got there. He was sitting on a chair, facing the front door, and he'd been shot through the chest." Again Levitt paused, and Pearl made no attempt to rush him.

Minsky took up the story. "There were two bullet holes in the door. Not fired from the outside, but from the inside. There was a gun on the floor by Landau's chair, two bullets had been fired. The police figure Landau had just enough strength left in him before he died to fire those two shots through the door. He must have fired as Moe left, after he'd closed the door on the way out. One of the shots . . . one of them hit Moe in the back of the head."

"Oh, God. Annie!"

"Yes, Annie," Levitt repeated. "Moe's gone as well as Jake, Pearl. Now you've got to be doubly strong because Annie's going to need your help."

"Have you told her? Has anyone? Does she know?"

Levitt shook his head weakly. "I can't tell her, Pearl." His hard blue eyes turned soft with begging, his voice became a whisper. "Will you?"

Pearl wanted to scream *why me?* But she knew the answer already. Only she could give the support and love Annie would need at a time like this. Police officers, when they broke such news, were brusque. They would hammer on the door, blurt out their devastating message, and depart immediately, leaving Annie clutching at the walls for support. Pearl must tell her—tell her and then stay with her to ease her through those first terrifying hours.

"Do it quickly," Levitt urged, "before the police get here."

Then, stoop-shouldered, feeling like cowards, he and Minsky left.

Cold and shaking, Pearl stood in the hallway. Laughing, red-haired Annie, who had always shown more confidence, more daring, than Pearl. Annie, who had always been at the forefront, ready with a sharp challenge to anyone who tried to put her down. That time in the janitor's shed when they'd caught the boys gambling, Annie had been the one to pull back the door. Annie had been the one willing to accept

Caplan's kiss. There had never been any man in Annie's life but Moses Caplan. And now, within two weeks of his friend's death, Moe was dead, killed while trying to avenge Jake.

How would Annie take the news? Pearl dreaded finding out. At the same time she felt a perverse sense of gratitude. No, not because of Caplan's death . . . God forgive her for even thinking of such a thing! But if Levitt had not chosen that exact moment to knock on the door, what would Pearl have done with Jake's revolver pressed to her head, the hammer cocked? Now she had more reason to live. Not just for the twins, for Annie as well. Poor, dear Annie who had been her friend for thirty years. The little girl who had tried running away from home with her and had gotten lost and dispirited in Washington Square. Annie with the bleach, Pearl's red hair the following day—all their schoolmates laughing, except Lou Levitt who had solemnly declared that there was nothing wrong with being different, and those who laughed were only fools. Well, they were both different now. Both young widows with children to raise. Only Annie didn't know it yet.

Steeling herself, Pearl opened the front door and went to the neighboring apartment. Would Annie be asleep, she wondered as she knocked on the Caplans' door. Could she sleep without her husband being there? Pearl had never been able to; she had always lain awake worrying.

Before she could knock a second time, the door was opened. Like Pearl, Annie was wearing a dressing gown. Her bright red hair was neatly brushed, and Pearl knew that she had been right: Annie was unable to sleep while her husband was away. She felt even sicker about the tidings she had to impart.

"Pearl, what's the matter?" Instantly, Annie felt fear for her friend. It was so soon after Jake's death, that she was still concerned for Pearl. Pearl had been too calm. She hadn't screamed, hadn't carried on as Annie would have expected any young widow to do. It was better to scream than to bottle grief and anger up inside where they could do damage.

Pearl said nothing. She walked past Annie into the apartment, and closed the door. Those few seconds were all Annie needed to know that her fear should be for herself. It showed in the grim set of Pearl's face, the hardness of her eyes as they turned that sharp amber, the thin, rigid line of her mouth. Annie felt her stomach lurch, her legs turn to jelly.

"It's my Moe, isn't it?"

"Annie. Moe's not coming home."

Annie sagged against the wall. Life fled from her face. The red of her hair framed pure white. She croaked one word. "How?"

"Moe found Gus Landau. There was a fight. They killed each other."

"How did you find out?"

"Lou was at my home a few minutes ago. He asked me to tell you before the police got here."

"Thank you." A wan smile drifted across Annie's white face as she pushed herself away from the wall and stood up straight. "That ends the chapter, doesn't it?"

"The chapter? What chapter?"

"The chapter that was started at school. Moe and Jake, they're gone. That leaves Benny and Lou, and they're both alone. Just like you and me, Pearl." She walked down the hall to the kitchen. Pearl followed, watching as Annie filled a kettle for tea. "I knew it was going to happen; I always knew," Annie said as she took crockery from the cupboard. "Every night he was away—on the liquor runs and now this—I always knew that one night he wouldn't come back. Silly, wasn't it?" She gave a tense, high-pitched laugh as if to show how silly she thought it was.

Pearl felt confused. When Annie had slumped against the wall upon first learning of the tragedy, Pearl had surmised that it was the beginning of a total collapse. Instead, Annie was bouncing back. She was showing a resiliency that Pearl had not expected. "How are you going to break the news to Judy? You won't be able to lie to her. It'll be in the newspapers tomorrow, just like Jake's death was."

"I know. I'll tell her the truth. A bad man killed her father."

"It won't work," Pearl said, hating herself for having to negate Annie's idea. "The police will tell the newspapers that Moe and Landau shot each other."

Obviously, Annie had not considered that. When Jake had been killed, the stories spoke of an unarmed man shot down outside a synagogue after his twin sons had been bar mitzvahed. There had been nothing but sympathy for his family. This was different. Caplan had been armed. He had shot first, and Landau had fired back as Caplan had left the apartment; that had been Landau's final act.

As if nothing were wrong, Annie continued making the tea. She filled two cups and carried them toward the dining room.

"Annie? Do you really understand what's happening?" Pearl asked cautiously.

The question triggered an explosion. Without warning, Annie raised her arms and flung both cups of tea at the wall. China shattered, hot liquid splashed back. "Of course I damned well understand!" she yelled at Pearl. "What do you take me for—

370

some kind of imbecile?"

Pearl was silent, stunned by the fury of Annie's outburst.

"Why did it have to be my Moe who found that bastard? Why couldn't it have been Lou or Benny or one of those bums who do their dirty work? Why did my idiot of a husband always have to follow your Jake so closely? He married me because Jake married you. He had a kid because Jake did. And now he's gone and gotten himself killed because Jake did! That idiot—my idiot—didn't have a damned mind of his own."

"Shut up, Annie, before you wake Judy!"

"So what? Let her wake up. She's got to find out anyway!"

Pearl stepped forward and swung her right arm. Her palm cracked across Annie's face, snapping her friend's head back. Annie's mouth dropped; her hand flashed to her cheek to touch the smarting spot.

"Now will you shut up?" Pearl demanded.

The moment of anger ended as abruptly as it had begun. Annie regained control of herself, picked up a rag to wipe the wall where tea dripped down. Pearl collected the pieces of broken crockery.

"How do you tell a young girl her father's dead?" Annie whispered.

"You begin by saying, 'Judy, I love you.'"

Annie dropped into a chair and gazed into Pearl's face. "Is that how you would have told the twins if they hadn't seen it for themselves?"

"That's what I told them afterward. It helped to ease the pain. Theirs and mine."

Annie tried it out. "Judy, I love you." They were four words she had said to her daughter hundreds of times before, but they seemed inadequate as a preamble to telling Judy that her father was dead. "What comes next, Pearl?"

"Whatever you want to come next. You can say that Moe was killed while trying to avenge his friend's death—"

"Will that make sense to a young girl?"

"Does this kind of butchery make sense to anyone?" Pearl rested a hand on Annie's head, felt the coarseness of her red hair. "Do you want me to stay here with you? I will, if you like. We can tell Judy together."

Annie shook her head, and Pearl removed her hand. "No, this is something I have to do by myself." She stood up and began to walk around the room. By a coffee table, she stopped and stared down at a wedding photograph of herself and Caplan. "Ever stop to think that we might have done better for ourselves by finding two other guys, Pearl?"

"I don't believe in what might have been, Annie, only in what is. Nothing can change that."

Annie picked up the photograph and kissed Caplan's face, smudging the glass. "I'll tell Judy when she wakes up. I just wish . . ."

"What do you wish?"

"That Moe was here to help me tell her. That's crazy, isn't it? If Moe was here there wouldn't be anything to tell."

Levitt and Minsky drove from the Granitz apartment to the West Side. The Jalo Cab garage bustled with activity, but above, where the gambling operation was based, there was only darkness. The bookkeepers had gone home for the night; the runners and collection agents were with their families. The two men walked up the stairs to the office Levitt had shared with Jake. Levitt turned on the light, locked the door, and sat down behind his desk. He paid no attention to the shortwave radio. For once, the news from Europe did not interest him.

For a minute, the two men sat quietly, staring at each other. Finally, Levitt said: "You appreciate irony, Benny?"

"What the hell's so ironic about this?"

"You and me being here together. We never got on since we were kids, and now we're stuck with each other. There's your irony."

"I don't like it any more than you do."

Levitt shrugged. "Like it or not, it's the truth and we've got to make the best of it. There're only two of us left, Benny. We've got to stick together, otherwise everything we worked for gets washed down the sink. You've got a son to take care of."

"And you?"

"I'll take care of the twins, they're my responsibility. I'll look after Jake's share of the business."

"And Moe's share. Who'll look after that for Annie and his daughter?"

"I'll make sure they don't go hungry. We owe that to Moe."

"Yeah, we do." Minsky shifted slightly in the chair. "Are you going to make a move on Pearl?" he asked casually.

Levitt looked up sharply. "What's that supposed to mean?"

"Exactly what I said. Maybe Jake wasn't smart enough to see how you feel about Pearl, but I saw it. I saw it all along, the way those big blue eyes of yours followed her wherever she went. Christ, you even look on those boys of hers like they're your own."

Levitt's voice turned dangerously low. "Benny, you surprised me once by having more brains than I gave you credit for. Don't push your luck and try to do it twice."

Minsky hid a smile. He *had* surprised Levitt, no doubt about that.

All these years that little son of a bitch had held the sword of David Hay's murder over Minsky's head. Until now, when the great man himself had slipped up by underestimating Minsky. He'd assumed once too often that Minsky's only attributes were strength and fearlessness, and Minsky was going to make him pay for that mistake for the rest of his life. It was a stand-off. Two fighters, not with trainers in their corners, but lawyers. Two lawyers, each holding a secret that could spell doom for the other counselor's client.

"How do we split up the business now?" Minsky asked.

"Right down the middle. Is that fair enough for you?"

"You're not going to haggle, say you should get more because you'll be looking after Pearl and the twins and Moe's family?"

Levitt shook his head. "Equal partners, that's what we always were and that's the way it'll remain. Because we've both got the same to lose. Expenses don't enter into it."

"Okay." Minsky offered Levitt his hand. "Equal partners."

After a moment's consideration, Levitt took it. "Just as long as you realize it doesn't mean we have to be friends."

"We never were. Why should we change now?"

Chapter Four

Pearl sat up all night, trying to imagine what was taking place on the other side of the wall separating the two apartments. She knew every emotion Annie was feeling now as she tried to come to grips with tragedy, but Pearl had been spared one of Annie's torments—she hadn't been forced to tell the boys that their father was dead. Gus Landau had taken care of that for her. How did you tell a child that its father was gone? Even at twelve, Judy was still a child. Would she react as Joseph had done, cutting off the world while she grieved in private? Or would she, like Leo, revel in being the center of attention?

At seven o'clock in the morning, the telephone rang. It was Lou Levitt, wanting to know what had happened. Pearl told him. "I wanted to stay with her, Lou, but she wouldn't let me. She wanted to tell Judy on her own."

"She seem all right?"

"As all right as any woman who's just learned her husband is dead could be."

"I'm sorry, it was a stupid question."

"It's okay, Lou. I know what you mean. If I don't hear from her by eight o'clock I'll go next door and see if she needs me."

"You're a strong person, Pearl," Levitt said. "Stronger than me."

"Experience has made me strong."

"Such experiences we can all do without." Saying he'd call back later, Levitt hung up.

The ringing of the telephone roused the twins. They dressed and came out to find the breakfast table all set and their mother in the kitchen. They didn't know she hadn't been to bed. She served breakfast and then sat down at the table with her sons. "Something terrible happened last night," she began.

"What?" Joseph asked.

"Uncle Moe was killed. He died when he found the man who shot your father."

While Joseph sucked in his breath at the news, Leo asked, "Did he

374

kill the man?"

"He killed him."

"I told the boys at school that they'd get him," Leo said with satisfaction. "And I was right, wasn't I?"

"Shut up!" Joseph snapped at his brother. "Uncle Moe's dead, don't you realize that?"

"So's my father," Leo responded.

Joseph turned to Pearl. "Auntie Annie? Judy? What about them?"

"I don't know. Annie was going to tell Judy this morning."

Joseph rose from the chair, breakfast forgotten. "We should be there, we should help."

"Sit down, Joseph," Pearl told him softly. She was as touched by the older twin's concern as she was appalled by Leo's seeming callousness. "I asked Annie if she wanted me there when she told Judy. She said no, she wanted to do it by herself." Pearl looked at her wristwatch, saw that it was seven forty-five. "In fifteen minutes, we'll all go next door. By then, Judy will know, and that's when they'll want help."

At precisely eight o'clock, Pearl got up, went to the front door, and stepped outside. Joseph and Leo followed. Pearl knocked. There was no answer. Again she knocked before trying the handle; it did not move. Beside her, face screwed up, Joseph sniffed the air as though he were trying to locate an offensive smell. "What's the matter with you?" Pearl asked.

"I think . . . I think I can smell gas."

"Gas?" Pearl dropped onto her hands and knees, face pressed to the bottom of the door. Joseph was right. She jumped to her feet. "Leo, run downstairs, find the doorman! There must be a spare key! Joseph, get on the telephone, call the police. No, call the ambulance first!"

"You call the ambulance!" Joseph answered. "I'm going in there." He threw himself at the locked door, bounced back as the slab of wood rejected him. Neighbors poked their heads out of other apartments. Pearl yelled that gas could be smelled, and two heavy men joined Joseph's assault on the door. It still refused to budge.

Pearl saw Joseph run back into the Granitz apartment. "Where are you going?" He did not answer. He rushed into the bedroom he shared with Leo, flung open the window, and looked out. A narrow ledge ran along the wall, no wider than nine inches. Climbing through the open window, he started to walk along the ledge toward the Caplan apartment. He did not look down, nor did he hear Pearl's anguished shriek as she leaned out of the window and saw him, a skinny figure with his back pressed against the wall, arms spread for balance.

Joseph reached the first window of the neighboring apartment, the

375

living room. Balancing on one foot, he kicked back with the other to break the glass. Slowly he knelt down to undo the clasp. It was only then that he saw the ground far below him, the people who stared up at the boy balanced on the ledge. His head swayed and his vision blurred. He clutched at the window frame for support. Judy was inside. Perhaps she was already dead—perhaps he was too late—but he couldn't stop now. Fighting off the dizziness, he slid up the window and fell onto the living-room carpet.

The smell of gas was overpowering. Holding his breath, he ran through to the kitchen. All four taps of the stove were turned fully open, hissing the poison into the air. Annie and Judy sat on the floor, backs against the wall. Annie, with one arm around her daughter's shoulders, was smiling peacefully. Joseph rushed past them, picked up a heavy kettle and heaved it through the kitchen window. Next he went to the stove and turned off all the taps. Only then did he take in the full scene. He pulled Judy away from her mother and dragged her upright, holding her face to the open window. Tears filled his eyes. He heard someone screaming: "Breathe, damn you! Breathe!" And he never realized that the voice he heard was his own.

Footsteps hammered along the hallway as the doorman arrived. He carried a crowbar and used it to force open the door. Kneeling down beside Annie, he felt for a pulse. There was nothing. He dropped her arm and switched his attention to Judy.

"Let her go, son," he told Joseph. "Let me have a look at her." The doorman took Judy from Joseph's protective grasp and pressed his head against her chest. "Sounds like we're just in time." While Joseph watched, the doorman set Judy on the floor, cupped his mouth to hers and blew as hard as he could. Judy's eyes flickered open, closed again as air forced its way into her lungs. Hands clenched, fingernails biting painfully into his palms, Joseph continued to watch. He knew that Annie was dead; he'd guessed as much from the manner in which the doorman had so callously dropped her arm. But Judy was alive.

He felt a hand on his shoulder, looked around to see his mother. "Come away," she whispered. Holding Joseph by the hand, she walked through the knot of people clustered in the kitchen doorway and led him into the living room. She didn't know whether to yell at Joseph or hug him, hit him or kiss him.

"You're a very courageous boy," Pearl told him. "Your father would have been very proud of you."

"I had to do it. I had to try to save them."

"I know." She let go of Joseph's hand, her attention caught by something on the coffee table. Propped up against the wedding photograph of Annie and Moses Caplan was an envelope addressed to

Pearl. Slowly she picked it up, opened the flap, removed the two sheets of notepaper.

"'Dear Pearl,'" she read aloud. "'Forgive me, but I'm not as brave as you are. I can't tell Judy. Nothing I could say would make sense. Carrying on makes no sense either. I loved Moe more than anything else in the world. He wasn't as handsome as your Jake. He wasn't as smart as Lou, and he wasn't as crazy as Benny. But I loved him all the same. Pearl, I don't want to live without him, can you understand that? And I don't want Judy to grow up by herself. I know if I asked you, you'd look after her like she was your own, but what kind of life would it be for a kid whose father was shot and whose mother committed suicide? It's not fair to leave her behind.'"

Pearl swung her eyes from the letter to Joseph, who was standing silently by, listening. She wondered whether to continue.

"Why did you stop?" he asked her. "If I'm old enough to save Judy's life, I'm old enough to listen."

"I suppose you are." Pearl sighed and returned to the letter. "'After you left last night, Pearl, I woke Judy up. I gave her a glass of warm milk and a tablet. I told her that was to prevent the influenza that's going around. Really it was a sleeping pill. I used to take sleeping pills on the nights Moe was away—they never worked. God only knows why I kept them all this time. I'm rambling. . . . Now I'm sitting in the living room, summoning up all the courage I can find. I'm going to close the window, carry Judy into the kitchen and turn on the gas. Pearl, please forgive me, but I don't see any other way. I'll always love you. Annie.'"

The letter dropped from Pearl's hands and floated to the carpet. Joseph picked it up. "Can Judy come and live with us?" he asked quietly.

"Of course," Pearl answered gently.

Judy spent three days in a hospital, under observation. During that time, her mother and father were buried next to each other. Pearl took the twins to the double funeral. She clutched Joseph's hand while Lou Levitt held onto Leo. To Pearl's left, Benny Minsky stood alone, his own son too young to attend. Silently, they watched the two caskets being lowered into the ground. The men stepped forward, waiting their turns to shovel earth into the pit. As Minsky, the last to do so, stepped away from the graves, Pearl took the shovel from where he had jammed it into the soft ground. Lifting up some earth, she stood over Annie's grave.

"Goodbye, Annie," she whispered. "God bless." Tears in her eyes, she stepped away.

"Each time we see each other there seems to be one less," she remarked to Levitt as they walked from the graveside.

Levitt ignored Pearl's observation. He told the twins to run on ahead to his car, then he tugged Pearl's arm. "You told me Judy's going to live with you, right?"

"That's what's best for her."

"Then get the hell out of that apartment, Pearl. The whole damned building is bad luck."

Despite the surroundings—and the subject—Pearl laughed. "Since when are you superstitious?"

"I'm not, but I'm realistic enough to face facts. You've lived in that place for fourteen years. You've sat *shivah* twice—for Jake, and for your mother—and now this. Get out of there before anything else happens. Do the twins know yet about you taking Judy in?"

"Only Joseph. It was his idea. I haven't gotten around to telling Leo yet."

"Good luck when you do. Listen to me, there are vacant apartments in my building on Central Park West. Come back with me now. We'll find a place this afternoon, sign a lease, do whatever we have to do. You'll move tomorrow morning."

"Tomorrow?" Pearl was stunned at the thought. You didn't leave a home you'd lived in for fourteen years just like that.

"Yes, tomorrow. Do you want Judy to go back to the building where her mother tried to kill her?"

"She doesn't know her mother tried to kill her. She doesn't know anything yet."

"And how long do you think that'll last? Take a good look at this." Levitt pulled a rolled-up newspaper from his coat pocket. Pearl turned cold when she glanced at the headline. "Gunman's Widow Kills Self, Tries to Gas Daughter," it read. "She's sure going to know once she gets out of that hospital," Levitt said bluntly.

Pearl read the story right through. Everything was there. Caplan had shot Gus Landau, the man police were seeking in connection with the murder of Jake Granitz, and had been killed himself. Shooting him was Landau's final act. Following that, Annie had committed suicide and had tried to kill her daughter. Only the bravery of a thirteen-year-old boy had saved the girl's life. "Where did they get all this information?" Pearl asked Levitt.

"Any reporter worth his paycheck will dig up that kind of information. From the police. From some hospital attendant. Take a look around, this place is crawling with cops and reporters."

Pearl did as Levitt told her. There were many faces she did not know. "Find me that apartment, Lou. Find it for me this afternoon."

Levitt did. He dropped the twins off at Fifth Avenue, and then drove Pearl to Central Park West. There, he located the building manager and explained that Pearl urgently needed a large apartment for occupancy the following day. The manager protested that leasing an apartment could not be done so quickly. Levitt produced two one-hundred-dollar bills and the protests stopped. An hour later, Pearl had selected a freshly decorated four-bedroom apartment on the floor above Levitt's. The building manager drew up a lease, and Pearl signed it, while Levitt made arrangements with a moving company to clear out the apartment on Fifth Avenue the following morning. The Caplan apartment would be left untouched; that could be seen to in the future.

With the lease and the moving settled, Levitt drove Pearl home. She invited him to stay for dinner. It was the last full meal she would ever cook in that apartment and she did not want to be alone with the twins. There were too many memories for her to face. Over dinner, she told Joseph and Leo the news. "We're moving tomorrow," she said with forced casualness. "We're taking an apartment in the same building as Uncle Lou."

"Good!" Leo clapped his hands enthusiastically. "I want to be near Uncle Lou!"

Levitt smiled at the response. "What about you, Joseph?"

"Does that mean we'll have to change schools?"

"Unless you want to walk fifty blocks each way each day," Levitt answered.

"Will Judy be going to the new school as well?" Joseph asked.

Before Pearl or Levitt could answer, Leo said, "Of course not. Didn't you hear what Uncle Lou just said? It's fifty blocks away."

"Don't be stupid—once she gets out of the hospital, she's going to live with us."

Leo dropped his fork and stared accusingly at Pearl. "What?"

"We were going to tell you," Pearl answered. "The best thing for Judy is that she comes to live—"

Leo cut his mother off by slamming a tightly clenched fist onto the table. "Why should she live with us?"

"Because she has nowhere else to go."

"She's got next door!"

Levitt waved at Pearl to be silent. Quiet logic was needed here, not heated emotion. "Leo, she's too young to live by herself. And she can't live in that apartment either, not after what happened there."

"I don't want her in our new home."

"Don't be so selfish," Levitt said. "Her parents were very dear friends of your parents. Judy's your friend."

"She's Joseph's friend! Not mine! I hate her!" His eyes narrowed, altered shade. "I wish—" He broke off abruptly and stared down at his plate.

"What do you wish, Leo?" Levitt asked quietly.

"Nothing."

"No, tell us what you wish. We want to know."

"Nothing, I said!"

"Do you wish she'd died in that kitchen with her mother?"

Leo looked up sharply. How did his Uncle Lou always know? He'd known about the dog, and now he knew about this. "Yes! I wish she had died! I hate her! I hate her more than I've ever hated anyone. She's always sticking her face in between Joseph and me!" Bursting into tears, Leo jumped up from the table and ran to the room he shared with Joseph.

Pearl rose from the table and started to follow him. Levitt stretched out a hand. "Leave him alone. You've pampered him too much already, Pearl, and now you're paying the price."

When Pearl remained standing by the table, undecided whether to heed Levitt's advice or her own heart—her feeling that Leo should be indulged—Levitt went on. "Something else you can do when you move. You can separate the boys. You've leased a place with four bedrooms, and they're old enough now to be in separate rooms. Would you like that Joseph?"

Joseph nodded.

"Leo's going to have to learn to stand alone, Pearl. He'll be much the better for it. Now sit down and finish your dinner. If he wants to return to the table, he will."

Ten minutes after storming from the table, Leo returned as calmly as if nothing had happened. He was about to sit down when Levitt pointed a finger at him. "What do you think you're doing?"

"Finishing my dinner."

"Not until you apologize to your mother, to your brother, and to me for the way you behaved."

"Apologize?" Leo's face turned red, his eyes a steely gray. "I'm not apologizing. I didn't do anything wrong."

"Leave the table and go back to your room."

Leo looked to his mother for help. She turned away.

"Go back to your room," Levitt repeated, "and stay there until you're ready to apologize."

Leo glared at Levitt, but the little man's blue eyes were every bit as hard and determined as his own. For ten silent seconds they stared at each other, until at last Leo retreated. Sulking, he went to his room, not to return.

That night, the family's last in the Fifth Avenue apartment, Joseph slept in the spare bedroom. It was the first time since Leo had had diphtheria that the twins had been separated. And as Pearl prepared for bed, after Levitt had left, a realization struck her. Levitt had assumed the role of man of the house. At the table he had even sat in the chair that Jake had always used. Not only had Pearl done nothing to stop him, she'd welcomed his move.

Was that the motive behind Levitt's suggestion that they leave the apartment? Why had he helped find her family a new home in his own building? So that he could be closer to them, could fulfill the role he believed was his? Was he doing it just for the twins' sake? Pearl wondered. Or was he doing it for her as well?

When Judy was discharged from the hospital, Levitt and Pearl drove her straight to the new apartment on Central Park West. During the journey, she seemed far different from the lively, happy girl Pearl had known. She was sullen, staring out of the window when she was spoken to, answering questions with curt replies.

"Is there anything you want from your old home?" Pearl asked her. Judy's clothing had been brought over during the move, but Pearl did not know whether there was anything of sentimental value the girl might need.

"I don't want anything from that place," Judy answered. "I don't want anything from the place where my mother . . . where my mother did what she did. I don't want anything that reminds me of her. I hate her!"

The outburst reminded Pearl of Leo's expression of hatred for Judy. "You shouldn't talk about your mother like that."

"Why not?" Judy wanted to know. "She left me! When I needed her most after what happened to my father, she left me!"

"She didn't want to leave you. She wanted to take you with her."

"And I shouldn't hate her for that? Some choice—either she left me all alone, or else she tried to kill me."

"You're not all alone. You've got us. We love you."

"Leo loves me?" Judy gave a bitter laugh.

"Don't you worry about Leo. I'll take care of him, but you have to bend a little as well. You have to try to like Leo."

Judy gazed morosely out of the window of the car. Her world had been ripped apart, her parents had been taken from her, her own life had nearly ended. And all she had to show for it was being told to like a boy she absolutely despised.

Three months passed before the new household began to settle down. The twins had been quick to adapt to the change of neighborhood. During the winter, there had been ice-skating almost outside their door; in spring, the park offered other attractions. Judy, as Pearl had expected, took longer to adjust. She went to school with the twins each morning, had dinner with them each evening. Then she would shut herself away in her room, ostensibly to complete her homework. Once, when Pearl had had reason to enter her room, she'd found Judy sitting at a small table, staring at the wall. Her homework lay in front of her, untouched.

Seeing the girl like that, her bright red hair tied in braids, noting her uncanny resemblance to Annie Pearl felt like crying. Annie might be dead, but her soul lived on in her daughter, constantly serving as a mirror to Pearl's own life, especially those days so long ago when everything had been so simple and carefree.

"Stuck with something?" Pearl asked gently. "I'm sure Joseph would help you if you asked him."

Judy answered without taking her eyes off the wall. "I'm not stuck on anything. I was just thinking about my mother. I think about her all the time. I try to understand why she acted the way she did, why she did what she did."

"To herself?" Pearl asked. "Or to you?"

"To both of us."

"Love. She loved your father so much that she didn't think she could live without him. She didn't want to. And she loved you too much to want to leave you behind to face things on your own."

Judy turned around to gaze solemnly at Pearl. "Did you love Uncle Jake?"

"Of course I did."

"And can you live without him?"

Pearl saw a mental picture of two ivory-handled revolvers inside a walnut presentation case. They were still in the locked bottom drawer of the bureau which now sat in her new bedroom; one of them, she remembered, was even fully loaded. "There was a time when I wasn't sure I could."

"And?"

"The moment passed."

"My mother's moment didn't pass," Judy said quietly.

"She had no one there to help her."

"Who helped you? Joseph?"

"No. Lou Levitt and Benny Minsky. They chose that exact moment to knock on my door."

Judy gave a thin smile. "God was watching over you more closely than he watched over my mother."

"Do you still hate her?"

"No. I'm beginning to understand what must have been passing through her mind. She thought she was doing the right thing. Is it true that Joseph climbed along the ledge to break into our apartment and save me?"

"Yes. The door was bolted from the inside." Pearl walked toward the bedroom door. She knew now why she'd been so open with Judy. Judy's resemblance to Annie was so strong that Pearl could easily believe she was talking to her friend. "I'm going to make some hot chocolate. I'll call you when it's ready."

"Thanks, Auntie Pearl."

Once Judy came to terms with her mother's reason for committing suicide, she settled in with her new family. The girl had always looked on Pearl as an honorary aunt, a good friend of her mother's who lived next door. Now she viewed her as someone much closer. Judy did not want to use the word *stepmother;* there was something repulsive to her about that title, it belonged to a woman who brought up a strange child because circumstances had forced her to. Pearl was not doing that. She had taken Judy into her home because she'd wanted to. So Judy began to call Pearl Ma, just as the twins did.

Pearl did not object. On the contrary, she encouraged Judy to do that, feeling that the girl was recovering from her loss and accepting her. Only Leo objected to Judy calling his mother Ma.

"She's not your mother!" he snapped at her one day when they were alone in the apartment. "She's my mother! Mine and Joseph's! Your mother's dead—she killed herself!"

The harsh reminder brought tears to Judy's eyes. She forced them back. Nothing Leo could say or do would make her cry. She knew he hated her, and she fought him with the same spiteful weapons he used. "She's not your mother either! You were switched at birth. You think you're Joseph's twin? Well I've got news for you. You couldn't be because you're nothing like him. You won't be anything like him as long as you live!"

When Pearl returned, Judy did not tell her what Leo had said. She did not want Pearl to be upset. Instead, she told Joseph. He rushed straight into his twin's bedroom and confronted him with the claim.

"You ever say anything like that to Judy again, and so help me I'll beat you to a pulp."

Leo taunted him. "She's making you soft in the head, that's what she's doing. She's nothing but a stupid girl. You should stand up for me, not her. You're my twin!"

"She's my friend!"

"You mean," Leo said slowly, "that you'd let a friend be more important to you than your twin?"

Joseph was lost for an answer. Since infancy it had been drummed into his head that it was important, unique, to be a twin. Yet at times he absolutely loathed his brother. He had never felt that way about Judy. He had always considered her special, and now that she lived with the family he was even fonder of her. He was starting to experience new feelings for her, strange, hot sensations that kept him awake at night. Sometimes he was glad Leo hated her. Because it meant that Leo would not be lying in his bed, thinking, feeling, the same. . . .

As Pearl became a mother figure for Judy, Lou Levitt assumed the role of substitute father to the twins. Now that they were all living in the same building, Levitt's presence was almost constant. Three or four times a week he ate dinner with the family, filling the position at the head of the table as though it were his inalienable right. On Friday nights, after Pearl had lit and blessed the candles, it was Levitt who poured the wine, broke the bread, and passed it around the table. When the twins wanted help or advice—especially with their arithmetic homework—they went to Levitt, who was clearly delighted to assist.

Those Friday nights were the only times that Pearl saw Benny Minsky and his son, William. Despite the upheavals, she continued to invite them for dinner. The sight of them was comforting, making her almost believe that nothing had really changed, that Jake . . . Jake . . . was still there with her. She noticed the improved relations between Levitt and Minsky. Levitt had told her they had split up the business, buried their differences for the sake of their own survival. It was a very thin silver lining, Pearl decided, to a crushing black cloud.

Minsky remained adamant about his son being bar-mitzvahed. He continued to take him to services every Saturday morning, made sure the boy attended Hebrew classes, and he never spoke about Kathleen. Even when the Hal Brookman production of *Broadway Nell* came out, he mentioned neither her nor the film. Out of curiosity, Pearl went with Levitt to see the movie when it opened in New York. They left the theater agreeing that the original Broadway show had been superior.

"You just wait and see," Levitt told Pearl as they drove home from

384

the theater, "pretty soon she'll be back in New York, broke and knocking on Benny's door. And he'll take her right back."

"No on all accounts, Lou. She won't come back. And even if she did, Benny wouldn't give her the time of day. He's changed too much to let her wrap him around her little finger again."

"Maybe you're right, who am I to say different?"

When they reached home, Levitt walked Pearl up to her apartment. At the door she asked him in for coffee. Judy and the twins were already asleep. Pearl and Levitt sat together on a couch by the living-room window. Then, out of the blue, Levitt said: "You know, the business . . . it doesn't only belong to me and Bonny. You've got a share in it. So have the twins. Even Judy, she's got a piece of it because she's Moe's daughter."

"Lou . . . what are you talking about?"

"I just want you to know that as long as I've got breath in my body, Pearl, none of you will ever want for anything. Never!"

Pearl stood up and looked out of the window at the darkened park. Scattered lights cast small pools of brightness, not enough to see the bench by the lake where she had sat that one time with Levitt. He had been this intense, this serious, on that evening. Because of it, Pearl knew exactly where he was leading, just as she knew exactly how she would respond.

Levitt got up and stood beside Pearl. "I'm asking you to marry me."

"I know. And I can't." The rejection was delivered in a flat, toneless voice.

"Why not? I told you once that I'd loved you ever since we were kids."

"I remember."

"Don't you feel anything for me?"

"Lou, next to Jake you mean more to me than anyone I've ever known, but being a widow once is enough for any woman."

"What's that supposed to mean?"

"Do you really think there's not another Gus Landau waiting around? Only this time he'll have a bullet in his gun with your name on it, Lou. You keep on with the gambling, with all the money that's involved, that's what's going to happen to you." Her eyes narrowed, stared accusingly at Levitt. "While we're on the subject, what happened to all those big deals you talked about? The move we were going to make once Prohibition was dead? I thought the idea was to get out of the gambling, to be one hundred percent respectable, leave legitimate companies to the children. Wasn't that the idea?"

"We've got interests in some companies—"

"But you're still operating the gambling."

"Pearl, there's a hundred—no, a thousand—times the money in gambling."

"Is there? Don't you really mean it's in your blood? Lou, I think I know you by now. Owning a hundred companies quoted on the stock exchange wouldn't give you half the thrill you'd get from organizing some nickel-and-dime crap game, would it?"

Levitt nodded modestly. "Pearl, what we set up—me, Jake, Moe, and Benny—rivaled any legitimated corporation. And it was a damned sight more fun."

"Because you had an edge."

"A gambler always needs an edge." He turned away from the window and looked at the coffee on the table as if undecided whether to drink it. "You changed subjects on me, Pearl. You brought up the gambling when I was talking about us. Those twins, they need a man to guide them. You saw that clearly enough with Leo the night before you moved out of the old place. You've let him get away with murder. Me, he listened to. You need help with those boys, you can't raise them by yourself."

"Nothing's stopping you from helping, Lou. You've always thought you're their father anyway. Maybe you are, I don't know anymore. I stopped thinking about it a long time ago. Help all you like, but don't ask me to make it official. I won't sit *shivah* for a husband twice."

"I'm stupid," Levitt said. "You need time to think about it. It's too soon after Jake. I'm sorry."

Pearl showed her gratitude for his retreat by saying, "In a little while, perhaps, I'll feel differently." She knew it was a lie. She wouldn't marry Levitt, no matter how much she cared for him; no matter how much she'd even come to depend on him, to love him. She would not marry any man who could send her back to that tiny wooden chair, make her tear her clothing and cover the mirrors again.

"Right now I'll settle for helping," Levitt said, "even if it's only as a godfather." He sat down again, lifted the cup of coffee he'd ignored. It was tepid but he drank it anyway. "Strange those two. Joseph—he'll score such marks at school that he'll walk into any university. But that Leo . . ." He pronounced the younger twin's name so oddly that Pearl was uncertain whether he was denigrating the boy or admiring him.

"What about Leo?"

"He's got a chip on his shoulder the size of the Empire State Building. He's going to be a handful when he grows up. He'll never be the equal of Joseph for brains, but he's got a different kind of cleverness. He can manipulate people. I've seen him do it to Joseph often enough—and to you. He's even tried it on me a couple of times."

"Is that good or bad?"

"I don't know. Like anything else, it's a talent. It all depends on how he learns to use it. And"—Levitt smiled broadly, as if congratulating himself—"who teaches him to use it."

Pearl looked out of the window again. She was disappointed and angry. Despite all of Levitt's fine speeches, all of Jake's promises to the boys regarding what they would inherit, she knew that Joseph and Leo were going to be guided into the gambling operation. Levitt had it all worked out. The twins would follow him, and she felt powerless, unable to prevent that.

Chapter Five

Benny Minsky saw his dream come true in the late autumn of 1942, when his son, William, was bar mitzvahed at the reform synagogue on West End Avenue.

Kathleen was not there to see it, although she was aware of the occasion. In a rare gesture of generosity toward his ex-wife, Minsky sent her an invitation. She never replied. The week before the bar mitzvah, Minsky telephoned her at the California home of Hal Brookman. A maid took the call. When Minsky announced who it was, the maid told him that Miss Monahan was not at home, nor was she expected. Minsky just shrugged and put the telephone down.

Miss Monahan! . . . So Brookman hadn't married her after all. Or was she just keeping the name for professional purposes? Minsky didn't know, and he told himself that he didn't really care. He had not even bothered to see her latest movie, a musical western—another Brookman production—that had been released three months earlier. He had read the reviews, though: acting with the "skill of a totem pole"; a voice that "no longer possessed the famous throaty lustiness." "Was her voice gone," the critic had asked, "or had Miss Monahan come across better as a young and sultry stage siren than a middle-aged singing cowgirl on film?" After reading that, and hearing Pearl, who had taken Judy, Joseph, and Leo to see the film, agree with the critic, Minsky was grateful that he had not gone. It was better to remember Kathleen as she had been when he'd first met her, a sexy-voiced manicurist in a barber shop.

Pearl took over the arrangements for the luncheon that followed the synagogue service. The fact that Minsky had no wife to perform such work was not the only motivation behind Pearl's offer to host the luncheon at her own apartment. Aside from Lou Levitt, Minsky was the only member of the old group left. She felt a strong attachment to him. Once, with his love of guns and action, she had been terrified of him. Now she admired him. He had set his mind to bringing up his son

388

by himself, and he had succeeded. That morning, when William had stood up in the synagogue, Pearl had looked at Minsky and seen the pride glowing on his dark face.

"Enjoy William's performance?" Minsky asked her when they arrived back at the apartment for lunch. Pearl figured it was the fourth time he had phrased the question.

"It was a lovely morning, Benny. Except"—she faltered for an instant—"except for one thing."

"Leaving the place afterward?" Minsky guessed. When Pearl nodded, he said, "I couldn't get over that feeling either, not after what happened to Jake. Every time I come out of a synagogue I get a chill down my back. But today especially." He shivered theatrically to make his point.

Levitt, who had stopped off to check his mail, entered the apartment. He was smiling and waving an envelope. "William's not the only one getting presents today," he said. "Look what Uncle Sam sent to me."

Pearl scanned the envelope and fear clutched her heart. "From the army?"

"From the draft board. I registered, just like I'm supposed to. They asked what I could do and I told them I had experience in bookkeeping work. Otherwise I could run a transportation unit." He paused while Minsky chuckled. "I got called in for the physical and"—he waved the letter he had taken from the envelope—"I failed the damned thing."

"You failed it? Why?"

"Don't make it sound like I've only got three months to live. I'm too damned short, isn't that one hell of a switch? Remember all those kids at school who made fun of me? They're going to be up to their armpits in mud on the front line, and I'm staying here because I'm too damned short. God has a way of righting wrongs, believe me."

"I didn't even know you'd taken the physical," Pearl said.

"I didn't tell anyone. What's the point of worrying about something until it happens?"

"Let's just hope this thing's over before our kids are old enough to put on a uniform," Minsky said.

"It will be," Levitt answered. "It will be. Those landings in Africa this week. It's the beginning of the end, you'll see."

"What about you, Benny?" Pearl asked. "Will you have to go in?"

"No, I'm a single parent. They want me, they'll have to provide a guardian for William."

"Not in a rush to pick up a gun anymore, Benny?" Levitt asked.

There was a smile on his face and a trace of the old mockery in his voice.

"I don't need a gun to protect myself, do I, Lou?" Minsky retorted. "I learned from you that there are better ways."

"I'm glad I managed to teach you something." The smile and the mockery had gone, and Pearl had no idea what the two men were talking about.

BOOK FIVE

Chapter One

Lou Levitt arranged the lives of the Granitz twins with all the care of a chess grandmaster deploying his pieces in preparation for the main attack. He knew the value of each twin, his strengths and weaknesses, which part of the board he should occupy for greatest advantage. Joseph was like a knight, able to cover each square of the board with intricate moves, deadly to every other piece because he could make moves they could not; and like a bishop, he could swiftly cut across a diagonal between ranks of other men. Despite such speed and trickery, though, he lacked the sheer bludgeoning power of a castle or a queen, the pieces which Levitt believed most typified Leo. The younger twin had none of Joseph's subtlety, none of his deftness. Just brute power. Not to worry, Levitt decided. The world had plenty of space for brute power as well as craft and guile.

When the twins finished high school in 1945, Levitt separated them. Joseph went on to Columbia to study business. Leo, who had barely graduated from high school, started work as Levitt's personal assistant. At first, the job consisted of acting as Levitt's driver, running him on innocuous errands or else hanging around the nerve center of the gambling operation above the Jalo Cab garage. Unlike Levitt, who treated cash strictly as a commodity, Leo was fascinated by the vast sums of money he saw. He gazed with awe as agents emptied their pockets of thousands of dollars, piling it on the desks in front of bookkeepers who counted it with a speed that dazzled Leo's eyes.

After a month, when Levitt asked Leo if he wanted to go out on one of the collection rounds, Leo eagerly accepted. Levitt immediately crooked a finger at a fair-haired man in his early thirties who wore an immaculately pressed blue suit, a sparkling white shirt and a deep red silk tie. "Phil, come over here and meet my godson."

Phil Gerson strolled over to where Levitt and Leo stood.

"Leo's learning the business," Levitt told him. "Why don't you take him under your wing for a while, show him around?"

"Sure, Lou." Gerson held out a hand which Leo accepted. Gerson's handshake was like the man himself, crisp and firm. "Come for a ride with me now," Gerson invited Leo. "It's payout time for the few lucky winners." After picking up a large cloth bag from one of the bookkeepers, he headed downstairs, through the Jalo garage, and into a shiny Lincoln. Leo settled himself in the passenger seat.

"You're one of Jake's boys, aren't you?" Gerson said conversationally. "Your brother also learning the ropes?"

"Joseph? No, he's going to Columbia."

"What's he studying for?"

"To be a businessman." Leo could not make up his mind whether or not he was jealous of his twin. Leo was out working for a living. He was earning money. He was finished with his youth, he had responsibilities now. What was more important, more prestigious, being a student, or being an earner? "That's what my twin brother Joseph's doing," Leo muttered. "He's learning to carry a briefcase like some goddamned businessman."

Gerson heard the disparaging note but made no comment. He sensed some dark hidden menace in Leo. The muscular body, the heavy, scowling face. He deemed it prudent not to mention that there was nothing wrong with further education; that he, himself, had a degree from Harvard Business School. His father had sent him there in the hope that Gerson would use what he'd learned to further the fortunes of the family's investment company. Instead, the business had fallen victim to the Depression. With his degree and a sharp mind, Gerson had gone to work for Levitt, starting as a bookkeeper, and now working in any slot where a clean-cut man from a good family was needed as a front.

"Your father always used to talk about you and your brother," Gerson said, "how you'd come into the business one day. Really proud of you both, he was."

"How long have you been working for Uncle Lou?"

"Ten years, must be." Gerson turned off Forty-second Street and headed south on Broadway.

"What do you do for him?"

"Whatever needs doing. Today I'm filling in for one of the collectors who's down with the flu. I'm picking up and delivering to all the downtown books."

"How many places?"

"Twenty. Candy stores, restaurants, bars. You'll see."

"What kind of a take do they pull in?"

"On a good day, maybe a couple of thousand apiece. Rarely below a thousand. That's turnover, of course, not profit."

Leo did some rapid mental arithmetic. Twenty books downtown; that worked out to be between one hundred and two hundred thousand dollars a week turnover just from downtown. Maybe ten million dollars a year. Such a sum was inconceivable. Or was it? He swiveled in the seat and fixed Gerson with an accusing stare, heavy eyebrows lowered, eyes a steely gray. "You ever stick to any of that money?"

Gerson laughed. "You think I'm crazy? Every penny's accounted for. Lou Levitt doesn't let a cent get away."

"That's the answer I wanted to hear." Leo turned forward again, satisfied.

Gerson's first stop was a small restaurant on Delancey Street. With Leo following, he walked through the dining area to the kitchen. Two people were there, a fat, middle-aged woman cleaning up from the breakfast period, and a painfully thin, balding man who sat at a table that had nothing on it but a telephone, a notebook, and a pen.

"Abe and Rachel Honick, husband-and-wife team," Gerson murmured to Leo. "She cooks while he takes the bets. That's how they're putting a couple of sons through medical school."

Gerson began to count out money to be paid to the previous day's winners. While he did so, three men came in to place bets on that day's races. Seconds after they left, the door from the restaurant opened again. This time the visitor was a red-faced, burly police sergeant. Leo clenched his fists. Gerson shot him a quick, calming glance. "Relax—cops have got to eat."

Abe Honick handed the sergeant a white envelope containing twenty-five twenty-dollar bills. The patrolman removed two bills which he placed in his own pocket.

"Now watch," Gerson whispered to Leo. "This is where it starts to come back."

Leo saw the sergeant leave a list of bets with Honick. They were immediately telephoned to the room above the Jalo garage.

"Who pays for the bribe?" Leo asked as he and Gerson left the restaurant and climbed back into the Lincoln.

"We do. Comes under operating overhead. An investment with a good rate of return."

"You ever had a cop turn on you?"

Gerson shook his head. "Everyone's got his price. The captain gets a C-note a week, the lieutenant seventy-five, the sergeant forty, and so on and so forth. Just from this one book."

"Sounds like you work to union scales."

"You've got it," Gerson said. For the first time he saw Leo smile, and he didn't know which expression bothered him more—the sullen,

393

threatening look or the dark smile that was laced with just as much menace.

With Gerson as his guide, Leo visited all the downtown books. He walked into the various locations and stood watching as Gerson conducted his business. Later that day, he made the rounds again as Gerson collected the new bets. That evening, he resumed the role of personal assistant to Levitt, driving the little man back to Central Park West.

"Learn anything?" Levitt asked.

"Plenty."

"Good. You stick close to Phil Gerson and you'll know all there is to know. You'll know where every book is, every numbers drop. You'll know the people who work for us, how much they take in."

Damned right I will, Leo said silently, because one day I'll run all of it. He drove on, his thoughts occupied with what he had seen. What power, to have the police on your payroll. He had never dreamed such things were possible. And Joseph . . . poor dumb Joseph . . . was going to Columbia to learn how to become a businessman.

What a jerk!

Levitt paid just as much attention to Joseph as he did to Leo, but he pushed him in a totally different direction. He was continually checking with the older twin on how his studies were progressing at Columbia. He exhibited, so Pearl thought, far more interest in Joseph's education than Jake had done; then she remembered that Levitt was more aware of the value of such an education.

In the first year, Joseph proved to be an average student. Levitt told him sharply that his grades weren't good enough. "Take a good look around you," he told Joseph, "and see how many average people there are. The world's full of average people, and you've got the brains to do much better than that. Use them."

Joseph did. He pushed himself to the limit in his studies, and by the end of his sophomore year he had climbed into the top five percent. Levitt was so pleased with the improvement that he went right out and purchased a gleaming pale blue Oldsmobile 76 for Joseph.

"She's all yours," Levitt said, handing the keys to Joseph. "Try her out."

Joseph jingled the keys in his hand while he looked at his mother, Judy, and Leo, who had all come down from the apartment to see the new car. At last, his eyes fixed on Judy. "Want to take a ride with me?" Before the offer could be repeated, she was in the passenger seat.

"Did you really expect him to ask you?" Levitt said to Pearl as Joseph drove away. He was certain that he'd seen a flicker of disappointment cross her face.

"If it had been me, I'd have asked you first, Ma," Leo cut in. He, too, had seen the sadness. He could read his mother just as well as Levitt could, and he believed that Joseph should have asked Pearl to take the first ride in his new car. Your mother was always the most important person in your life.

Pearl gave her son a patient smile. "Leo, you've got a lot to learn, you know that? When there's a pretty redhead available, you don't ask a middle-aged lady out for a ride." She stared after the car, feeling happy for both Judy and Joseph. They were content with life, with each other. Joseph's university work came first, but Judy ran a close second. They went out at least twice a week on what Pearl termed their formal dates. During the remainder of the week, they always found an hour or so each evening to go for a walk in the park. They might, Pearl reflected, just as well be married. She had little doubt that eventually they would be.

At Pearl's insistence, Levitt had even created a job for Judy. Although her school grades had been almost as high as Joseph's, she had exhibited no interest in furthering her education by attending a university. She'd wanted to find an interesting job, so Levitt had placed her with a dress company in which he'd owned a piece since Prohibition days. Judy had started by working in the office. Exceptionally quick to catch on, she was now in the sales department. Eventually, she wanted to use the knowledge she acquired to become a buyer for a big department store, but Pearl could never see that happening. She was certain Judy would be married long before then, with a couple of children to look after.

Seeing Levitt take care of all three youngsters, and thinking of Joseph and Judy together, Pearl wondered how long it would be before Levitt asked her to marry him again. The last time had been seven years earlier, just after Jake had died. She had rejected him then, told him that being a widow once was enough for any woman; minutes later, she had softened the rejection with the lie that she needed time. Now she was uncertain what her answer would be should he ask again.

During the past seven years, Pearl felt that her life had stabilized. Levitt, she understood, had been a major factor. He had stood by her, made the decisions, assumed the responsibility for bringing up the children. Without him, she was not certain how she would have managed. Joseph and Leo would have been enough of a handful without a man's direction. With Judy as well, life would have been impossible. Wryly, she recalled her thoughts of moments earlier about Joseph and Judy, the notion that they might as well be married. The same situation applied to herself and Levitt. They lived in separate apartments on separate floors, but she saw as much of Levitt as of any member of her family. More importantly, she relied on him more than she relied on anyone else. Just look at what he'd done with Leo.

In the two years that Leo had worked for Levitt, Pearl had noticed a distinct change come over the younger twin. He acted, for the first time, in a more mature manner than his brother. Joseph constantly displayed the worries of a university student, anxiousness about grades and examinations; and he was anticipating the day when he would finally graduate. Leo's appearance was far more worldly. He was always well dressed and was never without money in his pocket, even if he rarely went anywhere to spend it. Most nights he stayed in, indulging a new hobby: reading. Never a prodigious reader while at school, he now waded through heavy biographies of famous men. His favorites were Napoleon and Cesare Borgia. One, though of humble origins, had changed the face of Europe; the other, born with a silver cross in his mouth, had devastated Italy. To Leo they represented power. Not power earned, but power taken.

The infrequent times that Leo did go out always coincided with those nights Joseph dated Judy. Then Leo would take Pearl to dinner, treating her with the utmost courtesy, opening doors, holding chairs, spoiling her as she had never been spoiled before; not even by Jake. After one dinner and show, Pearl said to Leo: "Why are you wasting your time on an old lady like me, Leo? Find yourself a nice girl."

"When I find one who compares with you," he answered in a manner that reminded Pearl of Lou Levitt a lifetime earlier, "I'll take her out instead. Until then, you can be my girlfriend."

Pearl felt fortunate. How many mothers had such warm, loving sons? All her worries, all the care she'd given to Leo, were being amply repaid.

Chapter Two

Joseph graduated from Columbia in the summer of 1949. He received his results on a Saturday, and Pearl immediately began preparing a special menu for that night's dinner. Before she could pull a pan from the cupboard, though, Joseph told her that he had long ago planned to share this moment with Judy. A family celebration could come at a later date. As Pearl tried to hide her hurt at her son's rejection, Leo stepped in quickly with a dinner invitation for his mother.

Although Joseph missed the flash of pain in Pearl's eyes, Judy did not. Over dinner that evening, before seeing *South Pacific* at the Majestic Theater, Judy mentioned it. "I think Ma was very upset when you told her we were going out together tonight. She was busy planning a big menu for a celebration when you got your results."

Joseph shrugged it off. "You know she likes to cook. Tomorrow she can make her big dinner, but right now you're the only person I want to share this moment with."

Judy forgot about Pearl's injured feelings. Reaching across the table to cover Joseph's hand with her own, she said, "You mean it?"

"Every word. You're the most important person in the world to me."

Judy squeezed his hand and mused, as she often did, on how twins could be so different. One she loved, the other she absolutely detested. She understood how much she owed to Pearl, and she adored Joseph; but all of that combined barely compensated for her loathing for Leo. True, the younger twin had changed since leaving school four years earlier and going to work for Lou Levitt. He'd quieted down, grown out of his furious tantrums. Nonetheless, Judy could still sense his animosity toward her, a hatred based on the ridiculous belief that she was a divisive factor between him and Joseph.

"Now you've finished with Columbia, when are you going to start working for Lou Levitt?" Judy asked; she never referred to Levitt as

Uncle Lou like the twins did.

"A few weeks, I guess."

"Don't you ever wish you could do something else?"

"Like what?" Joseph asked.

"Why don't we"—she leaned across the table, her voice low and urgent—"go away? Just the pair of us. Let's go somewhere else and start on our own."

"Where do you have in mind?" Joseph was humoring her.

"Why don't we go out west? California. You could do anything you wanted to out there."

"Do you really object that much to my working for Uncle Lou?"

Judy gave an exasperated sigh. "It isn't just him, Joseph. I want us to get away from your brother."

Joseph leaned back in the chair and chuckled. "Don't worry about Leo. We'll get away from him when we're married."

"I mean clear away, Joseph. Leo's got a hold over you, or he believes he does," she added quickly, when she saw a denial forming on Joseph's lips. "He thinks this whole twins business is really something special. It's the most important thing in the world to him."

"Just because of the way he behaved when we were kids?"

"Even now. Oh, I know he doesn't carry on like he used to, but it's still there. One day he'll call on you, on your loyalty, and you'll respond because you've been taught to do that. I remember those times your mother made you do things you didn't want to do just to pacify Leo."

"Your imagination's running amok." Joseph's rebuttal lacked any real conviction. He could recall those times as well: at school when he'd been told not to shine so brightly because of Leo's injured sensitivity; the birthday party to which he couldn't invite friends because Leo had no friends to invite.

"I'm telling the truth, Joseph. Just remember, I'm on the outside looking in. I'm the spectator. I see more of the game than the players do."

"Maybe you do. And maybe you're also watching with a biased eye."

Judy did not think so, nor did she feel that Joseph really believed what he said.

After dinner, they went to the Majestic. Joseph became completely absorbed in the performance, but Judy's mind wandered. While they'd been dining, Joseph had spoken for the first time of marriage, had mentioned it matter-of-factly as though it were the natural progression of their relationship and did not require any special announcement. Judy did not know whether to be elated or disappointed. Her feelings for Joseph stemmed from childhood. First, she'd had a crush on him, a silly schoolgirl infatuation. Deep friendship had superseded that. Finally love. It had always been obvious to Judy that she and Joseph were meant for each other. How many times had she dreamed of the way it would be? Initially, those visions had been as clean and innocent as freshly fallen snow. As the years had passed, however, the images had changed. Now her dreams held to a constant theme: lying with Joseph, arms gripping his lean, sinewy body as he drove into her.

Quite suddenly, in the middle of the first act, Judy burst into a fit of laughter. Too late she tried to bury her face in her hands. Hisses erupted from those around her. Joseph turned in his seat and whispered: "What the hell's the matter with you?"

"Let's leave."

"Are you crazy? I had to pay a scalper for these tickets," he retorted, but already Judy was out of her seat, pushing past people's knees, then walking quickly along the aisle toward the exit. Mystified, and more than a little angry, Joseph followed her into the theater lobby. "Would you mind telling me what you're playing at?"

"A real couple of romantics, aren't we? You say we'll get married in the kind of tone you'd use to give directions, and I respond by talking about Leo."

"I meant it. Maybe it didn't come out right, or it was out of context, but I meant it."

"How much did you mean it?"

He gripped her shoulders and began to draw her close, his lips aiming for hers. Only at the very last moment, when less than two inches separated their lips, did Joseph remember where he was—in the lobby of the Majestic Theater, in full view of people lining up at the advance-booking window. "Let's get the hell out of here."

"Where shall we go?" Judy asked as Joseph opened the theater door and pushed her onto the street.

"Home."

"Home? There's even less privacy there than in the theater lobby."

"We'll go home and we'll wait," Joseph said as they reached the car. He helped Judy into the front seat and started the engine. "Leo and Ma'll be home soon from their dinner. Ma goes to bed early and we'll wait Leo out."

They entered the apartment building hand in hand, and in the elevator, Joseph pressed Judy against the wall, kissed her on the forehead, the tip of her nose, her chin, and lastly her lips. "When do we tell Ma about us getting married?"

"Tomorrow," Judy answered. "Let's keep tonight for ourselves."

The elevator door opened and they got out. Waiting for Pearl and Leo to come home, waiting for both of them to go to bed, seemed unbearable.

Pearl and Leo arrived at the apartment twenty minutes later. "You're both home early," Pearl said. "Show no good?"

"I didn't feel very well," Judy answered quickly. "We left in the middle of the first act."

"The theater was stuffy," Joseph added. "It gave Judy a headache."

"Would you like something for it?" Pearl asked.

"I don't think so. Bed's probably the best cure." Judy kissed Pearl good night, nodded toward Leo, and gave Joseph the briefest kiss on the cheek. "I'll feel better in the morning."

Pearl went to bed soon after, leaving the twins alone in the living room. Joseph was undecided as to what to do. Should he pretend to go to bed and hope that Leo, bored by sitting up alone, would also retire? Or should he just sit there and wait Leo out? Joseph decided on the latter course. Picking up a newspaper, he began to read. Every so often as he moved the newspaper, he could see Leo sitting rigidly in the chair, staring at him. Finally, Joseph dropped the newspaper to the floor and asked: "Is there something wrong?"

"You're damned right there is," was the surly response. "Don't you have any respect at all for Ma?"

"What?" Joseph did not have the faintest idea of what Leo was talking about.

"You know how much she's been looking forward to you getting your results from Columbia. I don't give a damn about it— businessman with a briefcase, big deal!—but it means a lot to her. Couldn't you have given her the pleasure of staying in for dinner tonight? You know she wanted to do something special."

"Leo, I didn't want a big dinner with everyone sitting around the table telling me how damned smart I am just because I've done what millions of other people in this country have done. I wanted to be somewhere quiet—"

"Somewhere quiet all right! With *her!*" Leo pointed wildly toward Judy's bedroom. "Ma should mean more to you than she does. She means more to me! All you worry about is Judy. That's all you've got eyes for—a stupid girl! She'll never give you a tenth of the love that Ma's given you!"

Joseph sat speechless as Leo ranted on. He wasn't even certain what lay behind this outburst. He just wanted Leo to go to bed so he could keep his tryst with Judy.

He got up, walked past Leo, and went into his bedroom. Moments later, Leo's fist crashed against the door. Joseph swung back the door and glared at his brother, their faces only inches apart.

400

"You're going to wake up everybody. Show some of that consideration for Ma you're accusing me of not having!"

The possibility that he might disturb Pearl had a dramatic effect on Leo. Instantly, his mood was transformed. From being red-faced and furious, he became deliberately calm. "All I'm trying to tell you is that you should show more appreciation for Ma. She hasn't had it easy, with Pa dying like he did. It wouldn't do you any harm to care for her a bit more."

"I care for her as much as you do. You just exaggerate how you feel because of the way Ma's always spoiled you." Despite Leo's conciliatory pose, Joseph's own fury was heightening. His thoughts over dinner, when Judy had reminded him of the past, began to spill out. "You ever stop to think how I felt when we were kids—you always getting your way because you'd been ill that one time? Maybe five millions kids had diphtheria. But you . . . you had to make a whole production out of it!"

Leo became defensive. "I *was* ill."

"So were a lot of kids. I've forgotten how many times I had to go without something just because it might hurt your feelings. So don't hand me this crap now about not caring for Ma. I care for her like a son should. You . . . you care for her like you're her damned lover!" Without another word, he closed the door firmly in Leo's face.

Leo stood in the hall, undecided what to do. The apartment was silent; somehow his mother and Judy had slept through the argument. He needed air. He needed time to think. Letting himself out, he went downstairs and began to walk north along Central Park West.

Leo knew exactly what the problem was. Judy. If Judy were not in the apartment, if she did not live with them, Joseph would have no distractions. All his brother cared about was that red-haired bitch who'd put poison into his mind, turned him against his mother and his twin.

Judy Caplan! Leo hated her with a passion that bordered on violence. He had always hated her because Joseph had spent so much time with her instead of with him. Now she was finishing off what she'd started when they were children. She had come between Leo and his twin brother then, tried to destroy that very special bond. Now she'd taken Joseph away from his mother, made him ignore his responsibilities and duties.

Judy Caplan! That filthy redheaded bitch!

Leo clenched his fists as he turned around and began to walk back to the building.

Joseph heard the front door close and mistakenly thought it to be the door to Leo's bedroom. He waited ten minutes, ears straining for any sound in the apartment. He heard nothing. Opening his own door quietly, he stepped into the hall. The apartment was in darkness. Walking on tiptoe, he checked the doors to the bedrooms of his mother and brother. Both were closed, no light shone from beneath. He tapped softly on Judy's door. It swung open instantly, as though she had been waiting on the other side, tensed, ready for his arrival.

She pulled him into the room, locked the door, and turned on the bedside lamp. "What was all that commotion?"

"Leo." Joseph wanted to give her a more comprehensive answer but his mind refused to function properly. All he could concentrate on was Judy. He had seen her in a nightgown before, late at night or first thing in the morning, when she walked around the apartment, but she had always worn a robe over the gown then, had never stood in front of a lamp as she was doing now. Joseph's eyes were riveted to the contours of her body: the flare of her hips, the narrowness of her waist, the swell of her breasts, the firm roundness of her thighs.

Judy felt her body begin to burn under Joseph's stare. "What was the matter with him?"

"He was mad"—Joseph placed his hands on either side of Judy's waist—"because I took you out tonight instead of having dinner here with Ma. He said I didn't care about her."

Joseph moved his hands upward until they were cupping Judy's breasts through the filmy fabric of her gown. She took a backward step. The edge of the bed pressed into the backs of her knees, and she fell back, arms open wide to receive Joseph. "I used to watch you all the time in school," she whispered, "and each time you got an answer right I fell in love with you a little more."

"You're the only reason I got those answers right," Joseph replied.

Judy's nightgown rode up as Joseph slipped his hands beneath the fabric, reveled in the softness of her skin. Her fingers tugged at his shirt, pulled it free of his trousers. Her lips pressed against his. "That's for the time you came first in the second-grade spelling bee," she whispered. She kissed him again. "And that's a reward for coming first in the history test in the eighth grade."

"Keep going."

Another kiss. "That's for coming first in geography in the tenth grade. And that"—as he parted his lips, her tongue darted in between—"that's for coming first in algebra in the eleventh grade."

"What about when I came first in geometry?"

"Don't be so impatient," she chided him. "We've got English, French, and physics to go through first."

Reaching out her left hand, Judy flicked off the bedside lamp.

Joseph experienced an instant of frustration at her modesty, but it was soon forgotten as she slipped off the nightgown and pulled him close to her. He did not remember taking off his shirt or slipping out of his trousers. All he knew was the warmth emanating from Judy's body, engulfing him. Even the scene with Leo was finally banished from his mind.

Leo returned to the apartment exactly twenty minutes after leaving it. He was no longer furious. Now that he was determined to resolve the problem, he was icily calm.

With slow, deliberate steps, he walked along the darkened hall toward Judy's bedroom. She was the source of conflict. She caused arguments. Worst of all, she had made Joseph ignore his responsibilities toward his mother. She had to go. Before she could stir up more trouble, Leo was going to throw her out.

Outside Judy's door he paused for an instant, steeling himself for the confrontation. What he was about to do would cause another rift in the family. Joseph would support Judy. So, too, might Pearl. Arguments would rage over Leo's decision to evict Judy from the apartment in the middle of the night. But eventually, Leo knew, his twin brother and mother would see that he was right.

His hand moved toward the door, stopped. Were his senses playing tricks? Had he really heard a muted giggle? Heart quickening, he placed his ear against the door. He heard words, whispers that he could not make out. A woman's voice. And a man's. Leo backed away, walked swiftly to Joseph's room. It was empty, the bed not slept in. Blood roared through Leo's veins like surging lava, boiling in his head, driving any remaining rational thought before it. He ran back to Judy's room, tried the door handle, rattled it. The door was locked. He heard the whispers again. Urgent this time, no longer full of pleasure as they had been moments earlier. Leo's wrath reached a crescendo. He took one step back, lifted his foot and drove it against the lock. Wood screeched and splintered. The door flew back into the wall with a roar like thunder. Leo leaped into the room, hand reaching out to flick on the light switch.

"You filthy slut!" he roared as he stood at the foot of the bed. "You goddamned filthy bitch!"

Judy had the sheet pulled up to her throat. Blood fled from her face. Her eyes were wide with fear and shock. Beside the bed, Joseph was scrambling furiously into his trousers which lay on the floor with the remainder of his clothing.

Only when his trousers were pulled up and buttoned did Joseph

403

face his twin brother, who remained standing at the foot of the bed, hatred burning in his gray eyes as he glared down at the terror-stricken Judy.

"What the hell do you mean by bursting in here?" Joseph demanded. "What right do you have?" He lunged forward and threw a punch. The blow ricocheted off Leo's jaw. Pain ripped through his face and he stumbled back. When he saw the next punch coming, he ducked and wrapped his arms around Joseph's body, pinning his brother's arms to his sides. Joseph lashed out with his bare feet. It was all Leo could do, even with his superior strength, to keep Joseph from breaking free.

"Don't you understand what she's doing?" Leo yelled. "That filthy bitch is breaking us up! She's wrecking our family!"

"Let go of me!" Joseph roared. He knew that if he ever got free, he would kill his brother. None of the things that had gone before compared with this outrage.

Leo refused to let go. He did not want to hurt Joseph—he only wanted him to accept the truth. No matter how much Joseph struggled, how much he injured him, Leo would not fight back. Surely that in itself would be proof of his love for Joseph; proof that whatever he did was only for Joseph's welfare.

A figure appeared in the doorway, hair in disarray, a face that registered total disbelief. "What is going on in here?" Pearl demanded.

Leo dropped his arms to his side. Joseph sprang free, whirled around, and threw a ferocious punch at his brother's face. Pearl shrieked Joseph's name when she saw his fist smash into the bridge of Leo's nose. Blood spurted, and Leo fell back against the wall, making no attempt to defend himself as Joseph charged in. There was a look of stoic acceptance on his face, the expression of a martyr dying for his beliefs.

Pearl forced herself between the twins. She had no idea why they were fighting. She only wanted to stop them before someone was seriously hurt. Never in her life had she seen such fury as that imprinted on Joseph's face. "Judy!" Pearl screamed as she felt herself being crushed between her sons. "For God's sake, help me!"

Judy rose from the bed. With the sheet wrapped around her body like a toga, she grabbed hold of Joseph's shoulders and, aided by Pearl, pulled him off his twin. Leo leaned back against the wall, dabbing at his bloody nose with the sleeve of his jacket. Pearl's eyes traveled from one twin to the other. "Would you mind," she said to Joseph, "telling me why you're beating the living daylights out of your brother? And while you're at it, you can tell me what the pair of you are doing in Judy's bedroom in the first place. You especially, without your shirt and shoes on." She looked around the room. "Is that them on the floor over there?

"I could hear you both screaming from my room," Pearl said when Joseph failed to answer. "Now you can't find your tongue." She turned to Leo. "You tell me what happened."

"Her!" Leo jabbed out an arm with such abrupt ferocity that he almost took Pearl's head off. "He was in here with her! He was in *bed* with her!"

Pearl looked again at Joseph's bare chest, at the clothing on the floor. She breathed in deeply, tried to settle herself. Calmness was needed now. Children you shouted at; adults you reasoned with. "Leo, go clean up your face. Then you can join us in the living room where we can discuss this situation sensibly."

Joseph picked up his clothes from the floor and then followed Leo and Pearl out of the room. As he passed through the doorway, he glanced back. Judy gave him a beseeching look which he understood only too well. Would Leo, she wanted to know, get his own way again? Was Joseph going to allow his twin brother to wreck their precious relationship? Joseph shook his head. Not if he could help it.

Leo returned from the bathroom ten minutes later to find his brother, his mother, and Judy waiting for him in the living room. Blood still dripped from his nose—Leo believed it was broken; Joseph hoped so—and the skin around his eyes was turning puffy and discolored.

"Now will someone tell me what happened," Pearl said.

"She's wrecking this family," Leo answered.

"Wait a minute," Joseph broke in. "Judy's not wrecking any family."

"What would you call it then, the way she makes you forget all about Ma?"

"I don't forget."

"Stop it at once!" Pearl snapped. Their arguing grated on her like chalk screeching on a blackboard, grinding the raw ends of her nerves. "I don't know what's got into the pair of you, carrying on like this. You're twins, you're supposed to be close. You're not supposed to be at each other's throats." She stared at the bloody handkerchief held to Leo's nose, the puffy eyes. A wave of sympathy swept over her. She had seen Joseph swing his fists, and all Leo had done was accept the beating. He hadn't tried to fight back. There wasn't a mark on Joseph. "Is this what you do to your brother?" she asked Joseph.

"He asked for it."

"May I say something?" The question came from Judy who had

405

replaced the sheet with her nightgown and robe.

"What?" There was such coldness in Pearl's voice, such anger in her light brown eyes, that Judy shivered.

"Tonight Joseph and I decided to get married. That's why we came home so early. It wasn't because I had a headache."

"Did you come back early to tell us, or to celebrate your decision in your own fashion?"

"We were going to tell you in the morning."

"After you'd found out whether or not you made each other happy in bed? Judy"—the bitterness left Pearl's voice, to be replaced by anguish—"I'd thought more of you."

"Ma," Joseph protested, "you're acting like we're a couple of fifteen-year-old kids who've been led astray. Judy and I are both adults."

"So I see." Pearl switched her attention to Leo. "And where do you fit into all of this?"

"I already told you. I wanted Judy to leave here, to stop splitting us up as a family."

"So you just burst in there?"

"He kicked in the lock," Judy interjected.

Pearl gave the red-haired girl another icy stare. "I'm glad you had the consideration to lock the door at least."

"I wanted a place of my own two years ago," Joseph stated. "If I had it, this wouldn't have happened."

"I told you then that I didn't leave home until I was married, and neither would you. Perhaps I should also have mentioned that I didn't go to bed with your father until I was married."

"Yours was a different generation, Ma. Things have changed since then. We've had a war that's altered—"

Pearl cut him off. "Morals and decency don't change, Joseph."

Judy dropped her gaze to the carpet. Leo, with all his craziness, was winning. Again. Either she got Joseph out of there right now, or she would lose him to his twin forever.

"Weren't you ever in love?" Judy asked Pearl softly.

"Yes, I was. But I controlled my feelings, Judy, until the appropriate time. It wasn't easy, believe me."

Pearl stood up and walked to the telephone. She was out of her depth here. Everyone was in the wrong. Judy and Joseph for being in bed together under her roof. Leo for breaking in on them, and for saying such terrible things.

"Who are you calling?" Joseph asked as Pearl's fingers spun the dial.

"Your Uncle Lou. He should be here as well."

Levitt came up five minutes later. He listened attentively as Pearl described what had happened: being awakened by the fight between the twins, learning that Joseph had been in bed with Judy. When Leo interrupted to explain that he was trying to preserve the family, Levitt cut him short with a curt wave of the hand and the admonition to let his mother finish what she was saying.

"Let me see if I've got this straight," Levitt said at last. "You two want to get married. And you, Leo, you figure that Judy's wrecking this household." Levitt nodded soberly as if in full understanding. It was the German shepherd puppy all over again. Joseph wanted something. Leo didn't.

"You both think you're mature enough to get married?" Levitt asked. When Joseph and Judy nodded, the little man continued. "I've never been married"—he caught Pearl's gaze—"so maybe I'm not really the one to offer advice. But why not wait for a few months? Give Joseph a chance to get settled in his work. How does that sound?"

Joseph looked at Judy. Despite Leo's wild interruption, his need for her was still violently strong. If he could, he'd marry her tomorrow . . . why couldn't he? They were both over twenty-one. Why listen to Levitt?

Suddenly guilt hit Joseph, deflating both his desire and his will to rebel. His mother! How could he have even thought of doing such a thing while in her home? Damn Leo! Because it was Leo, not Pearl, who had instilled that guilt.

"Well?" Levitt asked.

Slowly, Joseph nodded. He held Judy's hand, waiting for her answer.

"I'll wait," she said, "but not here." Tears brimmed in her eyes as she turned to Pearl. "I'm sorry. The last thing I wanted to do was upset you, but after tonight I can't stay here any longer."

"How does that sound to you, Pearl?" Levitt asked.

Pearl dabbed at her eyes. Were not Joseph and Judy simply going to do what she had always believed they would—marry? And who was she to question their feelings? Their actions? Their morals? Was she so pure? Was her own history so clinically sterile that she could be one hundred percent certain that the father of her twin sons was dead? That he was not sitting in the room with her right now?

Her son, and Annie's daughter. "A wedding would be nice," she murmured.

Leo got up from his chair and went to his room. His eyes, as he passed Levitt, were a hard, steely gray. Leo had lost this battle, but

Levitt had little doubt that the time leading up to the wedding would be stormy.

Two days later, Judy moved to her own place on West Seventy-second Street, a furnished one-bedroom apartment that she leased until the following January when she and Joseph planned to be married.

Pearl helped her to pack. When she was ready to leave, Pearl stood by the door, waiting. "Judy, I want you to know that I'm sorry about the other night. I got mad, and maybe I should have been more understanding."

"I'm sorry, too. I love you every bit as much as I loved my own mother, and to upset you like that . . ." Judy's voice broke as tears choked her. She reached out to hug Pearl.

"Perhaps it's better this way, darling," Pearl told her. "You and Joseph, you won't see so much of each other. When you get married, you might be in for some nice surprises."

Judy broke the embrace, kissed Pearl, and picked up one of her suitcases. Joseph was standing outside, holding two more. "Don't forget to call me when you get settled in," Pearl said. "And remember, every Friday night you come over here for dinner—and any other night when you haven't got food in your place."

As Pearl closed the door, her thoughts turned to Leo. How would he take these next few months? He would only see Judy once or twice a week, when she came to the apartment for dinner. But he would be with Joseph every hour of the day, now that both twins worked for Lou Levitt. Would he try to make Joseph change his mind about marrying Judy? Would Joseph listen? Or would Leo's dislike of Judy drive a wedge between the twins? Would Leo, in trying to keep the twinship such a special thing, shatter it into pieces?

When Joseph went to work for Levitt, Leo was already an established fixture in the operation. He had taken over the downtown book route that Phil Gerson had shown him on that first trip. Each morning, Joseph saw his twin go out with the winners' money, which Leo carried in a cloth bag; each afternoon, he saw him return with fresh money that had been bet that day.

Unlike Leo, Joseph did not go out on collections and deliveries. Levitt put him to work where his four years at Columbia would do the most good. "The bookkeepers who settle the bets, from now on they're going to bring them to you. Do spot checks—every tenth bet, every seventh bet. Switch it around a bit, make sure everything adds up right."

Joseph began his checking work. At the end of each day, the slips from his adding machine were placed in brown paper bags with the slips from the dozen other machines in the huge room. Levitt took them downstairs to the furnace that supplied heat in the winter to both the bookmaking center and the Jalo garage; and he burned the lot, carefully raking the embers to be certain there was nothing left.

At the end of the first week, Levitt went from man to man in the room and handed out wage packets. When Joseph received his, he saw that the advice detailing tax deductions had him listed as working for Jalo Cabs. He asked Levitt about it. "What am I supposed to be, a taxi driver?"

Before answering, Levitt took him into the office. "You can't be; you don't have a taxi license. Some of the other guys out there do, though. Didn't Leo ever tell you he was working for Jalo?"

"Leo never mentioned what he did for you."

"Good boy. Knows when to keep his mouth shut."

"Is everyone out there working for Jalo?"

"Some of them. Others are on B.M. Transportation's books, Benny Minsky's trucking company. I'll show you." He went to a file drawer and pulled out ledgers. Joseph ran his eyes down them, saw his own name and those of half the people working outside listed under Jalo employees. He was described as deputy office manager.

"What about the money you take in here? That must show up somewhere."

"Sure it does, in a bank in Zurich, Switzerland. We have a courier going over there every few weeks. He takes it by the caseload. Then, when we need money for a legitimate enterprise over here, we borrow it from that bank in Zurich."

"You borrow your own money?"

"That's right, and pay the interest to ourselves."

"And on top of that, you get a tax deduction on the interest you pay."

"Did you learn about that at Columbia?"

"Who takes the money?"

"You'll find that out in good time. One day you'll get to do a courier job yourself. You'll be able to meet some people, see how the system works."

"What about Leo?"

"That isn't Leo's end of the deal. You're an office man, Joseph; he's a street man. But always remember this: one can't work without the other. You're going to need Leo just as much as he's going to need you."

By removing herself from the apartment on Central Park West,
Judy avoided direct confrontations with Leo. She was, however,
unable to avoid his indirect assaults. In the first few weeks at the new
apartment, her telephone rang at all hours of the night, until she had
the number changed and specified that the new number be unlisted.
Next, she was pestered by a whole succession of salesmen representing companies to which she had allegedly written. Twice,
firemen came to her door in response to a call. At another time, the
police turned up in response to a burglary report.

Judy met each disturbance with a coolness that belied all myths
about redheads. She understood the situation perfectly. Leo was
making a last-ditch effort to keep his twin brother for himself. The
nuisance tactics were designed to wear her down. She refused to bend.
She kept telling herself that she was marrying Joseph, not his twin
brother. Joseph, who was as bright and straight and loving as his twin
was mean and hateful. She did not even tell Joseph about Leo's
actions; she didn't want to upset him, to incite another fight. But she
promised herself revenge. One day she would find some way to harm
Leo, as he was attempting to hurt her.

Arrangements needed to be made. After much soul-searching, Pearl
told Joseph and Judy that she would like them to be married in the
same Lower East Side synagogue in which she and Jake, and Moses
Caplan and Annie had been wed in that unusual dual ceremony.

"That's where Leo and I were bar mitzvahed," Joseph pointed out,
certain that his mother had made a mistake. "That's where Pa was—"

"Do you think I could forget? That's the very reason I want you to
be married there. Happiness should wash away the pain of that place."

Joseph agreed.

Next Pearl had to decide who would stand under the wedding
canopy with the bride and groom. Lou Levitt was the obvious choice
to stand beside Pearl on Joseph's side, but who would represent Judy's
parents? She called Benny Minsky and asked if he would take the
place of Judy's father. Honored by the gesture, he accepted instantly.
Pearl then contacted a woman who lived in her apartment building.
Now that Pearl was planning a wedding, a spark of matchmaking had
been ignited in her. When Fanny Jacobs' husband had been killed in
an automobile accident five years earlier, Pearl had busied herself
helping the widow over the early days of bereavement. A plump,

homely woman in her early forties, Fanny had occasionally been a guest at Pearl's home when Minsky and his son were there. Nothing more than simple courtesies had passed between them, but with a marriage coming up, Pearl felt it was a more opportune time to play Cupid. Being together at a wedding—standing in for the bride's parents—might be the push that Minsky and Fanny Jacobs needed. Pearl was determined to give it a try.

For best man, Pearl saw no alternative. Leo. What groom with a twin brother could possibly have anyone else fill such a trusted position?

Joseph was aghast at the idea. "What kind of best man is he going to be after what he's done? He's treated Judy like dirt."

Pearl would accept no argument. "What's happened is history. Ask him. It's a wonderful opportunity to patch everything up."

"Why ask him? How about asking Judy?"

"The best man is the groom's responsibility, not the bride's."

"Is that so? Well, I don't want him."

"Who would you choose then?"

"I was thinking of Phil Gerson." Of all the men who worked for Levitt, Gerson was the only one with whom Joseph had formed a friendship. Gerson and his girlfriend, a vivacious blond dancer named Belinda Rivers, often double-dated with Joseph and Judy.

"This Phil's closer to you than your own twin brother?" Pearl asked.

"He likes Judy, Ma. He's not against me marrying her. Isn't that a good enough reason?"

"No reason's good enough for excluding Leo," Pearl answered stubbornly.

Joseph knew he couldn't win. When he saw Judy that evening, he steeled himself, then broached the subject.

"Offhand," she said coldly, "I can think of a thousand other people I'd rather have, but the best man's your responsibility. Do you want him?"

"Ma wants him."

"Does Leo want to do it?"

"I don't think anyone's asked him yet."

"Maybe we'll be lucky and he won't be interested."

Then Joseph spoke the words Judy had been expecting. "Let's give it a try for my mother's sake. This is her day as well as ours."

Judy yielded. There was no way she could fight Pearl and Joseph as well as Leo. Thank God it would be over soon. She swore that once they were married she would cut the cord that held Joseph to his twin.

411

Leo was instantly suspicious when Joseph asked him to be best man. "Is this Judy's idea as well?"

"Does it really matter?"

"Ma told you to ask me, didn't she?"

"Okay, if you want the truth—yes, it was Ma."

"I'll do it," Leo said. "I'll be your best man. But remember this— I'm not doing it for your sake or for Judy's sake. I'm doing it because Ma wants it."

The next task was finding the couple somewhere to live. Pearl went apartment hunting with Joseph and Judy. Two months before their wedding, she helped them to choose a two-bedroom apartment across the park on Fifth Avenue, where their neighbors would be bankers and lawyers, doctors and company presidents.

Six weeks before the wedding, only one arrangement remained unsettled. Joseph and Judy had still not made up their minds about where to spend their honeymoon. Judy wanted to go far away from the wintry cold of New York. Cuba or some other Caribbean island tempted her; in January, she thought it would be nice to laze on warm beaches and be pampered. Joseph wanted something more. He wanted to see different countries, places he had only read about. After four years at the university and six months of working, he was ready to break free.

Lou Levitt offered a solution. "My wedding present to the pair of you," he said grandly. "A two-week trip to Europe. How does that appeal to you?"

"It'll be just as cold over there as it'll be here in January," Judy complained.

"So you'll stay in a warm hotel. You can go skiing in Switzerland."

"Switzerland?" Joseph repeated.

"Kill two birds with one stone. Take your honeymoon and see how the courier business works. I want you to meet our bankers over there."

Judy felt trapped again. She'd had Leo foisted on her as best man, and now Levitt was taking charge of their honeymoon.

Once Levitt had walked away, Judy said, "We might just as well live in your mother's apartment once we're married. He's still pulling his strings and making everyone else jump."

Joseph defended Levitt. "Judy, don't you realize how important it is that I learn about these things?"

"Learn to be just as big a crook as he is?"

The word stung Joseph. He'd never considered Levitt a crook.

Businessman was the term he'd use. "Is gambling such a crime, letting people have the thrill, the pleasure, of placing a few bets?"

"Your Uncle Lou picks his enterprises too discriminately to be labeled a criminal . . . the gambling and before that the bootlegging. He's clever enough to break the law by giving people what they want, but income tax evasion is certainly a crime, Joseph. That's what you'll be aiding and abetting if you take that case full of money out of the country for him."

"I'm not doing it just for him. It's our money as well. Everything Uncle Lou has is ours. Don't you realize that?"

"Maybe I don't want any part of it. It got my mother and father killed, didn't it?"

"What about my father? And my grandmother?"

Judy sighed. Like it or not, she was tied to it, the same as Joseph was. They had both been born into Lou Levitt's racketeering empire, and Joseph could see nothing wrong with continuing the dynasty.

Chapter Three

On the wedding morning things moved along with the precision of a fine Swiss watch. Benny Minsky and Fanny Jacobs, Pearl's widowed friend, went to Judy's home to stand in for her parents. Meanwhile Lou Levitt joined Pearl in the Granitz apartment. The ceremony was scheduled for three o'clock, to be followed by a reception, dinner, and dancing at the Waldorf-Astoria.

At two o'clock, Levitt made the final checks. "Leo, have you got the ring?"

"Right here." The younger twin patted his trouser pocket where the gold wedding band was wrapped protectively in a clean handkerchief.

"Show me."

Leo produced the ring, and Levitt nodded approvingly. The gold band was important to Levitt. In his own pocket was another ring. When the ceremony was over, when the excitement had abated, he was again going to ask Pearl to marry him.

"Your mother and I'll leave first. You and your brother follow us down."

"We'll be right on your tail," Leo promised.

Levitt knocked on the door to Pearl's room. She called him in and asked for his opinion on how she looked. He ran his eyes over the full-length green dress she had ordered for the wedding. "Too damned young to have a son who's getting married, that's how you look."

"I can't believe it either, but these gray hairs give me away." So did the lines on her face, she thought, the tiny creases of skin around her chin and throat. Levitt was too much of a gentleman to mention any of that.

"You could get rid of that gray easily enough."

"And look like I did at school the day after Annie bleached my hair? I made a vow then that I'd never have my hair colored, and I'm sticking to it."

"You want to call Judy's place, make sure everything's ready

414

over there?"

"I was just thinking about that."

While Pearl dialed Judy's number, Levitt went to Joseph who was standing in front of the full-length mirror in the hall. "You got the tickets and passports?"

"I've got everything."

"A briefcase will be delivered to you. From then on, it'll be in your hands."

Joseph nodded. The clothes he and Judy would take on their honeymoon were already in a suite at the Waldorf Astoria. As Pearl and Jake had done twenty-three years earlier, the bride and groom were spending their wedding night at the Waldorf. "How much'll be in that briefcase?"

"Not too much. A hundred and fifty thousand."

"How about being met in Zurich?"

"Don't worry, huh? Someone'll contact you within a day or so after you arrive."

"I just don't like the idea of carrying that much money around."

"It's been done plenty of times before, so quit giving yourself ulcers, okay?"

Pearl joined them. "I just spoke to Fanny. They'll be ready to leave in fifteen minutes."

Levitt checked his watch. "We'll leave now. The twins'll follow."

Joseph hugged and kissed his mother. "Don't start crying, you'll ruin your make-up," he said, sensing the tears that lay just below the surface.

"You make sure Leo drives carefully," was all she said.

When the twins left the apartment fifteen minutes later, a cold rain was falling steadily. Leo drove carefully toward the Lower East Side. As he pulled up in front of the synagogue entrance, he said to Joseph, "You go on in. I'll park someplace else, leave this spot clear for Judy."

"She'll appreciate not having to trail her dress through puddles." Laughing, Joseph went inside to where his mother and Lou Levitt waited.

For several seconds, Leo sat in the car, staring out of the window at the synagogue entrance. From his trouser pocket, he withdrew the gold band that Joseph had given to him. A ring. What was it? Nothing more than a piece of gold, yet its significance was terrifying to Leo. Once he passed that piece of gold to his twin brother, once Joseph placed it on Judy's finger, it would be all over. Leo would have lost— lost the battle and lost his twin. Ever since he'd been asked to perform the duties of best man, Leo had been torn apart, his deep love for his mother clashing with his hatred of Judy, who wanted to take his twin from him. For his mother's sake, Leo had repressed his feelings. But now, as he gazed glumly at the ring, he knew he could not go through with it.

A wild idea excited him. No ring . . . no wedding. He had been unable to stop it any other way. So he'd try this.

He pulled away from the curb. Instead of finding another parking space, he kept on going.

Judy sat in the back of the limousine that was carrying her to the synagogue. Sharing the seat with her was Fanny Jacobs. In the front, next to the uniformed chauffeur, sat Benny Minsky.

"Something old, something new, something borrowed, something blue," Fanny said. "Have you got all that?"

Judy lifted her veil to answer. "Something old's a necklace my father gave to my mother when they were first married. This is new." She showed Fanny a narrow gold bracelet she'd bought two days earlier, especially for the wedding. "I borrowed this from Uncle Benny," she said, displaying a dime.

"And what did you get that's blue?" Minsky asked from the front.

"This." Judy lifted her dress. Above her right knee was a bright blue garter.

Minsky roared with laughter. "Don't go doing that during the ceremony. You'll give the rabbi apoplexy."

"Ah, weddings . . ." Fanny leaned back in the seat. "Do you remember your wedding, Benny?"

"I try not to," he answered.

"Benny, what was it like being married to a celebrity? Did you get any privacy, or were you always being hounded?" Fanny asked.

Minsky looked straight ahead to hide his grimace. He had been delighted when Pearl had asked him to stand in for Judy's father, but now he could see the concealed reason for her request. He did not dislike Fanny; he had no feelings for her at all. He just wished that she would concentrate on the business at hand and not keep throwing Kathleen in his face. She'd been doing it all day, talking about the movies in which she had seen Kathleen, the shows.

As if to echo his thoughts, Fanny said: "The only thing I regret is that I never saw your wife—"

"My *ex*-wife."

"I never saw her in the Broadway production of *Broadway Nell*. I understand that was her greatest role."

Before Minsky could think of a reply, Judy said, "Do you think it might stop raining before we get there?"

Minsky turned around again, grateful to the bride. "This is going to turn to snow before it quits. You're lucky. When the evening's over, all you and Joseph have to do is go upstairs. We have to drive home again."

"Maybe, when William gets married, he'll have the sense to choose a better time of year."

"You can bet I'll make sure he does." Minsky wished the journey was over already, before Fanny could dredge up more memories of the times she had seen Kathleen perform.

Inside the synagogue, the bridegroom's party was becoming nervous. Ten minutes had elapsed since Leo had let Joseph off outside, and he had not reappeared.

"How long can it take to park a car?" Levitt muttered. Joseph made a move toward the door. Levitt stopped him. "You stay here with your mother. I'll go look for him."

Large strides took Levitt to the synagogue entrance. He pushed open the door to see Judy being helped from the bridal limousine by Minsky who held an umbrella over her head. "Have you seen Leo out here?"

"Leo?" Minsky shook his head. "I thought he'd be inside already. Didn't he bring Joseph?"

"He's disappeared since then. Said he was going to park the car."

Judy emerged from the limousine to stand beneath the umbrella. "Did I hear you say that Leo's missing?"

"Maybe he had trouble finding a parking space." Levitt knew how ridiculous the remark sounded the moment he said it. There was enough room to park a convoy of trucks on the street. "I'll go look for him."

"Take the umbrella." Minsky helped Judy into the protection of the doorway before passing over the umbrella. Then Levitt began his search. After ten minutes he was back.

"Find him?" Minsky asked.

"No. Where's Judy?"

"In the bride's room. Does Pearl know?"

"She must have figured out something's not right by now." Leaving the dripping umbrella in a stand by the door, he returned to the sanctuary. Guests filled the pews. Pearl and Joseph stood by the canopy. The rabbi was there as well now, the same man who had officiated ten years earlier at the twins' bar mitzvahs.

"Anything?" Joseph asked.

"Not a sign. Was he all right on the way here?"

417

"Didn't say much, just drove."

"You got the key to the apartment? Give it to me." When Joseph handed over the key, Levitt looked over the wedding guests; as yet, they were unaware of the drama. He singled out Phil Gerson. "Leo's run out on us. Drive back to Central Park West and see if he's there."

"And if he is?"

"Bring him back here. Take Harry with you." Levitt beckoned to Harry Saltzman who sat in the row behind Gerson.

The two men left, and Levitt returned to Pearl's side. "You'd better go tell Judy what's going on. I'll handle the rabbi."

"There's another wedding in an hour. He already told me that. We don't have that much time."

"Just go to Judy. Take Belinda with you." Levitt went over to Gerson's girlfriend and explained the situation. "Just keep her calm. Okay?' he said.

Pearl and Belinda went to the bride's room. Judy sat in front of a mirror, touching the ends of her wiry red hair. "Still no Leo?" she asked.

"Phil and Harry Saltzman have gone to look for him," Belinda replied. "If they can't find him, no one can."

"We don't need a best man," Judy said.

"We do," Pearl answered, "when he's got the ring."

Judy clamped her teeth down on her bottom lip. She should have expected something like this. Joseph should not have given Leo the ring until the ceremony was about to start, until it was too late for him to back out.

Gerson and Saltzman arrived back at the synagogue fifty-five minutes later. By then, the second wedding was about to start. Trapped spectators, the guests for the Granitz wedding had been relegated to the rear seats. Joseph stood in the synagogue lobby with Levitt, Pearl, and Minsky. Judy was back in the bride's room after having temporarily vacated it so the second bride could prepare herself.

"He'd been there, but he'd left by the time we arrived," Gerson reported. "His suit was slung across the bed like old rags."

"Okay," Levitt said. "We don't know where he is, we don't know where the damned ring is. Now . . . do we have a wedding, or don't we have a wedding?"

"You bet we do," Joseph answered. "Get Judy out of that bride's room and let's get on with it."

"What about a ring?" Minsky asked.

"Take this." Pearl wrestled her own wedding ring from her finger and passed it to Joseph.

"Are you sure, Ma?"

"Do you want to get married or don't you?"

"That's a nice gesture," Levitt said. He looked at Pearl's third finger, so naked without the wedding ring. He decided it was a good omen. Tonight, after all this was over, he would give her another ring to replace the wedding band.

Joseph weighed his mother's wedding ring in the palm of his hand. "Can I trust you with this?" he asked Phil Gerson.

"Maybe you should have given the ring to me in the first place," Gerson joked. No one laughed.

"Pearl, go inside to Judy," Levitt said. "I'll call the Waldorf, tell them we're going to be late."

Pearl returned to the bride's room. "We're going ahead without Leo."

"We still need a ring."

"I gave Joseph mine."

"Yours?"

"I don't have any use for it this afternoon. You can make the switch when Leo turns up."

"*If* he turns up."

The other wedding ceremony ended, and the Granitzes' guests reclaimed the seats they had given up. Joseph stood with Pearl, Levitt, and Phil Gerson. As he heard the door open, he sneaked a look back up the aisle to see Judy coming in on Benny Minsky's arm. Finally, he thought, it is happening. And just wait until I see Leo again.

Leo knew that Levitt would send men to the apartment to look for him. He drove back there quickly and changed from his formal suit, taking time only to transfer his money, wallet, keys, and handkerchief before he left.

He drove around aimlessly, seeing little of the road in front of him. The wipers swished back and forth in their never-ceasing battle against the steady rain. All Leo could think of was the wedding. Were they going through with it? Without him? Had he managed to stall the ceremony? They had no ring. Could they have a wedding without it?

He pulled out the handkerchief he'd taken from the other suit. The ring fell into his lap. Steering with one hand, he lifted the gold ring up to his eyes. Inscribed inside were the names of Joseph and Judy, the date. Rolling down the window, he tossed the ring onto the wet street.

Surely his mother would understand. She must realize how badly he felt about the marriage. Why had they insisted that he be the best man? Why had they forced such a responsibility on him when they knew his heart would not be in it? It wasn't his fault. It was theirs.

Leo's disappearance soured the wedding. When Judy and Joseph left the synagogue after the ceremony for the ride to the Waldorf-Astoria, an hour and a half behind schedule, they were both furious.

"He never had any intention of being best man," Judy said. "You and your mother wanted him to be. He strung us along and then he did this. It was his parting shot, his grand finale."

"If I'd have even thought . . ." Joseph shook his head. "How could he do such a lousy thing?"

"What did your mother have to say?"

"She was too upset to talk. But Uncle Lou . . ." Joseph whistled. "I've never seen him so mad about anything."

Slowly, Judy regained her composure. She could barely recall the ceremony, the drinking of the wine, the breaking of the glass, Joseph's slipping Pearl's ring onto her finger. Her smile when she'd kissed Joseph had been frozen on her face. "Joseph, are we going to let Leo ruin the party as well? Or are we going to forget him and enjoy ourselves?"

"What if he comes back to the party?"

"He won't," Judy said with conviction. "He won't show his face at all now. We won't have to see him until we return from Europe." She could not hide the relief in her voice at such a prospect. . . .

For Pearl, nothing had gone right. Leo's disappearance, the rescheduling of the wedding, the lateness of the reception. Even her attempts at matchmaking had met with failure. Benny Minsky and Fanny Jacobs had carried out their duties of standing in for Judy's parents, but nothing had happened between them. Even after dinner, when the dancing began, they didn't take the floor together. Deciding to learn what the problem was, Pearl told Levitt to ask Fanny for a dance. When Minsky was left alone at the table, Pearl approached him.

"Are you just going to sit there, or are you going to dance?"

He got up from the chair and took Pearl onto the floor. "You were trying to fix me up, weren't you?"

"I struck out. What happened?"

"Your friend seems to think it's some big deal that I was married to a show business personality. That's all she's been talking about."

"I'm sorry, Benny, I didn't realize she'd be like that."

"I don't want a woman who keeps reminding me about Kathleen. I can do that all by myself. I don't need any help. I want someone who can make me forget her."

Pearl was intrigued. "Benny, this probably sounds crazy, but are you still in love with her?"

"I don't know. I used to tell myself that I wasn't, but every woman I meet I compare with her. I remember the wild times, Pearl, like the night I threw all her clothing and all her jewelry out of the window. And damn it . . . remembering those times makes me smile!"

Pearl finished the dance in silence.

At eleven o'clock, thirty minutes before the party was due to finish, Joseph and Judy made their farewells. Once upstairs in their suite, Joseph dropped down onto the bed and raised his hands triumphantly in the air. "Hallelujah! Alone at last!"

"Don't you even want to open the presents?" Joseph's jacket was full of envelopes. Their other gifts would be taken to the new apartment by Pearl and Levitt.

"To hell with the presents. All I want is you!" He lunged at Judy, grabbed her around the waist, and pulled her down on top of himself. She screamed that he was ruining her dress. He laughed and tugged even harder until he found the clasps.

"Let's not go to Switzerland," Judy said. "Let's spend our honeymoon right here in this suite."

"Oh? And what about the briefcase Uncle Lou's having delivered to us?"

"We'll get it sent here instead. We'll spend it. We'll use it to take over an entire floor, hire every maid, every waiter, every porter the Waldorf's got."

Joseph fell back onto the bed, laughing. "I can just see Uncle Lou going along with that. It's bad enough that he's got one godson who's crazy."

"Ah, so you do admit it?"

"Let's forget about him. He ruined the last time we were together."

"And maybe . . . just maybe," Judy said as she slowly unbuttoned Joseph's shirt, "he did us a big favor."

"How's that?"

"If he hadn't barged in, we'd have nothing to look forward to now, would we?"

Pearl arrived home just after midnight. She invited Levitt in for coffee, then busied herself in the kitchen, while he sat in the living room, gazing at the engagement ring he had bought for her. For weeks he'd anticipated this moment, but now he questioned whether it was so opportune. Pearl was both worried about and angry at Leo. Levitt did not want to complicate her feelings further. As he heard her footsteps coming from the kitchen, he replaced the ring in its velvet-covered box.

Pearl set down the coffee and then seated herself opposite Levitt. "Glad it's all over?" he asked.

"I keep telling myself that it wasn't a disaster, but I can't quite make myself believe it."

Levitt patted her hand. "What was the purpose of the day?"

"To see Judy and Joseph married."

"Did they get married?"

"Yes . . . but all the other things that happened."

"Will those other things show up in the wedding album?"

"No, of course they won't. But neither will Leo. Do you think we should call the police, Lou?"

"What for?"

"In case something's happened to him."

"Nothing's happened to him, Pearl. He's just accepting Joseph's wedding with bad grace. When he's ready, he'll surface as though nothing's happened. Don't you remember that time after Annie died, when you told him that Judy was going to live with you? He stormed away from the table. When he came back, he acted as though nothing was wrong."

"And you threw him out. I remember."

"This is the same, Pearl. You just wait and he'll show up." He smiled at her, grateful when she responded with a weak smile of her own. He felt in his pocket for the velvet-covered box. Perhaps tonight would be the right time after all.

The telephone rang. Pearl got up to answer it. She listened for a moment before calling to Levitt. "It's Leo. He wants to speak to you."

Levitt forgot about the ring in his pocket. He took the receiver and motioned for Pearl to move away. "Leo? Where the hell have you been? Your mother's been worried sick about you all day. You almost wrecked your brother's wedding. What in God's name has gotten into you?"

Leo answered none of the questions. He just said, "I'm in terrible trouble, Uncle Lou. Come quickly, please come quickly."

When Leo left the apartment on Central Park West after changing from the suit he was supposed to have worn at the wedding, he drove around aimlessly, across the George Washington Bridge into New Jersey, then north up to the Tappan Zee and down through Yonkers, the Bronx, and back into Manhattan. He felt deserted. Never in his life could he recall being so lonely and miserable. The only two people in the world he really cared about, his mother and his twin brother, had turned their backs on him. They had betrayed him.

He drove all the way downtown. At seven o'clock, he was in a restaurant on Sixth Avenue, just north of West Fourth Street in Greenwich Village. He sat there picking at the meal, barely able to taste it. While everyone else was at a dinner and ball at the Waldorf-Astoria, he was eating some tasteless mush in a sleazy Italian restaurant. Dejected, he left the meal uneaten and walked outside.

Rain was still falling as he strolled aimlessly along Sixth Avenue. A bar attracted his attention. Never a drinker, he hesitated in the doorway. Behind the long polished counter, a bald man with a flourishing handlebar mustache was pouring drinks. Should he go inside? Jilted men always went to bars, he told himself . . . even if they'd been jilted, not by a girl, but by their own family. He entered, perched himself on a stool.

"What'll you have?" the barman asked.

Leo searched the display of bottles. The J&B label caught his eye. He ordered the Scotch. The barman set the drink down in front of him and walked on to the next customer.

Two hours later he was still there, hunched over the counter, in front of him a heap of bills and coins from which the barman took the price of a drink each time he ordered. Leo poked the money with his index finger. Five dollars and change. How much had he put down originally? He thought it was a twenty, but he wasn't sure. All he knew was that he must have drunk a lot.

Someone took the adjacent seat. Leo turned around to see a young fair-haired man. "Mind me sitting next to you?"

"Sit wherever you like; it's a free country." Leo saw that his glass was empty, and called the barman for a refill.

"Let me get it for you," the newcomer offered. "You look as though you could do with a friend."

Leo stared at the man again. The only person who'd spoken to him like a human being all day long, and he was a complete stranger. "How do you know what I look like?"

"Any man who drinks alone is looking for a friend."

"Oh, yeah, and what about you?"

"Maybe I'm looking for a friend as well."

"You know something? I've got a twin brother, and today he went out and got himself married. Can you believe that?" Leo asked.

"How come you're not sharing his happy day with him?"

"Because I'm not happy." The barman put down fresh drinks. Leo emptied his glass in one quick swallow. "If you had a twin brother and he got married, would you be happy? Or would you feel that he'd betrayed you?"

"Tell me about your brother."

"Why should I tell you about him? I don't even know your damned name."

"Tony. Call me Tony."

Leo began to laugh. "That's good. You're Tony the tiger, and I'm Leo the lion. My twin brother's name is Joseph. What shall we call him?" Leo didn't wait for an answer. "How about we call him Joseph the jerk?"

"That what he is?"

"I think so, marrying some stupid girl."

"You got a girlfriend?"

"Me?" Leo sounded offended. "What the hell for?"

"Some guys do."

"Well, I don't. How about you? You let some stupid bitch make a fool out of you?"

Tony grinned. "Not yet."

Leo lifted his empty glass. He banged on the counter. "Hey, how about a bit of service over here?"

The barman came back, saw the empty glass and looked at Leo. "Don't you think you've had enough, pal?"

Leo leaned threateningly across the bar. "Who gave you permission to count? Who do you think you are—my mother?"

"I can't count what you drink. I've only got ten fingers."

"Funny man. How funny will you be if I rip off your mustache?" He started to reach toward the barman. A hand gripped his arm.

"I've got a bottle at my place," Tony said. "Why don't we go up there instead?"

Leo froze halfway across the bar. "Where's your place?"

"Bleecker Street, couple of blocks from here."

Leo slid off the stool and followed Tony outside.

The rain had turned to wet snow, which was covering the sidewalk with a thin, glistening blanket. Twice, Leo slipped and had to be steadied by Tony.

They came to a narrow two-story building on Bleecker Street. Leo followed Tony up a flight of stairs, to an apartment above a hardware shop.

Tony unlocked the apartment door. "Here we go, a place where you can have a drink without anyone bothering you. Make yourself at home."

Leo dropped heavily onto an overstuffed beige couch. While Tony fetched a bottle of Scotch from a cupboard, he took in his surroundings. Pictures covered the walls of the small living room; paintings, sketches, and photographs all mixed together as though a child had hung them. Facing Leo was an easy chair that matched the couch he sat on. In an alcove was a small table and two chairs. Hearing the sound of running water, he turned to see Tony rinsing two glasses at the sink in the narrow kitchen.

"Like the place?" Tony asked.

"Gives me claustrophobia."

"Where's your fancy mansion then?"

"Central Park West."

"Excuse me for breathing." Tony carried the glasses to where Leo sat. Then he pulled up a small table and poured the drinks.

When he sat down, his thigh rested gently against Leo's knee. "You still mad at your twin brother?"

"Joseph?" Leo glanced at his watch. Ten-thirty. Were Joseph and Judy still at the party, or had they left already, gone up to their suite in the Waldorf? Were they . . . were they in bed together already? "Joseph the jerk, he's in bed with Judy the jackass right about now."

"Good place to be on a cold winter's night. Beats the hell"—very tentatively, Tony rested a hand on Leo's thigh—"out of drinking your troubles away in some bar."

Leo's muscles stiffened in an automatic reflex. Tony felt the tension, lifted his hand a fraction. As Leo relaxed, he replaced it. "What do you do when you're not cursing your brother out?"

"Work?" Leo tried to concentrate. The drinks had muddled his brain, he couldn't think. "I'm a messenger."

"For a bank?"

"Yeah." Leo found that funny. "For a bank, you could say that. What about you?"

"I'm a photographer, can't you see?"

Leo gazed at the walls again. Something struck him for the first time. All the photographs were of nudes. Not women, like the ones he'd seen pasted up in the Jalo garage, but men. White men, black men, front views, back views. He switched his attention to the paintings and sketches. They had the same subjects. "You photograph anything else?"

"Of course I do, I have to eat. But I'm selective about the way I decorate my walls."

Leo walked over to study a black-and-white photograph of a boy who could have been no more than sixteen. The boy had one foot resting on a log, an arm raised aloft as though waving. Leo's finger traced the boy's dark curly hair, his sloping shoulders and narrow waist. "He's beautiful."

"So are you." Tony stood beside Leo, an arm looped casually over his shoulder. Leo tore himself from the photograph and swung around. His heart pounded like a steam hammer. Tony's face swam in and out of focus. Only his eyes remained constant, a soft, liquid brown that promised so much understanding.

Leo felt a cry begin deep within him, funnel up through his throat until it burst from his mouth in a heart-wrenching sob. Tears sprang from his eyes. He threw his arms around Tony, warmed by the return embrace, strengthened by the knowledge that he had finally found someone who understood, who cared.

"Your brother deserted you," Tony whispered, "but it doesn't matter anymore, does it? He's having his big party and we'll have ours." He kissed Leo with a tenderness that only his mother had ever shown to him. Leo responded passionately, crushing his mouth against the other man's, searching with his tongue. The whiskey he'd drunk, the empathy this man had shown, combined to rid Leo of any inhibitions, to make him fully comprehend the needs that had burned unanswered within him.

Leo felt Tony take his hand, lead him slowly across the living room to a door that opened into the bedroom. More pictures decorated the pastel-colored walls. The bed was covered with satiny lilac sheets, a puffed-up quilt. Tony sat on the edge of it, his legs apart. Leo stood between them, pelvis thrust forward. Fingers darted across his stomach, picked at his bottom, shirt buttons, his belt, the clasp that held his trousers. He closed his eyes in ecstasy. . . .

The sour taste of stale whiskey filled his mouth when he awoke. He forced his eyes open. A small lamp glowed weakly on the night table, barely bright enough for him to see the figure lying next to him beneath the lilac sheet. Slowly, it all came back—the bar, the man who had befriended him, those pictures on the wall. He moved in the bed to look at the gold watch still on his left wrist. Just after midnight, the party would be over now.

Beside him, Tony stirred. "I've got to go," Leo said. He swung his feet onto the carpet. Eyes now more accustomed to the dim light, he saw his clothes folded neatly over the back of a chair. He hadn't done that. Tony must have put his clothes away after he'd fallen asleep. The thoughtfulness touched Leo. He angled his head to look back. "Can I see you again?"

Tony yawned and stretched his arms above his head. "Take my number, call me whenever you like, Leo the lion."

While Tony watched from the bed, Leo dressed quickly. After he'd tied his shoes, he walked toward the bedroom door. Tony called after

426

him. "You're not going to run away without leaving me a little souvenir of your visit, are you?"

Leo stopped. "What do you mean?"

"Well, a small token of your affection would be nice." Tony climbed out of the bed and stood in front of him.

Leo's eyes traveled down his body—the narrow, almost hairless chest, the tapered waist . . . just like the dark-haired boy in the photograph. Just like a girl. "You want some money?"

Tony smiled coyly.

For fully five seconds, Leo stared at the naked man in front of him. It took that long for the truth to register. "You brought me back here, you made yourself out to be my friend, and all because you wanted money?"

"Don't sound so shocked. You look like you can afford it. Central Park West, your hand-tailored suit, your gold watch. What's a few bucks to you? And just look what you got in return." He rubbed his hand against Leo's cheek. "What you might get in the future."

Twice in the same day Leo knew betrayal. This time the pain was too unbearable for him to face alone. It had to be shared, delegated. His hands moved like lightning, smashing aside Tony's arm, closing around his slender throat. "You bastard! I thought you wanted to be my friend! You're nothing but a fucking whore!"

Tony batted ineffectually at the strong hands that gripped his throat and choked off his air supply, but Leo lifted him from the floor by the throat, smashed his head against the doorframe, all the time screaming that he was nothing but a whore. The room began to spin as Leo squeezed even tighter, until there was no more flesh left to give.

Leo felt the body go limp in his hands, saw the head and arms drop, the legs and feet hang listlessly. For another minute he exerted the tremendous pressure. Then, like a man disposing of a crushed insect, he opened his hands and let the body fall to the carpet.

Comprehension came slowly. He backed out of the room, picked up his coat from where it lay in the living room, and let himself out of the apartment. In the street, the snow had thickened. Flakes swirled, limiting visibility. The cold cleared Leo's head of the whiskey's final traces. At last he fully understood what he had done. In the apartment above the hardware shop, he had left the corpse of a man who had first befriended him and then had betrayed him. He needed help. He couldn't just find his car and drive home. He couldn't leave the corpse there. Surely he must have touched things in the apartment, left fingerprints, some incriminating evidence that would tie him to the crime.

He found a pay phone. Fingers trembling with cold and anxiety, he slipped in a coin and dialed Lou Levitt's number. Uncle Lou would help. Uncle Lou would not let Leo face this situation alone. The telephone rang unanswered for two minutes. Each time a car passed, Leo glanced up nervously, expecting it to be the police. Where was Levitt? Why wasn't he answering? Surely the party must be over. Was Levitt with his mother? Had he gone back to the Granitz apartment from the Waldorf? Leo tried there. The telephone rang; then he heard his mother's voice.

"It's Leo. Is Uncle Lou there?"

"Where are you, Leo?"

"Never mind that, Ma. Please put Uncle Lou on. It's urgent."

Levitt came on the line. "Leo? Where the hell have you been? Your mother's been worried sick about you all day. You almost wrecked your brother's wedding. What in God's name has gotten into you?"

"I'm in terrible trouble, Uncle Lou. Come quickly, please come quickly." And then he poured out the story.

Levitt's anger fled. "Where are you now?"

"At a pay phone on the corner of Sixth Avenue and Bleecker."

"Where's your car?"

"I left it on Sixth Avenue, near the West Fourth Street subway entrance."

"Go back to it. Stay inside. I'll be there soon." He hung up and turned to Pearl. "He's been arrested."

Pearl's face turned white. "Oh, my God. What for?"

"Drunken driving. I'll go down there and square it. Get my coat, would you? It's in the closet." Pearl walked away and Levitt lifted the receiver again. He dialed the number of the house in Fort Lee, New Jersey, the place where they had all hidden out during the Fromberg crisis. Harry Saltzman lived in that house now. Levitt hoped that he'd gone straight home from the wedding party. He needed him. In a situation like this, no one measured up to Saltzman. He breathed a sigh of relief when the telephone was answered.

"Harry, it's Lou. Don't ask any questions, just meet me downtown at Sixth Avenue near the West Fourth Street subway stop as soon as you can. I'll be with Leo." Levitt hung up as Pearl returned with his coat. "I'll be back soon," he promised her. "Don't worry about Leo. He'll be okay, you hear me?"

He drove downtown as fast as he dared. Twenty minutes later, he pulled in behind Leo's car, got out, and joined him. Leo's hands were fixed rigidly on the steering wheel. When Levitt climbed into the car, he asked, "What are we going to do?"

"Wait for Harry Saltzman. While we're doing that, suppose you tell me exactly what happened? For starters, why did you run out on Joseph?"

Shocked because the question did not concern the apartment on Bleecker Street, Leo blurted out the truth. "I was trying to stop it. I figured without the ring, they wouldn't be able to go through with it."

"You're stupid, you know that? Rings are a dime a dozen." Levitt touched the ring in his own pocket. He thought of the use he should have found for it, the use he *would* have found for it tonight, had it not been for the actions of the young man sitting next to him. "They used your mother's wedding ring, that's how much you stopped it. Where is the ring anyway?"

"I threw it away."

Levitt made no comment. "So what did you do then?"

"Drove around for a few hours." Slowly, Leo related what had happened, right up until he'd left the bar with Tony.

"This guy got a last name, this Tony?"

"I never asked him."

"Who saw you with him in the bar? Who took any notice of you?" Leo thought hard. "Just the bartender."

"Okay. We can take care of him later. Now, this Tony, you never knew he was after money until you got ready to leave his place?"

"I thought . . . I thought he was like me."

"Like you?"

"All alone. I didn't realize—"

"Never mind that now." Levitt turned in the seat. "Leo, was this your first time like this? With a man?"

"It was my first time with anyone."

Levitt leaned back and closed his eyes. Twins, identical or fraternal, there was something strange about them. They'd both got laid for the first time on the same night; only one did it with his bride, and the other got it off with a fag! Levitt felt sick. Did this one time mean that Leo was queer? Or had it just been a one-off thing? Levitt knew he had to keep the truth from Pearl. Not only the murder, but Leo's liaison with this Tony character as well. It would break her heart if she knew.

"Leo." Levitt spoke with his eyes still closed. "Don't give me the details about what went on with you and this guy. I'm not interested. I just want to know one thing. Right now, are you ashamed of yourself?"

"No. I wanted to see him again until he asked me for money."

"Shut the hell up," Levitt said.

Harry Saltzman arrived a few minutes later. Levitt saw him coming and climbed out of the car. With Leo, they walked along

Bleecker Street to the hardware shop, up the stairs to Tony's apartment. At the door, Leo hesitated. He did not want to go back inside.

"Whatever's in there isn't going to bite you," Saltzman said. He pushed open the door, walked inside, and inspected the apartment. Tony lay naked on the bedroom floor.

"We need to make it look like an accident," Levitt told Saltzman.

"Got you." Saltzman knelt beside the body. "Be hard to make that look accidental." He pointed to Tony's throat. Livid bruises showed where Leo had squeezed out the dead man's life. "Still, whole piles of evidence have been known to disappear in a good fire." He looked up at Leo. "What did you touch?"

"The glasses inside . . . one of the photographs . . . lots of things."

Saltzman picked up Tony's shirt, ripped it twice, and then handed both Leo and Levitt a piece of it. "Split up and do the living room and kitchen between you. Wipe everything. I'll do it in here."

Wearing gloves, the three men set about their task. Every surface in the apartment was wiped meticulously. When they were finished, Saltzman carried Tony's naked body to the bed. Leo turned away, unable to watch as Saltzman clothed the man in a pair of pajamas he'd found beneath one of the pillows. Next, Saltzman searched through kitchen drawers until he found a candle. Setting it in a saucer, he lit the candle and left it flickering in the bedroom. As the three men prepared to leave, Saltzman went around checking that all the windows were tightly closed. His last act in the apartment was to turn on the gas taps of the stove. Then he closed the front door.

The three men returned to Leo's car. "Describe the barman," Levitt ordered.

"Bald guy, big handlebar mustache."

"Harry, go check if he's still on duty."

Saltzman got out of the car, opened the door of the bar just enough to peer inside, and came back. "He's there."

"Okay, we'll wait."

Twenty minutes passed. From the north side came the noise of alarm bells. Two fire trucks and a police car roared down Sixth Avenue and swung into Bleecker Street. Saltzman's gas bomb had exploded, tearing the apartment above the hardware shop to pieces. Strangulation marks would be the last thing the police would look for once the fire was extinguished.

At one forty-five, the bald man with the flourishing mustache emerged from the bar. As he walked toward the subway station, Saltzman slipped out of the car to follow. Both men disappeared down the stairs. Five minutes later, Saltzman returned. He nodded to the two men sitting in Leo's car before climbing into his own vehicle and driving away.

"Now we'll go home and you can face your mother," Levitt said.

"What did you tell her when I called?"

"That you got arrested for drunken driving. I came downtown to square it. That's the story you'll give as well."

"What about the reason I ran away? What do I say?"

Levitt thought quickly. "Say you lost the damned ring. You couldn't face them without it."

"Will she believe it?" That was important to Leo.

"Can you think of a better reason why you took a powder?" Levitt opened the passenger door. Halfway out, he stopped and turned around. "Leo, don't you ever let your mother find out about tonight. If she knew you'd been with a man, it would break her heart."

They drove back separately. Pearl was dozing in an armchair, but she woke up when Levitt entered the apartment. Leo followed a minute later. "Treat him gently, Pearl. He's suffering his first real hangover."

Pearl was still wearing the full-length green dress she'd had made for the wedding. It was creased now, no longer pristine as it had been when she'd left the apartment that afternoon. She walked a few steps until she stood in front of Leo. Then, without warning, she drew back her hand and slapped him hard across the face. "You pig! How could you run out on your brother like that?" She brought her hand back across his other cheek.

Watching, Levitt made no attempt to step between mother and son. If Pearl wanted to slap Leo silly, he wouldn't stop her. A lot of this might have been averted had she done it earlier, not waited until he was twenty-two.

Leo stood motionless as Pearl brought up her hand again. This time she touched the red mark on his left cheek where she had first hit him.

"I lost the ring, Ma. There was a hole in the trouser pocket. It must have fallen through. I couldn't come in and tell everyone I'd lost the ring. They'd have thought I was a fool."

Pearl touched his other cheek, and she wondered how she could have hit him. She should have known that he would not run away without reason. "Did the police treat you all right?"

"Uncle Lou fixed everything. There'll be no trouble."

Levitt spoke up. "Leo, why don't you clean yourself up and go to bed? You've got to work tomorrow. If you don't show up on time, I'll dock your pay."

Leo nodded meekly. He kissed his mother good night and walked toward the bathroom. Pearl watched him go before turning to Levitt.

431

"Lou, thank you for everything. For what you did for Joseph and Judy today, and for Leo tonight. I don't know what I would have done without you."

Levitt let his hand explore his pocket, caress the velvet-covered box with the ring inside. It occurred to him that he could still ask Pearl to marry him. He dismissed the idea. After doing such work with Leo and Harry Saltzman, he had no heart to talk of marriage. "Are you going to be all right?"

"I will be, now that I know Leo's safe."

"Go to bed. I'll speak to you tomorrow." He kissed her on the cheek and went down one floor to his own apartment. Taking the velvet box from his pocket, he opened it and looked at the ring. Twelve hours ago he had envisioned it on Pearl's finger. Instead, he had helped her younger son to cover up one murder and he had sanctioned another.

He closed the box and slipped it into a drawer. This wasn't the way Levitt had planned for the day to end. For once, his scheming had been way off the mark. Perhaps—the possibility dejected him—it was fated that he should never marry Pearl, never see his love for her fulfilled.

Joseph called his mother from the airport on the following day before he and Judy caught their flight to Europe. "Any word from Leo?"

"He came home early this morning. He was arrested by the police for drunken driving. Uncle Lou had to fix it."

"Why did he run away?"

"Joseph, he lost the ring. He was too embarrassed to come in."

Joseph did not know whether to believe the ring story or not. "I didn't want him as best man to begin with, Ma."

"I know. Perhaps it was my fault for insisting on it."

"No, it was mine. I let you persuade me to ask him." Before Pearl could protest, Joseph said that he had to check in. Promising to write, he broke the connection and rejoined Judy who was sitting in the waiting area. "Leo got arrested last night for drunken driving. Lost the ring, then went on a bender."

"Too bad he didn't drive into a brick wall," Judy answered, and Joseph did not feel inclined to argue the point. He picked up a newspaper and leafed through it, barely registering two items which were set side by side. One concerned an explosion caused by a gas leak on Bleecker Street. Fire had gutted an apartment and the hardware store below it; a burned corpse had been pulled from the ashes, that of a man identified as twenty-eight-year-old Tony Cervante. The other was about a knifing in the West Fourth Street subway station. The victim was a John Blackman, who had been on his way home to Elmhurst after finishing his shift as a bartender.

Their flight was called. As they filed onto the aircraft, Judy said: "What about that briefcase you're supposed to get from Lou Levitt?"

"Jesus Christ!" Joseph looked around, but now there was no way to telephone Levitt to find out what had happened.

Judy took her seat, as certain as Joseph that something had gone wrong. For once, there had been a foul-up in Levitt's scheming, and she was not unhappy. It showed that the little man was human after all, prone to mistakes like anyone else.

Strapped in, they felt the aircraft lumber to its take-off point, pick up speed, and climb into the sky. When their seat belts were undone, Judy said with a certain satisfaction: "Now we'll be able to enjoy our honeymoon without any responsibilities, won't we?"

Joseph was annoyed. Despite Judy's misgivings, he'd wanted to take the briefcase full of money, meet the contacts in Switzerland. He felt that he'd been cheated.

"Mr. Granitz?" The purser stood by Joseph's seat. "I think you left this in the lounge."

Joseph looked at the well-worn briefcase the man held, the baggage label with his name. "Thank you."

"You're welcome, sir." Leaving the briefcase with Joseph, the purser walked away.

"Open it," Judy said.

Placing the case between his feet, Joseph undid the clasp. It was filled with fifties and hundreds, neatly stacked and banded in shallow piles. At the top was a scrap of white paper. Written in Levitt's tiny hand was the figure, one hundred and fifty-thousand.

Joseph refused to let the case out of his sight. He and Judy passed through Swiss customs without incident. When they entered a taxi for the journey to the Hotel Savoy Baur en Ville on the Bahnhofstrasse, he pulled the case roughly away from the driver who wanted to put it in the trunk with the rest of the baggage. He did the same thing at the hotel when the porter carried their cases to their room.

"What if no one contacts us while we're here?" Judy asked. "We're only supposed to be in Zurich for a couple of days."

"I know." Joseph had the itinerary imprinted on his memory. Monte Carlo was the next stop, then Rome, Paris, and finally London. "Uncle Lou said the case would be delivered, and it was. He said we'd be met, and that's good enough for me."

When they went out to eat, he carried the case firmly in his right hand, and when they went to bed that night, Joseph wedged a chair beneath the door handle to prevent anyone from breaking in. Between bursts of laughter, Judy told him he was becoming paranoid.

"Are you coming to bed with me," she asked, "or are you going to sit up on guard duty all night long?"

"Are you worth a hundred and fifty thousand dollars?"

"I know damned well I am."

Shoving the briefcase under the bed, Joseph slid beneath the huge duvet with her.

When they went down for breakfast the following morning, they were met at the restaurant entrance by the maître d'hôtel. "Herr Granitz, I regret that we are unable to give you and your wife a table to yourselves this morning. There has been much confusion in the bookings. Could I prevail upon you to share a table with another charming American couple?"

"This is turning out to be some honeymoon," Judy murmured. "You're handcuffed to that damned case, and now we've got to share a table. They'll probably be big fat Midwesterners with rainbow clothes."

They followed the maître d'hôtel. Halfway across the restaurant, Joseph stopped in shock. Seated at a table for four by the window were Phil Gerson and Belinda Rivers. Gerson rose as Joseph and Judy approached. "I bet you're going to be glad to get rid of that case, aren't you?"

"You're our contact?"

"I'm the regular courier. Sit down, have some breakfast. There's no point in making your first deposit on an empty stomach."

"What are you doing here?" Judy asked Belinda.

"I'm between shows. Phil thought it would be fun for us both to come, maybe even make up a foursome if you don't mind sharing your honeymoon with a couple of strangers."

"You're hardly strangers. Have you got a deposit to make as well?" Joseph asked Gerson.

"Twice as big as yours."

"Where is it?"

"In my room, of course. I'm not as insecure as you are, carrying it with you wherever you go. Did he take it to bed with him last night, Judy?"

"He tried to. I told him that three was a crowd."

"So I got out and the case stayed," Joseph added, provoking laughter.

Belinda turned to Judy. "Why don't you and I go shopping while they do their banking business? You can buy some marvelous things here."

Judy looked at Joseph. He nodded, grateful for Belinda's unexpected presence in Zurich.

Directly after breakfast, Judy and Belinda went shopping along the Bahnhofstrasse. Joseph and Gerson, each carrying a case, walked in the other direction until they reached a building with an imposing black marble entrance. Written in raised gold letters was a single name: Leinberg.

"This is it?" Joseph asked, glad to be at journey's end with the briefcase. He took a step toward the entrance. Gerson pulled him back.

"Not so fast. We use Leinberg's back entrance." He guided Joseph past the building to a narrow street. Halfway along it was a heavy wooden door, very mundane in comparison with the main entrance. Gerson rang a bell. The door opened and the two men stepped inside. Joseph found himself in a narrow corridor. Utterly lost, he followed Gerson to an elevator which took them to the third floor. They emerged into an office area. A woman sitting behind a desk smiled at them.

"Herr Leinberg is expecting you, Herr Gerson."

"Thank you."

The woman knocked once on a heavy oak door, swung it back to reveal what looked to Joseph like a company boardroom. A wide oak table ran down the length of the room. Six chairs were placed on either side of it. Only the chair at the very end was occupied, by a tall, gray-haired man with thick horn-rimmed glasses. He wore a morning coat and gray striped trousers, and he rose as Joseph and Gerson entered.

"Joseph, meet Walter Leinberg, the president of Leinberg Bank."

"How do you do, sir?"

Leinberg accepted Joseph's handshake. "Is this a social call, or do you have a deposit for Blackhawk?"

"Blackhawk?" Joseph looked to Gerson for an explanation.

"That's the code name for the account your godfather and Benny Minsky share. The Swiss are the most discreet people in the world where money's concerned. Even so, it's asking for trouble to put the account in your real name." He hoisted a small suitcase onto the polished oak table. "Here's three hundred and fifty thousand dollars, and there's another hundred and fifty thousand in my friend's briefcase."

Leinberg pressed a buzzer. Within a minute, two men entered the boardroom. They were dressed exactly like Leinberg, in black jackets, stiff collars, and striped trousers. Without a word, they sat down at the table, divided the money between them, and began to count with a speed that made even Lou Levitt's bookkeepers seem arthritic. The total of both cases came to exactly half a million dollars.

"Correct as usual," Leinberg said, with a thin smile.

"My employer doesn't make mistakes," Gerson answered. "Not when it comes to money anyway. Let's go," he said to Joseph. "Our business here is finished."

Before Joseph knew what was happening, he was back in the elevator. "Don't you get a receipt?"

"We don't need one. Lou Levitt and Walter Leinberg know exactly what's been deposited."

"How do you keep track of interest payments and everything else?"

"A statement for the Blackhawk account is prepared every month. Sometimes I bring it back with me, at other times it's mailed in a plain envelope to a post-office box your godfather keeps under a false name. The statement's just a list of figures, no identifying words on it. But Lou Levitt knows exactly what it means." They reached the narrow street that ran along the side of the bank. "Let's go have a cup of coffee while the girls do their shopping," Gerson suggested. "Then I'll put you right in the picture like I was asked to by your godfather."

Over coffee, Gerson related the history of Lou Levitt's ties with Walter Leinberg. They stemmed from Gerson's own family's investment business. Gerson's father had dealt with Leinberg Bank, salting money away in Switzerland against the eventuality of his own business going bankrupt. When it had done so in 1935, there was more than enough set aside to keep the family living comfortably. "When I graduated and went to work for Lou Levitt, I saw this fortune in gambling profits. Your godfather couldn't afford to show it, not unless he wanted the revenue people and the police after him. He had to get rid of it. Walter Leinberg's late father was president of the bank then; he was the founder. My own father went to see him, set up the courier deal. When my father died, I took it over. Except for the war, of course, it's been a regular trip."

"Don't all those stamps on your passport raise any suspicion?"

"Frequent transatlantic crossings? No. When we leave here, I'll show you why not."

From the restaurant they took a taxi to the outskirts of Zurich. Their journey ended in front of a drab two-story factory. "This is A. G. Kriesel," Gerson explained, "an engineering company owned by Lou Levitt and Benny Minsky. It's never made a nickel. That's why I, as vice-president, keep coming over here, to shake it up. Want to go inside and look around?"

"Not particularly." Joseph had no interest in engineering companies. He was more concerned with the business the company fronted for. "How much is in the account now?"

Gerson smiled in anticipation of his reaction. "Around thirty million dollars."

Joseph whistled in surprise. "You trust Leinberg with that kind of money?"

"As much as I trust anyone. Leinberg's a shrewd bastard. Before the war he took money from Jews who could get it out of Germany. And during the war, he did the same for the Nazi bigwigs who could foresee what the end would be. Leinberg probably pays half the bills in Buenos Aires."

"Can anyone put money into Blackhawk?"

"Absolutely anyone. But only two signatures can get it out. One's your godfather's. The other belongs to Benny Minsky. I imagine that one day in the not too distant future your signature, your brother's, and William Minsky's will perform the same miracle."

Thirty million dollars. The sum was staggering. "Has any money been taken out?"

"Little sums so far, for small investments in the States. But your godfather's got his eye on a big scheme soon, down in Florida. He wants to build a couple of hotels down there, real fancy places, and run casinos from them."

"Why not Las Vegas where it's legal?"

"Too much competition there already. Don't you know Lou Levitt well enough by now? He likes that little extra edge. Besides, if you were a high roller, where would you rather play? In the middle of the desert, or in some subtropical paradise?"

Joseph considered the information. Was that where he was to go? Was he to take Judy with him to Florida to oversee the building of the hotels, spread money around to police and politicians so the gambling could continue unhindered, creating even more money to be smuggled out of the country to Switzerland, where it would rest in Walter Leinberg's vaults, side by side with the illegal funds of the fugitive Nazis?

Phil Gerson and Belinda Rivers accompanied Joseph and Judy from Zurich to Monte Carlo, and stayed in adjoining rooms at the Hotel de Paris. When they entered the casino on their first evening there, Gerson tugged at Joseph's arm. "Before you go in, get a feel of this place. This is what Lou Levitt's thinking about down in Florida. None of the meat-market approach they use in Vega. He wants a real classy place with dress rules—"

"I can't see everyone wearing a tuxedo in Florida."

"Not necessarily a tux. But proper dress, not strident plaid sportcoats and clashing trousers like the suckers wear in Vegas. He wants a place that reeks of class."

Gerson and Belinda Rivers stopped by a roulette table to play, and Joseph and Judy watched for a while before moving away. Neither had the desire to gamble.

"Did you know Phil's married?" Judy asked out of the blue.

"Who told you that?"

"Belinda, while we were out shopping. I asked her how long she and Phil had been seeing each other. When she said three years, I asked why they didn't marry."

"Nosy, aren't you? You're lucky she didn't tell you to mind your own business."

"I think she was looking for someone to talk to. Phil's got two daughters. They live with his wife in Riverdale. Estranged wife, I should say. He gets to see them once or twice a week."

"Why don't they get a divorce?"

"She won't give him one. He's left her, he's playing around with Belinda, so he has no grounds on which to sue for a divorce. Plus, his wife's told him if he ever pushes for a divorce, she'll make damned sure he never sees the girls again."

Joseph slipped an arm around Judy's waist. "And there was I, getting jealous of him because I thought he was a happy-go-lucky bachelor. Proves how wrong you can be, doesn't it?"

"Sure does. Let's go back and see how they're doing."

They returned to the roulette table. Gerson had a huge pile of plaques in front of him. When he saw Judy and Joseph, he gave them a beseeching look. "I'm the equivalent of five thousand dollars ahead. Belinda wants to risk the whole lot on one number. Tell her she's nuts from me, will you?"

"Isn't there a house limit?" Joseph asked.

"They'll lift it for one bet. They only use it to stop people doubling up until they win."

"It's seven," Belinda said. "My birthday. Seven, seven . . . the seventh of July. I just know it's going to come up."

Gerson let out a resigned sigh. "All right, but God help you if you're wrong." He shoved a pile of plaques into the center of the table. *"Sept, s'il vous plaît."*

The wheel spun. The ball dropped and rattled around the numbered slots. At last it lay still. *"Vingt-trois rouge,"* intoned the croupier. Gerson's pile of plaques was raked in with the other losing bets.

"Sorry, baby," Belinda whispered.

Gerson tried to look angry. But the scowl changed to a big, happy grin. "Ah, what the hell! Easy come, easy go, eh?" Turning from the table, he hugged her. "How about we find somewhere to dance?"

"Around her little finger," Judy whispered as she followed with Joseph. "Manipulates him any way she wants to."

"Are you jealous? Is that how you want me to be?"

"I'd shoot you if you lost money like that—even if it wasn't yours to begin with."

Joseph laughed. "You wouldn't have to. I'd blow my own brains out first."

Instead of writing to Pearl, Joseph telephoned her from their room that evening. He told her that Gerson and his girlfriend were with them, talked about the weather, the food. Pearl listened before starting to talk about Leo.

"He's really upset over what happened with the wedding, Joseph. He's been very quiet, very subdued. I can hardly get a word out of him."

Joseph was in a generous mood. He and Judy were enjoying themselves too much for him to feel angry. "Tell him we forgive him, Ma. He made a mistake. If he's genuinely sorry, that's okay."

"You mean that? I think it's important to him."

"We mean it, Ma." When he finished the call, he turned to Judy. "I told Ma that we both forgive Leo."

"Only on one condition." Sitting on the bed, Judy patted the space next to her. When Joseph sat down, she held him tightly.

"What"—he kissed her—"is the condition?"

"That if we"—the words were cut off as Joseph kissed her a second time—"ever decide to get married again"—another kiss—"Leo won't be asked to be best man."

Chapter Four

Lou Levitt's plan to organize gambling on a luxury scale in South Florida received a setback before it even got off the ground. While the money to be used to finance the venture continued to gather interest in Zurich, a senator named Estes Kefauver rose to national prominence. Levitt forced himself to wait patiently while Kefauver's organized-crime circus paraded around the country. He knew that the public would eventually tire of the constant hearings and exposures. When they did, he would be ready to move.

It wasn't until January 1953, after the election of Eisenhower, that the move was finally made. A corporation was formed. Its name was the Palmetto Leisure Development Corporation, and its business was to build hotels. Listed as chairman and chief operating officer of Palmetto was Philip Gerson. Gerson went south, to Florida, to inspect sites for the hotels the corporation would erect. He found two that he liked. The first was in Hollywood. The second, a mile farther south, was in Hallandale. Armed with a seemingly inexhaustible grease account, Gerson approached law-enforcement officials and politicians at the local, county, and state level; all recently elected to office, they would be in power for a long time.

Three weeks after he'd headed south, Gerson returned to New York, excited about the prospects. There would, he reported to Levitt, be no foreseeable problem in the construction of hotels or in the running of casinos in them. Levitt listened approvingly. Florida was a giant step away from the environs of New York where the idea of setting up such businesses had been conceived and nurtured. Gerson's success with the local authorities proved that the same tactics which worked in New York worked in Florida. Levitt had harbored little doubt that they would. Every man had his price, whether he was a slick New York politician or a redneck sheriff. It was just a matter of finding that price, deciding if it was worth paying.

"Phil, get together some ideas for"—Levitt looked at the wall calendar—"Friday."

"That's only three days."

"It's long enough to jot some thoughts down. We'll have a general meeting on it then. I think it's about time the next generation took a more active role in the running of this enterprise. I want to hear their opinions as well." Levitt had been musing on such a move for a while. The twins were now twenty-five; Minsky's son, William, was two years younger. It was time for them to shoulder their share of the responsibility. They had been carried long enough.

The meeting was held at five o'clock in Lovitt's office. Levitt sat at his desk, a large-scale map of Broward County spread out in front of him. The twins, Benny and William Minsky, and Phil Gerson sat crowded around the desk, on chairs that had been brought in from the main room.

"Phil, the floor's yours," Levitt said. "Go ahead."

The chairman and chief operating officer of Palmetto Leisure Development Corporation circled two points on the map, both along Highway A1A, the coastal road running north and south between the Atlantic Ocean and the Intracoastal Waterway. "Two hotels, that's what we're going to build down there. The Monaco in Hollywood, and the Waterway in Hallandale. These are quickly commissioned artist's sketches, just to give you a rough idea of what I'm talking about." He passed out sheets of paper to the men around the table. Levitt, who had already seen the sketches, glanced at them disinterestedly.

While the men admired the drawings, Gerson read out specifications. "The hotels are going to be similar. Luxury hotels, each one six stories, about three hundred rooms. We'll be booking great shows, and they'll have superb restaurants with top chefs hired from Europe, a ballroom, even conference facilities. And on the top floor of each hotel, accessible only by way of a special elevator, will be the casino."

"How much are these hotels going to cost?" Benny Minsky asked.

"For land, construction, materials . . . somewhere between four and eight million dollars apiece."

"Somewhere between?" The question came from Joseph. "That's a hell of a spread. Why can't we get a better handle on the price?"

Levitt jumped in immediately. "We're still groping in the dark. We haven't made an offer on the land yet, we haven't contacted builders, we haven't gone into anything. What Phil's giving is a ball-park figure, the low and the possible high." Levitt was pleased by Joseph's instant response. The older twin was thinking along the right lines—worrying about price, the lack of firm information. But then Levitt had never doubted that he would react in any other way.

441

For the past eighteen months, Levitt had given Joseph complete control over the bookkeepers who managed the financial side of the gambling empire. Simultaneously, he had appointed Leo to be in charge of the messengers who picked up and delivered the bets and the money. Both young men had slotted right into their new positions.

"These places are going to be something special," Gerson continued. "Every penny they cost will come back tenfold from the high rollers we'll get in there. I'm talking about the finest materials, marble floors from Italy, exquisite art—"

"Never mind all the fancy trimmings," William Minsky broke in. "What kind of a payback period are you talking about?"

Again, Levitt agreed with the quick question. The younger generation knew why they had been asked to this meeting. They were being measured, and each one was determined not to be shown wanting. William, too, had proved himself adept in the business world. Straight from high school, he had gone to work for his father at B.M. Transportation. For two years he had worked on the trucks, loading and unloading the merchandise that Minsky's fleet carried for Garment Center companies. Now, at twenty-three, William was seeing the business from a wider perspective. He understood that B.M. Transportation was just a respectable front, a façade which carried on its books men whose real work was in gambling. But that was no reason, he'd stressed to his father, for the firm not to expand into other areas. B.M. Transportation should stand independently, be a highly profitable concern on its own. When Minsky had given the boy his head, William had contacted furniture and appliance manufacturers, worked out terms to get their custom. Soon, he intended to negotiate for new premises, wanting to move the company out of Manhattan to a much larger—and cheaper—depot in Long Island City. Levitt concurred wholeheartedly with the proposed expansion. The bigger B.M. Transportation became, the more men it could carry.

"We haven't had adequate time to work out a payback period yet," Gerson said in answer to William's question.

Before he could say more, Leo hit him with a question. "These high rollers you keep talking about—where are they going to come from? Are you going to advertise in the *New York Times* what you're up to?"

"Word of mouth." Gerson looked to Levitt for help. Levitt had thrown him to the wolves, made him face a barrage of questions without enough time for complete preparation.

"If Phil's going to be tied up in Florida," Joseph said, "who's going to make the Zurich runs?"

"You will," Levitt answered instantly. "You know the route, you

442

know Leinberg. Phil can resign his fake position with A. G. Kriesel and you can succeed him. That'll give you reasons for traveling there."

"When will we have more concrete figures on these hotels?" Minsky asked as he checked the sketches again. "The Monaco and the Waterway?" He was concerned about the vast sums of money that Gerson had so casually mentioned. They'd worked damned hard for all that money, earned it when Gerson was still a snot-nosed kid in diapers. Minsky had never shared Levitt's faith in Gerson. The guy had been born into wealth; he couldn't possibly appreciate it like a man who'd worked and bled for it.

"When I've had time to look into it more," Gerson answered. "I only got back from Florida three days ago. I looked at sites, I cleared the way with the local bigwigs—"

"Okay, Phil, you can relax," Levitt told him. He turned to the others. "This thing'll get us out of New York, give us a whole new perspective. Phil's keen on it and he's the man we need up front. It'll mean his moving down there to supervise construction and run the hotels. What we have to do now is vote on whether we borrow some of our money from Leinberg in Zurich to finance this thing. What Phil's spent already—the incorporation of Palmetto Leisure Development, the grease—is peanuts. From now on, we start getting into the big bucks."

"Lou, how come William and the twins are here?" Minsky asked. For years, a vote was just him and Levitt.

"I was wondering when someone would ask that," Levitt answered with a smile. "I think it's about time they stopped being our employees and became our partners instead. Don't you?"

Minsky wasn't certain. It meant that Levitt, with the twins, would have two votes to Minsky's one.

After the meeting was over, Levitt and the twins drove to Pearl's apartment on Central Park West for dinner. Judy was already there, having come straight from her job at the dress firm. In the kitchen, where Pearl worked with a busy cheerfulness, small plates of chopped liver were set out on a counter, a saucepan of chicken soup bubbled merrily on the range, and the oven held a chicken in the final stages of being roasted. The entire apartment smelled of Friday night.

This was the night of the week that Pearl looked forward to the most, when her entire family was together for dinner in her home. Just like it used to be. Since Joseph's wedding three years earlier, the apartment had seemed empty, the family no longer a strong unit. Although her son and daughter-in-law lived just across Central Park,

Pearl often felt as though a high wall had been erected between her and them. Judy invited her to dinner at least once a week, but Pearl always went by herself. Leo never accompanied her. He refused to step inside Judy's home; he had as little to do with Joseph's wife as possible. Even when Judy and Joseph came to Central Park West on Friday nights, Leo would stay just long enough to eat dinner before disappearing for the evening, to return long after everyone had gone.

That Leo went out at all was a consolation for Pearl. She had been worried because he spent too much time at home, especially after the wedding when he had barely ventured out. Gradually, though, he had become more outgoing, more sociable. He told Pearl that he had joined clubs, made friends. Pearl sensed that working for Levitt had helped. Levitt had given the younger twin responsibility and trust, and Leo's confidence had bloomed. Deep down, Pearl hoped that he was seeing a girl. That was what Leo needed, a nice girl who would show him the love and kindness she had always given to him.

When darkness fell, Pearl lit the Sabbath candles and made the blessing. Levitt, sitting at the head of the table, poured wine into silver goblets, broke a slice of freshly baked bread, and passed the pieces around. As Pearl served the hors d'oeuvre, chopped liver, Levitt said: "You should be proud of your sons, Pearl. Today they became equal partners in the business."

"Oh?" She looked at Joseph and Leo.

Levitt started to talk about Palmetto Leisure Development Corporation. "We're moving into a totally new area, a new direction. Big respectable hotels."

Pearl disagreed. "Lou, it's the same area, the same direction. It's still gambling. Only instead of having everything tied up in small shops and restaurants, it'll be in some fancy hotels. What happens," she asked, "when they have the next elections down there? When the officials Phil Gerson bribes are voted out of office?"

Levitt smiled. "By the time that happens, we'll be so strong that we'll finance the campaign of candidates who'll know how to pay us back once they're in office."

"Indeed? And what about when the next Estes Kefauver turns up?"

Levitt dismissed the senator with a wave of the hand. "We won't get touched because we're not involved in interstate crime like those characters who were called up by Kefauver. We're strictly gambling, and we keep our noses clean."

The moment dinner was finished, Leo stood up. He went to his bedroom, returning ten minutes later after having changed into a fresh suit and shirt. "I'm going out," he said to his mother. "I'll be home late."

Joseph ran his eyes over his twin. "What's her name?"

Leo's face froze. "What's it to you?"

"Come on, Leo, you can tell us," Pearl said.

"Leave the boy alone," Levitt said sharply. "If he doesn't want to share his girl with the rest of us, he doesn't have to. Go on, Leo; go out and enjoy yourself."

Leo kissed his mother on the cheek, took a coat from the hall closet, and went downstairs to his car. As he drove south, he felt a spontaneous burst of warmth for Levitt. The little man had assumed the role of father in Leo's life. He had shown Leo trust by giving him responsibility in the firm; he'd shown reliability by extricating him from that situation on Bleecker Street. Most importantly, Levitt had shown him love.

After Bleecker Street, Leo had been terrified to leave his mother's apartment in the evening in case he should be drawn to another bar, meet another man like Tony. He remembered the fear he'd felt, while he'd waited in the car for Levitt to come and save him. No one else would have come that night; no one else would have arranged everything so neatly. Levitt, Leo believed, loved him as much as his mother did. Why else would he have done such a thing?

Gradually, that fear had passed. In its place had come a yearning for the physical and mental satisfaction he had found that one night with Tony. . . .

Leo parked his car near Washington Square, in the village. He entered a four-story building on MacDougal Street, climbed to the top floor, and let himself in. The apartment was fully furnished with an accent on antique pieces. Leo liked antiques; they gave him a sense of permanence. The apartment was a part of his new life, the life he had come to recognize so recently. Another part of that new life was the boy who would soon visit him, sent by an agency that specialized in such things.

After hanging up his coat, he turned the radio to a classical station. Humming along contentedly to Chopin's *Polonaise*, he sat down to wait.

In the summer of 1953, Phil Gerson was transferred south to Hallandale. He moved into a luxurious rented house on the Intracoastal, with Belinda Rivers who had given up her dancing to accompany him. With Gerson went twelve million dollars that had

445

been borrowed from the Leinberg Bank in Zurich, the final estimate he'd come up with for the construction and furnishing of the Monaco and Waterway hotels. He had completion dates from the builders— February for the Monaco, and the following August for the Waterway. Within a week of each completion, Gerson expected to have the casinos working, the money flow across the Atlantic reversed.

Gerson reveled in his role as head of the Palmetto Leisure Development Corporation. This was what a Harvard degree entitled him to, not doing bookkeeping for a gambling czar and shuttling across the Atlantic with cases of contraband money. Not that those days hadn't served their purpose. They'd added to Gerson's education, provided a learning experience that was beyond the scope of any university. Although Gerson understood that the real power of the corporation lay with its two hidden partners—Levitt and Minsky—that did not stop him from enjoying the respect his title merited.

When the foundation for the Monaco was laid in Hollywood, Gerson celebrated by throwing a party at his rented home. He invited the builders, local dignitaries, and his New York backers. Belinda was a gracious hostess, only too pleased to show guests the large house she'd had redecorated, and the fifty-foot yacht that was moored to the dock behind the place. But Gerson concentrated on introducing Levitt and Minsky to members of the county commission, high-ranking officers in the sheriff's department, and the local police force.

The two New York partners smiled and shook hands automatically, made small talk. The moment they were alone with Gerson, however, Minsky's attitude altered dramatically. He pushed the younger man roughly against the side of a grand piano that Belinda had installed when redecorating the house.

"Are you running some goddamned popularity contest down here, or are you putting together a couple of hotels for us?"

"One goes hand in hand with the other, Benny."

"When you're playing around with our money, Phil, you get the work done first. How much did this joint set you back? Hell . . . how much is it going to set *us* back for the year?"

"Take it easy, Benny," Levitt hissed. "There are people here who work with Phil, who respect him. Don't make him lose face."

Minsky released his grip, but not without adding another warning. "Don't ever forget you're down here to work for us, Phil."

"The foundation's been laid on schedule, hasn't it?"

"Sure, but that's only the start. Finish the Monaco and the Waterway, and then you can play all you want. You can be the sailor on the big fancy yacht, you can be the famous hotel owner, glad-handing everyone at the door, throwing all the goddamned parties you and Belinda like. But until you've done what you came here to do, you work. Understand?"

On the return flight to New York, Minsky was silent. He could see that Gerson was on schedule. The foundation for the Monaco had been laid right on time. It was the wasted money that bothered him, the way Gerson was throwing it around like it was going out of style.

"Lou," he said at last. "You figure that Rivers broad has got her hooks real deep into Phil?"

Levitt smiled bleakly at Minsky. "Like Kathleen had hers into you?"

"Forget Kathleen," Minsky said angrily. "She never had me blowing our money the way Phil's doing."

Oh, didn't she? Levitt thought. If Minsky had gotten his way, he'd have spent every cent he could get on Kathleen. His money and everyone else's. Only Levitt had stood in his way.

Still, Minsky's concerns did bear thinking about. The big difference was that Gerson had more brains than Minsky had ever shown. And important connections. Minsky could not have been entrusted with ferrying the money to Switzerland; he'd have found a way to get caught. Besides, the Leinberg Bank was a Gerson family connection to begin with.

Because Levitt liked the Harvard graduate, respected him, he was more tolerant. Belinda didn't stick in his craw like Kathleen had done. He thought some more about Gerson. Everything about the man was so right. His background. His appearance. His ability to get on with people when it mattered the most. He was the perfect guy to hold up the front end while others worked and schemed at the back. All the same, Levitt experienced the first nagging worry that perhaps he had made a mistake in trusting Gerson with quite so much.

With Gerson working in Florida, Joseph made the regular courier runs to Switzerland to bank the New York gambling profits. When he was away, Judy was at a total loss. Her job occupied her during the day, but in the evening she felt miserable without him. Since they were children, they had seen each other every day. To be married to him and not see him for three or four days at a time was unbearable.

Before leaving on the first trip, Joseph had made Judy promise that she would stay close to Pearl. "She'll be hurt if you don't eat over there every night," he'd said. "You know what Ma's like. She won't understand you wanting to stay home and cook for yourself. She'll expect you."

Judy had promised to go. She was glad that she did, because in Pearl she found a sympathetic ear for her complaints about Joseph's absences.

"You're going through exactly what your mother and I went through," Pearl told her daughter-in-law. "Your father and Jake were frequently away for long periods of time, just like Joseph is now. You should just be thankful that his work isn't as dangerous as theirs was."

Judy smiled. "Knowing he's sitting on a plane or sitting in some fine hotel—and not guarding a truck full of whiskey—doesn't make me any less lonely, Ma."

Despite Pearl's understanding attitude, Judy still had to cope with her brother-in-law during the visits to Central Park West. When Joseph was present, he acted as a barrier between Judy and Leo. Joseph had pardoned his twin's behavior at the wedding, and the twins now got on as though no disagreement had ever taken place. They both held responsible, if diverse, positions within the business; they were equal. Consequently, Leo acted in a civil, if cold, manner toward his sister-in-law. When Joseph was away, though, the barrier was removed, and all of Leo's dislike for Judy simmered just below the surface, ready to break out into hostility.

If her visit occurred on a night he was staying in, he would simply finish dinner and then lock himself in his room. He had a new interest to complement his biographies; he had discovered the melodrama of opera. While Pearl and Judy watched television after dinner, Leo sat in his bedroom and listened to records.

The times that he went out after dinner inspired both relief and curiosity in Judy. While Pearl was content to assume that Leo had a girlfriend he did not want to share, Judy was more inquisitive. She told herself that she didn't give a damn about Leo, but at the same time she wanted to know exactly where he went, why he was so secretive.

The next time that Joseph carried the currency-filled case to Switzerland, Judy had a plan all worked out. Joseph would be away for four days. Surely on one of the nights when she had dinner with her mother-in-law, Leo would go out. For the first two nights, he disappointed her by staying in with his books and records. On the third night, after they'd eaten, he went to his room to change. The moment he had gone, Judy turned to Pearl. "Would you mind very much if I didn't stay, Ma? I think I'm coming down with a cold."

Pearl was instantly concerned. "Would you like me to call a doctor?"

"It's not necessary. I'll go home, go to bed. Make sure it's gone before Joseph gets back. God forbid I should give it to him."

"Of course, darling. Do you want to take something home with you?" Pearl gestured at all the food left on the table; Judy had deliberately eaten little, as though she were really sickening. "And I've got plenty of chicken soup left over. It's in the refrigerator."

"No, thanks."

When Leo returned, he seemed surprised to see Judy preparing to leave. "Aren't you going to keep Ma company?"

"Why don't you?"

"I have other things to do."

"Leo, why don't you drive Judy home?" Pearl suggested. "She doesn't feel well."

"It's all right, Ma. I'll take a cab."

Outside, she found a taxi immediately. She made certain it was not a Jalo cab, a driver who might know Leo. Then, instead of telling the driver to take her across the park to Fifth Avenue, she instructed him to wait. "See that red car over there?"

"The Oldsmobile?"

"That's the one. I want you to wait until the driver comes down in a few minutes. Then I want you to follow him."

"Where to?"

"If I knew that, I wouldn't need you, would I?"

"I don't like being involved in some follow-that-car routine, lady."

"Will this make you more cooperative?" She offered him twenty dollars.

"For a while."

Leo came out of the building five minutes later, walked close enough to the taxi for both Judy and the driver to see his face clearly as he passed beneath a street lamp. He climbed into the red Oldsmobile and headed south on Broadway, switching to Sixth Avenue at Herald Square. The taxi stayed close behind, anonymous amid the many taxis that plied the streets. At last, Leo turned off on West Fourth Street, headed into Washington Square. He parked the car, got out, and strolled along the sidewalk.

"Now what, lady?" the driver asked.

"Please see where he goes." She passed across another twenty dollars.

"Stay here." The taxi driver followed Leo by twenty yards. Ten minutes later, he was back. "Your friend went into an apartment building on MacDougal Street."

"Which apartment?"

"I wasn't going to follow him inside."

"Take me there."

When the taxi parked outside the building, Judy debated what to do. Was this where Leo's friends lived? She'd never thought of him as being the Village type. A restaurant in the Village perhaps, but not friends.

"What do you want me to do, lady?"

"Just sit tight for a while."

"It's your money."

Fifteen minutes after Leo had entered the fourth-floor apartment, he heard a double knock on the door. Outside stood a rosy-cheeked, curly-haired teenager. "Leo?" the boy asked.

"You must be Alan." Leo's face beamed with pleasure as he held back the door for the boy to enter. "Come in, I've heard wonderful things about you." He took the boy's coat and hung it alongside his own. The evening stretched ahead of him like a journey through paradise. "Sit down, on the couch over there. Tell me all about yourself."

"Lady, we've been sitting here a half-hour already," the cabdriver complained. "Are you planning to stay here all night?"

Judy looked at her watch, amazed at how much time had passed. She still did not know what to do. Common sense told her to go home, but inquisitiveness forced her to stay. She wanted to damned well know about Leo's friend—this girlfriend Pearl was convinced he had.

"I want to find out what apartment he's in," she said.

"Why don't you hire a private eye instead of an honest cabdriver?" Turning around in the seat, the man looked at Judy. He noticed the engagement and wedding rings on her third finger and decided that the man inside the building was her husband. "Lady, if your husband's two-timing you, why don't you just accuse him of it when he gets home? You can even throw the address of this place in his face for good measure."

Husband? Two-timing? Judy hid a smile. She decided to make use of the cabdriver's misapprehension. "I have to know who's with him. I have a girlfriend who's always made eyes at him, even before we were married. I want to know if it's her."

"Is this where she lives, this girlfriend of yours?"

"No. I don't know who lives here, but they might have rented a place where they could meet."

"What does your girlfriend look like?"

450

"Tall, with wavy platinum hair and brown eyes," Judy answered, projecting an image of Belinda Rivers. She could think of no one else on whom to model her fantasy girlfriend.

The driver turned forward again, gazed through the windshield. "How much money you got on you, lady?"

"Another fifty dollars."

"Let me have it. I'll find out for you."

"How?"

"I'll bang on every door and ask who called a cab. If your husband opens the door, I'll try to see who's there with him."

Judy handed over the money. The driver left the taxi and entered the building. Checking the mail boxes, he saw that there were sixteen apartments, including the superintendent's. That one he ignored. He pounded with his fist on the door of the first apartment. Moments later a middle-aged woman in a housecoat peered out. "You call a cab, lady?" The woman closed the door in his face.

By the time the taxi driver reached apartment 4B on the top floor, seven doors had been closed in his face. Four had not been opened at all. Only one man had been polite enough to say that he had not called a cab. Anticipating another surly reply, the driver knocked on the thirteenth door. There was no response. He heard music coming from inside and knew that someone was home. If he was going to earn fifty dollars, he was going to earn it honestly. He knocked again.

The door swung back. Leo stood framed in the doorway, face glowering. He was barefooted and wearing a cotton dressing gown. "What the hell are you banging on my door for?"

The driver answered anger with anger. "I'm trying to find out who ordered a goddamned cab in this building!"

"It wasn't me!"

"That's all I've heard from everyone—it wasn't me! Have you got anyone else in this place who might have wanted a cab?" He tried to see past Leo into the living room.

"I told you that no one ordered a cab!"

Another door on the landing opened, an apartment the cabdriver had tried before Leo's. When he'd knocked before, it had stayed shut. The cabdriver swung around. "Was it you who ordered a cab, buddy?" he asked the man who looked out.

Leo grabbed the driver's shoulder and jerked him around. "Didn't you hear what I said? No one ordered a goddamned cab!" And there, over Leo's shoulder, the cabdriver saw a bedroom door crack open. He got the quickest glimpse of a rosy face and short, dark, curly hair. Then Leo slammed the door with a crash that almost deafened the cab driver.

The man trudged down the three flights of stairs to the street. He took his seat behind the wheel, started the engine and drove away.

"Well?" Judy asked.

"Apartment 4B, lady. That's where your husband is."

"Who was with him? Was it my girlfriend? Did you get to see her?"

The driver swiveled quickly in the seat to look back at Judy. "Lady, your husband's not up there with *your* girlfriend. He's up there with *his* boyfriend."

The discovery of Leo's homosexuality shocked and elated Judy. At last she had the weapon with which to wound Leo, disgrace him in front of his mother. No matter how much Pearl adored Leo—how much she spoiled him—she would be horrified to know that his secret assignations were not with a girl but with a man.

Judy waited until Joseph returned from Switzerland. To show how pleased she was to see him home, she prepared a special dinner. They went to bed immediately afterward, leaving the dishes on the table to be cleared in the morning.

"I should go away more often," Joseph said. He lay back and stared at the bedroom ceiling through half-closed eyes as Judy's long fingernails traced an exquisite pattern across his chest.

"You go away more often, and I'll find someone else to make candlelight dinners for." Should she tell him now, before they made love, or later when they would lie sleepily in each other's arms?

"Did you visit Ma while I was away?"

"Three times, for dinner."

"Was Leo there?" When Judy nodded, Joseph asked, "Did he run off on one of his secret dates again?"

Judy felt more relaxed. Joseph was making this easy for her. Of course, he was as curious about his twin brother's comings and goings as she had been. "They're no big secret anymore."

"No?" Joseph raised a querying eyebrow. "Don't tell me he finally admitted something."

"Not likely. I played detective." She waited to see the response.

Joseph started to smile, and then he burst out laughing. "What did you do? Follow him?"

"In a taxi."

"Where did he go?"

"Down to MacDougal Street in the Village."

"To a club?"

"No. To an apartment. A fourth-floor apartment."

"And he never spotted you?"

Judy shook her head, trailing long ginger hair across Joseph's face. "I got the cabdriver to do the legwork for me. I didn't have to get out of the cab."

"Let me see, what kind of a girl would my brother go for? Was she a brunette, a blonde, a redhead? I know . . . she'd have auburn hair like Ma had before it started turning gray. Leo would pick someone who looked like Ma."

"Wrong, wrong, and wrong again."

"What else is there? Don't tell me she was bald."

"Joseph." Judy's voice turned soft and earnest as she stared down at her husband. "Leo wasn't with a girl. He was with a boy."

"What?" Joseph sat up in bed so abruptly that Judy was flung back. "What the hell do you mean he was with a boy?"

"Exactly that." Suddenly Judy knew she'd made a mistake. It was all right as long as Joseph believed that she'd followed Leo to find out about his secret girlfriend, but not when she'd found out that his lover was a boy.

"Judy, do you have any idea what you're saying?"

It was too late to back out now. "I know what I'm saying."

"Why did you follow him?" Joseph's voice took on a note of hostility that frightened Judy.

"I just told you—to find out his big secret."

"Is that the truth? Or did you follow him in the hope that you could find something to hurt him with? To hurt us all with?"

Judy's answer was brutally blunt. "I wanted a chance to pay him back for every stinking rotten thing he's ever done to me, from jumping on my doll's house when we were kids, to breaking into my bedroom, and then trying to wreck our damned wedding! And, by God, he presented it to me on a silver platter."

"Wait a minute. You said the cab driver went into the building?"

"That's right."

"So you never saw Leo inside the building yourself?"

"The cab driver did."

"But you didn't. And you didn't see the boy either?"

"No."

"Then how do you know the whole damned thing wasn't dreamed up by the taxi driver so he could look like he was earning the money you were paying him to spy on Leo?"

"For Christ's sake, Joseph! The driver wouldn't make up something like that!"

"How do you know?"

Judy looked away, unable to hold Joseph's eyes. From being amused that she would take it upon herself to follow Leo, he had become furious with her. She understood why. Faced with a choice between his twin brother and his wife, Joseph was siding with his twin. Because of the way he and Leo had been brought up, Joseph would rather believe that his wife was a troublemaking liar than acknowledge that his brother was a pervert.

"Well . . . how do you know the driver didn't lie? You haven't even thought about that, have you?" Joseph demanded. "You believed the damned driver because you *wanted* to believe him!"

Judy slipped out of the bed, threw a robe around herself and opened the door. Joseph called out to ask where she was going. "To do the damned dishes!" she fired back before slamming the door with such force that the entire apartment reverberated with the shock.

As she began to collect the dirty plates from the dining-room table, she heard the bedroom door open. Moments later, she felt Joseph's strong arms around her. "Put down the plates," he whispered, "and come back to bed."

"What for?"

"I believe you about Leo."

She replaced the dirty plates on the table and turned around to face him. "Sudden, isn't it? A few seconds ago you were calling me a liar."

He shook his head. "You wouldn't lie."

"What about following him?"

"You've got every reason to hate Leo, every reason to try to find out something you can use against him. But Judy . . ."

"Yes?" She knew what was coming.

"Judy, if you ever tell Ma. If you ever tell her about Leo . . ."

He left the sentence unfinished, but Judy did not need to hear any more. She knew exactly what he meant. The only way to truly hurt Leo would be to expose his black little secret to Pearl; and Judy could not do that without breaking Pearl's heart.

Chapter Five

Benny Minsky threw a party in the offices of B.M. Transportation's new depot when it opened in Long Island City near the end of 1953. The party was as much to honor his son, William, as it was to commemorate the opening. William wasn't university educated like Joseph Granitz, yet in Minsky's eyes he had proven himself every bit as capable.

When Jake had been alive, Minsky had never harbored any jealousy of the Granitz twins. Jake had been his friend. Because of that, Minsky would never have begrudged his children anything. But the moment Levitt assumed the responsibility of raising the twins, guiding them in predestined directions, Minsky's attitude changed. He transferred some of his animosity from Levitt to the twins. The two men became competitive about which of the boys was the smartest. Minsky was fully aware that Levitt looked down on William, and he was determined to prove that William was as good as anyone else. So what if Leo organized the physical work of the bookmaking and numbers racket, and if Joseph handled the business end, made the trips to Switzerland, juggled the money and made it come out right? All the twins had done was pick up where someone else had left off, carry on operations that had always run smoothly. William had achieved much more than that. He had created something. He had taken a small trucking company and, through his own hard work and endeavor, had made it big and prosperous.

From the start in Long Island City, William worked until past ten every night. He only saw the Riverside Drive apartment he shared with his father for as long as it took him to fall into bed and sleep, and to wake up, shower and dress the following morning before returning to the new depot. William felt comfortable living with Minsky. He loved his father deeply, and understood how much he owed to him. Minsky had brought up the boy after his mother had left. From what William could now remember of his mother, he doubted that her presence during his formative years would have added anything

455

positive to his life. Mostly, that final raging argument between his parents stood out in his mind, when Kathleen had come back from the West Coast to find Minsky taking William to the synagogue on Saturdays.

Late one afternoon, during William's third week at Long Island City, his secretary came into his office. "There are two men outside to see you."

William checked his diary; it was blank. "Get rid of them, Susan. Tell them to make an appointment like everyone else." He was too busy going over dispatch records to see anyone.

"They're very insistent on seeing you." Susan Mendel had worked for William for six months, ever since he'd decided that he needed a secretary of his own. He had not hired her because of references or qualifications. Straight out of secretarial school, she had had few. Plainly and simply, he had been immensely attracted to her. Every other secretary who had applied for the job had been middle-aged and crusty. Susan's warm brown eyes, wide smile, and shining short brown hair had made up William's mind even before she'd spoken a word.

"Insistent?" he asked.

"Would you prefer rude? They told me they wouldn't leave until you'd seen them."

Before she could add anything else, the two visitors entered the office. One was middle-aged with a dark, lined face and oily graying hair. The other, William guessed, was around his own age, nattily dressed in a gray coat and gray hat, razor thin, with a gaunt face and gleaming black eyes that remained ice-cold despite the smile that played around an almost lipless mouth.

"I am Frank Scarpatto," the older man said, "and this is my nephew, Tony Sciortino. We have a business proposition for you."

"I'm busy," William answered curtly. "If you want to see me, make an appointment with Miss Mendel here." He looked down at the dispatch sheets again. A hand encased in a gray suede glove whipped them away and scattered them across the floor.

"I think you'll see us now," Scarpatto said.

Tony Sciortino looked at the secretary. "Take a long coffee break."

Susan gazed uncertainly at William, who nodded. When the door closed behind her, he said to the two men, "What do you want?"

Scarpatto motioned to his nephew who bent down to collect the dispatch records from the floor and replace them on William's desk. "A regrettable accident, Mr. Minsky. Unfortunately, such accidents can always happen when one is not careful."

"I asked what you wanted. What's this business proposition?"

"Insurance. Against bigger, more costly accidents taking place. Like damage to your pretty new trucks, for instance."

"Or your drivers," Sciortino added for good measure. He removed one of his gray suede gloves and slapped it against his hand. "Or even the expensive merchandise you carry for your customers."

"I've got all the insurance I need."

Sciortino's thin face sharpened. Scarpatto held up a hand, as though restraining his nephew. "There is insurance and there is insurance, Mr. Minsky. Just as there are trucking companies and trucking companies. Some are more reliable than others."

"You want to run a business around here," Sciortino said, "you run it on our terms. You buy our insurance on your trucks, on your drivers, on your premises, and on your loads. Otherwise nothing moves."

William jumped up from behind the desk, grabbed hold of Sciortino's arm and twisted it behind his back. "Get the hell out before I break your goddamned arm!" With one hand he pulled back the door. With the other, he shoved Sciortino out of the office. Sciortino sprawled onto the floor in front of Susan Mendel's desk. His gray hat flew off, his face was ground into the carpet. Hoisting himself on his hands and knees, he turned his head and glared at William.

"You'll regret this, Minsky."

William took one step and lashed out with his foot at the man's raised posterior. Sciortino flew forward again, landing on his hat and crushing it. "Come back again and you'll see how much I regret it!"

When the two men were gone, William rested his hands on the secretary's desk, breathing heavily. "I'm sorry, William," Susan began.

"Not your fault. Maybe it's mine. I might have expected something like this, new kid on the block and all that."

"Will they do anything?"

"I doubt it. They're probably small-time hoods who just try to push around every newcomer to the district. Some give in, I suppose, and that's where they get their money."

"And you won't give in?" she asked admiringly.

He smiled at her. "Damned right I won't. My father would eat those two clowns alive and not even have to chew on them."

"That's reassuring. Mind you, seeing you in action just now, I don't think your father would even be needed."

"Are you trying to make me blush?" He drew her into his arms and kissed her.

"Me? I don't think anyone could make you blush." She fingered the narrow dimple in the center of his chin and looked up into his eyes. "Will we be working late tonight?"

"No. We're just about caught up."

"Thank God for that. For once we can have dinner without having to come back here afterward and earn it."

William chuckled. Every night that he had stayed late, Susan had kept him company. Once the office staff had left, they had gone for dinner before returning together to work on cutting down the backlog of paperwork created by the move. William had never asked Susan to work overtime. She had volunteered. When he'd tried to pay her, she'd refused. "Buy me dinner," she'd told him, "and drive me home afterward, otherwise my parents will worry."

On their third night of working late together, when William had parked outside the Jackson Heights home in which Susan lived with her parents, he'd handed her a slender box. "There's your overtime." Inside was a slim gold watch. "Now you can keep a check on all those extra hours you're putting in."

"It's beautiful! Thank you!" Without thinking, she'd flung her arms around his neck and kissed him. The next moment, she'd drawn back, eyes wide, mouth puckered in embarrassment. "I'm sorry. . . ."

"Why?"

"Well, I shouldn't have—"

"Shouldn't have kissed the boss's son?"

"Shouldn't have kissed the boss."

"It's my father's company. Those initials, B.M., they're his."

"But he's hardly ever there anymore. You run it."

"He has other interests."

"Either way, I'm still sorry."

"Don't be. I was hoping you'd do exactly that."

"Would you like to come in? Have a cup of coffee, meet my parents? I'm sure they'd like to meet you."

To Susan's disappointment, he'd refused. "I have to get home. Another time."

Since then, she had asked him in every night after he'd taken her home. Each time he had refused. "Is it because you're frightened that my parents might think there's something between us?" Susan had asked.

"Isn't there?"

That night, after throwing out Frank Scarpatto and his nephew, Tony Sciortino, William decided that he would accept Susan's invitation. They would be going to Jackson Heights straight from dinner, earlier than usual.

"Coming in?" she asked automatically as he stopped outside her parents' home.

458

"Sure." Before she could register surprise, William was around to her side of the car, helping her out. As she entered the house, she called out that she'd brought a visitor. William forced a smile onto his face and followed her into the front room. Hettie and Benjamin Mendel were sitting in front of a television set. Only her father was watching the program. Her mother, by the light of a small table lamp, was knitting a long, shapeless yellow form which William took to be a scarf. The scene warmed him. It typified something he'd never really known—a family where both mother and father sat at home, comfortable in each other's company.

"This is my boss," Susan announced.

Benjamin Mendel switched off the television set. Hettie put down her knitting. "Welcome to our home," Mendel said. "Susan's told us everything about you."

"She has?"

"She said you were a gentleman, and in my book that's all that needs saying."

"Sit down, please," Hettie said. "Can I get you something?"

"A cup of coffee would be nice." He dropped onto a couch. Susan sat next to him, her thigh pressed against his own as if to give him confidence.

"That's quite some place you've just opened in Long Island City," Mendel said.

"You know it?"

"I see it from the subway each day when I go to work in Times Square."

William nodded; the elevated tracks passed within fifty yards of the depot. "What do you do there?"

"I work in the advertising production department of the *Times*."

William answered questions put to him by Susan's father, while Hettie Mendel returned with coffee and cake, then continued with her knitting. But he noticed that her eyes kept darting to him; he was sure she didn't miss a thing. Mendel was interested in the trucking company and William explained how his father had started it during the Depression. He phrased the story carefully. Instead of admitting that Benny Minsky had converted rum-running trucks to vehicles that transported garments, he told Mendel that his father had bought the trucks secondhand. Somehow, he did not feel that Susan's family's acceptance of him would be quite so warm if they knew that his father's wealth was derived from bootlegging and gambling . . . and he wanted her parents to think warmly of him.

After a second cup of coffee, he decided it was time for him to go home. "A pleasure to meet you, young man," Mendel said, shaking

William's hand. "Come by any time."

Susan saw him to the car. "They were impressed with you."

"Because I'm your boss's son?"

"Boss," she countered. "No, that had nothing to do with it. They liked you because you're one hell of a nice guy. The same reason I like you."

He kissed her good night and got into his car for the journey to Riverside Drive. He wondered if his father would be home. He hoped so. William wanted to tell Minsky that he had fallen in love. Then he remembered what had happened earlier, the two unwelcome visitors. Should he tell his father about Scarpatto and Sciortino as well? Or was he confident that he had killed any trouble before it could start?

By the time he reached home, William had decided to tell his father only about Susan. Minsky knew the girl already. It was time that he stopped looking on her as just a secretary, and started to regard her as a possible daughter-in-law. Mentioning Scarpatto and Sciortino would dampen the news, William decided. He doubted that they would be back, anyway.

Months after learning of Leo's homosexuality, Judy was wishing that she had never found out. Knowing such potentially damaging information about her brother-in-law, and being frightened to use it, was wrecking her peace of mind.

Then something happened to occupy her thoughts. New Year's Day fell on a Friday, and that evening, she and Joseph went to Pearl's apartment as usual for Friday-night dinner. Leo was there, so was Lou Levitt. Judy waited until the meal had been eaten and Leo had left to keep his appointment downtown. Holding Joseph's hand beneath the table, she said: "How's this for a New Year's surprise? I'm pregnant."

The most surprised one there was Joseph. "When did you find out?"

"When you were away in Zurich last week."

"Why didn't you say anything earlier?"

"I wanted to save it for today, start the year out with a big bang." Joseph kissed her. "You succeeded. Happy New Year."

Pearl rose from her seat to kiss both her son and daughter-in-law. "Now maybe you won't feel so lonely when Joseph's away," she told Judy.

"How about you? Will you feel different, being a grandmother?"

"How about someone asking how I feel?" Joseph broke in. "I am the father, after all."

"We all know how you feel," Pearl told him. "Immensely proud of yourself because you think no one's ever done it before. Well, I've got news for you—the only person we should be concerning ourselves with is Judy, because she's the one who's going to be doing all the work, before and after the baby arrives."

"How much work can there be? You didn't have much trouble with Leo and me."

"Sure I had no trouble with you two," Pearl said sarcastically. She looked at Levitt, sitting at the head of the table. He had been oddly quiet, not even congratulating Joseph and Judy on their news. "Lou, tell them how easy they were to look after."

Levitt seemed to consider his answer for a long time. Finally he said, "Joseph, if your mother had had four pairs of hands, she still would've been short two pairs. You and Leo were murder. And Judy, throw in what you and your mother were like as children and you've got the bloodlines for a real lively kid."

Soon after, Joseph took Judy home, leaving Pearl alone in the apartment with Levitt. She sat watching him for several seconds, unable to understand why he had been so withdrawn. The news of Judy's pregnancy should have made him happy, but he'd shown barely any reaction.

"What's the matter, Lou?" she asked at last. "You look like someone whose best friend just died, not a man whose godson is about to become a father."

A slight smile lit Levitt's face. "I'm sorry. Joseph and Judy having a kid is probably the only news guaranteed to cheer me up. It makes me feel like a grandfather-to-be."

She held his gaze. "You're entitled, Lou. You helped bring the kids up. Now what's the problem?"

The smile disappeared. Levitt rested his chin on his hands and stared glumly at Pearl. "Florida's the damned problem. I've been on the phone with Phil Gerson all afternoon, trying to find out what the hell's going on down there. He's running up bills like money's no object. That six million bucks we budgeted for the Monaco in Hollywood looks like it's going to be eight or nine million. And what's going to happen when he starts on the Waterway in Hallandale? How much will he go beyond the estimate with that?"

"What's causing the extra expenses?"

"That damned woman, Belinda Rivers. Benny spotted it long before I did, but I suppose he had the experience of living with Kathleen to go on. Belinda's got Phil dangling from a string. He's given her all kinds of responsibility in the decorating and she's going nuts."

"What did Phil say about it when you asked him?"

"He says that Belinda knows exactly what she's doing, and if we

461

want the best place imaginable, we've got to pay for it."

"Are you short of cash?"

"Of course not. I just don't like being taken for a fool."

"What about Benny? What does he have to say?"

Levitt laughed grimly. "What do you think? He wants to take the extra money straight out of Phil's hide."

"When were you last down there?"

"Five weeks ago. We're flying down there again, the pair of us, and it's going to take all my persuasion to stop Benny from killing Phil."

Phil Gerson met Levitt and Minsky at the airport three days later. The first thing they noticed was his deep suntan. After the bitter cold of a New York winter, Gerson looked remarkably fit and healthy. That made the two visitors from New York even angrier.

"What the hell is going to be the finishing price for the Monaco?" Minsky rasped the moment they were seated in Gerson's car. "At the rate you and your girlfriend are going, the only way we'll ever get our money out is for a hurricane to flatten the place and the insurance company to pay us off."

"Just relax, will you?" Gerson replied. "When you see what we've done to this place—even since you were last here—you won't have a worry in the world."

"I don't want to relax," Minsky fired back. "I want to see those two hotels open. And I want some concrete reasons for all the damned expenses."

"What was the place like when you were down here last, Lou?" Gerson purposely aimed the question at Levitt who, he believed, was more sympathetic to him than Minsky.

"The building was almost complete."

"Right, but the grounds were a mess, none of the amenities were finished. Wait until you see what it looks like now. Then you'll appreciate the investment."

They arrived at the Monaco just as the setting sun struck it with full force from the west. As Gerson passed through a portcullis-style entrance into the hotel grounds, Minsky and Levitt sucked in their breath. Built in a Spanish style and painted the palest shade of pink, the hotel resembled a shimmering palace. "Everything's finished but the inside," Gerson said, "and I've got double crews working overtime to get that ready for next month." He drove right around the hotel. "Three swimming pools, all finished. Tennis courts, all finished. And the dock"—he braked the car by the edge of the Intercoastal—"all finished."

"You can park an aircraft carrier here," Levitt said drily.

"Maybe we will one day, if the Navy decides to become our customer."

"Let's look at the inside," Minsky said impatiently. "I want to see the big hole that all the dough's been poured into."

Gerson drove from the dock and pulled up outside the hotel's main entrance, slipping his car in between three trucks that were unloading their cargoes. Workmen carefully carried a consignment of furniture into the hotel, treading on thick strips of matting that had been laid across the gleaming marble floor of the lobby. The three men followed the furniture inside. Standing in the center of the vast lobby, dressed in tight slacks and a cotton blouse tied around her waist, was Belinda Rivers. One hand held a clipboard. The other directed a group of men who were pushing a dolly on which rested a gigantic, ornate crystal chandelier. When they almost collided with the work crew moving in the furniture, she screamed at them: "Careful! For Christ's sake be careful! That chandelier cost twenty thousand dollars!"

"Since when did she become one of the staff?" Levitt asked Gerson. "You brought her down here as your girlfriend. No one objected to that. We didn't take into account that she was going to tear up the plans and write her own set."

"That's because I never realized how talented she was. She's had some great ideas."

"Yeah, we've been seeing the bills for her great ideas," Minsky muttered. "I don't eat off Royal Doulton or use real silverware at home."

"Maybe you should," Gerson told him. "The proper presentation makes the food taste better." He cupped his hands to his mouth. "Belinda, come over here! We've got visitors!"

She turned away from the men moving the chandelier. "Hi, I heard you were coming. What do you think of it?"

"The outside looks gorgeous," Levitt replied. "But this is where I don't like it." He pulled out his wallet. "Two hotels at this rate, and this is going to be empty."

"Gangway!" a voice yelled from behind. Levitt stepped aside and two men pushed past a pile of cartons on a dolly. "Where do you want these?" one of the men asked Belinda.

"What are they?" She checked the labels. "Lace tablecloths, take them through to the laundry. They've got to be unpacked and pressed before they go to the restaurant."

"Lace tablecloths?" Levitt repeated. He looked at the label. The shipment was from a company in Italy. He felt grateful that the price wasn't listed. "What the hell's wrong with linen tablecloths?"

463

"Everyone and his brother eats on linen," Belinda explained. "Lace adds something."

Gerson broke into the conversation. "I know what'll make you happy. Upstairs is all finished."

Leaving Belinda in the lobby, the three men rode the special elevator to the top floor. Plush carpet greeted their feet. High, arched ceilings gave a feeling of spaciousness. The walls were paneled in rich, restful oak. Set across the floor were ten tables for craps, blackjack, and roulette. Above each table hung a chandelier identical to the one Minsky and Levitt had seen downstairs. Another two-hundred thousand dollars, Levitt calculated.

"What kind of furniture's that?" Levitt pointed to dainty chairs and occasional tables set every few feet around the walls.

"French . . . some king or other, I forget exactly which one," Gerson answered. "Belinda did remarkably well at estate sales in Europe."

"Don't even think of telling me how much each piece cost."

"You'll make it back and more. This place will be able to stand on its own against the great casinos of Europe."

Levitt gave a slight shake of the head. Twenty-grand chandeliers, French antique furniture, solid silver tableware, a view of the ocean. And just down the road, hundreds of acres of tomato fields! . . . Levitt did not know whether to be flabbergasted or impressed. "Phil, when I was half your age, I was making a fortune on one craps table in the back of a joint on Second Avenue, underneath a restaurant Pearl's mother used to own. You do as well here as I did there, and we'll overlook the extra money."

"But God help you if you don't," Minsky added.

The first week of the new year was especially pleasing to William Minsky. Every truck in the fleet was out, hauling merchandise from manufacturers to retail stores to back up promotions. He could not have opened the new depot, expanded the business, at a better time. Nor, he congratulated himself, could he have chosen a better time to fall in love.

Since meeting Susan Mendel's parents, William had taken her home every night. Twice he had eaten dinner with the family. He was even considering having his father meet them once he got back from Florida. He knew that such a meeting would make his relationship with Susan virtually official, and that suited him fine.

"When's your father coming back from Florida?" Susan asked him one evening. "What's he doing down there anyway—wintering?"

"He's checking out a hotel his company's building."

"A hotel?" Susan was impressed. "He's got a lot of different interests."

"Can you keep a secret, especially from your parents?"

"A big, dark secret?"

"Nothing so romantic. Those trucks my father started out with twenty years ago. He didn't buy them secondhand like I told your father he did. He converted them from trucks he and his partners used for running bootleg liquor. That's where he got his start."

"Your father was a racketeer, like those people in the Kefauver hearings? Why are you telling me this, William?"

"Because I love you and I think it's only fair that you should know."

"Does he . . . does he still involve himself in anything?"

"He has gambling interests. So do I, Susan. I'm partners with him and his associates."

Susan stared at the floor. "I don't know what to say."

"Just say that it doesn't make any difference between us."

"But you work so hard here. I've watched you. You can't be involved in things like that."

"My father worked damned hard during Prohibition as well. He had to, if he wanted to get on." When she continued to stare at the floor, he wondered if he'd made a mistake by telling her. "Would you rather I'd kept you in the dark?"

At last she lifted her eyes. "I'm glad you told me. It's just a bit of a shock, that's all."

"Does it make any difference between us?"

Susan shook her head and smiled. "If you hadn't told me—if I'd found out some other way—it might have. But you've been honest. I appreciate that." The smile faded. "I'm not sure that my parents would appreciate it, though."

"That's why I lied to your father when he asked me about the company."

"Then we'll both have to lie in the future, won't we?" She looked at the wall clock. "We'd better hurry if we're going to have time for dinner before the movie starts. It's six o'clock already."

They got into his car and headed toward the Queensborough Bridge into Manhattan. Snow was beginning to fall, and as William flicked on the wipers he felt a bit jealous of his father. South Florida looked good at this time of year.

"William, watch out!" Susan shouted.

Ten yards ahead, a van pulled out from the side of the road and stopped dead. William stamped on the brake pedal. The car slid in the fresh snow and skidded to a halt less than a yard from the side of the van. The rear door of the van flew open. Three men jumped out and rushed toward the car. William's door was yanked wide open. Strong hands pulled him from the car. A massive fist exploded in his face. His arms were grabbed from behind. Helpless, he was shoved forward onto the battering fists of the man who had first hit him. From a great distance he heard a man's voice shout: "That's enough, let's get out of here!" Before he blacked out, he saw in the dim light from a streetlamp, a thin figure clothed in a gray coat and gray hat.

"William, are you all right?"

Susan's voice penetrated dark waves of pain. William opened his eyes. He was lying on the sidewalk, head cradled in Susan's arms. The snow was falling faster, covering his coat and legs. "How long . . ." Speech hurt. He raised a hand to his mouth; it came away bloody. "How long have I been like this?"

"A minute. Can you move?"

One by one he tested his limbs. The greatest pain came from breathing. His ribs felt like they were on fire.

"I'll help you to the car," Susan offered. "I'll drive you to the hospital. Then I'll call the police."

"No . . . no police. I don't need them. No hospital either."

"Of course you need the police. I recognized one of the men, the one giving the orders. It was the man you threw out of the office, Sciortino the nephew. He was telling the other men what to do."

"And I'm telling *you* what to do. Just drive me home. Wait a minute. . . ." He touched the left side of her face. The skin around her eye was red and puffy. "What happened to you?"

"I tried to stop them. One of them hit me. It's nothing."

She helped him into the passenger seat of the car, and while she drove, he held a handkerchief to his torn lip and debated the situation. He thought he'd quelled any problem by throwing Sciortino and his uncle, Frank Scarpatto, out of the office. He'd been wrong. He hadn't stopped them at all; he'd just declared war.

William understood perfectly what he was supposed to do now. The simple thing—tell his father and let Benny Minsky's friends handle the whole affair. Only William wasn't interested in the simple route. Whatever had to be done, he swore, he would do by himself. If he was responsible enough to build up B.M. Transportation, then he was damned well responsible enough to take matters into his own hands and deal with any problems that accompanied expansion.

Once in the apartment, Susan went to the medicine cabinet where she found iodine and bandages. William winced as she addressed his split lip, bathed a graze on his temple. "Do you think your ribs are broken?" she asked him.

"Just bruised. I didn't hear anything go snap." He held her face tenderly. "Who told you to be the brave one?"

"I couldn't sit there and watch you get beaten up."

"Look, maybe you'd better go on home. Take my car, or I'll get you a cab. I'm going to have to make some calls."

"To your father in Florida?"

"No. I'll handle this on my own."

She thought about that for a while. "I'll stay here with you. I told my parents that we had a date tonight. What'll they think if I turn up at eight o'clock, especially with my face looking like this."

William did not argue. He reached for the telephone. Before he could lift the receiver, it rang. "Mr. Minsky," a soothing voice said. "I just heard about your terrible accident this evening. You can't know how sorry I am."

"Who is this?"

"Frank Scarpatto. We met the other day to discuss insurance for your company. Perhaps you've changed your mind about your decision."

"I don't know about any accident," William said. "If you mean about me and my secretary getting driven off the road and then beaten up—"

"I'd prefer to describe it as an accident, Mr. Minsky," Scarpatto said placatingly. "We'll be by your office tomorrow evening to discuss the terms of the policy which I'm sure you'll wish to take out with us." He hung up.

William turned to Susan. "I don't want you coming into the office tomorrow."

"What's going to happen?"

"It's not necessary for you to know." Before she could protest, he switched his attention to the telephone. His father and Lou Levitt were the only survivors of the old generation. He was a member of the new, and his allies were the Granitz twins. Which one, though, should he call on for help? Joseph, the figures man, the university graduate who worked with a pen and a briefcase? Or Leo, the street man who had not even turned up for his own brother's wedding? William's fingers spun the number of Pearl Granitz's home.

Pearl answered. William fought down both pain and impatience to ask how she was. She had always considered him such a nice, polite boy; he could act no other way with her. At last, he asked if Leo was home.

When Leo came on the line, William explained what had happened. "I don't want to wait for my father to get back from Florida. Those two guys are coming by the office tomorrow evening, and I want to handle this myself."

"No problem," Leo answered. "We can take care of the matter ourselves." Leo breathed in deeply, felt the blood begin to flow faster in his veins. The elite society—those who had taken life. He was being summoned because he was a member. "Meet with these guys, William. Agree to whatever they want. It'll be the only time."

Leo replaced the receiver and walked into the kitchen where his mother was washing up after dinner. "What did William want?" she asked.

"Nothing much, Ma. Just some information." He put his arms around Pearl and kissed her on the cheek. He felt happy. Tonight he had a new boy coming to the apartment on MacDougal Street. He'd asked the agency to find him something different, and they'd come up with Gustav, an eighteen-year-old Swedish-American boy with platinum-blond hair and crystal blue eyes. Leo wanted to experiment, to learn which kind of youth, which looks, stimulated him the most. When he knew he would dispense with the agency's services and find his own boy. His own mistress to love.

Before he left the apartment that evening to drive to the Village, he telephoned Harry Saltzman in Fort Lee. Gave orders just as he had heard Lou Levitt do.

Susan Mendel defied William's order by turning up for work the following morning. Her left eye was almost closed. "What did your parents have to say about that?" William asked.

"I told them we'd been in an auto accident, and that you were in even worse shape than I was. Too banged up to be left alone in the office."

"I won't be alone."

William was torn. He didn't want Susan in the office because he had no idea what would happen. Nor did he want her to leave. "All right, Susan, you can stay. But any trouble, and I want you out of that front door in one big hurry. Get me?"

"Got you."

Just after midday, Susan entered William's office. "There are two men to see you."

"Already?" Scarpatto had said that he and his nephew would not be back until early evening.

"Not those two," Susan said. "But two others, just like them."

William came out of his office. Waiting in the reception area were Leo and Harry Saltzman. "Give us overalls and a spare truck," Leo said. "We're going to sit outside in the front, where this Scarpatto and Sciortino will pull in."

"What are you going to do with them?"

"When you go to a doctor with a cold," Saltzman said, "do you ask him what's in the pills he gives you?"

William was silent.

"Okay," Saltzman continued. "To business. We'll be outside in the truck. When these two characters arrive, William, your secretary can signal to us. Just stand by the window, honey; pull out a handkerchief and blow your nose. Me and Leo'll take care of the rest."

"Harry . . ." William's voice was low, urgent. "My father doesn't know about this. I don't want him to know."

Saltzman hid a smile. The first thing he'd done after hearing from Leo the previous evening was to contact Lou Levitt and Benny Minsky in South Florida. He didn't make a move without their approval, especially Levitt's. If Levitt had told him to leave it alone, he would never have gone near the Long Island City depot. Instead, Levitt had instructed him to work with Leo, assist him in whatever he needed. Levitt had made the next generation equal partners. Now he wanted to see how they reacted under stress.

It was dark by the time Frank Scarpatto and Tony Sciortino arrived at the depot. Flurries of snow whipped up to obscure vision, disappeared just as abruptly as the wind dropped. The Lincoln in which they were being driven pulled into the small parking lot in front of the company offices. Save for one truck parked by the side of the building and William's own car, the lot was empty.

"Wait here for us," Scarpatto instructed the driver. Pulling up the collar of his coat, he walked toward the building entrance. Sciortino, still wearing the gray coat and hat, followed. Inside the Lincoln, the driver pushed his hat to the back of his head and lit a cigarette. As an afterthought, he started the engine and swung the car around so that it pointed toward the street.

Scarpatto and Sciortino reached Susan's desk together. "I believe Mr. Minsky is expecting us," the older man said.

Susan looked from one face to the other. Something like a smile flashed across Sciortino's dark eyes. "Walk into a door?" he asked.

She didn't answer. "Your two visitors are here," she told William. She held the door open for them to enter, closed it after them, and then walked to the window behind her desk. The cab of the truck in which Leo and Saltzman were sitting looked right into the office. She took out her handkerchief and dabbed her nose with it. The truck doors swung open and she walked away.

In William's office, the two visitors made themselves comfortable. "Think of the trouble you could have avoided if you'd accepted our offer, Mr. Minsky," Scarpatto began.

"How much do you want?" William asked.

"Two thousand a month."

"That's preposterous! We don't have that kind of money."

"You've got more than sixty trucks. Are you telling us that you can't afford to spend a lousy five hundred bucks a week for insurance. That's just over eight bucks a truck."

"Eight dollars a truck, like hell! More like four hundred dollars per truck per year."

"So do what everyone else does," Scarpatto said disarmingly. "Pass it on to your customers."

"I give my customers good rates. I don't rob them to pay other robbers."

"Two thousand a month or you don't move a truck out of here," Sciortino stated flatly. "Pay that, and you can call us whatever you like."

"What if"—William leaned back in his chair—"I pick up this phone and holler cop?"

Sciortino stood up. "You look like a sensible man, Minsky. In fact, you look a damned sight more sensible today than you did when we first came in here. If you call the cops, you'll need the fire department as well, because your depot will burn down, with all your shiny trucks inside. And you'll need ambulances for all the drivers who'll have mishaps. After a while, they won't even want to work here—your accident record will be too high."

"Take your choice," Scarpatto said. "Two thousand a month and you stay in business. Cut us out, and you'll have no business."

William opened a desk drawer and counted out two thousand dollars in twenty-dollar bills. "Thank you," Scarpatto said. "That clears your account until the end of January."

"We're already a week into January!" William protested.

"Our accounts run from month's beginning to month's end. We signed you up as of New Year's Day." Scarpatto nodded to his nephew and the two men walked toward the door. Susan was still sitting at her desk outside William's office. She didn't look up as Scarpatto and Sciortino passed her.

A brisk flurry greeted the two men as they opened the front door. As it fell away, they saw the Lincoln waiting, smoke trailing from its exhaust as the driver ran the engine to keep himself warm. They walked toward the car, passing a tall, middle-aged workman who listlessly pushed a snow shovel in a losing battle to keep the parking lot clear.

Sciortino entered the back of the car from one side, his uncle from the other. As they closed the doors, the driver swung around, his gun pointed between the two men. "Should have been you two guys who took out the insurance," Leo said, grinning at them.

"Where's our driver?" Scarpatto asked.

"Taking forty winks in the back of that truck."

The front passenger door opened and the snowsweeper climbed into the Lincoln. Saltzman had discarded the shovel in favor of a heavy revolver. "Back up the car," he told Leo. "Get it close to the truck."

Leo put the Lincoln into reverse, guided it slowly until the rear doors were level with the back of the truck. Saltzman got out first, pulled open the back door of the car. "Out."

Hands in plain sight, Scarpatto and Sciortino left the Lincoln. When Leo threw open the loading door of the truck, they saw their driver lying on the floor, hands and feet tied, a gag stuffed into his mouth. "Step right in," Saltzman ordered.

Scarpatto and Sciortino entered the truck, moved right to the front as Saltzman prodded them forward with the revolver. "Lean forward, spread your legs and place the flats of your hands against the front wall. Take your weight on your hands."

As the two men obeyed, Saltzman stood behind one, Leo behind the other, each holding a weapon in his left hand, as his right drew a leather-covered blackjack from his coat. Two blackjacks arced through the air simultaneously. Scarpatto and Sciortino collapsed onto the floor of the truck. Leo and Saltzman picked up lengths of the heavy string that lay on the floor, bound the arms and legs of the unconscious men, and stuffed wads of rags into their mouths. Lastly, Saltzman felt inside their pockets until he found the two thousand dollars.

"I'll take the car. You take the truck and follow me," Saltzman told Leo.

The sound of the truck and car engines revving up could be heard inside the office. Standing with Susan, William looked out of the window. The Lincoln led the way out of the parking lot, followed closely by the truck.

"Take me home, please," Susan said. "I want to get out of this place."

"So do I." William said it as though leaving the depot would sever them from what had happened to the two men who had tried to cut themselves in on a piece of the company. He knew it wouldn't. William had built up a legitimate trucking company. But in its first scrape with trouble, instead of going to the police as any legitimate businessman would have done, he had used his father's contacts . . . his own contacts . . . to overcome the problem. It was a decision of great finality. He would never be troubled by Scarpatto or Sciortino again. At the same time, he would never be free of his father's past.

Saltzman checked continually in the rear-view mirror to make sure the truck was still following as he headed toward the Queensborough Bridge. Once in Manhattan, he turned north onto the FDR. The truck stayed behind, all the way onto Harlem River Drive and then the George Washington Bridge into New Jersey. On the Palisades in New Jersey, he finally came to a stop, switching off the lights but leaving the engine running as the truck coasted to a halt behind him.

"Turn them off," Saltzman told Leo, gesturing to the truck's lights, "and move over into the passenger seat." While Leo changed seats, Saltzman steered the Lincoln until it was pointing directly at the flimsy wooden fence on the edge of the cliff twenty yards away. He lifted the hood and jammed the accelerator linkage wide open. Slamming the hood closed, he reached in through the Lincoln's open window, jerked the gearshift from park into drive, and jumped back. The Lincoln rolled forward, engine roaring as it picked up speed in a mad dash toward the fence. The fence shattered. A grinding crash of metal erupted as the car went over the edge, its underside scraping against clumps of rock. Then it was gone, toppling end over end toward the river far below, engine screaming at full revs. Silence soon came when the lubricating system failed to cope and the engine seized up, piston rings welded to bores, journals fused to bearings. Saltzman jumped into the truck, thrust it into gear, and drove away. Only when he reached the road again did he turn on the lights.

"Where are we going now?" Leo asked.

"Paterson. I'll show you how I got rid of a troublesome union man a few years ago."

Leo fell silent. In school, the good students—boys like his twin brother, Joseph—had always been the quiet ones. They were too busy learning to talk, to play. Leo was learning now. He was studying with a master.

Saltzman pulled the truck into the parking lot of a funeral home, cut the lights, and steered around to the back where the hearses came and went. Only a small light showed in a window at the rear. After reversing up to a wide door, Saltzman killed the engine and jumped out. The door opened and a fat, bald-headed man peered out. Saltzman gave him the money he had taken from Tony Sciortino. "You all fired up in there?"

"Ready to go," the fat man answered. "How many?"

"Three." Saltzman flung open the cargo door, picked up the body of the driver and carried it through the door into the building. Leo lifted Frank Scarpatto from the floor. The body writhed in his arms, almost dislodging his grip. "Harry, this one's awake."

"Too bad. Where he's headed it's going to be hot anyway," Saltzman said as he returned for the body of Tony Sciortino.

Leo found himself in a chapel that was illuminated by a single lamp, the light he had seen from outside. The fat man led the way to a ramp where Saltzman had already deposited the body of the driver. As Leo set the wriggling Scarpatto next to it, Saltzman returned with Sciortino. "Hit your button," Saltzman told the fat man.

A low, steady hum filled the chapel. The ramp began to move. All three bodies were slowly transported toward a curtain that parted to give them passage. The first two bodies passed from view. The third writhed furiously as the conscious Scarpatto realized the fiery fate that awaited him.

Half an hour later, Leo and Saltzman were riding in the truck back to New York. Between Leo's feet rested a box containing the ashes of the three cremated men. Saltzman had suggested they give it to William Minsky as proof.

As they came off the Queensborough Bridge into Long Island City, a traffic light turned against them. Saltzman stopped. When the light turned to green, he put the truck in gear and pressed down on the gas. The drive wheels, stuck on a sheet of hard-packed snow, spun in place. Saltzman tried to get a grip in a higher gear, but the wheels continued to spin and the light changed back to red. Saltzman swore. "Give me that damned box," he said. Leo passed across the ashes. Saltzman climbed out of the cab and scattered the ashes beneath the drive wheels. He got back into the cab just as the light turned green again. Letting up the clutch, he gave the engine the tiniest squirt of gas. The drive wheels gripped on the ashes. The truck moved off.

Saltzman started to laugh. "Those three dumb bastards were more use in death than they ever were in life, eh, Leo?"

Leo joined in, leaning against the door, his body shaking with laughter.

*   *   *

When he returned to Fort Lee that night, Saltzman telephoned Florida. "Lou, it's Harry. The job went down okay."

"How was Leo?"

"Behaved like a champ. Never had a better assistant in my life."

"Thank you, Harry." Levitt put down the receiver and smiled to himself. He'd been right all along.

Chapter Six

Within two weeks of Judy's springing her New Year's Day surprise, she and Joseph started house hunting. After a month of feverish activity, the field was narrowed down to two choices, both on the north shore of Long Island. One house was in Great Neck, the other in Sands Point. The Sands Point place had been built by a film star in the 1920s, during Long Island's halcyon days.

One cold Sunday afternoon, Joseph and Judy called at the apartment on Central Park West. "Ma, come for a ride with us. We need your advice on something."

Pearl took a Persian lamb coat from the closet and went downstairs to Joseph's car. "Are you going to tell me where we're going?" she asked as they left Manhattan and drove through Queens.

"You'll see," Joseph answered. The house was only part of the surprise. The other part belonged solely to Judy. She'd suggested it, and Joseph had quickly agreed.

At last, Joseph drove into the semicircular driveway of a red-brick house in Great Neck. A brown Dodge belonging to the real-estate agent was already there.

"You've bought this?" Pearl asked. "Why do you need my advice if you've already bought a house?"

"We haven't bought anything yet. There's another one we're interested in as well."

With Judy and Joseph, Pearl followed the real-estate agent. The house had four bedrooms on the second floor, spacious rooms on the first floor and a long sloping lawn that was surrounded by carefully cultivated rose beds. "I don't know what advice you're expecting from me," Pearl said. "I've never lived in a house in my entire life."

Judy and Joseph winked at each other. "Get back in the car. We'll show you the other house."

Pearl made the short journey to Sands Point in silence. She'd be lost in a house, she thought. Her life had been spent in apartments, first above her parents' restaurant, then at the bottom of Fifth

Avenue, and finally on Central Park West.

"Here's the other place, Ma," Judy said.

Pearl looked out of the car window. They had turned off a narrow road to pass between tall wrought-iron gates. A winding gravel driveway led up to the largest house Pearl had ever seen. She noticed a tennis court, a stable, and a paddock where horses could be exercised. "You'll need a map and a compass to get around this castle," she said. "Even with a baby, the place'll be like an echo chamber. It's much too big for three people. The other place is better, in Great Neck."

"Who said anything about there being three of us?" Joseph asked.

"We want you to live with us, Ma," Judy said.

"Me?" Stunned, Pearl pointed to herself. "Why do you want me to live with you?"

"We want you with us, Ma, because we love you. Is there any better reason than that?"

"That's different."

Pearl marched toward the front of the house. The real-estate agent quickly ran to get ahead of her and unlock the front door. When Pearl stood in the center of the vast reception hall, she stared at the wide staircase that curved gracefully to the second floor. "How many bedrooms in this place?"

"Five upstairs," the agent answered. "Downstairs there's a formal dining room, a living room, a library, and a recreation room with a full-sized pool table that comes with the house. There's also a room that can be made into a children's playroom, plus there's a separate self-contained guest wing."

Pearl's eyes widened as she took it all in. She tried to remember the flat above the restaurant on Second Avenue . . . that place would have fitted into this entrance hall with space to spare. Yet hadn't she and her parents been thrilled to have such a home? "I want to see the kitchen," Pearl stated. "Please show me where the kitchen is."

"This way." The real-estate agent walked through the hall, into a large, airy breakfast room that overlooked the gardens at the rear of the house. "There's your kitchen."

Pearl walked back and forth on the tiled floor. Heavy oak cabinets were fitted to the walls. She opened the doors, peeked inside, ran her hands across the wide countertops. She pulled back the door of an enormous refrigerator that stood in the corner, inspected the huge range and oven. When she turned around to face her son and daughter-in-law, she was smiling. "Now this is what I call a kitchen. Buy this house. Cooking here will be a pleasure." Then concern replaced the smile. "If I live here with you, how will I look after Leo?"

Before Joseph could say anything, Judy answered, "Leo's a big boy, he's old enough to look after himself. He doesn't need his mother to fuss over him anymore.''

Pearl did not seem quite so certain. She still pressed Leo's shirts, cooked his meals, even made his bed each morning after he'd gone to work.

"Maybe if you stop taking such good care of him," Judy added, "he'll go out and find a girl to marry. You've made Leo too comfortable, Ma. That's his trouble. While you fuss over him, he'll never want to leave."

Pearl's smile returned. Judy was right. Hadn't Leo always treated her like she was his girlfriend instead of his mother? Leaving him to make his own bed, look out for himself, might just be the kick in the pants that he needed to make him go out and find a wife.

Touring the remainder of the house was anticlimactic. Even the bedroom with its own dressing room and *en suite* bathroom, the one designated for Pearl, aroused little interest. She had been sold on the kitchen. If the kitchen had not been to her liking, the house could have been a fairy-tale palace and she would have thumbed her nose at it.

As they prepared to leave, Joseph made an offer to the agent. "If it's accepted, when do you think we can close?"

"Let me call you tomorrow," the agent replied. "By then I will have spoken to my principal."

Instead of going to work the following morning, Joseph stayed at home by the telephone. At ten-thirty, the agent rang through to say the offer had been accepted and the closing could take place in four weeks. Joseph gave a yell of delight and hugged Judy who was standing next to him. Within ten minutes he was on the telephone to decorators, builders, painters; enquiring about estimates for the renovation of the house in Sands Point.

Leo was stunned when Pearl told him the news. "You're going to move in with Joseph and Judy?" he asked in disbelief. "What will I do?" Before Pearl could answer, Leo continued his protest. "How will I see you when you're all the way out there, Ma? Judy won't want me to come to *her* house. She talked Joseph into buying a house all the way out there so she could take him right away from me. She wants to take you away from me as well!"

"Of course she doesn't, Leo. You're just imagining it," Pearl said soothingly. Nonetheless, his wild accusation lodged in her mind.

*　　　*　　　*

Phil Gerson opened the Monaco in Hollywood at the end of February. The final cost was just over eight million dollars, two million more than it had been budgeted for. Levitt and Minsky went down to judge what kind of return they could expect from their expensive investment.

They did not tell Gerson they were coming. Arriving at night, they took a taxi from the airport to the Monaco, walked into the sumptuous lobby—"goddamned twenty-grand chandelier," muttered Minsky—and asked for Gerson at the desk.

The clerk recognized them, picked up the telephone, and made the call. Five minutes later, Gerson walked out of one of the elevators. Wearing a new hand-tailored tuxedo, he marched toward the two New York men, hand outstretched. "I must have known you were going to pay me a surprise call. I've got the place packed out upstairs."

"What about the rooms?" Levitt asked.

"Do you mean is there any place left for you two?" Gerson snapped his fingers. The clerk passed him the reservation book. "Ninety percent occupancy. Not bad for a first night, eh?"

"Not bad at all," Levitt concurred. The grand opening of the Monaco had been well advertised, both in South Florida and in New York. Top entertainers had been engaged for the floor show. Additionally, word had gone out to big gamblers about the casino on the top floor. For a moment, Levitt felt jealous of Gerson standing there in his new tuxedo, the king of the casino. It reminded Levitt of earlier days, the sweetness of running his own show in the back room of the Four Aces. "Let's go upstairs and take a look."

They took the special elevator that served only the top floor. The moment the door opened, Levitt's senses heightened. The sound of rolling dice, the riffle of cards being dealt, the rattle of the ball against the numbered slots of the roulette wheel was like a shot of adrenaline to him. He felt that he'd come home. Bookmaking, numbers . . . none of them had anything on this thrill. "How's the Waterway coming along?" he asked as he followed Gerson across the casino floor. From behind, he heard Minsky muttering sourly about more twenty-thousand-dollar chandeliers.

"They're putting down the foundation next week. With what we learned from this place—mistakes, short cuts—we'll be able to move much faster."

"Wait." Levitt stopped to watch a dark-skinned man place a thousand dollars on twenty-two at a roulette table, just as the croupier called out "No more bets." The wheel slowed, the ball jumped from slot to slot, eventually settling in thirty-six. No one at the table had it.

Levitt couldn't hide a smile as the dark-skinned man's thousand dollars joined the rest of the losing bets under the croupier's rake.

"Arab diplomat," Gerson whispered. "Came down from Washington for a couple of days."

"Good. Hope he loses some more. We'll be generous with his money at the next Israel appeal."

"Where's your girlfriend?" Minsky asked.

"Belinda? She had to go away for a few days."

"Where'd she go?" Levitt asked. "Off buying more stuff for the Waterway?"

Gerson laughed and slapped Levitt gently on the shoulder. "I told you, we learned from building this place. The Waterway'll come in on budget, don't worry."

Levitt backed off. He hated being touched. "You just get two thousand more players like that Arab at the roulette table and you'll make up the deficit on this place." It bothered him that Belinda Rivers wasn't on hand for the opening. It seemed so out of character for the blond dancer. She had played the gracious hostess the entire time Gerson had been down in Florida. Now, when the action started for real, she took off. It didn't make any sense. "When's she coming back?"

Instead of answering, Gerson assumed a sudden interest in one of the blackjack tables, standing to the side to watch the dealer play against three men. "What's the big secret with Belinda that he doesn't want to talk about her?" Minsky asked quietly.

"Beats me. You'd have thought she'd be here tonight, though. Grand opening and all that."

"Maybe they split up."

Levitt shook his head. "Doesn't it bother you that when the Monaco is finished, when the builders are paid off, she disappears all of a sudden? Just when all the final payments are made . . . when all the big bucks are on the table."

"You think—?"

"We've got our own ways of finding out, haven't we?" He broke off as Gerson left the blackjack table and rejoined them.

"If you're sticking around for a few days, I'll take you out on the boat. I finally took some sailing lessons."

"When did you find the time?" Minsky asked.

"I made it. This place got finished on schedule, didn't it?"

"We'll take a raincheck on the boat ride, Phil," Levitt said. "Benny and I have to get back to New York. Another time, maybe. When Belinda's here as well."

"Good idea . . . she does add something to the place, doesn't she?"

479

Add wasn't the verb Levitt would have chosen. He would have preferred to use *subtract*.

Levitt and Minsky returned to New York. The moment Levitt reached home, he telephoned Joseph and instructed the older twin to meet him at a restaurant close to the Jalo Cab garage. When Joseph joined him there, he said, "I want you to go to Zurich, make another trip for Kriesel Engineering Company."

"I was there last week. We've got nothing due for another three weeks."

"I want you to see Leinberg—not for a transaction, for some information."

"What kind of information?"

"About Phil. I think Phil's been skimming money off the top, that's why we're in so damned much of a hole over the Monaco."

"What?" The single word was filled with shock and revulsion at such an accusation.

"You heard me. All those trips Belinda's been making all over the place, buying up antiques in Europe, lace tablecloths in Switzerland. Every time she goes over there on a buying spree, I think she's been socking money away in some account. Our money. And now, when the Monaco opens, she isn't even there."

"So? What does that have to do with anything?"

"Joseph, have I got to spell it out for you? Everyone was paid off this week, all the builders, the contractors. There was a mountain of money flying around and no sign of Belinda. Benny and me, we asked Phil where she was. He wouldn't answer. I figure the reason she wasn't there was because she'd hightailed it to Switzerland again with what Phil's been skimming."

Joseph remained defiant, as though his own stubbornness could dissuade Levitt. "What if I go to Switzerland? Leinberg won't tell me anything. Even if Phil has stolen the money and Belinda's deposited it there for safekeeping, Leinberg won't admit it. Those Swiss bankers, they're sworn to secrecy about the accounts they hold. That's why you put Blackhawk there."

"Leinberg will tell you if you use your common sense. That's why you spent all those years at Columbia, so you'd be smart."

"Phil went to Harvard, that makes him smarter."

"Don't you believe it. You've got too much of me in you to get outfoxed by anyone, Harvard or otherwise."

"Too much of you?"

Levitt stiffened, realizing too late what he had said. "You know what I mean. I've spent too much time making sure you went in the right direction. You won't get conned by anyone, not by a Harvard graduate from a fancy family or by a stone-faced Swiss banker. Get over there and find out what's been going on. It's your money as well as mine."

Feeling troubled, Joseph returned home. He liked Gerson. He'd even wanted him as best man at his wedding. Was Levitt's claim true? Had Gerson, through Belinda, been stealing from them? For once, Joseph wanted the little man to be wrong. He didn't want Phil Gerson to be exposed as a thief, a man they had entrusted with a fortune only to have him betray them. He didn't even want to travel to Zurich and meet with Leinberg. Yet he knew he must. When it came to loyalty, his family—and Levitt was a part of that family—had precedence over friends.

Judy was disappointed when Joseph sprung the news of the trip. "I was hoping we could go out to Sands Point tomorrow, make some more decisions about what we're going to do."

"We don't close for another two weeks."

"Two weeks isn't long, Joseph. Besides, you went to Zurich only last week."

"Business is good." He saw no reason to tell Judy of Levitt's suspicions. Gerson and Belinda were her friends as well.

"Business is good, and this kid"—she patted her stomach—"is going to have a father who won't know whether he's on Eastern Standard Time, Greenwich Mean Time, or somewhere-in-between time!"

"You go out to the house. Take Ma with you. Between the pair of you, you can decide what should be done."

Judy knew it was the best she could hope for.

Joseph faced Walter Leinberg across the boardroom table of the Leinberg Bank. "What you are asking from me," the Swiss banker said slowly, "is unethical and out of the question."

"You shouldn't talk so glibly about ethics when you've got half the loot from the Third Reich stashed in your vaults," Joseph retorted. "We suspect that someone has had a finger in our till, and that the money—"

"Philip Gerson?"

Leinberg's instantaneous use of Gerson's name sounded a death knell to Joseph's faint hope that there might be no truth to Levitt's claim. Of course it was true. As if there had ever been any doubt! Once Levitt said something was so, it was gospel. "That's right, Phil Gerson.

And we think the money stolen from us has been brought over here and deposited in this bank or in another bank. What I want from you is information on whether an account has been opened here or in some other bank."

"What occurs in other banks is none of my concern," Leinberg replied tartly. "I doubt very much if other banks would allow me access to their records. You certainly would not want me to allow access to mine, would you?"

"Has Phil Gerson made any deposits here lately?"

"Philip Gerson has not been near our bank since you took over the courier run, Herr Granitz."

"That isn't what I asked." Joseph stood up and walked to the door. "I'll be at my hotel until midday tomorrow, after which time I will be flying home. Think about this. We have some twenty-five million dollars in Blackhawk. What's been stolen from us is two million at the most. You're a banker, you can work out balances. Which balance is more in your favor . . . our twenty-five million, or the missing two million?" He closed the door and left.

That evening, he telephoned Levitt in New York. "Uncle Lou, I told Leinberg we'd stop doing business with him if he didn't help."

"Good, that's a big hammer with which to hit someone over the head. Even a stone-face like Leinberg would feel it."

"I gave him until tomorrow, our time. What if"—an unwelcome idea had crossed Joseph's mind—"he threatens to expose our secret dealings?"

"He wouldn't dare. He'd blow his own bank to pieces if he did such a stupid thing. No one would go near him. And those more questionable accounts he carries, they'd carve him up into little pieces and feed him to the fish in Lake Zurich."

"If you don't hear from me tomorrow, you'll know I'm on the way home," Joseph said.

All the following morning he waited by the telephone in his room. At one minute to noon, it finally rang. "Herr Granitz, Leinberg. Would you come to my office, please?"

The two men faced each other across the boardroom table again. Joseph waited patiently for Leinberg to speak. "The name of the account is Dancer."

"How much is in it?"

"Just over a million and a half dollars."

"Who has signing rights?"

"Two people. Philip Gerson and Belinda Rivers. It was the woman who made the deposits."

"I know. You will receive notification from us when Dancer is to be closed and the balance transferred to Blackhawk. You may arrange the documentation any way you like to account for the transfer."

"As you wish, Herr Granitz."

Five men sat around Lou Levitt's desk in the office above the Jalo garage—Levitt himself, Benny Minsky, the twins, and William Minsky.

Levitt nodded at Joseph, who began to relate details of his journey to see Leinberg in Zurich. Halfway through, when Joseph mentioned the amount of money in the Dancer account, Minsky leaped to his feet. "Why are we just sitting around here talking? That fancy Harvard guy robbed us blind. Him and his damned girlfriend! We know what we've got to do, so why don't we just call up Harry Saltzman and let him get on with it?"

"Sit down, Benny," Levitt said. "And shut up."

Minsky dropped into his chair. "Since when don't you care about a million and a half bucks? You're the only guy I know who ever squeezed a nickel so hard the goddamned buffalo screamed in pain!"

"I was entitled to squeeze it. I was the guy who made those nickels, and the dimes and the dollars. Everything we have is of my making, and don't you ever forget it."

"Sure, you're so smart that Gerson pulled the wool right over your eyes. He didn't pull no wool over mine. I told you right from the start that there was something down in Florida that wasn't kosher."

Even to himself Levitt hated to admit that he'd been wrong and Minsky had been right. "Let's take a vote on it."

Minsky's decision was instantaneous. "Hit him."

"We know where you stand already, Benny. How about you, Joseph?"

Joseph sat there, uncomfortable as he weighed Gerson's friendship against the treachery. Finally he shook his head.

"That's right," Minsky said. "A university man stands up for another university man." He'd harbored little doubt that Joseph would vote against killing Gerson. The older Granitz twin was too immature to know any better. He hadn't learned yet that sometimes it was the only way. Minsky did not have the same feeling about Leo. Leo had killed already, and he'd helped to burn the men who had tried extorting money from B.M. Transportation. Allied with William, whose vote Minsky was certain of, the decision would be in favor of killing Gerson. Joseph's dissenting vote carried no weight at all.

"You, Leo?" Levitt asked.

"He deserves whatever he's got coming to him."

483

"Two for," Minsky said, "and one against."

"I can count," Levitt answered. "William?"

"No."

The single word of rejection hung in the air. Minsky swung around on his son, unable to believe what he'd heard. "What the hell do you mean, no?"

"How do we know that the million and a half in the Dancer account is our money? We've got no proof of it. Every penny that's been spent on the Monaco has a receipt to go with it."

"Receipt!" Minsky shouted. "That's the oldest dodge in the world. That broad could have had doctored receipts for all the junk she bought! Are we going to send people over to Europe and then check on every purchase? Phil could have pressured the contractors to give him a kickback for getting the work. All the contractors have to do is keep two sets of books, two sets of estimates, two sets of specifications. One for our benefit with figures that match what Phil's spent, and another set with the true figures for their own records and for the tax people!"

"I still don't want to see him killed," William said. "It's not necessary. We've got the money. Why kill him?"

"Two for, and two against," Levitt cut in quickly. "And my vote, the casting vote, is also no. You're outvoted Benny." Levitt had not been surprised to hear Leo vote with Minsky. He had thought he'd lost the motion on that vote alone. Then William had shocked him by going against his father.

Minsky argued with his son. "It doesn't matter whether we get the money back or not! It's the damned principle of the thing. Phil robbed us and he should be punished for it!"

"When a man talks about principle," Joseph said calmly, "he really means money."

"What?" Minsky turned his anger on Joseph. "Is that something you learned at the university?"

"Just something I once heard. A cute little phrase with a whole lot of truth in it."

Levitt rapped his knuckles on the desk. "Listen to me. Phil's been valuable to us in the past. He had that courier run down pat. The whole thing was his idea anyway, his and his father's. He's saved us plenty more than the million and a half he's swindled. He's also in the middle of doing a big job for us down in Florida. The Monaco's up and operating at a profit. The Waterway's under construction now. Let him get finished down there, and then we'll decide what should be done."

"Let him finish so he can steal more from us?" Leo asked.

"What does it matter how much Belinda ships over to Switzerland on her trips?" Joseph fired back. "We've got a lock on that Dancer account. It might as well be in our names because Leinberg will do whatever he's told to do with it."

"I don't care about the money," Minsky said. "This guy keeps stealing from us carte blanche, and I won't wait for Harry. I'll put Phil on ice personally."

"That's because you're taking it so damned personally," Levitt responded. "Stop thinking with your heart, Benny. Even your son can see what's right and what's wrong."

Minsky swung around to glare at William; he still couldn't accept that his son had gone against him. Like father like son . . . like hell!

Joseph broke in. "Let me say something. I agree with Uncle Lou. Phil's done a lot of good for us, in Florida and before he went down there. I think that makes him deserving of a second chance. Let me go down there. I'll speak to him—"

"You'll tell him to his face that we know he's been robbing us?" Leo asked.

"No. I'll tell him, friend to friend, that the people up here are upset over the cost overruns. There's a feeling that there might be something strange going on. I'm not going to tell him that we know. I'm just going to hint, that's all. If I'm right, that'll be enough. He'll toe the line from here on in. When the Waterway's up, and it comes in on budget, we'll just take the Dancer account from him. We won't be out of pocket. And if you want to punish him, you can throw him out on his ear. Losing the job he has with us will be punishment enough."

Slowly, Levitt nodded his head. "Good, logical thinking. Do we take a vote on Joseph's proposal?"

Minsky turned down the idea of a vote; he already knew what the count would be, the same as before. "I want to know one thing, Joseph. What if he pulls the same crap with the Waterway, doesn't take any notice of your hint?"

"How will we know," Leo asked, "unless we check every receipt?"

"Leinberg will inform us of any transactions on Dancer," Levitt answered. "I'll get onto him and make sure he relays news of any activity."

"Well?" Minsky pressed. "What if?"

Joseph had already considered that possibility before he'd made the proposal. "Then you can do whatever you want with him."

The deal on the house in Sands Point closed two weeks later. Joseph and Judy attended the closing, which was held at their lawyer's office, and then went to the house to meet with the decorators who were starting work that same day. Late in the evening, Joseph flew down to Florida to see Phil Gerson. He had purposely let two weeks elapse between the discussion of the theft and seeing Gerson. He did not want his warning to come right on the heels of the visit made by Levitt and Minsky. He needed Gerson to be at ease, free of the immediate worries of the hotel opening, receptive to a well-intended note of caution.

Gerson met him at the airport. Joseph had telephoned ahead to say he was coming, although he had not given a reason. Nor did he mention one as they drove from the airport to the Monaco in Hollywood.

"What do you want to see first?" Gerson asked when they entered the hotel. He assumed that Joseph had come south out of curiosity. "The casino or the books?"

"Show me both."

Gerson's office was on the top floor, accessible by a door that led from the casino. As they passed between the gambling tables, Joseph saw Belinda. She was so obsessed with playing blackjack that she didn't even notice him. "Is that good policy, Phil, having Belinda play?"

"It's quiet right now. A little action can lead to more action. People who are just watching might get the urge to play themselves. Here," he unlocked the office door, "sit down and I'll show you what's what." He set two ledgers on the desk in front of Joseph. One was full-sized, bound with a hard red cover. The other, smaller, thinner, with a flimsy blue cover, was more like a school exercise book. "The red one, that's the real accounts for the hotel operation."

Joseph flipped through the pages. Room occupancy was down to seventy-four percent from the original ninety. That was to be expected, Joseph supposed. The novelty of the opening had faded, and the winter season, when south Florida made its money, was drawing to a close. Room rates would drop during the summer months, and the hotel would take in the bulk of its income from the top floor. In November, when the season started again, the rates would go up. By then, the Waterway would also be open. Another luxury hotel, another moneymaking casino.

"The blue book, that's for up here."

Joseph opened it. There was not a single word, a single letter, written on its pages. Just figures, correlating to a code that Levitt had engineered. At the end of each week, when the casino profits were shipped to New York for the eventual journey to Zurich, the blue book accompanied them. Once Levitt had read the figures, the book

486

was burned in the furnace with all the betting and policy slips. "Over and above the payoffs, how much have we made so far?"

"A hundred and twenty thousand, that's the take for the first two weeks. We're not"—Gerson bathed Joseph with a tight smile—"billing up here for any share of the hotel's overheads, of course."

Joseph closed the book. "Phil, I didn't come down here to look at the accounts, to see how business was doing. I came down here as a friend to do you a favor."

"Oh?" Gerson pulled up a chair. "What kind of a favor?"

"New York isn't happy about the way this place went so far over budget, Phil. They've got a feeling—"

"Who's got a feeling?"

"Benny Minsky, mainly. He feels you've been deliberately inflating the costs to line your own pockets."

"He's crazy. Every goddamned penny we spent is accounted for. What does he think I'm doing, overcharging and sticking it in my pocket?"

Joseph didn't answer.

"That's fine gratitude," Gerson went on. "I bust my ass down here and Benny Minsky's sitting up there stabbing me in the back. You know why he's got it in for me, don't you?"

"I've no idea."

"Because I'm smart enough to have gone to university, the same as you. His kid wasn't."

The office door opened and Belinda walked in. Joseph could not help but notice how heavy the purse she carried was. It bulged so, it looked as if the seams might split at any moment. "Joseph, what a lovely surprise!" she burst out. "When did you get in?" Too late she tried to hide the swollen purse behind her back.

Joseph riveted his eyes on her face, pretended he hadn't even seen the purse. "Now I get the big greeting. Before, I walked by within three feet of you, and you didn't even notice me. You were too busy playing blackjack."

"You should have said hello."

"Did you win?"

She shook her head. "I never win."

"It's lucky she only plays minimum stakes," Gerson added with a laugh. Joseph did not share in the laughter. He had seen a mountain of chips on the table in front of Belinda. If she had been gambling with minimum stakes, it would have taken her the rest of the night to go through that lot.

Belinda clapped her hands. "Why don't we go out on the boat tomorrow?" she suggested. "Phil could do with a break from this

487

place for a few hours. How about it, Joseph?"

"Why not?" Maybe with no distractions other than the sun and the sea, he could drill some sense into Gerson's head before Benny Minsky got his way and drilled lead into it instead. . . .

The sun beat down the following morning, sending the temperature to eighty degrees by ten in the morning. By then, Joseph, Gerson, and Belinda were aboard the yacht, anchored two miles off the coast. The sun, as it rose toward its midday zenith, bathed the coast white. Joseph had no trouble in picking out the Monaco; it shone like a pink pearl.

"This is the life, eh?" Gerson said as he and Joseph sat in the stern of the yacht. Belinda was stretched out on a towel at the bow, sunning herself. "Now let's hear this again about Benny Minsky wanting my head on a silver platter."

"If you don't come in on budget for the Waterway, he'll have it, Phil. Right now, only Lou Levitt's standing in Benny's way. And he's doing that for services rendered in the past."

"Lou's the only one I'm worried about," Gerson answered. "But Benny Minsky? . . . That guy hasn't got the brains he was born with. Lou's carried him the whole time. Believe me, if Benny had been in charge of this operation, the Monaco would be ten million dollars over the projected price and they'd still be waiting to see the damned foundation!" Gerson's voice rose. "He can't talk about me. He's got no right to. And you've got no right to come down here acting as a messenger boy!"

"I'm trying to do you a favor."

"The hell you are. You're just relaying the message, that's all. You can tell that bastard if he's got any messages for me he can come down here in the future and tell me himself. Face to face, like a goddamned man!"

"Let's go back," Joseph said. "I'll catch an earlier flight." He had no wish to stay with Gerson any longer.

Joseph had no doubt that Gerson would bring the Waterway in for the right price. He wouldn't have to inflate it because he'd found another way to steal. With the Monaco casino open, he could help himself. How much did it take to bribe a dealer or two, especially when it was the manager who was doing the bribing? When no one was watching too closely, like last night, the dealer just paid out and paid out . . . to Belinda who filled her purse until it was fit to burst.

As Gerson guided the yacht through the inlet into the Intracoastal, Belinda joined Joseph at the stern. She'd heard every word the two men had exchanged. "You don't believe Benny Minsky and his crazy idea about Phil, do you?" she asked.

"If I did, I wouldn't have come down here to talk to Phil," Joseph answered. He decided to give it a last try. He'd work through Belinda. If she really loved Gerson, she'd put him straight. "Belinda, for Phil's sake, go easy on the spending for the Waterway. Buy a few less antiques. Buy a few less fancies that aren't really needed. Keep your decorating tastes less extravagant."

"You're a nice guy," she said and kissed him on the cheek. "If you weren't you wouldn't have come down here to warn us. You'd have just believed Minsky and left it at that."

"Friendship counts for something."

When Joseph left for New York that afternoon, both Gerson and Belinda saw him off. They waited until the aircraft was airborne before starting the return drive to the Monaco. "Joseph knows, doesn't he?" Belinda said.

"That we've been skimming from the building costs, giving in false receipts, padding the bills? Sure he knows. That's why he came down here, to warn us off. To tell us that everyone knows."

"What'll we do?"

"Just sit tight and put up the Waterway for what it's supposed to cost. In the meantime, we can still milk the golden calf in other ways. We put stooges in to play the tables, pay off a dealer, a croupier or two, and cash in that way."

"They won't find out?"

"How can they? I'm the manager. Security's one of my responsibilities."

"What about Leinberg?"

"Don't worry about him. His father and my father were buddies way back when. A connection like that is stronger than anything Levitt or Minsky can throw at him. I'll contact him anyway, make sure that no one's been asking awkward questions." Suddenly he slammed a clenched fist on the steering wheel. "Why the hell should I be a pauper when they're coining it in like they own the mint? I'm the guy who put Florida together for them. I'm entitled to a piece of the profits, a big piece."

"That's right, honey." She leaned across the seat and kissed him. The front of the car twitched as Gerson responded. Like he'd told her, there were a million ways to milk the golden calf and not get burned. He'd only started.

Chapter Seven

The work on the Sands Point house was completed by the last week in April. Joseph and Judy moved in immediately. By then, Judy was six and a half months pregnant. Both she and Joseph were anxious to be settled in their new house as quickly as possible. Pearl was to join them two weeks later.

As the time left before the move shortened, Pearl's trepidation increased. She compiled lists of what to take to Sands Point, what to leave at Central Park West for Leo who would continue to live in the apartment. Joseph pestered her about how much she really *needed* to take with her. "Ma, you don't have to drag all this stuff along. I'll buy you new."

"Why waste money on new when the old is still good?" Her own words made Pearl laugh. She sounded just like Sophie Resnick. Thirty years earlier, Pearl had been annoyed with her mother for being frightened to spend money when it was abundant. Now she was doing exactly the same thing.

"Ma . . ." Joseph tried again. "The moving men need to know how big a truck to allocate. Make up your mind!"

Finally, Pearl drew up what she termed her ultimate, irrevocable list. It was small, comprised only of her bedroom furniture and the bureau in which Jake had kept his valuables and important documents. These were familiar items she needed to see around her to make the transition more fluid.

On the day before the move, a Saturday, she went through the bureau's drawers. Purposely she left the bottom drawer until the very last. When she unlocked it, she saw the wedding and birth certificates. And there, beneath the documents, was the polished walnut presentation case that held Jake's twenty-fifth birthday present from Benny Minsky. She did not open the case. She simply sat there holding it, and she wondered if she were breaking the law by having the pair of ivory-handled revolvers with their ammunition, in her possession. Of course she was. Should she get rid of them? It would be

490

simplicity itself to ask Lou Levitt, or even one of the twins, to do it for her. She quashed the notion. Like the cuff links, tie pins, and collar studs still set out so neatly in the bureau, the two revolvers had belonged to Jake. She could not callously discard anything that had been his. . . .

At ten-thirty on Sunday morning, Joseph arrived with the moving van. While Pearl gave the moving men instructions, he rapped on the door of his twin brother's room. "Leo, are you awake?"

A minute passed. Still in pajamas, Leo swung back the door, hair awry, eyes gummy from sleep. "What do you want?"

"I'm getting ready to take Ma to Sands Point," Joseph began, but Leo interrupted him with an enormous, uncovered yawn.

"Tell Ma to wait a minute," Leo said. "I'll get dressed, come out to see her off."

"What about driving out with us?" Joseph asked. "You haven't seen the house. You haven't shown any interest at all."

"My invitation's got to come from Judy, not from you."

Joseph pushed past Leo into the bedroom and closed the door. "Listen to me, Leo. You've got it all wrong about Judy. You can come out to Sands Point whenever you want to. You don't need an invitation. Don't you understand that what happened at the wedding—and everything else before that—is all water under the bridge now?"

"Maybe it's behind you, but it's not behind Judy. She doesn't want me at her house. She never liked me, so why should anything change now?"

Joseph felt like grabbing Leo by the shoulders, shaking him hard. Did you ever, he wanted to yell, give Judy any damned reason to like you? Didn't you give her reason enough to want to find a way of hurting you? Despite the only answers such questions could elicit, Joseph knew that Leo was still his brother. His only brother. His twin. An accommodation had to be made, a compromise. By both Judy and Leo. Joseph had already told Judy that. Damn Leo's apartment in the Village, the boys he saw there, Joseph had said to Judy. If Pearl was to live with them in Sands Point, then Leo would have to be a welcome visitor. Judy had responded by promising to hide her antagonism toward her brother-in-law. Now it was up to Leo to make a corresponding move.

"For Ma's sake, Leo, you've got to make things change. If you don't come out to Sands Point, how the hell are you ever going to see her? She's not going to be riding up and down the Long Island Rail Road all the time to come and see you!"

"That's what Judy wanted," Leo answered. "She wanted to take Ma

491

away from me, and now she's done it."

"You might believe that but no one else does." Joseph stared sadly at Leo for several seconds. "For God's sake, you're my brother. I'm telling you that you're welcome at my home. Will you believe it from me? Because if you won't, when's the next time you're going to see Ma?"

Leo had an answer for that. "A week from today, when William Minsky marries that secretary of his."

In the rush of moving, Joseph had forgotten all about William Minsky's impending wedding to Susan Mendel. Now that he thought of it, it seemed ridiculous that the date could have slipped his mind. Ever since William had announced his plans to marry, just after the extortion attempt at the Long Island City depot, Benny Minsky had talked about nothing else. The marriage had even superseded Phil Gerson in Minsky's list of priorities. As a wedding present, he'd bought the young couple a house in Forest Hills Gardens, as if by doing so he could show that his son and daughter-in-law would live just as comfortably as Joseph and Judy.

"Fine," Joseph said. "So when someone gets bar mitzvahed, married, or buried, those are the times you'll see Ma. Is that what you really want?"

"No." Leo stared down at his bare feet which were protruding from his pajama trousers. "That's not what I want at all, and you damned well know it."

"Then make up your mind to let bygones be bygones. Whatever harm you *think* Judy's done to you, just forget it."

A knock sounded on the bedroom door. Pearl stood outside. "The men have taken down the furniture."

"Want to take one last look around the place?" Joseph asked.

"I've looked all I want to." She stared past Joseph. "Leo, I'm going."

A softness appeared in Leo's eyes as he walked toward his mother, a tenderness that Joseph could rarely recall seeing. It was as though his twin brother had a secret compartment of warmth and love that was reserved solely for his mother. "Ma, if they don't take good care of you out there, you know you're always welcome back here. I'll keep a light shining for you in the window."

"You keep it shining for some nice girl instead," Pearl told him. "You're going to find out that this apartment is a big, lonely place when you're all by yourself."

"I didn't let you get lonely in it, did I?"

"No, you didn't." It suddenly occurred to Pearl that perhaps Leo had not married—or even considered it, as far as she knew—because of her; he could not bear to leave her by herself. She could see so many things, so much goodness in Leo that seemed to be invisible to anyone else. She looked at Joseph, dismissal in her eyes. When he had walked out of the bedroom, she said to Leo, "Will you come out to Sands Point to see me?"

No matter what he thought of Judy, Leo could not refuse his mother. "Of course I will."

"Every Friday night, so we can still have our family dinner together."

"Every Friday night, Ma."

Pearl smiled; her worries over Leo dissipated. "And when you come, you bring me your shirts. I'll wash and press them just the way you like."

"I can take them to a laundry here."

"No laundry takes the care I do. You bring them to me. Leo"—she choked back a tear—"I'm going to miss you. And I'm going to worry about you being all on your own."

"Ma, I can take care of myself. Don't worry about me."

"Only when you find a nice girl," Pearl said, unable to resist getting her message across one last time, "will I stop worrying about you."

When Pearl left in Joseph's car to follow the moving truck out to Long Island, Leo stood staring through the living-room window. He was alone for the first time. The realization swept over him, but it did not bring the terror he had once thought it would. He had no reason to fear being alone. He had his work. He had his boys. He might even be better off than before. Without his mother he would not have to be so careful about keeping his second life a secret, dreaming up stories to answer her questions about where he'd been and with whom. He would not even have to return to Central Park West at all if he found a boy he really loved. He could just keep the apartment as a base, spend as much time as he liked at MacDougal Street.

His mood brightened. Every hour he had spent on MacDougal Street had been tinged with the fear that his mother would find out. With Pearl's departure, that fear was gone.

During the journey to Sands Point it wasn't Leo who occupied Pearl's thought, but Lou Levitt. She was surprised that he had not ventured up from the floor below to see her off.

She voiced those thoughts to Joseph. "You'd have thought Lou would have come by."

"You figure he's upset because you're moving out?"

"I don't know. He is the one who made me take that apartment."

"I remember. After Pa, and Judy's parents." Joseph drove on in silence for a mile, the moving truck fifty yards ahead of him. "Why did he do that, Ma? Did he just want to keep an eye on you? On all of us? Or was there more to it?"

Pearl gave a gentle smile. "There's a lot about Lou Levitt you don't know, Joseph."

"Such as?"

She considered how much to tell Joseph, how much he'd guessed already. "He asked me to marry him."

"When?"

"A couple of times. Once before your father asked me"—how glibly that rolled off her tongue—"and once after your father died."

"You turned him down both times?"

"I had to. The first time I was in love with your father. I was waiting for your father to ask me—he was a bit slow. And the second time . . . well, it was too soon after all the trouble. I told Lou I needed time to think."

"That's more than thirteen years ago, he's given you a hell of a lot of thinking time. Maybe he figured you'd turned him down twice, and he wasn't going to set himself up for a third rejection."

"You know"—Pearl touched Joseph's hand as it rested on the steering wheel—"I think he had it in mind on the day you and Judy got married. There was something about him that day, the way he fussed over us all before we left for the *shul*. I could sense that he was leading up to something."

"And then Leo stuck in his two cents worth," Joseph muttered. "Do you love Uncle Lou?" He could sense his mother's hesitation and added, "There's nothing wrong with being middle-aged and in love."

"Thanks. I'm glad you're allowing your mother to have feelings," she said, laughing. "I don't know how I feel about him, Joseph, and that's the truth. I've never been able to work it out to my own satisfaction. He's been like a father to you and Leo. He's done everything a father could have done."

"And he's done everything he could for you. You really think he'd forget to come upstairs and wish you luck with the move? He didn't come up to say goodbye because he's waiting for you at the house."

"He is?" Pearl's anxiety turned to delight.

"He came by first thing this morning. He wanted to be there to greet you, figured that saying hello would be more positive than saying goodbye."

Pearl sat back, smiling. That sounded just like Levitt, the tiniest detail given careful consideration.

When they arrived at the house, Levitt was waiting on the front steps, holding the largest bunch of roses Pearl had ever seen. "Welcome to your new home," he greeted her. "May it bring you as much pleasure as your old one."

She took the roses and felt Levitt's lips brush her cheek. "I'd given you up for lost this morning," she told Levitt. "I thought you'd washed your hands of me."

"Would I ever do that?"

"No, Lou, I don't think you would. You, above anyone else, would always stand by me."

"You never said a truer word. I've even got my eye on the guest wing here. Perhaps I can talk Joseph and Judy into renting it out to me."

Although he made it sound like a joke Pearl sensed an undercurrent. Like herself, Levitt was middle-aged; they were both closing in on fifty. She had Judy and Joseph, Leo. Who did Levitt have? It saddened her to think of him all alone. Since Jake's death, he had taken care of her. Who, in turn, would care for him? Or was he so alone? He had a family he could always rely upon. Her family.

They walked together into the house, stood in the large entrance hall and watched the moving men carry the bedroom furniture up the curving staircase. "How did Leo take it this morning?" Levitt asked.

"About my moving? Better than I ever imagined he would. He promised to come here every Friday night for dinner, just as usual. I was frightened that he might think I was deserting him."

"He's past that stage now, Pearl."

"He blew up when I first told him, when Joseph bought the house."

"He's had time to think about it since then. He knows it's the best thing for you."

"It might be best for him as well. Now that I'm not there"—Pearl's favorite subject surfaced—"he might start looking seriously for a girl to marry."

Levitt shrugged his shoulders and smiled. Pearl was wrong there, dead wrong, but he was not going to be the one to tear her apart by telling her. It was just as well that no one else knew. Leo's secret was safe only with him.

Two days after Pearl moved into the Sands Point house, Joseph made the courier run to Zurich to deposit money from the New York operation and from the casino profits that Phil Gerson had sent up from the Monaco Hotel in Hollywood. It was Joseph's first trip in more than a month, and with Pearl in the house he was comfortable about leaving Judy.

Carrying the small suitcase he'd been given after boarding the aircraft at Idlewild, he left the Savoy Baur en Ville and walked along the Bahnhofstrasse to the Leinberg Bank. He used the side entrance, rode up the elevator to the third floor. Walter Leinberg was waiting in the boardroom. Joseph opened the case and set two separate amounts of money on the table. The bookmaking and numbers take came to a fraction under half a million dollars. The casino profit for the month was just over two-hundred thousand dollars. Leinberg pressed his buzzer and the two black-coated bookkeepers filed in to count the money.

Leinberg drew Joseph away from the table. "We have had a deposit for Dancer."

"How much?"

"One hundred and seventy thousand dollars."

Joseph performed some rapid mental arithmetic. That was almost a third of what Phil Gerson had reported as total profits on the casino since its opening ten weeks earlier. The knowledge that Gerson was still stealing from the Monaco came as no surprise to Joseph. Only two weeks after he'd given Gerson and Belinda the warning, Levitt had heard from Leinberg that a letter had been received from Gerson. In it, Gerson had asked if any inquiries had been made from New York about dealings he might have had with the bank. On Levitt's instructions, Leinberg had replied that no inquiries had been made. To Gerson, that response had been a green light to rob his employers blind.

"What do you wish us to do with the deposit, Herr Granitz?"

"Let it ride. Pay interest on it as you would for any account. Don't give Gerson any reason for suspicion. When we're ready, you'll receive instructions on the disposition of the Dancer account." He turned to watch the bookkeepers flicking through the bills. "Who made the deposit?"

"The woman. But she did not come here. Perhaps she was afraid of a chance meeting with you. She paid for one of our employees to meet her in Geneva. He transported the deposit back to the bank."

Joseph's face blazed red with anger. It was one thing for Gerson to steal. They knew he was doing that, and had made plans so the money would not be lost. But to trust it to an unknown party for the journey from Geneva to Zurich! . . . No matter that the messenger was one of Leinberg's employees, he was still only a man living on a wage. What was to restrain him from succumbing to the temptation of walking away with the money?

Leinberg read Joseph's expression perfectly. "Would you prefer that we refuse to collect the money in future, Herr Granitz, and force the woman to come here to make the deposit instead?"

Joseph quickly shook his head. Such a move might alert Gerson. "You . . ." He pointed a quivering finger at Leinberg. "You pick up the money from the woman in the future. You I trust."

"A bank president does not normally perform a messenger's duties," Leinberg began. He saw steel in Joseph's eyes and his resolve wilted. "But I would be more than happy to make an exception to accommodate you."

"Thank you, Herr Leinberg. I never doubted that you would."

Joseph arrived back in New York late on Friday afternoon. When he reached home, the dinner table was set. The house was full of the smell of cooking. His mother had not taken long to settle in.

Lou Levitt and Leo arrived together from the office above the Jalo garage. Leo's arms were full, clasping a suitcase containing the week's dirty shirts for Pearl to launder and a large box of chocolates, wrapped with red ribbon tied in an enormous bow. Joseph waited for him to give the chocolates to Judy. Instead, he made a big show of presenting them, with his dirty shirts, to Pearl. It was obvious whom he had come out to Sands Point to see. He asked Pearl to show him around the house; he was especially interested in seeing her room, as if it were up to him to pass approval on the way she was being cared for. When he returned to the entrance hall, he was obviously satisfied.

"Some place you bought," he told Joseph. "You've got room for ten kids, never mind the one you're expecting." He walked to the window and looked out over the stable and paddock. "A place in the country, maybe I should buy one for myself. Get away from the rush of the city."

"No one's stopping you."

Leo turned to his mother. "If I bought a place like this, would you spend a few days a week with me?"

Pearl began to laugh. "I've heard of divorced parents sharing custody of a child, but never of sons sharing custody of their mother. I'll tell you what, Leo, you get married and give me grand-children . . ."

Before she finished, Leo turned away to look out of the window again. He was becoming tired of listening to his mother harp on that subject. . . .

After dinner, while Judy helped Pearl clear the table, Joseph led Leo and Levitt into the ground-floor recreation room. There he told them what he had learned from Walter Leinberg in Zurich.

"It comes as no surprise," Levitt said. "I'm afraid that your well-meaning advice to Phil fell on deaf ears, Joseph."

"Did you get any figures on the Waterway while I was in Zurich?"

"It's coming in on budget, not a cost overrun in sight. But what did you expect? Phil thinks we'll have our eyes on that and we'll never notice the rest."

"Almost a one-third share," Leo mused. "He thinks big."

"There is no other way to think," Levitt said, "but he shouldn't think so big when he's handling our money. I'll tell Benny when we see him on Sunday at William's wedding."

"He'll want to take care of Phil right away," Joseph said.

"So he should," Leo cut in.

Levitt looked sharply at the younger twin. "We know what has to be done to Phil. But before we sink him, let's get all the use out of him that we can. Let him put up the Waterway for us, get it running smoothly."

Judy went to bed that night at ten o'clock. When Joseph followed her an hour later, after Leo and Lou Levitt had left to return to Manhattan, he found her sitting up in bed, reading by the light on the bedside table.

"Baby keeping you awake?" he asked.

"No. I was waiting for you." She set down the book and watched him undress. "Your brother acted like I didn't even exist."

Joseph slipped into the bed, barely able to keep his eyes open. The journey to and from Switzerland, the changing back and forth of clocks—it was all catching up on him. On top of that, he had to cope with the knowledge that his information had passed a sentence of death on Phil Gerson. "Don't start now with Leo, darling," he pleaded. "I can't even think straight anymore."

"Joseph, you asked me to accommodate him. I did. The least he could have done in return was treat me with some respect."

"Judy, it's only once a week. You can put up with that, can't you?" He rolled over onto his side, facing away from her.

"Why should I have to put up with it? Joseph, I wanted your mother to live with us. God only knows, she's earned the right to have things a little easier now. But I didn't count on Leo totally ignoring me in my own home." She waited for Joseph to respond. When no sound came, she leaned over him and saw that his eyes were closed, his breathing was slow and regular. He was fast asleep. She snapped off the light and lay awake in the darkness, her fury at Leo mounting. It was not long before it expanded to include Joseph and Pearl as well.

*　　　*　　　*

William Minsky and Susan Mendel were married on the Sunday. Leo had been invited to bring a girl to both the ceremony and the dinner dance that followed. He came alone. When the dancing began, he ignored the single girls who were Susan's cousins and friends in favor of dancing with his mother.

Pearl was both flattered and flustered. "Stop wasting your time with me," she urged him. "There are plenty of pretty girls here. Ask one of them."

"I don't want to ask one of them. I want to dance with you."

"Everyone wants to dance with me tonight. You, Uncle Lou, even your brother because Judy's in no shape to go stepping out."

They bumped into someone. Pearl heard an "Excuse me" and turned to see Benny Minsky dancing with his new daughter-in-law. "How come you're dancing with your mother, Leo?" Minsky wanted to know.

"I just asked him the same thing," Pearl said.

"Susan's got all these cousins sitting around like wallflowers," Minsky went on. He looked at the bride. "Can't you fix Leo up with one of them?"

"He's old enough to find his own girls," was Susan's curt answer. She remembered Leo from the depot, with that other man who had also been invited to the wedding. Harry Saltzman, another of her father-in-law's business associates. She would not want her cousins dancing with either man.

"See, Ma," Leo said. "Only you're anxious about me. You're going to get more gray hairs than you have already."

The two couples separated, danced their way toward different sides of the floor. "You don't think too much of him, do you?" Minsky asked Susan.

"He enjoyed whatever he did that night at the depot. Him and that other man who's here—Saltzman."

"They were doing a job, that's all. A job that had to be done."

"Why couldn't William have gone to the police?" Susan had already asked William the same question; he'd avoided answering.

"The police are only good for writing traffic tickets. When it comes to trouble, we take care of our own." Minsky held his daughter-in-law a little tighter. "You're not thinking you made a mistake, are you?"

She shook her head. "William's not on the same level as those other two men."

"Damned right, he's streets ahead." Minsky's eyes drifted across the floor to where Susan's mother and father sat, surrounded by members of their family. There had been very little mixing of the bride's side and the groom's side, as if each group had recognized the other for what it was and had decided to have no part of it. That was all right. William wasn't marrying the entire Mendel clan, just Susan. "Do your parents know about that night?"

"Of course not. Do you think I'd tell them? I might be able to handle it, but they wouldn't." They danced in silence for a few seconds, then Susan said, "William told me how you got started with B.M. Transportation, converting the trucks you used to run bootleg whiskey."

"A lot of respectable people got started the same way."

"Name one."

Minsky was taken aback. He had expected the girl to accept his statement as absolute truth without demanding that he validate it. Deep lines furrowed his brow as he concentrated. "You ever heard of Patrick Joseph Rourke, a bigshot up in Boston?"

"The old ambassador?"

"That's the one." During the war, Patrick Joseph Rourke had served a short term as the American Ambassador to Ireland, a reward for his staunch support of the Democratic machine in Massachusetts. Minsky remembered the day he'd read of the appointment. Levitt had shown it to him, and they'd both laughed until they ached at the way the Irishman had bent over backward to become respectable. He'd invested his bootleg profits in real estate, buying up huge parcels of land at deflated Depression prices; he had even backed successful Hollywood movies, invested in utility companies, speculated successfully in engineering and automotive plants that surged to full production with the war. He had become a rich and powerful man, with every penny now emanating from a legitimate source.

It hadn't been all roses for the Irishman, though, Minsky thought. Rourke had lost one of his three sons in the war, an armor captain in the Battle of the Bulge; he'd been one of the American prisoners of war murdered by the SS at Malmédy. Minsky tried to remember which son it was. The middle son came to mind . . . Joseph, the same name as the older Granitz twin. "Old man Rourke had a big bootleg operation," Minsky told Susan. "He was the king of Irish whiskey. That's why he got that job in Ireland. All the big shot Micks had dealt with him before."

"Did you know Rourke personally?"

"We did business with him, that was all. What else did my son tell you?"

"Everything."

"Everything?"

"He told me about the bookmaking places you have, about the gambling in those hotels you're building in Florida. He said it was important that I knew everything before we were married."

"Would you rather he'd kept you in the dark?"

"No. I'm not sure how I would have felt if I'd found out later on."

"And how do you feel now?"

"Worried," was the simple answer. "William doesn't have to be involved in things like that. He's exposing himself to unnecessary danger. He can make a success of any business. I've seen what he's done with your trucking company. He could do it with anything."

"I know. That's what puts him one up on the Granitz twins. They just continued something that was already established. William created a business almost from the ground up."

"That's exactly what I mean. So why does he have to be involved in those other things?"

"Just because you're in a straight business doesn't mean you'll have no contact with hoodlums, Susan. You saw that for yourself when those goons tried to muscle in on the new depot. It doesn't do any harm to have some muscle on your own side."

The dance ended, and Minsky returned Susan to William. When he turned away, he saw Levitt beckoning. The men walked from the hall to the washroom. Levitt checked the cubicles to be sure they were vacant. "Leinberg told Joseph that Phil's girl made a deposit in the Dancer account."

"That's it then." Minsky drew a hand across his throat.

"We'll let him finish putting up the Waterway first."

"Okay, Lou. But once that hotel's up, Gerson goes."

"You're glad, aren't you?" Levitt accused Minsky angrily. "I can see that goddamned righteous I-told-you-so look plastered all over your ugly mug."

"Yeah, I'm glad, because you were wrong."

"That makes your son wrong as well, Benny. He also voted for giving Phil another chance."

Minsky's face clouded over at the reminder of William's treachery. "He's entitled to a mistake."

"So am I, Benny," Levitt said, clapping Minsky on the arm. "I don't make that many so I'm entitled to one now and again." He led the way back into the hall; then the two men separated. Minsky went to where his son and daughter-in-law stood while Levitt walked over to the Granitz table.

Midway through the evening, Judy began to complain of feeling tired. She had not enjoyed the wedding at all. The little food she'd eaten had lodged in her chest. The noise and excitement were making her irritable. Most of all she was still angry at Joseph for Friday night when he had stood up for his brother and tried to make her a party to a one-sided treaty of respect. Judy's only bright spot during the evening was her bitter amusement at seeing Pearl trying to persuade Leo to dance with one of the many single girls.

"Joseph, I'd like to go home," she said.

"You feel all right?"

"Tired. The noise and the heat's getting to me."

"Sure." He looked around. "Where's Ma?"

"Dancing with your brother, where else?"

"We'll wait until they've finished this dance; then we'll leave."

Judy derived some satisfaction from that. At least she could take Pearl away from Leo. It was a victory of sorts. When Pearl returned to the table on Leo's arm, Joseph said they were leaving. Leo appeared, momentarily, to be disappointed. Then he shrugged his shoulders and said he might just as well go home, too.

Joseph drove carefully, trying to pick out potholes in the glow of the headlights. He didn't want to jar Judy; with less than two months to go, he wasn't even sure that she should be in a car. In the back seat, Pearl kept up a steady conversation. She'd enjoyed William's wedding, just as she'd enjoyed his bar mitzvah. "Sometimes I feel that William's my third son," she mused. "Now if only Leo would find someone, then it would be three out of three."

"He's not going to find anyone dancing with you all night long," Joseph replied.

"He's too fussy, that's his trouble," Pearl said. "All those girls there tonight, and would you believe there wasn't one he liked?"

"Must we talk about Leo?" Judy asked. "I feel lousy enough without having to listen to his love life being discussed."

"Judy"—Pearl's voice was full of pain—"I thought that was all behind us."

"The hell it is! He comes to my home and treats me like I'm a piece of the furniture."

"Judy . . . knock it off," Joseph warned. "We can work this out without dragging Ma into it."

"Why didn't you try working it out on Friday night instead of turning your back on me and falling asleep?"

"I was tired, Judy. I'd just flown back from Zurich. I couldn't keep my damned eyes open."

Pearl leaned forward to touch Judy on the shoulder. "I'll speak to Leo. I'll tell him that he's upsetting you, all right? Next Friday, when he comes, you'll see the difference."

"Satisfied?" Joseph asked.

"No, I'm not. I'm sick and tired of everyone standing up for Leo by putting me down. I don't know whether he got dropped on his head as a baby or what, but there's something wrong with him."

"Judy, you've got to remember what happened when he was a child," Pearl began.

Judy cut her off abruptly. "The diphtheria? How the hell can I ever forget? Every strange action, every rotten thing Leo's ever done is supposed to have its roots in that damned illness! It wasn't the diphtheria that made him the way he is, believe me! He was born like that!" The last remnant of control fled from Judy, leaving naked anger and frustration. "You want to know why he didn't ask any of those girls to dance tonight, Ma? Do you?"

Joseph flicked his eyes nervously from the road to Judy. He'd never seen her like this before, fury mixed with total abandon—the need to spew it all out smashing aside consideration for anyone. He was terrified of what she was going to say. Of what only she could say! Yet the harder he tried to speak, the tighter his throat became, the drier his lips, the more swollen his tongue. It was all he could do to breathe, let alone speak to interrupt her.

"Well, do you want to know?" Judy demanded of her mother-in-law. "I'll tell you. Leo doesn't like girls. He prefers little boys to girls, and that's the goddamned truth!"

"Judy!" At last Joseph found his voice. His angry roar filled the car as he jammed his foot down on the brake pedal. The car slewed to a stop.

"Judy, darling . . ." Pearl's shocked whisper barely carried from the rear of the car. "Have you any idea of the terrible thing you're saying?"

Judy tried to stop but couldn't. All the poison she'd harbored against Leo spilled out. "I know exactly what I'm saying, and if you don't believe me I'll even give you the address of the apartment on MacDougal Street where he meets his little boys."

"Shut up!" Joseph yelled. "Not another word! We'll sort this out once we get home!"

Judy stared rigidly through the windshield as Joseph drove to Sands Point, his face taut, hands gripping the wheel like a pair of white claws. From behind, Judy could hear Pearl sobbing. Damn it . . . she hadn't wanted to hurt Pearl. She hadn't wanted to hurt Joseph either. But, dear God, didn't anyone give a damn about her?

By the time they reached the house, Pearl had regained some composure. Her face was streaked with tears when she confronted Judy in the entrance hall, but there was a resoluteness in her voice when she asked: "Where did you hear this terrible thing about Leo? Who would spread such a slanderous story?"

"She heard it from some cabdriver," Joseph answered before Judy could say a word. "She had a cabdriver follow Leo one night—"

503

Judy held up a hand for silence. If she was being interrogated, only she would give the answers. To her own surprise, she was icily calm. Finally, the secret she had withheld from Pearl since the previous year was out in the open. "Do you remember when I left your home early one Friday night while Joseph was away?"

"You were ill, or you said you were," Pearl recalled. "I asked Leo to drive you home, and you said you'd take a cab."

"That's right. I found a cab downstairs. I told the driver to follow Leo when he came out of the building. Leo led us to Washington Square. I gave the cabdriver money to follow him when he got out of the car. The driver came back with the information that Leo had gone into a building on MacDougal Street." Speaking evenly, Judy completed the story, right through the point where the driver had imparted his startling news.

Pearl looked at Joseph. "You knew about this already?" Joseph nodded mutely. "Why didn't you say anything?"

"There was no need for you to know."

"No? I'm only Leo's mother, have you forgotten that? Or is it because you didn't believe Judy that you didn't tell me?" Without waiting for an answer, Pearl marched to the telephone in the entrance hall. Joseph asked whom she was calling. "Leo," Pearl answered. "He left the hall when we did. He should have been home half an hour ago." The telephone rang forever in her ear. She replaced the receiver and turned to Judy. "Give me that address on MacDougal Street, the apartment number, everything. I'll get out of this long dress, and then I'll find out exactly what's going on."

"For God's sake, Ma!" Joseph burst out. "It's the middle of the night. I can't leave Judy alone here to take you to the Village."

"Who asked you to take me? I'm perfectly capable of telephoning for a taxi."

Joseph looked beseechingly at Judy. "Tell her that just because Leo hasn't gone straight home, that doesn't mean he's out with some little boy! Will you tell her you made up this whole damned story?"

"Did you, Judy?" Pearl asked.

Judy fervently wished that she could tell her mother-in-law the story was a lie. But she couldn't. "No," she said.

Pearl checked the directory for the number of the local taxi company and made the call. "He'll be here in fifteen minutes," she told Joseph, "and maybe then we'll start to find out the truth."

"What are you going to do once you get to the Village?" Joseph asked his mother.

"Learn the truth." Pearl left the living room and walked up the long, curving staircase to her own room to change.

"Happy now?" Joseph demanded of Judy. "You've got Ma running out in the middle of the night like there's some emergency. What in God's name made you come out with that garbage?"

"I didn't mean to come out with it, Joseph. You know I promised I never—"

"Some promise!"

Judy's anger heightened in the face of Joseph's sarcasm. "If I'd meant to tell her, don't you think I would have done it the moment I found out about Leo? I kept it here"—she beat her breast—"because I *didn't* want to hurt her. Tonight it just slipped out because I was so damned mad. All I ever hear is Leo, Leo, Leo! I'm sick of the sight and sound of him, of always being reminded about his attack of diphtheria when he was a kid and how it's affected him, and how we should overlook his ugliness!"

In Judy's outburst, Joseph heard his own words. Hadn't he said just the same to Leo that night the younger twin had accused him of not caring for their mother? Hadn't he accused Leo of making a career out of having had diphtheria? Using it all his life to get his own way? "Are you sure that cab driver told the truth?"

"You asked me that once before, Joseph. I told you then that the man had no reason to lie."

Joseph reached out to hold Judy's hands. "Then we'd better start figuring out a way to help Ma over the shock when she finds out about Leo for herself."

From the wedding party, Leo went straight to the apartment on MacDougal Street. He had made many changes in the week since his mother had moved to Sands Point. He had transferred some of his clothing from Central Park West to the apartment in Greenwich Village; he'd put food in the refrigerator, stocked the bar. He intended to use the small apartment as a proper second home, not just as an occasional meeting place.

Leo had left instructions for Gustav to come to MacDougal Street at midnight. That gave him enough time to enjoy a leisurely shower, after which he rubbed himself down briskly with cologne and then dressed in a pair of beige silk pajamas and a robe. He poured himself a drink and set a record on the turntable.

At five minutes before twelve, he heard a knock on the door. Setting down his drink, he walked across the living room. Gustav stood outside, tall and slim and platinum blond. Leo's heart leaped as he regarded his visitor.

"Hi, Leo, how was your wedding?"

The voice was the only thing about the youth that grated on Leo. A boy with Gustav's looks, the Swedish name, should speak like a Swede, not with a Midwestern accent. Gustav's parents had come from Sweden, but he had been born on a farm in Minnesota, from which he'd fled at the age of fifteen. "The wedding was boring. I only got through it by thinking of you. What did you do this evening?"

"Saw a movie."

Leo wanted to believe the youth. He didn't want to think that Gustav might have been seeing someone else on the agency's instructions. The only way to forestall that would be to take him over completely. Perhaps tonight he should broach the subject. "Was it a good movie?"

"It was like your wedding. Boring." Gustav's mouth curled in a sly smile. "Like you, I only got through it by thinking of what would come later. Are we going to stand out here talking all night, or are you gonig to invite me inside?"

"Come in, of course come in."

Leo was about to close the door when he heard the sound of footsteps ascending the stairs. Light steps, a woman's, and hurrying. Curious, he swung the door wide open and looked out . . . straight into his mother's amber eyes as she emerged from the stairwell. Leo's mouth dropped in shock. His stomach twisted itself into a tight knot. A confused babble of questions burst from his lips.

"What are you doing here? How did you get here?" And finally, an anguished "Why?"

"What's the matter?" Gustav asked, thinking that Leo was talking to him. Too late, he saw Leo's hand frantically gesturing for him to hide.

Breathless from the climb, Pearl marched up to the door and looked past Leo to see the slim, blond youth. "So it's true," was all she said.

"It isn't what you think—" Leo's voice broke as, without another word, Pearl swung around and walked back toward the stairs.

"Who was that?" It was Gustav's voice.

Leo whirled around. "Shut the fuck up! Get out of here!" He rushed past the startled youth into the bedroom, ripped off the robe and pajamas and clambered into trousers and a shirt. Tugging his belt tight, he raced after Pearl, clattering down the three flights of stairs like a runaway horse. He reached the sidewalk just in time to see her climbing into a taxi.

"Ma! Wait!" Leo's grief-stricken shout echoed along MacDougal Street. The taxi inched away from the curb, then stopped while another vehicle rolled past. Leo grabbed hold of the rear door handle and yanked it open. "Listen to me, will you, Ma? It isn't what you think!"

"What do I think, Leo?"

He reached into the cab as if to pull his mother out. She drew back, for the first time in her life rejecting any contact with him. Leo's hand hung motionless in midair, unable to again reach out to the shriveled figure of his mother in the far corner. "Who told you, Ma?"

"Does it really matter?" She watched as he withdrew from the taxi and closed the door. "Take me back to Sands Point, please," she told the driver. As the taxi moved off, she refused to succumb to the urge to look back.

Gustav was still in the apartment when Leo returned. "What are you doing here?" Leo demanded. "I thought I told you to get out!"

Bewildered, the blond youth refused to leave. "That old broad, who the hell was she?"

Leo smashed him across the face with the back of his hand. "That's my mother! Get out, you little bastard! Don't you see what you've done?"

Clutching his face, Gustav fled.

In the taxi, Pearl sat back quietly. Judy had been right. All those evenings Leo had been out, always refusing to divulge his destination, the names of his friends. And all the time he'd been seeing this blond-haired boy or one just like him. No wonder he'd brought no one to the wedding, ignored the single girls who'd been there, danced only with his mother. Pearl shivered at the memory. What had she done to deserve this? On top of everything else that had happened during her lifetime, why this?

Lights blazed in the house when Pearl reached Sands Point. Joseph flung open the front door the moment he heard the taxi drive up. He helped his mother out and paid off the driver. "Well, did you see Leo?"

"I saw him. Judy was right, he was with a young boy. Is she still awake?"

"I told her to go to bed. She wouldn't."

Judy was sitting in the living room, feet up on a low stool. When Pearl walked into the room, she avoided her eyes.

"Don't look away," Pearl admonished her. "You've done nothing to be ashamed of."

"Following Leo that night, spying on him, is nothing to be ashamed of?"

Pearl took hold of her daughter-in-law's hand and squeezed it gently. "I'd have found out some other way."

"Did Leo see you?" Joseph asked.

"Of course he did. I went up to the apartment."

"What did he say?"

"What could he say?" She let go of Judy's hand and began to walk toward the kitchen. "I'm going to make a cup of tea."

"Just make sure you don't start cooking a six-course meal," Joseph called after her.

Pearl returned to the living room with a tray bearing three cups. No one spoke for a full minute, each of them waiting for one of the others to say something. Finally Pearl broke the silence. "It's my fault, isn't it?"

"How do you figure that?" Joseph asked.

"I spoiled him."

Now that the whole matter was out in the open, Judy could afford to feel generous. "You brought Leo and Joseph up the way you thought was best. Don't blame yourself for this. It would have happened no matter what."

"Is that the truth, Judy? Or is that what you think I want to hear?"

"I believe it's the truth. You're not responsible for Leo's strange behavior. That's just the way he is."

Pearl felt grateful. Judy had suffered more than anyone from Leo's oddness. He'd treated her terribly, accused her of trying to drive a wedge between him and Joseph; he'd made her life a misery, especially after Moe and Annie had died and Judy had become a part of the Granitz family. "Whether I'm responsible or not, Judy, I think it's about time I apologized for the hell Leo's put you through. I never blamed him, and maybe I should have. I always blamed you."

Joseph breathed a long sigh of relief. At least, the immediate family unit had not been damaged. "What are you going to do about Leo?"

"What should I do?"

"While you were out, Judy and I talked it over. No matter what, he's still your son, Ma. He's still my brother. There's no reason—as long as he keeps his private life to himself—for anything to really change."

"If I know Leo," Judy said, "he'll be going crazy right now. He'll be trying to figure out how you learned; that's one thing. But most of all, he'll be torn apart because he's thinking you don't love him anymore. God only knows what he'll do."

"Ma," Joseph said. "I just told you that Leo's still my brother. Speak to him and show him that you're still his mother."

"If he wants to come here to see me, would he still be welcome?"

Instead of answering, Joseph looked to Judy. "Only if you'd want him to come," she said.

"I do."

"Then you'd better speak to him before he does something stupid."

Pearl finished the tea, washed up the cups and went to bed. Before she fell asleep, she decided to telephone Leo the following morning. She would have to learn to live with this as she'd learned to live with everything else that had happened during her lifetime. It was just another obstacle to be surmounted.

Benny Minsky was the last person to leave the hall. He'd waited until the last guests had drifted off into the night. William and Susan had departed an hour earlier, to spend their wedding night in a hotel before boarding the *Queen Mary* the following day for the voyage to Southampton, their first stop on a leisurely tour of Europe from which they would return six weeks later.

He reached Riverside Drive just before one o'clock. Parking the car thirty yards from the building entrance, he strolled along the sidewalk. The air was crisp, one of those gorgeous May nights when the sky was clear and every star visible. Minsky noticed a woman standing concealed in the shadows. Her back was stooped, her clothing shabby. Resting by her feet was a worn cardboard suitcase. Poor bitch, he thought as he felt in his pocket. Some broad down on her luck, probably looking for a handout. Tonight, fate had brought her to the right place. He was in a generous mood, ready to give where as normally he'd ignore a panhandler's approach.

"Here you are, honey," he said, without looking into her eyes. "Get yourself a meal and a place to sleep."

The woman felt a bill pressed into her hand. She looked down and saw twenty dollars, then she lifted her head and stared after Minsky as he walked on toward the entrance and the uniformed doorman on duty there. "Last of the big spenders, aren't you, Benny?"

Minsky stopped dead, turned around slowly. "What did you say?" Four large strides took him back to the woman. He ripped off the scarf that covered her head. Greasy hair tumbled down to the shoulders of her coat. Once that hair had been a shining blond color; now it was a stringy salt-and-pepper gray. "Kathleen? . . ." Minsky murmured.

Heavy footsteps approached from behind. The doorman pushed himself in front of Minsky, picked up the woman's suitcase and started to carry it away. "I told her to hit the road before, Mr. Minsky, when she came asking for you. I thought she'd gone. Sorry you've been bothered."

"Hold it right there!" Minsky rapped out the order. "Bring that goddamned case back here and mind your own business!"

"Whatever you say, Mr. Minsky." Uncomprehending, the doorman dropped the case at the woman's feet and returned to the building.

"Always the gentleman, Benny. Always the gentleman."

Minsky stared into Kathleen's face. It was gaunt and lined; folds of skin sagged at the bottom of her jaw. The green eyes had been robbed of their luster. She looked as though she had lost twenty pounds the hard way, not by dieting but through starvation. "Kathleen, what the hell happened to you?"

"Bad times happened, Benny."

"So you came back to me?"

"I had nowhere else to go."

A million times Minsky had played this scene over in his mind, what he'd do should Kathleen ever return to him. He'd always pictured her as begging to be taken back; that aspect of the scene had never altered. His own reactions had covered a wide spectrum. Sometimes he'd just slammed the door in her face. At other times he'd paid her off, drawn a fistful of bills from his pocket and flung them at her, telling her to use the money to hide herself from him. And just occasionally, he'd been honest enough with himself to know exactly how he would react. No matter how she came to him, how she looked, he'd take her back.

"So you had nowhere else to go," he repeated softly as he picked up her cardboard case. It was surprisingly light, as though it carried little.

"No one wants to know you when you're down, Benny."

"No one but your real friends, baby." He carried the case toward the building entrance. The doorman stared at him incredulously but was wise enough to say nothing.

"You've still got the same apartment," Kathleen said in wonder as Minsky inserted the key in the door. "I thought you would have moved."

"It suited me. Come in." He set down the case on the carpet just inside the door. In the bright light of the apartment, he got his first good look at Kathleen. What he'd seen outside was only a hint of how badly she'd fallen. Bones poked through paper-thin skin. The hands in which she'd once taken such pride were now a pair of skinny claws, the nails dirty and broken. The clothes she wore, expensive when new, were badly worn and fitted her poorly. Barely able to believe that this was Kathleen, Minsky could feel nothing but pity.

Gently he helped her off with her coat. "When's the last time you ate anything?"

"This afternoon, when the bus stopped somewhere in Pennsylvania."

"Bus?" Minsky asked as he walked toward the refrigerator. He and William both preferred to eat out, only kept bare necessities there. He found some bread, cheese, and tomatoes that the cleaning woman had bought. She came in twice a week, stocked the refrigerator as she thought necessary, and cleaned it out when the food started to turn.

"I took the bus from Los Angeles, and I had to beg, borrow, and steal the money for the fare." Hungrily, she watched him start to make a sandwich. "Do you want me to do that?"

"Go ahead, I'll fix some coffee." He found a tin of Nescafé, boiled water

Kathleen carried the sandwich into the living room, where she waited for Minsky to bring the coffee. "How's William?" she asked.

"William?" Minsky stared down at the tuxedo he was wearing. "William got married today, Kathleen—that's why I'm all dressed up like this. I just came from the wedding."

"William . . . married?" Monahan's eyes turned misty. "What's she like, Benny? William's wife?"

"Susan's her name, a lovely girl. You'll see them both when they get back from their honeymoon. They've taken a cruise to Europe. Be back in about six weeks. I'll show you the big house I bought for them in Forest Hills Gardens." He watched Kathleen begin to eat the sandwich. He could feel no animosity toward her. He could not even remember now how furious he'd been during their final fight. It all seemed so stupid. What was that fight really about? He'd wanted to see William bar mitzvahed, and Kathleen hadn't. "What happened with Hal Brookman?"

"Went bankrupt," Kathleen answered between bites. "Long time ago. Invested in a few bad movies. Some of them"—she laughed bitterly—"were even mine. I didn't have it anymore, Benny, but it took us a few movies to find that out. Truth is, when I quit the first time, I should have stayed quit."

"You left him?"

"Hell, no!" A spark returned briefly to the green eyes. "I never got the chance. The son of a bitch left me. I woke up one morning and found he wasn't in the house. Not even a goddamned note. Just the sheriff's men downstairs, come to repossess everything . . . the house, the cars, every damned thing he and I owned."

"Did you ever marry him?"

"No. Maybe that was the only smart move I ever made." She finished the sandwich and took a sip of coffee. Suddenly her face turned ashen. She stood up, looked around wildly as if trying to remember the layout of the apartment. Then she ran toward the bathroom. Minsky followed, watching through the open door as she knelt over the bowl and brought up the sandwich she'd just eaten. When she lifted her head, her face was gray and soaked with sweat. Minsky helped her up, guided her back to the couch she'd been sitting on. She leaned back, struggling for breath while Minsky stood by helplessly.

After a couple of minutes, she felt strong enough to speak. "Maybe I left it too late, eh, Benny?"

"Too late for what?"

"To see William. To tell him I'm sorry."

"I just told you—he'll be back in six weeks' time. Him and Susan, they're on their honeymoon."

Kathleen closed her eyes and let her head drop back onto the back of the couch. Her words were strangled, but their meaning held a startling clarity. "I don't have six weeks, Benny. When they let me out of the hospital—".

"Hospital? What hospital?"

"In Los Angeles. They opened me up, took one look, and closed me again. Cancer, Benny. I'm riddled with it. They think it started as cancer of the stomach or some such thing, and spread. They gave me three months tops then, and that was two months ago."

Minsky's eyes burned with tears. "I'll get you to a hospital here."

Weakly, Kathleen shook her head. "No more hospitals, Benny. No one's carving me up like a Christmas turkey again."

Minsky snapped his fingers. "William and Susan haven't left yet. They're catching their boat tomorrow. They're staying in New York for the night. I know the hotel—I'll call them."

He'd taken no more than two steps toward the telephone when Kathleen called him back. "Benny, I did my best to ruin that kid's life. Don't ruin his wedding night on my behalf, or his honeymoon."

"Don't be crazy, you're his mother."

"Some mother. You think I want him to remember me looking like this? Let him go, Benny. Perhaps if I'm still here when he gets back . . ."

She left the sentence unfinished. Minsky sat down on the couch, wrapped his arms around her painfully thin body. He could smell the sickness. It was on her breath, oozing through the pores of her skin; yet he was not deterred. Despite their fights, despite the way she'd run out on him—and the way he'd treated her!—she was the only woman he'd ever loved. After just seeing William married, that meant even more to Minsky. "Those quacks in Los Angeles . . . did they know what they were about?"

"Benny, it may have been a charity hospital, but the doctors knew what they were doing."

A charity hospital, Minsky reflected bitterly. If Kathleen had stayed with him, he'd have made sure she had the best attention possible. Would it have made any difference, though? Cancer . . .

"Can I stay with you, Benny?"

"Of course you can, baby."

Kathleen gazed around dreamily. "You know, this was the only place where I ever had any happiness. This building. The other apartment I had first, and this place when I played mother for a few years, until that bastard Hal Brookman turned up on the doorstep. You should have thrown him out that first day, Benny. Why didn't you?"

"Because I wanted you out of the way, that's why. It was the only way I was going to get William bar mitzvahed. With you on the West Coast, I could sneak him out for his lessons."

Kathleen's brittle laugh turned to a choking rasp. "Christ, you were a crazy bastard, weren't you, Benny?"

He gave her a big grin, as though she'd just paid him the greatest compliment possible. "You were some kind of a crazy bitch yourself, you know that?"

"How did William turn out? Crazy like both of us?"

"No. He's a good kid, just like I wanted him to be. Like you would have wanted him to grow up." He gazed around the room for a photograph, spotted one that had been taken during the party to celebrate the opening of the Long Island City depot for B.M. Transportation. While Kathleen looked at it, he told her how William had built up the trucking business, adding proudly that he was much smarter than either of the Granitz twins.

"You're all still tied up together then?" Kathleen asked. "You, that half-pint imitation Lou Levitt, Jake, and Moe?"

"Jake and Moe are dead. So's Annie."

"What happened?"

He brought her up to date. "Poor Pearl," Kathleen said when he'd finished. "Everything fell on her. And that poor kid of Annie's, I remember her—cute little red-headed thing."

"Perhaps I turned out to be the luckiest one," Minsky said. "I didn't lose anyone. My wife just ran away, found some fancy Hollywood producer and took off with him."

"She found a jerk," Kathleen countered. "Which shouldn't be so surprising, seeing she was just as big a jerk herself."

Minsky smiled. Kathleen had come back. All he cared about was making her comfortable, making her last days—Christ, it was tough to think in those terms—as easy as he could. He did not believe that she had come to him because she had nowhere else to go. She had come because, when all the cards were dealt, he was the only one she'd ever loved, the only one who'd ever loved her. Funny how forgiving you became as you grew older, as you realized that none of it was really important anymore.

Kathleen took another sip of coffee, swallowing along with it a large tablet which she took from a brown bottle in her purse. "Sleeping pill," she explained when she saw the question forming on Minsky's lips.

Minsky just said, "Oh," refusing to show that he disbelieved her. "Would you like to take a bath?" he asked.

"I'm not sure I could manage."

"Don't worry. I'll help." With a tenderness that surprised even him, he assisted her from the couch to the bathroom. After filling the bath, he undressed Kathleen and helped her into it. The sight of her naked body was like a stunning slap in the face. Once he'd worshiped that body, now he was repelled by it. Her breasts were wizened and sagging like those of a woman of seventy. Livid scars, still fresh from the surgery, crisscrossed her abdomen. Her arms and legs were withered. Only when he saw her naked did Minsky realize exactly how much weight she had lost. She resembled a parchment-coated skeleton.

"Sleeping pill working?" he asked as he helped her from the bath, wrapping a fluffy towel around her spindly shoulders.

"I'd like to go to bed."

"You can have William's room. Do you have a nightgown in that case?"

"Nothing in there but a change of clothes, and I changed them already."

"I'll get you a pair of my pajamas."

Kathleen was asleep the moment her head touched the pillow. For fifteen minutes, Minsky sat by the bed, watching anxiously. Kathleen's breathing was so shallow that her chest barely moved. He clenched his right fist and slammed it into the palm of his left hand. Damn it! Why the hell hadn't she come back to him when she'd first learned she was ill? A charity hospital! That was no place for the star of *Broadway Nell* to wind up. No place for the ex-wife of Benny Minsky, the mother of William Minsky! She should have come back, sought his help earlier on. She should never have waited just so she could return to die in his arms.

At last he stood up and tiptoed from the room. He opened the cardboard suitcase and removed the clothes. Like the ones she'd been wearing, they'd seen better days. Wrapping them in a bundle, he threw them down the incinerator chute. Tomorrow he'd buy her a new wardrobe, colorful dresses that would fit her and help to disguise the aura of impending death. He picked up her purse, opened the clasp and looked inside. The brown bottle of tablets caught his attention. He read the label: the name of a drugstore in Los Angeles, Kathleen's name, pharmaceutical terms he didn't begin to understand, and lastly the directions—one to be taken every four hours, dosage no more than four a day. Sleeping pills like hell! They were painkillers. God alone knew what agony she was going through. Minsky spotted a long white envelope. He opened it and extracted a single sheet of paper. The name of the hospital was on the top; the date was seven weeks earlier. The word *carcinoma* stood out starkly from the rest of the text. Other words—*exploratory* and *not treated*—jumped at Minsky's eyes. He shoved the sheet of paper back into the envelope and snapped the purse shut. Kathleen was carrying her own death warrant around with her.

He walked into William's room and sat down again. After Jake and Moe Caplan had died, Lou Levitt had asked if Minsky appreciated irony—the two men who'd been at each other's throat being the only survivors. What was happening now qualified as irony in its truest sense. William's bed, in which he'd slept until last night, was now occupied by the mother he had not seen for fourteen years. Nor would he ever see her. If Kathleen and those doctors from that damned charity hospital were right, she'd be dead and buried by the time William and Susan returned from their honeymoon in Europe.

Tears started to dribble from Minsky's eyes. He leaned forward, elbows on the bed, head resting in his hands. That was the way he finally fell asleep. . . .

The sound of coughing woke him at seven-thirty. He sat up in the chair, back aching, mouth sour and dry. "Benny . . ." Kathleen's voice was wracked with pain. "Please, get me one of those pills in the brown bottle, a glass of water."

"Sure." He ran from the room, returning moments later with the pill and a glass of water. With one hand he raised her head, with the other he held the glass to her lips. When she had swallowed the pill, he put another pillow behind her head so she could sit up.

"I heard you crying last night, Benny. You were crying in your sleep. Was it for me?"

"Since when have you ever known me to cry?" he asked in return.

She was touched by the way he tried to hide that moment of softness. She'd heard him crying, all right, but if he wanted to deny it she wouldn't push the issue. "You might have improved with age, you

515

bastard, learned a little compassion."

"If I'd turned compassionate, you'd never have recognized me. You want something to eat?"

"Later on, perhaps, when I feel strong enough to get up."

He stood up and walked to the window. "Looks like it's going to be a nice day. I'll put a chair out on the balcony for you. You can watch the river."

"A view of New Jersey's sure to make me feel better."

"You can't be that ill if you can make jokes. Those doctors must have been drunk when they said you were sick."

"I wish, Benny. I wish."

"So do I, baby." As he left the room, he found himself wondering whether Kathleen would have come back to him had she not been ill, not been dying. He shook his head to dispel the notion. It didn't matter what had prompted her to return. The important thing was that she had.

516

Chapter Eight

In the week since moving from Manhattan to Sands Point, Pearl had automatically assumed the responsibilities that fell to the first to rise. She had always awakened early on Central Park West, and moving out to the island had not changed her routine. By six-thirty she was downstairs, listening to the radio playing softly as she made coffee and prepared breakfast. She liked this time of the morning best, when she had the house to herself. She still found the greatest peace in the kitchen. There, among pots and pans, dishes and cutlery—items which had a familiarity that took her back to her earliest childhood days—she could think most clearly.

Both Joseph and Judy had advised her to be forgiving toward Leo. Judy's benevolence was especially surprising to Pearl. If anyone had reason to despise him, it was Judy. Yet she had urged Pearl to forgive. If Judy could feel that way, could Pearl feel otherwise?

At seven o'clock, she heard footsteps coming down the curving staircase. Joseph entered the kitchen. Although he was dressed for work, he would not be leaving the house for another hour and a half. Before the long drive into Manhattan he liked to take a walk with the Labrador he'd bought a few weeks earlier when they'd moved into the house. The serenity of the country setting prepared him for the hectic pace of the city.

Sitting down at the breakfast-room table, he sipped the coffee that Pearl had poured for him. "Have you spoken to Leo yet?"

"I was going to wait until later. He doesn't get up early."

"I doubt if he even went to bed last night, he must have been so shaken up. Stop putting it off, Ma. Get on the phone to him right now."

Pearl went to the telephone and dialed the number of the Central Park West apartment. The phone there rang unanswered. "Do you think he could still be at that other place?" Joseph asked. "With . . . with his friend?"

Pearl shook her head adamantly. "As I was going down the stairs, I

517

heard him scream at the boy to get out."

"Try, anyway. See if he's got a phone installed there."

Pearl called directory. The operator informed her that there was no listing for a Granitz on MacDougal Street.

Joseph finished his breakfast. Judy came down, her woolen robe blossoming out in front of her. "Before you even ask," Joseph said, "Ma hasn't spoken to Leo yet. There was no answer when she tried just now."

"Where is he?"

"That's what we've been sitting here, trying to figure out." Joseph got up from the table and announced that he was going out for his morning walk. He got as far as opening the front door before he came running back. "Leo's coming up the drive. Judy, go back upstairs. I'll slip out the back way, let Ma be here alone."

"Is that safe?" Judy asked.

"What's he going to do to me?" Pearl wanted to know. "Besides, it's better if he thinks no one else knows."

Judy saw the wisdom in that. Carrying her cup of coffee, she climbed the stairs as quickly as her condition would allow. Joseph waited until he heard the slamming of a car door, then the ponderous bang of the heavy knocker on the front door of the house. As Pearl walked from the breakfast room and then crossed the entrance hall, Joseph let himself out of the back door and whistled for the Labrador.

"Leo . . . I've been trying to call you for the past hour," Pearl said.

Leo looked terrible. Huge pouches hung beneath his eyes. His face was heavy with fatigue. A dark sheet of stubble covered his cheeks and chin. He hadn't slept at all. After his mother had appeared at MacDougal Street and Gustav had fled, Leo had remained at the apartment all night, alternately sitting down, then pacing around as he debated what to do. He was living through a nightmare . . . his secret exposed, and the blond boy, of whom he was extremely fond, gone. He had no doubt that Gustav would never return. No matter how much Leo pressured the agency, the youth would never consent to another assignation; getting slapped around wasn't part of the bargain. Leo cursed himself for his fiery temper, and for his stupidity. It was bad enough that his mother had come to MacDougal Street, that she had found out; he should have known better than to lose his temper so violently and blame Gustav for the catastrophe.

Slowly, his self-directed fury at losing Gustav had faded, leaving only the hopelessness of coming to terms with his mother's feelings. He tried to remember every second of the short confrontation, from the moment Pearl had appeared at the top of the stairs to when she'd shrunk away from him in the taxi. She'd pulled away from him when he'd reached out to her as though she'd wanted nothing to do with him. He knew he could cope with the loss of Gustav—there would be more boys—but the withdrawal of his mother's affection was far more heart-wrenching.

As dawn had filled the narrow streets of the Village with dim gray light, Leo had made up his mind to drive out to Sands Point. Pearl must be made to understand that she was accountable. She had created him, designed him. She could not wash her hands of him just because she had discovered something not to her liking. . . .

Leo stood in the doorway. "Why were you trying to call me?"

"I want to talk . . . to discuss last night with you."

He entered the house and walked through it to the breakfast room, noticing Joseph's dirty cup that was still on the table. "Where's Joseph?"

"Outside, walking the dog."

"And Judy?"

"She hasn't come down yet," Pearl lied.

"Do they know?"

"About last night? No," Pearl lied again.

"How did you find out?"

"It doesn't matter, Leo."

"It damned well matters to me. Was it Uncle Lou?" All night he'd debated who'd pointed the finger at him. Never mind that Levitt didn't know about the Village apartment; the little man was still the only person who was aware of Leo's diversions.

Pearl was so astonished to hear Levitt's name thrown at her that she could barely force herself to say, "No, it wasn't Uncle Lou." Why would Leo think it was? That could mean only one thing, and it shocked Pearl even more than learning about what Leo had done.

"Ma . . ." Leo reached out and grasped his mother's arm. Tears burned his eyes as he felt her stiffen involuntarily. "Whoever told you did so for only one reason—to hurt us, don't you see that? To turn you against me."

Leo's impassioned plea brought back to Pearl with stunning clarity memories of the child who'd come running to his mother for support in every crisis. She'd been incapable of refusing him then. This time was different. To give him comfort now would require putting on an act; there would be no heartfelt spontaneity. She tried. "No one's going to hurt us, Leo. No one's going to turn me against you."

Pearl's woodenness was evident to him. "If you really loved me, you wouldn't have listened to stories about me . . . you wouldn't have come down to the Village . . . you wouldn't have sneaked up on me."

"Leo, I do love you."

"Then tell me how you found out."

"It's of no importance."

"I want to know who's trying to hurt us."

"No one is. I wasn't hurt last night—"

"Of course you were. I saw you run away. You wouldn't speak to me, you wouldn't listen to me."

"Leo, I was shocked. How else could I feel? But since then I've done a lot of thinking. I love you, don't you understand that? However you want to live, I'll still love you."

Pearl's tone betrayed her. She might be saying that she could accept what he was doing, but Leo knew otherwise. "You're lying! I can hear that you're lying!"

The outside door to the breakfast room opened and Joseph appeared, with the Labrador tugging at the leash. Joseph had been crouching just below the open window, listening to every word. When he heard Leo's voice rise, he knew it was time to make an appearance. "I thought I heard a car," he said, feigning surprise when he saw Leo. "What brings you out here?"

Leo looked first at his twin brother, then at the dog which bounded toward him as Joseph undid the leash. Jumping back, he pointed a finger at the Labrador. "Get it away from me!"

Joseph snapped his fingers and the Labrador returned to his side. He bent down and rubbed the dog's head. "What's the matter with you? You can't find a more friendly dog than this."

Leo could not take his eyes off the Labrador. "I don't like dogs." The memory of the German shepherd puppy flashed before him— swinging it on the leash and smashing its head against the wall in the alley behind his parents' home. His fear of dogs hadn't abated since then; even a seemingly docile dog like the Labrador terrified him.

Judy chose that exact moment to come down the stairs. She, too, had been listening. "Come to join us for breakfast, Leo?" she asked sweetly.

Leo swung around, flustered. How much had Joseph and Judy heard? If they hadn't known before—if Pearl had told him the truth—did they know now? How much could they deduce from what they must have heard? He turned around, strode across the hall, and went out the front door, slamming it behind him. A minute later, the rear tires of his car spit gravel as he accelerated down the drive toward the road.

"Why would he think it was Lou Levitt who told you?" Joseph asked.

"I'd like to know the answer to that as well," Pearl replied. "Did Lou know all along about Leo's . . . Leo's . . ."

"Homosexuality?" Judy offered. There was no point in avoiding the word.

"If he knew, when did he find out?" Pearl asked. "And why didn't he tell me?" She started to walk toward the telephone. Joseph called her back.

"Don't call him up and ask him."

"Why not? I'm entitled to find out what's going on."

"You're entitled to nothing. However Uncle Lou knew—whenever he knew—it doesn't matter. Can't you see the reason he never told you? If he loves you as you think he does, would he tell you something like that about Leo? Or would he keep it to himself and hope that you never found out?"

"I tried to tell Leo I understood," Pearl mused, "but I couldn't put my heart into it. He knew I was lying."

"We heard," Joseph said.

"I don't understand, I never will." Pearl shook her head. "If anything made him the way he is, it was the diphtheria. That's what made him like this."

Benny Minsky did not go into work that day. He telephoned Lou Levitt at the Jalo office and claimed that he was feeling unwell. Once he'd finished the call, Minsky returned to the apartment's second bedroom to check on Kathleen. She slept peacefully, spared pain by the pill she had taken upon waking.

Leaving a note for her on the bedside table, he went downstairs to his car and drove to Bloomingdales. There he asked a salesgirl to help him assemble a wardrobe for Kathleen. An hour later, laden with bulging bags, he returned to Riverside Drive to find Kathleen just awakening. When she saw the clothes he'd bought for her, she clapped her hands like a small child receiving a birthday gift. She chose a light green cotton dress to wear that day. It hung on her emaciated frame, but she didn't seem to notice. The mere idea of wearing something new and colorful cheered her immensely.

After eating a slice of toast and drinking a cup of weak coffee, she sat outside on the balcony. Minsky left her there while he telephoned a doctor. Kathleen was still sitting outside, looking over the Hudson River to New Jersey, when the doctor arrived. Before taking him out onto the balcony, Minsky showed him the letter he had found in Kathleen's purse, the bottle of pills.

"I'd like to examine Miss Monahan for myself," the doctor told Minsky, "and draw my own conclusions."

Minsky walked out to the balcony. "Kathleen, I've got a doctor here. He'd like to talk to you."

"Talk to me, Benny, or examine me?"

"Both." Minsky didn't meet Kathleen's eyes as he answered. Instead, he looked south along the Hudson, wondering if the *Queen Mary* was making her tug-assisted journey down to the bay yet. William and Susan were out there, listening to the bands playing, watching the streamers arcing from the dock to the stately liner, while only a few miles away William's mother was sitting on a balcony, trying to find some enjoyment in the spring sun as she spent her final days.

"Benny"—Kathleen turned her head to look into the apartment. She saw the doctor standing there, a middle-aged man with a lined, compassionate face—"tell that fucking quack to take his little black bag and shove it up his ass. I don't want anyone treating me like I'm some damned guinea pig. Let me spend what time's left with a little dignity."

Minsky could not argue. He returned to the doctor and relayed Kathleen's wishes. "We can't force her to undergo an examination or further surgery," the doctor said. He wrote down the name of the Los Angeles hospital. "I'll speak to the doctors who attended Miss Monahan, learn what I can from that."

"Thanks, doc." Minsky saw the man out to the elevator before returning to the balcony.

"Benny, I'm sorry. I didn't want to be rude. I know you're only thinking of me."

He rested a hand on her painfully thin wrist. "I know, baby. I know exactly what you mean. Hey, even if you don't want a doctor, how about I hire a nurse to look after you?"

"Full-time?"

"Of course, full-time. What do you think I am—too cheap to get a live-in nurse?"

"Benny, I know you've got to work during the day, but you'll be here in the evening, won't you?" She gazed beseechingly at him, and there was no way he could refuse what he knew was coming. "I don't want a nurse here at night. I want you."

"Okay." He held her hand between his own. "When the doctor gets back to me, we'll see about getting a day nurse."

The doctor returned in the early evening, when Kathleen was asleep. He had spoken to the hospital in Los Angeles, discussed Kathleen's case with the surgeons who had operated. There was, he told Minsky, absolutely nothing to be gained by opening her up again.

All they could do was make her last few days as comfortable as possible. The doctor prescribed a diet that Kathleen would find easy to digest, and when Minsky asked about a nurse, he arranged for one to come the following morning.

"Toward the end, Miss Monahan's pain might become even more acute," the doctor told Minsky. "I'm going to prescribe a steadily stronger series of painkillers. These may, as they reach maximum dosage, render Miss Monahan almost unconscious. She will understand very little of what's going on, which is probably for the best."

When the doctor left, Minsky entered the bedroom and sat watching Kathleen. After half an hour of sitting by the bed, he went into the living room, and dialed the number of the house in Sands Point, where Pearl now lived. Joseph answered.

"Is your mother there?"

"I'll get her for you." Moments later, Pearl was on the line.

"Kathleen came home last night, Pearl. She was waiting outside for me. She came home to die."

"Oh, my God," Pearl whispered, as Minsky related the events of the previous night. "Where is she now?"

"In William's room, asleep."

"Are you going to let her stay?"

"What kind of a question is that, for Christ's sake? Of course I'm going to."

"Have you called a doctor yet?"

"He just left. There's nothing anyone can do. Just a nurse, that's it."

"Do you need anything, Benny?"

"Don't worry, I'll manage." He heard a sound from the bedroom and turned to see Kathleen standing in the doorway; his voice had roused her. "I've got to go, Pearl. I'll speak to you later." He replaced the receiver and looked at Kathleen. "Everything all right, baby?"

"I've slept enough, that's all. Who were you talking to?"

"Pearl."

"Does she know I'm here?"

"She does now." Minsky held out an arm for Kathleen to lean upon, and guided her to the couch. Tonight he'd live on toast and cheese and tomatoes. When the cleaning woman came the following day, he'd get her to fill the refrigerator properly. Maybe he could pay either her or the nurse to prepare meals as well. He'd work it out.

In Sands Point, Pearl rejoined Joseph and Judy at the dinner table.

523

"Kathleen's back. She was waiting for Benny outside his apartment building when he got home from the wedding last night." The ripple of excitement caused by that news abated when she explained Kathleen's reason for returning to Minsky.

"I think I should go over there," Pearl murmured. "Benny has a nurse starting tomorrow, but knowing him there's no food in the place. He won't go out to eat and leave Kathleen alone, so I'll take some of this." She gestured at the table full of food.

"How are you going to get there?" Joseph asked.

"The same way I went into the city last night. By taxi. You stay here with Judy." Without finishing her own meal, she went into the kitchen. She returned with a heavy saucepan, into which she ladled a generous portion of the goulash she'd made for that night. "Call a taxi for me," she told Joseph, "while I put together some more food for Benny and Kathleen."

"Are you doing this to help Benny," Joseph asked, "or just so you can forget what happened here this morning?"

"Both," Pearl answered candidly.

By the time the taxi arrived, Pearl had two shopping bags full of food. She assumed that Minsky had a stove on which she could warm it. "What time will you be home?" Judy asked.

"Whenever I get home. I'm visiting a sick friend."

Joseph handed money to the taxi driver. "Stay with my mother, wait for her and bring her back when she's ready."

Pearl sat in the back of the taxi as it headed west toward Manhattan. She could barely believe that she was taking her second hurried trip into the city in as many nights, first to learn the truth about Leo, and now this. Kathleen coming back! The idea was so impossible that all she could think of was Lou Levitt's prophecy that one day Kathleen would return and Benny Minsky would forgive her for everything. Again the little man had been proven right, but in circumstances he never could have imagined!

The taxi pulled up outside Minsky's apartment house. Reminding the driver to wait, Pearl walked into the building. The doorman was away from his post, so she went straight up to Minsky's apartment and knocked.

"I brought you a few things," she said when Minsky opened the door. "Is Kathleen awake?"

"Sitting in the living room. We're watching television."

"Sounds like an old married couple. May I see her?"

"Come in. Hey, Pearl . . . don't get a shock when you see Kathleen."

"I'll try not to." Despite the warning, Pearl was stunned when she stepped into the living room. Even in the dim glow of a small table lamp and the fuzzy glare from the television, Kathleen had an almost skeletal appearance.

"Hello, Kathleen."

Kathleen rose slowly. "Hi, Pearl. Good to see you."

"Am I interrupting a good show?"

"Nothing I won't miss. You look well. Nearly being a grandmother suits you. Benny told me," she added when she saw Pearl's mystified expression. "He's spent all of today bringing me up to date. I was sorry to hear about Jake, and the others."

"It was a long time ago, Kathleen."

"So was everything."

"What have you got in those bags?" Minsky asked.

"You show me what you had for dinner, and I'll show you what's in these bags."

Minsky took Pearl into the kitchen. A couple of crumb-spattered plates lay in the sink. "I made us some toasted sandwiches."

"Bread and cheese? For God's sake, Benny, no one can live on that." Pearl hoisted her bags onto the counter and started to take out the food. "There's goulash in this saucepan, vegetable soup in that one. Put them both on a low light. Here's some salad—"

"Pearl, I've got a nurse starting tomorrow. She can cook."

"That's tomorrow. First you've got to eat today."

"I'm glad you came," he said. "I hoped you would."

"Are you going to tell Lou about Kathleen?"

"I'm not in the mood for his sarcastic little speeches right now."

"I think he'd be sympathetic."

"I don't." Minsky was sure that Levitt would use Kathleen's return as a weapon with which to avenge himself for the humiliation of being wrong about Phil Gerson; Lou wouldn't be able to resist squaring the score. "If I haven't even told William—and I could have gotten word to him before the *Queen Mary* sailed—why should I bother telling Lou?"

"Different reasons. You don't want William to see Kathleen like this. You don't want to ruin the boy's honeymoon. With Lou, you're frightened that he'll get a laugh out of it, Kathleen coming back and you doing everything for her. He won't laugh. He's not like that."

Despite Pearl's assurances, Minsky was not so certain. Perhaps Pearl could recognize qualities in the little man that Minsky had never seen; but then, he reminded himself, she saw him from a different perspective altogether.

Pearl remained at the apartment for an hour. Minsky ate the goulash. Kathleen was able to get down only a cup of soup. At nine o'clock, when Kathleen's eyelids began to droop, Pearl decided it was time to leave. Minsky saw her downstairs to the waiting taxi. "Pearl, you don't know how grateful I am that you came."

"Could you imagine me not coming?"

"You must have been some kind of mother to the twins."

"You're turning out to be some kind of an ex-husband to Kathleen. Don't forget, if you need anything just let me know. If I can't get into town, I can always send it with Joseph."

"We'll be all right. You know, Kathleen really appreciated your visit. I think she looked on it as being forgiven, not just by me but by everyone. If you can find the time to come over again—"

"I'll be back, Benny." Pearl climbed into the cab, returned Minsky's wave of farewell, and gave the driver directions. Instead of returning to Sands Point, she told him to take her to the apartment building in which she'd lived until eight days earlier. While in the city, she had other errands to run.

Again, the driver waited while Pearl entered the building on Central Park West. Instead of going to her old apartment, however, she went to the floor below. There, she knocked on Lou Levitt's door. It was a chance call; she didn't know whether he'd be home or not.

He was.

"Pearl, what are you doing here all by yourself?"

"Making the rounds. May I come in?"

"Of course."

She stepped inside. Levitt's home had the same feel as the apartment she'd just left, that of a place cleaned by a woman whose only incentive was money. There was something missing in such clinical cleanliness. "I just came from Benny's place," Pearl said.

"What were you doing there—taking care of him because you heard he was sick today?"

"He wasn't sick. He was nursing a sick friend."

"Benny doesn't have any friends."

"How would you describe Kathleen then?"

"Kathleen?" Levitt threw back his head and roared with laughter. "What rock did she crawl out from?" Pearl told him the story and he continued to laugh. "What did I always say, Pearl? Didn't I tell you that one day she'd come back, and that mug would be eating out of her hand again? Didn't I say it?"

"You said it," Pearl agreed softly.

"What about his son? Did he go on his honeymoon?"

"Benny never told him. He didn't want to wreck the boy's trip."

"Considerate of him."

"Maybe you could learn a lesson, and show some consideration as well. Right now isn't the time to laugh at Benny's misfortune."

Isn't it? Levitt thought. He's ready to rub my nose into it over Phil Gerson, and I shouldn't make fun for being a jerk all over again? "What were you doing at Riverside Drive?"

"Benny called me with the news. I went over to see if I could help."

"Patron saint of waifs and strays . . . nothing changes. Is she really dying?"

"If you saw her, Lou, you wouldn't have to ask such a question." She gazed steadily at him for several seconds, plucking up the courage to go against the well-intentioned advice of Joseph and Judy. "Talking of questions, Lou, I've got one for you."

"Fire away." He was still smiling about Kathleen.

"It concerns Leo."

Amusement disappeared; tension took its place. "What about him?"

"Have you known all along that Leo's . . ." Words failed Pearl as she tried to think of a gentle way to describe her younger son.

Levitt offered no help at all. "Leo's what?"

"He's not right, not well. He . . . he goes out with men," she finally blurted out.

"Where did you hear that?"

"It's of no concern where I heard it. I just want to know if you were aware of it. You were, weren't you?"

Should he lie, try to protect Pearl from the truth when it was obvious that she already knew it? "I knew," he answered simply.

"For how long?"

"A few years."

"How did you find out?"

"Like you told me, it's of no concern. And before you ask why I didn't tell you, the answer's simple: one, it was none of your business what Leo did; and two,"—he reached out to hold her—"I didn't want to see you hurt, Pearl."

"I wasn't so much hurt as I was shocked, disgusted. But now, seeing Benny with Kathleen, it's made me take a second look at myself. If Benny can forgive Kathleen for what she did—"

"I always told you he would."

Pearl was glad to see that Levitt's attitude had changed. No longer did he sound as if he were enjoying Minsky's misfortune. "If Benny can forgive, then I can. Leo came around to the house early this morning—I found out last night, you see—and I think he wanted some sign from me, some words that indicated I understood, and I could pardon him. I couldn't give him those words this morning, Lou, but now I think I can."

"Before you go, Pearl, what made you think I knew?"

"Because he asked me if I'd learned from you."

"Are you angry that I didn't tell you?"

"No. You did what you thought was in my best interest. You always seem to."

"Go upstairs and see him."

Pearl climbed one floor. As she walked along the corridor, she heard music coming from the old apartment. Since moving out, she hadn't been back, and she wondered what changes Leo had made. The obvious one was that he'd moved the phonograph out of the bedroom into the living room.

She had to knock twice before Leo heard the sound above the roar of the music. Annoyed at the interruption, he flung open the door and stared, bewildered, at his mother. "Ma! Why are you here?" He looked up and down the corridor, expecting to see Joseph.

"I came alone, Leo. I want to talk to you. About last night . . . and this morning."

"I thought you'd said all you had to say."

"I've had time to think since then." She walked past him. Inside the apartment, the music was deafening. "Could you turn that down, Leo?"

Leo rejected the record. Silence returned to the apartment.

"Well?" he asked.

"Leo, I'm sorry about this morning. I had a big speech all prepared for when I saw you again . . . how I understood . . . that I'd love you come hell or high water . . . that whatever you choose to do is your own business. When you just turned up this morning, I hadn't had the time to rehearse it."

He stared stonily at Pearl, offering no help.

"Perhaps if we'd been alone, just you and me, I could have made you believe me."

"You sounded like you didn't believe a word of it yourself."

"It was hard for me to, Leo. What you were doing was something completely outside of my world."

"You demonstrated that pretty clearly. Your tone was enough—you didn't have to spell it out for me!"

"But that was this morning, Leo, only a few hours after I'd seen you in the Village. I needed time to adjust."

"You've adjusted now?" Leo sounded dubious.

"I had to make a choice. Either accept you as you are, or lose you. And you know I don't want to lose you. Leo, you're my son, just as Joseph is, and I love you both equally. It doesn't matter to me what you do, don't you understand that?"

Leo was quick to notice that Pearl's voice carried more sincerity than it had that morning. Something had happened to his mother. He had no idea what. All he knew was that she'd been turned around, made more receptive to his way of life. It was time to plead his case. "Ma, there's nothing wrong with loving another man."

"There's never anything wrong with love, Leo. It's hatred that injures people, not love."

"I tried to keep it a secret, Ma, because I do love you. If I'd told you myself, ages ago, would it have been easier for you?"

Pearl didn't answer immediately because she was uncertain how to reply. Benny Minsky's forgiving attitude toward Kathleen had opened her eyes. If she hadn't seen that, the wall between herself and Leo would still have been just as high, just as unscalable. "You just said it yourself, Leo. You didn't want me to know because you loved me. But now that I do know, it doesn't make me love you any less." She gave him a gentle smile. "Now . . . can you forgive me for what I did last night?"

Leo's answer was to reach out and hug his mother. Of course he could forgive her. She was still the most important person in the world to him.

Early the following morning, a nurse came to care for Kathleen. Minsky stayed in the apartment until eleven o'clock, when he was satisfied that the woman was capable. After kissing Kathleen goodbye, he drove to the B.M. Transportation depot in Long Island City, where he would fill in for William.

At midday, Pearl telephoned to ask how Kathleen was. Minsky reported that when he'd left, Kathleen had been sitting out on the balcony, while the nurse prepared lunch.

Thirty minutes later, Minsky had a surprise visitor. The temporary secretary who was filling in for Susan knocked on his office door. "There's a Mr. Levitt here to see you. He doesn't have an appointment."

Minsky was startled. Levitt never came out to Long Island City. Any business between the two men was always conducted at the Jalo garage.

"Is this a social call, or business?" Minsky asked Levitt, once he'd been shown in.

"Social. Got time for lunch?"

They drove, in Levitt's car, across the Queensborough Bridge and down to the Lower East Side, stopping outside Ratner's on Delancey Street. As they seated themselves at a table, Levitt said, "Pearl told me about Kathleen."

Minsky felt both angry and distressed. Had Levitt taken the time to drive all the way down here just to poke fun? So help him, if that were the case Minsky would commit murder right there in Ratner's, right in front of the waiter who was placing a basket of onion rolls on the table. "So she told you . . . so what?"

Levitt ignored the hostility. "Pearl said it was doubtful that Kathleen would still be here when William got home. That's tough. Look, Benny, I know you're stuck with minding the store while William's away, but if you want to take time off to be with Kathleen, I'll cover for you."

Minsky stared blankly across the table. "What do you mean?"

"I don't need to be over on the West Side. Joseph and Leo have got it down pat. If you want, I can stand in at the truck depot for you."

Finally, the impossible dawned on Minsky. Levitt was feeling sorry for him. In all the years he'd known the little man, Minsky could not recall him pitying anyone. He'd thought no kind of emotion was etched into his character, only a sharp brain that did not pander to the feelings others might have. Out of the blue, Levitt had learned about sympathy. "What's with the sudden change, Lou? I'd have thought you'd be the last person to care about Kathleen."

"Maybe we're all getting a little older, a little wiser. I never disliked Kathleen, Benny. I just thought she kept getting in your way. You weren't strong enough to draw a line between where infatuation had to end and work had to begin."

"But was I wrong? Did she have a great voice that time down in the Four Aces?"

Levitt laughed. "You were right. I just didn't have it in me at the time to understand how any man could get so messed up over a woman like you did."

"Now can you understand it . . . now that you're a little older, a little wiser?"

"I'm still not sure." Levitt dropped the subject while the waiter took their orders. Then he resumed. "What's going to happen after it's all over?"

Minsky stared gloomily at the basket of rolls. "After the wedding, on the way home, I was thinking about buying a place out in Queens, near the house I got for William and Susan. Now I'm not so sure. Maybe I'd like to get clean away for a while, out of town. William can run the trucking company, and you don't need me on the other side."

"How would you like to run a couple of hotels?"

"Down in Florida? The Monaco and the Waterway?"

"Someone'll have to—once Phil, well, you know."

Some of Levitt's sympathy rubbed off on Minsky. "Lou, you want to let him off the hook, perhaps I'll go along with it."

Levitt shook his head. "That wasn't why I came to see you today. The decision's already been taken regarding Phil. It's irrevocable. Someone's going to have to take his place, though. You think you can handle it—two hotels?"

"Florida," Minsky mused. "Yeah, it might be a good idea at that." It would be something to tell Kathleen when he returned home that night. Talking about a move to Florida would momentarily lessen the harshness of the days that lay ahead for both of them. Even if it was only Minsky who would be making the move.

For four weeks, Minsky's hopes regarding Kathleen remained on a level plateau. He had not expected her to improve—barring a miracle, there was no possibility of that—but he was delighted to see that she had not weakened further. At the beginning of the fifth week, however, Kathleen's condition suddenly deteriorated. No longer able to eat light foods, she became incapable of keeping anything down, and she complained constantly of pain. The drugs prescribed by the doctor seemed to have little effect. The dose was stepped up. The pain decreased, but so did Kathleen's awareness of her surroundings. Like a zombie, she sat out on the balcony, eating nothing, barely recognizing the nurse or Minsky. When Pearl came to visit in the evenings while Joseph stayed at home with Judy, she was a total stranger to Kathleen. Once Kathleen even mistook her for the nurse and said: "Are you going to give me another pill?" Pearl left the apartment, barely able to hold back tears.

Levitt came to the apartment just once with Pearl. Kathleen didn't seem to remember him at all. Neither his name nor his uniquely short stature meant a thing to her. She just smiled vacantly at him when he asked how she felt, and then answered, "I feel kind of tired, Irwin. Do we have to rehearse that number again?"

Levitt glanced at Minsky and Pearl. Kathleen's confused mind had mistaken him for Irwin Kuczinski. She could remember events from the past, but the present escaped her. Very gently, he rested his hand on hers. "Not if you don't want to, star."

"Thanks, Irwin." She looked out over the Hudson again, her green eyes following a barge as it made its way up toward the George Washington Bridge.

Minsky went back inside the apartment with Pearl and Levitt. "I was thinking she'd still be here when William gets home in ten days' time. All of a sudden, I'm not so sure. And even if she were, would I want my son to see his mother looking like this?"

Pearl had never seen him so distraught. He appeared as though he would burst into tears at any moment.

"I'd better take Pearl home," Levitt told Minsky. "She's got a very pregnant daughter-in-law to take care of."

That night, Kathleen didn't sleep at all. Despite the drugs, she lay awake, constantly crying, in pain. Minsky sat on the edge of the bed, cradling her in his arms, burying her face in his chest so that her screams would not be so strident, so heart-rending. When morning came, and Kathleen lay sobbing weakly, Minsky telephoned the doctor.

"Those pills aren't working worth a damn, doc. Haven't you got anything stronger?"

"I've prescribed the strongest safe dose, Mr. Minsky. Anything above that might kill her. Her body is in no shape to withstand more powerful medication."

"Anything stronger might be an act of mercy," Minsky grated.

"No, Mr. Minsky. It would be murder."

When the nurse arrived, Kathleen had finally fallen into a sleep of utter exhaustion, but she tossed and turned on the bed as her body responded to the pain that tore through her. "She was awake all night," Minsky told the nurse. "Those drugs aren't doing the trick anymore. I spoke to the doctor; he said anything more powerful might kill her."

"Have you given her anything yet today?"

"At seven o'clock this morning, just before she fell asleep. You can see and hear for yourself all the damned good it's done."

"You know, Mr. Minsky, it might be easier on Miss Monahan, and on yourself, if she were moved to a hospital for—"

"For her last days?" Minsky shook his head vehemently. "Nothing doing. She's not going to get better, so why the hell should she be taken away from me? Why should I have to drag myself up to some hospital ward to see her die when she can pass away with a little dignity right here?"

The nurse had no answer.

At midday the doctor visited the apartment. Kathleen was still asleep. Rather than wake her so he could conduct another examination that would tell him nothing he did not know already, he left her undisturbed. After speaking to the nurse, he took Minsky aside.

"I understand that the nurse suggested Miss Monahan be moved."

"You understand right, and my answer's still the same. If she dies—*when* she dies—it'll happen right here. Get it?"

"It's your decision."

"Damned right it is. Look, doc, I'm sorry. I just want to do what I think is best for her. Can you understand that?"

The doctor regarded Minsky sympathetically. "I think I can. Should you need anything, should you change your mind, please call me."

"I will." As Minsky escorted the doctor to the door, a firm resolve began to grow within him. The doctor couldn't help anymore. No medical person could. Even God couldn't help, because if God cared a damn he would never have let this terrible illness befall Kathleen. God had washed his hands of her, just like he washed his hands of everything. In the long run, mercy was left to man himself.

The nurse, as she did every evening, left promptly at six o'clock. Kathleen was asleep again, painkillers and sleeping pills giving her a temporary relief. Minsky sat watching her for a few minutes before picking up the telephone. He called Pearl out at Sands Point. After answering her inquiry about Kathleen with a curt "No change," he asked whether she had intended to visit them that evening. When she said yes, he suggested that she forgo the journey. "She's sleeping right now, Pearl. It's best that no one comes. That way she won't be disturbed, and she might sleep right through the night."

"Are you sure there's nothing I can do, Benny?"

"Nothing, Pearl." His voice softened. "I appreciate everything you've done so far, and Kathleen does too. She might not have seemed to recognize you these past few days, but I'm sure she did."

As Pearl replaced the receiver, all she could think of was the chilling finality that had underridden the softness of Minsky's voice.

Kathleen slept until midnight. Minsky was dozing in the armchair he'd dragged into the bedroom when her cries woke him. He sat up, startled. She was calling his name and looking at him. "What is it, baby?" he asked, after rushing from the chair to the bed. "What do you want?"

"Hold me tight, Benny."

He wrapped his arms around her and squeezed tenderly, scared that any greater pressure would snap her bones like twigs. He could feel her heart pounding, lungs laboring to bring oxygen to her failing body.

"How long is it until William gets back from his honeymoon?" she asked.

She understood what was going on around her! She remembered that William was away! Minsky was elated until he comprehended the reason. She was overdue for another of the painkillers the doctor had prescribed. She had exchanged the slight relief from pain that the drugs afforded her for clarity of mind. It was evident that she was in agony. Should he give her another pill? Or should he try to soothe her pain with caresses while he formed a mental bond with her?

"How long, Benny? How long before he gets back?"

"Seven, eight days." He wasn't sure anymore.

"I'm not going to make it, am I, Benny? I'm not going to be around to say welcome home to William."

"Sure you are, baby. If I have to carry you, you'll be down on that Cunard dock to give him one of the biggest, happiest surprises of his life." Yeah, some surprise, he added to himself, seeing his mother looking like a survivor of a hunger strike.

"You're full of shit, Benny. You never could lie worth a damn."

"*I* couldn't lie worth a damn? What makes you think you ever did better?"

She moved her head back and forth knowingly. "Every lie I ever told you, you believed. You were the easiest peron in the world to tell a lie to."

"Oh, yeah? Give me one example."

"Remember that sapphire necklace—the one I said I got from my mother?"

"The sapphire necklace I threw out of the window?" Minsky started to laugh. That had been the night of the double wedding—Jake to Pearl, Moe Caplan to Annie. Minsky's eyes had been riveted on the necklace all evening long, for he'd been certain that he hadn't given it to Kathleen. "Then I threw all your clothes out of the window as well, didn't I?"

Kathleen's body began to tremble. For an instant, Minsky was terrified, until he realized that, like himself, she was laughing. "And I pulled your gun from its holster—"

"And damned near blew my head off, you crazy bitch. Remember how I held you out of the window?"

"I really thought you were going to drop me. You were a mad bastard, Benny, you really were. And look at you now, as gentle as can be."

He kissed her forehead. "What's all this got to do with you getting away with telling me lies?"

"That sapphire necklace—it wasn't from my mother."

Minsky was in a dilemma. Should he admit to Kathleen that he knew, tell her the truth? Or should he just go along, pretend that he'd been taken in? Which alternative would be most beneficial to Kathleen?

"When you held me out of the window and I still yelled that it came from my mother, then you believed me, didn't you?"

"I never thought you'd have the guts to lie when you were a split-second away from being dropped on your head from five stories up."

"Guts had nothing to do with it, Benny. If I'd told you the truth"—her voice grew weaker as if she were finding all this talking, all this remembering, tiring—"you'd have opened your goddamned hands right away."

"The truth? That David Hay gave it to you?" The name sprang to Minsky's lips.

"David Hay . . ." Kathleen's body went rigid. For a moment Minsky feared that he'd gone too far. Then she asked, "How do you know about David Hay?"

Minsky chuckled. "That night Jake smashed up the car, remember? I was supposed to go down to the Jersey shore that night, but I didn't. Instead I went to the club where you were singing—"

"I was at the King High that night."

"You've got some memory. I went there but I missed you, and when I tried your apartment you weren't there either. So I figured something wasn't kosher and I waited. When that fancy chauffeur brought you home, I followed him. And that's how I found out about David Hay and his big palatial joint out on Long Island."

"Were you mad?"

"Damned right I was mad. I didn't know who to go after first, you or that rich creep Hay. So much for lying to me, eh?"

Kathleen's eyes slowly opened wide as she understood the implications of Minsky's smug confession. "Benny, just after that David disappeared. He went out riding. His horse came back but he didn't."

"I remember. I saw the story and his picture in the newspaper. I even pointed it out to you, just to see what your reaction was."

"What did I do?"

"You taunted me. You had the nerve to ask me if I recognized Hay as the same guy who threw you a rose that night. And then I taunted you right back by asking if he was the guy you were seeing behind my back. Was that why you remembered him, I said, because he'd given you the necklace?"

"Benny, it was you, wasn't it?"

A wide smile spread slowly across Minsky's dark face. "David Hay wound up as breakfast, lunch, and dinner for the fish off the south Jersey shore. One shot right through the heart while he was out riding."

Kathleen began to laugh again. "And I thought . . . oh, God, I thought he was so upset about me kissing him off that he just ran

535

away somewhere."

"You'd split up with him when I—?"

"When you killed him? Yes. We'd had a huge row. I'd told him he wasn't man enough to wipe your ass!"

"Oh, baby, and all the time I figured that your punishment would be wondering what had happened to him! And you couldn't have given a damn! Oh, Christ, if ever two people were meant for each other, it was us." He held her with his left arm, while his right hand clasped the pillow, drew it slowly toward himself. "I love you, Kathleen, you know that, don't you? I don't think I ever really stopped loving you."

"I love you too, Benny," she replied as he brought the pillow up and pressed it to her face.

At first she struggled. Minsky had no idea how long suffocation was supposed to take. In a healthy person it would require a few minutes at least. Kathleen wasn't healthy; she was a corpse looking for a grave. He wanted it to be over immediately; he didn't want her to suffer any more than she had already.

Gradually, Kathleen's body relaxed in his grip. Weakened by her battle with cancer, her heart could not stand the additional strain of being deprived of oxygen. Tears fell freely from Minsky's eyes as he replaced the pillow on the bed and set Kathleen's head upon it. For half an hour he sat looking at her.

At last, he stood up and walked to the telephone. "Doc, it's Benny Minsky. Sorry to call so late but I just looked in on Miss Monahan. I think she's gone."

536

Chapter Nine

The *Queen Mary* docked on the morning tide. Minsky was waiting to collect William and Susan, and drive them to their new home in Forest Hills Gardens. During the journey, the returning honeymooners excitedly told him of their trip. Minsky listened and occasionally nodded. His own news would keep until they were at the house.

"Susan, while you're unpacking I'm going to take William down to the depot," Minsky said once they'd arrived. "We'll be back in an hour or so; then I'll give him the rest of the day off."

"Keep him for as long as you like," she answered cheerfully. "I've got to get some food in the place."

Instead of driving toward Long Island City, Minsky headed in the direction of Glendale. "Where are we going?" William asked, puzzled.

"You'll see." Minutes later, they entered a cemetery. After parking the car, Minsky walked toward a newly opened section of the burial ground. Mounds of damp earth were piled high by open graves that waited to receive their occupants. At one graveside, a mourning party stood with heads bowed as a priest conducted the burial service.

"What are we doing here?" William demanded. "We're supposed to be at the depot."

Minsky held a finger to his lips before pointing to a freshly filled grave. There was no stone yet, just a modest wooden stake on which was written: Monahan/Minsky. "Your mother's resting there."

"My *mother?*" William went to the grave, knelt down to get a closer look at the stake. "When did this happen? How?"

"She came back. On the night you and Susan got married, your mother came back to me. She was ill, she'd come home to die."

"*Before* we left? Why didn't you get in touch with me? You knew where I was."

"Your mother wanted it this way," Minsky answered. "I was going to call you—she wouldn't let me. She said she'd made a mess of your childhood, she didn't want to wreck your honeymoon as well."

"What was the matter with her?"

"Cancer of everything. She found out about it in Los Angeles. Too late."

William picked up some of the earth, sifted it through his fingers. "Why did she come back to you? Because she still loved you?"

"I guess." There was no point in telling William about Hal Brookman or about Kathleen's dire financial straits; let him think his mother died a respectable, self-sufficient woman. "And I still loved her."

"When did she die?"

"A week ago. She died in your bed."

William brushed away a tear. "You know, all these years the only memory I've had of my mother is that last fight between the pair of you. And now . . ."

"Now what?"

"Why the hell couldn't she have lasted another week so I could have seen her? She came to you looking for two things—some love in her last days, and forgiveness. I think she would have wanted me to forgive her too."

"I told her you forgave her, William," Minsky said to his son. "Believe me, she went knowing that her own family loved her, and that was the most important thing in the world to her."

William climbed to his feet, dusted dirt from his hands, and started to walk back toward the car. "Are you going to stick around in that apartment?"

"For a while, then I'll be moving down to Florida."

William was surprised. "Why?"

"To run those two hotels. You don't need me up here, so why should I put up with crappy weather anymore?"

"It's still going on with Phil, is it?"

"Yeah. The smart Harvard boy's too damned dumb to take a hint."

William returned to the car in silence. He'd come back from six weeks of love and tenderness to find his mother dead and a death warrant drawn up for someone else. Welcome home.

A week after the return of William and Susan, Judy gave birth to a boy. The baby was named Jacob after Joseph's father. Although delighted that Jake would be remembered through his grandson, Pearl could not help sounding a note of caution.

"Is Jacob such a good choice for a name?" she asked when she went with Joseph to see Judy in the hospital.

"What's wrong with it?" Judy asked.

"What happens when you get mail that's just addressed to J. Granitz? How will you know who it's for?"

Joseph started to laugh. "We'll just do what we've always done. Judy'll open all the mail, no matter who it's addressed to."

Although tired from her ordeal, Judy found the strength to wrench the pillow from behind her head and throw it at him.

In the first week of September, the Waterway Hotel in Hallandale opened. Unlike its sister hotel, the Monaco, which had gone two million dollars over the original estimate, the Waterway came in on budget.

Lou Levitt and Benny Minsky traveled down for the opening of the Waterway. With the coming winter season, the two men knew that both hotels would be competing with each other, but there was more than enough money to go around. Gamblers were a superstitious lot. They'd lose at one casino and think their luck would change if they tried the other one. Levitt, especially, blessed the superstitions and systems of gamblers. Without them, he knew he'd be little more than a bookkeeper.

The first night at the Waterway, the casino was packed. Standing with Minsky, Levitt looked with satisfaction at the busy tables. When Gerson walked by, he pulled him over. "Glad to see Belinda's here tonight. Her absence was a bit conspicuous when the Monaco opened, especially after all the work she put into the place."

"She knew that if she missed this opening, there wouldn't be another one." Gerson looked hard at Minsky. "You happy now that this place came in on budget?"

"I'm happy," Minsky growled in reply.

"Well, I'm not. You made me sacrifice class for a few bucks. Look at this place—it looks like any other hotel that's going up nowadays. The Monaco reeks of class, and this joint looks like Hilton threw it up."

"If the customers aren't complaining," Minsky said, "why should you be?"

"Any imbecile can build a place like this. Only innovative talent can put up a class hotel like the Monaco."

"Innovative talent and a complete disregard for the damned budget, you mean," Minsky shot back.

"Still think I was skimming off the top, do you? Cooking the books?" Gerson had been in touch with Leinberg again; the banker had assured him that there had been no inquiries about him. He was confident that neither Levitt nor Minsky knew the truth. They might

539

suspect . . . but suspecting and knowing were two entirely different things. "Joseph came down here and handed me that line of crap a few months ago. I almost told him to take the damned project and shove it. What gives you the right to treat me like I'm some kind of cheap crook, after all the time and effort I've put into working for you?"

Levitt raised a placating hand. He understood Gerson's thinking. Reassured by Leinberg, he was capitalizing on injured innocence. "Phil, we made a mistake, okay? Everyone's entitled to make a mistake now and then. We got sore because of those gigantic cost overruns and we just grabbed at the most obvious reason. It was the wrong reason, and we're sorry."

"How sorry?"

"You've got nerve, you know that?" Minsky said. "You stick us with a two-million-dollar cost overrun on the Monaco, and when you bring this place in on budget you expect some kind of a special reward. This is what we're paying you to do. This is why we're picking up the tab on all your little luxuries down here."

"You still sailing around in that boat?" Levitt asked.

"Maybe one afternoon a week, when Belinda and I can take time off."

"That's a big boat, isn't it?"

"Sleeps six," Gerson answered proudly.

"An afternoon trip in a boat that size must be like using a Caddy engine to run a lawn mower," Levitt said, baiting the trap.

Gerson dropped right in. "Belinda and I keep planning to take a proper voyage on it, go to the Bahamas for a few days. We just haven't had the time."

"Take some time. You deserve a break." Levitt looked around the crowded casino, spotted Belinda in a long evening dress. She was watching one of the blackjack games. He called her over. "Sorry you got deprived of your shopping trips this time around."

Belinda regarded him coldly. She hadn't forgotten how Joseph had come down to spread the word that she and Phil Gerson were suspected of helping themselves. "You still think we've been dipping our fingers into your money?"

"We've just been through that with Phil. No, we don't think you've been robbing us. If we did, you wouldn't be operating this place now."

Gerson stepped in quickly. "Honey, Lou's just offered us a few days off, a chance to get away to the Bahamas. What do we do—take it, or stand here arguing about some misunderstanding that belongs in the history books?"

Belinda wasn't sure. While she and Gerson were away, what would happen? Would others be brought in to fill their places? No, the idea was ridiculous. She and Gerson had nothing to fear. The New York men were in the dark. "Let's take it."

"Stay around for a few days," Levitt said, "until the first weekend is over. Take off on Monday. Benny and I'll come back down to cover for you."

"Just remember," Gerson said, his confidence riding high, "that there's a world of difference between these two casinos and the back room of a club in Pearl's mother's basement on Second Avenue."

"We'll manage." Levitt touched Minsky's arm, and the two men walked away. They left the casino, but instead of going down to their rooms on the floor below they went to the parking lot. They drove north, eventually stopping outside a small, shabby hotel in Fort Lauderdale. Walking through the lobby, they banged on the door to one of the rooms.

"Harry, it's Lou. Open up."

Held by a chain, the door cracked open and Harry Saltzman's left eye appeared. Recognizing his visitors, he unhooked the chain and pulled the door wide open. The moment it was closed again, Levitt said, "It's all set up for Monday."

Saltzman rubbed hairy hands together. "It'll be a piece of cake. I'm going to need help, though. I can't control the boat and do the other things at the same time."

"You want Leo?" Levitt asked.

"Can Leo handle a boat?" Minsky wanted to know.

"Leo'll be fine. He knows what it's all about."

"You sure you know Phil's boat?" Levitt asked.

"I drove along the other side of the Intracoastal and eyeballed it pretty good. I even took some pictures. Are you guys staying on down here?"

"No, we're going back tomorrow. We'll come down again on Sunday. Anything you need?"

Saltzman gave both men a crooked smile. "Nice weather. Get the ocean to be like a sheet of glass that day. Not a ripple in sight, let alone a wave."

"I'll try to arrange it," Levitt said as he left.

On Saturday afternoon, Leo drove his car to the airport and left it in the parking lot. Removing a small suitcase from the trunk, he waited. Fifteen minutes later, Joseph drew up and removed a suitcase from the trunk of his own car. Together, the twins made the journey from the parking lot to the terminal. There they separated. Leo checked in for the internal flight to Florida. Joseph, passport in hand, checked onto the transatlantic flight to Switzerland.

Harry Saltzman met Leo when he arrived in Florida and drove him to the small Fort Lauderdale hotel. Maps were spread across the floor of Saltzman's room, and both men got down on their hands and knees. Leo watched intently as Saltzman's thick finger traced a route. "Phil and his girlfriend are going to be coming out of this inlet. We'll be waiting here, scanning the inlet for them. Once they come out and head east toward the Bahamas, we'll just tag along, maybe a mile away. We don't do anything until we're at least ten miles out, with no other boats around."

Leo felt an excitement begin to burn within him as he listened to Saltzman's plan. "How did you get the boat?"

"I hired it for a few days, nothing suspicious about that."

"Where did you learn to sail?"

Saltzman sat down on the floor and laughed. "Everyone from the old days can take a small boat out into the open sea. How do you think we used to bring in the booze? Magic? Snap our fingers and make it fly through the air from outside the territorial limit?"

"I forgot," Leo said.

"All I want you to do is hold the wheel and keep us on a steady course. I'll give you some practice at it when we go out tomorrow. If you don't think you can do it, let me know now. There's still time to get someone else."

"I can do it," Leo answered confidently.

"Good, because if you screw up, we'll never see hide nor hair of Gerson and his girlfriend again. That boat they've got can outrun everything but a Coast Guard cutter, and it carries damn near enough fuel to get them to Timbuktu. We're only going to get one chance, and we've got to use it."

On Sunday, while Saltzman and Leo practiced on the hired boat, Levitt and Minsky returned to the newly opened Waterway Hotel. Levitt carried nothing more than a small valise. Minsky had come prepared, with two large cases. When this was over, Levitt would be returning to New York. Minsky would not. Florida was about to become his home, and he looked forward to the change. Kathleen's death had soured him on New York. Even with William and Susan there, the grandchildren he was sure he'd have one day, he no longer wanted to live in the city.

That night, a tremendous thunderstorm smashed in from the west. Rain lashed down at crazy angles. Crashing explosions of thunder shook the windows of the Waterway, and lightning lit up the land for miles around. Gamblers left the tables to stand at the windows and watch.

"Will this take care of your boat ride?" Levitt asked Gerson.

"These things pop up all the time during the summer and early fall. They're usually afternoon or nighttime affairs. By morning, when Belinda and I leave, it'll be clear."

Levitt looked at his watch; it was past ten. "You'd better get away then, make sure you're awake enough in the morning to sail in a straight line."

"Thanks for standing in for me." Levitt's hand was perfectly dry and cool as Gerson shook it. It was the handshake of a man you could trust with a million dollars.

Levitt watched Gerson and Belinda walk into the special elevator that served only the casino. He didn't dwell on the fact that he would never see Phil Gerson or Belinda Rivers again; he had blotted them from his mind already.

Downstairs, Gerson and Belinda ran through the rain to their car. "How much do we have put away in Switzerland?" Belinda asked as Gerson drove away.

"Close to two million, maybe just over."

"Don't you think it's time to cut and run?" Belinda still was unsure about the future. With both hotels up, was Gerson really needed anymore? He'd gotten them into operation, set up the infrastructure. It would be easy for someone else to step in now.

"You worry too much. We're going to have a few lazy days on the boat, a great time in the Bahamas—and who knows, I might even come back and tell Lou that he should open a place in Freeport as well. If you think these politicians and cops are easy to bribe, wait until you see their Bahamian cousins."

"For Christ's sake, Phil, how many millions do we need to steal? How many before it's enough?"

"Don't use that word, Belinda," Gerson said angrily. "I'm not stealing a dime. What I'm taking from those two scrooges is rightfully mine. Without me, they'd have nothing."

They went to bed the moment they reached home. Outside, the rain continued to lash down, spilling from the tiled roof in waves. The noise was a stimulus, a swirling current with which to time their lovemaking. Tomorrow, under a baking sun, they would make leisurely love on the boat. Tonight, to the metronome of rain and thunder, they made love as though they were competing in a race.

Morning dawned clear and dry. While Belinda cooked bacon and eggs, brewed coffee, Gerson ran a check on the boat. At seven o'clock, they cast off from the dock at the back of the house and headed along the Intracoastal toward the inlet and the ocean.

From half a mile out to sea, Harry Saltzman trained a pair of high-powered binoculars on the mouth of the inlet. Boats emerged in rapid succession as weekend sailors took advantage of the fine weather. Suddenly Saltzman gripped the glasses tightly. "There she is."

"Let me see." Leo took the binoculars from Saltzman. Gerson's boat jumped into clear focus.

"Let's go." While Leo continued to watch Gerson's boat, Saltzman opened the throttle and moved further offshore. His intention was to keep a mile between himself and the bigger boat. Gerson might also have binoculars. Should he sweep the area with them and spot Saltzman or Leo, he'd know immediately what the score was.

"Stay out of sight, Leo," Saltzman ordered. "If he gives us the once-over, he'll just see me at the wheel. And with this"—he pulled a white cap down low over his forehead, shoved sunglasses onto his face—"he shouldn't be able to make me."

For more than an hour the game was played. Gerson's boat, with Saltzman and Leo always a mile ahead, ploughed steadily eastward. Soon, the morning rush of boats out of the inlet was left far behind; no one else was making the Bahamas run. Saltzman scanned three hundred and sixty degrees with the binoculars until he saw nothing but Gerson's boat. He throttled back, turned the wheel to bring the boat around. The distance between hunter and prey lessened.

On the bigger boat, Gerson noticed the maneuver and thought nothing of it. Obviously a weekend sailor who had reached his limit, or a fisherman who'd found a good spot to drop his line. "You see that boat?" he said to Belinda. "That's the kind of tiny thing we'd own if we hadn't helped ourself. Instead, we're flying high in this fancy craft."

"We don't own this one either," she reminded him. "It comes with the lease on the house."

Gerson laughed. "One of my earliest lessons at Harvard. Own only what appreciates in value—everything else you lease and let someone else carry the depreciation. Come over here and give me a kiss."

She stood next to him, both arms around his bare chest. Despite the heat, neither of them was sweating. The brisk breeze off the ocean kept them dry. She dropped her lips to his neck, then his shoulder and finally his chest, nibbling at the skin beneath the fair hair. Her left hand strayed down to the front of his shorts.

"Hey, I'm trying to steer this damned thing!" he protested.

"Let it steer itself for a while."

544

"You want to give the people on that boat a front-row seat?"

"We're in international waters. There aren't any laws here." The notion of making love in the gently rocking boat—in plain view of others—excited her. Her hand moved to the waistband of Gerson's shorts, tugged them down.

"I'm steering!"

Holding him with her left hand, she used her right to cut the engines. "Now you've got nothing to steer," she said triumphantly. "From now on,"—she felt him grow harder in her hand—"any steering's going to be done by me."

Half a mile away, Saltzman watched in amazement through the binoculars as the upper halves of Gerson and Belinda disappeared below the rail. "Leo! Quick, come and take a look!"

"What?" Leo put the glasses to his eyes. "Where the hell are they?"

"Where do you think? They've stopped in midocean to knock off a quick one." He adjusted course to bring them directly toward Gerson's boat and instructed Leo to take the wheel. "Just keep it steady."

While Leo maintained course, Saltzman crouched down and inspected the six capped one-quart bottles he'd placed on board that morning. Each was filled with a mixture of gasoline and paint—the gasoline would explode and burn, the paint would make the flames stick. He unscrewed each cap and inserted a long rag, shaking the bottles to wet the wicks. This was going to be easier than he'd expected. If he'd known they were going to stop dead in the middle of the sea to tear off a piece, he wouldn't have needed Leo. He glanced quickly at the younger twin. That would have been robbing him of a high experience, though. Saltzman understood Leo, knew he reveled in this kind of work. Saltzman had seen that at the B.M. Transportation depot. Like himself, the younger twin appreciated the qualities of fire. It was cleansing; done properly, it left no clues.

Finished with the wicks, he stood up. Only two hundred yards separated the two boats now. Saltzman pulled a Zippo from his trouser pocket, took it to the other side of the boat, and flicked the wheel. "Move a fraction to port so we come up alongside them." Leo turned the wheel until Saltzman said, "Enough." The small boat was now on a course that would take Saltzman and Leo to the starboard side of Gerson's boat.

Gerson heard the steady thud of an approaching engine and started to lift himself from Belinda. She clung to him voraciously, refusing to let him go. Her legs were wrapped tightly around his thighs, her arms crushed his ribs. "Let them watch!" she hissed. "Let them take pictures if they damned well want to. Kodak'll never dare develop them."

"Anyone home!" a voice yelled across the water.

"Shit!" Belinda swore as Gerson eased himself out of her grip. She lay back on the deck, feeling the sun bathe her body as Gerson stood up. Then she started to laugh. "Put some clothes on! Look at yourself!"

Gerson glanced down at his erection. He grabbed a towel and wrapped it around his waist before turning his attention to the small boat. "What do you? . . ." The question died as he recognized Saltzman standing by the rail, a bottle in one hand, the Zippo in the other . . . and Leo at the wheel. "Belinda! . . ." Gerson screamed.

"Got a case of the hots for each other?" Saltzman yelled across ten yards of water. "Here's a little something to keep the fires burning." The firebomb arced across the intervening space to explode on the rear deck. With machinelike precision, Saltzman lifted the next, lit and threw it, and the next and the next, raking the boat from bow to stern with the six bombs. As the last one left his hand, he roared at Leo: "Hit it!"

Leo gunned the throttle. The bow of the smaller boat lifted. Wake spilled out; its speed increased. Saltzman stood in the stern, watching in satisfaction as fire engulfed the larger boat. Through the flames he saw Belinda, hands beating furiously at her blazing hair, dive screaming into the sea. Of Gerson, there was no sign.

Four hundred yards away, Saltzman yelled, "Cut!" Leo killed the engine and came back to the stern to stand alongside Saltzman. A booming explosion tore through Gerson's boat as the fuel tanks went up. Pieces of flaming debris soared into the air, whirling like broken windmill blades to land, sizzling, in the sea. The two men watched impassively until, with a dying wheeze, the boat went down. Then they changed course and headed back toward the coast.

Leo and Saltzman were at the airport by the time a Coast Guard cutter spotted floating debris in the early afternoon. When the story of the sinking—"Probably a fault in the fuel system," a Coast Guard spokesman explained—made the news broadcasts, both men were halfway to New York.

The following morning, notices were sent to everyone on the staff at both the Monaco and the Waterway—hotel workers and casino employees. It is with great regret, the notice read, that Palmetto Leisure Development Corporation has learned of the tragic death in a boating accident of its chairman and chief operating officer, Mr.

Philip Gerson. Effective immediately, Mr. Benjamin Minsky will assume all responsibility for the day-to-day operation of both hotels.

As the notices were received and read, it was early afternoon in Zurich. Joseph Granitz had spent the entire morning in his room at the Hotel Savoy Baur en Ville, waiting for one phone call. Finally it came. The message from Levitt was short—go about your business.

Immediately, Joseph walked along the Bahnhofstrasse to Leinberg Bank, entered through the side door, and rode the elevator up to the third floor. In the bank's boardroom, he sat across the table from Walter Leinberg and told the bank president:

"Dancer is closed. Please see to it that all funds are transferred to Blackhawk."

BOOK SIX

Chapter One

The period following the birth of her grandson was the happiest time Pearl could remember since Jake had been alive. She felt that she had a purpose in life again, helping Judy to care for Jacob, bathing and dressing him, spoiling him at every opportunity. She experienced a supreme joy as he passed those red-letter times on a baby's calendar: first smile, first word, first step. It seemed to Pearl in those first two years of Jacob's life that nothing could make her happier. She was wrong. Her happiness increased a thousandfold when Judy became pregnant again.

In 1957, when Jacob was three, Judy gave birth to a daughter, a tiny, wrinkled bundle with a thick thatch of bright red hair. Pearl laughed the first time she went to the hospital with Joseph to see her granddaughter. "Little doubt whose child this is, is there?" she said to Judy. "Or who her grandmother was." She placed a finger in the baby's hand and felt tiny fingers grip with surprising tightness. "Have you and Joseph decided on a name yet?"

"Anne," Joseph answered. "We're going to name her Anne after Judy's mother . . . Anne Granitz."

"Another red-headed Annie," Pearl said, and made a horrified face. "God help us all."

Soon, the house in Sands Point, which Pearl had feared would be too big, too echo ridden for just Joseph and Judy, was filled with the nonstop noise of running feet, the shouting and laughter of young, exuberant voices. Pearl had her hands full helping Judy to cope with two normally boisterous youngsters who played and fought and constantly raced beneath her feet, but she would have had it no other way. Life, with its perpetual reversals of fate and fortune, had turned full circle to smile again on her.

Another source of pleasure for Pearl was William Minsky's family. William and Susan also had two children, both boys—Mark, a year older than Anne; and Paul, a year younger. William's sons were the closest Pearl's own grandchildren would ever come to having cousins.

Judy was an only child—there would be no cousins from her family—and there seemed little chance of Leo ever marrying. Pearl was pleased that such a strong friendship existed between the two young couples. The Minskys were frequent visitors to Sands Point, as were the Granitzes to William's home in Forest Hills Gardens. Sometimes, Benny Minsky would be in New York for a short visit from Florida, where he continued to operate the Waterway and Monaco hotels, and Pearl was always delighted to see him as well. She had reached a stage of her life in which contentment came easily, and she was grateful for it.

Contentment, yes . . . except when she thought about Leo. The younger twin still caused Pearl to worry. Time and again she asked herself if she would be so concerned if he were . . . were normal. Then she would become annoyed at herself for thinking of him as abnormal. Years after telling him that she could accept him whatever he wanted to do, however he wanted to live, she could still not bring herself to fully understand the manner of life he had chosen.

Pearl's anxiety about Leo was not eased when he bought a house out in Scarsdale. In the Central Park West apartment, he'd had Lou Levitt living below him. In Scarsdale, Leo was by himself. Pearl understood why he'd bought the house. He'd been impressed with the home Joseph and Judy had bought in Sands Point, and he'd wanted to prove that whatever his twin brother had, he could also have.

Several times Leo drove Pearl out to the house in Scarsdale, and she always left thinking the same thing—although it was not as large as Joseph's, the house was still far too big for one man to live in by himself. Especially a man who did not appear to have many friends. Leo's entire social life, as far as Pearl could ascertain, centered around a cinema he'd had built into the basement of the house. He would sit for hours watching old Bogart and Cagney movies, and then watch them again, speaking the dialogue with the characters, affecting their tough-guy accents.

"Leo, you can't spend all your time hidden away here," she protested one Sunday afternoon as she watched *White Heat* with him. "It's not healthy."

He chuckled at her concern. "Ma, all week long I work hard. I'm out on the streets for Uncle Lou and when the weekend comes I need some rest."

Pearl took advantage of the moment to ask another question, a far more searching one. "Now that you're living here in this beautiful house, do you still keep that apartment on MacDougal Street?"

Leo's gaze left the screen. Deep within him an angry spark glowed. He still needed to know who had turned his mother against him that time, who had wanted so badly to hurt her and him. It was unfinished business. Just as quickly his anger disappeared. "No, I don't keep the place on MacDougal Street anymore." As an expression of relief appeared on his mother's face, he added, "I moved uptown. I keep an apartment on East Fifty-ninth Street now."

Pearl turned her eyes to the screen. She was sorry now that she had asked. Sometimes ignorance was bliss. Even partial ignorance . . .

The start of the 1960s saw a long-held dream turn to reality for Pearl. To celebrate her fifty-fifth birthday, in November 1960, Lou Levitt arranged to take her out to dinner. Pearl, who had intended to commemorate the day by cooking a small family dinner at home— "After all," she'd said to Judy after Levitt's invitation, "who celebrates turning fifty-five?"—was mystified by the sudden invitation, even more so when Judy and Joseph pushed her into accepting the dinner offer.

"Maybe being fifty-five won't seem so terrible if you're with someone who's just as old," Joseph told his mother. "You ever think of that?"

"And did you ever think you're so big that I still can't give you a slap across the behind?"

"Have dinner with him," Judy pressed. "You'll enjoy being taken out more than you would cooking for us all—that's no special day for you."

Suddenly their motive became clear to Pearl. Levitt was going to propose to her again. And he had roped in Joseph and Judy to set it up for him.

Levitt came to call for Pearl on the evening of her birthday, a Saturday. As she opened the door, he kissed her on the cheek, said "Happy birthday," and handed her a small, gaily wrapped package.

Was this the ring? she wondered as she accepted the gift. Wasn't he even going to wait until the candlelit dinner was over, until the gypsy violinists had packed up their instruments and gone home? Stop it, she told herself. She didn't even know where he'd made reservations for dinner. How did she know there'd be candlelight and violinists? Probably there wouldn't. Levitt wasn't the overtly romantic kind.

"May I open this, Lou?" she asked.

"Why do you think I gave it to you? And while you're opening it, may I come inside? In case you haven't noticed, it's pouring out here."

She looked past him to see rain bouncing off the hood of his car. "Come in, I'm almost ready."

"Fine. I'll go talk to Joseph while you finish off."

Pearl stared at the package. He'd given her a ring and then walked away. She undid the wrapping to discover a flat, square box. Fingers trembling, she opened it. There was no ring inside, just a narrow diamond bracelet with a tiny card—"One stone for every year. Love, Lou." She ran after him into the living room, where he was talking with Joseph and Judy. "Thank you, it's beautiful."

"Next year I'll get you a bigger one."

"Where am I going to wear something like this?" she asked, slipping the bracelet onto her wrist and showing it to her son and daughter-in-law.

"Maybe it's time you started hitting a few of the high spots again," Levitt suggested.

"After dinner tonight," Joseph said, "go dancing with Uncle Lou."

"Oh, sure," Pearl answered sarcastically. "Can you imagine your fifty-five-year-old mother doing the wild and crazy dances the kids do nowadays?"

"We'd probably be able to find some place that plays old-time music," Levitt said. "Maybe a joint where you have to knock on the door and be admitted through some secret password. You know . . ." He lowered his voice to a growl and, in a rare flash of humor, added, "Charlie sent me."

Pearl smiled. Those had been the days.

As they left the house, Joseph and Judy saw them to the door. "You make sure you look after Ma," Joseph called out to Levitt. "You treat her like the lady she is." Levitt waved back, and Pearl was even more certain that he had another package in his pocket, another piece of jewelry. The bracelet had been part of the sell; the clincher would be the ring.

Pearl's suspicions were strengthened by the seeming sentimentality that began to overtake Levitt as he drove. "Mind if we go for a ride before we eat? I'd like to look around the old neighborhood."

Pearl gestured at the wipers swishing across the windshield. "You could have picked a nicer day."

Levitt's only answer was a gentle smile. Once he reached New York, he headed south along the FDR. Soon, they were driving on Houston Street, and then north along the first few blocks of Second Avenue. He pulled up outside a restaurant. "I wonder if they've got a club going in the basement, Pearl."

She stared at the door. Two dark-skinned men came out and ran toward a parked car, the collars of their jackets up against the rain. As the door closed slowly behind them, Pearl looked into the restaurant. The counter was still there, so were the booths, but the restaurant looked greasy and she wouldn't want to eat there. Remembering the wonderful food that had once been cooked on the premises by her mother and herself, she felt a wave of sadness sweep over her. Rain streaked the window, but she could discern the gaudily written menu card stuck behind the glass.

"I made cabbage *borscht, lockshen kugel,* and *latkes* . . . now they make hamburgers, french fries, and hot dogs. And look at those prices, Lou! Where do they get the *chutzpah* to charge such prices?"

"If you could have gotten those prices thirty years ago, we wouldn't have needed the club, would we? Or the books, or anything else."

They drove to midtown and entered an Italian restaurant close to where Seventh Avenue met Central Park South. Levitt told Pearl it was a restaurant he dined at frequently when he was alone; the fare was good, and it was within walking distance of his apartment. Pearl recalled walking past it when she had lived in the area, but she'd never been inside. The atmosphere was that of a family dining room, tables crowded together, diners who ate and talked simultaneously, waiters who bumped chairs without apologizing. It wasn't the kind of place where Pearl would expect to hear a marriage proposal.

She never got to hear one. Levitt's talk continued along the same sentimental lines as on the drive in from Long Island. She had to strain to hear him above the Saturday-night turmoil of the restaurant.

"I thought you'd get a kick out of seeing the old restaurant," Levitt said. "I knew you hadn't been down there for years."

"I didn't get a kick so much as I felt sad, Lou. I had beautiful memories of that place, except for when—"

He reached out to cover her hand with his own. "Your mother. I understand."

"But what they've done to it! Hamburgers and french fries." Genuinely outraged, she shook her head and made a disgusted face.

"And the prices," Levitt urged. "Don't forget the prices they've got the *chutzpah* to charge."

Her outrage vanished. Leaving her hand lying beneath his, she gave him a fond smile. "Did I really sound like my mother then, worrying about prices and money?"

"A little. Like I said, if you could have charged those prices, we wouldn't have needed the club in the basement, the books, anything. Pearl . . ." His hand tightened around her own. "The clubs were the first things to go when Prohibition bit the dust. And now the books have gone as well."

"What?" She could not keep the shock, and pleasure, out of her voice. Then the worry. "How did it happen? The police? . . ."

"No, not the police, although there are going to be a lot of cops who'll miss their weekly paychecks. We closed them down, that's all. Started about three months ago, phasing out one area after the other.

Joseph and Leo were sworn to secrecy. I didn't want you to know anything until the operation was complete."

"Lou, you don't know how wonderful that news is. I never thought—"

"That we'd close them? It was time, Pearl. We made a fortune out of those places, but there are other ways to go now."

"What ways?" she asked fearfully.

"Legal, respectable ways. One . . ." Levitt touched his left index finger to the thumb of his right hand. "Ever since Castro kicked everyone out of Cuba, there's been a lot of activity in the Bahamas. We were never in Cuba, Pearl, just as we were never in Vegas; the competition was too cutthroat. But we're moving into the Bahamas."

"We?"

"Benny and I, the twins, William. The Minskys and the Granitzes are still partners when it comes to gambling. We're moving into legitimate casinos. England's another place we're investing. They've got legal casinos springing up there—"

"Since when?"

"This year. They passed some law called the Gaming Act. Now they've got aboveboard places. Gaming clubs, the Limeys call them. Got a lot more class than the Vegas places—much smaller, dress codes—and to play there you've got to be a member."

"Do these London casinos make a lot of money?"

"Not as much as the places in the Bahamas will make, or even Florida. They're just a solid, silent investment."

Pearl considered the information. It had all come so abruptly that it took a while to digest. No more bookmaking, no more New York gambling. Levitt and her twin sons had become international. Did that mean that Joseph and Leo would be traveling often to those faraway places? Well, the Bahamas weren't that far away, but London certainly was. She voiced the question and Levitt shook his head.

"We're silent partners there, Pearl. We just put up the money and we take what we're given."

"What will Leo and Joseph have to do all day long?" She couldn't see them retiring at thirty-three. "The Jalo Cab company isn't enough to keep them busy—that runs itself anyway."

"There is no more Jalo Cab company." Levitt's face was wreathed in a big grin. He was obviously enjoying all the surprises he was springing on Pearl this evening. And she . . . she had thought that he was going to ask her to marry him! "At least, not as far as we're concerned. We sold it. We don't need the premises upstairs any longer, so why do we need the cab company?"

For some reason, that news caused sadness to Pearl. It took her several seconds to comprehend the reason. "Jake's name was a part of that company. Now it's like a tie with him is dead."

"I'm sorry. But if it'll make you any happier Joseph and Leo won't be sitting around doing nothing. Benny Minsky's boy, William, has his trucking business. Now the twins have got a business as well. Real estate. Granitz Brothers. Joseph can finally use that education he got. Now, how much more respectable can they be than that?"

"Where's the money coming from? Zurich?"

"Where else do we get such good rates?"

"You mentioned the London gambling clubs won't make as much as the Bahamas or Florida. Does that mean that you're continuing with Florida?"

"For the time being. It's a class operation. Besides, it makes Benny feel like he's important, being down there, running the places."

At the moment, Pearl was not concerned with Minsky. She sat back, her meal forgotten. The hubbub in the restaurant seemed to die; the interruptions by the waiters went unnoticed. The twins in real estate. Granitz Brothers. The books gone. And everything had been hidden from her. There had been a conspiracy to keep her in the dark about what was taking place until Levitt could present it as a *fait accompli*. From a lifetime of flirting with the law to total respectability. Well, almost. The only vestiges in the United States of the Granitz and Minsky families' unconventional past would be the two casinos in Florida. Levitt wanted those kept in operation. Not for Benny Minsky's sake, Pearl was certain of that. Nor was it for money. He wanted them kept as a memento of the old days. Although respectability might have its value, nostalgia also merited a place.

She didn't realize she was smiling until Levitt said, "Does that big grin on your face mean you approve of what's been done behind your back?"

"I was thinking, that's all. You know, Jake made a boast once . . . a lifetime ago . . . when you and he and Moe and Benny started buying into legitimate businesses. He said that not only would the twins own the clothing manufacturers who made their suits, but also the mills where the cloth was spun. Now that boast has come true. The only pity is that Jake's not here to see it."

"Pearl, you really think he doesn't know?"

"I'm sure he does."

As they left the restaurant for the return journey to Sands Point, Pearl felt sorry for Levitt. It was still raining, and after seeing her home he would have the long, lonely drive back to Central Park West, just walking distance from where they'd eaten. "Why don't you let me take a cab, Lou?"

"You heard what Joseph said to me as we left the house—that I should treat you like a lady. A gentleman doesn't let a lady take a cab home."

Pearl sat back, thinking about the birthday gift from Levitt, and what she'd originally believed it to be. She began to laugh. "Lou, you're going to think this is crazy, but the way you asked me out tonight, for my birthday, and the way Joseph and Judy pushed me into going with you when I just wanted to make dinner at home—well, I thought you were going to ask me to marry you tonight."

The moment the last words were out, she clapped a hand to her mouth, scarcely able to believe what she'd said. Her eyes moved sideways to see how Levitt was reacting.

He remained expressionless, eyes fixed on the road. "And instead I laid the big secret on you. Are you telling me that you're disappointed because I didn't ask you?"

"When I first thought that was the reason for the invitation, all I could think about was that no man in his right mind would ask a fifty-five-year-old woman to marry him. I never thought about being happy over the possibility or not."

"If I had asked you, Pearl, how would you have answered?"

"I don't know, Lou, and that's the God's honest truth."

"Pearl, many's the time I've thought about it. I've even got a ring at home. I was going to give it to you on the night—"

"That Joseph got married?"

Levitt looked startled. He swung his eyes off the road and stared incredulously at Pearl. "How the hell did you know that?"

"I guessed. And then that thing happened with Leo, where he ran away and you had to get him out of trouble."

Christ, Levitt thought, did I ever get him out of trouble that night! "A lot of times I've considered getting that ring out, dusting it off."

"Why didn't you?"

"Maybe I couldn't take another refusal. You turned me down twice, Pearl. Once before you married Jake, and again shortly after he died."

"Neither time was opportune."

"No, they weren't. And that third time, on Joseph's wedding day, when Leo pulled his number, I just figured that perhaps I was being given a message. I realized that you loving me—"

"I do love you."

"Let me finish. You loving me and being in love with me were two totally different things."

"Lou, I love you like a friend, like I loved Annie. It took me a long time to realize the difference as well." She saw an opportunity to

555

gently switch subjects. "You know, I often worry about you being all alone in that apartment. What if something happens one night? God forbid that it should, but just supposing? Who would know?"

Levitt had considered the same possibility himself, in those infrequent moments when he'd looked inward. He could fall ill and who would know until it was too late? "I'm not alone, Pearl. I've got a family. Your family. I get as much joy out of them as you do."

Too many memories had flooded through the gates tonight. First, the sight of the restaurant on Second Avenue. Jake's boast about being respectable. Levitt's proposals. And now this, which brought up the strongest memory of all. "Lou, do you still think they're yours?"

"The twins? Only God knows that, Pearl."

"I didn't ask if you *knew*. I asked what you *thought*."

"Yes. I still think Leo and Joseph are mine."

They drove the remainder of the way in silence, as if Levitt's admission had killed any contact between them. Only when they pulled into the driveway of the Sands Point house did Levitt speak. "Pearl, I'm sorry if the big surprise wasn't what you were expecting. I hope it didn't ruin the evening for you."

"It made the evening for me. I've dreamed for years of the day when all those places would be closed down. I'm just wondering if it's going to feel any different to be the mother of a couple of real-estate magnates."

"You mean you loved them less when they were just in the gambling?"

"No, I'd have loved them no matter what they did. You, too," she said quickly. "I'd have loved you just as dearly if you'd have kept on running a crap game beneath my mother's restaurant. Lou . . ." She reached out a hand to him. "I want you to know that if that apartment ever gets too lonely, there's a guest wing here where you'd be welcome to stay. I'm sure Joseph and Judy would welcome you as a tenant."

"Thanks, I'll remember that, Pearl." He leaned across the car to kiss her good night, watched as she walked quickly up the stone steps and swung back the door.

Levitt drove slowly back to Manhattan. He pulled up outside his apartment house on Central Park West but instead of entering the building, he walked south through the rain to a newsstand and purchased the early edition of the following morning's Sunday *Times*. He didn't feel at all sleepy; he might as well just sit up and read.

He turned to the week-in-review section, scanned through those stories which had made news during the previous seven days. Much of the emphasis was on the general election which had recently taken place. His blue eyes followed the lines of type automatically, taking in

556

details of Congressional and Senate victories. He hadn't taken much interest in the election at the time. Now, with a need to do something until he felt sleepy, he decided to rectify that lapse.

Suddenly his eyes sharpened. A familiar name leaped from the page. Rourke. Patrick Joseph Rourke. A loud chuckle burst from Levitt's lips. That Irish son of a bitch had finally reached the peak of respectability. Being named Ambassador to Ireland during the war hadn't been enough for him. Now he had a son, Patrick Rourke, Jr., who had been elected to the Senate.

Levitt read through the story more carefully. In a tight race, Patrick Rourke, Jr. had been elected Democratic senator for Massachusetts. There was even a photograph of Patrick, with his younger brother, John, who had acted as his campaign manager. The middle son, Joseph Rourke, Levitt noted, had been killed during the war, shot by the SS after being taken prisoner during the Battle of the Bulge. Levitt tried to guess how old Patrick Joseph Rourke was now. He had to be almost seventy. His son, Patrick, Jr., the senator, was in his mid forties. John Rourke was in his late thirties.

A third time Levitt read the story. John Rourke must have done one hell of a job as campaign manager for his brother, Levitt mused, run a tough campaign with millions of dollars thrown into the fight by old Patrick Joseph Rourke. Millions of bootleg dollars. There was no mention of that, though, not that Levitt expected there to be. Bootlegging was the skeleton in the Rourke family closet. They'd keep damned quiet about it.

Levitt found a pair of scissors with which to clip the story from the newspaper. He'd show it to the twins, let them know what had become of the man who'd contracted with Saul Fromberg to kill himself and Jake Granitz. Another thought struck him. He lifted the telephone and put through a call to Florida. Benny Minsky wouldn't read the newspaper, not past the front page or the sports section. He might not even find out about this unless someone told him.

"Hi, Benny, how's business?" Levitt asked when he reached Minsky at the Monaco in Hollywood.

"Pretty good. Both hotels are full, the casinos are busy. The season's just starting." Minsky's voice turned wary. "Why are you calling up in the middle of the night?"

"I want to read you something, from tomorrow's *Times*. Levitt read through the story, listened to Minsky's gasp of surprise. "See, Benny, there's hope for us all. Maybe we should get the twins and William to run for some public office."

"I don't have any grand ideas for my son," Minsky answered. "That Irish scumbag Rourke. Shall we send him a wire, congratulating him?"

"The hell with him," Levitt said. "I wouldn't waste the damned money. Besides, his son only won by a handful of votes. Maybe they'll have a recount and he'll lose."

Minsky laughed. "That sounds more like you," he said before hanging up.

Before placing the clipping in his wallet, Levitt read it through a final time. Senator . . . What he had done with the twins, what Minsky had done with William, none of it added up to a hill of beans compared with this. Old man Rourke must be reveling in his son's success, and Levitt begrudged the man every iota of the happiness he'd found.

Chapter Two

The next few years flew past Pearl, there one moment to be enjoyed and gone the next. Her grandchildren seemed to sprout a half-inch each time she looked at them, until she became scared to look at all, terrified that Jacob and Anne would be fully grown and another generation would have slipped past. By the time he was eleven, Jacob was taller than Pearl, showing the first signs of the transformation from boyhood to manhood—a sprinkling of hair on his upper lip, hands and feet suddenly too large for the rest of his body. Pearl was grateful that Anne was still a little girl, carrying that flaming head of red hair like a torch in memory of her grandmother.

As if to magnify the remorseless passage of time, Pearl witnessed the twins' real-estate company—Granitz Brothers, that respectable, legitimate business which Lou Levitt had surprised her with when she'd expected a marriage proposal—leap off the ground with the swift sureness that was the hallmark of any concern with which Levitt was involved. The first office building had been purchased on Broadway, just south of Forty-second Street. Further loans from Leinberg Bank in Zurich had followed during the next three years to facilitate the purchase of buildings on Madison Avenue, Sixth Avenue, West Fifty-seventh Street and East Thirty-fourth Street, across from the Empire State Building. At the start of 1965, the twins constructed their first building, a thirty-story edifice on East Forty-second Street called Granitz Tower. The entire top floor was given over to corporate headquarters. Pearl went there regularly to meet Leo for lunch. Always, she would stand by the huge picture window in his office and look out across the East River to Brooklyn and Queens. If only Jake could see it as she did, this view, owning all of New York. What pride he would have. . . .

When Granitz Tower was erected, Pearl expected the top floor to have an office with Lou Levitt's name on the door. It didn't. Nor was Levitt's name to be seen anywhere on the roll of company officers. As always he preferred to remain in the background, ever available for advice but wanting none of the fame that came with fortune. The same was true in the Bahamas and London, where Levitt's and Minsky's money had found willing takers. For Pearl's sixtieth birthday, Levitt took her to London. They appeared to be two friends sharing a vacation. First-class travel on a TWA 707; separate rooms in the Connaught; a formal good night, a chaste kiss on the cheek before retiring, and a happy greeting when they saw each other over breakfast the following morning.

In London, Levitt and Minsky owned shares in two gambling establishments, the Dominion Sporting Club in Knightsbridge, and the Embassy Club in the center of Mayfair. But when Pearl visited these clubs with him, they both had to take out overseas memberships, like any tourists, in order to enter. Once inside, Levitt was just one of many members. No one paid him any undue attention. He was simply a little sixty-year-old man in a smartly pressed mohair suit, accompanied by a gray-haired woman everyone assumed was his wife.

"You own a piece of this place," Pearl said to him when they were in the Embassy, "and no one has any idea who you are."

"That's the way I like it to be." He handed her a ten-shilling chip, the minimum stake, to place on the roulette table. When she dithered over which number to play, considering family birthdays and street addresses, the battle plan of any superstitious gambler, he whispered, "Put it on odd and even or red and black."

"But they only pay even money," Pearl protested. "A number's worth thirty-five to one."

"An even-money winner is always better than a thirty-five-to-one loser," Levitt answered with simple, undefeatable logic.

Pearl placed the chip on red. Black came up and the croupier swept the single chip into the pile of losing bets.

"Does Benny ever come here?"

"What for?"

"Well, he's as much a partner in these places as you are."

"So are the twins, so's William. None of us comes here. We just take the money and say thank you very much, like any stockholder who's happy to see in the annual report that his dividend's been increased."

Looking at Levitt, Pearl could sense that he missed the intimate involvement. Although he refused to risk another bet on the roulette table, he was watching the croupier intently. "You're jealous of him, aren't you, Lou?"

"Damned right. That guy's making a hundred bucks a week or

whatever these Limeys pay him in their pounds, shillings, and pence. We're making millions. Yet I'd give anything to be on that side of the table for an hour."

"You're incorrigible, you know that?" she said, linking arms with Levitt and drawing him away from the table.

No matter how wealthy Levitt became, he would always have a hankering to be back in that small room beneath the restaurant on Second Avenue, dressed up in a tuxedo while he managed his tiny gambling empire. Or to go back even further. He'd give up all the millions to be a teenager again, scrambling around in the dust of the basement floor like a little monkey while he operated a dice game. Those had been the happiest moments of Levitt's life, and, considering carefully, Pearl suspected that the same held true for her—those times had been the best.

When Pearl turned sixty-one in November 1966, she made a Sunday luncheon for family and friends at the Sands Point house. Benny Minsky flew up for the weekend to stay with William, Susan, and their two sons—Mark, now aged ten; and Paul, two years younger. The Minskys were the first to arrive.

Levitt turned up fifteen minutes later. For once, his greeting to Pearl was perfunctory. To her surprise, he seemed more intent on speaking to Minsky and William, but with four children running around the house and the final preparations being made for lunch, he had little opportunity. When Pearl asked if something was wrong, he shook his head and said, "I don't get much opportunity to sit down and talk with Benny and William these days, that's all."

Remembering Levitt's earlier antagonism toward Minsky, Pearl found that answer difficult to accept.

Leo was late.

"We thought you'd got lost," Levitt remarked lightly as Leo dropped into his chair and tucked a linen napkin into his shirt.

"Either that," Joseph added, "or you'd forgotten all about today."

"Me forget?" Leo shook his head. "Ma's birthday is one day I don't forget."

Across the table from Leo, Susan Minsky kept her gaze firmly down. For the others lunch became a relaxed, family affair which ended with the traditional presentation of a candle-studded birthday cake; Judy had stayed up late the previous night to bake it. "Are there really sixty-one candles there?" Pearl asked in wonderment. "How am I supposed to blow them all out in one go?"

"I'll help you, Ma." Leo positioned himself beside his mother, an arm around her waist. "Ready? One . . ."

Pearl found security and comfort in Leo's embrace. He was so caring, so fond of her. She knew that Joseph loved her just as strongly as Leo did, but the younger twin was unafraid to openly display his affection.

" . . . two . . . three . . ."

Under the joint assault, the mass of candles flickered and died. "Happy birthday, Ma," Leo said, hugging his mother tightly. "And many, many more."

"Did you make a wish?" Judy asked.

"Of course I did. Who blows out candles without making a wish?"

"What did you wish for?"

"If I tell you it won't come true."

"You can tell us," Joseph pressed. "It doesn't matter if you tell your family."

Pearl smiled. "I wished for all of us to live in health and happiness, okay?" Some wish, Pearl thought. But was it really too much to ask for? Neither of her parents had reached the age she was now celebrating. Nor had Jake. Or Judy's parents, Moe and Annie. Was Pearl fated to make up for all of them, to have a life that would be so long it compensated for the shortness of their lives?

When the cake was cut and passed around, Levitt held up a hand in refusal. "I'd love to, but I'm stuffed," he said patting his stomach.

"How about we go for a short walk to work off some of this food?" Levitt suggested in an easy manner to the twins, William, and Minsky. "Give the women a chance to clear up."

"Sure," Joseph answered immediately. Despite the casualness of the invitation, he had discerned an order. The five men took their coats from the hall closet and walked out of the front door, to stroll in a tight group along the gravel drive. The sky had clouded over and there was a strong hint of early snow in the air. Joseph pulled up his collar and huddled further into his coat.

As they turned around the side of the house, the barking of dogs shattered the silence. Bounding toward the men came a pair of Dobermans, a male and a female, which Joseph had bought when the Labrador had died two years earlier. Joseph glanced at his twin brother and saw Leo shrink back, face white with fear as he tried to disappear into his heavy sheepskin coat. Joseph clapped his hands sharply and called to the dogs. "Solomon! Sheba! Into the house!" Well-trained, the two Dobermans loped away toward the kitchen door, to wait there until they were told differently.

"Thank you," Levitt said to Joseph after the dogs had gone. He had important business to discuss, and he didn't want Leo or the others to be distracted. "Any of you read the *Times* this morning, the big political feature?"

As one, the other men shook their heads.

"Then you'd all better listen carefully, because there might be a whole pile of trouble coming down the road."

"What kind of trouble?" Minsky asked.

"To do with the next election."

"The next election?" Joseph repeated. "It was only yesterday that Goldwater got himself plastered all over the voting booths."

"It was two years ago," Levitt corrected the older twin. "And there's only two years until the next one. Johnson's got himself so deeply embedded in Vietnam that those couple of years are going to kill him, either physically or politically. There's already talk that he won't run again, which leaves a wide-open race among the Democrats to see who takes his place."

"Race? What wide-open race?" William wanted to know. "It'll be Humphrey. Humphrey's his vice-president. It stands to reason that he'll get the nomination."

Levitt shook his head. "Nothing stands to reason. Humphrey's more of the same, and the Democrats know that they aren't going to win the next election with more of the same. So the kingmakers are looking for new blood, a fresh face that can spark some interest among the electorate and prevent a Republican victory in 1968. One of those fresh faces belongs to Patrick Rourke, Jr. There's a move to run him."

"Rourke from Massachusetts?" Joseph asked.

"The Democratic senator from Massachusetts. More importantly, he's Patrick Joseph Rourke's son, which might make it tough for us."

Joseph mulled over the information in his mind. Levitt had not been this serious six years earlier when he'd cut the clipping from the *Times* about the election to the Senate of Patrick Rourke, Jr. He'd laughed about it then—the epitome of respectability for the son of an old bootlegger.

Levitt, certain that he had the undivided attention of the other four men, continued talking. "Patrick got elected six years ago because of the fortune his father spread around. Senator was the first step. Maybe that old bastard Rourke looked on 1972 as the year his son would run for the White House, because that would be the end of Johnson's second full term and he wouldn't be eligible to stand again. But now that Johnson's getting himself so bogged down in this Vietnam mess, the timetable's been brought forward by four years, to 1968. Also, the old man's in his seventies, so he might figure that he doesn't have the time to wait until 1972."

"How old is Patrick, Jr.?" Minsky asked.

"Fifty-one. His younger brother, John, a lawyer, acted as his campaign manager when he ran for the Senate six years ago. He'll probably fill the same slot for a shot at the White House."

Joseph tried to recall the clipping that Levitt had shown him six years earlier. "Wasn't there a third son?"

"Yes, with the same name as you—Joseph. He got himself killed during the war, so he's of no concern. We're just interested in Patrick, Jr. and John, and what old man Rourke's got planned for them. And for us."

"I don't like the way you say *us*," Minsky complained. "What exactly is *us* supposed to mean?"

Levitt heaved a silent sigh. He still had to spell everything out. "Old man Rourke has probably got it all figured out that Patrick, Jr., if he makes it to the White House, will appoint John as Attorney General, him being a lawyer and all that. But before they can take a crack at the Presidency, they've got the minor matter of the Democratic nomination to take into account. And that's where we, I think, come in. As sacrificial lambs. Patrick, Jr. isn't that well known outside of Massachusetts, outside of New England. He's sure as hell not a household name down in Arkansas or out in Utah, so he's got to be sold to the American public, and damned quickly. How much better can that be done than with a repeat of what Estes Kefauver did fifteen years ago? That's what was in the feature in today's *Times*. Another Senate investigation on organized crime is being planned."

Levitt gazed at his listeners, satisfied when he recognized the anxiety that appeared so suddenly on their faces. "The way I figure it, a move like that'll kill two birds with one stone for the old man. It'll get Patrick, Jr. and his lawyer brother known, just as it did for Kefauver, so when the big push starts for the primaries the Rourkes'll have a head start on Humphrey and whoever else is thinking of running. Secondly, and more importantly, it'll give the old man the opportunity to do what he's always wanted to do—hit back at us. At me. And"—he pointed a finger at Minsky—"at you. Because we're the only two left of the old group that almost bankrupted him."

"You mean the night his convoy was taken," Joseph said needlessly.

"That's right, the night Jake led a crew up to Massachusetts to pay old man Rourke back for participating in Saul Fromberg's plot against us. Rourke lost more than a shipment of booze that night. He lost twelve men. Those men had families; they had wives and scores of kids like all the Irish seem to have. Rourke had to pay out and pay out and pay out until he was tapped almost clean. He's been aching for some kind of revenge ever since. He couldn't hit back at the time with guns—he wasn't powerful enough, and he didn't want to court any more of that kind of trouble. So he went the respectable route instead. He waited all these years, and now that Patrick, Jr.'s all set to make a run at the White House the old man thinks he can nail us. Destroy us in full view of the public and make a name for his son . . . for his sons . . . at the same time."

Leo made his first contribution to the conversation. "Then kill him before he can do anything. Kill Patrick Rourke, Jr."

Levitt whirled around, his eyes gleaming with anger. "For Christ's sake, you don't kill United States Senators and presidential candidates! You don't team up with a Harry Saltzman and knock them off like cheap hoodlums. Maybe it's about time you took a break from watching those damned movies!"

William broke in. "If this Senate investigation gets off the ground, what real damage can it do to us? The books are closed, the people who ran them were paid too well to ever open their mouths. With the exception of the casinos in the Waterway and Monaco hotels, we're one hundred percent legitimate. Our interests in the Bahamas and London are well hidden. What do we have to fear?"

"We are *almost* one hundred percent legitimate," Levitt contradicted. "We've all taken a few liberties. Like I just said . . . remember those two jerks Leo and Harry took care of for you."

Benny Minsky ran his index finger along the bottom of his nose and sniffed at the crisp air. He did not like the New York cold, not when he could be sunning himself in Florida. "What about Harry Saltzman, Lou? You're still in contact with him. Can he be relied on to keep his mouth shut? He's been involved in enough stuff with us. He even lent us the men to knock off Saul Fromberg, and the men for the raid on Rourke's convoy. He's been tied in with us through the years."

Not to mention Saltzman's helping to cover up the murder of a man named Tony Cervante, Levitt thought and glanced at Leo. Saltzman could drop them all right into the crap, but Levitt had what he considered sound reasons for not worrying. "Harry wasn't directly involved with the convoy that night. He lent us the men for the raid, sure, but there's no way old man Rourke could have known that. Rourke just figured it was us—you, me, Jake, and Moe . . . we were the guys he'd contracted with Saul Fromberg to kill—and he was certain of it when his liquor started turning up in clubs we controlled. Forget Harry . . . Rourke doesn't even know he exists. Worry about us instead. The way I see it, once this investigation gets going, we'll be subpoenaed to appear. That might," he said to the twins, "include your mother."

Leo was instantly anxious, not for himself but for Pearl. "How will

Ma be able to stand up to some investigation?"

"Don't sweat about your mother. She's tough."

"Wait one minute," Joseph said. "If Patrick Rourke, Jr. starts throwing barbs about the old days, surely he's going to incriminate his own family right along with us. His father wasn't any better. He's not going to smear himself."

"Wrong. The old man was a bootlegger, straight and simple. The one time he got involved in murder for hire—with Fromberg—turned out to be a disaster for him, and no one knows about that anyway. As a bootlegger, he was a popular hero, helping people to circumvent an extremely unpopular law. He made his pile and he got out, turned respectable. He didn't stay in the rackets—"

"Like we did?"

"That's right, like we did. We still like to think that what we did, what we do, with the gambling is on the same level as bootlegging. It's not. Drinking's legal now. Bookmaking isn't. It's called organized crime. And that's what I figure old man Rourke wants to see us hit with. Our past will be gone over with a fine comb. Just thank God we're out of business in New York and we can pull the plug on Florida whenever we want to. Those casinos can always be set up again."

"We don't even need the money from them," Minsky murmured. At any other time he might have argued the point with Levitt. He did not want to see his small empire in Florida diminished, have himself made into nothing more glamorous than a hotel manager. Those two casinos gave him stature, but he was quick to see the problems they could cause should they be open during a Senate investigation. Buying cops and local officials in Florida didn't carry much weight in a Washington investigation.

"Don't say anything to your mother," Levitt cautioned the twins. "It might never happen, so don't worry her unnecessarily."

"Do *you* think it'll come about?" Joseph asked.

Levitt pursed his lips before answering. "Yes, Joseph, I do."

The five men returned to the house. Only Leo did not return his coat to the hall closet. He had to leave.

Judy watched through a window as he climbed into a new white Cadillac convertible and started the engine. As the car moved slowly down the driveway, she breathed a sigh of relief. Leo's visits were always traumatic for her. He still treated her like a doormat, and she tolerated him only for Pearl's and Joseph's sakes.

Hearing footsteps, she turned to see Joseph standing just behind her. "Sometimes I'm almost grateful for your brother's little boys. They mean he doesn't stay here too long."

"That's enough," Joseph said sharply.

He turned away and began to walk back to the living room. When it came to his twin brother, Joseph understood that he and Judy shared little common ground. God only knew, she had reason enough to hate Leo. He only wished she could find a reason to forgive him.

The white Cadillac convertible was two months old. Leo had not bought it for himself; it had been intended to be a gift, for a nineteen-year-old boy who had been Leo's lover for nine months. Originally from California, the boy had been referred to Leo through the agency. After a month, Leo had installed him in the apartment on East Fifty-ninth Street. That relationship had developed into the longest, most satisfying union Leo had ever experienced, as fulfilling, he was certain, as that shared by any couple. Three months earlier, though, the boy, a victim of homesickness, had started to talk of returning to the West Coast. Leo had pleaded with him to say, had showered him with gifts, all to no avail. One evening after work, Leo had gone to the apartment, hoping his new ploy would change his lover's mind: the keys to a brand-new white Cadillac convertible. The apartment had been empty. Nothing but a note on the dressing table, thanking Leo for nine months of generous affection. Leo had been heartbroken. For two months he had moped around his Scarsdale home, sitting alone in the basement cinema while he tried to conjure up some enthusiasm for his favorite gangster movies. Only now was he beginning to emerge from his depression. He had heard of a new restaurant in midtown named Oscar's Retreat, and his appetite was becoming sharp again.

From the outside, Oscar's Retreat resembled many other restaurants along the midtown stretch of Second Avenue. High, glass windows fronted the street; muted light spread from the outside. The windows were frosted, cutting off the curious glances of passers-by and allowing diners privacy. Leo checked his coat and settled himself on a barstool, using the time the bartender took to bring his drink to orientate himself. Of the fifteen tables in the restaurant, only three were occupied. The restaurant was still too new to have gained popularity. Leo decided that he would wait for half an hour. If business did not pick up, he would go home to Scarsdale, watch a movie in his basement cinema.

The bartender brought his drink. "Would you like to see a menu?"

Leo shook his head. "I don't know whether I'm staying. Is it always this quiet?"

"It's early," the bartender replied with a casual shrug of the shoulders.

Several times during the next thirty minutes the restaurant door opened and closed. Always Leo's eyes flicked over to the newcomers before returning to the drink in front of him. Men together, men and women, women together. Leo saw nothing to interest him. He would leave. Perhaps he would return to this place some other time.

As he swallowed the last of his drink in preparation for sliding off the barstool, the restaurant door opened once again. Two men entered. One was middle-aged and paunchy. Long brown hair was carefully waved off his face, and his hands were heavy with jewelry. Rings gleamed on his thick fingers; ostentatious gold cuff links peeked out from his sleeves. Leo dismissed him and concentrated on his companion, a slim youth with olive skin, jet black curly hair, and dark flashing eyes. Perhaps the evening would not be wasted after all.

After checking their coats, the two men passed close to the bar. Leo swung around on the stool to follow them with his eyes as they were shown to a table. The older man lit a cigarette and made a show of studying the menu. His companion, more interested in the surroundings, glanced around, sharp eyes darting here and there, until, at last, they met Leo's. Slowly a smile appeared on the dark face, an expression that both mocked and teased. Leo felt his pulse quicken. A sudden, giddy warmth spread through his body.

As if sensing what was happening, the older man lifted his eyes from the menu. He looked first at Leo, then at his companion. A few angry, muttered phrases ensued. Leo, unable to hear the words, could guess their gist. What was the arrangement between the two? Leo wondered. Did the older man pay for his companion's friendship, his favors? Did he keep the young man in a fancy apartment as Leo had done with his Californian? And would this young man one day jump up and leave, return to his home wherever that was? Studying the youth, Leo doubted that he was American. Italian, probably. Perhaps Spanish. His clothes appeared to be European; square-toed shoes, a narrow-cut jacket, the tightly fitting black leather coat he had left at the front of the restaurant.

Leo ordered another drink, nursed it while surreptitiously checking on the table where the two men sat. A waiter carried a menu to their table, stood waiting while they decided what to eat. Leo noticed how the older man tried to dominate his companion, suggesting what he should order. The youth seemed to take delight in ignoring the suggestions. A tease, Leo decided, and wondered whether the young man was really worth pursuing. Was the invitation in his eyes a tease as well?

After placing the order, the older man rose and walked across the restaurant to the restrooms. Leo swung around on the stool, locked eyes with the olive-skinned youth and then inclined his head toward the door. Grinning, the youth stood up, folded his napkin, and followed Leo out of the restaurant, stopping only to collect his black leather coat. Neither of them spoke until Leo stopped by the white Cadillac convertible.

"This is yours?" the youth said as Leo unlocked the passenger door. He spoke English with a harsh, almost guttural accent, and Leo felt jubilant because his assumption had been correct. The youth was not American. Guessing right seemed like a good omen.

Leo slipped into the driver's seat, inserted the ignition key but did not turn it. "Who was your friend?"

"No one of any importance. He is just someone I see occasionally. When I have nothing better to do."

Leo liked the answer. It meant that in him the youth had found a preferable alternative. He held out his hand. "My name's Leo. What do they call you?"

The youth took Leo's hand. He had the softest skin Leo could ever remember feeling. It was like a girl's, and his hand, lovingly manicured, was a hand that had never been insulted by manual labor.

"Mahmoud," the youth answered. "Mahmoud Asawi."

"What kind of a name is that?"

"An Arabic name. I am from Jordan."

Leo's hand still gripped Mahmoud's. Inside his head two voices raged. One, Lou Levitt's, was demanding to know what Leo was doing, shaking the hand of an Arab? The other, the voice he chose to heed, was his own. Why should he care about Levitt and his prejudices? What place did they have in his own life at this particular moment? He had been instantly attracted to this youth—so where did Levitt come off telling him who he could or could not see?

Mahmoud gazed around the interior of the Cadillac with undisguised admiration. "A Cadillac convertible! Fantastic! Ever since I came to America I have dreamed of owning a car like this. Of driving a car like this."

"You want to drive it?" Without waiting for an answer, Leo opened the door and changed seats with Mahmoud.

Sitting behind the steering wheel, Mahmoud turned the ignition key, flipped the gas pedal experimentally. Before driving away, he switched on the radio, selecting a station that was playing Beatles music. Leo winced at the choice but made no comment. He was content to let this slim Arab youth play whatever music he wanted.

"How long have you been in America?"

"Two years. My father—he lives in Amman—sent me here to study engineering at MIT. I preferred to have a good time, so I dropped out and came to New York. That was when my father cut off my funds."

"How do you survive?" Leo asked, although he already knew the answer.

"There are men more generous than my father, more understanding. They would rather see me enjoy myself than waste away in learning how to erect a power station."

Leo recognized the outright proposition. Like the man . . . what was his name now? Tony, that was it. Tony who had picked him up in the Sixth Avenue bar on the night of Joseph's wedding. This youth, this Mahmoud Asawi, sold himself as well, but unlike Tony he was up front. He was open about it, honest. In Mahmoud, there was none of Tony's deceit, the treachery that had caused his death.

"That man before, what was he to you?"

"I already told you. Someone I saw when I had nothing better to do. For a date with me"—Mahmoud spoke unashamedly about his way of life—"he would be very generous, sometimes paying as much as one hundred dollars."

"And there are others?"

"Of course."

Leo sat back. He had been entranced by this young man from the moment the restaurant door had swung open. Now he was jealous. He did not want to share him with other men. "Where do you live?"

"I have a studio apartment on West Seventy-second Street."

"Would you like to move from there?"

"Move to where?"

"To a beautifully furnished apartment on East Fifty-ninth Street."

"I will stay where I am. I like it there. East Fifty-ninth Street, is that where you live?"

"It's one of my homes."

"Where are the others?"

"I'll show you." Leo gave Mahmoud directions for Scarsdale, proud of the opportunity to show off his home. The man who had brought Mahmoud to the restaurant, Leo was sure, would have nothing like this with which to bewitch a potential lover.

The Cadillac's headlights picked out a high brick wall and concrete pillars. Leo gave the order for Mahmoud to pass between the pillars. Floodlights set into the garden illuminated the house Leo had bought. On Leo's instructions, Mahmoud parked the Cadillac in front of half a dozen, wide steps that rose toward a massive oak front door.

Awe was etched into the young man's voice when he asked, "You live here?"

"I live here." Leo climbed out of the car and walked up the wide steps. He inserted keys into two locks and then swung back the heavy door. Mahmoud followed, staring with admiration at the paneled entrance hall, the rich carpet, and the heavy crystal chandelier which hung from the center of the sculpted ceiling.

"Wow, some pad," he said, and Leo smiled, amused at hearing the Arab youth utilize American slang. It seemed so out of place, so charmingly unexpected.

"You like movies?" he asked Mahmoud.

"Are we going out to see one?"

Leo pointed to the floor. "I've got my own theater downstairs." He led the way through a door, down a flight of carpeted steps to the basement. A large screen was fixed to one wall. A projection booth was constructed into the opposite wall. Heavy leather furniture was scattered around the floor. Again, Mahmoud resorted to American slang, as though incapable of expressing his admiration in any other manner.

"Man, this is some setup!"

Leo slid open a closet door to reveal racks of film cans. The movie he chose was *White Heat*, the same one he had watched with Pearl. Of all the movies he owned, this was the one to which he could relate the most. Cagney's devotion to his mother was touching. Like Leo, Cagney understood who was the most important person in his life.

As images flickered across the screen, Leo and his newfound friend settled comfortably onto a wide leather settee. Knowing every moment of the film by heart, Leo closed his eyes. His right hand strayed to his side, across the cool leather of the settee. His fingertips questingly touched Mahmoud's thigh, stroked the smooth fabric of his trousers. He wondered what kind of an arrangement this youth would want.

Leo had already made up his mind to accede to whatever demands Mahmoud might make. He had never enjoyed a dark-skinned lover before. It would be fun, even more so when Leo understood that he had to keep it such a secret from everyone he knew. An Arab! But, after all, what did it really matter? Only in the Middle East did such taboos still hold sway. This was America. Biblical feuds had no place here. . . .

It was after midnight when Mahmoud returned from Scarsdale to Manhattan. Again, Leo allowed him to drive the white Cadillac, content to be a passenger and watch the Arab youth, to vicariously enjoy the thrill Mahmoud so obviously derived from handling the luxury convertible. Leo felt sated, even more so than he had with the boy from California. With any other boy. He knew that he had to reach an arrangement with this youth before they arrived at the studio apartment on West Seventy-second Street. Otherwise . . . the prospect chilled Leo . . . otherwise he might never see Mahmoud again.

"Mahmoud, I do not want to share you with anyone. Do you understand me?"

Mahmoud took his eyes off the road just long enough to smile at Leo. "That is up to you."

"You want a car like this? You want this car?"

Mahmoud drummed long, slim fingers on the steering wheel. "That would be very nice, Leo, but I cannot live in a car. I cannot eat a car. I cannot wear a car."

"You sure you want to stay where you are?"

"I am certain."

"I'll pay your rent—"

"And?"

"And a thousand a month."

Mahmoud's eyes sparkled. "Leo, I saw your house. I know about your other place on East Fifty-ninth Street. You are a man who is accustomed to pay for the very finest. Two thousand a month."

"From a hundred bucks a date to two-thousand-plus a month, that's quite some jump."

Mahmoud took one hand off the wheel and rested it on Leo's thigh. His palm made slow circular motions and Leo could feel his groin tighten. "Leo, you always have to pay for exclusivity."

"You promise me I'll get it?"

"I promise you."

On the return trip to Scarsdale, Leo's mind was full of Mahmoud. The secrecy would add a touch of conspiracy, a dash of excitement, to their relationship. Leo would pay him in cash, two thousand dollars a month, untraceable. And he'd give him cash to cover the rent so the lease would remain in Mahmoud's name. Instead of this Cadillac, he would give him cash to buy one in his own name. There would be absolutely nothing to tie him to the Arab youth, no clues that might give him away to Levitt.

How would he work out their meetings? Leo dare not be seen visiting Mahmoud's studio apartment. Mahmoud would have to journey out to Scarsdale. The house was secluded. Inside those high walls, their relationship would remain a secret. From Levitt. From

Pearl. From the world.

Always pay in cash . . . he'd learned that from Levitt. And now he would use what he had learned to keep Levitt in the dark while he enjoyed an affair so forbidden the very thought of it sent his blood bubbling through his veins.

So enthralled was Leo with his plotting, he did not even spare a thought for Levitt's concern over the Rourke family.

Chapter Three

Christmas Day dawned bitterly cold in Boston. In Jamaica Plain, to the south of the city, Patrick Joseph Rourke listened to the church bells from the comfort of an armchair placed by the drawing-room window. There, he could watch the wide boulevard that swept gracefully in front of his home, see the cars full of churchgoers all bundled up against the wintry weather. He was completely alone in the house, his chauffeur, butler, and cook having left ten minutes earlier to attend services. He, too, would have liked to go, but his arthritis was particularly painful. Even with a stick, he was barely able to walk half-a-dozen steps.

Glancing down at the hands which rested on his thighs, Rourke felt self-pity. The joints of his fingers were twisted grotesquely by the arthritis, swollen and misshapen. His right hip was almost destroyed by the disease. Once he had been strong and vibrant, a mover of mountains. Now he was an old and crippled man.

Leaving the window and the view of the boulevard, he hobbled over to a chair placed in front of a roaring fire. The warmth seemed to ease his pain more than any medication could, seeping into his joints to offer temporary relief. Behind thin wire-rimmed glasses, his watery blue eyes stared into the flames, then at the large, brightly lit Christmas tree that was set beside the fireplace. Gaily wrapped packages were scattered beneath, presents for his two sons, Patrick, Jr. and John; for their wives, Grace and Rose; and for Rourke's eleven grandchildren who would all be coming for the traditional Christmas dinner.

Rourke's mind slipped back to the Christmas of 1956, ten years earlier. It had been his wife's last Christmas. She had known she was dying from cancer, but at Christmastime she had forced a smile onto her face and had insisted on cooking the family dinner just as she had done every year since they were married. Two weeks later, she had gone into the hospital, never to come out. The following year, his daughter-in-law Grace, the wife of Patrick, Jr., had said she would take over the responsibility for Christmas dinner. She was now the oldest Rourke woman. Rourke had told her that as long as he remained alive, Christmas dinner would continue to be served in his home. And so the tradition had continued.

Another memory arose, a Christmas twenty-two years earlier. Not a white Christmas, but the blackest of the black. His three sons in the service. Patrick, a Navy pilot in the Far East. Joseph, an infantry lieutenant in Europe. John, in the Signal Corps. The Battle of the Bulge was taking place, Joseph's unit fighting in the very center of the disputed area. Christmas dinner that year was tinged with fear. The throbbing anxiety came when Joseph was reported missing. A cable. Confirmed dead. And only later, much later, a terrifying account from a survivor of how Joseph Rourke and seventy other American prisoners of war had been cold-bloodedly butchered by SS soldiers in a field in the Ardennes Forest. Rourke stared into the fire and saw his middle son as he had last seen him. Still freckle-faced at twenty-six, an enthusiastic lieutenant all ready to be shipped to Europe in preparation for the invasion.

The picture slowly faded as Rourke's eyelids dropped. Lulled by the comforting warmth of the fire, he fell asleep. . . .

"Sir . . . your guests, your sons and their families, are here."

Rourke jerked awake, head snapping around to see the butler's lined face only inches from his own. Rourke had not heard the servants return from church. They were all back, and now his sons were here. He must have dozed for more than two hours. While he had slept, the city of Boston had gone to church to celebrate the birth of the Savior. Now those same citizens were ready for their annual feast.

"Show them in, show them in." He struggled to stand and the butler lent an assisting arm. Rourke wanted to look alert, erect, when his sons saw him. He did not want them worrying about his health. They had more important matters with which to concern themselves.

The doorbell sounded a heavy chime that echoed through the house. Leaving Rourke standing in front of the fire, leaning on the cane for support, the butler went to answer the summons. Rourke heard shouts of "Merry Christmas!" and guessed that his sons were giving presents to the butler; all the servants were like members of the family. The drawing-room door burst open and a swarm of people rushed in. Rourke tried to separate the faces, the six children of Patrick and Grace, the five children of John and Rose. They all seemed so grown-up now, especially Patrick's two oldest girls, both married and both pregnant. The Rourke clan would be going strong for a long time to come.

"Merry Christmas, Dad!" Patrick and John reached their father simultaneously, enormous packages clutched in their hands. "You want to open these now or should we stick them under the tree?" John asked.

"Put them beneath the tree. We'll open all the presents later." Rourke gazed at his sons, thinking, as he always did, that there could be little doubt of their brotherhood. Patrick was much sturdier than John, but both men had unruly mops of thick, light brown hair, the same easygoing smiles on faces flushed with the cold. No doubt about their being Irish either. Rourke felt a twinge of regret when he realized that this would probably be the last family Christmas they would have, all together like this in the big house in Jamaica Plain. Next Christmas, Patrick would be unable to lead such a carefree life. He would be more than just a United States Senator. If everything went according to plan, he would be a front runner for the Democratic nomination for President.

Rourke's daughters-in-law, Grace and Rose, kissed him on the cheek, then the grandchildren took turns in wishing him a Merry Christmas. Halfway through the routine, Rourke had to sink back into the chair, suddenly tired.

The butler pushed a trolley full of bottles into the center of the room. "Sir . . ." He addressed Rourke. "Would you care for a drink?"

Rourke eyed the bottles carefully. "Jameson. For my sons as well. Nothing like good Irish whiskey to keep the cold out on Christmas Day, eh?"

The butler poured the whiskey into three highball glasses. When he started to add ice, Rourke waved him away. "For God's sake, man, you should know better than to give an Irishman ice in his whiskey."

When the butler passed the glasses to Rourke and his two sons, Rourke pushed himself to his feet again, faced Patrick and John, and raised his glass. *"Sláinte."*

"Sláinte," the two brothers replied before following their father's example of downing the whiskey in one swift gulp.

Rourke eased himself back into the chair. The fire and the whiskey and seeing all his family were doing him good. He'd do credit to the Christmas dinner the cook had prepared. And afterward, while the rest of the family opened presents, he would lock himself away in the library with his sons. They had much to discuss. . . .

Noise failed to penetrate the library. The book-lined walls acted as a sound barrier. Rourke sat in a deep leather armchair. His two sons sat opposite, in straight-backed chairs. Between them on a table rested the bottle of Jameson and three glasses.

Rourke opened the conversation. "If everything goes right," he said to Patrick, "this Senate investigation committee on organized crime is going to catapult you right into the nomination come convention time. The only thing that could stop you is Johnson and Humphrey bringing Vietnam to an end sometime in the next fifteen months. And we all know that's not going to happen. Vietnam's going to get a damned sight worse before it gets any better."

Patrick gazed thoughtfully at his hands. "I can't believe we start sitting in New York in six weeks' time. When I first sponsored the resolution for a special Senate committee on organized crime, it seemed like a million light years away. Now it's almost here."

"Are you nervous about it?" Rourke asked.

"No." Patrick gave his father the quick smile that newspapermen had termed a boyish grin. "I'll have to feel my way the first few days in New York, but by the time we sit in Philadelphia I'll have the whole thing down pat."

"I'm not interested in Philadelphia or any of the other places your committee will be sitting. I only care about New York. Who have you subpoenaed to appear in New York?"

"The names you gave us. Louis Levitt and Benjamin Minsky. Minsky's son, William. The Granitz twins, Joseph and Leo, and their mother. The subpoenas were served during the past week."

Rourke smiled back at his son. "That's what I call a Christmas present."

"Subpoenas went to a lot of other people as well," John cut in. Responsible for the campaign that had led to his brother being elected to the Senate six years earlier, and hopeful of repeating the feat when Patrick ran for the White House, John had thrown himself wholeheartedly into the Senate investigation, working behind the scenes with law-enforcement officials. He understood that this investigation would be the make-or-break for his brother's political ambitions—and his own.

"What other people?" Rourke asked sharply.

"Suspected mob figures. Italians with links to organized crime. We don't want to make it look like we're gunning for just one ethnic group."

"I don't give a damn about the Italians. Those Wops, they never cost me what the Hebes did—Levitt and Minsky and their damned partners, Granitz and Caplan, may they rot in hell! Those bastards almost put me out of business that night. And they killed your cousin, John McMichael. Don't forget they did that."

"We know," Patrick said. He glanced uncomfortably at his brother. "Dad, we've got to think about the Jewish vote. It swings a lot of weight in places like New York and California. We're going to need to win those states in the primaries and in the election, if we get that far, and we're not going to win them without the Jewish vote."

"If we make a name for Patrick by going after mobsters," John said quickly, "exposing these so-called respectable businessmen as nothing more than hoodlums, we'll win popularity. But if we make a name for just going after Jewish mobsters, it'll be too damned obvious where our priorities are. Not justice, but some kind of bigoted vendetta. It's one thing for this Louis Levitt to scream anti-Semitism when we're investigating gangsters of all faiths. If he does that, he'll be ridiculed. But if we're seen to be questioning only Jews and he waves the bloody flag of anti-Semitism, then people might start thinking that he's got a damned pertinent point!"

Rourke considered that. He knew his own vision was clouded by revenge. He couldn't give a damn about the Mafia, the Cosa Nostra, or whatever the hell the newspapers wanted to call it. Those dagoes had never done to him what the Jews had. First with that hijacking, a quarter of a million in booze and twelve families to support. Then the war, the Jews' war, that had taken his middle son, Joseph.

"But don't you understand what they did to me?" The question put to his sons was a whispered plea.

Again, Patrick appeared awkward. Ever since that terrible day more than thirty years earlier, when the convoy had been hijacked on the coastal road, he'd listened to his father spew this poison. The old man's reasoning was distorted by it. Patrick knew of the deal his father had cooked up with Saul Fromberg to supply killers to solve a dispute between two New York Jewish gangs, but Rourke never mentioned that. He had conveniently forgotten his own part in the devastation that had befallen him.

Both Rourke sons loved their father deeply. He had given them far more than most fathers could ever give their sons. Immense wealth. Position. And now this, the opportunity to walk among the most powerful men in the world. *To be* the most powerful men. Rourke had always been a staunch Democrat. His appointment as Ambassador to Ireland had been repayment for his work on behalf of the party. He had guided his oldest son into politics, put millions behind him in his bid for the Senate. And all the time he had been plotting his revenge on the Jews who had cost him so much that lonely night on the coastal road. He had kept tabs on what they were doing. When Jake Granitz and Moses Caplan had died, Rourke had rejoiced. Now, through his sons, he had, at last, the opportunity to close out all accounts.

Neither Patrick nor John had inherited their father's zealous hatred. In politics, where the secret to success was never to slam doors, bigotry could prove to be an expensive indulgence. But the sons also knew they owed an immense debt to their father. His work, his foresight, had given them incredible opportunities. They had to repay him, even if it was by conducting a witch hunt against his old enemies. At the same time, however, they had to protect their own positions. Hit their father's enemies, by all means, especially when doing so would achieve the publicity necessary for a successful presidential campaign. But not in a way that would brand them as the anti-Semites they were not.

Rourke stared at his two sons, unable to believe that they found his hatred so incomprehensible. Didn't his blood flow through their veins? Was not his cry for vengeance also theirs? "What have you got on them so far? On Levitt? On Minsky and his family? On the Granitzes?"

"We believe they own interests in overseas gambling ventures," John answered. "Two clubs in London, the Embassy and the Dominion Sporting Club. And a hotel casino in the Bahamas, the Belvedere."

"That's not illegal."

"No, it's not. But publicizing the connection might cause them discomfort. Their partnerships are silent. I doubt if the British or Bahamian governments are aware of the connection. Also, they own two hotels, in Florida, that have casinos. The older Minsky runs them."

Rourke nodded in satisfaction. "What about the bookmaking and the policy racket they had going in New York?"

"There's no longer any trace of it. Our people have asked until they're blue in the face and they can't get one positive answer. People have been paid too well to offer information—the police and the shopowners who ran those books and numbers drops."

"Minsky's transportation company . . . the Granitz Brothers real-estate corporation"—Rourke sounded desperate—"surely there's something there."

"Nothing. Everything's perfectly legal and aboveboard. Except—"

"Except what?"

"They don't borrow money from any American financial institution. They use a Swiss bank, Leinberg, in Zurich. We're looking further into that."

Rourke felt easier. He leaned forward and poured whiskey into the three glasses. Lifting his own glass, he said, "It's fitting that we drink this toast with Jameson. The cargo I lost that night was Irish whiskey."

"What is the toast?" John asked.

"To the Senate committee investigation. To its success."

"And to Patrick," John said. "To the next President of the United States."

"And to Levitt and Minsky," Rourke added. "May their souls be damned forever."

While Patrick Joseph Rourke spent Christmas in Boston with his family, the families of the men he'd damned were in Florida, staying at the Waterway Hotel in Hallandale, where Benny Minsky occupied a suite of rooms on the floor below the casino.

During the day, the temperature was in the low eighties; at night it fell back to sixty. The four children of the Granitz and Minsky families frolicked in the hotel pool all day long while their parents sunned themselves, except for Judy whose red hair and fair skin were ultrasensitive to the sun's rays. For that reason, she kept a cautious eye on her daughter, Anne. This was a vacation, a break from the New York winter, and she did not want to spend it dabbing calamine lotion all over Anne's arms, legs, and shoulders.

Neither Lou Levitt nor Pearl made use of the pool. Both agreed they were past the age where swimming was a pleasure. They seemed content to sit in the hotel lounge, reading or joining other older couples in games of cards. As on their trip to London, other people naturally assumed they were husband and wife.

Leo was the only one who was restless. Although he visited the casinos at both the Waterway and the Monaco during the night, he rarely stayed around the hotels during the day. He hired a car, explaining that he wanted to explore the area, see what the other beaches were like. In reality, he drove south to a hotel in Miami to spend time with Mahmoud Asawi who, at Leo's suggestion, had traveled down to Florida to be close to his lover. In keeping with the shroud of secrecy Leo had thrown over the affair, Mahmoud was not even registered under his own name. Leo was certain that no one knew of his affair with the Arab youth.

The purpose of the trip to Florida, however, was not pleasure. Pearl, the twins, Levitt, Minsky, and William had all been served with subpoenas summoning them to appear before the Senate Special Committee on Organized Crime when it sat in New York during the second week of February. What a month earlier had been a fear had become reality.

The six people who had been subpoenaed met late one evening in Benny Minsky's suite. Above their heads, dice clicked, cards were dealt, roulette wheels spun, but for once Levitt's mind was not on the action taking place in the casino, how much the house was making. It was the year's busiest season, and he could not care less.

"When we return to New York," he said, "we meet with our lawyers. Benny, you'll come back with us. We've got to fight this thing as one, cover every question we might be asked and make damned sure we all come up with the same answers."

"Do we have friends in the press who can throw some dirt on old man Rourke?" Joseph asked.

"We can try it. We can get stories printed about Rourke's bootleg dealings, but as I've said before, there are a lot of respectable people who started out that way."

"What about his tie with Saul Fromberg?" The question came from Minsky, who was disturbed at having to leave the sun of Florida for the cold of New York. He'd come to appreciate warm winters and was loath to give them up. "Surely that deal he made with Fromberg is pretty damning."

"You mean the way he contracted with Fromberg to commit murder? To kill me and Jake? I'd love to use that, Benny, to be able to use it. But if that story leaked out, it would harm us more than the Rourkes. Old man Rourke never did commit murder. That crew he sent down to New York failed. In return, we did commit murder. Twelve times. The twelve men who were guarding Rourke's convoy.

"This fight, on the surface anyway—what the public will see and hear about it—is between Senator Patrick Rourke, Jr. and us. It's not between old man Rourke and us. You can be damned sure the senator is going to tread carefully when he asks his questions. He won't expose his father's background if he can help it, so his questions are going to concern our more recent activities."

"Should we close this operation down?" Minsky jerked a hand toward the ceiling. "Here and the Monaco?"

Gloomily, Levitt nodded. He hated to do it, with the profitable winter season just under way; but he felt he had little option. "Let the casinos run until New Year's Day, Benny, then shut them down. Have all the stuff moved out. Turn the casinos into ballrooms or nightclubs. We can always go back into business again afterward. And be sure that you keep paying off all the sheriff's men, the cops and local authorities you've got on your list. That way, we'll be able to open again with no problem once this thing is over."

"How much will closing the casinos cost us?" William asked.

"Too much, but we've got to do it."

Pearl sat fidgeting on her chair, clasping and unclasping her hands. "What do you think they'll ask me?"

Levitt regarded her bleakly. He'd mentioned the possibility of Pearl being subpoenaed along with the rest of them, but he'd never thought it would actually happen. He remembered using the word *might*. Pearl might be included in the list of subpoenas, he'd told the twins. And then he'd cautioned them not to let her know anything about it. He didn't want her worried sick. Well, she was worried now. The moment she'd been served, she'd called Levitt. He'd told her to relax; they'd plan strategy when they all came down to Florida. Damn the Rourkes! he thought viciously. Where the hell did those Irish bastards come off dragging Pearl into this? A woman in her sixties! What goddamned right did they have to parade her in front of television, the press—brand her as a criminal?

"They'll ask you what you knew about Jake's business connections," he finally answered, putting as much gentleness into his voice as possible. "That's all. Maybe something aobut the New York book. I'm sure they know about it, but knowing and proving are two entirely different things. Believe me, Pearl, this thing might drag on for months, but in the end we're all going to walk away from it without a stain on our characters."

"Have you been in touch with Harry Saltzman?" Minsky asked.

"He didn't get subpoenaed. I've told you before, Rourke doesn't know Harry exists."

"I wish to hell he didn't know we existed either," Minsky muttered. And then, without thinking, he added, "Damn Jake for going up to Massachusetts that night!"

"Benny, shut your stupid mouth!" Levitt snapped. He swung around to look at Pearl, saw the shock on her face. He glanced at the twins. Joseph was sitting perfectly still, but Leo's eyes were undergoing that odd change of color. That hint of gray was becoming evident in them. Quickly, Levitt stood up. "We're all going to relax, okay? Senator Rourke's fishing, that's all. Fishing for the White House. This is not a criminal proceeding. He just wants to make a big name for himself by asking a lot of questions about organized crime, and he's hoping at the same time to show us up, square accounts for his old man. That's all there is to it. We're so clean, we squeak." His gazed turned hard. "And we stay clean!"

Without another word, he took Pearl by the arm and led her from Minsky's suite. "Don't get upset over Benny," Levitt said soothingly. "You know that jerk doesn't think before he opens his mouth."

"But he's right," Pearl said softly. "You begged Jake not to go. You said it would cause trouble down the road."

"I know. If I could turn back the clock, I'd find some way of stopping him. But that's not the way life works, Pearl." Seeing her tears, he felt a terrible fury toward the Rourke family. When this was all over, he'd find some way of paying them back again, maybe by keeping Senator Patrick Rourke, Jr. from making 1600 Pennsylvania Avenue his home.

He thought about Leo's remark at the house in Sands Point. *Kill him. Kill Patrick Rourke, Jr.* He'd screamed at Leo . . . a United States Senator wasn't someone like Phil Gerson who'd been milking the till. You didn't send a Harry Saltzman after a man like Patrick Rourke, Jr.! Or did you? Only if you were desperate, Levitt had thought at the time, and he hadn't been desperate. He still wasn't. But he was mad enough now to consider doing it. He'd consider killing anyone who caused Pearl this grief.

Christmas and the days that followed presented nothing out of the ordinary to Harry Saltzman. While the Rourkes celebrated in Boston by going to church and enjoying a warm family atmosphere, and the Granitzes, the Minskys, and Lou Levitt bathed in the Florida sunshine, Saltzman spent each morning working himself into a sweat in the basement of his home, finishing off a round of weight lifting with a five-minute session of pounding the daylights out of a punching bag. He would have preferred to be in Florida, enjoying the hospitality of the Waterway or the Monaco. Indeed, he had planned to be there. But Levitt had called him the moment the subpoenas had been served, with strict instructions to stay away from Florida, to avoid contact at all costs. Saltzman's name had avoided the scrutiny of the Senate investigating committee, and Levitt wanted to keep it that way. He did not want any connection to be found between Saltzman and himself.

"I just don't want to see you giving testimony, Harry," Levitt had told Saltzman. "Even with a battalion of lawyers sitting behind you, you wouldn't know what to say."

The rebuff hadn't offended Saltzman. He realized that his forte was strength, whereas Levitt's was brains. Saltzman eagerly anticipated watching the investigation on television. It would be just like the Kefauver hearings fifteen years earlier. People running for public office always thought they could get some kind of a lift by dragging up horror stories about organized crime. Maybe the Rourkes could garner popularity by tripping up some of the Italians they'd subpoenaed, but Saltzman was confident that Levitt would not get the Rourkes a single vote. He'd run rings around the investigation. By the time he was finished, Saltzman decided with a chuckle, the Rourke brothers would be investigating each other!

On Tuesday, two days after Christmas, Saltzman exercised as usual and took a long shower that finished with a startling burst of icy water that sent his blood tingling. He toweled briskly, dressed in a conservative gray suit, and prepared to leave the house. If he could not spend Christmas week in Florida, that didn't mean he had to remain idle at home. There was always work to be done.

He drove into New York, stopped in front of a brownstone in Murray Hill. A tall, middle-aged man waited on the sidewalk, hat pulled low over his eyes, coat collar wrapped around his ears, hands thrust deeply into his pockets. Saltzman leaned across the car to open the passenger door. "Hurry up and get in, Charlie, before all the heat escapes."

Charlie Jackson climbed into the car and slammed the door. "Merry Christmas, Harry."

"Merry Christmas, yourself."

"Is it this cold the other side of the Hudson?"

"Colder."

Jackson opened his coat collar experimentally as if to check on the temperature inside the car. Satisfied that it was warm enough, he unbuttoned his coat, then removed his hat, which he set on his lap.

Saltzman drove along East Thirty-fourth Street toward Madison Avenue. As he neared the intersection he saw a dozen men and women walking in a circle on the sidewalk. They all carried signs that screamed of unfair treatment and workers' rights. The target of their demonstration was a restaurant named Antonio's. Patrons who tried to enter the restaurant for lunch were confonted by placard-waving pickets. Rather than risk trouble, they turned away to find another restaurant. Ten yards from the demonstration, two patrolmen stood watching.

Saltzman parked the car; then he and Charlie Jackson walked toward the restaurant. The pickets broke ranks to allow them to pass. One of the men patted Jackson on the shoulder and shouted, "Give him hell, Charlie! Give him hell!" Jackson grinned at the recognition.

Pushing back the door, Saltzman entered the restaurant with Jackson following. From the kitchen at the rear rose an appetizing combination of smells. Only there were no customers present. Nor were there waiters, busboys, or dishwashers. Just one man was visible, and he stood in the center of the floor, hands clasped behind his back while he glared hostilely at Saltzman.

"You've got some damned nerve coming in here, you bastard!"

Saltzman ignored the greeting. "It's Christmas week, Mr. Berganza. I'm full of Christmas cheer, okay? I want to help you out."

"I don't need your help," Tony Berganza answered. "What I need is my staff back in here. I don't open for lunch today, I've got food back there that goes rotten."

"I understand that, Mr. Berganza, and this whole unfortunate situation can be resolved in just a few minutes. You know each other?" Saltzman asked Berganza and Jackson. "Mr. Berganza, this here is Charlie Jackson. He's the president of the waiters' local."

"They've got no reason to strike me. You know it and I know it. I pay good money, I don't take liberties."

Saltzman placed a heavy arm around the restaurateur's shoulders. "Mr. Berganza, I've got a lot of pull, a lot of influence with Charlie here. He and I, we've been friends for a long time. Right, Charlie?"

Jackson nodded. "Since we were kids."

"Charlie's open to doing me any favor I want, Mr. Berganza. If I asked him to, he'd go outside and tell those guys they've got to come back to work. He'd iron out your problems. But, Mr. Berganza, why should I ask Charlie for a favor like that, put myself in his debt, when you won't do anything for me?"

"Like join your goddamned association?"

"The New York Guild of Restaurateurs and Victualers." Saltzman reeled off the title proudly. He'd spent a lot of time dreaming up the name of the association he'd created two years earlier. A fancy title for a trade guild covering fancy restaurants. Fast food places and hamburger and pizza joints weren't worth worrying about; they didn't have the kind of money Saltzman charged as dues.

"Your guild's nothing but a protection racket," Berganza protested.

"So's Blue Cross," Saltzman answered with rare humor. "Your health-insurance people, they give you a tatty paper card that you show to the hospital when you get sick. Me . . . the New York Guild of Restaurateurs and Victualers . . . I give you this." He pulled a gilded plaque from his pocket on which was stamped the guild's logo. "Instead of showing this to the admission nurse at some hospital, you put it in your front window. Then, when you get a problem like you've got today, and if you're a member in good standing, all you do is contact me. It becomes my responsibility because I'm the president of the guild, and you're a member."

Berganza gazed through the window at the pickets. Even as he watched, more regular customers decided to eat lunch somewhere else that day. If this went right on to dinner . . . and then more of the same tomorrow . . . Berganza shuddered. "How much?"

"A joining fee of one thousand dollars—that's a one-off fee, Mr. Berganza, to cover paperwork and administrative details—and a yearly fee, up front, also of one thousand dollars. That's what gets you your benefits."

Berganza wanted to ask if it was tax deductible, but he did not have the courage. Of course it wasn't. Extortion wasn't an allowable deduction, and this was nothing short of extortion. But if he fought it, how would he survive? His restaurant would be struck for weeks. "Will you take a check?"

"Mr. Berganza . . ." Saltzman's voice was pained.

"I don't carry that much cash so early in the day. I work with a small float, just enough to make change."

"Then you'd better hurry to your bank before the lunchtime trade really picks up, Mr. Berganza. Two thousand dollars."

As he threw on his coat and hurried toward the door, Berganza already viewed the situation in a different light. Two thousand dollars was only forty dollars a week. He lost far more than that on the horses. And next year, after the one-time joining fee was paid, it would only cost him twenty dollars a week. Perhaps it wasn't so expensive after all.

Saltzman watched the door close behind Berganza, saw the pickets step back to let their employer through. "You go out and talk to them," he told Jackson. "Get them back inside, show Berganza that the guild keeps its word. In the meantime, I'll fix the plaque to the window." Smiling in satisfaction, Saltzman glued the plaque to the inside of the glass.

Berganza returned ten minutes later clutching a white envelope. The restaurant was not as he had left it. The waiters were back at work preparing for lunchtime; the busboys and dishwashers were at positions. Even as Berganza handed the money to Saltzman, two regular customers entered Antonio's to honor their lunchtime reservations.

"See how useful the guild is, Mr. Berganza?" Saltzman asked. He pocketed the envelope without bothering to count the money.

"Protection," Berganza muttered. "I'm paying you to protect myself from you."

Saltzman rested a hand on Berganza's arm. "You don't sound happy. The guild doesn't like its members to be unhappy." There was more menace in Saltzman's voice than outright threat would have contained. Berganza walked away to supervise the operation of a restaurant that was now a member of the New York Guild of Restaurateurs and Victualers.

Saltzman and Jackson returned to the car. Inside, Saltzman opened the envelope and counted out five hundred dollars which he gave to the union official. "How many does that make, Harry?"

"Members of the guild?" Saltzman consulted a dog-eared notebook which he pulled from his jacket pocket. "One hundred and thirty-five so far. Maybe we'll expand, take in northern New Jersey, Connecticut as well. Change the name and call it the Tri-State Guild."

"We've got enough potential members in New York," Jackson said. "It's just a matter of getting everyone else into line."

Saltzman nodded. The guild was not a spectacular fortune maker, but it was easy money and it gave Saltzman an entrée into the restaurant business. He understood that he could not squeeze the owners too tightly. If he levied unacceptable dues on them, they would go out of business and that would be the end of it. This way, he wasn't killing them. A thousand-a-year membership was affordable. More important, it wasn't worth the trouble of going to the police.

"Who else is causing us problems?" Saltzman asked as he started the engine.

"Mickey's Deli over on Seventh Avenue. We pulled a strike there last week, got all the waiters out on the sidewalk just like we did at Antonio's. So they fired everyone, closed up for the day, and opened the following morning with a whole new crew."

"That sounds like the kind of thing they'd do," Saltzman growled, with just a hint of admiration in his voice. Mickey's Deli was a large, well-reviewed delicatessen that Saltzman had been trying to incorporate into the guild for three months. The owner, a former lightweight boxer named Mickey Phillips, had refused, saying that he'd seen his fill of crooks and thieves while he was in the fight game; he didn't need to run a restaurant to encounter more.

"You giving the order to stink the place out?" Jackson asked.

"Not yet." Before Saltzman sent in men with butyric acid bombs, he wanted to try one more personal approach. Phillips was looked up to in the restaurant world. If he could be persuaded to join the guild, a lot of other holdouts would fall into line; and if he continued to put up a fight, others would take their lead from him. Perhaps it was time to offer the ex-boxer a loss leader. "I'm going to take you home, Charlie, then I'll drop by Mickey's Deli for lunch. See if we can't work something out there."

"I wish you luck."

After dropping Jackson off in Murray Hill, Saltzman drove slowly to Seventh Avenue. The delicatessen was full when he entered—a mixture of shoppers in town for the post-Christmas sales, theater people taking a break from rehearsals, journalists, and sporting folk. Plastered across the walls were signed photographs of athletes and entertainers, all wishing Mickey Phillips well on the opening of his delicatessen ten years earlier.

Instead of choosing a table or booth, Saltzman seated himself at the counter that ran almost the entire length of the delicatessen. A waiter slapped a menu in front of him. Saltzman let his eyes run down the cover—another photograph of an athlete, this one of Mickey Phillips in his prime, boxing gloves raised in a sparring stance. Below the picture was a story that told of Phillips carrying on a family tradition by opening the delicatessen. His parents, so it said, had owned a small delicatessen on Delancey Street, and it had always been Phillips' ambition to follow them into the family business. Saltzman smiled at the sickening sentimentality of the story. Some public relations writer must have had a ball coming up with that connection. About the only similarity between Mickey's Deli and any joint Phillips' parents may have owned on Delancey Street was that they both sold food. This place was the Waldorf of delicatessens. Phillips' old-world parents would have felt as out of place here as at a hog barbecue.

Before the waiter came back to take his order, Saltzman felt a strong hand grip his shoulder painfully. "See that sign?" a voice asked. A finger alongside Saltzman's face pointed to the wall behind the counter. In the center of the signed photographs was a sign that read: The management reserves the right to refuse admittance.

"I see it, Mickey," Saltzman said. He swung around on the stool and looked into Mickey Phillips' face. Despite the blue business suit, the white shirt and wine-colored tie, there was no doubt of Phillips' pedigree. His nose had been broken a couple of times, and scar tissue wove its way around his thin eyebrows. Much shorter, much lighter than Saltzman, Phillips still possessed the aggressiveness of a professional fighter, moving on the balls of his feet, his body lean and hard. He looked as though he could step back into the ring at a week's notice and give a good account of himself.

"That means you, ape," Phillips said. "I'm the management, and I reserve the right to refuse you admittance. Now get the hell out of here before I toss you out."

"Can't a man come in out of the cold for a cup of coffee and a pastrami sandwich?"

"I wouldn't serve you coffee if you were dying of the cold. Beat it, ape, before the zoo finds out you've escaped."

Saltzman ignored the insult. "I've got a proposition for you."

"Join your guild? Forget it."

"Honorary membership," Saltzman said grandly. He pulled a guild plaque from his pocket. "Stick this in your front window. No fee for joining, no membership dues."

A flicker of interest crossed Phillips' face. "Free membership, eh? And if I'm seen to join, how many others will also join?" Before Saltzman could think of an answer, Phillips continued. "If my being a member is worth that much, maybe you should be paying me to join. A free membership under those circumstances . . . why, that's almost an insult."

"Maybe I could—" Saltzman stopped speaking while he watched Phillips produce a gold lighter, hold the plaque in the air, and set fire to it. As the flames licked his fingers, Phillips dropped the burning plaque into Saltzman's lap.

"You son of a bitch!" Saltzman yelled, leaping up from the stool to beat at his lap with his hands. The burning plaque fell to the floor and Phillips stamped on it.

"That's what I'm going to do to you, you show your face around here again. Now get the hell out!" Phillips reached across the counter, felt beneath it, came up with a policeman's nightstick. Prodding Saltzman with the end, he shoved him toward the door.

Saltzman found himself out on the sidewalk, his trousers scorched, his pride shattered. He had hoped to get Mickey Phillips to join for nothing, a gesture that would encourage others to pay up. Instead, Phillips had humiliated him in front of a restaurant full of customers. If word of this got around, the guild would be a laughingstock. Other restaurateurs would start burning their plaques, and Saltzman's comfortable little business would be in jeopardy.

Saltzman could not afford to let that happen. It was time to consider more dramatic measures.

Chapter Four

The Senate Special Committee on Organized Crime convened in New York City the second week of February. The chairman of the committee, briefed and assisted by his brother John, was Senator Patrick Rourke, Jr. The other five members, all hand-picked for being outspoken opponents of organized crime and supporters of a presidential bid by Senator Rourke, were senators from New York, California, Pennsylvania, Ohio, and Florida. Each represented an area where the committee would hold hearings, and all hoped to reap political gain.

The committee was in session for a week, hearing the testimony of witnesses with alleged connections to organized crime, before any of the Levitt-Minsky-Granitz group was called to appear. Their order of appearance had been carefully planned. Lou Levitt was to be the final witness of the group. Senator Rourke did not want any of the others to take a lead from Levitt's testimony.

William Minsky was the first to be called before the committee. Accompanied by a lawyer, William identified himself and sat down to face the panel of senators. He was fully aware of the television cameras upon him, the tape recorders running, the reporters with pencils poised over their notebooks. With Susan, William had watched the news reports of the hearing the previous week. If anything, the questioning had seemed easygoing, almost conversational, but William had little doubt that once he and his associates appeared, the tempo would quicken.

Senator Rourke opened the questioning. "Would you tell this committee where you work, Mr. Minsky? Your position, and the nature of your work."

"I'm president of B.M. Transportation Company in Long Island City."

"B.M. stands for . . . ?"

"Benjamin Minsky, my father. He founded the company."

"When was that?"

"Back in the early thirties."

Senator Rourke inclined his head deferentially. "That was quite a tough time for starting businesses, Mr. Minsky. America was in the depths of the Depression. Businesses were going bankrupt, banks were being wiped out. Yet your father started what has become a well-known, highly successful company. In those hard times, where did he get the trucks? How did he pay for them? And where did he find customers who had goods to haul?"

William sensed that his lawyer was giving him a signal. He moved closer to the microphone on the table in front of him and said, "I was a baby then. I didn't even know how to spell the word *truck,* let alone ask my father where they came from. You'll have to ask him yourself."

"I intend to, Mr. Minsky. I intend to."

The senator from Florida raised a hand. "Do you have an interest in the Monaco Hotel in Hollywood and the Waterway Hotel in Hallandale?"

"Only by association. My father is chairman and chief operating officer of the Palmetto Leisure Development Corporation, which owns those hotels."

"Could you describe the hotels for us?"

"They're just regular hotels, what else can I say?"

"You speak very self-effacingly about two of the most luxurious hotels in South Florida. Would that be because each hotel has a casino, an illegal casino, on the top floor?"

"Not to my knowledge they don't," William answered evenly. "Casino gambling is against the law in Florida. I would have thought that you, who represent Florida in our nation's capital, would have known that."

Laughter erupted, and Senator Rourke pounded the table with a gavel. Not to be deterred, the senator from Florida said, "But casinos used to be there, right?"

William made no answer, and the senator repeated his question. The lawyer leaned across to William. "I refuse to answer that question on the grounds that I may incriminate myself."

William was questioned for another hour and then dismissed. Senator Rourke had never anticipated learning much from William, just as he expected to receive scant reward from questioning the Granitz twins. They, like himself and his brother, were of the second generation. The real answers lay with the first generation. With Benjamin Minsky, Louis Levitt, and Pearl Granitz. He called Pearl next.

Despite the calm appearance she tried so hard to maintain, Pearl's stomach was churning. Her legs felt weak, and she was glad of the chair she dropped into. She did not know how long she could have lasted if she had been expected to answer questions while standing up. Nervously, she patted her fresh hairdo, waved off her face and blue rinsed—the first time she had ever colored her hair since the escapade with Annie more than half a century earlier. The new hairstyle made her look like a sweet, little old lady. It had been Levitt's idea, along with the dowdy brown dress and plain shoes she wore. Levitt had spent the entire weekend with her, trying to soothe her nerves, giving her assurances that she would waltz through the hearing.

"Mrs. Granitz, you are the widow of Jake Granitz?" Senator Rourke asked.

"I am."

"How long ago did your husband die?"

"Twenty-six years ago."

"It was on the occasion of your twin sons' bar mitzvahs, correct?"

"It was."

"Would you explain to us how your husband died?"

Pearl wiped a tear from her eyes. There was no need for acting here. Any time she thought of that terrible day, she started to cry. "He was shot outside the synagogue, after the service."

"Shot by whom?"

"A man named Gus Landau."

Senator Rourke understood the perilousness of this line of questioning. It could bring an answer that might implicate his own father. He knew he had to elicit responses that would avoid doing that, while inflicting as much damage as possible on his father's old enemies. "Do you know what happened to Gus Landau?"

"He was killed a few days later."

"How?"

"He was shot by a friend of my husband." Levitt had told Pearl that the questioning would certainly cover Jake's death. He had instructed her to tell the truth. There was nothing in it that could harm her or the family; it was all public knowledge, splashed across the headlines when it had happened.

"The name of this friend, Mrs. Granitz?"

"Moses Caplan . . . Moe Caplan."

"What happened to him?"

"He was killed by Gus Landau. They shot each other." Pearl understood what Senator Rourke was doing—he was laying the groundwork for questioning that would come later from the other members of the committee. She decided to save him time by volunteering the remainder of the information she expected him to ask for. "The following day, Moe Caplan's widow, Judy—a childhood friend of mine—committed suicide. I brought up her daughter as my own. She is now married to one of my sons."

Senator Rourke smiled at Pearl's perceptiveness in answering the remainder of his questions. He looked to his colleagues, and the senator from New York took over.

"Mrs. Granitz, what do you know about the Jalo Cab Company?"

"It was a business partnership between my husband and his friend, Lou Levitt. The name was derived from the first two letters of their first names, Jake and Lou."

"I see. It was sold several years ago, I understand."

"In 1960."

The senator from New York leaned forward, chin resting on steepled hands. "There was a room above the Jalo Cab garage . . . a rather large room?"

"There may have been. I was never there."

"Do you know what took place in that room?" When Pearl was slow to answer, the senator continued, "Would it be safe to say that the nerve center for a large bookmaking and numbers racket was located in that large room above the Jalo Cab garage?"

Pearl felt her stomach churn. How was she supposed to lie about this? She'd never been up there, but she certainly knew what had gone on. She felt the lawyer touch her arm. "I refuse to answer that question on the grounds that I may incriminate myself."

The senator from New York carried on as though he had not heard her. "Would it also be safe to say that this highly illegal gambling operation was run through a chain of small mom-and-pop shops, cigar stores, restaurants, bakeries, and the like? And furthermore, would it be safe to say that the people employed in that operation were listed as employees of either the Jalo Cab Company or B.M. Transportation? Your son, Joseph, for example, who was employed as a deputy office manager for Jalo? And your other son, Leo, who was down on the books as a driver for Jalo?"

"Both of my sons went to work for Jalo when they finished their education."

Senator Rourke lifted a hand to signify that he wanted the floor. Pearl watched him warily, certain that he was going to lead her down that painful avenue of death again. Her intuition was perfectly correct. "Mrs. Granitz, let's go back to Gus Landau. He killed your husband, and he killed your husband's friend. Did he not also have a hand in your mother's death?" Rourke consulted a report on the table. "Your mother was killed in—"

"In the restaurant she owned on Second Avenue!" Pearl burst out. "Why do you have to bring my mother into this? Isn't it enough that you've already dragged up my husband's death?"

Finally, Senator Rourke thought with a savage wrench of joy . . . finally he had reached Pearl, torn through whatever defense she had built up. "There was a time period of seven or eight years between the deaths of your mother and your husband, yet they were both killed by the same man. What was the connection? For what reason did Gus Landau come back so many years after killing your mother to kill your husband?" He watched Pearl expectantly, waiting for an answer that never came. "Because, Mrs. Granitz, your husband was always Landau's target? And the intended victims on the night your mother died were Jake Granitz and his friend, Louis Levitt, but Landau missed?"

Pearl burst into tears and Senator Rourke banged on the table with the gavel. The hearing would adjourn for half an hour, he said, until the witness had regained her composure. Led by the lawyer, Pearl rose and went outside. The twins and Levitt waited for her. Leo was seething. He had seen his mother bullied, reduced to tears; and all he wanted to do was attack Senator Patrick Rourke, Jr. Not with words, as the senator had attacked Pearl, but with his fists. Levitt and Joseph worked hard to calm the younger twin.

"We've got to beat the Rourkes at their own game," Levitt stressed to Leo. "We'll fend off their questions, give them nothing. And that way we'll defeat them."

"Didn't you see what that bastard did to Ma?" Leo protested.

"He did what he's supposed to do," Joseph said. "We didn't expect him to do anything less. Ma handled him just fine."

"She cried! No one makes Ma cry and gets away with it!"

Levitt had a sudden vision of Leo running amok during the hearing. All the careful work that Levitt had done, all the briefing of the witnesses, would come to naught if Leo managed to get ahold of the senator. "I'll talk to him, Leo. I'll talk to Senator Rourke, okay?"

"You get him to lay off Ma, Uncle Lou."

"I will."

Before the hearing reconvened, Levitt sought out Senator Rourke. He found him cloistered in a small office with his brother, John. When Levitt was announced, the senator showed surprise.

"I don't expect witnesses to see me beforehand."

"And I don't expect a United States Senator to attack a defenseless woman the way you just did."

"Are you trying to persuade the senator to alter his line of questioning?" John Rourke asked.

Ignoring the younger brother, Levitt continued to stare angrily at Senator Rourke. "You know damned well that Gus Landau was trying to kill me and Jake Granitz the night Pearl's mother was shot. And you know why! It was because of your father. Your father contracted with Gus Landau and Saul Fromberg to kill us. That failed, and we all know what happened after that, don't we?"

"No, we don't, Mr. Levitt. I haven't the faintest idea what you're talking about."

"Then let me put it another way. It's no skin off my nose if you want to carry on with this Landau business, because when it's my turn to testify, I'm going to come back with the whole story. And all your gavel banging won't be able to shut me up. Your old man was a bootlegger . . . okay, that's nothing to be ashamed of these days. Lots of us started out the same way. But your old man's not going to look so smug and respectable once it comes out that he accepted a contract to kill people who were his good customers. We used to buy your old man's Irish whiskey, and he took money to bump us off. You think about that when you get back to questioning Mrs. Granitz."

"You wouldn't dare," John Rourke said as Levitt turned to leave. "You bring that up, and you'd better be ready to explain how twelve of my father's men got killed one night when a convoy was hijacked, or how Saul Fromberg died."

"Fromberg committed suicide because the IRS was going to nail him to a wall. His books were open on his desk when he jumped."

"Sure he committed suicide." John Rourke sneered. "He jumped out of the window a split second after he was thrown out. The IRS men were fakes—your men, dressed and trained to look like IRS agents. You think we don't know all that?"

Levitt's blue eyes followed the quivering finger he pointed at Senator Rourke. "You ask me whatever you like. You want to make some points for yourself, go right ahead and try to crucify me. But don't take cheap shots at Mrs. Granitz. She's got nothing to do with any of this."

"Were we right about you and Granitz being the intended targets on the night Pearl Granitz's mother was killed?" the senator asked.

"You're right."

"In that case," John Rourke said quietly, "how come only Granitz got killed outside the synagogue? Why didn't Landau go for you as well?"

"How the hell do I know? Maybe if I'd been standing with Jake, he'd have got us both. Landau was alone. He just fired the one shot and took off."

"You could say you were very lucky that day, the same as you were when Mrs. Granitz's mother got killed."

"I've learned not to question luck, just to accept it," Levitt said. He swung around and walked quickly from the room, leaving the Rourke brothers to ponder his threat about exposing their father's past.

"Why are we doing this?" Senator Rourke asked at last. "Are we doing it for Dad, to get his revenge? Or are we doing it for ourselves?"

"For ourselves," John answered.

"That's what I thought. What we know and what we can use here are two different things. I'm going to adjourn for the day, give the Granitz woman a chance to get herself together again. When we start again tomorrow, we'll either ease up on her or we won't call her back. We'll decide which course to take tonight. We can always come down hard on her sons, this Benjamin Minsky, and Levitt. They'll be able to defend themselves better, and we won't run the risk of having Dad embarrassed—or ourselves."

John nodded in agreement. The whole idea of a committee investigation was to gain popularity for his brother's run for the White House. No popularity ensued from making an elderly woman cry. And having their own father's criminal involvement publicized . . .

The hearing was reconvened just long enough for Senator Rourke to suspend proceedings for the day. Instead of going to their separate homes, the subpoenaed parties went to Granitz Tower. There, in Joseph's office, Levitt reviewed the day's proceedings.

"William, you handled yourself just great," Levitt said. "You didn't give those bastards a bone to chew on. I hope the rest of us do so well." He turned to Pearl. "What happened to you was unfortunate, but believe me when I say it won't be repeated. I spoke to the Rourkes. I made a deal with them. They're going to leave you alone on the condition that they can ask me whatever they like."

Leo broke in. "That doesn't make what happened any better. He had Ma crying. For Christ's sake, everyone and his goddamned brother will watch it on television. You think I want people to see my mother like that?"

"I don't want people to see it either, Leo."

"I want to pay them back."

"Vote for Humphrey in the Democratic Primary," Joseph quipped, "and you'll have paid them back."

Leo glared at his twin brother for a moment, and then he started to laugh. A vote for Hubert Humphrey . . . that was one way to pay back the Rourkes. But it wasn't enough by far.

Harry Saltzman felt disappointed in the television coverage of the Senate Special Committee. He had expected Levitt to be the first witness called to testify, and so far the little man had not been called. Saltzman found no pleasure in seeing William Minsky answer seemingly innocuous questions, or in watching Pearl being forced to tears. Levitt was the star of this spectacular. He was the witness Saltzman wanted to see.

Regretfully, Saltzman turned off the television. He was expecting visitors that evening and wanted to be ready for them. Six weeks had passed since his disastrous visit to Mickey's Deli on Seventh Avenue, when the offer of free membership had been rejected by Mickey Phillips. Other restaurateurs were taking courage from Phillips' defiance. That had to be stopped.

The doorbell rang. Saltzman admitted two visitors, men named Hymie Glass and Stan Kaye. He gave them money and a box that could have contained a pint bottle of whiskey. Instead, it contained a stink bomb. Not the kind a child bought at a novelty store and used as a practical joke, but a bottle filled with butyric acid, a chemical so strong that its vile odor of putrefaction seeped into carpets, furnishings, even into wood. Once there, it was impossible to remove. If Mickey Phillips wanted to stay out of the New York Guild of Restaurateurs and Victualers, he would do so because he no longer had a restaurant.

Hymie Glass and Stan Kaye timed their arrival at Seventh Avenue to coincide with the closing of Mickey's Deli at midnight. The last of the customers were leaving. Waiters pushed brooms across the floors, stacked chairs and tables. Phillips stood by the cash register, totaling the receipts. The black nightstick lay next to the register, in easy reach. When he saw Glass and Kaye enter, he said, "Sorry, fellows. We're closed for the night."

"We're not here for a meal," Glass answered with an easy smile.

"We're delivering a gift," Kaye added. He pulled open the box and showed the pint bottle full of butyric acid.

Phillips moved with the speed he had shown in the ring. Before Kaye could raise his arm to toss the stink bomb into the center of the delicatessen, Phillips darted from behind the cash register. In one quick movement, he picked up the nightstick and slammed the end of it into Kaye's stomach. Kaye doubled forward. Phillips grabbed the bottle with his left hand, using his right to swing the nightstick in a wide arc that kept Glass away. One of the waiters rushed forward, holding a broom like a lance. He rammed Glass in the back, sending him staggering. As Glass fought for balance, Phillips leaped forward, the bottle in one hand, the raised nightstick in the other. Glass merely whimpered as the nightstick cracked against the top of his head.

Breathing hard, Phillips leaned back against the counter. Glass was unconscious on the floor. Kaye was on his knees, clutching his stomach. Phillips set the bottle down gently on the counter. He had little doubt what it contained. If it was going to be smashed, that wasn't going to happen in the delicatessen he'd worked ten years to build up. He dropped the nightstick, stepped forward, and lifted Kaye up by the lapels of his coat.

"Who sent you? Saltzman?"

Kaye groaned and Phillips slammed him against a wall. "I'm going to ask you one more time, and then your head is going to start making a pretty stucco pattern on my walls. Who sent you?"

"Harry Saltzman!" Kaye's voice was a shriek as he felt Phillips' grip tighten.

"Where do I find him?" Phillips jerked his arms straight, and Kaye's head banged off the wall. "Where?"

"Fort Lee. New Jersey." Kaye sputtered out the address. Phillips memorized it, then dragged Kaye to the front door and threw him out onto the sidewalk. With the help of the waiter who had wielded the broom, he sent Glass after him.

"What are you going to do?" the waiter asked. "Call the police?"

Phillips thought about it. "What can the police do that I can't?" he asked with a grin. Carrying the bottle of butyric acid, he left the restaurant and walked to his car which was parked in a lot on West Fifty-fourth Street.

Twenty-five minutes later, Phillips was in Fort Lee. He felt tense, excited and confident, just like he had the moment before he'd stepped into the ring. He found Saltzman's house at the end of a cul-de-sac. A large wrought-iron gate prevented him from driving further. Lights shone inside the house but no cars were parked in the driveway. Phillips guessed that Saltzman would be out, probably with somebody who would vouch for his whereabouts this night. Even if he had sent others to stink-bomb Mickey's Deli, he would want an unshakable alibi of his own. That suited Phillips perfectly.

Letting himself in through the wrought-iron gate, Phillips walked along the driveway until he reached the front door. To make sure no one was about, he rang the bell. There was no answer. Satisfied, Phillips made a quick inspection of the outside of the house. All the windows were locked. Entrance was impossible without breaking glass. He did so, shoving his gloved hand through a large pane of glass in the living-room window. The sound barely carried for the broken glass fell onto soft carpet inside the house. Working carefully, Phillips picked all the glass out of the pane. Then he stepped back, wound up like a baseball pitcher, and flung the bottle of butyric acid, as hard as he could, through the opening. The bottle sailed across the living room and shattered against the opposite wall. Even as Phillips ran back toward the wrought-iron gate and his car he caught a whiff of the acid. The stench almost made him gag.

After tonight, Harry Saltzman would be more interested in looking for a new house than in increasing the membership of his guild. . . .

Harry Saltzman arrived home at three in the morning after playing in a poker game that would alibi him against any charges Mickey Phillips might want to level. The moment Saltzman stepped out of his car, he knew something was wrong. He could smell butyric acid everywhere. Faint traces wafted across the grounds, carried by the light breeze, to hit Saltzman like the smell of a sewage farm close up. He guessed immediately what had happened. Hymie Glass and Stan Kaye, the men he'd sent to soften up Phillips, had failed. Phillips himself had paid a return call.

The moment he opened the front door, the full force of the smell hit him like a bomb-burst. He staggered back, hands grabbing at his stomach as he threw up. Every piece of furniture would have to be thrown out, burned. The house itself was a total loss. No perfume sprays, no coats of paint would ever hide that offensive odor. As he got back into his car he could smell the putrefactive odor on his clothes. Leaning out of the window, he retched again and again, until his stomach was empty. And then he retched painfully, bringing up nothing at all.

Face covered with a cold sweat, he drove like a wild man across the George Washington Bridge into Upper Manhattan. Stopping at the first pay phone he saw, he dialed Hymie Glass's home number in the Bronx. The telephone rang unanswered for fully thirty seconds before Saltzman slammed the receiver down. The dime dropped. He reinserted it and dialed Stan Kaye's home in Queens. Kaye answered.

"What the hell happened?" Saltzman yelled. "I get back to my house and the place stinks like an overflowing shithole!"

"He jumped us, Harry."

"What do you mean, he jumped you? There were two of you!"

"He jumped us with a nightstick. The waiters joined in. We never had a chance. Hymie's in the hospital. They're keeping him overnight for observation, possible concussion."

"You get him out of that hospital and you meet me tomorrow night."

"Where?"

Saltzman's mouth dropped. They couldn't come to his house; he didn't have it, couldn't use it. "Wait until I get settled in a hotel, get myself some new clothes. Then you, me, and Hymie are going to wait for Mr. Phillips one night. You understand?"

"We'll be there, Harry. We've got a score to settle with him as well."

"Not half as bad as mine," Saltzman growled. He hung up the telephone, got back into the car, and headed toward midtown.

When the Senate Special Committee reconvened the following morning, Pearl was not called back to testify. The next witness was Leo, and his fury at Senator Patrick Rourke, Jr. was evident from the moment he opened his mouth to identify himself.

"Leo Granitz!" he spat out with such force and venom that Senator Rourke, playing to the press, mentioned facetiously that there was no need for the witness to shout since he had a perfectly adequate microphone on the table in front of him. Leo glared at the microphone, as though it were an extension of the senator. He placed his hands on either side of it, clenched into hard, angry fists.

"Would you tell the committee where you work, and your position there?" Senator Rourke asked.

"Granitz Brothers. I'm a vice-president."

"Responsible for what?"

"The day-to-day maintenance operations of our properties."

"You give orders to the maintenance crews?"

"I do."

Senator Rourke tapped the end of a pencil on the tabletop. "When you left high school, you went to work for the Jalo Cab Company. What was it like to drive a cab?"

Leo looked at Senator Rourke as though he were mad. What kind of question was that? What was it like to clean sewers . . . what was it like to sweep streets . . . what was it like to sew clothes or repair shoes? "All right, I guess."

"It's quite a switch from driving a cab to being vice-president of a thriving real-estate company. I must congratulate you."

The senator from New York took over the questioning. "While you were driving your cab for Jalo, did you make frequent stops at small restaurants, candy stores, places like that?"

"I stopped wherever I had a fare."

"And were there fares, every single day, to these small shops? Morning and evening?"

"I don't remember. It's been a long time since I pushed a cab."

"Let me see if I can jog your memory," the senator from New York said. "You weren't driving a cab. You've never driven a cab for hire in your life, although you do hold a license to do so. You were going out every morning and every evening from the Jalo offices to pick up bets and betting slips and to deliver payout money. Is that true?"

"I drove a cab," Leo reiterated stonily.

"Have you ever been involved with bookmaking?"

"I've placed bets at the track."

"That does not answer my question. Have you ever been involved with bookmaking? Was a bookmaking operation run from the room above the Jalo garage? Were you a collector? Were you in charge of all the collectors? Is that where you received your experience in supervising, giving orders to other people?"

When Leo sat with his lips compressed in a thin, angry line, Senator Rourke told him, "You must respond to the questions, even if it is only by saying you refuse to answer."

After a brief consultation with his lawyer, Leo pled the Fifth Amendment.

"What do you remember about your father's death?" the senator from New York asked.

"It was a long time ago."

"What do you remember about your grandmother's death?"

"It was even longer ago. I was a small child."

"Your mother, when she testified yesterday, could give us no connection between the same man shooting your grandmother and your father. Can you give us a connection, Mr. Granitz?"

The fury, which had been bubbling just below the surface while Leo sat at the witness table, finally broke through. He shot to his feet and jabbed a fist in the direction of the committee. Immediately, two police officers hurried toward him. "You had no damned business dragging my mother into any of this! What kind of a man are you, picking on a widowed woman?"

Senator Rourke watched impassively as Leo's lawyer hissed something to his client. Leo sat down before the two policemen could reach him. What with Levitt's visit yesterday after Pearl's breakdown, and now this, they certainly stuck together, Rourke thought. An insult to Pearl Granitz was an insult to them all. He wondered if he would encounter the same fierce loyalty when Joseph Granitz was called to testify. Perhaps it would be just as well to lay off Pearl altogether. Her inclusion in this resulted in nothing but hostility. Besides, Senator Rourke already knew the answer to the question that had enraged Leo. Gus Landau had been after the same target both times. "Mr. Granitz, I promise that this committee will not

601

mention your mother again," he said.

Joseph was the next to testify. Senator Rourke led him through the background with the Jalo Cab Company, ascertained that he had been deputy office manager and, as he had done earlier with Leo, congratulated him on rising to such a prestigious position with Granitz Brothers. Joseph's face remained devoid of expression.

"I think we know all there is to know about the Jalo Cab Company," Senator Rourke said, "so we won't bore you any further with it. Let's talk, instead, about Granitz Brothers."

"Talk about whatever you like," Joseph invited the senator.

"Thank you. Tell me, Mr. Granitz, why do you finance your deals in this country through a Swiss bank?"

Joseph's eyelids flickered, but that was all. "Because they offer us the most competitive rates."

"I see. Leinberg Bank offers you the most competitive rates. You must like Switzerland as well. I understand that while you were deputy office manager for Jalo you made a number of trips there. Would you tell us the reason for all these trips? Were they job connected?"

Joseph took a deep breath. "My first trip to Switzerland was for my honeymoon. Zurich was one of the many places my wife and I visited."

"And the succeeding trips?"

"I was vice-president of an engineering company in Zurich called A. G. Kriesel."

"Deputy office manager of a New York taxi company *and* vice-president of a Swiss engineering company. Quite a combination. I am impressed. Who owned this A. G. Kriesel?"

"Lou Levitt and Benny Minsky."

"For the record, that is the Louis Levitt who was a partner with your father in the Jalo Cab Company, and the Benjamin Minsky who founded B.M. Transportation and who is now chairman and chief operating officer of the Palmetto Leisure Development Corporation. Have I got it all correct?"

"You have."

"Why did you make such regular trips to A. G. Kriesel?"

"The company was experiencing difficulties. I was attempting to straighten out these difficulties."

The senator from Ohio raised a hand. "Mr. Granitz, what is the difference between a sun gear and a planet gear?"

Joseph stared dumbly at the senator from Ohio; he might just as well have asked for the secret of eternal life.

"Does your silence mean that you don't know?"

"I don't know."

"Isn't it rather odd that a vice-president of an engineering company does not possess such basic engineering knowledge?"

Joseph sought frantically to retrieve the situation. "My degree is in business, not engineering. Kriesel's difficulties weren't concerned with engineering. Their problems stemmed from mismanagement."

The senator from Ohio seemed not to hear. "Isn't it also rather coincidental that this engineering company in Zurich, this A. G. Kriesel, should be so close to the Leinberg Bank, which has financed your real-estate corporation? As it has also financed the Waterway and Monaco hotels in South Florida."

Joseph chose not to answer. He suspected the senator was not anticipating a reply.

Senator Rourke picked up the thread of the interrogation. "Would it be closer to the truth to say that your real purpose in visiting Zurich so often was to deposit money with the Leinberg Bank? Money that represented the profits of the vast gambling operation that was run from the Jalo Cab Company building. Money that could not be deposited in this country because you wished to avoid paying taxes on it."

Joseph felt the warning touch of the lawyer's hand. "I refuse to answer that question on the grounds that I may incriminate myself."

"Thank you, Mr. Granitz," Senator Rourke said. "That will be all." He knew he'd scored points with that line of questioning. He would score even more when he got Benny Minsky and Lou Levitt in front of him.

When the hearing recessed for the day, another meeting was held in Joseph's office in Granitz Tower. This time, the mood was not so upbeat. Levitt was worried. Senator Patrick Rourke, Jr. and his brother, John, had done their homework well. They knew every date that Joseph had made the trip to Zurich. They must have checked with airlines, the immigration people, to be so thorough. Levitt wondered what surprises the committee would have for him and Benny Minsky when their turns to testify came.

"Okay," Levitt said when everyone was seated in Joseph's office. "So they've knocked us back on our heels a bit. They're making assumptions, but they haven't got a damned bit of proof. If they had, we'd all be facing criminal charges by now. To get us, they've got to have corroborating witnesses, and there's no way they're going to pull that off."

"What do you think they're going to ask me?" Benny Minsky

wanted to know.

"Probably questions about the trucking company. And about the hotels. You went down there after Phil was out of the picture."

"They haven't brought up Phil's name," Joseph mused. "Think they missed something? They know all about me going to Zurich, they know all about the hotels in Florida; but they haven't mentioned Phil."

"Don't worry about it, they will," Levitt said with grim certainty. He noticed Leo agitatedly checking his watch. "You got a date or something?"

"We'll miss the news," Leo answered. "I want to see how I look on television."

Levitt grinned at the answer, and some of their tension disappeared. "You looked like someone who was mad enough to kill a whole bunch of United States Senators. Go on, get out of here. We'll see you back at the hearing tomorrow."

Leo left. Instead of returning to Scarsdale, he went to his apartment on East Fifty-ninth Street. The news was just starting when he turned on the television. He pulled a chair close to the screen and sat down to watch. The Senate hearing was the fourth item to be covered. The emphasis was on Joseph's testimony about the trips to Switzerland and Leo felt disappointed. Then his mood lightened when his own angry face filled the screen, shouting at Senator Rourke that he had no damned business persecuting a widowed woman.

The moment the piece finished, the telephone rang. Leo answered. "I just saw you on the news," an accented voice said. "Such anger, such fury . . . I do not think I would want to cross you."

Leo smiled as he recognized Mahmoud Asawi's voice. "Where are you calling from?"

"A pay phone, of course, outside of where I live. Do you want to see me tonight?"

"Come to the other place." Leo even refused to mention Scarsdale by name. "I'll be there by nine o'clock. No, better yet, I'll pick you up at the northeast corner of Columbus and West Seventy-second Street at eight-fifteen." With the investigation, he had no way of knowing if his house was being watched. Someone might see the number of the car he'd given to Mahmoud. Secrecy! . . . Secrecy! . . .

"I look forward to seeing you," Mahmoud said before breaking the connection.

Benny Minsky was the first witness to be called the following morning. Levitt sat watching, holding Pearl's hand as Minsky was sworn in. Neither the twins nor William Minsky were present; they were back at work, their roles in the committee hearing finished. Levitt had not wanted Pearl to come either—Senator Patrick Rourke, Jr. had put her through enough aggravation already—but she had wanted to be present for when Levitt's time came. Like himself, she had little doubt that he was really the star attraction. She wanted to give him all the support she could.

"How do you think Benny will do?" Pearl whispered.

"As long as he listens to the lawyer and keeps his mouth shut when he's supposed to, everything'll be fine. The last thing we need is for him to go bursting a blood vessel now because he gets riled up."

"He isn't that way anymore," Pearl said. "He's grown out of it, matured."

Levitt gave a cynical laugh. "Everyone else matures at twenty or twenty-five. Our Benny, bless him, he has to wait until his mid-sixties."

At the witness table, Minsky sat perfectly still, confident that he could field any question that the committee threw at him. "Mr. Minsky," Senator Rourke said, "let's go back to a question I asked your son. When you started B.M. Transportation, where did the trucks come from?"

"I bought them, fitted them out with rails, and started by hauling dresses for manufacturers in the Garment District."

"But *where* did you buy them?"

"From a truck shop!" Minsky exclaimed. "Where else do you buy trucks . . . from Gimbel's or Macy's?"

Senator Rourke's voice turned to ice. "Please remember where you are."

"Some guy sold them to me. He had trucks and no money. I had money and no trucks. So we struck a deal."

"Were they trucks that had been used to haul liquor—illegal, bootleg liquor—during Prohibition?"

"They could have been," Minsky admitted grudgingly. "I didn't ask their pedigree. I was buying transportation, not championship dogs."

"These manufacturers you hauled merchandise for—dresses—did you have a financial interest in any of them?"

"I may have. I had a lot of interests in those days."

"How did you acquire those interests?"

"I bought them."

Senator Rourke quickly realized that he was getting nowhere by asking about the origins of Minsky's transportation company. More than thirty years had passed; a man could be forgiven for having a sketchy memory of events that happened so long ago. He looked to his left at the senator from Florida, who had his own questions to ask.

"You head the Palmetto Leisure Development Corporation now?"

"I do."

"I shall not ask you about casinos in the two hotels operated by the corporation. You would undoubtedly tell me, as your son did, that casino gambling is illegal in Florida. What I would like to hear from you is something about the man who built those hotels. Tell me about Philip Gerson."

Minsky licked his upper lip clean of the beads of sweat that had suddenly appeared. "A smart cookie."

"A smart cookie," the senator from Florida repeated. "What happened to this . . . this smart cookie?"

Minsky's upper lip was sweaty again. So was his entire body. "He died."

"How?"

"He was in a boating accident, him and his girl. The boat burned up while they were out at sea."

"And immediately afterward, a memo stating that you were taking over Gerson's responsibilities was sent to the staff at both hotels. The memo was sent out so quickly that one could almost believe it had already been prepared."

"That memo was sent out the morning after the Coast Guard spotted the wreckage of Phil's boat. The moment we heard about Phil, we had to move into action fast. Sure we grieved for Phil, he was too clever a guy to lose like that, but the hotels had to keep on running. So I stepped in." Damn! Minsky thought, what the hell was the matter with him? He never sweated as a rule. He was never scared. Yet these questions were making his sweat glands work overtime, his heart beat like a jackhammer.

"And you've been there ever since?"

"Ever since."

The senator from California motioned to Minsky. "I believe that a former associate of yours was once a resident of my state."

Minsky regarded the man blankly.

"Your wife, Mr. Minsky."

"My late wife. She died a lot of years ago."

"Miss Kathleen Monahan. She started her career by singing in a club, did she not?"

"Sure. A club me and my partners owned."

"A club that served illegal liquor?"

"That may have been one of the attractions, I don't remember."

"Never mind that. When Miss Monahan got her big break on

606

Broadway in"—the senator from California consulted notes—"*Broadway Nell*, was it solely because of her voice, her talent, or was it because you coerced a certain producer? *Leaned* on him to give Miss Monahan the role?"

"I leaned on Irwin Kuczinski?" Minsky burst out laughing and his heart pounded even more wildly. He swung around to look back at Levitt and Pearl. They were smiling, they could see the joke as well. "It was Kuczinski who did the leaning! He leaned so far over the goddamned stage that he had Kathleen's boobs stuck in his eyes!"

Senator Rourke hammered with his gavel. "Mr. Minsky, I must ask you again to remember where you are. Such language will not be tolerated—"

Minsky cut the senator off. "Can I help the way I speak? I wasn't educated all fancy like you were. I came up the hard way, in the streets. When you and your hoity-toity family"—Senator Rourke banged again with the gavel and Minsky jumped to his feet, shouting—"were being wheeled around by your goddamned governesses, I was sweating blood to make a nickel or a dime so my family could eat and pay the rent on the shithole tenement we lived in! Maybe if I'd have had a rich father to send me to Harvard or Yale or wherever, I'd be a senator too. But I didn't, and I'm not! I came up the hard way, and I'm goddamned proud of it!"

Again and again, Senator Rourke slammed the gavel down. It was hopeless to continue. Minsky had made a mockery out of the entire proceedings. All Senator Rourke could do now was adjourn, take a break during which he'd discuss with his brother and fellow committee members how to approach the next and final witness, Louis Levitt.

The adjournment was called. Minsky started to walk away from the witness table, hands clasped above his head like a triumphant boxer. Levitt himself would not be able to do any better when his turn came! Minsky took no more than half-a-dozen steps when his legs buckled. His arms flailed for balance, and emitting a muted cry of pain as the searing bar of fire ripped across his chest, he fell to the floor. Within twenty minutes, he was in intensive care, the victim of a massive heart attack. . . .

The television news that night concentrated on the final confrontation between Senator Rourke and Benny Minsky, the six steps Minsky took before the heart attack hit him. Patrick and John Rourke watched the report together in the hotel where they were staying. Neither brother thought their case had been well served by the day's events.

"It's a goddamned circus," John said disgustedly as he watched a close-up of Minsky being carried from the hearing. "The press is making out that it's our fault for pushing a man with a heart condition."

"I never knew he had a weak heart!" Patrick exclaimed.

"And that bit about governesses and Yale and Harvard . . . a rich father!" John slammed his fist against the palm of his hand. "We're trying to get you the Democratic nomination, and that bastard Minsky rams it down everyone's throat that we're members of a privileged class!"

The telephone rang. The caller was old Patrick Joseph Rourke, from his home in Boston. "I suppose I should congratulate the pair of you on your first success," the old man said sarcastically. "At least, you put one of those bastards in the hospital. You'll cost him medical bills if nothing else."

"Dad, we're doing all we can," Patrick protested. "But the stuff we've brought up, it means nothing. There's a statute of limitations."

"What about Switzerland?"

"We can't get proof! Swiss banks don't talk about their depositors."

"For God's sake, are you going to let those Jews walk away after what they did to me? To our family?"

"We'll get Levitt when the hearing resumes."

"You'd better!" Rourke snapped. "Or else you're no sons of mine!"

Patrick heard the receiver being slammed down in Boston. He stared helplessly at his brother. "If we don't get Levitt, we're no sons of Dad."

"We'll get him," John said. "We'll get him good."

Lou Levitt took his seat at the witness table. Although he appeared outwardly calm, he could not rid himself of the previous day's scene, the sight of Minsky falling to the floor. Pearl had been tremendously upset by it, and Levitt had stayed with her at the Sands Point house, both waiting for news of his condition. Early in the morning, William had called to say that his father was resting comfortably, and Levitt had promised Pearl that if visitors were permitted he would take her to the hospital after this session of the hearing.

Senator Rourke's first question knocked all thought of Minsky clean out of Levitt's mind. He had expected the senator to start off with innocent queries about his background, his early days, perhaps draw some references to the clubs and liquor business. Instead, the senator went straight for the jugular.

"Mr. Levitt, do you have financial interests in foreign casinos?

Specifically, the Embassy Club and the Dominion Sporting Club in London, England, and the Belvedere Hotel in the Bahamas?"

Levitt shifted uncomfortably on the seat. The Irish son of a bitch had dug deeply. "I have no financial interest in these establishments whatsoever. Nor do I have any financial interests in any other casinos, in the United States or overseas."

"You are under oath, sir."

"I am perfectly aware of that." Levitt made a rationalization to himself. A lie under oath was only a lie if it could be proved to be so. There was no way that Senator Rourke could prove his allegations. He could suspect the truth, but there was no black-and-white evidence. The financial involvement was too well concealed, money put up on a handshake, a verbal promise. Nothing anywhere in writing.

"Have you ever been to any of the places I mentioned?"

"I have. I went to London on vacation with Mrs. Granitz some time back. I took out overseas membership at the Dominion Sporting Club and the Embassy Club for the period I was in London."

"Did you gamble?"

"I did not."

"Did Mrs. Granitz gamble?"

"Yes." Levitt smiled coldly. "She lost ten shillings."

"Why would you take out a temporary membership at a gambling club and not gamble?"

"I find enjoyment in watching gamblers. I find no enjoyment in being one of them. They always lose eventually."

"In how many places have you watched gambling? In Florida? In the room above the Jalo Cab Company garage? In the clubs you controlled during Prohibition? How many places, Mr. Levitt?"

"I watch gambling wherever I can. I admit to being fascinated by it."

"Let us forget London and the Bahamas for a moment, Mr. Levitt," Senator Rourke said. He no longer needed to dwell on those casinos. The damage was already done. The British authorities were so strict about granting licenses that they would look hard at those two clubs now, as would the Bahamian government with the Belvedere Hotel. Senator Rourke had little doubt that the three casinos would lose their licenses because of being associated—albeit only through allegation—with Levitt. How much more could his father want? "How much are you worth, Mr. Levitt?"

"Offhand? I can't say."

"A rough guess, a ballpark figure, will suffice. One million dollars . . . two million . . . five million?"

"That's being ridiculous. I live in a rented apartment. I drive a

Pontiac. I buy my clothes off the rack. Does a man worth that much live in such a frugal manner?"

"Mr. Levitt . . ." Senator Rourke's voice was condescending. "You don't have to live high off the hog to prove you're wealthy. How much is in that account you have in the Leinberg Bank?"

Levitt felt sweat begin to trickle down his armpits. "What account?"

"The account you keep in Switzerland. The account from which you borrowed money to finance the hotels in Florida, the buildings owned by Granitz Brothers. You're borrowing your own money, aren't you, and paying interest to yourself?"

For one icily terrifying instant, Levitt lost his composure. Had Walter Leinberg, or someone else working at the bank in Zurich, been reached? No! . . . Levitt relaxed. If Senator Rourke knew the truth, if someone had broken the vow of confidentiality, he would throw the code name in Levitt's face, demand to know what Blackhawk was. "I have no idea what you are talking about, Senator Rourke."

"Let me enlighten you a little." Rourke knew the value of such innuendoes. He didn't need to have proof. Allegations alone would cost Levitt his interest in the foreign casinos, just as allegations about a Swiss bank account would bring acute embarrassment. "Before Joseph Granitz became your courier to Switzerland, Philip Gerson made the regular run. Was Mr. Gerson also continually *sorting out problems* with an engineering firm in Zurich called A. G. Kriesel? You must have squirreled away a considerable sum of money during all those years, Mr. Levitt. Is it thirty million dollars . . . forty million . . . a hundred million? And all of it tax-free, all of it from illegal ventures."

"I repeat my last statement. I have no idea what you're talking about." Levitt wasn't going to plead the Fifth. That route was for cowards, for people with little faith. He was going to keep on lying until he was blue in the face, brazen it out, dare the committee to prove him a perjurer. He knew they couldn't, otherwise they would have done so already.

"Mr. Levitt, will you tell this committee how much you are worth?"

"If you wish, you're perfectly welcome to inspect all of my holdings," Levitt offered. "I'll have bankbooks, lists of stocks, an inventory of personal possessions all ready for your scrutiny. You can figure it out for yourself."

"Tell us about Switzerland, Mr. Levitt. Tell us about the Leinberg Bank."

"Ask the Leinberg Bank."

"We did," Senator Rourke admitted. "They refused to yield any information about their depositors. They refused to say anything about you having an account there."

"Did you ever stop to think that was because I don't have an account there? Or isn't that what you wanted to hear?"

Senator Rourke never answered. He did not need to say any more; there was no need to ask another question. Whatever Levitt's character was like, this hearing had besmirched it. No matter what Levitt did or said in the future, the allegations made against him in this hearing would stick. He would never be free of them. The respectability he had labored so hard to build up was destroyed. Senator Patrick Rourke, Jr. had paid off his father's debt. Now he could concentrate on his own ambitions, take the Senate Special Committee across the country to give himself nationwide fame.

"Thank you, Mr. Levitt. You have been most helpful. You may step down."

Levitt left the witness table and returned to Pearl. She could see him holding back his temper. "Let's get out of here," he muttered. "I stay here any longer, I'm going to explode."

Pearl followed him outside. "How bad is the damage?"

"Bad enough. Rourke dug deep and he came up with a ton of dirt. None of it can be proved, but the allegations are enough. We dare not open the casinos in Florida again, and mark my words it'll be just a matter of time before our places in the Bahamas and London lose their licenses. The smell of scandal alone will be enough to set the ball rolling on that."

"What about the Granitz Brothers? What about B.M. Transportation?"

"Oh, they'll be all right. They're rock-solid."

"Is that so bad, Lou? The respectable businesses will still be there. We'll live more than comfortably from them."

"Respectable!" His voice was venomous. "You still want respectable? Is that all you're interested in?"

"Maybe London and the Bahamas will be all right," Pearl said as she tried to placate Levitt. "Maybe nothing will happen to them."

"Maybe," Levitt said, but he didn't believe it. He'd already lost the Florida casinos. The Waterway and the Monaco would have to remain as they were now—legitimate luxury hotels. And soon, he'd lose London and the Bahamas. He was certain of it, and he was just as certain that if such a thing happened, he wouldn't rest until he'd made Patrick Joseph Rourke and the whole damned Rourke family bleed again. Bleed until their veins ran dry.

Pearl and Levitt went straight from the committee hearing to see Benny Minsky. They found William and Susan already there, sitting in the waiting room, holding hands as if to give each other strength.

"How is he?" Levitt asked William.

"We haven't seen him yet. The doctor says we might be able to spend a few minutes with him in half an hour or so."

"Did the doctor give you a prognosis?"

William made a rocking motion with his hand. "My father's a strong man, that's the biggest thing in his favor. The doctor said anyone else would have been blown away. It was a major heart attack."

Pearl went over to Susan. "Who's looking after Mark and Paul?"

"A baby-sitter. How are you, after your ordeal this week?"

Pearl shrugged and smiled. Her own troubles seemed minor now.

"While William and I were sitting here, we watched the news." Susan indicated a television set in the waiting room. Pearl had not even noticed it. Now some man was pointing a stick at weather charts and talking about a cold front coming down from Canada.

Pearl dropped her voice to a whisper. "Don't mention anything about it. Lou's very upset over what happened, to Benny, and to himself today."

"I saw," Susan whispered back. "That senator made a big show of it. He won all the points he wanted to."

A doctor entered the waiting room, a young man with shiny black hair and horn-rimmed glasses. "Mr. Minsky, Mrs. Minsky, you can go in now, but only for a few minutes."

As William and Susan left to go to Benny, Levitt noticed the young doctor staring at him. "You want something from me?" Levitt asked.

"No . . . no . . ." The doctor was flustered, but unable to tear his eyes away from Levitt's face.

"See me on television before, did you? Want an autograph?"

"I'm sorry. I didn't mean to stare."

Pearl stepped in. "May we see Mr. Minsky as well?"

"Are you family?" the doctor asked, relieved by her intervention.

Pearl was about to say no, until she realized that a man in intensive care would only be allowed visits from immediate family. She was no longer under oath. "I'm Mr. Minsky's sister."

"I didn't realize he had a sister."

"Ask his son, William, my nephew."

"And you, Mr.? . . ." the doctor asked.

"You know damned well what my name is," Levitt said. "And you know what my connection is. I'm his business partner. I want to see him as well, to talk about all those millions we've got stashed away in some Swiss bank."

"Two minutes. After his son and daughter-in-law come out." The doctor walked away quickly.

"Marvelous, isn't it?" Levitt said to Pearl. "I spent a lifetime staying out of the spotlight, and that bastard makes me into a celebrity overnight."

"People'll forget, Lou. Next week no one will know you."

William and Susan returned to the waiting room five minutes later. To Pearl's surprise, William was smiling, although Susan appeared downcast. "He's sitting up in bed, talking about how he made a fool out of that committee," William said.

The doctor reappeared. Looking just at Pearl, ignoring Levitt completely, he held two fingers in the air. "Two minutes, that's all. He needs rest."

Pearl and Levitt entered the private room. Minsky was propped up on a pillow. His face was gray, but life sparkled in his dark eyes. "Did you see how I took care of that son-of-a-bitch senator? I put him in his goddamned place, didn't I?"

"You put yourself in this place as well," Pearl said. She looked at the equipment adjacent to the bed, machines that meant nothing to her, only that they were registering Minsky's condition.

"I heard what happened to you as well," Minsky said to Levitt.

"How?"

"The doctor told me."

"Which doctor? The one who showed us in here?" When Minsky nodded, Levitt said, "That little snot-nose was looking at me like I was something out of a freak show."

"How long will you have to stay here?" Pearl asked.

"Maybe a week."

"Then what? Will you stay with William and Susan?"

Minsky shook his head. "I'm getting the hell out of this cold weather. That's what did it to me, having to be in New York during the winter. A couple of days in that Florida sun, listening to those dice click up profits, and I'll be as good as new."

"I thought you said you heard what happened," Levitt muttered. "There won't be any dice. Ever again. We're all washed up. Those hotels stay as hotels from now on. We'll lose our London licenses, we'll get kicked out of the Bahamas. We're out of business altogether."

"So I'll just sit in the sun," Minsky answered, refusing to let Levitt dampen his enthusiasm.

Levitt glanced at Pearl. "Leave me alone with Benny for a moment, Pearl. We've got things to discuss."

"Get well, Benny. I'll see you tomorrow." She bent to kiss him on the cheek. Despite his protestations of how well he felt, his skin was cold and damp. Pearl wanted to wash the clamminess off her lips.

The door closed quietly behind Pearl. "William said you had a real big heart attack, Benny. Maybe you're kidding yourself about how good you feel."

"Forget it, shrimp." Minsky purposely used the derogatory nickname he'd called Levitt when they were young. "You're talking me into nothing. I feel fine because I am fine."

"Benny, don't kid yourself about your health."

Minsky struggled to sit up. A little of the color returned to his face. The pulse on the machine that measured his heartbeat jumped into urgent action. "Listen to me, Lou, and listen good. You know what's going to keep me alive? You . . . you're the best medicine I could have."

"Me?" Levitt's tight little smile was totally bereft of humor. "How do you figure that?"

"If it wasn't for you, I'd say pull the plug, God, I'm ready. I've done all I ever wanted to do. I've had one hell of a good time. Most importantly, I've watched my son grow up to be the man I always wanted him to be. But he's no match for you, Lou. No man living is, not even that fancy bastard Senator Patrick Rourke, Jr. He may have made a monkey out of you today, cost you some—"

"Make your point, Benny," Levitt said impatiently.

"No one's a match for you, Lou, except me. I'm going to stay around to see you don't rob my son blind and give everything to those twins of Pearl's."

"You're crazy, Benny. You always were."

"I'm crazy?" Minsky laughed, and the pulse on the machine jumped again. "You think after all these years I don't know what you're like, Lou? You always figured you were the only one with any brains, and because of that you were entitled to everything. If I go, you'll screw my son out of that money we've got socked away with Leinberg. Not because you need it, or the twins need it, but because you think you deserve it more than anyone else."

"Why shouldn't I think that way? Every deal that ever made money was my idea. What did you contribute, Benny? Name one thing."

"Get out, Lou, before I ring for the nurse and have her throw you out."

"Nothing, Benny. You contributed nothing! I did it all."

"Maybe you did, but so help me God, I'm staying alive to see you don't get it all. I'll beat you by outliving you."

Levitt left the room. "I'll drive you home," he told Pearl.

"What happened in there? You look awful. What did you and Benny have to talk about?"

"Nothing. I have nothing to talk about with Benny at all."

Chapter Five

Benny Minsky was discharged from the hospital eleven days after the heart attack. There was no question of his returning to Florida to look after himself, so he moved into the Forest Hills Gardens home of his son and daughter-in-law to convalesce for four weeks under the care of a nurse. Despite being so close to his family, especially his two grandsons, Minsky hated it there. The weather was still too cold for him to be allowed outside, and the nurse's constant ministrations made him complain that he might just as well be incarcerated in a maximum-security prison.

Minsky had been in Forest Hills Gardens for two weeks when Levitt received the bad news from his English partners. Following the allegations made by the Senate Special Committee in New York, a government inquiry was being launched in Britain to determine the extent of the infiltration of gaming clubs by so-called "undesirable American elements." Levitt took small comfort from the fact that neither the British press nor the government referred to him outright as a gangster or a criminal, just as an "undesirable American element"; he wasn't even named. As a first step, the licenses of the two London clubs referred to in the hearings were suspended. The principals were given thirty days to prepare arguments as to why they should be allowed to continue operation.

Levitt knew it made no difference to himself whether the clubs reopened or remained shut. His interest in them was no longer welcome. Nor, a week later, was it welcome in the Bahamas. Taking a lead from the British government, a Royal Commission of Inquiry ordered the Belvedere Hotel's gambling license to be revoked. Senator Patrick Rourke, Jr. had repaid his father's debt in full.

At home in his Central Park West apartment, Levitt flicked on the television set and tuned in to the late news. As if to mock him, the first topic was the Senate Special Committee on Organized Crime. It was sitting in Cincinnati that week, interviewing men who operated clubs along the Ohio River on the Kentucky border. Small people, Levitt thought as he watched. The clubs they ran, the illegal casinos, were pocket change when compared with the operations he'd had swept away from him. Rourke's main objective had been achieved when the damned committee had convened in New York. He had destroyed the empire Levitt had built up over the years.

News on the committee hearing finished with an interview of Patrick Rourke, Jr. The camera zoomed in on that Irish face, and Levitt inched the chair closer to the television set. "The people of this country," the senator was saying, "have an unfortunate habit of forgetting quickly, and those who fail to learn from history are, as we well know, doomed to repeat it. Senator Kefauver exposed all this fifteen years ago, and people were interested for a while . . . but only for a while. Then they forgot, and the very people they had seen exposed as criminals of the worst kind slipped back once again into positions of power. This time, I am praying that their interest in the thieves and vandals who have stolen this country lasts a little longer."

For thirty minutes after the end of the late news, Levitt sat staring at the television screen. Commercials, programs, more commercials flickered meaninglessly in front of his eyes. All he saw was that Irish face. That stinking, hateful Irish face with its unruly mop of hair. He became as obsessed with the Rourke family as old Patrick Joseph Rourke was obsessed with him.

While Levitt was staring at the television, Mickey Phillips was preparing to close up for the night. Leaving the cash register open, so that anyone peering through the window could see it was empty, Phillips checked around the delicatessen one final time before turning off the lights and locking the front door. As he walked briskly along Seventh Avenue, enjoying the cold wind that shook off some of his sluggishness, he started to feel more awake. Just as well, he decided. He had a long drive to his home in Paramus.

Leaving the bright lights of Seventh Avenue behind him, he turned into West Fifty-fourth Street where his car was parked. At first, he thought that the footsteps dogging his own were nothing more than an echo. When he decided otherwise and turned around, it was already too late. Hymie Glass had a piece of iron pipe raised high in the air. Phillips tried to duck and weave as he had once done in the ring. The pipe cracked down across his shoulder. Only the thickness of his coat saved him from having the bone broken. Nonetheless, the blow made him stagger. He came up quickly, fists clenched. He never saw Stan Kaye slip out of a shadowy doorway, a sawed-off baseball bat clasped in both hands. The weapon smashed into the side of Phillips' head.

Without a sound, he dropped to the sidewalk. Glass and Kaye half-carried, half-dragged him to a black Cadillac that waited at the curb, its engine purring. Behind the wheel sat Harry Saltzman. The moment the doors slammed, Saltzman dropped the car into gear and sped away.

Phillips regained consciousness to see a bright light glaring into his eyes. He was tied to a wooden chair. His feet were cold and damp, difficult to move. Squinting against the light, head throbbing, he looked down. Saltzman was squatting in front of him, gazing raptly at an old tin bath into which Phillips' feet were wedged. The damp coldness Phillips felt was freshly mixed cement that oozed above his ankles. He tried to wriggle his feet to break the cement's hold before it could set.

"Move all you like, Mickey," Saltzman said in a genial tone, "because where you're going soon, you won't be moving for a long, long time." Phillips watched in horror as Saltzman lifted a bucket and poured more fresh cement into the bath. Slowly, the level crept up to the midway point of his shins, reaching the bottom of his rolled-up trousers.

"You ruined a house for me, Mickey, stunk it out so it smells like some shithole in a Bowery flophouse. Had to burn everything. The house still stinks, and I've got to spend good money to stay at the Statler Hilton." Saltzman ran a finger across the surface of the wet cement, leaving a groove. "Should be hard in a couple of hours, Mickey, and then you're going for a swim. Any preferences? East River? Hudson River? Harlem River? The condemned man's final wish."

Phillips struggled in the chair but Hymie Glass and Stan Kaye held him still. All he could do was watch. And wait.

"Could have been so simple, Mickey. All you had to do was join my guild. For nothing I offered to let you join. But no, you were too hardheaded, too much the tough guy. You had to do things your way, didn't you?"

Phillips wanted to shout that Saltzman would never get away with it, that no one got away with murder. But the gag stuffed into his mouth cut off all sound. He looked around, wondered where he was. The place looked like a garage, or maybe a warehouse. Was it a warehouse? Was he on the docks already? He thought he could smell the water.

"You're just going to disappear, Mickey. All people are going to remember about you is your ring career. And soon they're even going to forget that."

Saltzman looked up and gave an almost imperceptible nod. Behind the bound and gagged man, Hymie Glass lifted the iron pipe. It

618

descended in a short, swift arc, and Phillips' consciousness departed once again.

When he came to the next time, he knew he could smell water. Arms and legs still bound, feet fixed firmly in hard cement, he was on a dock. The opposite shore was far away, almost pitch black, only an occasional light lifting the gloom. He made a guess. The Hudson, high up, close to the Tappan Zee Bridge. There was a small rowing boat. Hymie Glass and Stan Kaye lifted him into it, held him fast on a narrow bench. Saltzman took hold of a pair of oars and began to row swiftly into midriver.

"This'll do," Saltzman said. "Tip him over, boys."

The gag was ripped from Phillips' mouth and he heard Saltzman say, "You can save your last words for the fish, Mickey." Strong hands gripped his arms and legs. The boat rocked. Before he could gather strength for a scream, the freezing water shocked his system.

He tried to flail his arms, and couldn't. He tried to move his legs, and couldn't. The icy water closed over the top of his head. He sank rapidly. His eyes were open, his mouth jammed closed in one final, desperate attempt to avoid the inevitable. Blood roared in his ears. His chest pounded as he settled onto the bottom of the river, and his eyes burned as he sought oxygen and found only water. The darkness became even blacker as his sight dimmed. Slowly, the roaring subsided to a dull hum. And finally, mercifully, he drowned.

Benny Minsky returned to his suite of rooms at the Waterway Hotel in mid-March. Both his son and daughter-in-law were reluctant to let him leave, but he assured them that he felt well enough to travel. A doctor who examined him expressed surprise at his recovery. Minsky's strength and resiliency had made a mockery of a heart attack that would have destroyed many weaker men.

Minsky took life easy when he reached home. With no casino gambling to oversee, he was in bed each night by eleven o'clock, and rose promptly at seven each morning to walk along the beach before eating breakfast. He knew that he was nothing more than a hotel manager now, and Palmetto Leisure Development Corporation had a more than competent management staff. Minsky had all the free time he could want. He took up golf, spending hour after hour with a professional at a local course as he tried to acquire in weeks the experience it had taken other players years to gain.

Under a doctor's direction, he went on a special diet to lose twenty pounds, the excess weight that Pearl had noticed on her sixty-first birthday four months earlier. More than anything, he wanted to remain healthy, to realize his boast that he would outlast Lou Levitt. That was the only thing Minsky had to live for. Anything else, he had already accomplished.

Harry Saltzman had never worked on a building site in his life, and that led to his downfall. Reading the directions on the bags of cement he'd bought from a hardware store was not enough. Experience would have told him to let the cement set longer.

The Hudson River, which Saltzman believed would serve as the last resting place of Mickey Phillips, went to work on the bathful of cement the moment Phillips sank beneath the surface. At first, the deterioration of the cement was virtually unnoticeable. The water did nothing more than weaken the top layer, certainly not enough to free Phillips' corpse from its anchor. After a couple of weeks, the damage became more apparent. The top surface of the cement began to break up, and the water probed deeper. The cement began to split, small pieces initially, then larger chunks, were swirled away by the Hudson's undercurrent. Finally, the tin bath floated free. Phillips' body banged along the river bed like a sodden log, hands and legs bound, skin bloated, hair rising from its scalp like fine streamers. The current carried the body toward the ocean. Past Yonkers on the New York side of the river. Past Alpine and Englewood Cliffs on the New Jersey bank. Under the George Washington Bridge. Past Fort Lee and Washington Heights. Until finally, abreast of the Cunard Docks on the West Side of Manhattan, it popped up to the surface.

A sergeant on board a New York police launch was the first to spot Phillips' body. It was after midnight, and the launch's spotlight picked out a white disc floating in the water fifty yards away, a paper plate discarded by some litterbug, or a frisbee skimmed across the water by kids. The sergeant looked closer, ordered the boat to be swung around. Paper plates and frisbees did not have the bloated features of a face that had been underwater for a month. Engines cut back to a low rumble, the launched edged nearer. A boathook was thrust into the water. It ripped through coat, jacket, shirt, and flesh. Phillips' body was hauled on board, and the men on the launch radioed in that they were bringing home a floater for identification.

Identification was simple. The murder was not connected to any robbery. Harry Saltzman and his two henchmen had not bothered to go through Phillips' pockets. Even the roll of cash he'd taken from the cash register at Mickey's Deli was still in his trousers. Identification papers, driving license, and Social Security card—all wrapped in protective plastic—were dried off. Within an hour of fishing the body from the Hudson, the police knew that the drowning victim was a man who had been reported missing almost a month earlier by his wife. The corpse wore no shoes, his hands were tied and fragments of dried cement clung tenaciously to his trousers, so the police were certain that the drowning was not accidental.

Inquiries began, and ended, early the following morning at Mickey's Deli on Seventh Avenue. The delicatessen was still open, managed by Phillips' widow. The waiters were only too willing to talk of the heavyset man who had been thrown out by Phillips when he'd tried to coerce the delicatessen owner into joining the New York Guild of Restaurateurs and Victualers, and of a later visit by two men who had a bottle of butyric acid. Finally, they described Phillips' poetic if ill-conceived revenge.

Saltzman was easy to trace. After checking at the house in Fort Lee, the police learned there was a forwarding address: the Statler Hilton in New York City. Before noon, two detectives—Lieutenant Derek Mulholland and Sergeant John O'Brien—arrived at the hotel to make the arrest. Showing their shields to the desk clerk, they asked for the number of Saltzman's room.

"He's out," the clerk said.

"How do you know?"

"He goes out every morning, a gymnasium in Times Square. He's a fitness nut, comes back in a huge sweat each day."

"Give us the key."

The clerk did so, and Lieutenant Derek Mulholland and Sergeant John O'Brien went up to Saltzman's room, let themselves in, and looked around. There was nothing in the closets but three suits and some shirts. The bureau contained only the underwear and socks Saltzman had bought to replace the clothing he'd lost at the Fort Lee house. They went into the bathroom, closed the door, and waited. . . .

Saltzman returned to the hotel an hour later. He entered the room, closed the door, and sat down heavily on the edge of the bed. The sound of the bathroom door opening made him swing around, and he found himself looking down the barrel of a revolver held by Mulholland. Behind the lieutenant stood O'Brien. "Harry Saltzman, you're under arrest for the murder of Mickey Phillips."

"Not a chance," Saltzman said without even getting off the bed. "I didn't murder any Mickey Phillips. I don't even know a Mickey Phillips."

"Is that so? Then how come you were so gung ho about getting him to join your restaurant guild?"

"*That* Mickey Phillips!" Saltzman exclaimed. "He's dead?"

"You know damned well he is." Mulholland waited while O'Brien

621

stepped forward with a pair of handcuffs. Saltzman stood up, held his hands out unresistingly. "We've got witnesses who saw him throw you out of Mickey's Deli, witnesses who saw him beat up the two men you sent to stink-bomb his place, witnesses who saw him on his way to your home in Fort Lee with the same stink bomb."

Saltzman started to laugh. "If you've got witnesses to all that, why the hell aren't you arresting Phillips? I'm the injured party, not him!"

"I already told you . . . he's dead. Murdered."

"Says who?" Saltzman asked belligerently.

"We fished his body out of the Hudson this morning."

"That's crap!" Saltzman burst out. "He had enough cement around his—!" He gulped as he realized what he was saying. He looked at the handcuffs, felt himself being pushed from the room. His mind started to race down avenues of escape. Not physical escape, that was out of the question. A trade-off! Who could be traded for his own benefit? Hymie Glass and Stan Kaye? Why should the cops be interested in the helpers when they had their chief? Money . . . could he bribe these two cops? Money always worked, everyone had a price. Saltzman had learned that from Levitt. But who else would he have to bribe? The whole goddamned police department? If it were just these two, perhaps . . . but everyone? Even a clever little bastard like Levitt wouldn't be able to subvert an entire police department.

Levitt! . . .

The gleam of an idea began to shine in Saltzman's mind as he was helped into an unmarked car outside the hotel.

Levitt . . .

Saltzman wouldn't have to use money to bribe his way out of trouble. He'd use Levitt. Levitt was a much more valuable commodity than mere cash, certainly in some quarters. Didn't the Federal Government carry more weight than mere city cops? Saltzman tried to remember the television newscast he'd seen the previous evening. Where was the Senate Special Committee on Organized Crime sitting now? Where was Senator Joseph Rourke, Jr. campaigning for votes with his little circus? Los Angeles, that was it. The committee was sitting in Los Angeles.

"I've got a right to make a phone call," Saltzman said the moment he was taken into the precinct house.

"You'll get that right," Mulholland assured him. "No one's going to stop you from calling your lawyer. Just make sure you get the best lawyer money can buy, because you're going to need him."

"You're wrong," Saltzman said. "I'm not going to call a lawyer. I'm going to call someone with more pull than F. Lee Bailey and Clarence Darrow put together."

"Who?"

"I want to make a long-distance call. To Los Angeles. To Senator Patrick Rourke, Jr. I've got a deal to offer him that's going to make anything you've got on me seem like a parking violation." Saltzman bathed both detectives with a smug smile. "I'm going to walk right out of here, boys. And there won't be a single thing you can do to stop me."

Lou Levitt ate dinner that night at the home of Joseph Granitz. During the meal the children, Jacob and Anne, were present at the table, so the conversation ran the gamut of inconsequential subjects. The moment dinner was finished, and the children went to watch television, the topic switched to Harry Saltzman, whose arrest for the murder of Mickey Phillips had made the front pages of the late editions. Even Pearl and Judy delayed clearing up from the meal, so shocked were they at the news.

"Is there anything you can do for him?" Pearl asked Levitt.

"Like what? According to the story in the paper, they've got witnesses that he tried everything to get this Mickey Phillips to join his restaurant association racket. Phillips hit back by wrecking Saltzman's house with the stink bomb that had been intended for the delicatessen."

"Couldn't you talk to some of the waiters, perhaps?" Pearl asked. "Maybe you could get them to change their minds, lose their memories?"

"Bribe them?" Levitt shook his head. "Pearl, believe me when I say that if I could do anything for Harry, I would. God knows, he's helped us enough in the past. But I can't afford to get involved in anything now, not so soon after those damned committee hearings. Harry carried on like he was still living in the twenties. He didn't use his brains, whatever little God gave him. He's going to go down the river, and there's nothing anyone can do for him."

"Does he present a danger to us?" Joseph asked.

"No. We never got ourselves involved in those stupid protection rackets like Harry did. The New York Guild of Restaurateurs and Victualers . . . where the hell does he come up with a name like that? He must have eaten a dictionary before he dreamed that one up. No, Harry's no danger to us at all. He's just going to draw a life sentence, and at Harry's age that shouldn't last for too long." For a moment, Levitt wondered who would now be available for those special jobs at which Saltzman had been so efficient. Then he struck the worry from his mind. After the mess the Senate Special Committee had made of the gambling empire, there would be no need for a man like Saltzman again. . . .

Levitt's belief that Saltzman posed no threat changed dramatically when he arrived home later that night. The telephone was ringing. He lifted it from the hook. "Hello?"

"Lou, Derek here. I've been trying to get ahold of you all evening. I've got to see you. It's urgent."

Levitt's eyes sharpened as he pictured the caller. Derek Mulholland. Tall, gray-haired, distinguished-looking. Always turned out in fine custom-made suits, which was hardly surprising for he had been on Levitt's payroll since he'd been a patrolman along Houston Street when the bookmaking and numbers action had been heavy. Mulholland had risen far since then, to detective lieutenant, but he still received two hundred dollars a week from Levitt just for keeping his eyes and ears open. It was a ten-thousand-dollar-a-year investment that was about to pay enormous dividends.

"What is it?" Levitt refrained from using any names. Because of the Senate Special Committee hearings, no man knew what line was safe anymore.

"Meet me. I'm parked on the east side of Second Avenue, just south of Fifty-second Street. A white sixty-four Impala."

"I'm on my way." Levitt left the apartment immediately and drove to the meeting place. He saw the white Impala and pulled in behind it. There were two men inside. Derek Mulholland behind the wheel, a younger, solidly built man with jet black hair in the back seat.

"This is my partner, John O'Brien," Mulholland greeted Levitt. "We made the arrest today—Harry Saltzman."

"So?"

"Saltzman made a phone call."

"He's entitled."

"We thought you might be interested in knowing who he called," O'Brien said from the back seat. "He made a long-distance call to Senator Patrick Rourke, Jr. in Los Angeles, California."

"We've got special orders, Lou," Mulholland said. "All of a sudden, Saltzman's no longer a prisoner facing a first-degree murder rap. Now he's a goddamned VIP. He cut himself a deal with Senator Rourke."

"What kind of a deal?"

"I was there when he made the call. He didn't seem to want any privacy, like he wanted the whole wide world to know how powerful he was. Like he wanted us to know that the cops, the evidence we had, didn't mean shit to him. But your name came up, Lou—"

"What kind of a deal?"

"Saltzman told Rourke that if he got a break with this Phillips murder rap, he could deliver you, Benny Minsky, Minsky's son, and the Granitz twins to Rourke on a silver platter, with apples stuffed in your mouths."

Levitt did not need to hear more. He knew exactly what Saltzman could say about them all. He'd been associated with them too long. He knew too much. He'd been involved in too many heavy things. "Where is he? Rikers Island? The precinct house?"

"Neither place. He's been billeted in some fleabag hotel on Times Square. Under guard the whole time. A couple of detectives always with him."

"How come?"

"Rourke apparently can't get back from the Coast for a couple of days, this investigation of his. He wants us to keep Saltzman on ice."

"Has he made a statement yet?"

"No. He's saving it for the senator."

Two days, Levitt thought. Today was Monday. Rourke would be in New York on Wednesday, Thursday at the very latest. He'd see Saltzman, get his statement, and have himself a witness far more powerful than any he had subpoenaed during his entire committee hearings. A witness who could explode a bomb under Levitt, the Granitzes, and the Minskys—put them all behind bars from now until the Messiah came. "This hotel he's in . . . can he be reached there?"

Mulholland gave Levitt a grim whisper of a smile. "I thought you'd never ask. John and me, we've got the four P.M. to midnight shift. Cushy detail because we were the arresting officers."

"How much?" Levitt said. He was on firm ground, offering a price for a service.

"How much for what?" O'Brien asked from the back seat.

"What do you think? For tucking him into bed? For reading him a bedtime story? For putting him out of his misery, of course."

"That's putting us both on the line," O'Brien complained. "I've never received a red cent from you."

"Okay, consider yourself on the payroll as of now." Levitt knew he was being shaken down. He didn't care. All that mattered was that Mulholland had come to him, had offered him this one golden opportunity to redeem everything. "Fifty thousand dollars apiece. I'll pay you fifty grand each to shut Harry Saltzman up before he has the opportunity to spill his guts."

"You've got it," Mulholland said.

As Levitt started to leave the Impala, O'Brien said, "That's a lot of dough for doing away with a slug like Saltzman. What's he got on you?"

Levitt swung around and impaled O'Brien with his sharp blue eyes. "I'm paying you to commit murder for me, not to be my confessor."

"Hey, I was kidding around, that's all. None of my business what's between you and Saltzman."

"Kid around all you like when you're taking from someone else. When you're on my payroll, you're serious the whole damned time!" Levitt slammed the Impala's door and hurried back to his own car. Saltzman, who'd been connected with him for forty years was going to die because he was trying to use what he knew to save his own skin. Through some perverted reasoning, Levitt felt no blame, no disgust for Saltzman's action. He would do exactly the same in a similar situation, bargain someone else's neck for his own. If there was any blame, it rested with the Rourke family. Like some ancient curse, they'd risen to plague him.

Sitting behind the wheel of his own car, Levitt watched the two detectives drive off in the Impala. The name of Rourke thundered through his mind, distorting his vision, shutting out the noise of the street. Cars and buses drifted past silently, like ghosts on Halloween. Lights flashed on and off in front of Levitt's eyes. Rourke! . . . It was only because the Rourke family had tried to use Levitt as a political stepping stone that Saltzman possessed such a powerful negotiating tool. Levitt could imagine the bargain Saltzman would strike. In return for spilling everything he knew, Saltzman would want a huge payment, a change of identity, the opportunity to live out his remaining years in some spot where no one would ever find him. The Rourkes would have no problem in putting up the money. Plastic surgeons could do wonders with a man's appearance. Saltzman would just vanish.

And still Levitt could find no fault in Saltzman's actions! Levitt had just contracted the murder of a man he'd known for forty years, an ally from the old days. He'd arranged to have Saltzman killed, all because of the goddamned Rourke family! Destroying his entire gambling empire, sullying his reputation in front of the entire nation—that was not enough! Now they were forcing him to kill Saltzman!

Levitt knew that if he returned home he would never sleep. He would sit up all night, thinking, imagining the worst. Imagining Senator Rourke changing his mind, returning immediately to the East Coast, getting to Saltzman before Mulholland and O'Brien could earn their money. Would the senator do that, drop his precious committee work, the opportunity to gain a few more votes, just to rush back and destroy his father's enemies forever? For once, Levitt's mind was unclear. Inside his head, a jumble of confusing thoughts clashed against each other. He was unable to make any sense of it all.

He started the car. Instead of returning to Central Park West, he headed out to Long Island again. Misery and uncertainty, like happiness, should be shared around. To share his troubles would lighten the load on his own shoulders. It was time for others to carry some of the responsibility; he'd carried it alone for far too long.

Twice he had to hammer on the door of Joseph's home before a light came on. Levitt heard the barking of the two Dobermans, the scratching of paws around the base of the door. Footsteps. The door cracked open to reveal Joseph in pajamas and a heavy woolen dressing gown. Behind his legs, the Dobermans strained to see the identity of the late-night caller.

"What are you doing here?" Joseph asked.

"I've got to talk to you."

Joseph shooed away the Dobermans and Levitt entered the house, heading toward the library. As he walked across the entrance hall, Pearl appeared at the top of the stairs. She asked the same question Joseph had, and Levitt beckoned for her to come down. It would lighten his load even more if he could share his misery with two people instead of just one.

They sat down in the library. "It's Harry . . . Harry Saltzman," Levitt began. "I just passed a death sentence on him."

"You did what?" Pearl's voice was hushed.

"He made a deal with Senator Rourke to save himself. Spill his guts on what he knows about us to get himself off the hook for this Mickey Phillips murder. The senator's flying back from the West Coast in a couple of hours to meet with him."

"How did you arrange it?" Joseph asked.

"Saltzman's locked up in a hotel, under guard. The two cops who made the arrest are pulling one of the shifts. For fifty thousand each, they'll arrange a suicide."

"Lou, Harry helped to save Leo's life when he was ill," Pearl protested. "How could you do this?"

"You think I've forgotten all the things Harry's done for us?" Pearl's face swam in front of Levitt as he looked at her. He was losing control of himself, control of the whole situation, and he did not know how to regain it. He only understood that he had carried them all for years. They'd ridden to prosperity on his coattails, on his brain power. And still they wanted more. They couldn't lead themselves, they couldn't help themselves. Babes in the goddamned wood! If he weren't there to guide them, they'd be lost, floundering. Suddenly Levitt felt nothing but contempt. He wanted them to know how much they owed him, how much they'd been made to rely on him. "Would you rather," he asked Pearl, spacing out his words, "see Leo in jail for life instead?"

"Leo? What do you mean? What did he do?"

"Harry could give testimony that Leo helped to get rid of Phil Gerson and his girlfriend."

"Get rid of them?" Pearl's face wrinkled in puzzlement. "They . . . they died in a boating accident, didn't they?"

"That was no accident. Phil and his girlfriend took the boat out. Harry and Leo were waiting for them."

Pearl did not know which shocked her more—that Phil Gerson and Belinda Rivers had been murdered, or that Leo had participated in such a terrible thing. All she could say was: "What did Phil and his girlfriend do to deserve . . . to deserve being killed like that?"

"Why don't you tell your mother?" Levitt asked Joseph. Let the older twin get a piece of the grief that was going around wholesale tonight!

"They stole a couple of million dollars from us," Joseph said softly. "They were given warnings and they continued to steal."

"*You* knew? Joseph, you knew about this?"

"Of course he knew!" Levitt snapped. "He's on the board of directors, isn't he? We all took a vote on what should be done to Phil."

"Joseph, Phil was your friend. You wanted him as best man at your wedding. And you knew? You voted?" When Joseph turned his face away, unable to look his mother in the eye, she swung back to Levitt. "And you . . . Leo is your godson. How could you allow him to be involved in something so terrible?"

"Because he was good at it, that's why!"

"Good at murder?"

Levitt wanted to grab hold of Pearl, grab hold of her and shake her, ask where she'd been living all these years, where she'd been hiding. But it wasn't her fault. She hadn't known any of this. Levitt had made sure that the dark side of the business was kept from her. She'd known only what he'd wanted her to know. And maybe, just maybe, that had been a mistake! "Just before William and Susan got married, some Italian thugs tried to muscle in on the trucking company. William got badly beaten up. I was down in Florida at the time with Benny, trying to get to the bottom of the Phil Gerson mess, so William went looking to Leo for help."

"That night William telephoned me, when I was living on Central Park West," Pearl recalled.

"Leo got hold of Harry Saltzman and they took care of the problem between them—they burned three guys in a crematorium over in Jersey."

"Lou, what's happened? What have you done to my family? To my sons? What have you done?"

"I've done nothing. I just carried on business the way it was always carried on."

"But Leo . . . Did you have to drag Leo into it?"

"Leo dragged himself into it!" Levitt shot back. He knew that Pearl had always blinded herself to Leo's pecularities, but he didn't see how she could have blocked out everything else as well. How in God's name did she believe they'd all got on so successfully? By going to work from nine to five every day, taking two weeks' vacation a year, attending the company Christmas party and the annual softball game? "If it hadn't been for me and Harry, Leo would have been where Harry is now thirteen years ago!"

Pearl's face turned ashen. In the center of her forehead, a tiny vein began to pulse. "Did Leo kill someone thirteen years ago?"

"If he did," a woman's voice said, "it wouldn't surprise me in the least." The three people in the library swung around to see Judy standing in the doorway, a robe covering her nightgown.

"This is a private conversation," Levitt said.

"Then you should have closed the door. I heard every word upstairs."

"Okay, you want to hear more? Come in. You might as well know, seeing as it happened on your wedding night. Leo was missing, remember? He wound up in the Village, drunk, and got himself picked up by some queer. They went back to the guy's apartment. Afterward, he tried to put the arm on Leo for some money. Leo went crazy and strangled him. That's when he called me, to come and bail him out. I contacted Harry, and Harry made the whole thing look like a gas leak. A big explosion which blew the apartment to pieces, burned it out along with the hardware shop that was downstairs. A little while later, he killed a barman who'd seen Leo with the queer. And I invented some story for you, Pearl, about Leo being drunk and getting into trouble with the cops."

"Why did you bother helping him?"

"You think I'd let that kind of trouble come home to roost? I bothered for the same reason I just paid a couple of cops a hundred thousand dollars to take care of Harry. To keep us . . . this family . . . out of trouble." Levitt suddenly felt very tired. The wild emotions that had shattered his logic were dissipating. "That barman could have fingered Leo. Harry can point the finger at us all. One kind act done for Leo as a child doesn't balance the books."

Pearl breathed deeply to steady herself. Her younger son was a killer, a murderer, a man who took life. Joseph had the brains, the education, the skill to run a large corporation. Leo possessed the strength and viciousness to make sure no one got in the way. They were equal partners. Levitt had made them so. What was it he'd once said . . . would he give one lox and the other pickled herring? He'd made certain to treat them equally, pushing each in the direction dictated by character. And without Levitt? . . . Would Leo have been convicted of murder thirteen years earlier, of a killing done on his twin brother's wedding night?

"This business with Harry, having to do what you did—it would never have happened without those hearings, would it?"

"I don't know, Pearl." Levitt closed his eyes, wanting only to rest. He could not even be certain of what he had told Pearl. The urge to sleep was overpowering, making him forget.

"No, it wouldn't," Pearl stated firmly. "The Rourke family set out to destroy us. They think they failed because they couldn't make anything stick at the hearings. They won't get Harry to talk now, either. But they succeeded all the same, didn't they, Lou? They succeeded beyond their wildest dreams."

"They succeeded," Levitt agreed softly. He opened his eyes, forced them to focus on Pearl. At that moment, Joseph and Judy did not exist for him. Only Pearl, a tiny, tearful figure who had seen her cherished illusions shattered into a million fragments. Levitt knew he should never have told her everything, but he'd been too distraught to use cold reason, common sense. It wasn't his fault, just like Harry Saltzman wasn't to blame for trying to save his own skin. It was the fault of the Rourke family. No one else. Just the Rourkes, those goddamned stinking Irish bastards!

The ten-story hotel in Times Square where Harry Saltzman was installed under guard had been chosen because it catered to a transient trade. Rarely did its guests stay more than two nights. Usually, they stayed only one, military personnel on passes, salesmen on overnights. The different faces of three shifts of detectives on guard detail would not stand out among a sea of changing faces.

Saltzman was located on the eighth floor, at the very end of a long corridor leading from the elevators. He had what the hotel termed a suite—a bedroom barely big enough for the double bed it contained, a toilet and shower, and a tiny area with a table, three chairs, and a television set. This last was referred to as the living room.

When Lieutenant Derek Mulholland and Sergeant John O'Brien arrived for their watch, Saltzman was sitting at the table, playing cards with the two detectives who shared the eight-to-four shift. The two newcomers exchanged notes with their predecessors before settling down for their eight-hour watch.

"Play some cards?" Saltzman said to O'Brien.

"Sure. Why not?" O'Brien pulled himself in toward the table while Saltzman shuffled the deck. Mulholland took a chair over to the door, sat with his back against it as he read the newspaper.

"Hope you guys aren't sore at me," Saltzman said conversationally.

O'Brien picked up his cards. "Why should we be sore at you?"

"Well, you made a big murder arrest and it's not going to stand up. I'm going to walk."

"Don't worry about it. If you've got enough pull to slip out from under a murder-one charge, more power to you. Right, Derek?" he asked Mulholland. The lieutenant just grunted, without even lifting his eyes from the newspaper.

At six in the evening, when the shift was two hours old, Mulholland ordered dinner from a take-out restaurant. Prisoner and guards ate in silence, using plastic cutlery and paper plates which were discarded the moment the meal was over. Afterward, Saltzman watched the news on television, while the two detectives started a game of gin rummy. When a report of the latest hearing of the Senate Special Committee on Organized Crime came on, Saltzman seemed more attentive, as though he now had a personal stake in the proceedings.

"You must really have some clout with that guy," Mulholland commented as Senator Rourke's face was displayed on the screen. "Fancy accommodation like this, the finest food."

"Never met him in my life," Saltzman answered. "Never thought I would. Just shows you how things work out, eh? A big guy like that thinking so much of a little guy like me. America . . . the land of opportunity!"

"Don't knock yourself, Harry," O'Brien said as he dealt cards to his partner. "I hear the Romans thought a lot of Judas as well. I just hope you get more out of the deal than he did."

"What did he get?"

"Thirty pieces of silver."

"What's that worth?"

O'Brien chuckled and started to sort out his hand.

Saltzman spent the entire evening watching television. At ten-thirty, he covered a yawn with a beefy, hairy hand and announced, "I'm going to hit the sack."

"Wish we could do the same," Mulholland replied. The lieutenant was feeling the first twinges of nerves. The shifts changed in ninety minutes; he and O'Brien did not have that much time. They had to get Saltzman now, as he was preparing for bed. His defenses would be lowered. They could not risk a frontal assault while he was in the living room. With the damage such a ploy would cause, there would be no way of faking a suicide.

"Yeah, we've got to stay on our toes for another hour and a half," O'Brien added. "Make sure your ex-pals don't come looking for you with a machine gun."

"You make sure you do that," Saltzman said. "Senator Rourke won't be very happy if he loses his star performer."

Mulholland and O'Brien continued to play cards while Saltzman went into the bedroom. There, he slowly undressed, slipping his thin snakeskin belt out of his trousers and hanging it with the suit he would wear the following day. Wearing only his underpants, Saltzman returned to the living room where the two detectives were still playing cards. He watched a couple of hands and then went to the bathroom. He did not bother to close the door. If the cops wanted to play nursemaid, they'd have to put up with the sound of his taking a leak.

He was standing in front of the toilet bowl, looking down at the water as he shook himself free of the last few drops, when he heard a sound. As he started to turn around, the snakeskin belt was looped over his head and pulled tightly around his throat. Eyes bulging, he fought against the belt held by O'Brien, while in the living room Mulholland turned up the volume of the television. Voices singing the praises of Coca Cola drowned out the sounds of struggling coming from the bathroom.

O'Brien dug his knee into Saltzman's back and pulled as hard as he could. It was like fighting a bull. Despite his strength and the thirty years difference in their ages, O'Brien wasn't sure he would win. He called out Mulholland's name. The lieutenant came and joined him in the struggle, pinioning Saltzman's arms while O'Brien continued to apply pressure with the belt. Slowly, the resistance diminished. Saltzman's eyes rolled up into his head. His body collapsed, his knees buckled, and he dropped to the floor. O'Brien went down with him, continuing to squeeze tightly with the belt for another full minute.

"Is he dead yet?" O'Brien whispered.

"If he isn't now, he never will be," Mulholland answered as he checked Saltzman's pulse. "Get him in the shower stall."

Together the two detectives hoisted Saltzman into the stall. Mulholland pulled on the shower head, grunting in satisfaction when it held his weight. He pulled the snakeskin belt tightly around Saltzman's neck and tied the free end around the shower head. When

O'Brien let go of Saltzman, the heavy body swayed from side to side, knees bent, weight on the toes.

"Determined guy to hang himself like that," O'Brien muttered. "He must have been scared shitless of what his pals would do if they ever caught up with him."

O'Brien left the bathroom. Mulholland locked the door from the inside and knocked gently on the wall. Moments later, O'Brien's size thirteen oxford smashed into the lock from the other side. A second time, then a third. Wood splintered. The lock gave, the door smashed back. Mulholland came running out of the bathroom, heading for the telephone.

"Saltzman just locked himself in the bathroom and hanged himself!" he yelled when he got through to the precinct house. "You'd better get a blood wagon up here quick!"

633

Chapter Six

For six weeks after Harry Saltzman's death, Levitt lived in the depths of depression. Not because of Saltzman; the inital shame of ordering the killing soon passed, replaced by the certain knowledge that it had been the safe, logical decision to make. It was Pearl who lay at the root of Levitt's misery, her shock at learning of Leo's involvement in murder. All these years Levitt had managed to hide the truth because he wanted to protect her. Until, in one violent outburst, he had blurted out everything.

During those six weeks, Levitt spent much of his time around the apartment, reading, watching television, listening to music. He ventured out only for meals in local restaurants and daylight walks in Central Park, where he would sit by the lake and talk to the elderly men who always seemed to be there, watch children sail boats, or wander through the zoo and stare at the animals. It crossed his mind that this was how it must feel to be retired. Nothing to do but eat and sleep and walk. Retired! . . . He detested the idea, and he despised himself for even thinking of it. He wasn't retired. He was simply taking a break, a vacation, that was all. Soon he would pick up the pieces and start to live again.

Several times Pearl telephoned with invitations to dinner, as though she understood the pain Levitt was suffering. Each time, he refused. He could not return to the house in Sands Point. Not yet. But Pearl remained insistent.

"Lou, I don't blame you for anything, can't you understand that?" she asked after yet another refusal.

"You asked me what I'd done to your family, to your sons. If that isn't blaming me, what is?"

"Whatever I said was due to the heat of the moment, just like what you told me about Leo."

"Have you spoken to him at all?"

"Yes." A pause followed before Pearl said, "He took me out to dinner over the weekend."

"Did you say anything to him?"

"Of course not. He's still my son. Judy left the house before Leo came to collect me," Pearl volunteered. "She took the children with her and returned after he'd left."

"Did she say anything?"

"She didn't have to. It was obvious that she didn't want to be around Leo. Didn't want him near the children."

Levitt was not at all surprised. Judy had always claimed that there was something wrong with Leo; now she had all the proof she would ever need. "What did Joseph say?"

"She told him and he accepted it. She refuses to be in the house when Leo's around. Have you spoken to Leo at all?"

"No. I haven't been to Granitz Tower. I haven't done anything. I may as well take up golf like Benny."

"You?" Pearl laughed. "You and I, we could never play golf, Lou. Too many people would mistake us for the clubs."

Levitt laughed as well. Knowing that Pearl held no animosity made him feel a little better; some of the self-pity he'd been nurturing began to dissipate. "Maybe I'll come over to dinner one night soon."

"Good. You let me know when and I'll make something special for you."

Levitt hung up the telephone and went to the window. Looking out over the lake in the park, he recognized two frail old men sitting on benches. The two men were always there, just sitting, whiling away the time. Suddenly, Levitt sensed that he was looking at himself. He must have appeared just like that these past few weeks. Perhaps not so old, but certainly just as aimless, a man with no motivation, no reason to get up in the morning. He had to change. . . .

The change came a week later when war erupted in the Middle East. Pearl and Judy instantly became busy with the Hadassah chapter to which they belonged, organizing fund-raising events for Israel. Levitt took another direction completely, one with which he was quite familiar. Although he had the reputation for carefully watching every cent, he had always been a philanthropist where Israel was concerned, constantly claiming it was the duty of every Jew in the world to help the Jewish state. At the start of each fall, around the time of the Jewish New Year and the Day of Atonement, Levitt would send a percentage of the casinos' take to agencies acting for Israel, much like a man in a synagogue would make a pledge on a UJA card. The casinos were not in existence anymore, but the hotels were. Even if it was the wrong time of year for all the big spenders to be down from New York, Levitt was certain he could make a success of a gala night for Israel.

News of the war reached the United States first thing on Monday

635

morning. By early afternoon, Levitt was in Hallandale, marching into the Waterway Hotel and demanding to see Benny Minsky. When he was told that Minsky was out playing golf, Levitt went looking for him. He found him lining up a putt on the third green.

"What are you doing out here?" Levitt yelled.

His concentration shattered, Minsky dropped his putter onto the grass. "What does it look like I'm doing? What the hell business have you got down here anyway?"

"There's a war on."

"I listen to the radio, I read the papers. You didn't have to come all the way down from New York to tell me that."

"You're running a hotel corporation, Benny. You've got the facilities for dances, shows, banquets—anything to raise money for Israel."

Minsky's enthusiasm was aroused by golf, not by benefits for Israel. "You want to put on a dance? You want to arrange a show? Fine! Help yourself, just let me get on with my game." Minsky picked up the putter and lined up the shot. Levitt snatched it from him and tossed it clean off the green.

"Up in New York, Pearl and Judy are busting a gut with their Hadassah work. I dare say your daughter-in-law, Susan, is doing much the same. I've flown all the way down here to make use of the hotels, and all you can think of is your damned golf game?"

"Lou, we've got a banqueting manager, we've got an entertainment director. We've got managers for this, directors for that. They're all overpaid. Go see them. Leave me alone to play my damned game, will you?"

Levitt marched off the green, disgusted with Minsky. This was the man who, twenty-five years earlier, had moved heaven and earth to see his son bar mitzvahed. Being a Jew had been important to Minsky then. For the first time in his life he'd found some pride in it. Now, when his fellow Jews were fighting for their very existence in a land they'd carved from the desert, all Minsky wanted to do was play golf! Ah . . . what did you expect from a man who'd married a blond *shikse* anyway?

In the Waterway, Levitt located the banqueting manager, the entertainment director, and the public relations man. "This Saturday, five days from now, I want the Waterway to put on the biggest dinner dance and show that's ever been seen in Florida. Get the top stars from Vegas. I don't care how you do it, I just want it done. The cost is coming out of the hotel's pocket, and every penny we make is going to Israel, so you know what kind of people we want as guests." He turned to the PR man. "Get something in the Miami *Herald*, the Fort Lauderdale and Palm Beach papers, tomorrow. A big advertisement. A story. And run an ad up in New York. Maybe some of our old customers will come down for it."

"What about applying for a license to run a Monte Carlo night?" the entertainment director asked.

"Are you crazy? This place and the Monaco couldn't get a license to hold a horseshoe pitching contest. No gambling. Just good food, good music, and good entertainment. A gala for Israel, five hundred dollars a plate. How many people can we fit in?" he asked the banqueting manager.

"At a pinch? Four hundred. Forty tables of ten."

"Make the necessary arrangements." Four hundred people at five hundred dollars a plate. That was two hundred thousand dollars. A good sum. How many bullets would that buy? How many guns? How many gallons of fuel for tanks and aircraft? Suddenly, Levitt felt blood surging through his veins. His head was clear. He was alive again. "I'll take the first table, right by the stage," he told the banquet manager. "And put Benny Minsky down for one. The other thirty-eight tables are your responsibility. See they're filled."

Levitt left the banqueting, entertainment, and public relations people feeling that their jobs were on the line.

Minsky heard the news when he returned from the golf course after completing a full eighteen holes. He found Levitt settled in a suite of rooms, avidly watching the news reports of the first day's fighting. "You've got some nerve putting me down for a table."

"Are you hard up for five grand, Benny, or haven't you got enough people to invite?"

"What's the point? You're not going to put all this together in five days. It can't be done."

"We need to raise money, Benny. We used to do it. Remember in nineteen fifty-six, the Suez Crisis? We raised money for Israel then."

"We passed the hat around the two casinos. The big winners felt generous. This isn't the same. You're not holding your hand out to gamblers now. You're asking five hundred bucks a head from regular people."

"Gamblers are regular people." Levitt held up a hand for Minsky to be quiet as the newscaster gave the latest details of the first day's fighting. Each side claimed to have inflicted heavy losses on the other; the number of aircraft destroyed was estimated to be over one thousand.

"Jesus," Minsky murmured. "They're slaughtering each other. They go on at this rate, and there won't be any need for you to hold a gala night on Saturday. There'll be no one left to send the money to."

"You believe the Arabs' claims?" Levitt asked. "Or do you believe our claims?"

"*Our* claims? I'm no part of this."

"You're a Jew, that makes you a part of it."

"I'm an American," Minsky countered. "I hope the Israelis win because they're in the right. I don't hope they win because I think I'm one of them. I'm not."

"You don't know what you're talking about," Levitt said angrily.

"I know that I don't make a living out of being a Jew like you do."

"What's that supposed to mean?" Levitt swung away from the television to stare at Minsky.

"You've been playing a game all your life, or haven't you realized it yet? Always you've been stressing how important it is to remember that you're a Jew. You've been using it as a weapon, as a defense, as a crutch. Anything ever went wrong, like this Senate Special Committee on Organized Crime, and you brought it up. I knew we got investigated because of the gambling, because of what happened to old man Rourke years ago. But you . . . you had it fixed in your mind that the whole thing was cooked up because the Rourkes were a bunch of Jew-hating bastards."

"They are."

"Maybe the old man is, but you've got no proof that says you can hang that label around the necks of his sons."

"Are you sticking up for them?"

"No way. I'm just pointing out the truth to you. For God's sake, Lou, if a damned dog bit you in the ass, you'd say it was because its owner was an anti-Semite. You thought you were better than me because I fell in love with Kathleen, and then you sneered at me because I wanted to see William bar mitzvahed. You were the one who was so hot to see Pearl's twins get bar mitzvahed . . . the stories you told them about standing up and being counted. You haven't used being a Jew as a religion. You've used it as a goddamned career!"

Levitt arranged for Pearl, Joseph and Judy, Jacob and Anne to fly down from New York for the weekend as his guests. Minsky made the same arrangements with his son, daughter-in-law, and grandsons.

By Thursday night, the banqueting and entertainment heads were ready to face Levitt with grim news. "We think you'd better cancel this gala night," the banqueting manager said. "Out of thirty-eight tables, we've sold three."

"What about the show?" Levitt asked the entertainment director.

"I've been on the telephone for two days solid. You don't get top-rate singers and comedians on five days' notice. Every Jewish entertainer—even every entertainer who claims he's sympathetic to Israel—is already booked doing some charity show, helping some Israel Bond drive."

"How come they got booked up so quickly for other Israel functions? How come you were so slow?"

"The war may have started this week, but there's been a threat of war out there for more than a month. All the Jewish stars have been taking bookings for the past four weeks."

"Wait until tomorrow," Levitt said. "Give it one more day. I'll make a decision tomorrow night."

When the Granitzes and Minskys arrived on Friday evening, Levitt was in a jubilant mood about the progress of the war, but his spirits were dampened by the continuing failure of his big gala night. Only three more tables had been filled, sold to wealthy Floridians who had once been regular patrons at the gambling tables on the top floors of the Waterway and Monaco hotels. All the entertainment director had been able to book were second-string acts, and even then he'd been forced to promise exorbitant fees for their services.

Pearl was quick to spot Levitt's disappointment. She knew him too well for him to be able to hide his feelings. When he told her the reason, she urged him to do what the entertainment and banqueting heads had already suggested. "Cancel it, Lou," she advised him gently. "Admit it was a mistake and walk away."

"It should have worked. There's no reason for it to flop like this."

"Cancel it," Pearl said again. "You let your emotions override good sense. You didn't have a remote chance of putting something this big together in just five days."

On Saturday morning, Levitt held one more meeting with the department heads. Including his own table and Minsky's, ten tables of the forty had been taken. Grudgingly, he gave the order to cancel. Whether he had thought for once with his heart or not, failure in any form did not sit well with Levitt.

Instead of attending a gala on Saturday, Levitt settled for dinner with Pearl and her family. Minsky, who had spent the day on the golf course with his son, took his own family to Miami for dinner. Levitt was glad that his partner was absent. He could not have stood Minsky's rubbing in the failure of the gala night or, even worse, God forbid, commiserating with him, offering sympathy.

Late that night, Pearl sat with Levitt in his suite, watching the news on television. The main story was still the Middle East where, after six days, the war had ended with Israeli forces having achieved the strategic objectives of the Suez Canal, the Jordan River, and the Golan Heights. Levitt watched dispassionately as reports were made from the capitals of the combatant countries. Next, the focus switched to the huge drive for funds in the United States. Feeling that his own inadequacy was being thrust in his face, Levitt started to get up to switch off the set.

He froze in midstride as a scene was flashed on the screen. A gala dinner, just like the one he had planned. Only this one was in Boston. There were no singers, no dancers, no comedians. Just a solitary speaker.

"What is *he* doing at a dinner to honor Israel?" Levitt shouted at Pearl while his finger pointed at the screen.

"Quiet, Lou," Pearl said. "Let's hear what he has to say."

Quivering with rage and indignation, Levitt dropped back into his seat. He could not believe his eyes. There, standing in front of American and Israeli flags, was Senator Patrick Rourke, Jr., pledging to a hall full of people his support of Israel, his willingness to fight in Washington for increased aid in money and armaments. As the camera swung around the hall, Levitt saw that there were no empty spaces. Here, in Florida, there were vacant tables, but in Boston every seat was taken.

The newscaster's face returned. Levitt heard the man say that more than one hundred thousand dollars had been raised at the two-hundred-dollar-a-plate dinner. Further pledges by those attending were expected to increase the amount to more than a million dollars.

"That shitbag!" Levitt yelled out. "That anti-Semitic Irish bastard has got the goddamned nerve to show himself at a fund raiser for Israel! It's because of him that we raised no money here tonight!"

"Lou," Pearl said softly. "Don't you think you're becoming a little obsessed with him?"

"Obsessed?" Levitt laughed. "I've every reason to be obsessed. If he hadn't stuck his face into our business, the casinos would still be open. We'd have gone around with the hat again, just like we did in fifty-six. We'd have taken in a fortune. And now he's got the damned nerve to stand up in front of five hundred people, five hundred Jews, and say he supports Israel!

"He should rot in hell!"

In the basement of his Scarsdale home, Leo watched the news with Mahmoud Asawi. He sat back comfortably on the leather couch, barely interested in what was happening in the Middle East. He felt it did not affect him at all. Only if the Arab nations cut off the supply of oil would he feel involved. Mahmoud, however, was tense. Positioned on the edge of the couch, chin resting on his clenched hands, he watched and listened.

When the focus of the report switched to the Jordanian capital of Amman, Mahmoud rose from the couch and stood right in front of the television, as if he could enter the screen, travel along the airwaves and be home.

"What are you getting so wound up about?" Leo asked.

"My family."

"I thought you didn't give a damn about your family."

Mahmoud swung around angrily. "Just because my father does not send me money anymore does not mean I have no feelings for him. I have a mother as well, and a brother who is in the army. He is a captain of infantry."

"It's over. It only lasted for six days. How much harm could have come to your captain-of-infantry brother in six days, for crying out loud?" Leo wondered why Mahmoud had never mentioned his mother and brother before. Had the abrupt ferocity of this odd little war stirred his memory, shaken up his emotions? Even after seven months, Leo felt that he knew little about Mahmoud's inner feelings. The Arab youth was a hedonist, interested in nothing but his own pleasure for which Leo paid dearly, and now that he'd caught his first glimpse of Mahmoud's inner self, he was not very sure that he welcomed it. Mahmoud's preoccupation with the war was throwing a wet blanket over the weekend. Leo wished he would forget his family until he was back in his own West Side studio apartment, where he would impose his feelings on no one but himself.

"It is easy for you to say the war is over," Mahmoud said hotly. "Your side won."

"My side?" Leo was puzzled.

"Your side. The Israelis. You are a Jew; they are your side."

Leo stared blankly at the young man. In seven months, Mahmoud had never made any reference to Leo's being Jewish, or to his being an Arab. Nor had Leo ever commented on the fact. Now, suddenly, everything was changing and Leo didn't like that.

"Switch off that garbage," Leo said at last. "Let's watch a movie, have a little fun."

"Your movie is the garbage. You live in the world of your movies. This"—Mahmoud's eyes flashed as he pointed agitatedly at the screen, at a reporter speaking from Damascus, "this is real life. *My* people are dying so *your* people can steal their land."

Again the *your*. *Your* side . . . *your* people. What was it that Lou Levitt had once told the twins? It didn't matter if they forgot they were Jews because sooner or later a *goy* would remind them. "Mahmoud, you're beginning to bore me. I pay you well for your company. I don't pay you for your neuroses."

"Am I not permitted to show some concern for my family?"

"Of course. Go ahead, watch the news. Afterward I can show the movie." He clasped his hands behind his head, staring at the back of Mahmoud's slim body. The word *your* kept going around in his mind. Your . . . your . . . your . . . For seven months he'd felt as close to Mahmoud as he had ever been to anyone. Mahmoud had been the lover, the mistress, Leo had always dreamed about. Their basic differences, the knowledge that the relationship must remain secret, had added spice. Now Mahmoud was displaying the width of the rift that really existed between them. Leo had mistakenly believed that he had bought and paid for the Jordanian youth, and now Mahmoud was telling him that money meant nothing. Perhaps seven months was long enough.

Mahmoud took one step to the side, allowing Leo to see the screen. The newscaster's face was back again. Leo caught words about fund-raising drives in the United States, and he wondered how Levitt had gotten on with his gala night in Florida.

A picture of a hall full of tables flashed onto the screen, and Leo heard a familiar, hateful voice. Instead of saying, "It's quite a switch from driving a cab to being vice-president of a thriving real-estate company," the voice was now pledging support for Israel, promising to fight in Washington for increased financial and military aid.

"There!" Mahmoud spat as he spun around to face Leo. "That man who tried to disgrace you! Even he is on your side!"

Leo sat gaping at the picture. Only when it finally faded did he seem to notice Mahmoud glaring at him. "Did you hear what I said? That man who tried to disgrace you is on Israel's side. He wants to fight in Washington to get the Israeli expansionists more guns, more bombs, more planes with which to kill my people!"

A spark of sadistic mischief took fire in Leo. He wanted to tease Mahmoud, see how far he could push the young man. "Oh, he'll do it. He carries a lot of weight in Washington. He wants to be the next president of this country and he's got a lot of friends in influential places. When he gets in, this country will supply Israel with nuclear weapons."

Mahmoud's lips were stretched tight. His eyes blazed and his body trembled. He had no idea that Leo was poking fun at him; he took everything at face value. "My people get no help at all. Israel gets help from everyone. Do you know what my people call your President Johnson?" Leo shook his head. He didn't know and he didn't really care. "They call him Johnson the Jew because of all the support he gives to Israel. And this man, if he becomes President, you say he'll give even more."

"No. I didn't say *if*," Leo replied, fanning the sadism into fresh flame. "I don't think there's any *if* about it. Senator Rourke will be our next President."

Mahmoud spat drily at the television. "That for Senator Rourke. And that for his influential friends in high places. My people will fight on forever to regain the land that has been stolen from them. We will kill the Israelis and we will kill those who aid them. Even those in high places in America. That way we will show the Americans how costly is their support of Israel."

Leo turned the screw another notch. "It wouldn't show Americans a thing. Murders here are a dime a dozen. Even if you shoot the President, ten seconds later the vice-president steps into his shoes and nothing really changes. The policies remain the same."

"Maybe nothing would change here. But in my country it would change. It would give my people great strength to know that they are not completely impotent."

"It would give them a hero, is that what you mean? What use is a hero if he's locked up in jail?"

"So he would be a martyr. A martyr to a worthwhile cause."

Abruptly, Leo's streak of sadism burned itself out. Replacing it in his mind was a picture of his mother, her anguish at the Senate Special Committee hearings. He had seen her reduced to tears and he had been unable to do anything about it. And the casinos in Florida, London, the Bahamas . . . "Would you," he asked Mahmoud softly, "want to become such a hero?"

Mahmoud gazed stupidly at Leo for several seconds. "Are you proposing what I believe you are proposing?"

Leo just smiled.

"Why would you want to see a friend of your people killed?"

"I keep telling you . . . the Israelis are not my people. My people are right here in this country."

Mahmoud turned toward the television again. When he saw an advertisement, he snapped off the set. "You, yourself, pointed out the difference between a hero and a martyr. I do not wish to become a martyr for anything."

Leo appeared crestfallen. His face fell and his voice, when he eventually spoke, was laced with sorrow. "I thought I saw something in you, Mahmoud. I thought I saw fire, a desire for justice, the courage to right a wrong no matter what the cost."

"You would like to see that man dead, would you not?"

"Whether he lives or dies is of little concern to me," Leo lied easily. "He tried his hardest to hurt me and my family, and he failed miserably."

"Nonetheless, you would like to see him dead."

"Let's just say I wouldn't wear sackcloth and ashes for him."

"That is what I thought. I have no desire to be a martyr. The robes of a hero would suit me well, but not the rags of a martyr. I have too much living to do, and I do not intend to waste my life behind bars."

"No one said you had to be a martyr."

Interest flickered in Mahmoud's dark eyes. "Escape would be possible after committing such a deed?"

"It would be possible."

"How?"

Leo shrugged his shoulders. "There are ways."

"You are serious, are you not?"

"Only if you are."

"A man who did such a thing and escaped would have to leave this country. Where would he go?"

"With a half a million dollars, such a man could live anywhere he chose." Leo was certain that the Jordanian was motivated by money, and he was not wrong.

"A half a million dollars." Mahmoud relished the sound of the amount on his lips. "A very wealthy hero. But if such a thing came about, what would happen to us? There would be a connection."

"There would be a connection only if you were caught and identified. And there are ways to avoid that."

Mahmoud stood in front of the television set, rubbing his index finger across his bottom lip. Leo watched expectantly, then his optimism plummeted when Mahmoud shook his head and grinned. "No, Leo, no. Why are we even discussing such a thing? Let us watch your movie instead. What was it tonight? *Scarface?*"

He sat down on the couch while Leo turned on the projector. . . .

Mahmoud left Leo's home late on Sunday night to return to his studio on West Seventy-second Street. Leo stayed awake, sitting in his basement cinema while *White Heat* unfolded on the screen in front of him. He had seen the movie countless times, and still that ending never failed to thrill him. The last of the great old-fashioned gangster films, a blazing, roaring apocalypse of a finale.

The telephone rang and Leo stared at the instrument with annoyance. Who could be calling at this hour? Despite the many times he'd seen the movie, he was loath to stop the projector and answer the call. Leave it alone, he told himself. Half-a-dozen rings and the caller would give up.

Half-a-dozen rings were followed by another half-dozen. Disgusted, Leo answered with a petulant "Yes!"

"I am coming back to see you."

"Why?"

"My brother . . . my brother Hussein is dead."

Leo could hear the tears in Mahmoud's voice. After a week of watching reports on television, Leo felt that the war had struck home. Not with the death of a friend, but with the death of an enemy.

When Mahmoud arrived, his face was streaked with dried tears. His hands clutched a Western Union telegram.

"From your father?" Leo asked.

Mahmoud nodded. "The first time he has contacted me in almost a year. And this is what he has to say." He repeated the words he'd memorized. "Your brother Hussein killed Jerusalem June Seven."

"Were you and your brother close?"

"He was my brother," Mahmoud answered in a tone that inferred nothing more needed to be said. "Were you serious before?"

"About Senator Rourke?"

"About the enemy of my people. About the half-million dollars. About the escape."

"I can arrange it all."

Mahmoud stood silently for several seconds. "Show me how well you can arrange it, Leo, and then I will give you my answer."

Leo contacted Lou Levitt the moment he returned from Florida. "Uncle Lou, I've got to see you right away. Can you come into Granitz Tower?"

"Is it really important, or can it wait?"

"It's important, Uncle Lou. You'll want to hear this."

"In that case, I'll come right over."

Levitt arrived at Granitz Towers forty minutes later and was shown into Leo's office. At first he looked around, expecting to see Joseph. "He's not here," Leo said. "This isn't Granitz Brothers business. It's strictly between me and you."

"What's between you and me?"

Although there was no one who could overhear, Leo dropped his voice to a mere whisper. "Did you see the news on Saturday night, Senator Rourke at that fund-raising dinner in Boston?"

"What about it?" The question was snapped out. Levitt didn't need to be reminded.

"How would you like to see him dead?"

Levitt regarded Leo as though he were mad. "Don't you ever listen?

I've told you a thousand times that you don't kill a United States Senator."

What Leo had to say next took courage, because it could destroy the veil of secrecy with which he'd protected his affair with Mahmoud Asawi. "I know someone who'll do it for us, provided he's assured of half a million dollars and an escape."

"Who is this someone?"

"A young man named Mahmoud Asawi."

"An Arab?"

"A Jordanian. He's from Amman. He came over here to study."

"How do you know him?"

"He's a friend."

"You're friends with an Arab?" Levitt's eyes registered total disbelief. "How the hell could you be friends with an Arab? Wait a minute. Have you been—?"

"Having an affair with him? Yes, I have." Leo saw no shame in admitting it now. Levitt would overlook such an indiscretion when he fully realized its ramifications.

Levitt's reaction was exactly as Leo had imagined it that first night with Mahmoud. "How could you . . . how could you have? . . ." Levitt's voice trailed off. He was unable to put into words the horrifying thoughts that pounded his brain. Finally he went on.

"Been his lover? The lover of an Arab?" Leo asked. There was nothing wrong in using the term, he realized.

"You said it, not me. How could you do it? He'll stab you in the back as soon as look at you. He'll cut your stupid throat while you're asleep. Has he called you a goddamned filthy Jew yet?"

"No. Nor will he."

"How come you're so sure about that?"

"Because I've shown him sympathy. Because I've pointed out that Senator Rourke is my enemy as well as his enemy."

"And just because of that," Levitt said disbelievingly, "he'll go out and kill the senator for you."

"No, not because of that. Mahmoud spent Saturday night with me. I put the idea to him then. He toyed with it, interested but not committed. When he left to return home, something happened that made up his mind." Leo told Levitt about the cable that had been waiting for Mahmoud, and the little man's skepticism changed to intrigue.

"You told him you could arrange the escape?"

"Yes."

"He believed you?"

"I think so."

646

Levitt stroked his chin. "I don't know. Half a million dollars, that's a lot of money, Leo."

"It cost us a hundred thousand to shut Harry Saltzman's mouth. Surely a United States Senator, a presidential hopeful, is worth five times what Harry was worth. Especially when that half-million is only in the form of a nonrecourse promissory note."

"What about your connection to him? How many people have seen you together?"

"Uncle Lou, if I kept this relationship secret from you, even God wouldn't know about it."

"I want to meet him. I want to make the final judgment for myself."

"I can have him over at my place whenever I want. I pay him enough."

"You do that. Let me see if this Arab boyfriend of yours is really as gullible as he sounds—or whether you're the gullible one."

"Not me, Uncle Lou," Leo said proudly. "There's nothing gullible about me."

We'll see, Levitt thought, still unconvinced that Leo could have manipulated the Arab into such a position. We'll see.

Mahmoud approached his meeting with Levitt cautiously. He had seen the little man on television during the Senate Special Committee hearings and knew that he, like Leo, wanted to see Patrick Rourke, Jr. dead. But Levitt was another Jew, and since learning of the death of his brother Hussein—killed by Jews while defending East Jerusalem against the invading Israeli army—Mahmoud was very wary.

The meeting was held late at night in Leo's home. Watching Mahmoud's car swing right into the grounds where no one would be able to see the license plate or the driver, Levitt was able to appreciate firsthand the careful manner in which Leo had gone about the relationship. Levitt had never even guessed that such an association could be taking place. Leo and an Arab. For seven months yet! Leo had even got the Arab to go to Florida over Christmas, register in Miami under a false name. If I don't know about it, Levitt mused, even God doesn't know. The deception gave him a new understanding of Leo. He could plot and scheme with the best of them. Even with me, Levitt thought, and he could conjure up no finer compliment for anyone.

After Leo made the introductions, both men stood facing each other silently. At last, Levitt offered his hand. He wasn't happy about shaking the hand of an Arab, but it was a small price to pay if Leo's claim was true. The final, devastating blow to the Rourke family. A blow struck not by an American, but by a Jordanian. A blow struck by an Arab at a United States Senator who was loud in his support of Israel. A double-edged sword. A shattering disaster for the Rourke family, and the reason for a wave of anti-Arab sentiment in the United States. Levitt did not know whether Leo had foreseen this added benefit. It didn't really matter. Leo had laid the groundwork, and for that alone he deserved Levitt's admiration.

"I was sorry to hear about your brother," Levitt said.

"Do you really care?"

"I do. War is a waste, and this is a war that should never have happened."

"All I understand is that you hate this Senator Rourke as deeply as I do," Mahmoud said. "And you would pay me half a million dollars to do this thing."

"We would pay you. We would help you."

"Help me? How?"

"Before I can tell you that, we have to decide where this act will be committed. Only after we learn that—see the surroundings, the area involved—will we know." He saw doubt begin to flicker in Mahmoud's eyes, and added quickly, "I am a man of my word. If I say these things will be done, they will be."

Mahmoud looked to Leo, who slowly nodded his head. They had Mahmoud exactly where they wanted him. Revenge and greed, an infallible combination, had him dangling at the end of a thread.

"Leo will stay in touch with you," Levitt said. "When the time is right, we will meet again." He offered his hand. Mahmoud shook it more readily this time. "To our mutual ambition, to our mutual revenge."

The moment Mahmoud left the house, Levitt turned to Leo. "Drive me to Flushing."

"Why?"

"It's time to see a friend in the police department, Lieutenant Mulholland."

The two men made the long journey from Scarsdale to Flushing. Mulholland lived with his wife in an unprepossessing duplex, half of which was rented out. At the end of the street was a pay phone. Levitt fed it a dime and dialed the detective's number. Mulholland's voice was coated with sleep when he answered, but he snapped alert the moment he recognized Levitt's voice.

"We're parked at the end of the street. Come out, we're going for a ride."

Mulholland threw on some clothes, let himself out of the house, and walked quickly along the street. Leo's car was parked in the shadows, far from the nearest streetlamp. The detective climbed in.

"I've got a proposition for you," Levitt said as Leo drove. "It'll make you look like the biggest hero since George Washington."

"I've already got a chest full of citations."

"There's a hundred thousand dollars that goes with this particular citation."

"Maybe I can find space for one more."

"First, I want you to find out for me if Senator Patrick Rourke, Jr. is making any appearances in New York. He was at a big fund-raising dinner for Israel in Boston the other night. Find out if he's going to be doing anything here."

"That should be easy enough."

"Next, I want you to be near him while he's in New York."

"If he's somewhere in midtown, I can always find a legitimate reason to be there."

"Good. Then I want you to meet a friend of ours."

"That's it?"

"The rest comes later. Leo, drive Lieutenant Mulholland home and let him get back to sleep."

The detective was dropped off at the end of his street and left to wonder what the meeting had really been about. A hundred grand to be a hero? Levitt must have something big up his sleeve this time.

Three weeks passed before Mulholland discovered the information Levitt needed. A pro-Israel rally was scheduled to be held the following Sunday outside the United Nations Building on the East Side of Manhattan. Among the speakers would be the Israeli Ambassador to the United Nations, the Mayor of New York, and several congressmen and senators. A late addition to the list of speakers was Senator Patrick Rourke, Jr.

Leo was told to summon Mahmoud to the house in Scarsdale. When Levitt arrived, he had Mulholland with him. "This is the man who will help you to escape," he told the Jordanian youth.

Mahmoud regarded the detective quizzically. "How will you do that?"

Mulholland gave him an easygoing smile. His looks had always been his biggest asset: carefully groomed gray hair; tanned, open face; and tall, athletic build. Three of the commendations he'd earned during his twenty-nine years with the department stemmed from his ability to talk an armed man into surrendering. "I'm going to show you," he said, and pulled a hand-drawn map from his pocket.

"This is United Nations Plaza. There'll be a platform erected there;

that's where all the hotshots will sit. We figure there are going to be about fifty thousand people there on Sunday. That's a lot of people, a lot of confusion and noise. To get to the platform, the speakers will have to walk from their limousines which are parked here." Mulholland's finger jabbed the map at the point where First Avenue and East Forty-sixth Street intersected. "There'll be police barriers up to protect the speakers from the crowd, but they'll stop to shake a few hands on the way. Never knew a politician who could pass up a handshake."

"Where will I be?"

"Right here, right at the start of the aisle that the police barriers will form. With this." Mulholland lifted the small case he'd brought to the house. Opening it, he displayed a double-barreled shotgun. The butt had been shortened and shaped like that of a handgun. The two barrels had been sawed right down. "Ever use one of these?"

Mahmoud took the weapon, examined it. "Never."

"Don't worry. Even a blind man couldn't miss with one of these. All you've got to remember to do is press down with your front hand. Don't let it kick up and spray into the air. Now, as Senator Rourke passes close to you, you call his name. Everyone's going to be calling him, wanting to shake his hand. You do the same. And when he looks in your direction, you do this." Mulholland took the sawed-off shotgun from Mahmoud, leveled it at the wall and pulled both triggers. The click of the hammers falling onto empty chambers was deafening. Mahmoud jumped back. Even Leo flinched. Only Levitt showed no emotion, other than a grim smile as he envisioned Mahmoud squeezing the triggers on a loaded gun, with Patrick Rourke, Jr. right in front of him.

"Where does that gun come from?" Leo wanted to know.

"Evidence room. Used in a bank holdup a long time ago."

"Can it be traced?"

"No way."

"What happens after I fire?" Mahmoud asked.

"There'll be pandemonium like you never saw before. I'll be standing within a couple of yards of you and I'll arrest you. You'll hand me the gun. I'll put the cuffs on you, get you out of there. Only you'll never see a squad room. You'll be in my car so quickly, no one'll know what really happened."

"What about the money, the half a million dollars?" Mahmoud asked Levitt.

"It'll be waiting for you. Name a bank, name a drop-off point. Wherever you want it to be."

Mahmoud took the shotgun from Mulholland and examined it

650

again. His heart was racing, his brain in turmoil. Was it really this simple to kill such a powerful figure in America? Walk right up to him, call him by name? Watch, as hand outstretched, his face collapsed in shock and disbelief? And then this policeman would perform the fake arrest, spirit him away before anyone had a chance to work out what had really happened.

"Well?" Levitt asked. "You wanted your chance to make a hero out of yourself. A rich hero. We've given it to you."

Mahmoud looked past Levitt to Leo. In Leo's eyes he would find the truth. Leo had loved him. Leo would not lie. What he saw in Leo's eyes was trust and tenderness, a reflection of the love they had shared these past eight months. It was enough. Clasping the shotgun tightly to his chest, Mahmoud said, "I will do it."

Sunday dawned bright and clear. By midday, three hours before the rally was due to start, the first listeners drifted in to claim a good position. Many carried flags, Israeli and American. There was a carnival atmosphere to this outpouring of support for Israel that would undoubtedly be seen by those inside the United Nations Building who were hostile to the country; that was part of the idea of staging the rally there.

Mahmoud Asawi approached the United Nations Plaza at twelve-thirty. He wore heavy sunglasses and a white cotton hat. Pinned to the front of the hat was an enameled pin composed of crossed American and Israeli flags. From his left hand hung a bulky shopping bag. Hidden in it, beneath a sweater, a thermos of cold juice and a book, was the sawed-off shotgun Mulholland had provided. A single shell rested beneath each hammer.

Instinctively, Mahmoud felt out of place the moment he reached the edge of the gathering throng. He found himself surrounded by men and women, young and old. Some of the men wore hats or yarmulkes; a few even sported the flourishing beards of the orthodox. Mahmoud realized instantly how dark his skin looked in comparison with everyone else's. Surely it would be an immediate giveaway. All the police had to do was look at him and they would know he was an Arab. He would be dragged from the crowd, his bag searched. The shotgun would be found. He would be flung into jail. What kind of a hero would that make him? And how would Leo and the little man he referred to as Uncle be able to help him then?

A yell ripped through the air to Mahmoud's right. He spun around, expecting to see accusing fingers pointed at him. Instead, he saw a group of young people, arms resting on each other's shoulders. They were dancing! Singing at the tops of their voices and dancing! Were these people utterly mad? He had come here to commit a political assassination, and all around him these maniac Zionists were dancing.

Slowly, Mahmoud's panic passed. The dancers, the singers, they all signified that his own arrival had gone unnoticed. He even saw men and women with skins darker than his own. Oriental Jews, Jews who had fled from Arab countries to live in Israel. Now they were in New York, demonstrating in front of the United Nations. Mahmoud prayed that none of them spoke to him.

The crowd grew larger as Mahmoud pressed himself toward the police barrier in the exact spot that had been pointed out to him on the map. He felt bodies crushing in behind him and looked around wildly. He saw a snap-brimmed hat made of straw with a wide, colorful band around it. Beneath the hat were sunglasses. Despite them, Mahmoud recognized the face he had seen in Leo's Scarsdale home, the police detective who would escort him from this crowd, assist in his escape. He felt Mulholland's gaze sweep over him and then move on. Mahmoud tore his own eyes away from the tall detective. There was to be no liaison between the two men, no opportunity for anyone in the vast crowd to notice a connection, to remember. . . .

At two forty-five, the limousines started to arrive. The Mayor of New York was first, passing along the narrow aisle within two feet of where Mahmoud stood. Hands were thrust out, and the mayor took pains to shake every single one. Mahmoud saw a light brown hand reach out in front of him; the mayor's white hand grasped it over the police barrier. Only when the handshake had been broken, the mayor had moved on, did Mahmoud realize that the hand had been his own. He had shaken the hand of the Mayor of New York. The mayor had accepted him as one of the crowd. So, too, would Senator Rourke when he arrived. He would reach out to shake Mahmoud's hand just as the mayor had done. It would be the last hand the politician would ever attempt to shake.

More people passed along the aisle between the police barriers. Mahmoud had seen their photographs in newspapers, on television, but he could not put names to the faces. It didn't matter; he was interested today in only one face. Anger suddenly gripped him as he identified one of the speakers, the portly, bespectacled figure of Israel's Ambassador to the United Nations, the man who lied so eloquently in front of the General Assembly. It took every ounce of Mahmoud's self-control not to reach into the bag there and then, and abort his mission by killing the wrong man. The moment passed as the ambassador continued on up to the platform and took his seat.

Mahmoud looked around to see that the straw hat and sunglasses had moved closer, no more than five yards away. Only half-a-dozen people separated the detective from himself. His confidence grew until he could feel it bursting through his chest. He was on wings, soaring above this crowd, untouched by all the madness, the noise, the Broadway atmosphere. He was a man with a mission that would rectify all the injustices his people had ever suffered.

He heard a roar of applause, the clapping and cheering of thousands; saw another limousine disgorge its occupants. Two men, obviously brothers, both with bushy light brown hair and fresh, ageless Irish faces. Mahmoud had seen both men on television; he had no trouble recognizing them. Senator Patrick Rourke, Jr. and his brother John. Mahmoud's hand snaked into the bag, past the book, the thermos flask of cold soda, past the sweater, until it gripped the smoothly shaped wooden handle of the sawed-off shotgun. . . .

The narrow aisle between the gray-painted police barriers stretched before the Rourke brothers. The crowd crushed forward on either side but the space remained intact, leading up to the platform like Moses' parting of the Red Sea. Bodies hung over the barriers, hands were outstretched. Senator Rourke felt an overwhelming flow of emotion. All these people, these thousands of people, were cheering him. So what if the primaries were still almost a year away? The popularity he was gaining here would not fade by then. Nor would the positive publicity he'd achieved through his Senate Special Committee hearings across the country. The Six Day War could not have occurred at a better time, right on the heels of those hearings. He'd been able to use it to keep his name firmly in the headlines. He'd get the Jewish vote, whether his father approved or not. To a degree, he could understand his father's bitterness, but all that had been so long ago, in the thirties. This was the sixties. It was a different world completely, and Senator Patrick Rourke, Jr. was different from his father.

"Make it good," John Rourke whispered to his brother as they started the walk toward the narrow aisle leading to the platform. "Fifty thousand votes right here. And don't forget to shake a few hands on the way up there."

Senator Rourke reached out to the first hand that came close to him. An Israeli flag was thrust in his direction. He took it, waved it above his head to draw even more cheers. Vote-getting had never been so easy. Everywhere he heard his name being called. Wherever he turned he saw a smiling face, felt a hand in his own. Never had the senator seen such an enthusiastic crowd. Even if it had poured that day, he was sure the crowd would have been just as large, just as cheerful. American support of Israel was a highly emotional issue.

Votes were given, denied, because of emotions. And the senator, when he finally spoke to this wonderful crowd from the flag-festooned platform, would be as emotional as any Oscar-winning actor had ever been.

"Senator Rourke! Over here! A big smile!"

The senator looked to his left, straight into a camera lens. He waved his hand, made his smile even broader as the shutter was released. Cameras seemed to be appearing everywhere. He looked directly ahead into the beckoning lens of a television camera and gave his big confident smile for the six o'clock news.

"This way!" another voice called out. "This way!"

Senator Rourke looked to his right, into a light brown face, eyes that were shaded by sunglasses, hair that was covered by a white cotton hat. He saw the enameled pin of the American and Israeli flags pinned to the hat. What kind of camera was that the young man held? Twin lenses. He hadn't seen a stereo camera for years; he didn't know that people still used them. In all the excitement, the senator did not even recognize the twin barrels of the sawed-off shotgun for what they were.

Mahmoud's lips parted in a wide, victorious smile. His teeth gleamed in the sunlight. Two barrels. Two brothers so close together. Remembering to hold the weapon down, he pulled both triggers. Two booming explosions, so close together they sounded like one, rose above the shouting of the crowd. The senator flew back against the police barrier, his chest and stomach ripped open. His brother, John, fell on top of him. On the dry, baked concrete, their blood mixed in an ever-widening scarlet pool.

Next to Mahmoud, a girl screamed. All around him the crowd scattered. Suddenly he had space in which to move, in which to escape. Everything was happening just as he had been told it would. He swung around, the shotgun still held in front of him. Five yards away, now separated by no one, was Mulholland in the straw hat and sunglasses. He was crouched in a shooter's stance, a heavy revolver gripped by both hands in front of his face.

Mahmoud's fingers started to open. The revolver in Mulholland's hands roared, flame spurted from the muzzle. Mahmoud felt no pain as the bullet smashed into his head to give him a tiny blue-rimmed eye directly between the other two. He felt only surprise. His final thought as he crashed through the barrier and fell onto the bloodied corpses of the Rourke brothers was *why?*

Chapter Seven

News of the assassinations of Senator Patrick Rourke, Jr. and his brother interrupted regularly scheduled radio and television programs, including the Sunday afternoon concert to which Leo was listening. An announcer, voice charged with emotion, broke in to say that Senator Rourke and his brother, John, had been shot to death by an assassin during a pro-Israel rally in front of the United Nations Building. The unidentified assassin, while trying to escape, had been shot and killed by a New York City detective who had been on the scene.

Leo felt no sadness about the death of Mahmoud Asawi. His fling with the Arab youth had run its course. Mahmoud, like Harry Saltzman before him, had served a purpose; then he had become dispensable.

The announcement ended with the promise of an update later in the program. The music picked up again. Leo leaned back and hummed along, quite content with the world.

He had planned, he had schemed, and he had succeeded. With a smug smile wreathing his face, he wondered how high he had climbed in Lou Levitt's estimation. Leo understood that his twin brother, Joseph, had always held the edge. He'd had the education, and he had the ability to manage a large corporation, keep his finger firmly on the pulse of every department. But that edge was blunted now. Surely Uncle Lou would recognize Leo's value as well. . . .

Lou Levitt heard the news while at Joseph's home in Sands Point, where he was spending the day. He was sitting outside with Joseph and Judy, watching the children, Jacob and Anne, play on the grass with the Dobermans, when Pearl came running out of the house. She had been in the kitchen preparing dinner. As was her custom, she had a small radio on, playing popular music.

"Someone just killed the Rourke brothers, the senator and his brother John!" Pearl exclaimed.

"Where?" Joseph asked.

"In front of the United Nations Building. There was a rally today; they were speaking at a pro-Israel rally. Everyone was there, the mayor, the Israeli Ambassador to the United Nations, everyone."

"Was anyone else killed?" Joseph asked.

"No. Just the Rourkes."

"Did they catch the murderer?" Levitt asked.

"He was shot by a policeman. Killed. How terrible."

Levitt led the way inside the house. Bending over the radio, he paid rapt attention. Pearl, Joseph, and Judy crowded in close.

"Who could have done it?" Pearl asked.

"Don't tell me you're sorry they're dead," Levitt said.

"Lou, how can you say such a thing at a time like this?"

"You won't see me crying for them. They tried to pillory us, why should any of us be sorry?"

The four of them remained in the kitchen for another fifteen minutes until an update was given. The assassin had been identified as Mahmoud Asawi, a Jordanian national living in the United States as a student. The detective who had shot him down was Lieutenant Derek Mulholland, a twenty-nine-year veteran of the force with many commendations for bravery.

"So now he'll get another one," Judy remarked drily. "He'll be called a hero, and no one will ever know for sure why this Jordanian student killed the Rourkes."

"Don't you know that already?" Levitt asked.

"Do you?"

"Of course I do. These Arab bastards, they aren't satisfied with trying to push the Israelis into the sea, so they come over here and murder our leaders who are sympathetic to Israel."

"*Our leaders?*" Joseph asked incredulously. "You just said you wouldn't shed any tears for Senator Rourke, and now you're calling him your leader."

"You know what I mean. The Arabs bring their dirty war over here. They got their butts kicked in face-to-face battle, so now they come here and gun down unarmed politicians who've said they were wrong to start the war in the first place. It's going to backfire, Joseph, you mark my words. By this time tomorrow, there'll be so much revulsion, so much anti-Arab sentiment in this country that the Arabs will need a microscope to find a friend over here in the future."

When the news was repeated, Levitt announced he was going for a walk on the grounds. A stiff breeze was blowing in from Long Island Sound, cooling the air and bringing with it a hint of the sea. As the breeze swept over him, Levitt experienced an enormous wave of satisfaction. With Leo's help, Levitt had put to eternal rest a ghost which had haunted him viciously. It seemed that at every turn these past few months, the Rourke family had been waiting—the hearings, the forced closure of the casinos in Florida, the loss of the gambling licenses in England and the Bahamas, and finally, the fiasco of the fund-raising dinner at the Waterway. While Senator Rourke had been speaking at a dinner in Boston which had been successful, Levitt's attempt at fund-raising had been an abysmal failure. That was all paid off now.

Levitt turned and looked back toward the house, Joseph's house. All these years he had been convinced that only Joseph had his own traits—the quick mind, the attention to detail, the ability to grasp any situation immediately. Now, with one deft piece of thinking, Leo had placed himself on the same plateau. Leo was ready, Levitt decided, to be told the truth about the death of the man he believed to be his father.

That night, as Leo was preparing to drive into town to begin the search for Mahmoud's successor, the telephone rang. It was Levitt, extending an invitation to his apartment on Central Park West.

Leo had little doubt that the summons concerned the events of that afternoon outside the United Nations Building. Shock waves were being felt throughout the country, throughout the entire world. As one, politicians on both sides of the House had risen to cry out against the killing of the Rourke brothers. It was even rumored that President Johnson was going to make a condolence call at the Boston house of Patrick Joseph Rourke.

Levitt had the television on when Leo arrived. Silently, they sat down in front of the set for a few minutes to stare at the footage taken by the cameraman who had been preceding the Rourke brothers along the aisle toward the platform. Levitt showed no emotion as the drama unfolded, but Leo watched hungrily. Mahmoud's outstretched hand . . . instead of a handshake, the sawed-off shotgun's double blast . . . the senator and his brother reeling back. And then the finale, Mahmoud turning around to face Mulholland, believing that the detective in the straw hat would afford him escape. Another roar of gunfire, and the drama was over.

"Sweet," Leo said, surprised to find himself breathing hard.

"Revenge always is," Levitt remarked evenly. "It's the purest motive in the whole world, and when you achieve it, you can actually taste the sweetness. Too bad your mother couldn't taste that sweetness, you know."

"What do you mean?"

"When she heard this afternoon, she was upset. Can you believe that? Upset that two bastards like that should have died. But you . . ." Levitt leaned forward and patted Leo affectionately on the knee. "You, you're like me. You know how to take enjoyment from the sweet things of life. I've been waiting a long time to see how you and Joseph turned out," Levitt continued, unaware of the consternation his approach was causing. "I've been waiting a long time to see which one of you was the man to tackle an important task. A task that will right a wrong committed many years ago and restore the honor of your family."

"Restore the honor of my family? I don't understand, Uncle Lou."

"Listen to me, Leo, and you will understand. It's appropriate that I should tell you this on the day that Patrick Joseph Rourke's sons died, because this story begins with Patrick Joseph Rourke. That old Irish bastard, he contracted with Saul Fromberg to kill me and Jake." Levitt was unable to describe Jake to the twins as their father, not when he firmly believed himself to be; he always used Jake's first name. "The men Rourke sent to do the job, they were Irishmen like himself. No brains. They blew their chance and we all went into hiding."

"That time I had diphtheria."

Levitt nodded. "While we were in hiding, we arranged the murder of Saul Fromberg. Bogus Internal Revenue agents threw him out of his office window, faked a suicide, just like we did with Harry Saltzman. Only Gus Landau, the man who was Fromberg's lieutenant, he escaped. We thought he'd run and we made the mistake of forgetting all about him while we evened up the score with Patrick Joseph Rourke."

"That night my father went up to Massachusetts?"

"That's right, the night Jake hijacked old man Rourke's convoy and killed a dozen of his guards. But Gus Landau came back. He tried to get me and Jake again, outside of your grandma's restaurant on Second Avenue. Instead, he killed her."

"Uncle Lou, I know all this. Landau ran again. He disappeared, until the day of my bar mitzvah, when he came back."

"No!" Levitt allowed the sharp rejection to hang in the air while he studied the amazed expression on Leo's face. "That is not what happened at all. What I'm about to tell you is the truth of what happened. Landau was hiding out for years in Canada, in Toronto. You remember Canada entered the war two years before we did; they were with England. So in 1940, Landau wanted to come back. But he was scared to show his face in New York because he knew we were still looking for him. He was between a rock and a hard place—Canada, a country at war, or the United States where we'd get him. So he came up with a deal to buy his way back here."

"What kind of a deal?"

"In Canada, he was involved in a new business. He had good drug connections. The stuff used to come into Canada from Spain and some of the Middle Eastern countries, countries that were neutral during the war or on the Allies' side. In September nineteen-forty, a few weeks before you were bar mitzvahed, Landau contacted Benny Minsky and asked for a meeting. A one-on-one meeting to discuss this deal he wanted to make."

"And Benny Minsky met with him?"

Somberly, Levitt nodded. "Benny didn't tell any of us beforehand. He just took off one day, met Landau in Niagara Falls on the Canadian side. Only when he came back to New York and met up with me, Jake, and Moe Caplan did he have the balls to say he'd been with Landau."

Leo clenched his teeth in anger. The man who'd killed his grandmother—and Benny Minsky had met with him! Left the country to meet with him! The man who had eventually killed his father!

"The deal Landau offered to Benny was this: we would forget what had happened in the past, let bygones be bygones, and Landau would turn over his drug connections to us. We could sell the stuff in New York through selected small shops that handled the betting for us. Benny was all for it. There was a vote. We voted on everything in those days, the four of us. Jake was dead set against it, and me and Moe, we voted with Jake. But that didn't stop Benny. To him, the democratic process didn't mean a damned thing."

"You mean, he kept pushing for this deal with Landau?"

"You bet he did. There were tremendous arguments between Benny and Jake over Landau's offer. It reached a point where Jake, one day, stood up, jabbed a finger at Benny and said, 'So help me God, if I ever see one packet of white powder in any of our books, I'm coming looking for you with a gun!' That's how Jake threatened Benny, Leo, and he meant it."

"Why was my father so against drugs?"

"Two reasons. Landau himself, obviously. Landau had killed Jake's mother-in-law, your grandmother. He wasn't going to let that be forgiven and forgotten. And the second reason was you and your twin brother. Jake said that kids got hooked on dope and he wasn't going to be involved in anything that preyed on kids. Jake wanted to know if Benny didn't give a damn about his own kid."

"Obviously he didn't."

"Benny said he could control what his own kid did. The truth is, Leo, Benny was more interested in making bucks than he was in his own family. As if the money we made from the gambling wasn't enough."

"What happened then?"

"I acted as peacemaker. I persuaded Benny to cool it. I kept saying we had a good enough business without drugs—why did we need something that could get us into hot water? Things quieted down, returned to normal. I never thought Benny would double-cross us. But he did. While Benny was sitting next to Jake in the synagogue that day, listening to you and Joseph do your bar mitzvah pieces, he had Gus Landau cruising up and down the street outside. He'd brought him down from Canada, accepted his proposal with a rider . . . Benny would let Landau come back to New York in return for the drug connections if he killed Jake."

"Why? Why was it so necessary to kill my father?"

"Benny knew that Jake meant every word of his threat. Jake would have gone looking for Benny with a gun in his hand once drugs started popping out of those small shops. Benny was just protecting himself. And Landau wasn't shy about that part of the deal. He hated Jake like the plague. He had orders from Benny to hit Jake as he came out of the synagogue after your bar mitzvahs."

Leo's eyes burned with fury. "That bastard! He brought William around to our apartment. He got me and Joseph to explain how important it was to be bar mitzvahed because he wanted William to be bar mitzvahed. And then on our bar mitzvahs he had our father murdered!"

"Now do you see what I mean about restoring the honor of your family?"

"What about Moe Caplan and Landau shooting each other?"

Levitt answered the question obliquely. "Once Moe and I realized that it was Landau sitting in that car outside the synagogue, we knew what Benny had done. He'd gone against the vote. So Moe and me had a choice—we either threw in with Benny, or we fought him. We pretended to throw in with him, that way we could pick our own time to even Jake's account. Only Benny wanted a sign of good faith. He wanted Moe to go with him to some abandoned building in the Bronx where Landau was holed up. Benny wanted Moe to help him kill Landau. Moe went along. They killed Landau, and as Moe walked out of the place, Benny fired a shot into the back of his head. Then he stuck the gun in Landau's hand. The scenario was easy for the police to understand. Moe Caplan had shot Landau. Landau, with his dying breath, had squeezed off a shot through the door and gotten lucky."

"How do you know all this? Were you there?"

"No. Benny came to see me right after."

"To kill you?"

Levitt shook his head. "I was the one person he couldn't kill. I was the person he had to make his peace with."

"Why?"

"Because I could have sent Benny to the electric chair any time I wanted to. I still could, if this state practiced capital punishment, and any jury would convict Benny for a murder he committed forty years ago." Levitt stood up, walked to a table where he picked up a folded sheet of paper. "This is a photocopy of an affidavit I swore to forty years ago. It concerns the death . . . the murder . . . of a man called David Hay."

Leo read through the photocopy of the affidavit. It was all there— Levitt being suspicious of Minsky's desire to rush down to the Jersey shore, following him to Flushing Meadows, the eventual disposition of David Hay's body. Leo was uncertain how much weight the affidavit carried now, forty years after the event, when both men were in their sixties. He had little doubt, though, that at the time of Jake Granitz's death, the affidavit had been pure dynamite. He handed the photocopy back to Levitt.

"He knew he couldn't kill me, not without going to the hot seat himself because of my insurance, so he put a deal to me," Levitt said. "If I didn't fight him, we'd split fifty-fifty on everything. Two weeks later, drugs started getting pushed from twenty or so of the small shops where we had the book and the numbers drops."

"You went in with him?" Leo asked in disbelief. "He killed my father, he did all this, and you *went* in with him?"

Levitt lowered his head a fraction as if admitting shame. "Leo, what could I have done? What choice did I have? I never made a living with these"—he lifted his fists—"like Benny did. Violence was second nature to Benny. I made a living with my head. I had to go in with him because it was the only way I could protect you, your brother, and your mother. Who knew what that maniac Benny would do if I went against him?"

"But you still went in with him." It was no longer a question. It was an accusation filled with regret.

"I'm sorry, Leo, but there was nothing else I could do."

"There were no drugs when I started working for Jalo. When I began making the rounds with Phil Gerson, none of the places was pushing drugs."

"Five years, that's all Benny did it for. That's all the time he needed to make a killing."

"Why five years?"

"Benny was bringing his son up on his own then, and maybe wha Jake had said about drugs had lodged in his mind. He didn't wan William seeing his father make money with drugs. I didn't want you and Joseph seeing it either. We agreed that the moment the first boy left school and started working—that was you—the drug busines would cease. Benny kept his word. As you were finishing high school the drug trade was killed off."

"That money in Zurich?"

"A lot of it came from drugs."

"And I thought it was all from gambling."

"That's what you were supposed to think. I didn't want you or Joseph believing that the money rested on filth like drugs."

Leo stroked his chin with his hand. "All this time you waited. Al this time you did nothing. My father was murdered by Benny Minsky and you did nothing."

Levitt's temper flared with sudden fire. "I did plenty, damn you! kept you, your brother, and your mother alive! And I kept tha memory alive!"

"What is it you want me to do?"

"Make Benny crawl and scream. Do you remember your mother after Jake was killed? Do you?" When Leo nodded, Levitt said, " want Benny just like that. I want him climbing the walls because the son he had with his blond *shikse,* his precious son, is dead."

Leo looked up sharply. It had never occurred to him that William would be the means of vengeance. "Why not just go after Benny?"

Levitt dismissed the suggestion with a wave of the hand. "Too easy He'll hurt for a minute, maybe not even that, and then it'll be all over Like the Rourke brothers hurt for a minute. But their father's pair will go on for the rest of his life, and I hope he has a long life in which to remember and regret. That's the revenge we want against Benny.'

Leo turned to gaze at the television set. He was surprised that the set was off; he couldn't remember either Levitt or himself flicking the switch. But Leo's imagination provided the only picture he needed. A scene outside a synagogue, Leo and Joseph admiring the gold watches Levitt had given to them. And Jake, walking on ahead with Isaac Cohen, the elderly man who had taught the twins their bar mitzvah portions. Jake leaving Cohen to come back and look at the watches His name called, just as Mahmoud Asawi had called the name of Seantor Rourke. Even the same weapon, a shotgun.

There was a chilling coincidence to that. The use of a similar weapon to kill both Jake Granitz and the Rourke brothers. Leo's mind explored another coincidence. A bar mitzvah. Benny Minsky's older grandson, Mark, was due to take the step into manhood in two years' time.

"How's Benny's heart, Uncle Lou?"

Levitt looked at Leo in some shock. "How do I know?"

"Will he last two years?"

"Why is it so important that he should?"

Leo told him. At first, Levitt just nodded in agreement. Then he began to laugh, a low chuckle that finally erupted into a loud, appreciative roar of laughter. "It's poetic, Leo. Snatch the joy from Benny's mouth, just the way he snatched it from Jake's."

Leo just smiled. He had two years in which to prepare. When a man had that much time to plan, he rarely made a mistake.

BOOK SEVEN

Chapter One

Richard Nixon's defeat of Hubert Humphrey in the election of 1968 gave rise to a string of haunting hypothetical questions. What would have happened if Senator Patrick Rourke, Jr. had been alive? If he had won the Democratic nomination? Would the slim margin of victory that Nixon enjoyed have been transformed, instead, into a margin of defeat? The assassination of Senator Rourke and his brother by a fanatical Jordanian youth named Mahmoud Asawi had left an indelible question mark over the immediate course of American politics.

A side story to the election was the death in his Boston home of old Patrick Joseph Rourke. When the butler went into Rourke's bedroom to rouse him on the day after the election, he found the old man dead in bed. Rourke's two daughters-in-law, Grace and Rose, both agreed that it wasn't old age that had killed the former ambassador. He had died from a broken heart after having seen his dreams swept away in a hail of gunfire.

Despite her own harsh feelings toward old man Rourke, Pearl was saddened when she read of his death in the *New York Times*. Rourke had allowed his life to be compelled by two driving forces: vengeance and the need to see his sons in Washington. She wondered if he had actually taken any joy in his family, real joy as she did in her own, or was his familial concern based only on self-serving interest?

When she mentioned seeing the story to Lou Levitt, he advised her not to waste her sympathy. "Remember, Pearl, he took money to kill Jake and me."

Pearl supposed that Levitt was right. Still, she continued to dwell on what she considered Rourke's wasted life. What had he really gotten out of it? Nothing; he had just reaped the hatred he'd sewn. For that reason she felt sorry for him. And she felt a trace of sympathy for Lou Levitt. She felt sorry for him because Levitt's hatreds seemed just as strong, just as long-lasting as Rourke's had been. Levitt had allowed his loathing of the Rourke family to become an obsession. Even after the tragedy which had befallen the Rourkes, Levitt could find no compassion for them.

As old age approached, Pearl was seeing shortcomings in Levitt that she had never recognized before. Or did the fault lie within herself? Was her willingness to forgive, and not Levitt's continuing hatred, the real flaw?

Had Pearl asked those questions of Levitt, he undoubtedly would have answered yes, the fault was her own. You never forgave, and you never forgot—that was the maxim by which he had lived. To forgive, he would have told her, was simply an invitation to those you had forgiven to go ahead and hit you again.

Pearl, Joseph, Judy, and the two children spent the Christmas holiday and the New Year's Day following the election at the Waterway Hotel in Hallandale. Benny Minsky's family was also there. Only Lou Levitt and Leo refused to travel south for the holidays.

Minsky was a genial host. During the day, he played golf with William and Joseph. In the evenings he took everyone out to dinner, and when the Waterway celebrated New Year's Eve with a gala party, Minsky reserved a table for his family and the Granitzes. All four children stayed up until midnight, holding hands with the adults in the center of the dance floor as "Auld Lang Syne" was sung.

"That makes two years since the casinos were closed, Benny," Pearl said as she clutched his hand on one side, Joseph's on the other. "Do you miss them?"

"I thought I would, but I don't. This is like a retirement for me. I'm sixty-six, Pearl, I've earned it."

The singing of "Auld Lang Syne" ended and it was 1969. The hotel guests returned to their tables on which bottles of champagne had been placed. Minsky picked up a bottle. "Can the kids have champagne?"

"Why not?" Joseph asked. "Jacob's fourteen. Anne's eleven. A drop of champagne once a year isn't going to hurt them."

"William . . . Susan?" Minsky looked at his own son and daughter-in-law, then answered the question for himself. "Mark's getting bar mitzvahed in less than six months. Of course he can have a glass of champagne. And if we give Mark, we can't leave out Paul. Let's just check it's the real stuff, the good stuff—fresh off the boat." He pulled a pair of glasses from his pocket and slipped them on. "Taittinger, *Comtes de Champagne. Blanc de blanc Chardonnay*," he read from the label, and everyone laughed at his atrocious pronunciation. "Don't make fun of the way I talk," he protested. "Remember what I told

Senator Rourke, *olova sholom*. I was brought up on the streets, not in some fancy university with a grim-faced governess."

"They certainly weren't the streets of Paris," Susan said.

"Never mind what streets they were." Minsky bent forward to pour the champagne. The glasses slipped off the end of his nose and dropped onto the table. Setting down the bottle, he retrieved the glasses, drew them back toward his face. Pearl watched, puzzled, as he placed them upside down on his nose.

"Are you playing games, Benny?" she asked uncertainly. Minsky's mouth worked as he tried to answer. His words were slurred, running into each other. Horrified, Pearl watched as a sag blossomed on the left side of his face. Muscles collapsed to drag down the eye. The entire left side of his body seemed to shrink and he began to fall.

As realization dawned on Pearl, she reached out to grab Minsky. Simultaneously, William held him from the other side. Together, they lowered him into a chair. "Get a doctor, quickly!" William hissed at Susan. "My father's had a stroke."

Pearl saw Minsky the following day in the hospital. He was sitting up in bed, the left side of his face twisted as though he had no control over it. He recognized Pearl and tried to smile at her when she entered his room. As Pearl sat down next to the bed, he said something which she had to ask him to repeat. His words were still slurred, malformed by his inability to control the muscles on the left side of his body.

"I . . . said . . ." Slowly, Minsky forced the words out of the side of his mouth, and Pearl could see frustration in his eyes at having to speak like this, at not being understood. ". . . Happy . . . New . . . Year."

"You sure started it off on the wrong foot," Pearl answered, and realized that she, too, was speaking slowly, pushing out each word with extreme care.

Minsky said something more and, again, Pearl did not understand. She felt terrible as she watched him reach out his good right hand for the notepad and pencil which rested on the bedside table. Pearl mouthed the words he'd written in big block capitals.

"'It'll go away'? The paralysis will go away?"

Minsky nodded, pleased that he had got the message through. The pencil started to move again, and Pearl read out each word. "'The . . . doctors . . . told . . . me . . . that . . . the . . . paralysis . . . is . . . temporary.'"

Minsky set down the pad, ripped off the top sheet, and started on a fresh page. "Exercise. Therapy. Good as new."

"By when?"

"June," Minsky wrote. "Got to be June. Bar mitzvah. Mark."

Pearl patted his hand and removed the note pad. Even writing a few words was exhausting Minsky. He needed to rest, otherwise his dream of being fully fit again when his older grandson was bar mitzvahed would remain just that.

Pearl returned to New York that night with Joseph, Judy, and the children. When Levitt met them at the airport, Pearl told him of Minsky's stroke. Levitt's concern upon hearing the news surprised her. "Is he going to be all right?"

"The doctors say he is. With therapy, the paralysis on his left side should disappear."

"Will he get back the use of everything? What about his mind? Is that affected? Does he understand what's going on around him?"

"He recognized me when I went to see him."

Levitt relaxed, but only a little. Leo had wanted two years, and Levitt had been content to wait because Leo's scheme would snatch away Minsky's pleasure in his grandson's bar mitzvah—take that pleasure and turn it into the most devastating grief. But it would all be wasted if Minsky wasn't fully cognizant of what was taking place. A stroke! . . . Was nature—was God?—going to snatch away the revenge that Levitt so desperately wanted?

Minsky's recovery was a slow, frustrating affair. Only after a month of rigorous exercise was he able to bring back some movement to his left side. He was able to stagger a few steps with the aid of a walker, but the prognosis of a virtually full recovery had been toned down. If Minsky was fortunate he would regain eighty percent of his physical faculties. He would be able to walk, but not without a cane. He would be unable to drive, and he would never be able to play golf again.

Minsky accepted the news stoically. Since the stroke he had resigned himself to living one day at a time, and it was most important to him that his brain had not been damaged. He remembered everything—people, places, dates. Even if he had to be helped into the synagogue when his grandson Mark, was bar mitzvahed, he would be happy. Just as long as he could see and hear.

In Minsky's mind, the bar mitzvah of his older grandson became as important as that of his son, William, had been. It was the coming of age of the third generation, just as William's bar mitzvah had signified the coming of age of the second. And more. Whenever Minsky thought back to those days he could feel a lump forming in his throat, a churning of the stomach, a wetness in his eyes. If he could point to one act he had committed during his lifetime and say he was proud of it, it was that.

His physical improvement continued slowly. Four months after the stroke, Minsky could walk fifty yards with just a cane for support. His left hand and arm were sufficiently strong to grasp the cane. He was realistic enough to understand that this was probably the best he would ever achieve. That there had been improvement at all was cause enough for gratitude.

Only Minsky's facial muscles showed no improvement. The downward, twisted slant remained on the left side of his face, as though his expression had been frozen into a grimace.

Despite Minsky's protests, William flew down from New York to spend every weekend with his father. He watched while Minsky took his few steps, listened attentively as his father spoke slurred words. At the beginning of May, four months after the stroke, Minsky asked, "Are you planning on coming down every weekend until I fly up for Mark's bar mitzvah?"

"Of course."

"In that case, I'll come up to New York for the month before, otherwise Susan's going to be citing me as the reason for a divorce. You're married to her, William, not to me."

Minsky flew to New York in the middle of May. An elderly man, obviously the victim of a stroke, he was assisted onto the aircraft, pampered during the flight, and helped off. William was waiting by the baggage carousel. "How was the flight?" William asked as he carried his father's two bags to the car.

"Everyone was wonderful. They treated me like I was some bone-china ornament."

Words were still difficult for Minsky to form, so William listened with extra care. The last thing he wanted was to aggravate his father by asking him to repeat something.

"That's how we're going to treat you when we get you home," William said. "Susan's made up a room for you on the first floor. You won't have to climb any stairs, you'll be able to get around just fine."

Minsky settled himself into the car. "Do me a favor, William. When you go into Long Island City to work, take me with you."

"What for?"

"I only came up here to stop you flying down all the damned time. But I'll go crazy if I'm stuck around the house all day long. Besides," he added with a twisted grin, "I want to see what kind of a mess you made of that business I gave you."

"Sure." William reached out and squeezed his father's arm. It would do Minsky good to hear the rumble of trucks again. Be like old

668

times, Benny Minsky and Son.

When William took his father to the depot the following morning, Minsky hobbled around on his cane, inspecting the fleet of trucks. For half an hour he watched a mechanic working on an engine, until William came over to see how he was faring.

"In my day, all you needed to strip an engine was a screwdriver and a monkey wrench," Minsky told his son. "For these damned complicated things you've got to have a degree in nuclear physics!"

"They might look more complicated, but they sure work better."

"Do they?" Minsky asked dubiously. "Let me tell you something— if we ran out of gas, damned thing would run forever on the booze we were hauling. Can this?"

"We don't haul liquor."

"Too bad. Make sure your drivers keep an eye on the fuel gauge."

Smiling, William suggested they go have lunch. He took his father to a diner close to the depot. It was a diner that Minsky had frequented when he was working in Long Island City, and he was pleased to see it was still in business. Even the owner, Minsky noticed, was the same; fifteen years older, but the same man nonetheless. When Minsky called him by name, though, the man just stared uncomprehendingly.

"You remember my father, surely," William said quickly to the diner's owner. "Benny Minsky, he used to come in here all the time."

"Benny Minsky, sure, but . . ." The man's voice trailed off in embarrassment. One side of the face he recognized; the other, the deformed side, was that of a total stranger. "Hey, Mr. Minsky, I know you now. I thought you were living down in Florida, running those hotels we heard all about during the Senate investigation."

"I am, but I came up for my grandson's bar mitzvah," Minsky answered proudly.

The owner of the diner was Greek, but he knew enough of Jewish culture to wish Minsky *mazel tov* and shake his hand.

Minsky sat back, satisfied that he had not been forgotten.

After eating lunch, father and son left the diner to return to the depot. As William swung his car into the parking lot, a motorcycle roared past, its rider swathed in leather, his face concealed by a black helmet with a dark visor. The rider turned at the end of the street and coasted to a halt beside a pay phone. Taking off his helmet to reveal a sharp face topped by long, curly blond hair, he dropped a dime into the phone and began to dial.

In Leo Granitz's office at Granitz Brothers, the telephone rang. Not the line that came through the switchboard, but a private direct line that Leo had ordered installed four weeks earlier. He answered it immediately.

"Chris here," the motorcyclist said. "Our friend just had lunch at the Pantheon diner close to the depot. Now he's gone back to work. By the way, he wasn't alone."

"Who was with him?" Leo asked.

"Old guy, walked with a cane. Had a bad limp on his left side and his face was all out of whack." Chris talked the slow speech of North Carolina.

Benny Minsky, Leo thought. He knew about the stroke, but he hadn't been aware that Minsky was in New York. "Call me again if anything happens. I'll be here until six." Leo hung up and leaned back in his chair, hands clasped across his stomach. Perhaps Minsky's coming north early was an added benefit. Instead of hearing about William over a long-distance telephone call and then having to make the hectic rush north, he'd be on hand. The shock would be that much greater.

Leo wondered if this was how Napoleon had felt at the outset of a campaign. Or Alexander the Great, Patton, Rommel, or any of those military leaders. Receiving intelligence reports, sifting, evaluating the news brought in by the spies. That was all Chris was, a twenty-two-year-old spy. Leo did not even know his last name, nor did Chris know Leo's. He had met the young man a month earlier in a bar and had bought him a drink. Chris was just out of the army, drifting while he looked for a way to make some money. Leo had offered him the means to do so. A game, he explained to Chris—a game that would last a couple of months or so. Follow a man during the day, let me know where he goes. Call me every time he makes a move. Chris hadn't asked any questions; he didn't even know the location of the telephone number that Leo had given him. Nor did he know the identity of his quarry, only that he worked at a trucking firm in Long Island City that traded under the title of B.M. Transportation. All he cared about was the money Leo gave him, the promise of a large bonus when the game was over.

Leo decided to see Levitt that evening and apprise him of the situation. . . .

When he went to Levitt's home, the little man suggested they walk in the park.

"Benny's come up from Florida," Leo said. "He was in the depot with William today."

"How do you know this?"

"My spy." Leo answered with a smile. "Young guy on a motorcycle who keeps me informed on everything William does during the day."

"Such as?"

Leo decided to boast. "Did you know that he goes into Manhattan every Tuesday morning, takes a cab over to an address on Madison

Avenue in the Fifties?"

"Advertising agency that handles B.M. Transportation's account," Levitt answered. "Figured out how you're going to do it yet?"

"Kidnapping. Make Benny bleed three times that way. Once when he finds out William's been kidnapped. Second time when he pays the ransom. Third time when he doesn't get William back."

"Three-time loser," Levitt said approvingly. "And then we pray that Benny has a long time left in which to think about it. Not like that old bastard Rourke. A year, fifteen months, wasn't enough for him. He should have been tortured for all eternity thinking about his sons."

They walked some more, then Levitt asked, "Can you trust this spy of yours?"

"Could we trust Harry Saltzman to keep his mouth shut?"

"In the end we could."

"We'll be able to trust my spy as well."

"Funny thing . . . I got my invitation to Mark Minsky's bar mitzvah the other week."

"So did I. How come you were sent one?"

"Keep up appearances. Minsky's son and daughter-in-law don't know what's between Benny and me. Anyway, I returned the invitation, able to come. Even sent the boy a gift already. Too bad there won't be any bar mitzvah."

"Too bad," Leo concurred. "Think the kid'll return the gifts?"

Levitt laughed and clapped Leo on the shoulder. Together, they made their way toward the park exit. It was beginning to get dark, and there was no sense in hanging around longer than necessary.

Chapter Two

Mark and Paul Minsky, William's two sons, loved having their grandfather around. He fascinated them with stories of how New York City had once been, told them, to their disbelief, of the manner in which he had lived when he was their age. He wove tales of bitter poverty, rats and roaches, of more people crammed into a single building than now lived in an entire street. Having known nothing but the secure comfort of Forest Hills Gardens, the boys found their grandfather's stories of the Lower East Side difficult to accept. So one Sunday Minsky made William drive the entire family down to the Lower East Side. There, he showed his grandsons the streets and buildings, and when he saw them grimace at the dirt and squalor of the area, he was quick to point out that in his day the people who lived there had shown more pride than the current residents.

"It sure as hell wasn't heaven," he told the boys, "but we didn't turn it into no garbage pit either. There . . ." He indicated a shop that sold luggage. Suitcases were piled high inside the shop and on the sidewalk outside. "That place there, it used to be a bakery. Me and the other kids, we'd each bring our family's dish of *cholent* down there, and the baker would leave it in the oven overnight to cook. We'd pick it up the following day. We used to pay the baker a nickel for that."

"What's *cholent*?" Mark asked.

Minsky looked at the boy as though he came from another world. Then he stared at William and Susan. "This kid's going to get bar mitzvahed soon, and he doesn't know what *cholent* is?"

"Who cooks *cholent* anymore?" Susan asked in return.

"I bet you Pearl Granitz still does."

"Pearl Granitz is your generation, not ours."

Minsky dismissed his daughter-in-law's rationalization with a wave of the hand. He turned back to his grandsons. "*Cholent* was meat and potatotes and onions and hard-boiled eggs, baked overnight." He lapsed into silence, staring at the grimy buildings that were simultaneously so familiar and yet so strange. For a moment he could even smell the dish of *cholent* he had so often carried back from the baker for the Sabbath feast.

Another Sunday, Minsky took his grandsons to a ball game. Because the loss of movement in his left side precluded him from driving, William had to chauffeur them the short distance to Shea Stadium and pick them up after the game. While the boys watched the baseball players, Minsky just sat back in the spring sunshine and smiled. He reached out and hugged both boys, marveling at the wonderful joy of being a grandfather. That was something Lou Levitt would never know. The little man's preoccupation had always been with turning a buck. He'd done that well enough, but in doing so he'd cheated himself of everything else.

For three weeks after Benny Minsky's arrival in New York, his son's working habits were monitored by the young blond-haired man named Chris. Sometimes Chris would wear motorcycle leathers. At other times, when the sun shone warmly, he would be dressed in blue jeans and a cotton shirt. Always the helmet obscured his face and hair. Often he would change two or three times during a single day, just so William would never become suspicious of the motorcyclist who dogged his every move from the moment he arrived at work each morning until he went home at night.

Leo carefully studied the information he received from Chris. William's daily trips to the diner with Benny Minsky were useless. Leo needed William to be alone. Also useless were visits William made to a barber in Long Island City, to a dry cleaner, and to an employment agency in Manhattan. All these journeys were irregular; there was no way of knowing in advance when he would make such trips again. Only one activity stood out to Leo. William's Tuesday-morning taxi ride to the Madison Avenue advertising agency. According to Chris's information, you could set a clock by that. It had to be a standing appointment, a regular weekly meeting with the account executive who handled B.M. Transportation's advertising. Every Tuesday morning at ten-thirty, William would climb into a taxi. The meeting was for eleven. At eleven-thirty, he would be outside the building on Madison Avenue, looking for a taxi to take him back to Long Island City. Maybe he was frightened to drive in Manhattan, Leo mused. Or perhaps he just didn't need the aggravation of battling the heavy traffic. He had to be fresh for his meeting at the advertising agency; he didn't want to walk in there looking like he'd just been through a mangle.

Tuesday morning it would be then.

On the Tuesday before Mark's bar mitzvah, William drove his father to the truck depot as usual. While Minsky wandered around, talking to drivers and mechanics, William went through some paperwork. At ten-fifteen, he instructed his secretary to order a taxi for ten-thirty.

"I'm going over to Manhattan," William told his father. "I'll be back at midday for lunch."

"Your advertising people? That's a side of the business I never knew much about. It's something new, all these advertising types with their statistics and charts."

"I know. In your day all you needed to run a trucking company were some trucks, a serviceman, and a place to park them. Times change."

"It might be time I changed with them. Today I think I should come with you. In all my business life, I never so much as went inside an advertising agency."

William considered the idea. He shook his head. "You'd be bored out of your mind."

"I would, wouldn't I? Go. Go ahead and see your advertising people. I'll be waiting for you when you get back." Minsky returned to watching the mechanics at work, while William, briefcase in hand, walked out to the parking lot where the taxi was just pulling in. It was beginning to rain, and he wondered how much trouble he would encounter in finding a cab to bring him back.

Leo was nervous. Sitting in the back of a Cadillac limousine with darkened windows, he looked along the length of Madison Avenue, trying to spot one yellow taxi among the many that would be carrying William Minsky to his regular Tuesday-morning appointment. At the wheel of the Cadillac sat Chris. He no longer wore the motorcycle outfit. He was dressed that day in a dark gray chauffeur's uniform, the long blond hair seeming out of place as it dropped below the peaked cap to hang just above his shoulders.

"Maybe he put it off today," Chris said. "Didn't like the rain."

"Was it raining any of the times you tailed him here?"

Chris tried to remember. "Once. It was coming down in buckets."

"Then he'll be here today." Leo glanced at his watch. Ten fifty-five. A taxi pulled up in front of the building where the advertising agency was based and Leo leaned forward eagerly. To his disappointment, a woman alighted. Two more taxis pulled up. Neither carried William.

Leo swiveled agitatedly on the seat, trying to cover the street and both sidewalks in one sweeping glance.

"There he is," Chris said.

Leo swung forward again. Another cab had stopped. William jumped out and ran through the rain to the building entrance; a woman who had been waiting for a taxi took his place, and the vehicle moved away into the stream of traffic.

"Now we wait," said Leo. He dug his hand into his coat pocket and pulled out two lengths of string which he ran between his fingers. All his planning was about to be put to the test. Leo was confident that he had overlooked nothing. What did military leaders do while they waited for the battle to commence? Did they review their plans a final time, make sure they had taken every possibility into consideration? It was a strange question. No matter how certain each general was, one of them had always overlooked something. That was why he lost. What was the quote he had once read in the biographies of great military men? Leo tried to remember. A battle wasn't won by the most prepared army—it was won by the least confused? Something like that, he couldn't remember it word for word, but he had the gist. Well, he wasn't confused right now as he sat in the Cadillac limousine and waited. His mind was clearer than it had ever been before.

"Eleven-thirty," Chris said from the driver's seat. "Should be surfacing any minute now."

Leo craned forward. The Cadillac's engine was ticking over. The transmission was in drive, ready to roll forward at a moment's notice. The wipers swished monotonously across the windshield. Fifty yards away was the building that housed the advertising agency. How long would it take to cover that distance? Five seconds? Ten? Would William have found a cab in that time? The first doubts started to eat away at Leo's confidence. "Move up a little bit," he told Chris.

"If we get any closer than this, he'll see we've pulled out from a parking spot," Chris answered.

Leo opened his mouth to rebuke the younger man until he realized that Chris was right. The general having something pointed out to him by the lieutenant. It happened. The whole idea was that William would believe the Cadillac was just passing by—not that it was waiting for him.

"Here he comes," Chris said. In a quick movement, he slipped his foot off the brake pedal and onto the gas. The Cadillac surged forward. As William glanced along the street for an empty cab, Chris braked the Cadillac to a halt in front of him, and Leo threw open the rear door.

"William, which way are you heading?"

William stared blankly across the wet sidewalk at Leo and the invitingly open door. He'd been looking for a cab, cursing the rain because it would be that much more difficult to find one, and the sight of the chauffeur-driven limousine with the darkened windows threw him completely off balance.

"Get in!" Leo called across the sidewalk. He was grateful for the rain. Not too many people were out. Those who were walked quickly, or ran, heads down, as they tried to dodge the rain. No one seemed to take any notice of the limousine. "You'll never find a cab in this lousy weather, William."

William darted across the sidewalk and slid into the Cadillac. "You're a godsend, Leo. I'm heading back to Long Island City if you're going in that direction."

"No problem," Leo said grandly. He leaned forward to give Chris directions for the truck depot. "What are you doing in town?"

"Meeting with our ad people. You sure this isn't taking you out of your way?"

"Don't worry about it. I'm early for a lunch meeting."

William laughed. "If you hadn't turned up, I'd be late for one. I told my father I'd be back at the depot by midday, we'd go to lunch together. He's a stickler for having lunch exactly at noon. Must be something to do with getting old, having to eat at regular hours."

"You'd know that better than I would. I never saw my father get old."

William appeared not to hear. He was staring through the windshield as Chris headed north along Madison Avenue. At the intersection with East Fifty-seventh Street, he swung west. "Hey, where's this driver of yours going, Leo? We need the Queensborough Bridge."

Leo slammed his right elbow hard into William's chest, right over the heart. Above William's sudden gasp of pain, Leo shouted: "Did you hear what I said about my father?" His elbow slammed into William's chest again. The snap of cracking ribs could be heard clearly. "He never got old, and do you know why?" Leo swung around in the seat to send a huge fist smashing down into the side of William's face. William slid across the seat to crack his head against the darkened window. "He never got old because your father double-crossed him and set him up for Gus Landau! That's why my father didn't get old!" Leo dived across the seat, lifted William up by the lapel of his raincoat and smashed his right fist into Minsky's face again and again.

After the fourth punch, William's eyes rolled up in his head. Leo released his hold and dropped the unconscious man onto the seat. He glanced frontward, saw that Chris was concentrating on the driving, and then pushed William onto the floor. Kneeling beside him, Leo pulled out the two pieces of string with which he had been playing earlier. He tied William's wrists and ankles, pulled the string tight until it bit harshly into flesh. Lastly, he stuffed a rag into the unconscious man's mouth.

The Cadillac sped through the Holland Tunnel and into Jersey City. The rain began to fall more heavily, and by the time the limousine reached an old warehouse close to the river there was hardly a pedestrian to be seen. The warehouse doors were open. Chris drove right inside, stopping when he reached the far wall. Leaning against the wall, hidden by a tarpaulin, was Chris's motorcycle.

"Get the door," Leo said. While Chris ran to drag the warehouse door closed, Leo slipped on a pair of gloves. He lifted William from the limousine and carried him up a flight of wooden steps to a room that had once been an office. Its windows were broken, rain blew in to wet the debris that covered the floor. Without any ceremony, Leo dropped the body onto the floor. Returning downstairs, he found Chris removing the chauffeur's uniform. Leo watched as the young man slipped into the black leather trousers and jacket he wore when he rode the motorcycle.

"You know what you've got to do?"

"Sure," Chris answered. "Tonight at six o'clock, I call the number you gave me. Then again at seven."

"Do everything just like I told you. It's foolproof. Once we get the money, a third of it's yours. That's your bonus."

Before slipping on the crash helmet with the dark visor, Chris nodded. He'd thought he was in on a kidnapping, nothing else. Meeting Leo in the bar had been an answer to a prayer. Just out of the army and needing some easy money, and opportunity had knocked. A partnership in a quarter-million-dollar abduction. He'd never realized when he'd accepted the proposition that his partner wasn't in the least interested in the money, or that his own participation was only intended to be a very temporary affair.

Leo watched Chris sit astride the motorcycle and kick it into life. He roared across the warehouse, stopped by the door to push it open far enough to pass through, and then disappeared into the rain. Leo walked after him, and pulled the door closed. He then went back upstairs to where William lay. William's eyes were open. His breathing, forced through the rag stuffed into his mouth, was ragged. Leo stuck in two fingers and pulled the rag free. William immediately coughed up blood from a lung that had been punctured by his broken ribs.

"Why are you doing this?" William asked. Each word was an

677

effort. Each movement of his lips sent pain searing through his chest.

"Why did your father have my father murdered?" Leo asked in return. "That's the question you should be asking. Not of me, but of your father."

"I don't know what you're talking about. My father thought the world of Jake Granitz."

"Did he? Or did he think more of the money he could make from the drug deal he set up with Gus Landau?"

William coughed again. Blood and saliva dribbled down his chin. "You're crazy, Leo. You're as mad as they come if you believe that."

Leo's eyes altered shade. "Don't . . . call . . . me . . . mad!" he spat out, punctuating each word with a savage kick to William's chest. "It's your father who was mad! Mad to do what he did! Mad to think he could get away with it! And now you're going to pay for what he did. You ever hear about the sins of the fathers being visited on the sons? That's what this is, William. With your last breath, you can curse your goddamned father for what he did!" Leo stuffed the rag back into William's mouth. On the floor was a ball of twine. Leo picked it up, looped it around William's ankles, drew it tightly around his neck, then around the ankles again before tying a knot.

Leo rose to his feet and stared down. William lay on his stomach, body arched into a bow, the twine running from his ankles to his neck. He could still breathe, but any relaxation of his muscles would cause the twine to tighten around his throat.

"Strangle yourself, you bastard," Leo said, and closed the door.

At twelve o'clock exactly, Benny Minsky stood sheltered from the rain in the doorway of the B.M. Transportation office. William was supposed to be back to accompany his father to the diner for lunch. Minsky glanced anxiously at his watch, then at the rain. Maybe he couldn't find a cab. You never could when it was raining like this.

Going back inside, he forced himself to sit down and wait. When twelve-thirty came, however, he began to panic. If William was going to be half an hour late—if he'd been delayed in his meeting with the advertising people, or if he'd been stuck looking for a cab—he would have called.

"What's the number of that advertising agency?" Minsky asked William's secretary. The woman dialed the number and Minsky waited for the telephone to be answered. "I'm looking for Mr. William Minsky of B.M. Transportation," he said. "He had an eleven o'clock appointment with someone at your place."

"He left an hour ago."

"Thank you." Minsky replaced the receiver and went back outside. Even allowing for a half-hour wait for a cab, William should have returned already. In his bones, in his stomach, in his heart, Minsky knew that something was terribly wrong.

At one o'clock he telephoned the police, only to be told that a man could not be listed as missing after only an hour. "I know that!" Minsky snapped back. "I just want to know if there have been any accidents in Manhattan that might have involved my son." He was advised to try the hospitals. Every admittance desk he contacted had no record of a William Minsky. At three o'clock, he tried the police again.

"I know something has happened to my son!" he yelled into the mouthpiece. "I want your people to do something about it!"

"Mr. Minsky, three hours doesn't warrant a police investigation. I'm sorry."

Minsky went back to the secretary. "Is there anywhere else he could have gone? Any other business meeting he might have forgotten to tell me about?"

The secretary scanned through William's appointment book. Only the advertising meeting was scheduled. Nonetheless, she telephoned every business contact William had—insurance agents, the bank, parts suppliers. No one had seen or heard from him that day.

At four-thirty, Minsky telephoned Susan in Forest Hills Gardens. Somehow, he managed to sound reasonably calm. "Susan, I'm worried about William. He went to his advertising meeting this morning, and he hasn't returned yet. Do you know of anywhere else he might have gone?" The wild notion that William might have a girlfriend crossed Minsky's mind. No . . . even if his son were fooling around, he'd be more discreet than to give his father reason to suspect. Minsky felt ashamed for even thinking of such a thing.

"I don't know of anywhere. What places have you tried?"

Minsky reeled off the list. "There's no record of him being involved in any accident or crime. He's just disappeared."

"That's not like him," Susan said. "Every time he goes anywhere, he tells his secretary."

"There's probably a reasonable explanation behind this whole thing," Minsky assured Susan. "But just in case, I want you to stay at home until you hear from me. Something might have happened, an accident perhaps, and there'll be a call to the house. In the meantime, I'll stay here in case someone tries to contact the depot."

At six o'clock, Minsky was alone in the depot office. He had sent the secretary home, telling her that there was nothing she could do, no point in her staying. Now he wished she were in the office with him.

Facing the unknown alone was terrifying.

The telephone rang. It was Susan, her voice a mere whisper that was filled with fear. "William's been kidnapped."

"What?"

"I just had a phone call. A man. He said William's been kidnapped. I tried to ask him what he meant, but he hung up."

"I'll be home as soon as I can find a cab."

The uncertainty was gone. His only son had been kidnapped. A ransom. Money didn't mean a damned thing. Minsky would pay it and not even bother calling the police, just to get William back. And afterward, when William was returned to his family, Minsky would take his own revenge. He still knew people. He'd find out the identity of these kidnappers just as surely as the police would. More surely. All the police could do was dig for clues. Minsky could do much more. He could offer such a reward that the kidnappers of his only son would never be safe from treachery. That was it, he decided as he waited for a taxi. Keep the police out of it. Do it all on his own.

Such hopes were dashed the moment the taxi swung into the driveway of the house in Forest Hills Gardens. A police car was parked there, a garish advertisement that something was amiss. Tucked in behind it was an unmarked Plymouth. Minsky paid off the cab and hobbled toward the front door. It was opened before he could reach it by a man in a dark blue suit. Minsky had seen enough federal agents in his life to be able to recognize them at first glance. "Who the hell called you here?"

The agent showed no response to Minsky's hostility. "You would be William Minsky's father, I take it. I'm Frank Hopkins, from the New York office of the Bureau. Your daughter-in-law called the police the moment she received the telephone call. They informed us."

Pushing his way past the FBI agent, Minsky came face to face with a uniformed sergeant. "Where's my daughter-in-law?"

"In there." The sergeant pointed to the front room. Minsky opened the door and saw Susan sitting on a couch. Her sons were on either side of her.

"Why did you call the cops?" Minsky demanded. "I could have handled this."

"It's a kidnapping," Susan answered. "A police matter."

"The hell it is. I can take care of it, just like I've taken care of everything where William's concerned."

"This isn't the twenties anymore!" Susan retorted. "You don't just pick up a gun like you used to do and go out looking for someone to shoot full of holes."

Minsky started to say something in return, then closed his mouth when he noticed his grandsons staring at him. Both were frightened, uncertain. So was he. But he knew he had to take charge. "Don't worry about a thing," he told them. "Your father'll be home safe and sound for the bar mitzvah on Saturday. You'll see."

There was a knock on the door. Frank Hopkins entered. "Mr. Minsky, I'd like to speak with you and your daughter-in-law. Just the two of you, please."

Reluctantly, Susan sent the boys out of the room.

"Is your husband a wealthy man, Mrs. Minsky?" Hopkins asked. He felt it was a rhetorical question; the house alone told him the answer.

"He's comfortable."

"And you, Mr. Minsky?" Hopkins asked.

"I can put together a couple of bucks." Minsky wondered when the FBI agent would point a finger and say he remembered Minsky from those damned Senate hearings.

"You've been contacted once, Mrs. Minsky. No demands, nothing but a short message to let you know your husband's been abducted. The kidnapper will call again. When that happens, we'd like to trace the call."

"Supposing you do?" Minsky butted in. "Supposing you catch the kidnapper that way? What happens to my son then? The kidnapper keeps his mouth shut, and my son rots away somewhere. Nothing doing."

"It's more than likely that we could reach an agreement with the kidnapper once he was in custody. A trade-off. He could lessen his own problems by helping us."

"Sure. And just supposing he's got a pal who's guarding William? That pal doesn't want to get caught in a double-cross, so he takes it on the lam . . . after taking care of William. Forget it. When we get a ransom demand, I'll come up with the money. Once we get William back, it's your affair. But only then."

"I think I should point out that many kidnappings end up with the abducted party being killed after ransom is paid. That's if he hasn't been killed before the payoff, sometimes before the first contact was even made."

"If you're trying to scare me into letting your guys take this thing over, you're doing a lousy job."

"Why don't you listen to him?" Susan pleaded. "He knows what he's talking about. He's been involved with kidnappings before."

"Not where my son's concerned, he hasn't."

"You're forgetting that he's my husband as well."

Hopkins stepped in between them. "Nothing is going to be solved by the pair of you arguing." Before a word could be spoken, the telephone rang.

"Answer it," Hopkins said.

Susan hesitated, fearing what the call would be. Minsky touched her on the arm and walked over to the telephone.

"Hello?"

"That's not Mrs. Minsky, is it?" a man's voice asked.

"This is Benny Minsky, William Minsky's father."

"You've got until tomorrow morning to come up with two hundred and fifty thousand dollars, Benny Minsky."

"Who is this?"

"Two hundred and fifty thousand dollars. Tens, twenties, and fifties. Used bills. No consecutive numbers. We'll be in touch again at ten o'clock tomorrow morning." A sharp click was followed by the dial tone. Minsky stood staring at the mute instrument for a few seconds before replacing it.

"They want a quarter of a million dollars by ten in the morning."

"Can you arrange for that?" Hopkins asked.

Minsky nodded. "I'll get hold of the bank my son's company uses."

"If you'd prefer, we could handle the money. We have funds we can call on for these emergencies."

"And mark it? Stick a tear-gas bomb or some dye spray in the bag? No thanks. You're not getting my son killed."

The FBI agent tried one more time. "Let us tap your line. When he calls tomorrow morning, we'll trace it."

"What the hell's the use? You couldn't have traced that call. It was too short."

"Tomorrow morning's call will be longer. They have to supply details on where the money is to be taken."

Minsky looked at Susan. He knew what she wanted. To let the police, the feds, in on the act. She didn't come from the same background he did. To her, the police symbolized security. Not to Minsky they didn't. If he was ever going to see William again, this would have to be done on his terms.

"You don't tap anything," he told the FBI agent. "Afterward you can do whatever you damned well like, but until that money's delivered, until William's safe back here, you keep your face out of it."

The story of the kidnapping was in the following morning's newspapers. Before eight o'clock, Lou Levitt telephoned the house in Forest Hills Gardens.

"Benny, is this true? About William? It says in the paper that he's been kidnapped."

"It's true, all right."

"How much money do they want?"

"A quarter of a million."

"You need help in raising it?"

"No. I was on to William's bank manager last night. They're shipping the money up here before ten."

"Okay. If you need any help, you know where to reach me."

Despite himself, Minsky felt a sudden burst of warmth toward Levitt. Sometimes trouble brought out the best in people. "Thanks, Lou. I'll remember."

On Central Park West, Levitt hung up the telephone and smiled to himself. It was always easy offering another player an extra card when you held all the aces yourself. . . .

Pearl telephoned at nine-thirty, shortly after a bank messenger had delivered the ransom money. "Benny, this is terrible."

"You don't have to tell me that."

"How's Susan?"

"Bearing up."

"And the boys? What's happened to them?"

"Susan sent them to a friend's house last night. Look, Pearl," Minsky said as he saw the agent gesturing toward his watch, "I've got to get off the phone. We're expecting a call soon from the kidnappers."

"All right. Benny, if there's anything you need, let me know. I'll come over and stay with Susan if that'll help."

"I'll let you know." He hung up.

At ten o'clock, the telephone rang again. It was the same voice, the same Southern accent as the previous night.

"Have you got the money?"

"I've got it."

"Listen good. By ten-thirty, be at the pay phone on the corner of Jewel Avenue and Queens Boulevard. By yourself. You'll be under surveillance the whole time. We see a cop within half a mile of you, and you can kiss your son goodbye."

"I can't drive," Minsky said, suddenly remembering his own condition. "I'll have to have someone with me."

"Take a taxi." The caller broke the connection. Minsky snatched the directory from beside the telephone and looked up the number of a taxi company. As he started to dial, Hopkins pressed down the receiver rest.

"One of our men'll drive you. He'll be the cab driver."

"Forget it. This guy so much as smells a cop and my son's dead."

"How do you know your son isn't dead already?"

"I don't. I'm just praying that he's not."

"Think of yourself then. Have one of our men as a driver for your own protection. You'll be carrying a fortune around with you."

"Screw my protection! Can't you get it through your fucking thick head that I want you and your FBI to butt out?"

The taxi came. Minsky handed the driver two one-hundred-dollar bills and said he was hiring the vehicle for the day. "I don't know how long I'm going to need you. I've no idea how many miles we'll cover. Let me know when that two hundred runs out."

"What is this—some kind of a mystery tour? A treasure hunt?"

"It's a kidnapping. I'm delivering a ransom." He pointed to the small blue suitcase he had brought into the taxi. "That's what's in there, two hundred and fifty thousand bucks worth of ransom money. And just in case you get any crazy ideas, there's a whole gang of cops and FBI men inside that house who've got your license number. Understand?"

"Where to?"

"Corner of Jewel Avenue and Queens Boulevard."

The taxi reached the pay phone with five minutes to spare. Precisely at ten-thirty, the telephone rang. The voice Minsky had come to know so well was mocking as it said: "Glad you could make it. Now I want you to go to Jackson Heights." Minsky scribbled feverishly with a pencil on the back of an envelope. "Thirty-seventh Avenue and Eighty-second Street. There's a pay phone outside a men's clothing shop. Be there in twenty minutes."

Returning to the taxi, Minsky gave the new destination to the driver. He understood perfectly what William's kidnappers were doing. They were going to run him all over the city, follow the taxi to make sure he wasn't being tailed by the police. Minsky hoped the cops weren't stupid enough to totally disregard the kidnappers' and his own demand that he be left alone.

From Jackson Heights, Minsky was sent to another pay phone at Queens Plaza. There, he received instructions to go into Manhattan, to Grand Central Station. Slowly, the voice at the other end of the line drew him west across the borough, and then north, until, at just after two o'clock, Minsky was laboriously climbing the stairs from Broadway to the George Washington Bridge bus station in Upper Manhattan. He prayed this was the last stop. He was exhausted, his heart beating wildly, sweat covering his face and body. Twice during the long walk up the stairs—cane and small suitcase clutched in his right hand, while he used his left to claw at the rail—he stumbled.

Both times he just wanted to sit there on the cool stairs, let the case and cane go tumbling down to Broadway. He didn't care anymore, he was too tired to worry. Until he thought about William, and remembered the promise he'd made to his grandsons. *William would be home.* In three days' time, on the Saturday, the entire family would be sitting in the synagogue for Mark's bar mitzvah—sitting there as if nothing had happened! He hauled himself up and continued the climb, praying to God for the strength to see this thing through. William was relying on him like never before.

As he reached the top of the stairs, Minsky reviewed the last set of instructions he had received, at a pay phone on Amsterdam Avenue. Go to the George Washington Bridge bus station. Climb the stairs. You'll see two banks of telephones, one with six booths, one with only two. On the smaller bank will be a telephone with an out-of-order sign hanging from it. That is the telephone where you will receive your next orders.

Christ, Minsky thought, as he headed toward the bank of two telephones; whoever was behind this had planned the whole thing like some kind of military campaign. Under surveillance . . . all the fine details. What next? His heart leaped when he noticed that one of the two telephones was in use. A man in motorcycle leathers was standing there, his back to the second telephone as he talked into the mouthpiece. He was wearing a crash helmet with the dark visor lifted so that he could hear and speak. Between his feet was a red suitcase, slightly larger than the blue case Minsky carried. Was that the telephone he was supposed to use? Had something gone wrong? Then Minsky spotted the out-of-order sign hanging from the telephone next to the leather-clad man, and he breathed easier. Standing next to it, he waited for the summons.

In the adjacent booth, Chris had seen Minsky emerge at the top of the stairs, face flushed and sweaty. "He's just arrived," he said softly into the mouthpiece. "Looks like he's going to have a heart attack at any moment."

In his office at Granitz Brothers, using the direct line that bypassed the switchboard, Leo digested the information. Everything was working like a charm. He'd planned as carefully as any tactician had ever done. Chris had made all the telephone calls so far, had watched while Minsky sped by taxi from one destination to the next. With the mobility of the motorcycle, Chris had always been there first, ready to put the next step of the plan into operation. Now, Chris's participation was almost over. The next voice that Minsky would hear would be Leo's. Minsky would spot the difference immediately, the switch from the slower speech of North Carolina to the abruptness of

New York City. That would throw him enough to avoid recognition. But just in case . . . Leo draped a handkerchief over the mouthpiece.

"You sure no one followed him?" he asked Chris.

"What's the matter with your voice? I can hardly hear you."

Leo removed the handkerchief. So much for that worry. He repeated the question. Chris said no; he'd watched the stairway leading down to the street carefully. By the wildest stretch of his imagination none of the people who had reached the top of the stairs after Minsky could have been police or federal agents. Old women, young women struggling with baby carriages, kids, old men. But no cops.

"I'm going to hang up now and call the other line," Leo said. "You stay on, pretend you're still speaking until I've given him the instructions."

"Okay. Anything else?"

"No. We'll meet tomorrow night as planned."

"Got you." Chris heard the line click, the dial tone return. Leaning against the wall, he engaged in a one-sided mock conversation, pausing as though listening to someone, then talking again. Beneath the crash helmet, his ears strained for the ringing of the out-of-order telephone.

Thirty seconds later it rang. Minsky leaned forward to lift the receiver from the rest. "I'm here!"

"Good. What I want you to do now," Leo said through the handkerchief, "is leave your suitcase on the floor right where you're standing. I want you to walk away. On the other side of the bus station are local bus schedules. Go over to them, pretend you're studying them. Whatever you do, don't look back. Stay there for five minutes. After those five minutes are up, you go home. The message regarding your son will reach you at home. Once we've got the money and are certain that you've kept your end of the bargain, you'll be told where to find your son."

"Is he all right?"

"Walk away. If you look back, your son's going to wind up looking like Lot's wife when she looked back. Understand?"

The line went dead. Minsky replaced the receiver and looked down at the blue suitcase. Dare he leave it there, right in the middle of the busy bus terminal? There was a quarter of a million inside. He glanced at the adjacent booth, at the back of the man in leather. The man was still carrying on his conversation, totally unaware of anything that was going on outside his own little world. Minsky left the case on the floor and walked toward the local bus schedules. It took all the willpower and determination he possessed not to turn his head and look back.

Still clutching the receiver to his ear, Chris angled his head just enough to see Minsky's back as he walked toward the local bus schedules. His foot snaked out, caught the edge of the blue case. With a deft movement, he lifted his own, slightly larger, red case and dropped it over the blue one. The red case was hollow and had no bottom. It fell over Minsky's blue case like a glove fitting a hand. The handle of the blue case came through a space in the top of the red case. Chris gripped it, replaced the receiver, and walked quickly toward the stairs. As he started down, he risked one backward look. Minsky stood at the schedule board, apparently engrossed. Quickening his pace, Chris reached the street, strapped the red suitcase and its load onto the rack of his motorcycle, jumped aboard, kicked the engine into life, and sped off along Broadway.

A quarter of a million dollars! Excitedly, Chris gripped the handlebars of the motorcycle as he thought of the vast sum. In thirteen months of risking his neck in Vietnam he'd barely made one percent of that! Now he could head anywhere, keep the money for himself, do whatever he liked. The man he knew as Leo would never find him. Who the hell was Leo anyway? Just a fag who prowled the bars to see who he could pick up. Fags always got taken once in a while. It went with the territory, a little risk in return for their fun and games. Chris grinned . . . if he split with the entire quarter of a million, Leo would get taken for a lot.

For a minute, while he battled the Broadway traffic, slipping in and out of different lanes, Chris ran the idea through his mind. Leo would turn up at the meeting place tomorrow evening, expecting to be handed the ransom so he could turn a third of it over to Chris. Why, Chris asked himself, should I get only a third of it? Sure, Leo did all the planning, but I did all the work.

A stop light loomed red in front of him. Chris slowed to a halt. To his left was a police cruiser. He gave the vehicle the once over, and the two police officers surveyed him through narrowed eyes. Come on and change, Chris whispered to the traffic light. He froze as the police car's siren suddenly burst into life. Lights flashing, it moved into the intersection, swung left, and sped away to an accompaniment of squealing tires. Chris wanted to laugh. A traffic accident, probably, and those stupid cops had torn off to that when they'd had the biggest crime of the week sitting right beneath their noses.

The light changed and Chris rolled forward. Steering with one hand, he felt quickly beneath his leather jacket, caressed the butt of the automatic that was stuck in his waistband. Souvenir from Vietnam. Now it would come in handy. Chris knew he had to go back to Leo, keep the appointment with him. Leo was the only link between Chris and the kidnapping. The man they'd abducted and left in the Jersey City warehouse was someone Leo knew. Chris had seen that much when they had picked up William outside the building on Madison Avenue. But there was no link between that man and Chris. No connection at all, except for Leo.

Chris would keep all of the money, and when he met with Leo the following night he would sever the connection completely.

Minsky counted off seconds while he stared at the bus schedule board. All around him, people jotted down platform numbers and departure times, but Minsky just stared. And counted. At two hundred and forty, he glanced down at his watch. Three minutes and fifty-three seconds had passed since he'd arrived at the schedule board; he was only seven seconds out with his count. Dare he look around yet? He had little doubt that the case would be gone, its collector long since departed from the bus station. The five-minute waiting period was meaningless. He could be on his way back to the taxi already, heading back to Queens, to Forest Hills Gardens to learn where William was being held.

"Hey, mister . . . are you going to stand there all day?"

Minsky felt an elbow dig him in the back. He swung around, and a tiny middle-aged woman dived past him to the board. The bank of two pay phones flashed before Minsky's vision. Both were empty. The blue suitcase was gone. Gripping the cane in his left hand, he walked toward the stairs.

"Where to now?" the cab driver asked.

"Back to where you picked me up."

"You finished running around for the day?"

"I've finished."

"Where's that case?"

"Why don't you just shut the fuck up and drive?" Minsky leaned back as the taxi moved off. His breathing was still coming hard and he could feel his heart pounding through his chest. That would be the final irony, another goddamned heart attack or stroke. He closed his eyes and, by some miracle, went to sleep.

He awoke just as the taxi pulled up behind the unmarked Plymouth belonging to FBI agent Frank Hopkins. Minsky climbed out and walked toward the front door. Hopkins opened it. Behind him stood Susan.

"Did you make your delivery?" the agent asked.

"At the George Washington Bridge bus station. They ran me all over town, one telephone to the next. Have they called here yet? They're supposed to let me know where William is."

"No calls at all." Hopkins stepped aside as Minsky entered the house.

"Are you okay?" Minsky asked his daughter-in-law.

"When William comes back, I will be."

"He'll be back. I did everything they told me to do. Where are the boys?"

"They're still away." She noticed how tired he seemed. "Do you want something? A cup of coffee, a sandwich?"

"Coffee'll be fine." Minsky went into the living room and sat down, hands clasping the top of the cane in front of him. Where were they? Why didn't they call? Any time he had made a bargain in his life, he'd kept to it. Weren't these bastards cut from the same damned cloth?

Susan brought in cups of coffee, for Minsky, the FBI agent, and herself. Over the top of his cup, Minsky glared at the agent. "I suppose you're going to tell me how I should have let someone from your office drive me around. That way we'd have the pickup man by now."

"I'm not going to say anything, Mr. Minsky. You made your choice, did what you thought was best for your son. My active participation will commence the moment your son is released."

"Look, I'm sorry. I know you've got a job to do. . . ." Minsky was suddenly aware of how badly he'd mistreated the FBI agent.

"Don't apologize, Mr. Minsky. Believe me, I understand perfectly what was going through your mind. You didn't care about the kidnappers being caught, all you wanted was your son back. That's fine. I just hope they keep their word." Hopkins lifted his head inquisitively as the telephone began to ring.

Minsky put down his coffee and took the call. It was the same voice that had told him to walk away from the money in the suitcase, the muffled New York accent.

"Welcome home, Mr. Minsky," Leo said.

"Where the hell's my son? I paid you the damned money just like you said. I kept up my end of the bargain."

"We know," Leo said. "Here's where you'll find him. In Jersey City, there's a warehouse close to the river. . . ."

Minsky scribbled down the address on the pad next to the telephone. The moment the call ended, he ripped off the piece of paper and handed it to the FBI agent. "I'll call this in," Hopkins said. "My people will be waiting when we get there. With a bit of luck, they might be able to pick up something."

Feeling far better than he had earlier, Minsky kissed Susan goodbye and climbed into the back of Hopkins' Plymouth. As the car began to move, he rolled down the window and called back to Susan, "Get the boys back! William's going to want to see them. They're going to want to see him."

As they exited from the New Jersey end of the Holland Tunnel, the Plymouth's radio crackled into life. Hopkins picked up the microphone. In the rear of the car, Minsky was unable to hear what was being said above the hum of the tires, the sound of traffic. But he knew it was bad the moment Hopkins pulled the car over to the side of the road and turned around.

"What is it? My son? What's happened? Isn't he there, at the warehouse?"

"He's there all right, Mr. Minsky, or a man answering his description is. But he's dead." He stared sympathetically at Minsky for a few seconds, then swung around, put the car in gear, and continued the journey.

Four cars were parked at the deserted warehouse when Minsky and Hopkins arrived. Two displayed the insignia of the local police department. The other two, like the Plymouth, were unmarked. Minsky got out of the Plymouth and walked toward the entrance. Hopkins pulled him back.

"Are you certain you want to go in there, Mr. Minsky?"

"Someone's got to identify the body, right?"

"Someone has to, yes. But you don't have to do it right away."

"I may as well get it over with."

Accompanying Minsky into the warehouse, Hopkins decided that his haste was prompted by the slender hope that the body might not, after all, be that of his son.

A medical examiner was at work in the small room upstairs that had once been an office. The twine had been removed from William's ankles and neck. A vivid red line encircled William's throat. His eyes bulged sightlessly, the skin on his face was dark, his swollen tongue protruded grotesquely from his mouth. Minsky walked into the room and rested his weight on the cane as he stared down at the body.

"Is that your son, Mr. Minsky?" Hopkins asked.

"That's William." He shifted his gaze to the medical examiner who, totally oblivious to the grief of the man standing next to him, continued with his work.

"Been dead a full day, I'd guess," the examiner said to no one in particular. "Be able to get a better handle on the time of death when we do an autopsy, but twenty-four hours seems like a reasonably accurate estimate."

A reasonably accurate estimate . . . that was how they talked about

William now, Minsky thought. Been dead a full day . . . get a better handle on the time of death . . . autopsy. "He was dead when they first contacted me," Minsky murmured. "All this time they had me running around, and he was dead all along."

"Come away, Mr. Minsky," the agent said. He had been proven right, yet he felt no pleasure. Seeing this elderly man just standing there, gazing numbly down at his son, he could derive no joy from being correct.

Minsky refused to move. He remained in the room until William's body was taken downstairs to a waiting ambulance. As the medical examiner prepared to leave, Minsky touched him on the arm with the cane. "Excuse me, sir. How long will it be before I can bury my son?"

"There has to be an autopsy. It shouldn't take long, though. A formality, really. Perhaps we'll be able to release him to you by tomorrow."

"Thank you."

All the way back to Forest Hills Gardens, Minsky tried to think of a way to tell Susan and the boys. He had broken his promise to his grandsons. He'd told them William would be coming back, and it wasn't true. They would not all be at the synagogue this coming Saturday for Mark's bar mitzvah. They would be mourning William instead.

Susan knew the truth the moment Minsky stepped out of the Plymouth in front of the house. She had been watching through the front window, her mind made up about what was about to happen. If the telephone rang, everything would be all right. Minsky would call the moment William was found unharmed. He would put William on the line to reassure her. But if Minsky did not telephone . . . if he returned to the house without calling first . . . it would be because he had bad news. News he could only impart personally.

She came running out of the house before Minsky could reach the front door. One look at the iron set of her father-in-law's dark face was enough to tell her the worst. "He's dead, isn't he? William's dead."

There was no way to soften the blow. "Yes, Susan," Minsky answered in a voice that was as expressionless as his face. "William's been murdered. He was dead all the time. Where are the boys? I should be the one to tell them."

Chapter Three

The meeting place chosen by Leo Granitz was a tiny rest area with no facilities on Route 17, close to the Wurstboro exit in Sullivan County, some eighty miles northwest of the center of New York City. Late at night, the road was lightly traveled. A car and a motorcycle with lights off, parked well away from the road, stood a one-in-a-thousand chance of being noticed.

Just before midnight on the day following the discovery of William Minsky's body, Chris sped west along Route 17 on his motorcycle. As he followed the road illuminated in the white beam of the headlight, he considered the impending meeting with Leo. They hadn't collaborated on a kidnapping—they'd collaborated on murder. The discovery of William's body had been in all the newspapers, on radio and television. It became even more imperative for Chris to sever the link that bound him to the crime. Not that he should have been surprised at learning William was dead. It was the obvious outcome of the whole affair. Leo and William had known each other. You didn't kidnap someone you knew, and then let him go when the money was paid. The first thing he'd do was identify his abductors.

When had Leo committed the murder? While Chris was still in the warehouse, changing from the chauffeur's uniform into his leathers? String tied around William's ankles and neck so he'd choke himself. Despite the cloudy, humid June night, the heavy clothing he wore, Chris shivered. It took a certain cruel bent to kill a man that way, leave him to choke himself to death. Chris knew he would have to be extra careful when he arrived at the meeting place. He had underestimated Leo, thought he was just some middle-aged fag. Now he knew better.

Chris passed the exit to Wurtsboro and started to look for the rest-area sign. Glancing down at the luminous hands of his watch, he saw it was a few minutes after twelve. Was Leo there already? Waiting for him? The sign for the rest area loomed up, flashed past. Chris cut his lights and touched the brakes. At the beginning of the entrance ramp, he killed the engine and coasted silently.

The rest area did not even boast a light. It was nothing but a narrow paved area set well back from the highway with dense trees to its rear. For a moment, the cloud broke and the moon shone through. Parked right at the far end of the rest area, off the paved surface and almost in the trees, Chris saw a white Cadillac convertible, its top up. Chris braked and ran the motorcycle up onto the grass at the entrance to the rest area. He jumped off, dropped the motorcycle silently onto the grass, following it with his helmet. Then, gun in hand, he started to run. Not toward the Cadillac, but toward the trees.

Ten yards into the trees, he cut left, using what he had learned in the army to find his way in the darkness. Each step was an adventure, foot and hand thrust out in front, used as a blind man uses a white stick. He made agonizingly slow progress. After eight minutes, he estimated that he must be level with the white Cadillac. He turned left again, moving by inches in case he snapped a twig, disturbed an animal. Was he being overcautious? Leo was just sitting in the Cadillac, waiting for him. Or was he? The brutal killing of William Minsky was forcing him to be careful.

He reached the edge of the trees, stayed in their shadow while he surveyed what lay ahead. The trunk of the Cadillac was only five yards away. A single shot—he raised the gun to eye level—through the rear window. A single shot and his connection to the kidnapping and murder of William Minsky would be cut. Wait! . . . Again the night was dark, the moon once more concealed by clouds. The rear window of the Cadillac's convertible roof was now obscured. Chris could not be certain there was anyone sitting in the Cadillac.

Emerging from the cover of the trees, he took a step closer. He dropped down onto his knees and elbows, crawled like they had taught him to do in the army. He could feel the warmth of the Cadillac's exhaust system. Skirting the side of the car, he made his way to the driver's door.

From behind Chris came a soft whisper. "I knew you'd come here tonight, Chris. And I knew why."

Chris spun around in his crawl position, the gun coming up. Before he could raise it fully, exert pressure on the trigger, a heavy steel bar crashed down across his right shoulder. He screamed in pain. The gun clattered onto concrete. His scramble for it was stopped when Leo slammed his foot down on the young man's wrist. The steel bar descended again across the side of Chris's head, and blackness followed it.

Leo picked up the pistol, slipped it into his coat pocket. He ran toward the other end of the rest area where Chris had left the motorcycle. After unstrapping the grip full of money, he returned to the Cadillac. Chris was just beginning to regain consciousness. Leo squatted next to him, took out the gun and pointed it at Chris's face. The metallic click of the hammer being pulled back could have been the sound of a cricket.

"I must have looked like a real fool to you, Chris. I let you pick up a quarter of a million dollars from the bus station, didn't I? You could have just cut and run. But I knew you'd come to this meeting. You know how I knew?"

"If you're going to pull the trigger, get it over and done with, you fucking fag!" Chris spat out.

In the darkness, Leo's smile was barely visible. "Quarter of a million. Easy pickings. But no, you wanted to get rid of me first, didn't you? You had to. I could connect you to what happened in Jersey City. You didn't want that, did you? That's why I knew you'd come, to kill me before you took off with the money."

Chris tried to black out the waves of pain that pulsed through his entire body from his shattered shoulder. The gun was so close. If he could gather the strength, time his move, push himself up, make a grab for it . . .

"You know what makes you even more stupid, Chris? This money, it doesn't mean a damned thing to me. Here . . ." Leo unzipped the grip, felt inside and pulled out a fistful of bills. He threw them up into the air like confetti, let the wind carry them away toward the road. "Little windfall for someone. I'm going to burn the rest. This money doesn't mean shit to me." He broke off, lifted his head curiously as the sound of an engine carried through the night air. A truck in low gear struggling up a hill. Headlight beams danced across the sky like searchlights. The beams leveled out, and Leo turned toward the source of the noise. There, approaching the far end of the rest area after having completed its climb up the hill, was the truck.

Chris took a deep, silent breath and lunged at Leo. His left hand slammed against the gun barrel, shoved it back and up. A booming explosion echoed across the rest area. Leo catapulted back, hands clutched to his head. For a few seconds he lay writhing and groaning, then in one convulsive movement his body jerked straight and he became perfectly still. As Chris approached him, the truck rumbled past the rest area, engine revolutions dropping as the driver shifted into a higher gear.

The gun lay on the ground. Chris picked it up, leveled it at Leo's head, then lowered it. Even in the dim light supplied by the hidden moon, Chris could see the copious flow of blood that cascaded from Leo's temple, filling his right eye before running off his cheek onto the ground. He dropped the hammer, slipped on the safety, and concealed the weapon in the waistband of his trousers. Taking the grip full of money in his left hand, he spent a few seconds looking around to see if he could spot any of the bills Leo had tossed into the wind. They were gone. Why did he need them anyway? He had more than enough in the grip.

The moment he started to lope toward the motorcycle at the far end of the rest area, his right shoulder screamed in agony. Excitement—danger—had acted like an anesthetic, killing the pain caused by the break, numbing the ache in his head. Now the anesthetic had worn off. The pain in his head he could live with, but every movement was like having sharp knives thrust into his shoulder and right arm. He gritted his teeth, tried to remember what it had been like in airborne training at Fort Bragg before he'd ever gone to Vietnam. Mind over matter . . . that's what the drill sergeants had said. If he could live through the hell of airborne training, the further hell of Vietnam, he could live through this.

He reached the motorcycle, struggled to raise it. After strapping the grip onto the luggage rack, he jumped up and down on the kick start. The engine roared as he opened the throttle. Every degree of steering, every gear change, every braking motion, was rewarded with a spasm of agony that ran from his fingers to his head. How many bones had that fag son of a bitch broken with the damned steel bar? He pointed the motorcycle toward the rest-area exit, lights off until he reached the sanctuary of the highway. He'd fake an accident, that's what he'd do. Find someplace to stash the money and then fake an accident to explain away his injuries while he sought medical help.

The motorcycle picked up speed. Chris passed the Cadillac, the motionless figure of Leo. Reaching the highway, he flicked on the lights. He'd keep heading west, get well away from this spot. Try to hold on for a couple of hours. Ditch the gun, hide the money, then fake the accident. A hospital would set his shoulder straight.

The front wheel wobbled uncertainly. Chris caught it just in time. He was having difficulty steering. Despite the pain, he gripped tighter with his right hand. He could hang on. A couple of hours, that was all. Two hours to put a hundred and thirty miles between himself and Leo's body. He could tough it out for that long. Sure he could, when he had a quarter of a million dollars to look forward to spending.

After five miles, red lights danced in the blackness ahead of him. The tail lights of the truck that had passed the rest area when Leo had held the gun on him. The truck that had saved his life—and cost Leo his. Chris pulled out to overtake. As he roared past, he raised his good left hand in the air. He was thanking the truck, thanking the driver, not that the man would ever understand. The front wheel wobbled again and Chris dropped his left hand back onto the handlebar.

He saw no more westbound traffic until he reached the long hill leading up to Monticello. Halfway up the incline, he spotted a battered old truck staggering along in low gear. Chris sped by as if the truck were stationary. He reached the crest of the hill. Down to his left was Monticello Raceway. Ahead was a steep downward gradient. The needle of the speedometer swept up to eighty miles an hour as Chris opened the throttle. Caution fled on the wings of excitement. He was aware only of the speed of the powerful motorcycle on the open road, the knowledge that he had defeated a man who'd thought him outwitted.

The gun! . . . He still had to get rid of the gun! Steering with his right hand, feeling the pain shoot up his arm to his shoulder, Chris plucked the gun from his waistband and flung it as far as he could to his right, aiming for the dense undergrowth that bordered the highway. The sudden movement cost him balance. He felt the motorcycle sway sickeningly. Too late he tried to correct the situation. The back end of the motorcycle swung out. At eighty miles an hour, the motorcycle skidded off the road, across the hard shoulder and into a deep ditch filled with shrubs and small trees. Flung off, Chris soared through the air like a tree uprooted by a tornado, arms and legs flailing as though trying to fly. His attempt at flight was stopped abruptly by the sharp, spiky tree branch that impaled him through the center of the chest.

Hanging upside down, ten feet above the ground, Chris's final thought was of waste—the criminal waste of a quarter of a million dollars he had carried on the back of the motorcycle.

Leo had been right all along. The money didn't mean a damned thing.

Leo wasn't dead. The bullet from Chris's gun had only grazed his forehead, leaving a deep furrow across his right temple that merged into his hairline. All around the cut were minuscule black dots, powder burns from the weapon that had been discharged so close to his head.

The noise of the motorcycle starting permeated through to Leo's brain. Lying on his back, face covered in blood, he listened to the sound and knew that he should do something. He had to stop Chris, kill him as he'd intended to do before the solitary truck had diverted his attention for a fraction of a second. Urgently, his brain sent out messages to his body. They went unheeded. He heard the motorcycle pass by where he lay, and he could do nothing but listen to its engine

696

grow fainter and fainter. For another five minutes he lay on his back, moving only to dab away some of the blood that closed his right eye like glue.

Chris was gone. There was nothing Leo could do about it now. He had to save himself. Summoning all his strength, he rolled over onto his hands and knees. The effort sent hammers ringing inside his skull and he almost passed out again. Screwing his eyes shut with pain, he pushed himself onto his knees. Next, he attempted the most difficult feat of all. Standing up. The world swayed. Feeling his legs starting to buckle, Leo guided himself in the direction of the white Cadillac. He fell against the door, fingers clawing for support. Gradually the dizziness passed. He opened the car door, fell onto the seat. He'd left the key in the ignition. He turned the key, listened gratefully to the engine crank into life. Home. He had to get home to Scarsdale. There, in the safety of his own house, he would clean up his head, wash away the blood, clean the wound. He couldn't go to a hospital. No matter what lies he told there, no one would believe him. Even a first-year medical student would be able to spot the gunshot wound. The police would be summoned. Leo could not afford that.

He turned on the headlights, put the Cadillac into drive, and headed slowly toward the rest-area exit. Leo turned the steering wheel to the left and headed east, back to New York City. He had no idea which way Chris had gone. He just hoped that the young man got clean away. Next to being dead, the safest thing for everyone was for Chris and the money to disappear completely.

The journey home seemed to last forever. Entering the house, he went to the bathroom and took the first-aid kit from the cupboard. First he washed the blood from his face and right eye. Gritting his teeth, he cleaned the wound. The iodine caused even more pain than the bullet had done, burning its way into open flesh. As Leo looked at the raw furrow in the mirror, he realized for the first time that he had been shot. Shot, and he'd survived. Not only that, but here he was, standing in his own bathroom, cleaning the wound. Someone had been watching over him tonight.

Once the wound was clean, he covered it with cotton gauze and a large patch of plaster. The powder burns still showed. He picked at them with a pair of tweezers, ripping off the burned spots of skin, leaving the area with a raw, shredded appearance. He would say he'd stumbled, slipped on the gravel driveway of the house and grazed his temple. That would account for the raw patchiness. No one would suspect that he lied; no one would have reason to.

After taking aspirin, he went to the telephone. Two o'clock in the morning or not, Leo knew that he had to tell Lou Levitt what had happened. He dreaded apprising the little man of his failure.

William was buried on Friday morning. Pearl rode with Joseph to the chapel in Forest Hills. Lou Levitt traveled in Leo's Cadillac. Minsky rode alone. Susan did not attend the service, nor would she be at the interment. She remained at home, with Judy keeping her company. Susan's two sons, Mark and Paul, were staying with friends of the family, as they had during the period of the abduction; they were considered too young to attend the funeral of their father.

Leo's head still throbbed excruciatingly from the gunshot wound. Regular doses of aspirin had done little to alleviate the pain. The patch of plaster was partially concealed by the hat he wore. Nonetheless, questions were asked when he arrived at the chapel. He responded with the story he had concocted—a fall on the gravel driveway of his home, a bad graze. Everyone offered him sympathy. Everyone except Levitt.

"You're damned lucky you didn't get yourself killed," Levitt said as they took their seats in the chapel. "How could you let yourself be distracted like that?"

"I thought the truck was coming right into the damned rest area," Leo replied in an angry whisper. "That's all I needed, for some truck driver to see me there with a gun."

"You've no idea where this Chris went?"

"He just took off, that's all I know."

"While we're here, you'd better pray that he gets swallowed up by some hole in the ground. Him and the damned money."

Some of Levitt's anger abated as he looked at Benny Minsky leaning on his cane. Minsky seemed to have aged dramatically since the last time Levitt had seen him. He looked like a man in his eighties, not his late sixties. He wore his grief like a piece of clothing, on the outside for the entire world to see. When Levitt had gone over to shake his hand, he had seen tear stains on Minsky's dark, wrinkled cheeks.

When the service was over, the funeral procession headed out to the cemetery on Long Island. Leo drove behind his twin brother's car, in which Pearl rode. At the cemetery, he parked next to Joseph. Levitt took Pearl's arm and walked with her toward the freshly dug grave. "Your place isn't here," he said gently. "You should have stayed with Susan and Judy at the house."

"Benny's my friend, Lou. I couldn't let him face this alone."

"I know. He thought the world of that son of his. What happened to William makes me worry about the twins. Some lousy place we live in, eh? A guy puts together a few bucks and immediately he becomes a target for animals."

"The police said William was killed even before the ransom demands were made. He was tied up and left to choke to death." Pearl's voice faded. Levitt held her arm tightly and turned to the twins.

"Why don't you get your mother out of here? Let her sit in the car until it's over."

Before either Leo or Joseph could move, Pearl said, "I'm all right."

Levitt felt her arm stiffen and he let go. When she marched on ahead to join Minsky at the side of the grave, Levitt's eyes turned bleak as he watched her. She had no business standing next to that bastard.

The prayers were said, the coffin lowered. One by one, the burial party stepped forward to shower a spadeful of earth into the pit. Levitt followed Joseph. He lifted the spade to send earth cascading down onto the top of the casket. To his ears, the noise of earth and stones hitting the wood was like applause. Biting back an expression of satisfaction, he turned around and passed the spade to Leo.

Leo dug the spade in deeply, twisting free a huge mound of earth. He straightened up too abruptly. Blood roared, his head felt empty. Levitt and Joseph reached out simultaneously to grab hold of him as he tottered back and forth at the edge of the grave. The spade fell from his hand into the pit, bouncing off the top of the casket.

"Carry on like that and you'll join him," Levitt said. "You'd better get yourself home, get some sleep."

"I'll be okay." Leo breathed in deeply, waited for the moment of dizziness to pass.

While Joseph took his mother back to the Minsky home in Forest Hills Gardens, Leo drove Levitt to Central Park West. Levitt no longer talked about the young man named Chris. His worry over Leo's mistake had been replaced by a sensation of victory. "You see Benny's face back there?" he asked Leo. "That's what you call defeat. Total, utter defeat. When you can do that to a man, you've crushed him like an ant."

"I saw. He looked so bad I thought we were going to get two funerals for the price of one."

"Don't wish that, Leo. Wish instead that the bastard lives for a long time yet, so he can think about this. He set Jake up for Gus Landau, and now he's going through what you, your brother, your mother all went through. What I went through as well."

"You?"

"Sure me. Jake was the closest friend I ever had. From schooldays, even. Too bad your mother can never know the truth, never know who was responsible for Jake's death, never know how we paid him back." He shook his head at the injustice of it all. "How's your head holding up?"

"Still there." Leo took one hand off the wheel, touched it to his temple. Was it his imagination or were the aspirins beginning to have some effect? The pounding seemed to have lessened. Gunshot wound. It was an injury, just like any other. It was nothing special. Given time, it got better.

After dropping Levitt off outside his building on Central Park West, Leo drove north to Scarsdale. He removed the dressing on his temple and inspected the wound. The tiny tears where he'd ripped off the spots of burned powder were already beginning to fade. The bullet wound also was paler. He applied a fresh patch, took two more aspirin, and lay down in his bedroom. He'd do as Levitt had suggested, get some sleep. If he felt better when he awoke, he'd go into town.

Just because Benny Minsky was in mourning, it didn't mean that Leo had to forgo his own pleasure.

Pearl, Joseph, and Judy stayed the remainder of the day at the Minsky home. At five o'clock in the afternoon, Minsky's two grandsons were returned to the house. The family sat in a somber group in the living room, while Pearl busied herself in the kitchen. They had to eat. Cooking dinner for them would take Pearl's mind off the tragedy. It was a tried and trusted remedy. She only wished that she could prescribe a similar cure for Minsky, Susan, and the boys. As she prepared the meal, she wondered how well Susan would stand up to the loss. It had happened so close to her older son's bar mitzvah. There was something uncanny about that. Pearl had lost Jake immediately following the twins' bar mitzvahs twenty-nine years earlier. Now, history had repeated itself.

Pearl prepared dinner, but she did not stay to share it with the Minskys. Promising to be back the following day, she left the house with Joseph and Judy to return to Sands Point.

Susan served the meal, which was eaten quietly, without enjoyment. Afterward, when the boys helped Susan clear the table, Minsky walked out to the patio in the rear of the house. He wanted to be alone, to review the day he had buried his only son.

Sitting there in the warm June night, Minsky questioned how he could have changed his life in order to avoid this dreadful day. Why— he gazed up to the heavens as though asking God—had it ended in this manner? Minsky had taken more pride in his son than in anything he'd ever done. In fact, William was the only thing in Minsky's life that he was truly proud of. And to have it end like this! A stupid, senseless murder when he'd been prepared to hand over the money for William's release. A quarter of a million dollars. He would have given ten times that much for William's safe return; he would have given every penny he could beg, borrow, or steal.

Footsteps sounded. Minsky swiveled around in the chair to see Susan standing by the French windows that led to the dining room. "The boys have gone to bed."

"Already?"

She gave him a weary smile. "You've been sitting out here for almost two hours."

Minsky looked at his watch, surprised to see it was almost ten o'clock. "So I have."

"They want you to go up and say good night to them."

"Of course." He eased himself to his feet, entered the house, and laboriously climbed the stairs. First, he went into Paul's room. The younger boy was sitting up in bed. "Good night, Paul." Minsky bent forward to kiss his grandson on the cheek. "I'll see you in the morning."

From Paul's room, he went to Mark's. The older boy was not in bed. Wearing pajamas, he was sitting in a chair by the window, looking out over the street. When he heard Minsky enter his room, he turned around.

"I can't believe it, Grandpa. I can't believe my father's dead."

Minsky sat down next to him. "Neither can I, Mark." He hoped the boy wouldn't remind him about the promise he had broken.

"I keep looking out of the window, expecting to see his car pull into the drive. Like when he'd worked late at the truck depot, and I'd be watching out of the window for him."

Minsky put an arm around the boy's shoulders, held him tightly. "I know how you feel, Mark. Each time I hear a car, I think it's him."

"Will the police ever catch the people who did it?"

"I don't know."

"I hope they do," Mark spat out with sudden vehemence. "I hope they catch them and kill them."

Minsky said nothing because he was in agreement with his grandson. He just kissed Mark good night and then went downstairs. Susan said that she, too, was going to bed and she asked if he needed anything. Minsky told her no. He just wanted to sit, to be alone.

Instead of returning to the patio, he sat downstairs in the room that had been turned into a bedroom for him while he was in New York. Looking through the window, he understood only too well how Mark felt. Each time a car came along the road, Minsky could easily think it was William returning home after working late. Soon, he felt, one of the cars would turn into the driveway. Its lights and engine would die. The driver's door would open and William would step out. He'd see his father sitting in the window and give him a cheerful wave, and the nightmare would be over.

Another set of headlights probed the darkness of the street. Minsky's imagination took over completely. The car did not go past the house. The headlights turned full on the window through which Minsky was looking, illuminating his face, almost blinding him. He had to shield his eyes with his hand until the car had swung around in front of the house. The lights dimmed. The sound of the engine died. The driver's door opened. Minsky almost cried out William's name. He stopped himself only when he realized it was not William who was stepping out of the car. It was Frank Hopkins, the FBI agent who had stayed at the house, who had begged to be allowed to tail Minsky when he'd made the ransom drop; the man who had driven him to the warehouse in Jersey City to identify William's body.

The agent saw Minsky sitting in the window and lifted a hand in greeting. Minsky opened the window. "What do you want?"

"I need to speak to you, Mr. Minsky. We have information, important information."

"Come around to the front door. I'll let you in. Please be quiet, my daughter-in-law and grandsons are sleeping." Minsky limped to the front door and opened it. The agent stepped inside and led the way to the front room where Minsky had been sitting.

"What is this important information?"

"Do you know of a man named Christopher Latham?"

"Christopher Latham?" Minsky repeated the name mechanically. "Never heard of him. Who is he?"

"Was. He's dead. A Vietnam veteran, out of the army two or three months. From Sanford, North Carolina, originally, but he'd been living in a hotel in Times Square. He was killed in a traffic accident either late last night or early this morning on Route 17 up in Monticello. Drove a motorcycle. Came off it at high speed and was impaled on a tree."

"What does this have to do with me?"

Hopkins held up a hand, signaling for Minsky to be patient. "It may have everything to do with you, with your son. Latham's motorcycle was wrecked, but at the scene of the accident the state police recovered a leather grip. Inside it was almost a quarter of a million dollars."

Minsky's dark eyes sharpened. "Wait a minute. When I went to the George Washington Bridge bus station, I was supposed to wait by a telephone that had an out-of-order sign hanging from it. In the next booth, talking on the telephone"—Minsky recalled the scene clearly, every single detail—"was a man in motorcycle clothes. You know, the leather pants and jacket, the helmet. He had a suitcase on the floor by his feet. A red suitcase. I didn't pay any attention at the time, but now I remember."

"The state police also found this among Latham's possessions." Hopkins produced a slip of paper. It was a photocopy of a list of telephone numbers, eight in all.

"What's this?"

"The first seven telephone numbers correspond to the pay phones where you were sent. This one"—Hopkins pointed to the first number—"that's the telephone at the corner of Jewel Avenue and Queens Boulevard. The next one's Jackson Heights, and so on and so on. We've located seven of these numbers. It's the eighth number that's interesting."

"How come?" Minsky ran over in his mind the information about Christopher Latham. Sanford, North Carolina . . . how could he have missed that? "The man who spoke to me most of the time, he had a Southern accent."

"That's right," Hopkins said. "But let's get back to this eighth number. There's no area code to tell us which city it's in, so we assumed it was two-one-two like the rest of them, a New York number. This number in New York presents us with an intriguing scenario. It's a recently installed business line, but it doesn't go through any switchboard. It's a direct line to an office in a real-estate company called Granitz Brothers."

"Granitz Brothers?" This time, Minsky's repetition of a name was filled with amazement.

"The installation order was placed by Leo Granitz." Hopkins sat quietly while he watched a whole flood of expressions flash across Minsky's face. Surprise came first, dumb amazement as though Minsky could not comprehend such an involvement. Shock. That gave way to a bland expression of acceptance, and then, slowly, Minsky's face clouded over until it was filled with nothing but rage and hatred. His body started to tremble, and he grasped the cane until his knuckles turned to ivory.

"Mr. Minsky, we don't know what the connection is. We don't know why this Christopher Latham would have Leo Granitz's private office number in his possession. We don't even know if it is Leo Granitz's number that Latham had. The two-one-two is just a guess."

"It is," Minsky said with grim certainty. "It's Leo's number. And that money is the ransom money."

"Please allow us to do our job. Our men are at Scarsdale now, at Leo Granitz's home. We want to question him. He's away at the moment, but when he returns we'll question him. Believe me when I say we'll arrive at the truth of this matter."

"Have you tried looking anywhere else for him?"

"At his twin brother's home in Sands Point? Yes, we've been there."

"What about Lou Levitt, Central Park West? He might be there."

"I'll get onto that right away. When we learn anything, I'll be in touch." Hopkins stood up, ready to leave. As he looked down at Minsky sitting in the chair, he felt a perverse gratitude that the man was a partial cripple. The agent had never seen such fury as that which was etched on Minsky's face. If Minsky were fit, the agent was certain he would take matters into his own hands.

Minsky remained in the chair for ten minutes after the FBI agent had left the house. Christopher Latham, fresh out of the army with a quarter of a million dollars and the direct-line number to Leo's office in his pocket. Was Latham—the Southern-accented voice on the other end of the line—the murderer of Minsky's son? If so, he had already paid the penalty. Minsky felt cheated, the bastard had gotten off too damned easily. Or was it Leo who had tied the string around William's ankles and throat, left him to choke to death? The hell with what Hopkins said about finding the connection between Latham and Leo! Minsky did not need a degree in criminology, or whatever education modern-day cops had to get before they could strap on a shield and a gun, to know what the score was. He could see the connection perfectly. Not the connection Hopkins was chasing, but the *real* connection. A little runt of a double-dealing bastard named Lou Levitt!

He rose from the chair. Very cautiously, he climbed the stairs to the upper level of the house. By each door he stopped to listen. Susan and the boys were sleeping soundly. He returned downstairs and went into the kitchen. On a hook above the counter were Susan's keys. Minsky took the key to her car, and prayed that he could drive without full control and strength in his left arm and leg.

The driver's seat of Susan's car felt strange. Minsky had not sat behind a steering wheel since the stroke on New Year's Eve. Six months without driving. For a moment he came close to getting out of the car, leaving the police to do the job they were paid to do. No! This was something he alone had to do. Levitt! That sawed-off, two-faced little shitbag had even had the gall to come to the funeral, to walk right up to Minsky, shake him by the hand, and offer condolences. Minsky turned the ignition key and peered up at the house. No lights came on.

Carefully, he guided the car along the driveway to the street. The power-assisted steering and automatic transmission made driving feel easy. He did not even need his left hand and foot.

Confidence deserted him the instant he reached Queens Boulevard. The heavy Friday-night traffic swept at him from all directions. Horns assaulted his ears as he dithered over which direction to take. He was a stranger in the city where he had been born, grown up. Headlights flashed as he wandered from lane to lane. He followed signs to the Long Island Expressway. A car horn screamed when he entered the eastbound side without first checking for traffic. A sports car flashed past, its driver punching the air angrily with his fist. Minsky ignored him. He stayed in the inside lane, slowly picking up speed until he reached forty-five miles an hour. His was the slowest vehicle on the road, but he was not prepared to go faster. Driving was a new experience; he felt like a learner approaching his test.

Leaving Queens behind, he entered Nassau County. After a while, he saw signs for Sands Point.

He reached Joseph's house. Lights blazed in almost every window. The Minsky house was black with mourning, and here, the Granitz home looked as though a party were in progress. Climbing the steps to the front door, Minsky rapped on it with the head of his cane. Immediately, the hollow barking of the family's two Dobermans echoed from inside.

Joseph swung the door open and let the Dobermans run out. "Benny, what are you doing here? How did you get here?" He looked past Minsky, expecting to see someone else. "Who brought you?"

"I brought myself. Where's your mother?"

"In the library with Judy and the children. I thought you weren't able to drive."

"Never mind that." Minsky waited for Joseph to stand aside and let him enter.

Pearl appeared in the large entrance hall to confront Minsky as he stepped into the house. "Benny, the police were here, men from the FBI. They were asking about Leo. They wanted to know where he was."

"Do you know?"

"I thought he'd be at home. He wasn't well. You saw at the funeral, the bandage on his head, the accident he'd had."

Minsky hadn't even noticed what Leo had looked like at the funeral. He'd had eyes only for the casket that had contained his son. "Leo's not at home. The police have already checked Scarsdale."

"How do you know what the police have and haven't done?" Joseph asked.

"I just left an FBI man at Forest Hills Gardens, that's how I know. He came to tell me that the ransom money has turned up. A motorcyclist who got killed in an accident upstate had it. He also had Leo's office number on him."

"What number was that?" Joseph asked. When Minsky told him, Joseph shook his head and said, "That's not one of our numbers. The police have made a mistake."

"Don't sound so pleased, they didn't make any mistake. It's a direct line to your brother's office, only installed recently. Even you, his goddamned twin, don't know what he gets up to, do you?"

"Do you believe the police?" Pearl asked fearfully. "Do you believe that Leo could possibly have been involved in William's? . . ."

"In William's murder?" Minsky finished the question for Pearl. "You're damned right I do. I believe Leo had something to do with my son getting killed, and I know why. It's that bastard Lou Levitt. In all the world, I'm the only person who ever got the better of him, and he never forgave me for it."

"What the hell are you talking about?" Joseph demanded.

"Your godfather, that's what I'm talking about! The slimiest son of a bitch who ever drew breath! Lou put your twin brother up to this. God alone knows what lies he told him, but your brother's nuts enough to listen to anything. To believe anything!"

"Benny, William and Leo were friends!" Pearl protested. "Leo would never have done such a thing!"

"Don't bet on it." Judy's voice came from inside the library. "You know full well what Leo's done in the past. Lou Levitt told you himself. Phil Gerson and his girlfriend, Belinda. Those men who beat up William." She touched a hand to her mouth as she mentioned the name of Minsky's dead son. "And the man who picked Leo up on the night Joseph and I were married."

Joseph swung around on his wife. "Don't be satisfied with saying it in front of the kids! Take a full-page ad in the *Times*, let the whole damned world know!"

Judy bit her bottom lip. Grabbing her son and daughter by the hand, she led them through the entrance hall to the door that connected the house with the guest wing. Both Jacob and Anne kept their faces averted from the people standing in the hall. They were confused, unable to comprehend what was going on. They only knew that voices were being raised, and that their Uncle Leo and the man they regarded as their grandfather were the cause of the argument.

Minsky looked from Pearl to Joseph. "The police are convinced that Leo's mixed up in William's murder, but I don't blame Leo, can you understand that? I know what he's like. He was always a little crazy, not really responsible for his actions. A child who could be persuaded to do bad things. That's why I blame Lou Levitt, because he could manipulate Leo like some kind of a hypnotist. For twenty-nine years Lou's had a grudge against me, he's hated me because I wasn't as dumb as he liked to think I was. That's why I'm still alive. That's why I didn't die that week Jake and Moe Caplan died, and Gus Landau. I stayed alive because I had more smarts than Lou gave me credit for. And what he's always thought should have been all his, he's had to share with me all these years."

Joseph glanced at his mother. Both wore the same puzzled expression. Neither could make any sense out of what Minsky was saying, yet they made no attempt to interrupt him.

"That two-faced little worm, he wanted to see me crawl. My heart attack, my stroke—they weren't enough for Lou. He wanted to take away the only thing I ever did that was worthwhile. He wanted to take my son. Pearl, call him . . . call Lou. Have him come over here now and explain to you and Joseph what he's done. Have him come over here and face me, if he's got the guts to do that."

Pearl found her voice. "I don't have to call him. He's on his way. The moment the police left here, I telephoned him."

"You told him they were looking for Leo?"

"Yes."

"And? What did he say?"

"He told me not to worry. He said he'd keep Leo out of trouble just as he's always done."

"And you asked me if I believed that Leo was involved? There's your proof right there!" Minsky walked into the library and sat down. "I'm going to wait right here because I want to hear the lies that scheming bastard uses to explain away why he got your son to murder mine. And when he's finished his lies, I'll tell you some truths."

Leo drifted from bar to bar, staying only long enough to have one drink while he surveyed the young men who stood alone. He didn't know whether it was the dull ache in his head that was responsible, but his appetite was blunt that night.

At eleven-fifteen, he began the drive home to Scarsdale. Was he growing old? He would be forty-two this year, the start of middle age. Did a man's sexual drive start to fade when he reached the middle period of his life? He knew that the answer was no. Only three days earlier, as he had watched Christopher Latham change from the chauffeur's uniform into his motorcycle leathers, Leo had felt a tremendous sexual urge. It was just a bad day, that was all. He should have stayed in, perhaps watched a movie in the basement cinema. That would have done him more good. He'd put one on when he got home.

He had his first inkling of trouble when he neared the house. A police car was parked at the corner of the street where he lived. Instead of turning into the street, Leo drove straight on. The car could be out on regular patrol, or answering a call. But why were its lights off? Why was it tucked away, almost out of sight, behind a clump of bushes? The sight of the car unnerved him. He had to find out for certain.

He drove back to the center of town, found a pay phone, and dialed the number of the local cab company. Ten minutes later, a taxi collected him. Leo instructed the driver to take him down the street on which he lived. One look at the house was all he needed. Lights were on inside. Cars were parked about with little care for concealment. He instructed the taxi driver to return him to his point of origin.

Back in his own car, Leo sat quietly for several minutes. If the police were at the house, it meant they had a warrant. A search warrant . . . and a warrant for his arrest? He began to perspire. The ache in his head increased. He had to run. To where? The police would be looking for his car. A white Cadillac convertible, it was conspicuous. How many of them were around? Damn . . . why hadn't he bought a Chevy or a Ford like everyone else? Why did he have to be different?

He drove the Cadillac into a dark alley and left it there, running away as though it carried some disease. He entered another telephone booth and dialed the same taxi company he had used earlier. "I want to order a cab."

"Destination?" asked the woman dispatcher.

"Sands Point, out on Long Island." The woman told him there would be a special rate for a journey of that length. "I don't care!" Leo yelled back. "Just get me the damned cab!"

"One'll be with you in fifteen minutes."

Leo stood in the shadow of a shop doorway while he waited. Sooner or later, the police would find the white Cadillac. By then he'd be long gone from Scarsdale. He would be hiding in the only place where he would be safe, the only place in the entire world where he had ever felt safe.

He would be with his mother.

Chapter Four

Benny Minsky sat immobile on the chair, hands clasping the top of the cane that stood between his parted legs. He was thinking about a New York socialite named David Hay. More than forty years had passed since he had killed David Hay, and for all that time Lou Levitt had dangled the specter of that murder over Benny's head. For the past twenty-nine years, since the death of Jake Granitz, the weight of Levitt's blackmail had been excruciating, forcing Minsky to loathe himself. Tonight he hoped to cleanse that stain from whatever soul he had left.

Pearl sat on a couch on the far side of the library from Minsky. Her thoughts concerned both Levitt and Leo. Was it true what Minsky had said—that Levitt had told Leo lies? What lies? Why? And what did that have to do with William's being killed? She no longer knew what to think. She could only hope that Levitt, when he arrived, would explain the situation to her. Just like he always did.

Joseph stood, arms crossed, in front of the library door. He could have been a guard, ensuring that none of his charges escaped.

Pearl and Joseph swung their heads toward the window as they heard the sound of a car drawing up. Only Minsky failed to move. He remained sitting like a statue, unmoving, unblinking. A car horn sounded. Joseph, walking toward the hall to let Levitt into the house, swung around and looked out of the library window. Levitt was sitting in his car, pointing at the two Dobermans which stood by the driver's door.

"Call off these hounds of yours."

Joseph went to the front door and whistled for the dogs. While he held onto their collars, Levitt left the safety of the car and hurried into the house. The moment he was inside, Joseph pushed the dogs out and closed the door.

Leaving Minsky sitting alone in the library, Pearl walked into the hall to join her son and Levitt. When Levitt saw her, he said, "Pearl, I don't want you to worry about a thing. Leo's going to be all right. I'll

709

get him the best defense lawyer, I'll fix him up with rock-hard alibis that'll prove he was nowhere near where William was found. He'll have an alibi for every moment of the time William was missing. You can rely on me."

"Just like I've always relied on you, right, Lou?"

Levitt angled his head. Had he detected an odd tone in her voice? "Sure. Have I ever let you down? For one moment since Jake died, did I ever do wrong by you or the twins?"

"Why, Lou?" was Pearl's plaintive question. "Why did you have to get Leo involved in something like this?"

"For Jake, that's why. Leo was evening the score for what Benny did to Jake."

Finally, Minsky moved. The motion was minimal, just a slight turn of his head so he could see Pearl as she stood in the hall talking to Levitt. The real action took place in his eyes. The hatred and fury that had frightened FBI agent Frank Hopkins were again lending Minsky's eyes a dark fire.

"What Benny did? . . ." Pearl asked.

Levitt's voice became softer, and Minsky had to strain to hear the words. "Who do you think set Jake up outside the *shul* that day? Who do you think arranged for Gus Landau to come back to New York from Toronto? Who do you think cooked up a drug deal with Landau to grab ahold of that business? It was Benny, that's who! And who do you think was responsible for Moe Caplan's death?"

"Liar!" Minsky screamed from inside the library. "Goddamned filthy lying bastard!"

"Benny?" Levitt's voice dropped to the faintest whisper as he stared at Pearl. "Benny's here?"

"In the library," Joseph said. "He's waiting for you."

Levitt walked to the library door and looked inside. Minsky was struggling to his feet. In his right hand, the cane was brandished like a sword. "Liar!" Minsky screamed again. "Is that the poison you told Leo to make him kill my William? To kill him, and make it look like a kidnapping? Is that how you get back at me after all these years?" He stumbled toward Levitt, thrashing the air with the cane. Levitt ducked, and the cane cracked against the doorframe. Minsky lost his balance and toppled to the ground. When he tried to get up, Joseph stepped between the two elderly men.

"Look at yourself," Levitt sneered. "A foolish old man who still can't accept the truth about the evil he did."

"The truth? What would you know about truth? Every time you open your mouth, a lie pours out."

"What was it you told my brother?" Joseph asked Levitt.

"I told him what this piece of garbage did to Jake. What he did to Moe Caplan, and what he would have done to me if he could have gotten away with it. Leo took that truth and used it to avenge Jake, to avenge this family." He swung around to face Pearl. "That's why I used Leo. That's why I involved him. Because it was his duty to pay this maniac back for what he did."

"You paid me back for still being alive!" Minsky shouted. "You paid me back for outsmarting you. Your ego couldn't stand that, could it? You couldn't cope with someone who was as smart as you."

"If you lived to be a thousand," Levitt shouted back, "you wouldn't have ten percent of my brains!"

"What about Gus Landau?" Joseph asked Levitt. "What about Benny bringing him back from Toronto? Tell me the whole story you told my brother."

"Tell us all," Minsky invited. "Let us all hear your lies, and then we might go out and kill innocent people for you as well."

"I told Leo only what happened," Levitt said to Minsky. "I told him how you met with Landau, Benny. I told him how Landau offered you the drug business if he was allowed to return unmolested to New York. I told him how the offer was put to the vote, and you were outvoted, three to one. But you still went ahead with it. You brought Landau down and you set Jake up for him, because Jake had sworn to kill you if he ever saw drugs being pushed from our shops—"

"Don't listen to him!" Minsky shouted at Pearl and Joseph. "He's lying. All his life he's been a liar, a cheat, a thief. And now he's telling the biggest lie of all."

"Am I, Benny?" Levitt asked softly. "You remember, surely, the way you took Moe to that place where Landau was hiding out after shooting Jake. You were going to close Landau's mouth. And you closed Moe's mouth as well." He turned to Pearl. "Me he couldn't kill, because I'd protected myself."

"How?"

"Years before, Benny murdered a boyfriend of Kathleen's. I found out about it, made out an affidavit that I kept in a safe place, because I didn't trust Benny. If anything happened to me, that affidavit would have been sent straight to the police. Benny would have burned, just like he should have."

Pearl remembered the night she had sat in the bedroom she'd shared with Jake, toying with the ivory-handled revolvers, contemplating suicide . . . the knock on the door that had saved her life. Minsky and Levitt waiting outside to tell her that Landau was dead, killed by Moe Caplan who had died himself. They had wanted her to break the news to Annie. She had, and the news had made Annie take her own life. "The pair of you came around to see me. You told me that Landau and Moe had killed each other. What is the truth? How did Moe die? And what is all this about drugs? And Landau . . . who was it who arranged for Landau to come back to New York?"

"Do you have to ask that, Pearl?" Levitt wanted to know. "Didn't you just hear what I said?"

"I heard Benny as well."

"Who are you going to believe? Him or me?"

Pearl shook her head. "I don't know anymore, Lou." She placed a hand to her temple. It was burning. Within seconds, a blinding headache enveloped her. Movement was pain, but that pain gave her thinking a clarity she could never recall having had. Suddenly, everything in her thoughts, in her vision, seemed so sharply defined. She could see things to which she had been blind.

Without a word to anyone, she left the library and climbed the stairs to the second floor. In her own bedroom, she approached the heavy bureau which stood against a wall. She opened the bottom drawer and pulled out a polished walnut presentation box. Lying on top was the card signed by Benny Minsky more than forty years earlier—"If you need protection," Pearl read, "then protect yourself with style." One ivory-handled revolver was still loaded, from that night she had contemplated suicide. She inserted ammunition into the second weapon, wondering if it would still be good all these years later. Of course it would. Bullets weren't milk or bread; they did not turn sour or go stale.

When she returned downstairs, she was carrying a large handbag. Minsky and Levitt were just as she had left them, as though her temporary absence had suspended life. Minsky stood in the center of the library, leaning on his cane. Levitt stood just inside the doorway, glaring at the dark-skinned man. Even Joseph had not moved. He remained between the two men, keeping them apart.

Pearl's right hand dipped into the bag. When it emerged, she was holding a revolver. "Sit down, both of you."

"Ma, give me that!" Joseph reached out a hand to remove the revolver from his mother's grasp, but she snatched the weapon away from him. "Where did you get that thing?"

"It was your father's."

"It's been in this house all the time?"

"Under lock and key."

"Hey, that's one of the guns I gave to Jake for his twenty-fifth birthday!" Minsky exclaimed. "A matching pair—"

"I said, sit down." Pearl motioned toward the couch, and Minsky sat. Next, she pointed the gun in Levitt's general direction. "You, too." She watched him take a seat on a straight-backed chair. Pearl switched her gaze from one seated man to the other. "All I've heard tonight is a single word. *Truth*. Now I'd like to hear some."

"I just told it to you!" Levitt's voice had lost some of the calm reasoning quality that Pearl had always associated with it.

"I've listened to you already, Lou. I've listened to you all my life. Now I want to listen to Benny."

Minsky sat back. He had no fear of the revolver in Pearl's hand. All he felt was relief. After all these years, he could finally tell the truth to someone. As damning as it would be to himself, the truth would hurt Levitt even more.

"Well, Benny?" Pearl said.

"Lou came to us with a proposal," Minsky said. "He called a meeting late one night in the office above the Jalo garage on the West Side, and there he told us he'd come to an arrangement. An *arrangement*, that's what he called it, with Gus Landau."

Pearl listened, and as Minsky went further into his story she felt acid burn her stomach. . . .

It was raining the night Levitt called the meeting above the Jalo garage. The big room was empty, the bookkeepers and runners gone for the night. While Levitt waited for his three partners, he sat behind his desk and listened to the radio with its war news from Europe.

Jake and Moses Caplan arrived together, having driven in Jake's car from their apartment building on lower Fifth Avenue. The three men sat listening to the radio for ten minutes until Benny Minsky walked in. The moment Minsky sat down, Levitt flicked off the radio.

"You know, I've been doing some thinking," Levitt began. "Those small shops where we run the books, the numbers—we could push a million different kinds of things through them."

"Such as?" Jake asked. He doubted that Levitt was fishing for ideas; he probably had one of his own already.

The answer came back in one word. "Drugs."

"You're crazy."

"Am I? What we're making in those shops right now is *bupkes* compared with what we could be making. I don't mean use every single shop. Maybe twenty, that's all. One in each area."

"And those twenty shops would get raided by the cops so fast we wouldn't know what hit us," Caplan argued.

Levitt dismissed the objection. "We'll make more money pushing drugs through those twenty shops than we do taking bets, so our payoffs to the cops will be proportionately larger. They'll be paid well enough to look the other way."

"Where are these drugs coming from?" Jake asked.

"Gus Landau."

"Landau?" It was Minsky who repeated the name, in his voice a mixture of surprise and disgust. "Where the hell did you drag up that scumbag from?"

"Canada. Landau's been living up there since he ran from New York. In Toronto. He's worked himself up a good little business with junk. Now he's willing to turn it over to us as long as we let him come back to New York. He's paying for his safety with his drug connections."

"How do you know all this?" Jake asked.

"I met with him."

"You met with Landau?"

"In Niagara Falls last weekend. I went across the Canadian border to see him. He drove there from Toronto."

"How did you know where to go to see him?"

"He wrote to me."

"How come you never said a word to us?"

"Because I wanted to see what he had to say. Landau wants to come back here badly. Canada's fighting a war and he doesn't want any part of it. Turning over his drug connections in New York will be worth a fortune to us."

"When you get around to giving him an answer," Jake said quietly, "make sure you tell him no. If he shows his face in New York, I'm going to blow it off for him!"

"Jake, think with your head, not with your guts. Don't you know how much this money could mean to us? Landau has built up a whole business. He'll turn over his connections so we can do the same thing down here."

"Is money the only damned thing that matters to you? He killed Pearl's mother, remember? And just in case you've forgotten, he killed her while he was trying to kill you and me!"

Levitt regarded Jake with an icy stare. "It's just as well that there are four of us. Maybe Moe and Benny won't think the same way you do."

"Go ahead and put it to a vote," Jake responded. "I couldn't care less how much I'm outvoted by. If Landau comes back here, I'll kill him. And I'll fight you all if you decide to push drugs from those shops. We don't need any part of that business. It stinks. It's the kind of filth that only a rat like Landau would get involved in. What the hell do you want to get mixed up in it for?"

"Money," Levitt answered simply. "The same reason I get involved

714

in any business." He looked at Caplan and Minsky. "Well?"

"Count me out," Caplan said.

"Me, too," was Minsky's answer.

Levitt looked like a man betrayed, a man who finds himself cuckolded by his best friend. "Christ, where are your brains? We've been offered a fortune on a silver plate, and all you can do is shake your stupid heads. If I'd have thought this was how you'd react, I wouldn't have gone all the way up to Canada."

"Who asked you to go?" Jake said. "You had no damned business going up there without talking to us first."

"I had plenty of damned business! Remember, everything we ever did that made money was my idea. The three of you would still be living in some shithouse on Delancey Street if it wasn't for me."

"Maybe we would," Jake concurred. "I'll tell you one thing, though, little man. We just took a vote here, and you were outvoted, three to one. That puts an end to it. Maybe you've got some other ideas, but if I ever seen one ounce of Landau's junk coming out of one of our books, I'm going to come looking for you with a gun in my hand." He stood up, glanced at Caplan and Minsky, and the three men left the office. . . .

When Minsky paused for breath, Pearl turned her attention to Levitt. As small as he was, he had shrunk even more, and was pressing himself against the back of the chair as though trying to become a part of it. His face was devoid of color, his eyes were nothing more than slits through which icy sapphires gleamed with hate.

"It was the first time I'd ever seen an argument between Jake and Lou," Minsky continued. "The first time Jake had ever raised his voice to any of us. But he had a thing about drugs. He was scared of them because of the twins. And he hated Landau because of what the man had done. But he couldn't believe that Lou would have gone to see Landau to talk about such a deal."

Pearl tried to recall those weeks leading up to the twins' bar mitzvahs. "Jake was edgy," she said. "I couldn't understand why. I put it down to nerves, getting worried for the twins' sake. But Lou kept on coming around to the apartment for dinner just like he always did. He seemed to get on well with Jake."

"That's right. The day after we had the meeting and the vote, Lou called us all together again. He apologized, said we were right, he'd been outvoted, and that was the end of it. He even apologized for what he'd said to us, claimed it was all done in the heat of the moment. But," he glanced over at the still figure of Levitt, "you saw what happened outside the *shul* as well as I did, Pearl."

"Landau. So Lou did bring him down."

"Lou went right ahead and disregarded the vote. He got back to Landau, told him it was okay. But turning over the drug connections wasn't enough anymore. He wanted Landau to do something else. He wanted Landau to kill Jake."

"Why, Benny? Why?" Pearl pleaded. "Jake and Lou had been friends since they were small, just like you all were. Why would he turn on him like that?"

"Why don't you ask him yourself?"

Levitt found his voice, and when he focused his eyes on Pearl the sheen of hatred had softened. "I was in love with you, Pearl. You're the only woman I ever loved, you know that."

"To prove you loved me, you killed Jake? Had him killed? For me, and for the money this drug deal with Landau would have made?" Levitt fell back into his motionless, silent stare. Pearl knew the truth now, there was no point in going on. Levitt's admission of love had proved it. She again turned her attention to Minsky. "You and Moe, didn't you know what had happened?"

"We knew, all right. Once that old boy who taught the twins their bar mitzvahs said he'd never seen such a scar on a man's face, we knew exactly what had happened. Lou had double-crossed us. There was chaos outside the *shul*, people running everywhere—"

Pearl interrupted. "I can see it as though it's happening right now. I ran to look at Jake, and Lou"—she gave him the briefest of glances—"caught hold of me. He buried my head in his shoulder so I wouldn't be able to see what had happened . . . what he had caused to happen. Annie, she was holding the twins. And Benny, you were holding William and Judy, pulling them away."

"That's right. Lou pushed you onto Harry Saltzman—"

"Did he have anything to do with it?"

"Nothing. Harry was an outsider; he had no role in our business. Lou pushed you onto Harry and yelled at Moe to get on the telephone for an ambulance. Moe made the call, and while he waited for the ambulance, Moe went up to Lou and told him he knew the truth. There and then, outside the *shul*, while Jake's blood was pouring onto the sidewalk, Moe told Lou that he was going to kill him. He didn't know where, he didn't know when, but he was going to kill him for what he'd done."

"Why didn't you just turn him over to the police when they arrived?"

"What evidence did we have? An argument about drugs? Lou would have waltzed his way around any murder charge based on that.

You saw what he did at the Senate hearings. This was a family affair, something we'd sort out between ourselves. Moe wanted justice, and so did I. And all Moe got"—Minsky dabbed at his eyes; Pearl was surprised to see he was crying—"was a taste of what Jake got. Betrayal by a friend. Me. . . ."

Throughout the week-long *shivah* for Jake, Levitt was constantly at Pearl's side, doing all he could to help her through the painful time. Whenever Caplan and Minsky were present in the apartment, Levitt ignored them. Only when the mourning period ended, did he acknowledge their existence. As Pearl removed the cloths that covered the mirrors, Levitt noticed that Caplan had returned to his own apartment next door. The little man inclined his head toward the twins' bedroom, indicating that Minsky was to follow him.

"What's on Moe's mind these days?" Levitt asked.

"Nothing new. He's going to kill you."

Levitt didn't seem in the least perturbed. "Too bad he feels that way."

"I'd sound a damned sight more worried if I were you."

"Worried?" Levitt laughed. "I don't have to be worried, Benny. Not when I've got you on my side."

"Me? I wish Moe luck. A bullet in the back of the head's all you deserve."

"Is it? And what do you deserve, Benny? A few thousand volts of electricity running through your veins? I've got my affidavit about you and David Hay all locked up nice and safe, but it won't take much for someone to turn a key and bring it out. Remember, Benny, something happens to me, and something just as bad is going to happen to you, whether it's you who pulls the trigger or whether it's Moe."

Minsky flinched as though he could already feel the current coursing through him. Levitt smiled. "That's better, Benny. Now you look like a man who's ready to act sensibly. I know where Gus Landau's hiding out. Do you think Moe will be satisfied with Landau? Do you think if you led him to Landau, he'd call it quits?"

Minsky was powerless. He remembered a stupid poem from schooldays, about a Pied Piper who cleared the town of Hamelin of rats. He felt like one of those rats right now, dancing to a tune played by Levitt, unable to do anything but follow. Nevertheless, he tried to wriggle free of Levitt's spell. "That affidavit isn't going to stand up in any court so long after David Hay's murder. Where's the body, for one thing?"

"At the bottom of the Atlantic. Just a skeleton now, Benny. But are you prepared to take a chance on my sworn testimony *not* standing up in court? If you are, all you've got to do is walk away from me right now. Let Moe put a bullet in me. That's all you've got to do."

"Where is Landau?"

"Sensible, Benny. Sensible. He's holed up in an apartment in the Bronx, off Fordham Road." Levitt handed Minsky a folded slip of paper. "There's the address. Not tonight. Wait three or four days. Let me get it set up. And while you're at it, keep Moe off my back."

The three or four days that Levitt asked for, that was the only thing Minsky liked. He knew there was more to it than just killing Landau, closing a mouth that could incriminate Levitt, trying to satisfy Caplan's desire for justice and revenge. Minsky was being asked—asked, hell!—he was being forced, coerced, blackmailed into setting up Moses Caplan, removing another threat to Levitt. In three or four days, however, he could create a barrier of protection for himself from the little man. Levitt had always sneered at him. No brains . . . crazy Benny. But he wasn't that dumb that he couldn't learn a thing or two parrot-fashion from the master of deceit. . . .

The building in which Landau was hiding was slated for the wrecker's ball. The last tenant had left a month earlier. There was already an air of decay about the place; it hit Minsky and Caplan the moment they entered the lobby, a damp stench that caught in their noses and their throats.

"Third floor," Minsky said, and led the way to the stairs. The handrail was loose and trembled in his grip.

"How did you find out about this place, about Landau being here?" Caplan asked.

Minsky pretended not to hear the question. He could be forgiven for being temporarily hard of hearing. He was about to betray a friend, and his heart was pounding loudly enough to drown out any other sound.

"There." Minsky reached the third floor and pointed to a door at the end of a long hallway. A gun appeared in Caplan's hand and he crossed the intervening space in long, running strides. His foot smashed into the lock to send the door flying back. Caplan charged into the apartment with Minsky on his heels. There, right in front of them, sitting in an armchair that faced the door, was Gus Landau. His eyes were fixed wide open, and a crimson stain covered his shirt front. Caplan's hopes of revenge were smashed, for Landau was already dead. But standing next to the chair, holding a silenced Colt automatic that seemed almost as big as himself, was Levitt. The weapon was pointed unerringly at Caplan's chest.

"You son of a bitch!" Caplan shouted as he spun around to confront Minsky. "You double-crossing son of a bitch! You're in this with him!"

More than anything, Minsky wanted to tell Caplan the truth. He wasn't allying himself voluntarily with Levitt. He was being forced to do this. But his sense of self-preservation overrode that urge. He knocked the gun from Caplan's hand and shoved him away. Caplan banged against the open door and bounced out into the hallway. As the door rebounded off the wall, Levitt fired two shots with the silenced automatic. Both bullets tore through the wood of the door. The first ripped through the fabric of Caplan's coat as he fought to regain his balance and run. The second bullet smashed into the back of his head, killing him.

The gun in Levitt's hand described a slight arc until it was pointing directly at Minsky. Levitt's index finger tightened, and Minsky wondered how much more pressure was needed before the hammer dropped. He tried to find his voice, but his throat and mouth were dry. The words that could save him refused to come.

Just when it seemed that the hammer must slam forward, Minsky managed to croak: "You pull that trigger, Lou, and you go right down the drain."

Levitt's hand remained rock steady. The gun never wavered. But a flicker of interest—or was it apprehension?—appeared in his blue eyes. "How's that, Benny?"

Minsky's voice became stronger. "I know lawyers as well, Lou. I know what an affidavit is, just like you do. You taught me."

"I taught you what?"

"How to cover myself. I know how you set up Jake, and I knew you were using me to set up Moe. I couldn't fight you, Lou, not with what you've got hanging over my head. But I could make damned sure I had something just as heavy hanging over yours."

"You swore out an affidavit about Jake, about this?" Levitt couldn't believe it. Never in a million years would he have credited Minsky with such forethought.

"Damned right I did. Once I brought Moe here, there was no way you were going to let me walk. Not unless I had protection."

To Minsky's surprise, Levitt laughed. "I underestimated you, Benny. I never even gave you credit for having the brains to copy anything I did. What do you know? . . ." While he spoke, he wiped the automatic clean of his own fingerprints and pressed it against Landau's hand. Then he dropped the weapon onto the floor beside Landau. Next, he took another gun from his pocket, a revolver; wiped it clean and then went into the hallway to press it against

Caplan's fingers.

"Is that the gun you shot Landau with?" Minsky asked as he watched Levitt slip it into Caplan's pocket.

"That's right. The police will think they shot each other," Levitt answered. "Now let's get out of here and leave the police to clear up this mess."

"Where are we going?"

"We'll drive around for a while, we've got things to discuss. We're partners now, partners always talk about what they're going to do. After a while we'll go see Pearl. She might want to know that Jake's killer is dead. Too bad about Moe, though." Levitt shook his head sadly. "He should never have gone looking for Landau on his own. Landau was too tough to be taken by one man alone. Moe should have called us first." He walked past Minsky, heading toward the stairway. Minsky followed automatically.

Late at night, they knocked on the door of Pearl's apartment. Both men wore expressions of mourning. Like each other or not, they were bound to each other for life, each protected by sworn testimony that could send the other straight to the electric chair. Neither man had any idea that by calling on Pearl to tell her of the deaths of Gus Landau and Moses Caplan, they had prevented her suicide.

Pearl opened the door and flung her arms around both men. "Lou . . . Benny! . . . What are you doing here?"

"We found Landau," Levitt said after kissing her on the cheek and entering the apartment. Minsky followed him inside.

"Where?"

Levitt checked that the twins were sleeping, closed their door, and walked on into the kitchen. "Landau was holed up in some apartment in the Bronx, off Fordham Road. He's dead, Pearl."

"Lou, it doesn't make me feel any better. I don't feel anything at all."

Levitt took her in his arms as she burst into tears. He waited for a minute, until the crying tapered off. "Pearl, look at me. This is very important, and I want you to listen carefully. I didn't come here to make you feel better, Pearl. I came because I need your help."

"What is it?"

"It was Moe who found him, Pearl," Minsky said softly. "We had a tip that Landau was hiding out in that apartment. Moe went in after him, all by himself."

"Maybe he wanted to pay him back real bad for what he did to Jake," Levitt said. "Who the hell knows why he did it on his own? We don't know all the details yet, only what our friends in the police

720

up there have told us. It looks like Moe surprised Landau, burst into the apartment and shot him. That's the way the police found Landau when they got there. He was sitting on a chair, facing the front door, and he'd been shot through the chest."

"There were two bullet holes in the door," Minsky added. "Not fired from the outside, but from the inside. There was a gun on the floor by Landau's chair, two bullets had been fired. The police figure Landau had just enough strength left in him before he died to fire those two shots through the door. He must have fired as Moe left, after he'd closed the door on the way out. One of the shots . . . one of them hit Moe in the back of the head."

"Oh, God. Annie!"

"Yes, Annie," Levitt said. "Moe's gone as well as Jake, Pearl. Now you've got to be doubly strong because Annie's going to need your help."

"Have you told her? Has anyone? Does she know?"

"I can't tell her, Pearl," Levitt replied. "Will you?" When Pearl hesitated, Levitt urged, "Do it quickly, before the police get here."

Leaving Pearl to tell her best friend that her husband was dead, Levitt and Minsky departed. They drove to the Jalo garage on the West Side, walked up the stairs to the office that Levitt had shared with Jake.

"You appreciate irony, Benny?" Levitt asked.

"What the hell's so ironic about this?"

"You and me being here together. We never got on since we were kids, and now we're stuck with each other. There's your irony."

"I don't like it any more than you do."

"Like it or not, it's the truth and we've got to make the best of it. There's only two of us left, Benny. We've got to stick together, otherwise everything we worked for gets washed down the sink. You've got a son you've got to take care of."

"And you?"

"I'll take care of the twins, they're my responsibility. I'll look after Jake's share of the business."

"And Moe's share? Who'll look after that for Annie and his daughter?"

"I'll make sure they don't go hungry. We owe that to Moe."

"Yeah, we do." Minsky fidgeted on the seat, uncomfortable as he thought of Moses Caplan and his own part in his friend's murder. Better to think of something else. "Are you going to make a move on Pearl?"

Levitt looked up sharply. "What's that supposed to mean?"

"Exactly what I said. Maybe Jake wasn't smart enough to see how you feel about Pearl, but I saw it. I saw it all along, the way you had those big blue eyes of yours following her wherever she went. Christ, you even look on those boys of hers like they're your own."

"Benny, you surprised me once by having more brains than I gave you credit for. Don't push your luck and try to do it twice."

"How do we split up the business now?"

"Right down the middle. Is that fair enough for you?"

"You're not going to haggle, say you should get more because you'll be looking after Pearl and the kids, and Moe's family?"

"Equal partners, that's what we always were, and that's the way it'll remain. Because we've both got the same to lose. Expenses don't enter into it."

"Okay." Minsky offered his hand to Levitt. "Equal partners."

"Just as long as you realize it doesn't mean we have to be friends."

"We never were," Minsky said. "Why should we change now?"

Minsky fell silent again, gazing at Pearl and waiting for her questions. He felt as weak as a baby. Confessing the betrayal of his friend had drained him of every ounce of physical and emotional strength. Pearl watched him for a while before looking at Levitt. Some of the color was returning to his face. He was beginning to recover from the traumatic shock of having his life exposed as one gigantic lie. Minsky, too, had lived a lie. Both of them in an unholy partnership based on the murder of Jake and the subsequent murder of Moses Caplan. Pearl could feel a degree of sympathy for Minsky. He hadn't acted out of greed, out of envy. He had become entangled in the web of Levitt's deceit—just as they all had, Pearl thought. One way or the other, Levitt had ruled their lives. They were all his victims.

"Ma, please let me have that thing." Joseph stepped forward to remove the revolver from Pearl's hand. She looked down, surprised to see that she was still holding the weapon. While listening to Minsky she had forgotten all about the gun she had taken from the walnut presentation box.

"Take it, Joseph. Take it away from me." She handed the revolver to the older twin, relieved to be no longer encumbered by its deadly weight. She could not even remember now why she had gone up to her bedroom to fetch it. Joseph held the gun as though it were something distasteful, thumb and forefinger around the barrel, letting the butt hang down by his knee. He retreated to his former position beside Levitt's straight-backed chair.

"That affidavit you made out," Pearl said to Minsky, "is that what you meant when you said you were the only one who had ever gotten the better of Lou?"

Minsky nodded. For an instant his eyes met Levitt's. The gleam of hatred was back in those blue eyes. "I had him tied down just like he had me, and he hated me for it. I'd proved to him that I was his equal in deceit, in trickery, and he couldn't handle that. The only thing that mattered to Lou was being smarter than anyone else, being a step ahead. Some crazy drive to prove he was the best. It robbed him of every feeling, except what he felt for you."

Joseph spoke up. "He must have felt something when he killed my father and then Moe Caplan. You don't kill without emotion."

"Lou does. It was just business to him."

"What about those drugs Landau offered?" Joseph asked.

"They went on sale through the small shops. Lou took care of the police just like he said he would. He carried on with the drug trade until Leo was getting ready to finish school, and then he stopped the supply. He didn't want Leo—or you, when you joined the firm—to know where the money was coming from. He considered drugs too dirty for you and your brother to be involved with."

Levitt interrupted in a low, hollow monotone. "That was because my sons' interests were always closest to my heart."

The three other people in the room swung their heads to look at him. Minsky and Joseph were stunned, perplexed. Pearl's face was a picture of fright. It was her turn to have her past exposed, to face the shame she had concealed for forty-three years.

"What did you say?" Joseph's voice trembled as he asked the question.

"My sons!" Levitt's voice gained strength and authority. His body grew stronger. "You, your twin brother Leo. Jake wasn't your father. I am!"

"You're crazy," Joseph whispered.

"Ask your mother! Ask her about the night Jake was in the hospital after he'd smashed up the car on the drive down to the Jersey shore! Go ahead, ask her!"

"Ma . . . what happened that night?" Joseph asked.

Pearl composed herself. So much else had come out that her own moment of indiscretion appeared trite in comparison. It didn't even seem worth admitting. "Lou came around to the apartment with the news that *your father*"—she stressed the words purposely, a deliberate snub to Levitt—"had been injured in an automobile acci-

723

dent. I . . . I was upset, how else would you expect me to be?"

"Tell him everything," Levitt urged. "Tell him why you were upset. Not because Jake was in the hospital, but because you believed that you had put him there. Remember? Trying too hard for children, pushing Jake too much! And then you made love with me. I'm the one who got you pregnant with Joseph and Leo. It was never Jake!"

Pearl stared in horror at Levitt. She had been his friend for over fifty years, but only now was she beginning to know him. And she despised what she saw. "Lou, you're absolutely mad."

"I looked after you, after the twins, better than Jake could ever have done. You never married me, but I was still the head of your family. I guided the twins. I brought them up to be something." Levitt rose to his feet, stood beside Joseph, clapped him on the shoulder. "Didn't you ever wonder where you inherited such brains? Was your mother good with figures, with organizational work? She was a cook. Was Jake? No, he was a truck driver. It was me. My genes run through you."

"They must run through Leo as well," Minsky said in the same kind of sneering tone that Levitt had perpetually used when addressing him. "You turned Leo into a murderer. Did he inherit that from you?"

With a movement so swift it took everyone by surprise, Levitt snatched away the ivory-handled revolver that Joseph held by his side. "Your gun, was it, Benny? You gave this to Jake for his twenty-fifth birthday, did you?"

The sight of the revolver in Levitt's hand threw Minsky back into the labyrinth of memories he had navigated that night. The revolver changed into a Colt automatic with a longer barrel threaded for a bulky suppressor. He was no longer sitting in the library at Sands Point, partly crippled with a stroke. He was back in a condemned apartment building in the Bronx. Moses Caplan was dead in the hallway, and Levitt's gun was swinging around to seek a new target. Minsky knew that all he had to do was speak. Find his voice, tell Levitt of the reverse blackmail. Instead of death, Levitt would reward him with a partnership . . . and Minsky would have to live with the shame of the betrayal for the remainder of his life.

He thought about it. He'd gone that route once. He didn't want to take it again. The last time, the gun in Levitt's hand had been a threat. This time it promised blessed relief. "Fire, you twisted little bastard. Pull the trigger, and I'll be waiting down in hell for when you come."

Levitt squeezed the trigger. The explosion rocked the library.

Minsky's body slammed back into the couch. The cane skipped out of his grasp and rolled across the floor.

"You're mad," Pearl murmured, her eyes riveted to the spread of crimson across Minsky's chest. "You always called him crazy Benny, but you were the crazy one all the time. It's not Joseph your genes run through. It's Leo. He's mad, like you."

Levitt continued to hold the revolver, the barrel pointing harmlessly down at the floor. He began to smile. "Pearl, what's happened to you?"

"To me? Nothing's happened to me."

"But it has. What about the diphtheria, Pearl? Every time Leo did something, you found refuge in the diphtheria. Diphtheria was to blame for everything. All his craziness. Don't you remember the things he did? Bursting in on Joseph and Judy in the bedroom when you all lived on Central Park West? The scenes he would throw, the temper tantrums. And each time you said it was the diphtheria."

"What did you expect me to say, that he was crazy?"

"I recognized what he was, Pearl. On his tenth birthday I knew exactly what he was. Remember the dog I brought for a present?"

"The one Leo lost?" Joseph asked. He kept his eyes fixed on the revolver in Levitt's hand, hoping for an opportune moment to take it away.

"He didn't lose it. He took it for a walk to prove he wasn't scared of it. And then he smashed its head to a pulp against the wall of a building."

Joseph blanched. He had known that Leo had done something to the dog. He'd thought Leo had deliberately lost it, but this! . . .

Levitt kept on talking. "I promised you, Pearl, that I would make something of Leo, and the only way I could do that was to understand him, understand what drove him. I knew about his homosexuality long before you did. I accepted it, and because of that Leo trusted me. He trusted me enough to let me turn his craziness into a weapon."

"You made him kill for you."

"No! I made him strike against those who would harm this family! My family! Behind his craziness was my ability to scheme, to plan!" Levitt licked lips that were suddenly dry. His heart was racing, the gun trembled in his hand. "The whole world thinks the shooting of the Rourke brothers was just the random act of some Arab student. It was me who was behind it. With Leo. That boy who shot them, he was one of Leo's lovers. The Rourkes hurt us, and we paid them back!"

"You were behind the Rourke killings? Leo as well?"

Levitt nodded. "The policeman who was on the scene, the one who killed that Arab, he was paid by us to be there." Levitt saw Joseph's hand reach out to take the revolver from him. He relinquished his grip on the weapon, no longer needing it. He had done what he should have done twenty-nine years earlier.

The library door flew back on its hinges. Judy stood framed in the doorway. "I heard a gunshot—!" Her hand flew to her mouth when she spotted the revolver in Joseph's hand, the body of Minsky on the couch. "My God!"

"Where are the kids?" Joseph asked.

"I left them. You . . . ." She pointed at the gun. "Why?"

Joseph dropped the revolver onto the floor. "Not me. I didn't do it."

"Lou did," Pearl said. "He killed Minsky, just like he killed Jake, just like he killed your father when they went against him." Her voice was calmer than it had been all night. She felt wonderfully serene as she sat down in an armchair. The large handbag was on the floor beside the chair. She slipped her hand inside.

"Lou, did you hear what Benny said before?" she asked.

"About what?"

"He recognized that revolver. He gave it to Jake." Her hand began to come out of the bag. "It was one of a pair, a matching pair. Here's the second one."

Eyes bright like amber, she lifted the matching revolver clear of the handbag, aimed it at Levitt's face and squeezed the trigger.

Leo could not believe how long it was taking to go from Scarsdale to Sands Point.

"For Christ's sake, can't you go any faster?" he asked as the taxi sped west through Queens on the Long Island Expressway.

"Take a look at my speedometer, mister," the driver answered. "I've been doing sixty-five, seventy, all the way. You want to get there any quicker, hire yourself a Phantom jet the next time, not a damned taxi."

Leo sat back and checked his watch for what he knew must be the fifth time in as many minutes. One-thirty. His mother would be in bed. She always went to bed early. He wanted, needed, her to help him, and she was asleep. A sweeping wave of self-pity washed over him. He was in trouble like never before, fleeing across New York in a taxi while police turned his home inside out, and the only person who could help him didn't even know of his plight. And he had only acted out of concern for her. He had killed because his love for her was so strong. She didn't understand. She didn't care. She was asleep.

"You all right back there?" the taxi driver asked. He peered nervously into the rear-view mirror as an oncoming car's headlights lit up the inside of the taxi. His passenger had his hands to his face; tears were streaming down his cheeks.

Leo made no reply. He didn't even hear the question. He glanced out of the window, saw the sign that told him the taxi was entering Nassau County. He sniffed, wiped away the tears. Soon he'd be there. His mother wouldn't be asleep. She'd know that something was wrong. She'd feel it. She'd be waiting to comfort him like she had always done. She'd hold him, and all of his troubles would just disappear.

No embrace, not even those of the young men he had loved, could ever match the security that a hug from his mother brought.

Chapter Five

For fully a minute after shooting Lou Levitt, Pearl remained sitting rigidly upright in the armchair, the revolver pointing down to where Levitt had fallen. Joseph and Judy stood perfectly still, too terrified to move. Finally, the gun dropped from Pearl's hand onto the floor and she leaned back in the chair.

"Call the police," she whispered. "Tell them what's happened."

Joseph leaped forward to snatch the revolver from beside his mother's feet. He saw Judy lift the telephone receiver and dial the emergency number. When the call was answered, she asked for both police and an ambulance.

"What about the children?" Pearl asked after Judy had made the call. "You should see about the children."

Judy glanced at Joseph, who nodded. Jacob and Anne must be terrified, alone in the guest wing, hearing the two shots, wondering what had happened. Judy left the library to return a minute later. Both children were asleep; by some miracle they had slept through everything.

Joseph squatted down beside his mother's chair. "When the police come, what are you going to tell them?"

"The truth, of course. That I shot Lou after he killed Benny." Pearl made it sound so childishly simple that Joseph worried about his mother's sanity.

"Ma, before the police get here, I can put that other gun next to Lou. Judy and I, we'll say you shot him in self-defense. We'll say he was threatening everyone. We'll swear to it on a stack of bibles."

"We'll back you up," Judy assured her mother-in-law. "We'll say whatever will keep you out of trouble."

Pearl smiled at them both. "What kind of trouble can an old lady get into? I just did what should have been done years ago, that's all. While we're waiting for the police," she added, "perhaps I should make some coffee. Would anyone like a cup?"

Joseph stiffened at what he considered the oddity of the suggestion. Two corpses, one killed by his mother, and all she could think of was making coffee. Judy cut in quickly.

"That's a wonderful idea. I know I could do with some." She caught Joseph's eye.

Slowly, he understood. It was his mother's way of coping with a crisis, any crisis. Feed the crisis until it went away. Joseph watched his mother walk out of the library, heard her footsteps as she crossed the entrance hall to the kitchen. "Is she all right?" he asked Judy.

"She's in shock. She just killed someone, a man who was very close to her."

"Closer than you think," Joseph whispered. He told Judy Levitt had claimed that he was his father, and Leo's. Judy's eyes widened.

"Do you think that could be true?"

"What? His claim that he . . . he made love to Ma, or that I'm his son?"

"Both."

"Ma didn't deny that she'd . . . you know." He was unable to think or talk of his mother in those terms. "But being his son? . . ."

"You're not," Judy assured him. "You couldn't be."

"Thanks."

"Go into the kitchen, stay with her. Show her she's not alone."

Joseph left. Rather than remain alone in the library with the two bodies, Judy walked into the entrance hall. She'd listen for the police. After a couple of minutes, she heard the sound of an engine, a car door slamming. Before the bell could be rung, she pulled open the door—and stopped dead. There was no police car or ambulance outside. Only a taxi pulling away, and Leo climbing the steps toward the door.

"Where's Ma?" he demanded. "I've got to see her!"

Judy stepped outside, pulled the door closed behind her. "What do you want?"

"I want Ma. Wake her up. Tell her I'm here."

"Go to hell. You're not setting one foot inside this house ever again."

Halfway up the steps, Leo froze into immobility. His mouth gaped. He stared in disbelief at Judy. "You can't stop me from seeing Ma."

"She doesn't want to see you, don't you understand that? She knows what you did. She knows what you're like. She knows what you are. She never wants to see you again. Now go away, before you bring her even more grief."

"I've never brought Ma grief!" Tears started down Leo's cheeks

...s he voiced the denial. He'd never hurt his mother. Judy was lying, just like she always did. "She loves me. How could I ever hurt her?"

"You've hurt her with every breath you ever took, you bastard." Standing in front of the door, denying Leo entrance, Judy felt no fear. Only jubilation. At last, after years of having to accept his abuse, his insults, she could confront him. No longer would his twin brother or his mother stand up for him. No more would Pearl find excuses for his barbaric behavior. On this night of tragedy, Judy was experiencing a heady triumph. "She doesn't want to see you, don't you understand that? She doesn't love you, Leo. She hates you. Like poison, she hates you."

Leo wiped his eyes with the sleeve of his jacket. Then a cunning look appeared on his face. At last he understood. "You made her hate me, didn't you? All along you worked on her with your lies to make her hate me. And my brother, my stupid brother who's supposed to be my twin—supposed to be closer to me than to anyone else—he let you fill Ma's mind with your lies." He started up the steps again, determined to push Judy aside to gain entrance to the house. Determined to kill her if that was what it took.

"Lies?" Judy laughed. "I didn't have to tell her lies." She stopped talking for a moment, squinted as she tried to peer into the bushes behind Leo. Surely she had just seen something move out there. What was it? There, again. The bushes moved. Then she relaxed. It was Solomon and Sheba, that was all, the Dobermans, foraging around in the bushes until they were called back into the house. She looked back into Leo's heavy face, noted the patch of plaster across his temple. "Who do you think told your mother all about your place down on MacDougal Street? That wasn't a lie, was it? I didn't lie about your meeting your pretty little boys down there, did I?"

"You? It was you?"

"Damned right it was me." From inside the house, she heard Joseph call her name. He didn't know she'd gone outside, or that Leo had arrived. He called her name again, and she ignored him.

"You're the one who told Ma about me? You're the one who told on me?" Leo's voice rose to a tortured scream. He ran up the remaining steps, hands reaching out for Judy's throat. She heard Joseph call her name again, but now that she wanted to answer, she could not. Leo's strong hands were around her neck, cutting off sound, cutting off air.

"I'll kill you!" Leo shrieked. The pressure around Judy's throat became greater. "I wish you'd died with your fucking lousy mother. You should have died, you bitch!"

The bushes parted. Judy heard a deep growl, saw nothing more than a dark blur flying through the air. The pressure on her throat eased. She leaned back against the door, chest heaving as she watched Leo stagger down the stairs, Solomon, the male Doberman, hanging from his right arm.

"Get him off me!" Leo screamed. He punched wildly at the large dog with his left fist. Despite the assault, the Doberman continued to hang by its teeth from Leo's arm.

Another blur of movement. Leo's screams soared to a peak beyond human hearing as Sheba, the Doberman bitch, joined the attack, snapping its fangs into Leo's left thigh. Judy stood on the top step, frozen in fear and fascination as the two powerful beasts worried and tore at Leo as though he were nothing more than an old blanket, a toy.

Pulling and ripping, Solomon and Sheba dragged Leo onto his back. Then the larger dog released its grip on Leo's right arm and backed off, tongue hanging out as it panted for breath, blood dripping from its mouth. Staring at Leo lying helplessly on his back, Judy understood perfectly why Solomon had given up the arm. Leo's white, unprotected neck presented a far more tempting target. Judy closed her eyes, but not quickly enough to avoid seeing Solomon leap forward and sink gleaming fangs into Leo's throat.

At the far end of the driveway, lights appeared. Headlights, and the red-and-blue flashes of emergency vehicles. Behind Judy, the door opened, and she fell back into Joseph's arms. The nightmare was over, and she was just grateful that those she loved had lived through it.

Pearl refused to go to bed. She insisted on staying up all night to make coffee and serve homemade cake to the many officials who tramped through the house, taking photographs, asking questions, and making copious notes.

"Do you think my mother really understands about Leo?" Joseph asked Judy nervously. "She's walking around like she's the hostess at some party."

"She understands all right. She's just treating this crisis the way she treats any other. Be more worried about yourself."

"It hasn't sunk in yet, none of it. Benny Minsky, Uncle Lou, Leo. It's all like a dream." Joseph shuddered as he recalled the bodies being removed, two from the library, and Leo's from the front teps. Of all three bodies, Leo's, savaged by the dogs, had been the hardest to look at. "Judy, why did Solomon and Sheba attack Leo?"

"Because he attacked me. He tried to strangle me."

"Why?"

When Judy did not answer, Joseph repeated the question. "Did you provoke him at all, knowing the Dobermans were out there?"

"Of course not!" she fired back.

"He just tried to strangle you?" Even while Joseph asked the question, he tried to understand his own feelings about what had taken place. As if the deaths—the violent deaths—of three people so close to him weren't enough, he had to come to grips with the sickening betrayal of the entire family by Lou Levitt. Three deaths? . . . Four deaths! He'd forgotten all about William Minsky, whose abduction, whose murder, had started the chain of events leading to the carnage in the Sands Point house. But the betrayal, and Levitt's absurd claim about being his father, and Leo's? No matter which way he tried to approach it, he could not even begin to comprehend that.

"Since when did your brother need to have a reason to wish me harm?" Judy wanted to know. She would never tell Joseph that she had deliberately taunted his twin brother by telling him that she'd been the one who'd told Pearl about his homosexuality. If she did, he might think she'd done so knowing that the two Dobermans were foraging in the bushes, that Leo would assault her, and that the dogs would come to her aid.

A police officer approached Joseph and Judy. More questions were asked. Judy knew the rush of official activity was acting like a buffer for those involved. Only after the inquiries ended, the outsiders left, would she and Pearl and Joseph be able to sit down and think about the future. They'd have to move, of course. This house, once the home of so many happy memories, was now a horror chamber of ghosts.

One by one, the policemen and the technicians finished their work at the house in Sands Point. The last to leave was the medical examiner. As he placed his black bag in the trunk of his car, Pearl approached him.

"Excuse me, you are a doctor, aren't you? A regular doctor?"

"Yes, ma'am," the medical examiner replied. "Would you like me to prescribe something for you? A sedative?"

"No, thank you. I have my own family doctor should I need anything like that. It's just that I was wondering if you could answer a question for me."

More than anything else, the medical examiner wanted to ge home and go to bed. It was already six in the morning; he had been at work for four hours. Later that day he had to perform three autopsies. Yet he could not bring himself to be abrupt to this sweet little old lady who had supplied coffee and cake all night long, who had treated all of those in her house on official business as though they were her own flesh and blood. "What is it, Mrs. Granitz?"

"It's about twins. Not identical twins, mind you, but fraternal twins."

The medical examiner appeared startled. He had expected something far less ordinary, especially from a woman who had suffered what Pearl had. "What about fraternal twins?"

"Is it possible . . . oh, this must seem like such a silly question to a doctor like yourself . . . but is it possible for fraternal twins to have two separate fathers?"

"There's nothing silly about the question at all, Mrs. Granitz. They can."

"They can?"

"Yes. You see, the difference between identical twins and fraternal twins is this: identical twins are formed when a single egg splits in the mother's womb, whereas fraternal twins are formed when two eggs are fertilized separately. It's possible that a woman could have sexual intercourse"—the medical examiner spoke in a crisp, dry tone, without any hint of embarrassment at having to explain such things to an elderly woman—"with two separate partners within a very short period of time, and the sperm from each partner could fertilize a single egg. She would then be pregnant with twins from different fathers. Does that answer your question?"

"Yes, thank you, it does." Pearl walked back toward the house. When she passed Joseph and Judy standing in the doorway, she gave them a slight smile and said she was going to bed. She was feeling tired, and she would sleep well now that she knew Lou Levitt had been wrong. Imagine that, little Lou Levitt being wrong. And being wrong about the most important thing of all.

As she climbed the stairs to her bedroom, she recalled the times Levitt had claimed he was the father of the twins. Tonight, of course, when he'd caused enough confusion to snatch the revolver from Joseph's hand. And more than forty years earlier, just after Pearl had given birth. When everyone had come around to see the babies, and Pearl had warned Levitt that Jake would kill him if he ever learned the truth. And all those intervening years he'd believed it. He'd been wrong, Pearl thought with a savage joy.

Levitt wasn't the father of the twins. He was just the father of one twin. Of Leo, who had inherited Levitt's madness. Joseph's father was Jake. Joseph was the only true child of her marriage to Jake. The only child that mattered.

Dawn flooded the room as Pearl climbed into bed. If only she'd known that snippet of information more than forty years earlier, she reflected as she closed her eyes.

Who would have thought it possible that twins could have different fathers?

SEARING ROMANCE

REBEL PLEASURE   (1672, $3.95)
Mary Martin
Union agent Jason Woods knew Christina was a brazen flirt. But his dangerous mission had no room for clinging vixen. Christina knew Jason for a womanizer and a cad, but that didn't stop the burning desire to share her sweet *Rebel Pleasure*.

SAVAGE STORM   (1687, $3.95)
Phoebe Conn
Gabrielle was determined to survive the Oregon Trail and start a new life as a mail-order bride. Too late, she realized that even the perils of the trail were not as dangerous as the arrogant scout who stole her heart.

GOLDEN ECSTASY   (1688, $3.95)
Wanda Owen
Andrea was furious when Gil had seen her tumble from her horse. But nothing could match her rage when he thoroughly kissed her full trembling lips, urging her into his arms and filling her with a passion that could be satisfied only one way!

LAWLESS LOVE   (1690, $3.95)
F. Rosanne Bittner
Amanda's eyes kept straying to the buckskin-clad stranger opposite her on the train. She vowed that he would be the one to tame her savage desire with his wild *Lawless Love*.

PASSION'S FLAME   (1716, $3.95)
Casey Stuart
Kathleen was playing with fire when she infiltrated Union circles to spy for the Confederacy. But soon she had to choose between succumbing to Captain's Donovan's caresses or using him to avenge the South!

Available wherever paperbacks are sold, or order direct from the Publisher. Send cover price plus 50¢ *per copy for mailing and handling to Zebra Books, Dept. 2086, 475 Park Avenue South, New York, N.Y. 10016. Residents of New York, New Jersey and Pennsylvania must include sales tax. DO NOT SEND CASH.*